DON'T GIVE UP ON ME

Part 1

Sam Douglas

Copyright © 2025 Sam Douglas

All rights reserved

This is a work of fiction. Names, characters, places, and events are the product of the author's imagination or used fictitiously. Any resemblance to actual persons, living or dead, is purely coincidental.

No part of this publication may be reproduced, stored in a retrieval system, or transmitted in any form or by any means including electronic, mechanical, photocopying, recording, or otherwise, without the prior written permission of the author.

Cover design by Sam Douglas.

Dedicated to everybody who adores these characters as much as I do.

CONTENT WARNING

Don't Give Up On Me is a contemporary romance drama that explores the complex relationships between a drug dealer, his high-powered mogul brother, and a young woman with a troubled past.

This novel contains mature themes and emotionally intense content that some readers may find distressing.

Topics include, but are not limited to:
- Substance abuse
- Domestic violence
- Abortion
- Miscarriage
- Murder

This book is intended for adult readers. All characters are fictional and over the age of 18. The author does not endorse or glorify illegal activity, abuse, or violence.

CONTENTS

Title Page
Copyright
Dedication
CONTENT WARNING
Connect with me
Soundtrack

Chapter 1	1
chapter 2	57
chapter 3	95
chapter 4	137
chapter 5	191
chapter 6	228
chapter 7	270
chapter 8	320
chapter 9	356
chapter 10	395
chapter 11	431
chapter 12	475
chapter 13	519
chapter 14	576
chapter 15	621
chapter 16	656
chapter 17	697

Thankyou

CONNECT WITH ME

Thank you so much for your support.
I'd love to hear from you.
Follow & Connect:

- TikTok: @sam.douglas_author
- Instagram: @sam.douglas_author
- Email: sam.douglas11@outlook.com
- Website: samdouglas11.wixsite.com/mysite

Loved the book?

If you enjoyed this story, please consider leaving a short review on Amazon. Your feedback helps more readers discover Chloe and Romeo—and it means the world to indie authors like me.

Thank you for being here.
Stay wild, stay fierce, and I'll see you in the next book.

With love,
Sam

SOUNDTRACK

To bring you even closer to their world, I've created a playlist **Don't Give Up On Me Part 1** featuring the songs woven into their journey. You can listen as you read or after, letting the music pull you deeper into their story.

Scan the QR code below to access the playlist.
(Available on Spotify. You can also search for the song wherever you stream your music.)

CHAPTER 1

"Romeo? Romeo, are you awake?" I whispered into the darkness.

The air, too still, held its breath with me as I stared into the black.

Another faint sound made my heart race. Something shifted outside, too deliberate to be the wind.

"Hmm?" he grumbled. "What time is it?"

Adrenaline spiked through my fingertips as I reached for my phone on the nightstand, clicking the button to wake the screen.

"A little after one." I turned to gauge his reaction.

The soft glow from the display cast an eerie light over Romeo's face. He was already drifting again.

Was I imagining it? I could've sworn I heard something...

My grip on the bedcovers eased—until another noise crept in from beyond the walls, this time more deliberate.

Shit.

This time, I was sure.

I grabbed his arm with both hands and rocked him hard enough to tilt the mattress.

"Romeo, wake up!"

He shot up instantly, hand moving lightning-fast as he reached under his pillow.

"What!?" he barked into the stillness, shifting in the shadows as he gathered his bearings.

I placed my cold, jittery hand over his, gently lowering the gun. He protested a little, then relented.

"I heard a noise outside. Should I turn on the light?"

The faint rustle of leaves. A swirl of wind sweeping across the gravel. Then the crunch of footsteps.

He threw back the covers and sprang from the bed—naked—and padded to the window, twitching the drapes aside.

It was like watching a scene from a police interception. His back pressed to the wall, gun low by his thigh as he peered through the curtain's edge.

"Queen, you need to start rememberin' what I tell you." He released the safety on his favourite gun. The metallic click announced its deadly intent. "Light stays off."

My pulse quickened when the length of his penis retracted slightly—barely a quarter of an inch.

He was on high alert.

"Can you see anything?" I held my breath. Sweat broke across my skin as he scanned the grounds.

Seconds passed.

I gulped, shoulders stiffening. "Well? Can you?"

He threw a quick glance my way. Then zeroed in again, focus as sharp as crosshairs.

"Yeah. Five bitches in balaclavas next to my Rolls."

The weight of his words stole my breath.

"Another burglary? Romeo, this is the second time this month!"

Those footsteps—different this time, yet eerily familiar.

Anxiety clung to the edges of my sanity at the thought of going through this again.

The timbers creaked in the eaves, as if the house remembered. As if it were bracing for another fight.

Instinctively, I peeled back the sheets, morbid curiosity drawing me in. A cold draft kissed the back of my neck as my toes touched the carpet. Goosebumps rippled down my spine, chasing the chill of memory.

Last time, they'd evaded our best men and made it to the patio door. Torchlight flickering through the glass, pooling across the kitchen floor. Hushed voices rattling the silence as I peered through the slats in the banister.

Last time, they were so close.

I inched across the carpet, needing to see them, to watch the thieves at work. To see just how close they were to breaking in *this time.*

Romeo's voice hit like a wall, stopping me dead.

"What the fuck are you doin', Chloe?" He blinked against the gloom. "After last time? You know the drill. Panic room. Now."

Pale light skated across his skin, lending warmth to the cold edge in his voice. But if he thought I was going back into that glorified prison, he was mistaken.

Instead, I snapped my exposed foot back under the covers, yanking the duvet up to my eyes like a child hiding from a monster.

If I closed my eyes and counted to three, it would all disappear.

One… Two… Three…

My lids fluttered open.

It was still dark. And he was still staring—relentless in his pursuit of my safety. He looked worried this time. And that was unnerving.

Regardless, there was no way I was spending the night locked in a damn box.

"So, what are we going to do?" My voice barely made it past the linen, but my husband's ears were sharp.

"We?" He scoffed, gripping his gun tighter. "Your pregnant ass is stayin' put. I'm gonna go handle it with my boys."

The vibration of his phone on the nightstand pricked both our ears—a little beacon casting light against the ceiling, ready to make all of this real.

Reluctantly, he tore himself away from the window, snatching up the phone.

"Yeah?" he said aggressively to the caller, then nodded. "Aight. Now."

He hung up and tossed it onto the bed.

My fingernails dug into my palms.

"Romeo, please, don't go. I can't bear it when you leave me like this. It's like you're going off to war—like this is our last goodbye."

His pecs flinched. "Come on, Chloe. You know I protect what's mine."

I watched, almost in slow motion, as he pulled on his sweatpants, T-shirt, and sneakers. Then, like always, he moved to his jewellery box. The crucifix necklace was the final touch. My husband was preparing to kill someone.

I cradled my stomach, mustering authority. "You better put on the bulletproof vest I bought you. Remember? The one you've never worn? Romeo, I'm not kidding."

With a sharp click, he dropped the half-full magazine, slid a fresh one into place, and racked the slide—loading a round into the chamber of his loyal friend.

"Yeah, yeah, I know." He edged toward me. His glare shone through the murk of uncertainty. "Panic room now. Let's go."

Being locked inside a luxurious, Kevlar-lined safe room should've been reassuring.

But it wasn't.

Padded walls softened with draped fabric and feminine accessories did absolutely nothing to ease my fears. No matter how many times Romeo had coaxed me inside to acclimatise, I still hated this place.

Just like a prison cell, there were no views of the outside world. No fresh air. Nothing to anchor me to reality.

All I had was a hope and a prayer that Romeo would come back for me. That I wouldn't be forgotten.

Sure, the keypad on the wall meant I could leave if I had to, but Tommy's countless safety drills echoed loud and clear: stay put until someone comes for you.

The moment I stepped inside, cool with artificial air and scented faintly with new leather upholstery, my fight-or-flight instincts kicked in. And I struggled to hold myself together.

Just knowing that, while I was in here staring at four walls, Romeo could be lying dead somewhere, pushed me beyond my tolerance.

Last night's cigarette floated between us when he stepped in beside me.

"Aight, you good?" he asked, already knowing the answer.

He flicked on the lights. They spluttered to life, like they too had been rudely awoken.

My reply came with an arm fold and a pout.

He ran a hand through his hair.

That warm coconut scent clung to him, familiar and sweet—but it didn't cancel out the fact he was about to abandon me.

"Come on, Chloe. I don't wanna be worryin' about you when I'm out there."

My pout instantly softened, hands falling by my waist, fingers flexing with an ache.

Worrying my husband at a time like this was the exact opposite of what I wanted.

I sighed, flicking my wrist, looking anywhere but at him.

"Go on then. Handle your business."

He paused for a beat before pulling me close, kissing the top of my head. The dampness of his lips and the warmth of air puffing from his nose tingled my scalp.

"I'll be back soon, baby."

I clung to him like the childhood teddy bear that had once guarded me from bad dreams.

We'd done this too many times. And every time became even harder.

"Be safe, Romeo," I murmured against his chest. "I love you."

He shifted, tipping my chin until our eyes met. The heat of his finger, the scent of his skin—I imprinted every last beat, as if this might be the last.

"*Ti amo da morire.* Until death, my Queen."

Hopeless. Helpless. Distraught, even. I watched him leave. His broad back. The black sweep of his hair. The last fragments of him vanishing before the door sealed shut with a heavy, safe-like thump.

Just like that, I was alone again.

Instinctively, I curled into the bedding like a foetus, wrapping the alien scent around me—a cocoon. But no matter how hard I fought the panic. No matter how many times I blinked the thoughts away. Fear returned in ghostly figures, casting mocking silhouettes across the walls.

I screwed my eyes shut, took a minute to follow my therapist's advice: focus on breathing. Focus on something—anything—to keep me tethered.

And then, like always, Romeo appeared behind my eyelids.

That playful wink.

That smile.

The perfect vision of the man I loved more than anything.

Since our wedding day six weeks ago, we had grown stronger in ways neither of us had expected.

From the exchange of vows to the re-gifting of Nonna's ring, the entire day had unfolded flawlessly.

And to top it off, the brothers hugging it out, finally forgiving each other, was all anyone could've hoped for.

A new beginning. Exactly what the doctor ordered.

Before our big day, I'd worried I was bringing a child into a hopeless relationship—with a man I feared was incapable of self-control, or even the ability to show human emotion.

But now? Now, I couldn't be more excited for the day I made my husband a father.

My eyes blinked open, and the room rematerialised.

The images shifted along the walls again. This time, the ghosts morphed into Romeo, like a reflection in warped glass. His gun raised. Worry carved across his face. Shots fired. My breath hitched.

Somewhere, right now, I knew this was happening. I drew my knees in as far as my bump allowed, rocking gently as the scene played out, like a film I couldn't look away from. I never wanted to feel this again. This sick, helpless waiting. Wondering if he'd survived whatever fresh hell he'd walked into.

For the umpteenth time in our relationship, I was stuck in limbo. And if he hadn't put that bloody vest on, I'd kill him myself.

◆ ◆ ◆

"Chloe? Chloe, baby, wake up."

"Hmm?"

My eyes flickered open to find my husband sitting on the edge of the bed beside me.

The smell of conflict, outdoors mixed with metal, clung to the artificial air around us like a warning.

I rubbed my eyes, surroundings unfamiliar, until I realised I was still in the panic room.

I kicked off the covers and sat up fast, the haze of sleep melting away. My focus snapped to his face.

"Are you okay?" I asked, scrambling upright, limbs still tangled in the duvet.

He cocked his head, breathing calmly, brow furrowing.

"Why wouldn't I be?"

Did he seriously just ask why?

My battle with myself simmered down. A frown settled on my face as the sleepy fog filtered back.

I yawned into my fist, wondering how the hell I'd managed to sleep at a time like this.

"Did I dream what happened last night, or was someone actually trying to steal your car?"

"Nah, it was real," he murmured softly, like this was pillow talk.

His finger traced a slow line down the centre of my cleavage, sending an electrical current through my core. With a glint in his eye, his mouth twisted into a wry smile as the connection between us crackled like embers.

He licked his lips, stealing another peek. The fire smouldered, the temperature in the room rising further.

I swatted his hand away, throwing a bucket of ice water on the heat of the moment.

"Romeo, please." I turned my back toward him. "I don't like how you always want sex after you've killed someone. It's weird."

His jaw tightened, eyes glistening in that way they always did when I pushed back.

"Come on, Chloe. Gimme a lil' somethin'. I need it."

I yawned again, this time until my eyes watered.

"Jeez, I'm so tired."

"You are?" he asked casually, plucking a piece of imaginary lint from his shirt. But the sudden dilation of his pupils caught my attention.

"What?" My whole body tensed.

He lifted his head, brows knitting in mock confusion, then pushed off the mattress to straighten the misaligned frame of the scenic artwork hiding the concealed safe.

"Huh?" he mumbled, now at least six feet away.

My scalp prickled when he took it a step further—pressing a finger into the padded wall like he was gauging how much of the aftershock it'd absorb if I started swinging him round by his curls.

"Oh, please. Don't play dumb. Why did you act weird when I told you I was tired?"

Casual Romeo was a side character in his own story. One who rarely made a convincing appearance.

He shrugged, hands buried in his pockets, eyes fixed on his feet as he kicked at the floor.

"Just put a little anaesthetic through the air vents," he muttered. "No big deal."

That woke me up.

The bucket of ice water I'd tossed at his libido had come right back at me—square in the face.

"You did what!?" I leapt off the bed to join him.

My eyes locked on his, drawing in breath like I was stuck in a vacuum. I had to get out. I needed real air.

I yanked open the safe room hatch, almost blinded by sunlight that spilled in through the gap in the curtain, catching me full force.

"Are you crazy?" I turned on my heels as he emerged from the closet.

My anxiety was already at fever pitch. This just shoved it right off the edge.

He dragged a hand through his hair, brows drawn in quiet thought.

"Be real, Chloe. You fuckin' hate that room. I had that feature installed to keep you calm. I didn't want you and the baby stressed."

With daylight pouring in, there was no shadow left to hide his intentions. And that only made me angrier.

"You fucking drugged me!?" My voice crashed off the walls like a thunderclap. "What was it? An add-on special? Free tote bag with every fogger?"

Just when I thought he couldn't possibly do worse…

Defensive. Backed into a corner, he jutted a finger at me. The bass in his voice rose in an attempt to outdo mine. "Don't make it sound like I forced a fuckin' needle into your arm. It's all been cleared by a doctor. It's safe. Chill out!"

Words failed me. Hell, even sound failed me.

A tiny squeal was all I could muster from the depths of my soul.

We stood there a moment, chests heaving, shoulders rising and falling like a pair of NPCs.

The echoes of our yelling finally dispersed, tension ebbing as we both pulled it back under control.

He cracked a small smile. I kept my game face on.

Then, like a reset button had been pressed, the world crept back in—the melodic trill of birdsong and the distant hum of a lawnmower slipped through the window.

"Come here, baby," he purred in that sexy way that usually had me melting, reaching his hand out to me, fingertips twitching their invite.

But this time, I couldn't quite shake it off.

How could he betray my trust like that? How could he even think of doing something so reckless?

My lips drew tight, guarded. But he didn't seem to notice.

He closed the tension-fuelled space between us and took a misinformed finger, running it down my cleavage again.

The sensation ignited my skin like flame to a fuse, but I wouldn't let him detonate us this time.

I smacked his hand away, hard, then slapped his chest for good measure before retreating into the hollow of our bed.

Persistent by nature, he followed.

"You're getting nothing from me, Romeo. I cannot believe you did that."

Already hard, his sweatpants pitched like a tent. Flustered by his own arousal, he flailed his arms in frustration.

"You panicked so fuckin' hard the last time you went in there that you passed out! I did it to help you out!"

Oh.

Silence descended. Even the birds paused, heads tilted like they were listening in.

I mean, sure, it was no secret my last failed attempt to acclimatise had been... dramatic. Even Britney accompanying me hadn't helped.

I'd never been particularly claustrophobic before, but I guess my time in the punishment room under the stairs, combined with the night I spent in a jail cell with Frankie-Jo, had really taken its toll.

"Fine!" I snapped, realising I might've overreacted, just a little.

My reluctant surrender reignited the sparkle in his eyes, and, believe it or not, he went in for a third try.

"No, Romeo." I caught his hand before it made contact with my skin. "I'm too wound up for sex. Leave me alone!"

"Okay then," he huffed. "Guess I'll have to jerk off again! Remind me why I married you? 'Cause I ain't gettin' any of the perks!"

Ugh. Here we go again.

How many more times was he going to bring this up?

I turned my back on him. "You're a selfish son of a bitch, Romeo. You really are."

His eyes narrowed as his fingers curled into fists.

"You used to be a filthy little slut who couldn't get enough of my dick." He grabbed himself, gave a sharp tug. "What the fuck happened?"

My mouth fell open. "You got me pregnant, ass-hat. That's what happened!"

The mattress shifted as he pushed off the bed, stalking toward the bathroom. He slammed the door with enough force to make me wince—and the whole house rattle.

For a brief moment, a flicker of guilt pricked at my conscience that I wasn't meeting his needs.

But should I feel guilty? Was it my fault my husband was a sex-crazed deviant? *And* a selfish prick?

I'd have to ask Nelly at our next therapy session. Maybe I'd leave out the part where he kills people first... Or maybe I wouldn't if he kept being a damn baby about things.

Eight minutes later, Romeo emerged—cheeks tinged pink, expression softer.

My man got his nut, eventually.

The soft fragrance of last night's shower oils clung to him, at complete odds with the masculine, post-orgasm flush he wore like a victorious warrior.

Checking my overdue manicure, I cast him a quick glance. The heat of the day pressed through the open window, warming the undercurrent between us.

"That took you a while. You usually come a *lot* quicker than that." A giggle bubbled beneath the surface, half-stifled by a crooked finger to my lips.

Only God knew why I was still poking the bear.

The bathroom door clicked shut behind him—quiet, almost apologetic.

"Well, I had nothin' to look at, did I?" He threw his hands up. "Gone are the days when the man of this house could look at his woman while he beats it. I can't do nothin' in this fuckin' place anymore."

I rolled my eyes, jaw still tight from earlier, recalling our last heated debate over his constant wanking.

It wasn't that I cared that he did it—it was how often. Always playing with himself when his time could be put to better use.

After I made it a rule that all solo activities be confined to the bathroom alone, he'd cut down. Slightly.

I sighed, rolling onto my back, eyes following the hairline cracks snaking across the ceiling—fitting, considering the state of my nerves.

"Anyway." My tone softened. "I want to know what happened."

Romeo stopped at the foot of the bed, his jewellery glinting against his body like a ray of hope.

He kept the bed frame between us. Intentional distance.

"Well, I used some of your shower cream on my nuts and then started workin' the shaft—"

"What?" I lifted my head, blinking. "No, you idiot. I meant what happened with the burglary. And I wondered why my cream was running low already!"

"Oh." He chuckled, cupping his crotch like it needed consoling. "We lost two men. But all five of the bitches tryin' to take the Rolls got dropped. So I figure it's about even."

His hand shifted to his hair, and that's when I spotted the wound on his knuckle.

Shit.

It was real. It really happened. Two more of our crew gone. How many more could we afford to lose?

The hum of a lawnmower swelled in the distance, its blade slicing through grass with a clean, relentless rhythm. Jack and his team were out on the grounds, keeping the place ticking over. Probably clearing more bloodstains.

If I'd been keeping a list of everyone we'd lost, the first page would be full by now—and I wasn't ready to start the second.

The ceiling above became a shifting mural—every crack and shadow, another fragment of the scene Romeo painted of last night.

I held my breath. Waiting for the next brushstroke.

"How many of them did you kill, Romeo?"

He squared his shoulders, chest puffing. A subtle adjustment of his crucifix told me everything I needed to know.

"Chloe, I thought we agreed not to talk about this shit. All it does is start an argument, and I'm done."

We were both running on empty. But only one of us had blood on their conscience.

I blinked back the weight in my throat, my own brush dragging across the canvas.

"Do you think it's connected to Benny English?"

A gust of wind pulled at the voile—nature's reaction to a question I dared to ask.

It was no secret that Romeo's European business partner had started hitting below the belt, testing our evasion tactics with low blows and calculated pressure.

So, it wasn't unreasonable to think he was behind this. Toying with us. Tightening the screws until we had no choice but to give in.

Romeo flicked his lighter, the tiny flame catching in his eyes. A reminder he liked a smoke after an orgasm.

"That counts as askin' questions." He snapped the lighter shut, extinguishing the flame. "Just kids lookin' for a quick buck."

But he wasn't fooling anyone, least of all me. There was more to this than he was letting on.

"What about Detective Saxon?"

The curtain stirred again—a restless whisper that cinched the knot in my stomach tighter at the sound of that name. Ever since he'd threatened me outside the courthouse, I'd been waiting for him to strike.

We both had.

Romeo chuckled. The crucifix around his neck winked in the light—a holy symbol worn by a man who answered only to himself.

"Tell me how, in your crazy-ass mind, it makes sense that a bent cop would try to steal my Rolls?"

Slightly affronted, I narrowed my eyes. Arms folded.

"Jeez, Romeo, I don't know. Why would anybody want to take your damn Rolls when we've got more security than the White House?"

The whir of garden machinery had faded, replaced by the buzz of a fly thumping against the windowpane. Desperate for a way out of this mess. Just like me.

His smile hardened. The humour vanished. He flicked the lighter again—restless hands meant a restless mind.

"Like I told you the last time you asked." His voice dropped. "I dealt with that cop."

Hmm.

We both knew Saxon was the snake in the grass.

Romeo had claimed before that he was no longer a problem, only for that cop to rear his ugly head again. And again.

My brow arched. "How exactly?"

"Stop." He raised a hand like a traffic cop. "No more questions. We're done here."

But I wasn't letting him off that easy. Not yet.

I gave a dry look, already bracing for the answer I knew was coming. "Did you wear that bulletproof vest I bought you?"

His all-telling eyes widened before flicking down—like something fascinating had just appeared on the carpet. If I had my way, it'd be something I could use to hit him over the head with.

"Err... yeah, of course," he muttered.

The vein in his forehead pulsed, matching the twitch at the tip of his nose. His lies always did bloom like steam off a fresh dog turd.

"Romero Giannetti, you're a fucking liar."

He could never meet my eyes when he wasn't being truthful. And without fail, he always scratched the tip of his perfectly sculpted nose.

Sure enough, his finger lifted to his face.

"Queen, come on. That shit's for girls. We've been through this."

Right then, I wanted to unclasp his necklace and shove the point of that cross right up his arse. I wanted to scream that he was a selfish, arrogant son of a bitch who needed to grow up for the sake of his unborn child.

But I was practising the art of decorum. Barely.

With as much self-control as I could muster, I took a deep, cleansing breath.

Today was too important for a full-blown row. This could wait until tomorrow.

"Are you ready, Chloe? We gotta go now if we don't wanna be late," Romeo's voice echoed up the stairs, heavy with impatience—tapping his watch like I was the one who always kept us waiting.

This afternoon was our baby's first official scan, and I was anxious as hell. Romeo was too; I could feel it. But he was trying hard not to show it, for my sake, as much as his own.

My hand lingered on my bump as I took one last look in the mirror, turning to the side and smoothing my T-shirt over the gentle swell. It was definitely getting harder to hide now. The fabric stretched tight, clinging to the curve.

Did I just look fat? Or was it finally obvious I was carrying a baby?

"Queen! Now!" His voice cut through the house, sharp and on edge.

He could stand to practise the art of decorum himself.

The low, sultry growl of the engine beneath our bedroom hummed through the walls, pulsing along with his impatience.

"Okay, relax!" I called back, grabbing my purse and pausing for a final glance at the pale-faced woman staring back at me.

I flicked off the closet light and closed the bedroom door with a firm click, taking in a deep breath before facing the music.

Tommy was already at the front door. He opened it and stepped aside, giving me a curt nod.

Amidst the fragrant scent of Jack's freshly cut grass and sun-kissed dew clinging to the flower beds, the Rolls-Royce stood gleaming in all her glory.

Glossy baby blue, chrome flashing like a declaration of war—it was just as imposing as its owner.

I paused at the passenger side, arching a questioning brow at my impatient husband. "The Rolls? Really?"

Romeo leaned against the hood, taking a final drag of his cigarette with that smug look I hated.

As I reached for the handle, he took over—gesturing me inside with a push just a little too firm for my liking, then shutting the door with haste, like a gag around my mouth.

The interior smelled just like him.

New leather. Black Ice. Control.

His cars meant more to him than most things. Maybe even more than me.

Sliding into the driver's seat, a faint waft of smoke brushed my skin as he flicked the smouldering butt to the ground, then shut the door with an expensively muted thud.

Before settling in, he adjusted the Glock at his waistband, like it was an extension of him, then leaned back, clicked his belt into place, and gave the already purring engine a sharp rev.

The car crept forward. Itching to move. Just like him. His fingers tightened around the wheel, a self-satisfied grin creeping across his lips as he pressed the gas again.

Then he turned to me.

"You hear that?" he asked, expectant.

I glanced over my shoulder. "Um… hear what?"

He revved it again.

"My other cars growl, but this V12? It's got that sexy-ass moan."

I didn't blink. My lip curled as I watched him enjoy himself a little too much.

"I've no idea what that means. Why the hell would we use the Rolls after what happened?"

He flipped down the sun visor and unhooked his Ray-Bans, sliding them onto the bridge of his perfect nose like he was posing for a campaign.

"Why wouldn't we use the fuckin' Rolls?" He adjusted his hair around the black frames, smirking. "Gotta make a statement. Any bitches try to play with King, they lose."

He scrolled through his playlist and hit play on a Jay-Z track, then tossed the phone into the cup holder.

"Difference between me and Jay?" He jabbed a finger at the album cover on the dash. "He said he had 99 problems, and she wasn't one? Must be nice."

The sunglasses acted like armour against the sunlight and against his emotions.

He wasn't ready to talk about last night.

Maybe he never would be.

"Haha. Very funny." I drummed my fingers on my thighs.

To fight or not to fight—the age-old question…

"Whatever," I sighed in defeat, resting my head in my hand. "Let's just get there. I'm really anxious."

Since the scare, I'd been checking my underwear for blood every time I peed. This whole pregnancy felt like walking a tightrope over broken glass, and I was desperate for something—anything—that felt like certainty.

He peered at the satnav. "We're twenty minutes out."

A fogger-laced yawn took hold. Romeo's parting gift from the panic room.

"I'm taking a nap. Wake me five minutes before we arrive. I'll need time to freshen up."

Of course ass-hat hadn't woken me at the time I'd specified. He'd waited until the engine cut in the parking lot before nudging me out of my slumber.

I'd been stewing on it for the past seven or eight minutes while we sat inside the private doctor's facility in the swankiest part of LA.

It was unusually packed with suited businessmen and their even more elegant wives. Most were grouped in throuples, and I could only assume the third wheel was the surrogate.

Too much money had overridden people's sense of purpose, and I doubted there was a stretch mark to be found among any of the mothers in this place—except me.

To make groggy, anxiously irritated matters worse, some overweight air-con contractor, dangling one-legged on a ladder, was still fiddling with the vent on what felt like the hottest day of the year—winter or not —leaving the air thick with body odour and impatience.

His exposed butt crack had hair. His light grey polo clung to his back, a dark sweat patch trailing his spine.

Trying to relax felt like waging war with a toothpick. My nausea didn't stand a chance.

"Are you hot?" I asked Romeo, wafting my cheeks with a discarded leaflet on yeast infections.

All casual, one leg crossed over the other ankle. He shrugged. "Not really. Can't be more than sixty-five in here."

Maybe it was anxiety boiling me like a furnace. Or maybe I was still pissed he hadn't woken me up. Either way, the bead of sweat creeping down the back of my neck had me praying the A/C would kick in and save me.

To distract myself, I played a silent round of Raise the Toe inside my sneakers—a private game I'd been using for years when grounding failed.

I was deep into level five, trying to move my little toe independently, when Romeo leaned in and whispered, "You good, Queen? You kinda look like you need a shit."

The air-con sparked to life, then died again almost instantly. A flicker of hope… followed by a waft of despair.

Yes, he'd whispered it. Pretty sure no one had heard. But that didn't stop me from feeling like every eye in the room had turned my way.

I snapped my head toward him, clutching the hem of my T-shirt. "What do you mean?" I hissed, heat rushing behind my ears. "I'm just sitting here."

He shrugged. "You've had a look on your face the last ten minutes like you're pinchin' a loaf."

Oh God. Was he serious? Had anyone else noticed?

A pulse fluttered in my throat. My feet shifted against the slick tiled floor.

I could've died of embarrassment. I'd been playing Raise the Toe since I was a kid.

The static crackle of the overhead speaker came to life.

"Miss Adams?" a female voice called into the sophisticated hum of the room.

Moments later, a white-coated woman stepped into view, her warm smile framed by casually tucked hands in her jacket pockets—before vanishing back into the shadows of her darkened office.

Instinct kicked in before logic. I looked up, startled.

"Who, me?" I pointed to myself. I hadn't heard that name in what felt like forever.

Romeo's cheek twitched as he shot up from his seat, snapping every single gaze in the room from me to him.

Fresh white sneakers carried the weight of his silent outrage as he stormed toward the reception desk.

By the time I'd taken the four or five strides to her office, my stomach was practically in my mouth. I hovered there, handle biting into my fingers.

"Can you not do that later, Romeo?" I whispered sharply, catching the glare of a suited man who seemed far more interested in me than his newspaper.

I just wanted to see our baby.

He shook his head, a low growl rumbling in his throat like distant thunder.

"No. Now."

His fist clenched too tight as he tapped the glass partition—rattling it in its frame and snapping the receptionist out of her pile of photocopying.

She looked up with a neutral smile. Until she saw him.

Then came the giggles.

"Afternoon, sir. How may I help you?"

She was sweet. Friendly. Everything Romeo hated in a woman.

"She's married now." He pointed at me, then at his diamond wedding band, just in case she wasn't entirely sure. The thick chain around his neck glinted like a dare, offering her more visual stimulation than her clit was ready for.

Her smile widened. That told me everything.

His handsome features had clearly tickled her fancy. At this point, it was boring. He tickled everyone's fancy.

The muted conversation of the wealthy echoed behind us—a soft soundtrack to her flirtation as she propped her chin on steepled fingers and fluttered her lashes.

"Oh! I'm so sorry about the mistake, sir."

Romeo's pecs twitched. His rage seeped into the space between them like invisible threads pulling tight.

"Handle it." He didn't raise his voice. "Now."

One minute she was aroused—the next, on high alert. Flustered, she fumbled for a pen, eyes darting for paper.

"Could you write the correct name down, please, sir?" Her fingers trembled as she slid the page across the desk.

This woman acted like she'd walk over hot coals for him.

If I had the energy, I'd have tapped on her glass myself and told her he wasn't worth it—on account of him being a massive pain in the arse.

But then, as she handed him the pen, it hit me.

This was a normal request for most people. But for Romeo? This was huge.

My heart skipped a beat. Even the low murmur behind us seemed to hush, like the whole room paused to witness his personal growth and the unwavering support of his life coach, Tim, bringing him to this pivotal moment.

My grip loosened, and my hand fell from the handle.

I edged closer.

Should I help? Was he even capable of doing this?

Since he'd executed his wedding vows so beautifully, I'd kept my nose out of his business when it came to learning to read and write. Whatever happened in Tim's company stayed between them. But moments like this reminded me just how little I actually knew about his newfound capabilities.

Before I could ask, Romeo placed the pen to the paper, tongue slipping out between his plush pink lips.

With slow, deliberate strokes, he wrote my married name:

~~Clo e Gia nn ett i.~~

C h l oe Gia nn ett i.

I peeked over at his handiwork with a grin.

Yes, he spelled Chloe wrong the first time, and yes, his writing was a little childlike—but that only made it more precious.

His time with Tim was worth its weight in gold.

"There. Change it right now." He jabbed the paper. "I mean, now. Please."

He thrust it at her and tossed the pen onto the desk, punctuating the moment with cool finality.

Happiness bloomed. He'd remembered to say please. Just one word, but in Romeo's world, it meant everything. It meant he'd listened to me. To all those little reminders about manners.

"Sure. No problem. Thank you," she purred, already scanning the paper like it held the coordinates to his boxers. "I'll get right on it."

Romeo turned on his heel, mission accomplished, and caught me smiling at him.

He smiled back. Then narrowed his eyes.

"What are we smilin' at?" His attention flicked to my breasts, like he was trying to distract me before I could answer.

"I'm just proud of you, is all."

He rolled his eyes. "Woman, please. Don't start with that soppy shit in public."

"Chloe Adams?" The doctor's voice cut through. "Sorry, guys," she added with a light laugh. "I need to hurry you. I'm on a tight schedule."

We stepped into her office, the clinical sting of bleach hitting my nostrils instantly.

My senses were so sharp these days, I could even smell the curl of steam rising from her cheap hospital coffee—cradled in a Best Mommy of the Year mug. One hand on that, the other clutching my hospital notes.

The room was dim, lit only by the bluish glow of the large monitor on the wall. Furniture was minimal. A couple of chairs. A hospital bed dead centre. Nothing about it was familiar.

We hovered in the doorway. I took a dry swallow, clenching the fabric of my shirt between my fingers.

"Please lie down for me and get comfortable," she said, patting the bed and fluffing the standard-issue pillow like that would somehow help.

Romeo took my hand as I lay back gingerly, anticipation coiling tight in my stomach—a feeling that, judging by his grip, mirrored his own.

The faint hum of the monitor mingled with the soft squeak of her sneaker as she shifted with clinical efficiency, sharpening the low whir of chilled air as the filtration unit finally kicked back to life.

My senses clung to the details, desperate for something—anything—to anchor the panic rising in my throat.

"Ahh, the A/C's finally back on. 'Bout gosh darn time. My pregnant ladies need it, right?"

She patted the vent like it had done a job well. "Though I read online, we were in for some snow. Can't see that happening, can you?"

I giggled nervously, fingers tightening around the bedframe.

"Okay, guys." She took a seat on the swivel chair and cranked it up a notch. "Since this is my first time seeing you, let's go over the information I have in my notes."

She flipped a page on her clipboard. Then another. Pen dragging along the lines, she paused. "So, we have Mom and Dad here today?"

We looked at each other, then nodded in unison.

Romeo might've been playing it cool, but his sweaty forehead told a different story.

"Perfect." She turned to the computer screen and began to type. "We have Chloe and Daniele."

Just like that, the room fell silent, the air turning ice cold. So cold, I could've sworn Romeo had frozen solid.

Sheer panic twitched in my toes like my body was gearing up to run.

What should I say? What could I do?

Why the hell did they have *Dan's* name?

I never gave them his name... Did I?

"Oh, um—no. Not Dan!" My voice splintered. "You mean Romero?"

My eyes darted toward Romeo, hoping—praying—he somehow found the mix-up amusing.

He did not. His face was stone.

The ghostly glow of the monitor blackened his eyes, casting a haunting shadow across his features.

This was where he kicked off. I felt it in the sharp intake of his breath. In the sudden halt of his thumb against the back of my hand. The only sign of life from my husband was a single bead of sweat rolling down his temple—and the faint twitch of his eyelid.

He stayed eerily still, lips parting just before the words cut loose in a clipped tone.

"My wife forgets which brother she's married to." He looked at me. "Don't you, Chloe?"

Fuck.

Sinister Romeo. The worst version of him.

I shook my head quickly. "I don't know what happened, Romeo. Honestly—I never made any changes to the record."

He snatched his hand from mine and cracked his knuckles like he was already preparing for revenge.

My palms were damp. The heat of his hand, now gone, was replaced by a hollow chill, like he'd already given up on me.

"Sorry about this, guys." The doctor's tone shifted into damage control as she cranked the lever on her chair another notch as if slightly higher ground might give her the upper hand.

"Let me have a look at these notes. Let's see what's gone on here."

The silence that followed stretched for hours—even if it was less than a minute.

A stuffy voice crackled over the tannoy. Footsteps approached... then faded into the next room.

My throat tightened like I'd swallowed tar.

But amidst the insanity, one question pulsed through the fog: How the hell did Dan's name end up in my file?

"Ahh, here we are." She turned the monitor towards us. "There was an in-person visit made to update the records on October 4th."

Wait—

October 4th?

Why did that date sound familiar?

My hand shot to my mouth.

Romeo and I locked eyes, the realisation slamming into us both like a head on collision.

His court hearing. That's when Dan did it.

The only evidence I'd found while snooping through Dan's nightstand was my hospital letter.

"Your brother is behind this, Romeo. I'm so sorry."

He said nothing.

His shoulders stiffened. Eyes drilled a hole into the wall ahead.

Was he even listening to me? Or already plotting his next victim?

The doctor didn't acknowledge our issue. She didn't need to. The tight press of her lips said it all.

She blinked once. "Err... should I carry on?"

I glared at Romeo, waiting for him to respond.

He didn't.

Even waving my hand in front of his face did nothing to bring him back to the room.

There was no way I'd waited this long to see my baby just to give up now.

My toes uncurled. Sanity slowly returning.

"Yes, please carry on." I smiled tightly at the doctor.

Her shoulders dropped slightly as the room released its held breath.

"Okay, great. I can see here that you went to the emergency room with a bleed?"

I nodded, and Romeo's reflexes kicked in. He took my hand again, his grip tightening in reaction to the traumatic memory.

"All good since?" she asked expectantly.

Her Texan drawl was oddly comforting in such uncomfortable circumstances.

"Yes." I hesitated. "I think so."

"Super." She slipped her pen into the top pocket of her white coat. "All right, let's get right into it, then."

Without wasting a second, she gathered a few supplies from the trolley, gave a bottle a vigorous shake, then popped the lid and squeezed a line of cool gel onto my stomach.

"This'll be cold," she added—after the fact.

She wasn't wrong. It was so cold it instantly made me need to pee. Cold enough to feel like a reality check.

Minutes passed as Romeo and I watched her squint at the screen.

"Okay, first off—here's your baby," she said, sounding a little distracted.

She tilted the monitor back our way. Its pale wash fell across our faces like a spotlight.

And there it was. A grainy black-and-white landscape shifting beneath the wand gliding across my stomach.

For a moment, the fear quietened. Just a moment.

Just long enough to fall in love all over again.

Shaped like a little bean. A tiny leg flinched. One hand almost waved. That was our baby.

The doctor inched closer to the image. Then leaned back. Then closer again.

This was taking too long. Much longer than last time.

Why wasn't she saying anything?

"Okay," she said at last, clicking a few buttons on the keyboard, offering no further information.

Oh God.

I couldn't go through this again.

"What's wrong? What is it?" I gripped Romeo's hand tighter.

The doctor peeled her eyes from the image and glanced down at her notes.

"Hmm. Interesting. This is your first official twelve-week scan, right?"

Panic surged again. The hum of the screen. The whoosh of the air con vibrating in my eardrums.

"Um, well, yes." I swallowed hard.

"That's what I thought." She nodded. "We have you down for twelve weeks, but you're actually measuring twenty. That's around five months pregnant."

... Huh?

My brows pulled together. My chest tightened like armour. "Is that bad?"

"No, not at all. It just means you're further along than we thought—so conception happened a little earlier than originally estimated."

Hope vanished.

Romeo's hand crushed mine as the cogs in his primitive mind began to turn. Pain flared beneath my skin, hot and immediate, as his grip only tightened.

"Ouch, Romeo! You're hurting me!"

He let go like I'd shocked him, but his veins still bulged, anger pulsing beneath the surface.

Suddenly, I was in a state of surreality.

Secrets have a way of warping reality. Carry them long enough, and they become the truth. And somewhere along the way, I'd convinced myself—without question—that Romeo was the father of my baby.

So how the hell was I supposed to explain myself now, when I'd built my entire truth on a lie?

"Are you sure everything's okay, guys?" The doctor's hand was anything but reassuring as it settled gently on my shoulder.

"Um…" I smoothed down my hair. "It's just, the dates seem a little off." My throat closed, the weight of my choices pressing down like concrete.

She offered comfort in her nod, like she'd heard this story before.

"Sometimes, it's just in God's hands, honey." Her smile held no judgement. "Regardless, the baby looks fantastic. The measurements are great. Would you like to find out the gender?"

A jolt of adrenaline zipped through me.

"Wait—we can find that out today?"

I cast a glance at Romeo for his reaction.

His nostrils were flared. His posture, rigid. That eyelid twitch still hadn't abated.

He was pissed. Really pissed.

"Sure we can." She glanced between us, fingers poised on the scanner, ready at my word. "Shall we?"

A complex knot of emotion coiled.

Not only had I just seen our baby. Now I was about to know who they were.

A pretty little girl. Or a handsome boy.

"Yes, please." I whispered, blinking back tears as I silently willed Romeo to acknowledge me.

The doctor turned her attention back to the image. She rolled the mouse, clicked a button, then swivelled to face us again.

With a flicker of excitement in her tone, she peeled off her gloves.

"You ready?" she asked, eyes lit with quiet excitement.

I nodded. Romeo didn't flinch.

The room seemed to dim around us. The screen, now glowing brighter, cast shadows over everything.

A breath caught—suspended between us all.

"You're having a... boy. Congratulations."

A boy? We were having a son?

Elated, I smiled at him, momentarily forgetting our problems, praying for him to say something. He still didn't look at me.

She rolled up the power cord and dropped the supplies into the trolley, already wrapping up.

"Alright, then. We're all done. Your due date is April fifteenth."

My smile fading to black.

"April?" I squeaked.

I really was five months pregnant already?

If anything, it explained the weight gain. But not who my baby's father was.

"Mm-hm. You'll be a mommy earlier than expected. Here's a photo of your boy. We'll see you again in a couple of months."

Specks of light danced across my vision as I sat up, wiping myself down with a paper towel—clumsy, distracted, my mind spinning.

Romeo stood stock still with his chin high, doing a valiant job of pretending I didn't exist.

Then, as if summoned, his fists emerged, bunching at his sides. Each stomp hit the floor like a weapon as he stalked toward the door. He threw it open, a wash of light flooding the room.

I stared, stunned.

He walked away. Didn't wait. Didn't even look back.

He left me.

As I stepped sheepishly back into the open air, the sun's heat scorched the sensitivity of my emotionally heightened skin. The weight of the doctor's office clung to me like fog as I tried—and failed—to rationalise what had just happened.

Nature's breath whispered in my ear as the breeze swept my hair in its rhythm. A taunt. A chill. It prickled my skin as reality snuffed out my hope like someone pulled the plug on my last breath of air.

Not only was I going to be a mum sooner than expected, but now I wasn't the only one who knew Romeo might not be the father. And as if that wasn't enough, Dan's little stunt had made everything so much worse.

Each step toward the parking lot thickened the dread. The ground felt uneven beneath my feet. Heart pounding. Chest tight like a death grip. Any second now, I'd find out if he'd actually left me. And if he had—could I even blame him?

I turned the corner, eyes down, counting my steps.

Four… five… six…

My nose twitched, pupils dilating as the scent of tobacco smoke hit the air.

His broad shoulders framed the sinew of his back, a cigar clamped between his teeth—nearly swallowed whole, like he was inhaling life support.

For a split second, I braced for him to reach for the axe.

But he didn't.

No words. Not even a glance.

He stared off into the distance, nostrils flaring as he inhaled. One hand rested on the car roof, his fingers gripping with restraint.

Sinister Romeo was still in operation.

We stared at each other in silence as I watched him unravel. The hollow of his cheeks with each drag, the way the smoke framed his face, only deepened the pain etched into the dark circles beneath his eyes.

Reaching for the only comfort I had, I toyed with my watch—the links clinking softly as I rolled the loose strap around my wrist. I checked the time like it mattered. Like I was counting down the seconds left to save my marriage.

Running had always been my instinct, but we'd come too far. Whether he was the father or not—I'd keep believing my son belonged to Romeo.

"Please believe me." My voice cracked, the threat of tears burning the back of my eyes. "You are the father."

But he gave me nothing.

He looked down at the dying embers of his cigar. Then re-lit it, taking another drag. Then another.

Thick plumes of smoke curled from the corners of his mouth, wrapping around him like a shield.

I rubbed my arms, hugging myself tighter as I stepped closer into the haze.

The bite of the smoke caught in my throat, stopping me dead—his first line of defence.

"I'm sorry about Dan. I had nothing to do with the records. I swear."

That's when he finally looked at me.

Only for a second.

He tossed the cigar to the ground like the comment meant nothing, grinding the lit end beneath his heel with unnecessary force. Stamping out more than the smoke trail.

"How do you know I'm the dad?"

I didn't. And that was the problem.

But when you're cornered, arms forced out wide, back against the wall, there's only one way out.

My chin trembled. "Are you calling me a liar?" I hissed, masking fear with fury.

Every second I stalled was borrowed time.

Time to make the impossible make sense.

He grit his teeth, eyes flicking to the shadows.

Paparazzi. A horde growing by the minute.

A camera lens clicked. Then another. Flashes strobed like warning lights. They were watching. Waiting for their payday.

"We ain't doin' this out in the open. Get in."

The car door slammed so hard it echoed in my skull. The sun pressed through the windshield like an uninvited guest. Sweat gathered beneath my shirt. The leather stuck to my skin.

Tempers flaring. Breaths shortening.

Still, he didn't push start.

No engine.

No music. No air.

Just the stale silence. And the crushing weight of everything we weren't saying.

I caved first.

"Romeo, you are the father. Please… just believe me." My voice splintered, the lie clawing its way toward the surface.

I reached for his hand.

My fingers barely grazed his before he pulled away like I'd burned him.

Then he turned to face the window. A move I knew too well.

His reflection offered me a glimpse of the sadness in his eyes. The emotion he wouldn't let me see directly.

I touched his shoulder. "Look at me. Please."

He didn't flinch. Didn't give me a single piece of him.

An eternity passed before he finally faced me.

His irises were glossy. Damp with betrayal.

"Is Daniele the father? Did you know all along? Is that why you changed the name?"

Air punched from my lungs. My chest hollowed.

There wasn't a single word I could say to reassure him—or myself.

"What? No! Please, Romeo."

He jerked back like I was poisoned to him, a pulse hammering at the base of his throat. "I don't believe you."

The moment I'd feared for so long was happening.

Right here.

Right now.

I was losing him.

Think, Chloe. Think.

Five months pregnant. Unprotected sex with both Romeo and Dan… around the same time.

But Romeo didn't need to know that.

Did he?

"Believe what you want." My voice trembled. "But I always used protection with clients. Always. No exceptions. The only time I didn't... was at my audition. With you." I lied.

I met his eyes—burning, broken, furious.

"Remember that night?" I panted. Adrenaline igniting the tips of my fingers. "That was five months ago."

He didn't argue.

Not yet.

The heat inside the car had turned unbearable, our fired tempers bringing it to a boil. I cracked the window, desperate for a breeze.

"Dan doesn't matter." I clutched my stomach. "This baby is yours, Romeo. I know he is."

The faint clatter of lens shutters echoed through the gap in the glass.

His jaw ticked. He chewed the inside of his cheek like he needed the sting—like pain was the only thing keeping him grounded. For a second, just a flicker, I thought he might believe me.

But it didn't last.

"Bullshit," he spat, both hands white-knuckling the steering wheel. "That proves nothin', you fuckin' whore."

I flinched.

The glint in his eyes sharpened like a fresh blade.

He leaned in, his lips grazing my cheek—close enough to set the fuse.

"You've fucked Daniele more times than you've fucked me."

The toxic tang of smoke lingered on his breath, curling past my lips like punishment.

"Don't call me a whore." A tear slipped down my cheek, betraying everything I'd fought to hold in. "I'm your wife."

He let out a laugh—harsh and humourless.

"I'm just keepin' it real. One of us has to."

He leaned even closer.

My breath hitched.

His fingers twitched by my face—then reached across me to flick the window switch. The faint hum of glass rising was the last sound before silence fell once more.

Behind the dark tint, the click of cameras faded into shadows again.

"Whore," he muttered, before sinking back in his seat.

It hit like an axe to the chest. No, worse. A slow puncture to the heart.

Just when I thought he'd changed. He hadn't.

I caught sight of my own reflection. Sorrowful. Forlorn. Almost unrecognisable.

Another tear fell hot down my cheek.

"Fuck you, Romeo." I swiped the evidence away. "I slept with you first!"

His arms crossed his chest, muscles twitching with resistance.

"Don't give me that bullshit. Why would I risk catchin' the clap by nuttin' in a whore at an audition? That didn't happen."

His leg jiggled with rage.

He'd lost all sense of himself. Of us.

Outside, a cloud swallowed the sun. Darkness crept through the windshield like a cloak on our fate.

"Excuse me?" My voice pitched higher. "Yes, you did! How dare you sit there and deny it?"

He cracked his own window this time—like the rules didn't apply to him—and lit another cigar. Dragged deep. Exhaled a thick plume of smoke that filled the cabin with contempt.

A tension-fuelled minute passed before he finally eyed me.

I eyed him right back.

His blown pupils locked onto my pinpricks. Then he glanced at my stomach.

"I want a DNA test."

My breath snagged. The smog burned my lungs, his words fusing with the toxic air.

A DNA test? The beginning of the end.

"Fine!" I choked, slicing through the thick wall of his rage. "You can fucking have one!"

I waved a hand, coughing harder, and did the opposite of what he wanted—rolled my window all the way down in protest.

He hadn't smoked in front of me in months. Now it seemed the baby, and I, were no longer his priority.

A smug glint flickered in his eyes as he hit the controls on his door, raising both windows together.

A camera lens nearly caught in the gap, the pap leaning too close.

Then he fired up the engine. The vents spat heat before the air-con took over. He cranked up the radio, drowning out the silence.

Without a word, he shifted into reverse, swung the car from the spot, and skidded off the lot—narrowly avoiding a photographer.

Reckless. Completely unhinged. Dangerous.

Where did we go from here?

How the hell could I rescue this?

The tyres peeled against the tarmac, ripping free like duct tape from skin.

That's when the universe decided to mock me—

First with a familiar jingle drifting through the speakers.

A few guitar chords. Piano keys.

♪ *"Giannetti Haulage—built on trust, driven with care."* ♪

My stomach dropped.

♪ *"Wherever you go… we're already there."* ♪

Romeo's fingers clamped onto the steering wheel.

Then his voice exploded. "You gotta be fuckin' kiddin' me!"

The sound jolted me in my seat.

"I can't catch a fuckin' break with you two, can I!?" His words shook with fury as he slammed his fist into the car's touchscreen.

The first punch clearly wasn't enough to drain his anger, because the second came harder. And the third… even harder still.

I didn't breathe. Didn't move. Just stared as pixels bled and glass shattered like ice.

I lowered the volume with slow fingers, wary of provoking him again —ironic how even Romeo's fists couldn't knock the cheer out of Dan's voice.

His chest heaved. Foot on the gas. Trees blurred past the windows in long, angry streaks.

"Your hand is cut, Romeo. You're bleeding."

He retook the wheel like always. One knuckle was bruised, the other raw. The cream leather wasn't so cream anymore.

Beads of blood slid down his wrist, trailed his forearm, and dripped from his elbow in slow, deliberate beats. Each one tapping the armrest in a menacing rhythm.

He didn't even flinch.

"Romeo… that needs looking at." I softened. "There's probably glass in your skin."

Instinct took over. I reached for his hand, just to check. But he snatched it away, as if my touch was a toxin he didn't want in his bloodstream.

Our entourage followed close behind. Headlights glinted in the rear-view mirror, growing brighter as the SUV closed in.

They must've seen it happen. They had to know something wasn't right.

Already defeated, I let my hands drop to my lap and laced my fingers together—trying to ground myself in the silence he'd weaponised between us.

"I'm sorry Dan humiliated you in front of the doctor. I had no idea he changed the records. But that doesn't change the fact you're having a son."

My voice cracked. My heart cracked harder.

He let the words sit.

Toyed with them like prey.

Then his lip curled.

"You are," he corrected, voice cold as steel. "This ain't nothin' to do with me anymore."

My jaw dropped.

That punch to the console practically echoed in my chest.

"Don't be such a fucking arsehole!"

My chin wobbled as I stared into his eyes.

But they were hollow. Dead.

Lifeless.

A bitter huff slipped from his lips, followed by a smirk that didn't reach his eyes.

"That's me," he sneered. "Don't you fuckin' forget it, whore."

Aside from my erratic breathing and Romeo's deep, nostril-flaring inhales, the silence screamed all the way back to the mansion.

The dips in the road, the judders from potholes—barely noticeable in the Rolls—hit me like bruises I somehow deserved to feel.

As soon as the car's wheels ground to a halt over the loose gravel, I unbuckled my seatbelt and curled my fingers around the chrome of the door handle.

I waited a beat for him to say something.

Do something. Anything.

Nothing.

No word. No arm across my chest. Not even a glance in my direction.

He just sat there, eyes fixed on the valet—who'd already started polishing the hood with a chammy, like it wasn't already gleaming enough. And that was all the confirmation I needed. My husband didn't love me anymore.

His refusal to speak made the decision for me. I shouldered open the car door and stepped out into the humidity.

A single look in my direction could've undone me. But he didn't even give me that.

I paused, the sun burning into my back, giving him one last chance.

Still nothing.

The slam behind me echoed longer than it needed to—but not louder than the ache in my heart as I stormed inside.

"Britney!?" My voice bounced down the hallway like the opening to a cave.

She was somewhere in this house. But where?

"I'm in the living room, Chloe," she called back, cautious.

I tossed my purse on the console and stormed in, breathless and sweaty, to find my best friend chatting with a few of the girls.

"Cash on the table," I barked at the room, eyes locked on Britney. "Then all of you back to work. This isn't social hour."

Her cheeks flushed as she scrambled to her feet. The other girls followed. Except one. Candy.

Reclined on the couch, legs slung over the arm, she slowly unfolded herself and sauntered over, filing her nails as she walked.

Amid the stale mix of cigars and cheap perfume held within the walls, hers was the worst—sickly sweet and offensive as it curled in my sinuses.

"Everything okay, Mrs Giannetti?" she asked, syrupy as ever.

Afternoon light streaked across the room, warm but missing the chill in her intentions completely.

I folded my arms, arching a brow.

Her fake concern crawled over me like cockroaches. Sure, she'd behaved lately since our little run-in—but I was still watching her.

"None of your business," I spat. My patience hung by a thread, dangling between her scissors.

She folded her arms, defiant.

All eyes were on me. The small gathering of women waited for my reaction. One wrong move, and I'd lose their respect.

"Britney." I gripped her wrist. "Come with me. Now."

Like a loyal dog, Britney was at my heel in a blink. Her gentle touch on my arm melted the edge off me just a little.

We turned to leave—but I glanced back once, just in time to catch Candy dragging that file down her talons with smug slowness, like she knew a secret I didn't.

Before I did something I might regret, I stalked out of the room, needing space from pretty much everything.

Britney didn't hesitate, trailing behind me through the kitchen, quiet and obedient, right on my tail.

Out into the garden we went.

Birdsong. Fresh-cut lawn. Peace.

I dropped onto the old wooden bench by the roses, breathing in floral air like it might fix everything.

Britney sat beside me, her sweetness washing away Romeo's sour.

"What's wrong, Chloe?" she asked, her fingers brushing my arm again

—raising the fine hairs, hanging on my every word.

She knew me too well to pretend this was nothing.

"The short version?" I paused. "King thinks the baby isn't his."

Her hand flew to her glossed lips.

"No!" she gasped. "Why?"

A breeze rustled the rosebush beside me, brushing my skin—reminding me this was real.

"The dates are messy. And Dan… changed the name on the paperwork. To his."

Her eyes widened. Fingers tightened on the edge of the seat. "Really?"

I pinched the bridge of my nose and screwed my eyes shut. Romeo's face was right there, waiting behind my lids again. Only this time, he looked angry. Disappointed. Empty.

"He said things I can't un-hear," I whispered. "I don't want to be here right now. Come out with me? I just need space."

She hesitated, glancing back toward the house. Its size stretched like a barrier.

"But I've got clients—"

"Cancel all of them."

Her lashes fluttered. The ghost of a smile curved her lips when she saw I truly meant it. "Okay. If you're Sure."

That was easy enough. We both knew she hated her job.

I stood, brushed myself down, and nodded toward the driveway at the back of the house.

After everything I'd said about not running… this was survival.

The clatter of tools. Sparks from a rotary saw. Then the thick scent of oil and grease settled on our skin like a second layer as we reached the bustling workshop.

And there he was. The man I'd hoped to see. Snake.

Clean shaven, razor sharp buzz cut. Loyal to a fault. My favourite of King's crew.

"Hi, Snake," I hollered over the noise, giving him a small wave.

Wrench still in hand, he took a final drag and flicked his cigarette to the gravel, stubbing it out with his boot.

"Err… hi, Boss." A trail of smoke followed his words. "Everything alright?"

He continued fiddling beneath a raised car—cranking something, tightening bolts.

I smiled at the nostalgia of our situation.

"Gimme the keys." My fingers curled around the command. "To one of his good cars."

His shoulders sagged. The wrench dropped to his side as he emerged from the shadow beneath the wheel.

"Not this again? Boss, please…"

I twitched my fingers, coaxing him. "I don't have time for this. Come on. Keys."

He took his time placing the wrench into the toolbox—just so—with a satisfying clink. Then ran his hands through a rag he somehow kept almost impossibly clean.

"You don't wanna take your own car?" He eyed me sideways. "She's all washed and ready to go."

His suggestion wasn't out of line. There was absolutely no reason I shouldn't take the G-Wagon. Except I wasn't doing this for convenience. I was doing it to piss him off.

To make him come looking for me.

I shook my head. "Keys. To his car. Now."

He glanced up at the sky just as a flock of blackbirds swept overhead in a uniform sheet, blocking the sun and darkening the mood completely. Their shadow lingered longer than it should've—like the light might never come back.

I stood there, unmoving, watching the darkness lift. Then, as if someone had flipped a switch, the sun re-emerged just as he flicked open the key safe beside the shop's shutter and unhooked a set of keys.

With clenched teeth and an even tighter grip, he handed them over.

G1ANETTI1. A satin red McLaren.

Fancy as hell.

Britney hovered at the passenger door, eyes darting between me and

Snake—who looked like he was silently begging her to talk me down.

"Are you sure about this, Chloe?" she asked, chewing the gloss off her plush bottom lip.

Poised at the entry, I gave her *the* look. "Yes. Don't question my judgement. Get in."

We slid into the car together. Spaceship didn't even cut it.

The deep suede bucket seat sucked me in as I stared at the pulsing dashboard.

I flipped down the sun visor like it might reveal a manual.

Nothing.

There had to be a button somewhere—

"Ahh. There it is," I murmured, hovering my finger over a low-profile switch just above the D-N-R control.

Britney clung onto her seatbelt. A silent scream flickered in her eyes.

My finger twitched.

I paused.

One last moment to change my mind.

Then I pressed it.

The flutter of danger in my chest exploded as the engine fired with a sharp, aggressive roar—snapping to life like a woken lion.

The growl echoed through the lot before dropping into a low, rumbling idle that vibrated through the carbon fibre.

This wasn't a car. It was a bloody weapon.

"Ready?" I asked, revving the engine until the vibration danced up my spine.

Britney gulped. Pale. Eyes wide. Thighs clamped shut.

"I guess?" she murmured—barely audible beneath the sound.

Foot down, I tore up the drive as fast as the stones would let me. The air con whipped our hair as the back wheels snaked, dragging us left, then right. Each gear shift launched us forward like a rocket.

"Where are we going?" she called over the noise, nerves tightening her voice—like she half-expected me to kidnap her.

We weaved from side to side, her hair whipping across her face. The intensity of it all reminded me of how I'd felt when King first took me to the cottage. I couldn't help but think of him—of the mess I was running from.

"Honestly? I don't know." My shoulders slumped as the adrenaline drained from my system.

All I knew was that I needed to get away from everything Romeo.

"It'll work out, Chloe. It always does with you two."

Normally, her words would've soothed me, but not today. Because the only thing that could solve this mess was a DNA test—And if that test came back wrong, everything I'd fought so hard to keep would be gone.

We ended up at a rooftop bar on the other side of town and slid into a secluded booth, parasol flaring in the breeze, safely out of sight from paparazzi.

I'd just wrapped my fingers around the stem of a mocktail, cherry garnish bobbing gently, when my phone lit up.

It jolted across the glass tabletop, skittering forward with each tremor like it had something urgent to say.

Romeo's topless, tanned body filled the screen. His smile in the photo... so at odds with our current shitshow.

"You should answer that." Britney sipped her coffee—cupped between both hands like a barrier.

I flipped it face-down with a grimace.

"Nah. Fuck him."

If I couldn't see him, I couldn't hear him. And if I couldn't hear him, he couldn't tell me he didn't love me anymore.

My untouched drink sweated on the table, soaking the coaster—like it felt my anxiety too.

The buzz of nearby conversation blurred into static. A bottle cap popped. A glug of something fizzy poured into a glass.

The phone's vibration seemed to grow louder. My nails dug into my palms, willing me not to answer his call.

Then—stillness.

I stared at the phone like it held the key to our marriage.

Was that really all I was worth to him? Just one lousy phone call?

We sat at our quaint little table for at least an hour, chatting about nothing in particular—girl talk, as if there wasn't a care in the world between us. But of course, it was all pretend.

While I plastered on a fake smile, elbow on the table, chin resting on the back of my hand, my insides were splintered. Utterly broken.

Laughter amongst a few guests over at the bar caught my attention. Even more so when the young server—about my age—seemed to be looking our way.

I leaned across with a girlish giggle.

"That cute guy is so checking you out." I nodded towards the bar.

He'd been polishing the same glass for the last five minutes.

Britney, not-so-subtly, peeked over her shoulder.

"Pretty sure he's looking at you," she whispered back, then caught the straw of her third cocktail with her tongue, taking a long, lazy sip.

Discretion had never been our thing.

The same cute bartender clocked our interest. Tossing his polishing cloth over one shoulder, he strolled over—all swagger and confidence, dark brown eyes flickering with intent.

"Holy shit, he's coming over." I panicked, fussing over my windswept hair.

The hustle and bustle faded to a hush as he closed in.

Eyes—female and male alike—followed that tight little tush, hugged by skinny jeans, as he wove between their tables.

"Can I get you ladies a top-up or anything?" His eyes locked on mine.

Bulge front and centre, he leaned in like he owned the place, whipping the cloth back down to buff the already spotless surface between us.

His slim build suited his boy-next-door looks—cute, with a justified arrogance. And just enough edge to suggest he wasn't a strictly vanilla kind of guy.

Matching the energy between us, I slid the cherry off my mocktail stick with slow, deliberate teeth, offering a sweet smile as I chewed. "No, we're good, thanks."

Up close, he was even more attractive. Fresh cologne. Chiselled jaw.

Freckles dusting the bridge of his nose.

He grinned wide, playful—confirming Britney's suspicions.

"No problem, beautiful. If you need anything, you know where I am." He winked, tossed the cloth over his shoulder again, and strolled off with a swagger and a whistle.

Sheesh.

The sound of other guests crept back in as the mist of bad decisions began to lift. The old me would've flirted more. Might've even invited conversation. But I wasn't that girl anymore.

I shook off the wayward thought and turned my attention back to Britney, who was doing her best to relax through the whole ordeal.

"So anyway. Come on, Brit. How're things with Dan?"

Was I asking to see whether Dan was still a viable back-up?

Probably.

But she didn't need to read the fine print.

The sun dipped lower behind cotton-thick clouds, casting soft light over the rooftop. A gust of wind swept across the parasols, sending them into synchronised motion.

Britney tugged on her jacket, then jabbed her straw into the ice at the bottom of her glass like she'd had enough.

"Are you sure you want to talk about him after he sabotaged your appointment?"

My lips thinned as Dan's handsome face filled my mind—those soft chocolate curls, his piercing green eyes. Us, laughing at the kitchen island. The way he always looked out for me...

Honestly? I wasn't even mad at him.

"Dan and I were together when he did that." I shrugged. "So, come on. Spill."

Britney beamed, her whole face lighting up like she'd just been waiting for permission to gush.

"Oh my God, Chloe. He's so sweet!"

I sighed as his face and my back-up plan faded into the dark.

"You met the mother yet?"

A new image replaced the last—me, wielding an axe, chasing that woman through the woods, hoping she might trip.

Britney took a long sip, visibly more relaxed now. "She's awesome, isn't she?"

I'd just taken a gulp of my drink when that sentence smacked the back of my throat like a brick.

I coughed into my fist, eyes watering, frowning at her through the burn. "She's awesome? Dan's mom?"

She nodded, giving a small, delighted clap. "Yes! Angela's been so welcoming!"

Angela. So that was her name.

Was it bad I didn't even know my own mother-in-law's name until now? No wonder the woman hated me.

"That's great, Britney," I lied through my drink, the chilled liquid of my fourth mocktail sliding down like frozen treacle at the thought of her and Dan thriving.

Making love. Cuddling. Kissing. Touching.

But the reasons, of course, were obvious. Britney was stunning. My best friend turned heads wherever she went. If I could see it, then of course Dan could too. And apparently, so could his family.

I watched her twirl a strand of hair around her finger, her gaze drifting somewhere over my shoulder.

My widening smile pulled her focus.

"What is it?" She reached into her purse for her compact mirror. "Do I have something around my mouth?"

"No." I giggled, watching her fuss. "You're fine. How's work going? Did you take Tonya out with you like I suggested?"

She folded the compact closed with care and slipped it away.

"I hope you don't mind," she hesitated, "but I decided against it. I don't mean to be unkind, but she's not really my type of girl."

We both sniggered in unspoken agreement.

"It's alright—I get it. So… how is work?" I nudged.

Crates clinked behind the bar as someone unloaded bottles. Daytime was slipping toward evening, the hum of customers slowly fading.

Britney sighed and threw back her final drop of courage.

"Well, I had a really creepy guy the other day. Mr X, I think he was called."

I sat up straighter.

"Hold up." I cut her off. "The agency gave you Mr X?"

She nodded, cautious.

My hand found a napkin, locking it in an iron grip.

"What did that creepy son of a bitch do to you, Britney?"

She took a breath, running her own napkin between her fingers—soft, slow.

"I mean, sex-wise, it was mostly just hitting him. It was afterwards that got me worried."

I nodded, white-knuckling the napkin. Twisting it around my fingers into a rope I'd have gladly used around his neck.

"He chased you, didn't he?"

"Yes! How did you know?"

My eyes flicked over my shoulder, half-expecting him to be standing there. "Did the same to me. You won't be seeing him again, so don't worry, okay? You should've told me sooner."

She shrugged. "You've got a lot on your plate. But I will from now on. I promise."

Time ticked by slower than Britney would've liked. Her constant fidgeting, eyes darting to her watch, fingers tapping—too much movement for comfort.

"Should we go back now?" She nodded toward the staff, lifting chairs onto tables.

A tired-looking server swept the floor, dragging the broom halfheartedly along the tiles while her co-worker trailed a mop over the same path. Dust particles spiralled up, blending with the sharp tang of bleach.

My stomach coiled at the thought of facing my problems. But at some point I had to.

I pulled a fifty from my purse and slid it beneath my empty glass. "Come on, let's go."

Truth was—I'd hoped he'd come for me. But ultimately, it was down to me to fix this.

With Nelly's guidance, we'd promised to face our issues head-on. And running off, ignoring his call, wasn't exactly what progress looked like.

The car spun like an off-road daredevil as I tore a sharp left into the driveway, narrowly missing the wrought iron gate—nearly taking out a pap or two in the process.

Loose gravel pinged against the bodywork, clinking like shrapnel as we skidded toward our spot.

Britney clutched the dashboard like she was bracing for impact. But I had everything under control.

Aside from my marriage.

Tommy, already waiting, waved his arms wide like he was guiding a jet on the runway.

We locked eyes through the glass—frozen in a game of chicken. Seconds from collision, my foot struck the brake like a reflex. The car lurched to a violent stop inches from his boots.

He trudged round to my side and tugged on the driver's door handle.

"You good, Boss?" he called over the rumble of the engine.

A quick glance at Britney as I unclipped my seatbelt gave her the nod of approval.

I stepped out into the cool evening air—and straight into Tommy's judgement.

"Yes. I am, thank you." I brushed my T-shirt down with a flick—only then noticing the pink mocktail stain splashed across the front.

Britney closed her door carefully and lingered beside me, unsure, waiting for direction.

A valet was already sliding into the driver's seat, edging the McLaren into position as Snake and his crew swarmed it with polishers and cloths.

I placed a hand on her shoulder. "Thanks for today, Brit. Go do what you want—relax, or whatever."

She studied my face, scanning for any micro-expression that might betray the part of me that didn't want to let her go.

"You sure, Chloe?" Her arms wrapped tightly around herself.

I gave her a small wink and pulled her into a brief hug.

"Yes." I held her a moment longer. "I've got business to attend to."

Cutting the cord like a balloon lost to the wind, I turned on my heel, ready to face the fallout.

Tommy caught my elbow.

Wind stilled. Tension crackled between us as the feel of his rough fingers on my skin made my patience prickle.

I snatched my arm back.

"What is it, Tommy?"

The flex of his hand tipped the boil of my anxiety. He never touched me. Not unless something was seriously wrong.

But he wasn't done there.

The sheen on his bald head gleamed beneath the driveway spotlights. His thin lips. That shift in his breathing.

None of it eased my concern.

He knew something.

"Just wanted to, err..." His pupils bounced left, then right. "Check that you were all right, Boss." He glanced sideways at his crew.

Snake was already polishing the rims, erasing every trace of my rebellion.

"You're acting strange, Tommy, and I don't like it. Where's my husband?"

He buffed the car with his sleeve—but the quick flick of his eyes toward the mansion gave him away.

"Not sure, Boss." He dropped his gaze back to the paintwork.

I stared him down, then pushed past his bulk. If he wasn't going to tell me, I'd find out for myself.

The front door was already open, so I lost the chance at a dramatic entrance.

Feet planted at the bottom of the stairs, I paused with two options. The gym. Or the bedroom.

And something told me this wasn't leg day.

Tommy's presence practically heated my back as he hovered behind me on the climb. Three steps up, my chest tightened, breath snagging halfway. Swollen feet dragged beneath me, one hand on the banister doing most of the work.

By the time I reached the landing, I was bent over, panting. One deep breath in. One out. A second to compose myself.

Only the faint glow from the landing lights spilled across the carpet, casting my shadow against the closed bedroom door. I gave my shirt a final swipe, trying to mask the stain. Looking my best while I saved my marriage was non-negotiable.

The latch clicked as I turned the knob and pushed open the door with a flourish.

Greeted by dark, stale air. I could barely see past my feet on the threshold.

I skimmed the wall for the switch.

Click.

The lights burst on.

My pupils shrank as my eyes adjusted—and in one split second, my world imploded.

There, in our bed, was my husband.

With Candy.

Naked.

Ankles locked. Fists clenched. I squeezed my eyes shut, begging the image to vanish. But when I opened them again, heart thudding, pupils blown, they were still there.

Mingled, sweaty bodies. Her hands gripping his biceps. His torso pressed against hers.

They both stared at me, wide-eyed, mouths open—like a nightmare that had just materialised right in front of them.

"What the fuck is this!?" I slammed the door shut behind me—only for it to ricochet back open on the rebound. "Just when I thought you couldn't be any more of a prick!"

Pain tore through my chest and up my throat. A sharp, metallic tang stung my tongue. My heart thudded so violently it hurt.

Romeo leapt off her instantly—still hard, cock curved as he grabbed his T-shirt and yanked it over his head.

Thick bands of sex clung to the air, suffocating me with the stench of betrayal. Bile rose up, bitter and hot.

The glint in his eye didn't waver when he cast a glance at Candy. "Get out, slut." His voice came low, lethal.

Then he locked eyes with me as he tugged on his shorts draped over the nightstand. Right next to the tipped photo from our wedding day.

Candy hesitated, still sprawled across my bed, thighs parted, lips slightly open—like she'd rather finish what she started, with me watching, before obeying.

Romeo turned his head slowly, fixing her with a glare that could wither stone.

"Now!"

The air shifted. Sex turned to danger. His tone fired a warning shot she couldn't ignore.

Her manicured fingers trembled as she fumbled for her things. A red lace bra dangling from the bedpost, matching panties balled in her fist.

The second I saw that bra, I knew she'd planned this. And to think I gave that bitch a second chance...

She made the mistake of thinking I'd let it slide. Tried to sneak right on out of the room without eye contact.

But I blocked her. Hand splayed on the doorframe, fingers locked like iron. My shoulders squared. I grew an inch taller, towering above her with disgust.

"Leave tonight—and don't come back. You will *never* set foot in this house again." I dragged my gaze down her body. "You pathetic little slut."

I waited long enough to let it sink in—then stepped aside.

She fled, that sickly-sweet perfume of hers trailing behind like rot.

However, I wasn't finished.

Slamming the door successfully shut, loud like a gunshot, I strode into the centre of the room. Spot light on me.

Close enough to feel King's heat. Far enough not to be burned by it.

"Why?" I asked bluntly.

Any more words than that, and I'd break.

His cock, still swollen, was a half-mast betrayal.

Jaw twitching, he toyed with his lighter, eyes pinned to the floor. Then he swallowed and dragged his eyes up, lingering on my body before settling on my stomach.

"That baby ain't mine." He jabbed a finger at me like punctuation.

My hand flew to my belly. My whole body quivered as I cupped the child he'd just denied.

"I'm getting a DNA test. And when it proves you *are* the father..." I looked him dead in the eye. "I want a divorce."

His head snapped up. Irises blazing.

The curtain twitched behind him. Night air hissed through the crack like a sigh of pity slipping in from the dark.

"That don't make fuckin' sense." His fingers tightened around the lighter enough to shatter it.

"No, Romeo—what doesn't make sense is you fucking a whore before even finding out!"

My gullet throbbed. That copper taste bloomed, bitter and raw, as tears streamed down my face.

His eyes shone, glassy as emotion began brimming beneath the surface.

"We ain't gettin' a divorce," he said thickly, like it killed him to say it out loud.

I folded my arms.

The breeze died.

The air turned heavy—sex and deceit still clinging to the walls.

"What, even if the baby isn't yours?" I sneered.

He stepped closer.

"You sayin' it ain't mine?" His voice rose—an invisible pulse of grief vibrating between each word.

Liquor on his breath fanned my cheeks, drenching me in his sadness. I turned my head away, exposing the pulse of my neck.

"That's not what I'm saying. I think we're done here. There's nothing else to say to you."

I made to leave.

The first step had barely landed when he called out.

"Chloe, wait!"

I spun back around, hardly able to see him through my tear-blurred vision.

"I don't know why I did that." He collapsed onto the bed, burying his face in his hands like the gravity of it had just hit him.

"Too little, too late." I pivoted again.

"Please. Don't go." His voice cracked.

I froze mid-stride.

Was he crying?

Hesitantly, I stepped back into enemy territory—closer to him. Instinct more than choice.

I'd never seen his vulnerability laid this bare.

"You've given me no choice, Romeo."

He wiped his nose with the back of his hand. "Why? I didn't give up on you."

Just like that, his words stopped me cold.

"So, this was payback? For me sleeping with Dan?"

He hesitated, rubbing his hands together as if conjuring a lifeline in his palms.

"I guess," he muttered. "I dunno."

"That's real fucking mature."

He raked a hand through his dishevelled curls, chest rising and falling too fast.

"Chloe… Shit." He wiped a trembling hand across his face. "I'll die if that baby ain't mine."

My lungs stalled.

His words, unfiltered and raw, suddenly made a kind of terrible sense. Why? Because that was how I coped too.

Self-sabotage.

Did I care that he'd fucked Candy? Yes. More than I wanted to admit. But this wasn't about her. Not really. This was revenge. Retribution for my mistakes. Punishment because he'd convinced himself Dan was the father.

I lowered myself beside him, clenching the duvet just to stop myself from touching him. Still warm. Still tainted with her stench. "Find someone to do the DNA test... and I'll do it."

At this point, the marriage was broken—represented perfectly by the wedding photo still facedown on the nightstand.

The only shot we had left... was the truth.

His shoulders sagged.

His head dropped into his hands—his whole body hunched.

"I'm sorry, Chloe. My head is fucked up."

I wrapped an arm around his shoulder, my own emotions bruised. His skin, heated by betrayal and shame, almost scalded me.

"This should've been the happiest day of our lives. We're having a baby boy." My voice wavered, tears stinging all over again.

"I know," he whispered—so close, I could almost taste his grief. "The son I always wanted."

He rubbed his temples in slow, deliberate circles.

A shift passed between us. A flicker of hope clung on to the dying flame.

Outside, a distant siren wailed—too far to matter, yet close enough to remind us that life beyond this room still existed. This was real. We had to make it.

I nudged him gently. "The therapist will have a field day with this one."

Tears no longer fell in clean tracks. They clung and itched, drying sticky against my cheeks.

He let out a soft chuckle and placed his hand on my thigh—the same hand now wrapped in a plaster, tiny dots of blood seeping through the gauze.

I knew instantly what he wanted. His way of gluing us back together. Sex.

"Don't touch me like that. Please." I flinched, turning my knees away from him, needing space.

He was my weakness—and right now, I couldn't afford to let my guard down.

"She's just a whore, Chloe. It meant nothin'."

Laughter echoed from the landing. It riled me. Like the house was on his side.

"That's beside the bloody point! When you phoned me earlier, was it to tell me you were sleeping with Candy?"

His eyes, usually fire, looked waterlogged. His brow furrowed, like he couldn't even understand how we got here.

"I had no plan to fuck anyone. You didn't answer my call, so I went for a smoke. She followed me out and… seduced me."

That laughter still echoing now felt like mockery.

I rolled my tongue over my teeth, glaring at him.

"This isn't her fault, Romeo. Take responsibility for your own actions."

He nodded at the floor. "Yeah, I get it. I fucked up."

Now I knew exactly how it felt to be on the receiving end of a fuck-up. And by God, did it hurt.

Exhaustion crept in—heavy and unforgiving. A yawn took hold as I lay flat on the bed, staring up at the ceiling. A witness to it all. No matter how hard I looked, I still couldn't see the bullet hole. But that didn't mean it wasn't there. Just hidden—beneath a fresh layer of paint.

Patched over. Like us.

"Romeo?"

He lay down beside me, his pinkie brushing mine. "Yeah?"

"I get why you did what you did with Candy. But why didn't you have one of the crew follow me when I left?"

Romeo scrunched his nose like he'd caught a whiff of something rotten. If we were hedging bets, I'd say it was Candy's pussy lingering in his moustache.

"What you on about? I sent Tommy."

I threw him the same look right back.

"You must've been too busy with Candy's tits to execute the order. No one followed me. I met him in the driveway when I got back."

He tugged on his necklace like a noose that had just doubled in weight.

"For real?" He swept a glance at the door. "I'll deal with him later."

I bit my thumbnail, processing. Tommy was the least of our concerns.

And with the state Romeo was in, it seemed far more likely he'd forgotten than Tommy had disobeyed.

I watched him fiddle with the blood-soaked dressing.

"How are you gonna explain your hand to Tim?"

He scoffed, flexing the knuckle like the injury was a fake.

"Pretty sure he'd shake my hand when I told him why I did it."

Ugh.

There he went again—outsmarting me with that quick wit.

Well, if he was studying sabotage, I had a PhD in deflection.

"Anyway…" I stretched, lacing my fingers behind my head. "Did you wear a condom, or did you go the whole hog and come inside her just to prove a point?"

He let out a low chuckle, adjusting himself inside his shorts.

"I still got the rubber on now."

The sound of wet latex rolling off the tip sparked a tickle in my throat —escalating to a dry heave when he waved it.

"Don't waft it around like that. What's wrong with you?" I swatted his arm. "Toss it in the bin."

He followed the order, launching it across the room and straight into the trash with casual precision.

Relief that he'd even used one settled me like a cold compress.

I found myself softening.

"When the DNA test proves the baby's yours—we're even. Got it? And I don't want your dick inside anyone else. Ever. Again."

He leaned in, brushing a kiss on my shoulder. One kiss. Then another. His grin widening like he thought he had a shot.

"Yes, Ma'am."

It seemed, in a twisted way, Candy's manipulation had only strengthened us.

"You sure you don't wanna?" He flashed that dangerously sexy smile as he took my chin between his fingers, forcing my gaze.

My eyes dropped to the erection still straining in his shorts—thick, long, pulsing with need.

Now it was my turn to be angry.

"No, I don't wanna." I jerked my chin from his grip. "And that's your punishment. No orgasm. Until at least tomorrow."

He bolted upright, shifting the whole damn bed frame.

"But I always get a nut before bed! You know it helps me sleep."

His arousal fogged his thinking. He eyed my cleavage, sliding a finger beneath my top like that would earn him a pass.

"I don't give a shit." I slapped his hand away and yanked my shirt back into place.

He pouted.

I plotted.

Candy wasn't necessarily a threat to our marriage—but that didn't mean I wanted him thinking about her. That hard-on belonged to me. I needed her erased.

With one arched brow and a flicker of inspiration, I rose to my feet. Slowly, deliberately. I undressed.

T-shirt first—dragged over my head, hitting the floor with a whisper.

Then my bra. I eased down one strap, then the other. Letting it slink down my body in a slow tease.

My nipples stiffened against the raw air, stinging sweetly as my palm swept over them.

Romeo's eyes followed. Up, then down. Circling. His jaw clenched, thighs twitching.

He got up slow, stopping just shy of contact.

Only hours ago, he'd let me walk away. Now he was fighting not to explode.

I hooked my fingers into my panties, dragging them down—nails grazing my thighs.

Like a predator, he tracked my every move, eyes dark, need radiating off him in droves.

His hand twitched near his dick, tilting his hips like that alone might get him off. His arousal swelled, aching to burst.

Smirking at my own performance, I rode his tension like a surfer catching the last wave—then hopped off at the final crest, climbing into bed and leaving him to ebb alone on the shore.

He blinked, white knuckles loosening as the reality of my game set in. Now that hard-on was mine.

I won.

Lost on his own island—no map, no compass—he stood over me with not a single thought beyond the next nut.

I tapped the empty space beside me, feeling a little guilty… but mostly triumphant.

"Come on, big boy. Let's have a cuddle."

A flicker of hope stretched his smile wide. Maybe all wasn't lost. He kicked off his shorts, tossed his T-shirt aside, and dove beneath the covers. The tented sheet betrayed his suffering. He tried to be discreet, rubbing himself through the fabric.

"By cuddle, do you mean…?" His eyes dipped low again.

"I mean cuddle, yes," I teased.

I stifled a giggle, relaxing into the pillow as he curled into me. His head resting on my chest, breath warm against my skin. That familiar coconut scent in his curls reached me. I pressed my nose to his scalp, erasing every last trace of Candy's pussy.

"I didn't think much of that red car of yours," I murmured through a yawn, reaching over to click off the light.

The weight of his arm across my stomach tightened. He kissed the heave of my breast.

"My wife loves to play games with me. Why'd you take my McLaren when you've got your own car?"

I pressing another kiss into his roots, the curls soft against my cheek.

"Because I can." I sniggered.

He laughed, too.

Then silence.

"Chloe?"

The room had fallen dark. Only our voices remained.

"Hmm?"

He brushed a finger over the hump of my pregnancy, stroking back and forth.

"I hope he's mine."

I placed my hand gently on top of his, kissing his head once more. "He is, baby. I know it."

Please God, let him be.

CHAPTER 2

I hadn't ever imagined spending Christmas Eve getting a blood test to prove who my unborn son's father was, but here I was, preparing to do exactly that. Turned out, the same man we'd hired had also handled other medical services in our mansion—abortions among them, along with a list of black-market offerings I didn't care to know about.

Neither one of us needed a reminder of those darker chapters in our relationship.

Still, the one thing this doctor guaranteed was anonymity, and with Romeo's celebrity status, that was non-negotiable. The last thing we could afford right now was the press catching wind of our situation.

Palms sweating, ears ringing, I poured another coffee. Just me and my thoughts in the kitchen, while Romeo buried his emotional wounds in the gym.

I sat for a moment, running my fingertip around the rim of my mug—caught in the same loop as my thoughts.

I stared out the window ahead. Really stared. The trees swayed in the wind, branches waving like fans with front-row seats to the show.

My show. The shit show that was my life.

Old Man Jack, overalls and cap, pottered in his flower beds—hitching his trousers, crouching, hobbling upright. His crew hurried across the grounds with wheelbarrows and pitch forks. The hum of real lives carrying on around our crisis. All of them working to keep their boss happy.

We were never alone. Yet somehow I felt so lonely.

The patio door swept open, ushering in a gust of air that brushed my ankles as the housekeeper bustled in, cleaning trolley in tow.

Silver cropped hair and a genuine smile. She began spritzing her bottle across the counters, misting everything in sight—including my pulse.

My nose twitched. I loved that smell. A warm summer breeze laced with whatever magic she used, but never revealed. I could've sat there all day, just sipping and watching.

"Ma'am." She gave a quick nod, already scrubbing the bottom cabinets.

I had half a mind to ask her to climb inside my skull and scrub my thoughts clean while she was at it.

"Hey, Mrs Knowles." I smiled, lifting my mug so she could wipe away the ring.

Four strokes in, the faint musk of heat and hard work drifted between us.

She tilted her head at the look I was failing to hide. "You alright, sweetie?" she asked. Then paused, scowling at a stain that wouldn't budge before switching tactics on the granite countertop.

"I'm good." I nodded convincingly enough, but the lie stung.

An ache bloomed like a virus. For my baby. For the truth I'd buried so deep, it felt like digging up the dead.

The real truth was: our marriage was on the line. A line I'd been toeing since the day that ring slid onto my finger.

And if this baby wasn't his... It was game over.

"Any plans for the holidays?" she added, now working her way across the tabletop.

My chest huffed silently. "Just the usual. You?"

If only she knew what was really going on.

Her smile broadened. "Seeing my granddaughter for the first time in three years. My daughter emigrated to Australia, you see. Long story, but she's back, and I'm thrilled."

She moved round to the far end of the table.

I gave her a nod as I continued to watch her work. Each sip of my coffee pulled me another second closer.

Our appointment was set for 5:00 PM.

Since Romeo's call to the doctor this morning, I'd gripped my phone so tightly it nearly drew blood.

I clicked the screen awake again. 4:25 PM.

Just over half an hour to go...

The weight of it, the knowledge that this DNA test could change everything, twisted my nausea into something darker. A pressure that clawed at the edge of my sanity.

I hadn't eaten all day. Just coffee and a single whiff of the breakfast Chef made for the girls. That was it. All I could stomach in this haze of disbelief that one test result—positive or negative—could tear my life right down the middle.

Regardless of our situation, Romeo's appetite, on course, remained unaffected, but communication since last night's incident with Candy had been minimal—strained, at best.

Yes, I'd cuddled him in the wake of it. Held him close. Tried to let him touch me without recoiling. Tried to forget. But the image of the two of them tangled in our bedsheets had burned into my mind like a laser. I hadn't slept a wink.

See, I understood why he did it... but that didn't stop the replay in my brain. Over and over. Endlessly on repeat.

And if I was really honest, what hurt the most now was knowing how it felt to be the one betrayed.

The tension in the living room was stifling, pressing in with every passing minute.

Strips of light bled through the big window overlooking the gardens— but even that wasn't enough to brighten our darkness.

Romeo sat on the couch, legs spread, one arm slung over the back, brooding in the shadows with a glass of whiskey in hand, chewing gum with slow, menacing intent.

Uncomfortable and unsure of our connection, I kept my distance— standing by the fireplace like the unlit logs might offer some warmth. Some comfort. But, of course, they were as lifeless as I was.

I breathed deep and exhaled hard, fists trembling at my sides, pulse throbbing at the tips of my fingers, bracing for the knock that didn't come until 5:07 PM.

At the first echo through the hallway, Romeo downed the last of his liquor, slamming the glass onto the table without care. He rose to his feet and gave me a detached nod—as though I was nothing more to him than an inconvenience. Then, adjusting the thick chain around his neck, metal links shifting like armour, he strode out of the room in long, heavy steps.

I followed.

Strong liquor brushed past my ear as we both reached for the front door handle at the same time. I flinched at the contact. He got there first, gripping it tight—as if controlling this one small action might steady everything else spiralling around him.

The house creaked. Floorboards popped. We stood at ground zero. Together, yet anything but.

His fingers twitched on the handle before he pulled open the heavy oak door. Its weight matched only by the weight of what might follow.

Sunlight spilled in around our visitor, his silhouette casting a black mark across an otherwise beautiful winter's day—like the first shadow of a storm. The bearer of what could be bad news.

"Afternoon, Romero. Nice to see you again. It's sure been a while."

Leaves bristled like a melody. Workshop noise fell quiet. He half-smiled at us both, like he already knew the outcome.

Shifting his weight, the sleazebag doctor extended his hairy-backed hand for Romeo to shake. Chubby fingers jutted from a palm so small it looked borrowed from another body. That hand had sealed more crooked deals than I dared imagine.

"S'up, Arnold." Romeo's tone was flat. Hands buried in his pockets, he made no move to reciprocate.

They stood in the doorway, Arnold's gesture still hanging mid-air. The atmosphere thickened—heavy as the LA winter breeze curling into the hall. A fallen leaf skated in, settling on the doormat like even nature knew to wipe its feet first.

"Don't leave a man exposed here, Romero." He flicked his hand again, refusing to drop the act.

Another gust slipped up my dress, fanning the fabric. The cold bit at my bare skin as the door hung open like an invitation to disaster.

Romeo finally caved.

They shook.

Ten more seconds passed before I broke—just as one of the girls sloped into the living room in nothing but a robe, clutching a bucket of popcorn.

"Okay then." I planted a foot on the first step. "Shall we take this upstairs?"

The ceiling bulb hummed in its bid to flood the room with a fierce wash of overexposure. Cheeks flushed, thoughts tangled, I pulled the drapes closed with frayed nerves, sealing us in tighter.

Romeo, unusually quiet, dusted off his old poker table and chair set from the closet. It had been a while since he'd gambled in our bedroom—a boundary I'd once set, never expecting him to honour it. But lately, he was full of surprises. And if I had to choose between card games and sex with Candy, I'd take poker every time.

Arnold gave the room a slow, knowing once-over. Hands clasped behind his back, he strolled to the drinks cabinet, swiping a finger across the polished wood like he was inspecting an old crime scene.

"I tell you what, Romero, the last time I was in here was—"

Romeo snapped open the chair. The crack echoed like a whip, the hinge nearly tearing clean off.

"Take a seat," he cut in, jaw tight, nostrils flaring as he white-knuckled the chair's back.

Not much got past me. This was no exception. He was hiding something.

That was the problem with Romeo. I hated how easily he kept things from me. And knowing Arnold, he'd probably had a hand in at least one of the deaths that had taken place in this room.

With a groan and a wince, the doctor sank into the chair, trusting its worn frame to hold his weight. His ominous black holdall dropped into his lap with a dull thump. Whatever was inside remained to be seen.

He ran a hand through his thinning hair, the sheen on his exposed scalp glistening with sweat. Old Spice and something sterile—like he'd walked straight out of theatre—hit the back of my throat with an aftertaste that didn't leave on the next swallow.

"Alrighty then." He flipped open the bag's leather flap. "Fancy making me a cup of coffee, Romero?"

Too casual. Like time ran by his watch. He tugged the zipper and started rifling through the contents.

I locked eyes on Romeo.

As if the bulb above had swung on its pendant, the light angled straight at him.

In all our time together, I'd never heard anyone speak to him like that. Not even me. Which only raised the question—what the hell did Arnold have over him? Something big, clearly, because my knees nearly buckled when Romeo turned and walked out without a word. No protest. No comeback. He just did as he was told.

Wow.

It didn't take Arnold long to settle in once Romeo closed the door behind him. He tapped the tabletop like a salesman about to pitch a lie.

"So, Chloe, is it? Romeo says we've got a sticky situation that needs ironing out?"

His arrogance grated. My marriage to Romeo had handed me power, an element of control—but right now, with Arnold parked at my husband's poker table, he held the Royal Flush.

I busied myself smoothing the bed linen. Each crease I pressed down ironed out another chink in my armour.

"Yes. We need a DNA test."

I knew he was peeking at my cleavage when I leaned over to plump the pillow. I let him enjoy the view for a moment, then straightened.

Caught red-handed, he switched focus—digging in his bag like it owed him answers.

I shifted around the bed. "You have my husband's email for the results, right?" I asked, knowing full well Romeo didn't have access to email on his phone.

He paused. Head tilted, eyebrows pinching.

"I usually call Romero with sensitive information."

Son of a bitch.

Footsteps pattered down the hallway—light, quick. Too soft to be Romeo's.

My heart thudded.

What else had Arnold called him about in the past?

Sweat slicked my palms. I swept a hand across the sheets one final time.

"Email him this time. Please."

But Arnold smelled blood. Shadows twisted across his face. His grin turned sly as he sniffed once.

"Sure, no problem… but it'll cost ya."

A door across the hall creaked open, then snapped shut. Footsteps moved elsewhere. The house shifted around me. My chances of not getting caught slipped through my fingers.

I locked onto the door. Any second now, it'd open.

Heart pounding, I flicked my gaze back to the blackmailer.

"Fine. How much?"

He leaned back in the chair. The frame groaned, almost as if bracing for what was coming.

He gave one slow blink, hand drifting to his chin.

"An extra thousand oughta do it."

I swallowed the urge to laugh. Clearly, this doctor's qualifications extended beyond medicine. Scamming came naturally to him.

I peered at the door again, nerves flaring—like Santa was coming and I hadn't fallen asleep yet.

There wasn't time to barter or crack the panic room safe.

Rushing to Romeo's nightstand, the charged air cooled the heat in my cheeks. The point of the frame dug into my hip as I yanked open all three drawers, one after the other—cigars, magazines, and other crap posing as cover for a bundle of cash buried at the bottom.

My hands trembled, fingers clumsy, as I made a banker's attempt at counting the total.

Seven hundred. Eight. Nine…

I practically threw the wad at him—straight to the chest, like a threat.

Arnold was a pro. Didn't even flinch. He rolled the bills once, tucked them smoothly into the inside pocket of his blazer, not missing a beat.

Shoulders bobbing, blood pumping, I panted through the final stretch—waiting for confirmation.

It never came.

"So…" I folded my arms. "Can we get the results today, then?"

As if the exchange hadn't happened, he pulled out a tangle of medical equipment, each piece clattering as he laid it in a neat row on the table—like prepping for surgery.

"I mean, it's possible," he murmured, inspecting one of his tools. "But for the test to be fully conclusive, we really need a DNA sample from both potential fathers."

Heavy stomps climbed the staircase, raising every hair on my scalp.

Romeo.

The freshly pressed sheets crinkled again as I perched on the edge of the bed, legs crossed, quickly fixing my hair—hoping he wouldn't notice.

He re-entered, curls dishevelled, lungs working overtime, clutching Arnold's coffee like a butler late to his shift. All that was missing was an apron and a plate of cookies. Domesticated Romeo was someone I could get on board with.

Fresh tobacco from his sneaky cigarette gave him away in an instant.

"What did you just say about Daniele?" Romeo asked, his voice more bite than question.

"I was just saying that the test would be most accurate with a sample—"

"No! No fuckin' chance am I gettin' Daniele over here." He placed the coffee down on the table with the kind of restraint that looked like it hurt. "This shit stays between us."

It seemed there was nothing wrong with Romeo's hearing when it suited…

Arnold raised both hands in placation.

"No sweat, Romero. I'm just saying—especially with sibling DNA in question, having both samples makes the results cleaner."

Romeo pulled out his lighter, flicking it open and shut, as if he hadn't already reacquainted himself with it while waiting on the coffee machine. The metal click filled the silence while we watched Arnold prep his swabs.

"Right, first things first." Arnold scooped up the steaming mug and gave it a sniff test. Lip curl. Head bob. Then came the taste.

"Ooh, this coffee's a little dark for me, Romero… but I guess it'll have to do."

Romeo didn't rise to it. Didn't say a word. But the comment hung in the air like unfinished business.

There was no question—he owed him. Big time.

"Okay, Romero, take a seat." Arnold peeled open the first packet.

Romeo dropped into the opposite chair, both hands braced on the table like this was an interrogation.

"Open wide," Arnold instructed, carefully running the swab along the inside of Romeo's cheek. "Once I've done this, I'll need to draw your wife's blood."

I swallowed past a tethered knot at the thought of a needle slicing through my skin.

Arnold sniffed the air between them.

"Did you just smoke a cigarette?"

Romeo paused mid-swab, mouth still open, shook his head.

Arnold replaced the swab in the vial, screwing the lid on with a disapproving look.

"Okay, next."

Specks of light danced in my vision as I took my seat at the table.

And breathe.

"Alright, Chloe. This rubber band will pinch your arm for a moment, but I won't be long."

Eyes fixed on the wall ahead, one leg bobbing, I retreated to my happy place. Sun. Sea. Sand. Bliss. But no amount of mental escape could stop the storm clouds from creeping in.

Truth was, I hadn't even begun to make plans in case the baby wasn't Romeo's. I couldn't bear the thought.

As I wrestled with it, I caught a glimpse of Romeo—who, judging by the mileage he was clocking pacing laps around our bedroom, looked like he was training for an expedition up Mount Everest.

Arnold's wielding of the needle sent my anxiety into overdrive.

"Ready?" he asked, tightening the tourniquet.

Romeo froze for the pivotal moment.

"Come hold my hand!" I snapped—voice wavering, panic closing in.

It was clear he was waging his own internal battle when he stalked toward me, mumbling under his breath.

Reluctantly, he scooped up the chill of my hand in the heat of his, gripping tight enough to crush bone.

My heart pulsed out of rhythm. Sweat clung to my back.

Arnold tapped the vein. "Sharp scratch." Then leaned closer.

That Old Spice cologne, coiling with the metallic sting of blood, left my pulse fading to a whisper.

I screwed my lids shut.

One Mississippi. Two Mississippi. Three—

Then click. The band released, just in time to spare my fingers from the tingle.

"And you're all done," he said, like that was the hardest part.

In an instant, life rushed back to my fingertips—but it wasn't enough to ease my worry that this might be the beginning of the end.

On the last word, Romeo dropped my hand and steamed toward the bedroom door.

"So, you'll call me tonight with the result?" he asked, propping it open with his foot. He produced a fresh packet of cigarettes from his shorts pocket, taking a moment to choose the next victim.

Arnold glanced over his shoulder at me, that smug little smirk playing on his lips—a silent nod to our secret thousand-dollar agreement.

"I might have the result tonight," he said, weighing it up. "Or, because of that cig you just smoked, most likely tomorrow."

This man had double-crossed Hanna. I had to hope he wouldn't do the same to me.

"You mean on Christmas Day?" I cut in, frowning at the thought.

What kind of doctor worked on Christmas?

"Sure, for the right price." He winked, flashing that greasy charlatan smile.

Ah. Of course.

Arnold zipped up his bag, pulled the flap over, and gave himself a pat-down.

"Alright—keys, wallet, supplies. We're all done here. Just the bill to settle, my old friend."

He held out his hand, fingers curling in invitation.

Patience thinning, the atmosphere fraught, Romeo took flight toward the nightstand, rushing past me close enough to nearly knock me sideways.

He pulled on the handle...

The room drew breath when the squeak of the drawer's runner set my teeth on edge. My stomach clenched as he reached for the same wad of cash. But he froze for a beat, shoulders tensing as he dug beneath the surface.

My eyes darted to Arnold—his flicked straight back at me.

The unspoken secret crackled between us.

Did he notice the roll was a little lighter than before? If he did, who do I blame?

Arnold?

Me?

One of the whores?

Do I plead innocence? Or denial?

Pack my bags now? Or ride it through?

Romeo turned his head slow. Serious.

"How much this time?" he asked, slipping off the rubber band with practised ease.

The walls leaned in to witness the deceit.

"Call it an even three," Arnold replied, cautious.

Romeo counted the total with swift precision before handing over the eye-watering three grand. The rest, he balled up and tossed into the open drawer.

My lungs deflated. Arnold's eyes shifted. The bright light above seemed to simmer.

We'd made it.

After an awkward handshake, we saw Arnold on his way. All three of us lingered at the front door with nothing more to say.

He stepped outside, tugging his long coat tighter as he braced against the wind that rolled into the house like an uninvited guest.

"This weather's something else," he said, blowing into his hands and rubbing them together. "Yesterday, I was sippin' piña coladas on my porch. Mark my words—tonight we'll get the first snow California's seen in a long time."

I offered a cursory smile at the small talk. Romeo gave a single nod.

Branches rustled. Bushes shivered in the stiff breeze.

Arnold gave one last tip of his cap. "Merry Christmas to you both."

Just before disappearing into the night, he turned, waved, and climbed into his classic car.

The engine spluttered to life, its chrome catching the floodlights as he eased down the gravel drive. Two soft beams stretched across the grounds, lighting his way.

I rose onto my tiptoes and watched him leave, as if sheer will could fix what was broken.

He hooted the horn, one last goodbye, as the gates swung closed behind him.

With the echo of the horn still ringing in my chest, I pressed my back to the wall and exhaled a long, weighted breath. The cold surface helped dial down the furnace burning inside me.

Romeo shoved the heavy oak door shut like he meant to wound it, taking with it the last sliver of natural light that had softened the space between us.

He looked at me with unwavering focus—like I was the target. One slow sweep of his eyes, followed by a scratch to his crown, like he'd just drawn back his bow.

"Goin' for a smoke," he muttered, hand already dipping into his pocket.

"See you later."

◆ ◆ ◆

We sat in the kitchen—but at opposite ends of the table. If conversation had tried to exist, it would've died at the centrepiece.

One or two of the girls were likely in the gym. Maybe another in the pool. The house would hum again soon. But for now—just silence.

Cold air. Shrivelled hearts. No appetite for anything more. Silence pressed like frost on glass.

Between toying with a sandwich I couldn't stomach and sipping water I didn't want, I kept glancing his way, hoping to catch his eye. He didn't look up. Just tore off pieces of leftover bread, popping each chunk into his mouth, phone screen reflecting in his pupils.

So much had happened.

The burglary, Dan, Candy. The DNA test.

Now, Christmas Eve, and we were both sick with nerves, wondering if this was it. The end before we'd even begun.

The fridge hummed too loud. The wall clock ticked too slow.

Fairy lights blinked against the window, tapping at the glass like they wanted to come inside.

Our first Christmas Eve together.

God willing, not our last.

I opened my mouth to speak, but soft footsteps tugged my attention. Each one kissed the marble like a song played slow and sweet.

The door cracked open.

"Hey guys," Britney's voice fluttered like a fresh-winged butterfly. "Can I come in?"

For once, her interruption was welcome.

"Of course." I set the sandwich down and brushed crumbs from my lap.

Her perfect smile entered first. Beautiful as ever, in a charcoal coat buttoned to the chin. Her long golden waves fell down her back like she'd walked straight out of a winter photo shoot.

"Hey bestie," she said, peeking into the fridge. "What've you been up to?"

I glanced at Romeo. Still no acknowledgement.

"Um… nothing," I replied, biting down the urge to say more.

She mumbled something and shut the fridge with a nudge of her hip. Grapes in hand, she popped one into her mouth and chewed with puffed cheeks.

"Are you off out, Brit? That jacket's cute."

"Aww, thanks!" She twirled. "I need to grab some last-minute Christmas presents. Can you believe I've not bought Angela anything yet?"

Christmas presents.

Romeo's gift.

Shit.

The realisation struck like a slap.

I looked over at him again. Still scrolling.

"You're going now?" I asked, checking the time. 6:30 PM.

She nodded. "Mm-hm. Wanna come with?"

I tossed my napkin aside, chair legs scraping as I rose.

"I'm going into town with Britney," I announced.

That got Romeo's attention. His gaze lifted. Suspicion sharpened.

"Town?" He stood, eyes darting between us like he'd replaced Britney's name with Dan's.

My defences flew up.

I stepped closer to Britney as he moved in.

"I just need to collect your gift," I said, pulling on my coat. Phone zipped into my bag. Keys rattled in my pocket. "I'll see you later, Romeo."

My voice landed like goodbye.

Maybe it was—if that email came through tonight.

"Hold up." He caught my arm by the door.

The sting of his grip made me flinch. "Yes?"

He eased off.

The scent of too much liquor clung to his clothes as he pulled me closer. His gaze swept down me like he was memorising what might be lost.

"You don't kiss your husband anymore?" His voice softened. Eyes dropped. Hands restless.

There he was. My Romeo. He hadn't given up on me just yet.

◆ ◆ ◆

Britney and I had parted ways three stores ago—right after she insisted on spending over two hundred dollars on an antique vase for Mother Giannetti.

My patience with her had worn sugar-paper thin. Her relentless need to impress a woman unworthy of breathing the same air as me grated on my last nerve.

I pulled my coat tighter. The night drawing in hadn't yet quietened the city's hum. People rushed by; car horns flared; cheerful music spilled from shop doors as the next customer, bags in hand, hurried back to their family. A cruel reminder that, soon enough, I'd know whether I still had a family of my own.

Security kept their distance. Tommy and a couple of his crew idling by the curb in one of the more discreet blacked-out SUVs. I couldn't see them, but I knew they were watching me. Someone cared. At least this time, Romeo had remembered to give the order.

The last few places I'd checked had nothing even remotely suitable for a zillionaire, drug-dealing pimp.

Store after store of the same generic crap—ties, underwear, the usual. What the hell do you buy for the man who has everything?

About a quarter-mile down the row of storefronts, a hot dog cart sizzled with leftover sausages along the sidewalk, charcoaled meat clinging to the frost.

A busker strummed nearby, making his last few bucks before the lights dimmed and shutters rolled down.

I passed a jewellery shop, its soft golden light glowing through the window like an invitation.

Shielding my eyes from the glare, I cupped my hands around my face and leaned in for a closer look.

Amidst the diamonds, watches, and bracelets, something caught my eye dead centre: a silver-plated photo frame.

Simple. Personal. It took me straight back to those sentimental gift ideas I'd saved on Instagram months ago.

A little bell above the door jingled gently as I stepped inside. The bustle of the street fell away like a flipped switch, replaced by a hush that settled instantly over my skin.

Familiar Christmas carols played softly through the speakers—sweet, nostalgic melodies that felt both comforting and cruel. Like I'd stepped into someone else's holiday. One that didn't carry the threat of pure hell.

A beautifully decorated Christmas tree in reds and golds twinkled in the far corner, smiling at me. Offering its own kind of hug. Reed diffusers dotted the space, releasing warm cinnamon that curled softly through the air. The spirit of Christmas, captured like a photograph.

A sharply dressed assistant greeted me from behind a sleek, modern counter. His pinstripe suit was as immaculate as the polished glass surrounding him.

"Good evening, ma'am," he said brightly. "How's this weather, huh? The guy on TV earlier said snow for Christmas. Crazy, right?"

I laughed softly. "I've never seen snow here before."

He nodded. "Once, when I was a kid. Never stuck, though."

With a charming flick of his hand, he brushed down his lapel. "Anyway—welcome to Kelly-Annette's. I'm Christopher, but please, call me Chris. Can I help you with anything today?"

He pressed his palms to the glass, leaning forward with just enough warmth not to overstep.

"The photo frame in the window?" I asked. "Can I take a closer look?"

He sprang into action, sliding around the glass cabinet between us.

"Ooh, sure thing! A present for someone?"

He glided across the floor with the grace of a salsa dancer, an elegant little sashay in his walk.

No more than a minute later, he was back.

"Here we are. Sterling silver, Tiffany & Co." He placed the frame gently in my hands.

I hadn't expected it to be so heavy.

The soft lighting glistened off the polished metal—a little wink at me, like this was the right choice.

"It's a little extra gift for my husband."

Chris folded his arms and leaned into the counter, relaxed. No sales pitch. Just that warm, unforced smile.

"Gorgeous choice. Take a seat by the tree, and I'll gift wrap it for you. There might even be a chocolate or two left hanging on the lower branches—please, help yourself."

The next carol kicked in, bells jingling just enough to bring joy, not enough to be tacky.

I hadn't realised how uncomfortable my feet were—strained by pregnancy and the weight of Arnold's looming email—until I finally took a load off. Twinges flared in new places. A dull ache settled in my back. A throb pulsed through my ankles.

The high-backed, velvet-covered chair welcomed me with a sigh of its own, like it understood my struggles.

I unbuttoned my coat, easing the tightness around my waist, then peeked at the tree's offerings. Sure enough, a solitary foil-wrapped chocolate remained amidst the fairy lights. It looked so lonely, all on its own.

Childlike excitement sparked as I took it. Peeling back the foil, my mouth flooded with saliva. Stomach growling. Now I was hungry.

I'd just popped it in when the now-familiar door chime sang out again.

A curl of chilled wind swept in, disturbing the cinnamon-sweet air with a sharp hint of fumes from outside.

I turned in my seat, rolling the foil into a little ball, expecting another last-minute shopper.

What I didn't expect was to lock eyes with someone tall, dark, and devastatingly familiar.

Daniele Giannetti.

The breeze thickened into a gust that tangled my hair.

My fingers froze mid-roll.

My throat tightened.

Mouth dried like desert heat as I tried to swallow the chocolate now stuck in my teeth.

Even Santa's cheerful *'ho'* in the background suddenly sounded sinister.

What the hell was he doing here?

Chris did a double take, abandoning the wrapping mid-task and dropping his scissors to shake Dan's hand.

"Mr Giannetti! Great to see you again!"

A regular. Figures.

I made a poor effort to fix my hair discreetly as Dan strolled past me—all Tom Ford citrus freshness—stealing one final glance without a word.

There I was, sat by the tree, eating chocolate like I was waiting for the elves at the grotto. I may as well have had it smeared all over my damn mouth.

His lean, muscular frame moved effortlessly through the boutique, already mapped out, quiet confidence rolling off him like he was home.

That foil ball rolled fast between my fingers, knees pressing together, heart in my mouth as my hopes faded—that he might acknowledge me.

Say something. Anything, really.

But he didn't.

Oh.

Dressed in dark, fitted jeans, a turtleneck sweater, and a trench coat, he looked like he didn't even have to think about it. But that was nothing new.

He moved along the glass cabinets, a stray coil of chocolate curl falling across his forehead as he leaned closer to inspect the display.

Chris said something funny. Dan laughed.

That laugh, like a warm cuddle, brushed over my skin, igniting something deep inside me.

He stepped toward the next cabinet, closer now. Close enough that I could smell that citrus cologne all over again.

He was always summer, no matter the time of year.

My knees pressed tighter.

Eventually, he pointed at a piece that caught his eye.

"That bracelet looks good. I'll take it."

Christopher folded over the same cabinet, both of them admiring the selection.

"Very nice, sir." He slipped on a pair of white cotton gloves and presented the bracelet in the palm of his hand. "A gift for a lucky lady?"

My teeth clenched so hard I nearly cracked a molar.

Why was I so mad about this? Was I jealous?

He was supposed to be my backup. My plan B. If Romeo wasn't the father... would Dan still take me back?

Would he choose Britney over me?

Dan's voice was exactly how I remembered—silky smooth, with a hint of gravel.

"A little something for the girlfriend," he said, pulling out his platinum AMEX and tapping it against the counter.

Girlfriend. And he didn't mean me.

"Super. That'll be an even fourteen thousand dollars plus tax."

The tree lights blinked beside me, too cheerful for this moment.

Fourteen grand? On Britney?

My knees dropped apart. The air vanished from my lungs.

A tremble of adrenaline loosened my grip on the foil ball. It practically jumped from my hand and rolled away, landing by Dan's foot with finality.

Dan's role in my escape plan was slipping through my fingers like dry sand. If Romeo wasn't the father... what the hell was I going to do now?

Before I could fully process it, Dan turned to leave, gift bag in hand. The foil glinted beneath the lights like a marker.

He stopped—as if he'd spotted gold. Then knelt right in front of me.

A proposal?

My heart pounded like a drum. Pupils blown.

I swallowed.

"Here," he said softly. "You dropped your..."

He frowned, lifting it to eye level. "Little ball?"

Those eyes—so green, so warm. That hair, soft as hazelnut whip. His smile. The way his fingers brushed mine when he handed me that stupid chocolate wrapper. Electrically charged. A bristle of connection.

I wanted to cry. And I had no idea why.

"Thanks," I murmured, just as Santa Claus Is Coming to Town blared through the speakers—Loud and brash to match my pulse.

His smile tipped into a grin as he rose to his feet, sighing, like he'd needed that connection too.

"Merry Christmas, Chloe." He fastened the top button of his coat and turned to leave.

I opened my mouth to respond, but the words caught in my throat.

He took a step away from me.

"Merry Christmas, Dan," I managed—just as the song faded. My words rang out like a declaration, hitting his back like a snow ball.

He turned one last time and paused.

Tree lights twinkled in those emerald eyes.

He nodded at me, then at Chris, and the bell above the door jingled as he stepped out, taking his extortionately priced gift for a woman he barely knew… along with my hopes.

The static air simmered as the door swung shut, blowing out the last of the fire.

Then he was gone.

A slow burn crawled up the back of my throat as I tried to swallow down the rising sting.

Was there still something between us? Or was I losing it? After all the times he'd refused to give up on me… would he be there when it counted?

The track moved on. A beautiful carol played through the speakers. Holy. Traditional. Silent Night.

Christopher let out a hum of appreciation as Dan strolled past the window, his silhouette fading into the winter's night.

The mood seemed restored.

"Sorry about that, ma'am. I'll get right on with wrapping your frame. Total is three hundred dollars."

My cheeks flushed with embarrassment at my paltry little purchase—especially compared to the filthy rich man who'd just graced the store like

Richard Gere.

But that wasn't what had me spiralling. It was the feelings swelling in my chest after seeing Dan.

I felt jealousy twist in my gut over his generosity toward Britney. But was it even about her?

Or was it just a reminder that Dan, in all his thoughtfulness, kindness, generosity… held the missing pieces to Romeo's puzzle? And now, out of nowhere, I found Dan attractive again? Was it just because he'd moved on—while I'd been secretly clinging to the idea that I could always run back to him if things went to hell?

I couldn't ignore the gnawing thought that the truth about my baby's paternity was still hours away. Was it a coincidence that my body chose now to react to Dan? Or was it trying to tell me something—some deep, primal instinct I hadn't dared admit? Was the lack of intimacy with Romeo part of it? Did I already know my baby was Dan's?

The tissue paper crinkled as Chris wrapped the gift. He said something too quiet to hear above the white noise roaring in my head.

"Ma'am?"

My fingers tightened around my purse. My eyes widened, darting side to side as I pictured the email. The result.

How was I supposed to process all this—push down the anxiety-fuelled knot in my stomach that whispered I'd known the answer all along?

Could Dan really be the father?

"Ma'am? Hello?"

The noise lifted. I blinked away the panic.

My eyes refocused on the concerned, half-smiling face in front of me.

"Oh. Yes. Sorry." I gave a small, apologetic giggle, handing over Romeo's card.

"Ahh, welcome back to the room. You totally zoned out." Chris chuckled, holding out the wrapped frame.

"All set. That'll be just the three hundred."

By the time I left the jewellery store, I'd made a promise to myself—anything to do with Daniele Giannetti would be locked in a box within my subconscious, labelled: DO NOT OPEN UNDER ANY CIRCUMSTANCES.

That was—unless the result said otherwise…

The hotdog vendor had long since packed away. The busker was gone too, leaving behind nothing but a faint memory and a scattering of copper coins. Aside from that, the streets were getting pretty empty.

I checked my watch. 8:47 PM. Ten minutes until the final store I needed to visit would be closing.

I gestured ten fingers toward the SUV. The headlights flashed once in approval.

No time to waste.

The place was empty, the mezzanine level lights switched off by the time I reached the counter at the sports store with just minutes to spare, a little sweaty and lightheaded.

The buzz of the overhead lighting seemed sharper now the chatter of customers had faded.

A young man, blond, tattooed, with a few piercings, popped up from behind the counter with a pricing gun and a wish for his day to be done. He clicked the trigger. It spat another sticker onto a box.

"Evening, Mrs Giannetti. You here to collect the customs?"

The slight quiver in his voice betrayed his nerves. He, like all the other staff in the store, knew exactly who I was. And who this gift was for.

"Yes, please." I nodded enthusiastically, unzipping my coat, wafting the fabric to cool myself down. "I'm excited to see what you've done."

The vacuum hummed across the carpet. A scrape of hangers echoed as staff made final adjustments to the rails, preparing to close.

Five minutes later, he returned—box in hand and a tight smile on his face. He looked a little paler than before.

"Are you ready?" he asked, lifting the lid with caution.

Butterflies fluttered in my stomach as I peeled back the packing paper. The faint scent of rubber soles and fresh cardboard lingered in the air.

My breath hitched. A masterpiece sat nestled inside the box, now trembling slightly in the designer's unsteady hands. My vision had come alive.

"Oh, wow. These are perfect." I shot him a look of amazement, grinning as I took in the work of art he'd created for my husband.

I ran my fingertips softly along the hand-painted lettering. Felt every stitch. Every brushstroke. Exactly what I'd envisioned.

Outlandish to some, I'd ordered a pair of Nike Air Force Ones customised using gold paint. This particular style of shoe meant a lot to both of us—Romeo had worn them on our wedding day. The second time.

"Did I get it right?" he asked, narrowing his eyes. His grip on the box was so tight, the sides had begun to bow under the pressure.

The vacuum silenced. Another light flicked off. Distant footsteps of a staff member tapped across the floorboards.

I peered up at him through my lashes. "Yes. I love them. Thank you."

His shoulders slumped. Eyes closing with relief.

"Thank God. I'll take them to the register for you."

"You needn't have worried about taking on this commission. You nailed it," I said, as he printed the paperwork.

"I mean... it's Romero Giannetti, ain't it?" He shrugged. No further explanation needed. "You still cool to leave me reviews on my socials?"

"Of course." I passed him my credit card.

Figures had been mentioned loosely, but I didn't care how much he charged for something that said what I wanted to say better than I could.

He slid the receipt across the counter, hands still a little unsteady—just as the penultimate light went out.

"All set. Merry Christmas, Mrs Giannetti."

I smiled. "Merry Christmas."

The frost in the air bit at my heels as I closed the big oak door behind me, shutting out the wind with it.

I'd made it home just in time, arriving as the girls were heading out to visit their families for the holidays.

Romeo and I had argued about this at least a hundred times. I wanted the house to ourselves for Christmas, and the more he resisted, the more stubborn I became. But beyond craving alone time, I also wanted to give the girls a chance at something close to normality. A family Christmas of their own.

Unlike his brother, Romeo didn't have much capacity for empathy, but I'd managed to talk him around eventually.

Suitcase wheels rolled along the stone, coming toward me at an excited speed.

The first to leave was one of my favourites.

"Thank you again for this, Chloe," Lala said, pressing a grateful kiss to my cheek. "I haven't seen my mom in months." Long brown hair kissed the base of her spine. All wrapped up like a gift herself in a fluffy long coat—her mom was about to be thrilled.

"You're welcome." I smiled, squeezing her hand. "I want you to enjoy yourself."

As the crowd gathered in the hallway, chatter hummed around me.

I cleared my throat.

Silence.

"Listen up, ladies. Go have fun. I'll see you back here on the 27th. Got it?"

Old habits had me using my authoritative voice, but these days, I didn't need to.

That chilly bite snapped right back the moment the door swept open. I waited at the threshold as each of them left, handing them an envelope.

"Each of you gets a bonus. You work hard, and I appreciate you."

Eyes glittered as grateful hands took their parting gift. A conveyor belt of happy women.

Britney was the last to leave—and the first girl I opened my arms to. I pulled her in. Sweet perfume. Sweeter nature.

"Take care, Brit. Enjoy it. Are you still staying at Dan's?"

Her hold on me slackened.

"Err, yeah." She peeled back. "Is that okay?"

My pulse quickened.

"Of course!" I forced a smile, eyes darting. "I'll see you soon."

She tilted her suitcase and rolled it along the drive like I was seeing the future. In a few hours, that could be me—though I'd be leaving this place for good.

My heart sank all over again.

Romeo was waiting at the far end of the hall, hands in his pockets as he oversaw their departure.

As soon as the latch clicked on the last whore, he strode forward. The central heating kicked up a gear in a bid to warm the cold. But I was frozen to the spot, watching him closely.

Watched his hands for fists. Watched his gun for the draw. Those eyes, a window to his soul, showed no mercy.

To my surprise, he stopped close enough for the whiskey on his breath to flare my nostrils, pulling me into his body, closing around me in a hug. The strength of the embrace, my chest to his, felt more like a promise than a connection. Almost as if he wasn't yet ready to let me go.

"Our income has doubled since you took over the whores," he murmured into my hair.

My fingers curled tighter around the gift bags, the weight of the handle suddenly digging into the crease of my fingers.

I tilted my head with a shy smile. "Really?"

My success wasn't a complete surprise. I had the upper hand, knowing how they thought, what they went through daily. They respected me for that.

He ruled with fear. I ruled with compassion.

His arms fell away, neck craning, a crooked finger hovering over the bag's opening.

"What you got in there, then?"

The softness in his tone, paired with the tightening sinew of his muscles, showed the depth of his battle.

I took a small step back, moving the bags behind my back.

"You'll have to wait and see. I'm going upstairs to wrap them. You wait down here, okay?"

His sad smile through the slits in the banister was all the confirmation I needed. As the distance grew between us, so did the weight of unspoken emotions. He was hurting just as much as I was.

I took the stairs two at a time, my mirrored smile fading as I fed off the panic curling in my stomach. If the result came back that Romeo wasn't the father, would I need to leave the house immediately? Would he give me a grace period to find somewhere? Or would he throw me out without another word?

My biggest concern was that I already knew the answer. If I was lucky enough to escape death, he'd throw me out before I even had a chance to put my shoes on.

Did I have a backup plan? I thought I did. Dan. But that ship had sailed. Or had it? Should I call him? Drop a hint?

Don't be stupid, Chloe.

Now was not the time for making reckless decisions fuelled by crazy ideas.

Gifts toppled in their bags beside me. The drapes parted just enough for a small twinkle of Christmas lights to shine through the gap, right on the spot on the carpet I'd chosen to sit. Waves of light and dark kissed the pile, hung in the balance as if it couldn't quite make up its mind which way my fate lay.

The longer I sat there, the shadow seemed to stretch wider, flickering on the ceiling like it was ready to engulf the room in flames. As if the spark had yet to ignite. The real disaster hadn't yet begun.

I sat there, legs folded beneath me, refreshing Romeo's emails like my life depended on it. Each swipe of my finger across the screen grew slippier. More clumsy. Fraught. My foot had gone to sleep—not that I cared. The tingling made everything feel more real. Like I wasn't actually floating.

Drenched under my arms, beads of sweat forming at my temples, this was a living hell. Bile rose. I swallowed it back down. I had no time to vomit now.

I kept replaying the same scene in my mind—me opening that email, Romeo not being the father. The air in the room seemed to starve my lungs more than replenish them.

Overcome with urgency, I scrambled to my feet, threw open the closet, and pulled out a holdall. In a flurry, I tossed in a couple of dresses, underwear, a pair of sneakers. The more I added, the harder I panicked.

A whistle of wind tapped those lights against the glass harder. Nature's knock. But was it a comfort—or a warning?

If the baby wasn't Romeo's, I had no choice. I would need to leave quietly. Slip out before he even noticed I was gone.

It was the safest way. The only way. What I'd do after that—I wasn't sure. But I was pretty certain it would involve a knock on Dan's door.

◆ ◆ ◆

10:30 PM landed.
I swiped to refresh.
The little loading circle spun—longer this time.
His inbox pinged.
The sound rang loud enough to echo round the room.
My heart lurched.
Air—gone.
Throat so tight I felt the strangle.
I scrambled to my feet, stars flooding my vision.
My whole hands juddered as I stared at the sender's name.

From: Dr Arnold Jacobs <arnoldlab@medencrypted.com>

The letters shifted almost out of order.
Blinking at me. Threatening to show me the result too soon.
This was it.
Fuck.
Oh God.
My hand shot to my mouth.
Bile surged again, burning the back of my throat.
The twinkle of light turned into a taunt of shame.
I scrolled to the next line.

Subject: DNA Test Results Re. Mr and Mrs Romero Giannetti

My eyes scanned the dense email, running up and down the paragraphs of scientific jargon—accuracy percentages and whatnot—but I scrolled straight to the bottom.

Then paused.

I stood closer to the window. The words *Statement of Results* pulsed under the twinkle—one second lit with hope, the next shadowed by dread.

Statement of Results:

The alleged father cannot be excluded as the biological father of the unborn child.

Based on the analysis of STR loci, the probability of paternity is 99.999999999%.

To conclude, Romero Giannetti is the biological father.

The vice cinching the room snapped. The walls expanded. The air—breathable again.

There it was, in black and white. Bold lettering.

Romeo was my baby's father.

My knees buckled, and I dropped to the floor as adrenaline surged through my entire body. I drew in too much breath. Drank in too much relief. I teetered on the verge of blacking out.

That's when I saw the holdall. Unzipped. Half-packed. No longer needed. A remnant of my worst fear—now obsolete.

Romeo was the father.

Elated. Relieved. Saved. My hands shook as I forwarded the email straight to the printer. A physical copy would complete my gifts. The hum of energy dancing through my body had me wanting to float again. But this time, on cloud nine.

Was this real?

I pinched myself three times—each one harder than the last. I was still here, still in shock. The cloud was still right beneath my feet, holding strong.

Romeo was the father.

I snuck out of the unused office across the hall, the email now printed and trembling in my grasp. With the house empty, not a single girl saw me creep back into the bedroom. Not a single person yet knew just how I felt.

A stray tear fell as I folded the result and slipped it inside a Christmas card, along with words I knew he could now read.

The baby scan photo was the final piece. I slid it into the silver frame, its shine catching the light like proof that hope had been restored. I wrapped it alongside his new sneakers.

Gifts wrapped and stacked, I kicked the holdall back into the closet before carrying the bundle downstairs.

Loaded with love, I placed them beneath the tree the girls had dressed together, each ornament a mark of growing trust between them.

Sounds from the kitchen—the cheer of Chef's music, the sizzle of his pans. Each sound, each sensation, belonged to me.

Romeo was the father.

This was my home.

I stepped back, admiring the scene. A quiet room filled with a festive glow. Just me and my son, waiting to share the day with the man sitting in the other room.

Tomorrow morning would be the best Christmas I'd ever had.

I found Romeo in the kitchen, knocking back the remains of a whiskey while he waited for our dinner to be served. Judging by the flush on his cheeks, it wasn't his first glass of the hour.

The room was thick with steam—warm from the oven, damp from the pans—condensation dripping down the window in thick beads against the freeze outside. But the tension between us somehow made my skin cold.

Caught in the joy of my news, my smile had stuck a little too brightly when he looked up. So at odds with the atmosphere, he frowned as he swallowed another mouthful.

"What took you so long?" He eyed me with unease, scanning me up and down like my body might carry a confession.

"Oh, nothing," I replied with a knowing smile, sliding into the seat beside him at the beautifully presented table.

The vision of the tree, the gifts, him tearing open the wrapping—I couldn't have been any happier.

He gave me a sideways glance. The chill he was creating turned Baltic.

"You're supposed to sit at the other end," he murmured, gesturing with his glass toward the place setting opposite.

His thumb rubbed the rim of his tumbler, eyes unfocused.

Oh—

"You don't want me to sit with you?"

The glinting centrepiece suddenly felt mocking. Gold napkin rings fit for a banquet seemed like a practical joke.

He chuckled into his refilled glass. "My mother's right about somethin'. You make a shitty Italian wife."

The sound of bubbling pans and clinking dishes filled the silence. A carving knife dragged across the sharpener.

The joy inside me began to slip away. I clung to it for dear life.

"Are you saying you wish I was Italian?"

His knee bounced beneath the table.

He shook his head, exhaling hard.

"No, Chloe. I was jokin'."

I see—

"Oh. Okay." My voice vanished into the background.

The knife made its final pass before the carving began. It was ready. So was I.

I wasn't sure if he'd meant it. Nor did I understand how a wife's seat at the table could define her worth. Embarrassed, I scraped my chair back louder than I meant to, then did as I was told, taking my place what felt like half a mile away.

All I could see now was his silhouette, thrown against the backdrop of his gilded throne.

He cracked his neck.

A sense of foreboding settled over me as I sipped my orange juice, fingertips tapping the tabletop while we waited for our meal—the one far too late to be eating, in my opinion, but I'd agreed to it, anyway. His family's tradition, apparently. A full stomach to welcome in Christmas.

At one point, I half-expected the kitchen doors to swing open and a couple of strippers to appear. But they didn't.

"Are they not eating too?" I nodded toward Tommy and Snake, still posted at the kitchen island. Locked, loaded, ever ready.

"They'll eat after us," Romeo said, holding out his tumbler for another refill.

My eyes followed the glass as the server poured right up to the rim. "You're going heavy on the liquor tonight?"

With narrowed eyes, he accepted the pour and brought it straight to his lips.

"Are you the alcohol cops?" He glowered, swirling the liquid before throwing it back in one.

I suppose, under the circumstances, he had every right to take the edge off.

His Adam's apple bobbed with a hard gulp.

Suddenly, it felt cruel to make him wait.

"Never mind," I relented.

The atmosphere between us was shifting fast, and not in the right direction.

◆ ◆ ◆

"Jeez, I can't eat another bite." I wiped my mouth with a beautifully folded cotton napkin and dropped it onto the empty plate.

My already swollen belly was fit to burst after the incredible meal Chef had served us. A traditional British Christmas dinner—turkey, pigs in blankets, thick, rich gravy—the whole nine yards. Exactly what I'd needed.

Romeo, of course, had finished long before me. And while I ate, he kept drinking. The strain between us had deepened with every silent minute. I couldn't take much more.

"Right, that's it. Change of plan. I want to give you one of your gifts now." I shoved my chair back, hands slapping the table and clinking the cutlery.

Then I marched the length of the room, reaching for his hand. He didn't resist—dropped an uncoordinated hand into mine like I was his saviour. The sway in his step dragged me sideways with him.

"Does it involve this?" he mumbled, groping my arse with little strength. He was nearing his limit.

I swatted his hand away. "No. Come with me."

I led him into the living room, where the Christmas tree waited —glowing with warmth and welcome. Fairy lights bounced off glass baubles, brushing everything with magic. The pine scent fought off the kitchen smells. There was no place for those in here. This room was Christmas. And beneath the tree, his gifts waited.

My hands trembled slightly as I passed him the card, our fingertips brushing—igniting that familiar spark.

The howl of the wind faded. Frost feathered waiting patterns across the windowpanes.

"Open this first," I said, my voice thick with emotion.

His lips thinned as he took the envelope, a wary look sobering his eyes.

"And then this," I added, handing him the small box containing the frame.

Tucking the box under his arm, he peeled open the envelope with fingers trembling more than he'd admit.

Inside, a Christmas card. The illustration showed a big family gathered around an oval table—a glimpse of the future he longed for. Children. Belonging. Joy.

I held my breath as he flipped it open.

"What is this?" He frowned, his fingers curling tighter around the paper.

"Read it."

He exhaled slowly, unsteadily, then followed each word carefully, his finger tracing the lines.

By the final word, he looked up at me. His eyes were alight.

The whiskey coil snapped clean.

A single tear gathered in the corner of his eye.

His breath caught.

"I'm the dad?" The words barely made it out—testing the meaning aloud.

I nodded, grinning, placing my hand over his heart. It thudded beneath my palm.

"Yes, Romeo. You're having a son."

Him reading the result for himself was its own kind of gift. A testament to how far he'd come with Tim.

That knowledge fuelled him. He tore open the box and pulled out the photo frame, fingers gripping the silver edge.

"I love my daddy," he whispered, his voice catching on the words etched into the metal, his tone heavy with awe.

Shivers rippled over my skin. I watched as the most powerful man in America crumbled—undone by a truth he'd barely let himself believe.

His bottom lip quivered. A second tear fell.

"That's my son? Our son?"

His thumb traced the outline of the scan photo nestled inside the frame.

Peace. That's what I saw. Not triumph. Not power. Just peace.

He glanced up at me, the tear trailing a jagged path through his stubble.

The rawness of it rocked me.

Last night, he'd been close to crying. But this—this was something more.

He wiped his eyes with his forearm, sniffing.

"Don't look at me. Shit."

I ignored the shame, gently pulling his hand away from his face. "Merry Christmas, Romeo. I love you."

The connection bloomed like a match strike.

I kissed him, soft and slow, our lips salt-streaked from tears. My arms wrapped tightly around him. His grip was tighter still. Our tongues entwined.

The heavens didn't open with tears of rain. They snowed.

A thick white sheet fell beyond the window—flurries descending like blessings, ticking softly against the glass.

"Let me love you, Chloe." His voice broke against my neck, breath hot, words urgent. "Let me take what's mine."

I knew exactly what he meant. Romeo sought comfort in the only way he knew how—and tonight, I was more than willing to give it.

My pulse fluttered. "Take me, Romeo." I kissed him back. "I love you so much."

We'd just shared a life-changing moment, but for him, love had always been most real when it was raw and physical. He didn't just need connection. He needed me.

And outside, the snow fell so thick it cloaked the earth in magic.

Without hesitation, he dropped his shorts.

But neither of us expected what we saw.

His cock hung soft. Lifeless.

My heart clenched as he cupped himself, shielding his body in shame. His worst fear—here, now, when everything was supposed to be perfect.

"Why is my dick broken?" He sank into the couch, gripping his hair like he could pull the answer free. "What the fuck!?" His chest heaved, panic swallowing his breath.

The panic in his eyes mirrored the moment he'd opened the card. That flash of vulnerability replaced by dread.

He gripped himself, tugging in frustration—desperation mounting with every second his body failed him.

I laid my hand over his, gently stilling his frantic movements. "Shh. It's okay, Romeo. Let me take care of you."

When a man's mind starts drowning, it takes more than words to pull him back. I sank to my knees, hands trailing over his tense thighs before parting them. I settled between. Then, I cradled his balls in my palm, rolling them slowly, warmth against warmth, teasing every inch except where he ached most. If I could bring him back without even touching his cock, I'd have him completely.

A long, shuddering breath escaped his lips. His shoulders eased. His head slumped back. His body softened beneath my touch, surrendering to something deeper.

But it wasn't enough.

His cock began to swell—then faded again.

My tongue swept along the base of his shaft, slow and deliberate. My fingers curled around him, coaxing, stroking, urging him to respond. I kissed the tip, massaging with my tongue, revelling in the way he twitched beneath my mouth.

"You sexy little slut. Fuck, I've missed this."

His hand tangled in my hair, gripping tight at the roots.

The tree lights glowed beside us, their soft halo casting warmth over the tension in his face.

This wasn't just desire. It was need.

I kept going—lips, tongue, devotion.

But again, I felt it. So did he.

His arousal faded like smoke.

A tortured groan tore from his chest. Raw and broken. His jaw locked. His whole body braced. And it crushed me. Because I knew why.

I looked up at him.

His chest rose and fell in uneven heaves, his eyes glassy.

"Don't stop, Chloe. Please." Another tear rolled down, catching in the rough stubble of his jaw. *"Don't give up on me."*

My grip on him tightened. Giving up on the father of my child was never an option. Not now. Not ever.

If there was ever a time, my past life could serve me. It was now.

My focus sharpened.

Jasmin returned.

The girl who once seduced strangers for survival. The woman who now used that power to save the man she loved.

I peered up at him through my lashes, a wicked smile curving across my lips. "Do you want it dirty, Romeo?"

The snowfall thickened outside like my promise.

His breath hitched.

Condensation trickled down the glass, the air thick with lust. And just like that—he was back.

"Fuck—yeah," he rasped. "Always."

Flashes of our beginning consumed me. The lust. The chaos. The hunger of two damaged souls clawing their way back to one another. Somewhere along the way, Romeo had softened for me. But not now.

Now, he needed to feel us again. And I was going to pull him back from the edge. Remind him who the fuck we were.

"If you want it dirty, you know what to do." I teased, aiming his dick at my bare chest.

Memories of one of our first times in his bed flickered through my thoughts, reigniting a spark of desire.

His urine had claimed me then. I wanted him to claim me that way now.

"And when you're done, I want you to come in my mouth."

His entire body tensed—every muscle, every sinew coiled like a loaded gun. His dick thickened in my grip, pulsing against my tongue as I coaxed him closer to the edge.

Fuelled by my fire, his fingers regained their strength, gripping my hair tighter until it stung.

"Oh, fuck! Holy shit, Chloe."

A wicked smile played on my lips as I dragged my tongue across the swollen head, watching, waiting—ready to take whatever he gave me.

His body reacted instantly. His breath faltered. His erection hardened to full, aching thickness in my grasp.

He loved to call me a filthy slut, but the truth was, no one was filthier than him.

I bit my bottom lip, then flicked my teasing tongue relentlessly, tasting the salt of his arousal.

"Claim me," I panted, stepping out of my dress. "Take me. I'm yours."

Fortunately for Romeo, the five whiskeys in his system ensured he wasn't short on ammunition.

Within moments, the warm golden liquid seeped from the tip in controlled bursts. His cock twitched with each release. He groaned with relief.

Clenched tight in my hand, his offering washed over me—a golden shower fit for a queen. His groans of appreciation sent a pulse of need straight between my legs, spurring me on. My lips wrapped tightly around him, sucking until his thighs clenched beneath my fingers.

"I can't wait any longer, Queen. I gotta come for you."

His jaw tensed. His eyes squeezed shut as he let himself get lost in the pleasure I gave him.

"Finish in my mouth, baby." I cranked him like a water pump. "Come for me."

The world around us faded to nothing.

Just us. This moment.

But unexpectedly, his hand gripped mine, halting my movements.

The beads of moisture dripping down the window stilled.

"No," he murmured. "I want to make love to you."

Oh—

Before I could react, he gathered me into his arms and laid me where he'd been, the cushions still warm with the lingering heat of his arousal. His touch turned reverent. He caressed my body, cradling my swollen, aching breasts.

He made quick work of my bra, then hooked his fingers into the waistband of my panties, sliding them down my legs.

Now we were bare. Nothing between us.

Romeo positioned himself above me, his dick resting hot and heavy against my body. His breaths came in deep, uneven pulls as he stared into my eyes—searching for something.

I threaded my fingers through his dark curls, bringing his face to mine until our lips met. The kiss was soft, unhurried. Yet laced with a hunger that threatened to consume us both. His tongue teased mine as we unravelled beneath each other's connection.

"You've got me so fuckin' hard. I might come as soon as I put it in. You good with that?"

It only made me crave him more.

I panted into his open mouth. "I don't care. Take me. Please."

With a guttural groan, he pushed his red-hot length inside me, stretching my swollen, delicate flesh. My insides clenched in response. A sharp pleasure coiling tight, ready to snap.

His pace was controlled—rolling his hips in slow, sensual movements, savouring every inch of me.

In and out. Deeper. Hotter.

Fuck—I was close.

"I can feel your pussy tighten for me, Chloe. We'll come together. You ready?"

My eyes closed, head tilted against the cushion. I moaned. The warmth spread through my core, pooling between my thighs, swelling into something uncontrollable.

"Romeo..." I writhed in ecstasy. Clutching his arms. Gripping his hair. "Romeo, I'm coming!"

A snowflake melted against the glass—melting just like us as our universes collided. A shared climax that shattered every barrier between us. A release of all the wrongs we had done to each other—now made right.

Kisses tangled. Breath mingled. Our hearts became one.

Romeo was the father.

We lay there so still. His weight pressed down, but he wasn't heavy.

I kissed the bruised knuckle of his wounded hand, my heart too full.

"It really snowed." I beamed. "Look."

He peered over his shoulder. Inches of snow covered the grounds.

"Holy shit, it did. First Christmas with snow. First Christmas with you."

Emotion swelled in the back of my throat.

"Same," I whispered.

Neither of us true Americans. Different stories, yet the same ending.

"I love you so much, Romeo."

There were no tears now. Just the white blanket beyond the window to cushion our fall.

Our home. Our tree. Our son. Us.

He smiled, brushing a strand of hair from my face.

"Not as much as I love you. *Ti amo*."

CHAPTER 3

"Queen, wake up." Romeo's whisper stirred the air just before he flipped the switch, bathing the room in soft light.

My eyes fluttered open, met by the handsome smile of a man already out of bed.

"Hmm?" I yawned, stretching. "Did I sleep in?"

Grey sweatpants, socks, and a crisp white T-shirt clung to his tall, defined frame—his trademark. There was something about the way those sweats hugged the outline of his cock that never failed to make me smile. Especially after last night's lovemaking had reaffirmed that every inch of him was mine.

He glanced at his phone screen, the glow highlighting the perfect angles of his face.

"Nah, it's a quarter past seven. Merry Christmas, baby."

Crouching beside me, he leaned in for a kiss. Yesterday's lingering sex and heavy drinking clung to his skin, softened only by the fresh mint on his tongue.

Clearly, he'd been awake for hours.

Reluctantly, I kissed him back, too aware of my morning breath. Not that he cared. He deepened the connection the moment our lips met, one hand slipping round the back of my head as his mouth parted mine.

I broke away first, yawning again, my eyes refusing to stay open.

"Ugh, it's too early," I mumbled, throwing an arm over my face, shielding myself from the glare of the bedside lamp.

He leapt up like a coiled spring. "I don't give a shit. I wanna give you your gift."

A gift, he says? That got me peeking.

With the lack of presents under the tree, I'd started to wonder if he'd even bothered at all.

After our latest rollercoaster of emotions, this morning's energy stood in stark contrast, almost electric. I giggled beneath my forearm, last night replaying in my mind in Ultra HD.

"If the gift is your dick." I smirked, licking my lips. "Then I already had it."

I waited for his laugh, but it didn't come.

He peeled my arm away.

The light flooded back with a vengeance.

"What do you mean, you already had it? This ain't a one-time deal, Queen. This dick's for life."

His hand found its usual resting place—cupping his favourite toy. A move he always made to protect his masculinity.

When I stole another glance, his face had fallen, like he'd just found out that first prize was a pair of socks. It never took much to bruise my husband's fragile ego.

His grip help firm, tugging at the crotch of his sweats. But I was feeling playful. I couldn't help but keep it going.

"Don't remember 'dick for life' being in our vows?" I sniggered.

It was about time we had some fun. But he stayed stone-faced, unamused. Dick jokes never did land well with him.

"Okay, fine," I relented, sitting up. "I'm up."

The urgency in his twitching made me smile. He crossed to the window and tossed open the blackout drapes.

"Check that out," he said, placing both hands on the glass. The heat of his breath clouded the cold pane.

The entire lot—acres of property—was blanketed in snow. Thick, untouched, glistening like something out of a fairytale.

My breath caught. "Oh my God, it's beautiful!"

A chill crept up my calves as I padded barefoot to stand beside him. Unusually cold for LA, my toes curled against the cold settled deep in the carpet fibres.

He pulled me into a hug, pressing a kiss to the top of my head. "Ain't it somethin'?"

"It's incredible." I placed my hand on his chest, peering up at him.

He smiled, eyes still fixed on the scene below.

The crew was light, most on rotation, spending a day or two with family for the holidays. Old Man Jack was shovelling a clean path past a car that Tommy and Snake were prepping for something. The rhythmic, muffled scrape of his shovel through the snow sounded almost comforting.

The men worked in sync, circling cloths over the car's bodywork—methodical, focused—while thick engine fumes curled upward, drifting over the rooftops.

Mesmerised by the magic of it all, I watched as closely as Romeo did.

"What are they doing down there?" I asked, wrapping my arms around his waist. His body radiated heat, warming the near-frozen air leaking through the window frame.

"Their job." His lips twitched at the corners. "Get dressed, woman. I wanna give you your gift now!"

He swatted my arse. I yelped, dodging the second swing, laughing as I darted into the bathroom.

He tugged on his sneakers, zipped up his hooded jacket, spritzed on some cologne, then leaned against the doorframe with one foot propped, arms crossed like his patience was running thin. That woody leather scent drifted between us, making my mouth water and my focus waver.

He tapped his watch with a playful smirk. "Three minutes."

In front of the mirror, I ran a brush through my hair, watching him in the reflection as he watched me. His excitement lit up the whole room.

I reached for the toothpaste. "Are we going somewhere?"

Cold porcelain pressed into my thighs as I spat out the minty foam and scrubbed again.

"You'll see." He checked the time again. "You've got one minute."

Snake wiped the chammy over the hood one last time. Tommy gave all four tyres the kick test as we climbed into the freshly prepped car.

From the pre-heated cabin, we had a panoramic view of the white scene outside—trees feathered in snow, branches heavy as if they'd been iced like a cake. Christmas had well and truly arrived.

As usual, Romeo adjusted his gun and ran his hands around the steering wheel. This one had that rearing stallion stamped in the centre—theatrical, just like its owner. Leather seats, brand new, like they'd never been sat in. Yellow stitching that felt more like a warning than a welcome. This car wasn't one of my favourites, but he sure seemed into it.

We'd barely been seated a minute before he lifted his hips and rummaged in the front of his sweatpants.

"Here, put this on," he said, handing me a balled-up piece of fabric.

I unfolded it cautiously, lip curled. "What the hell is this?"

His sexy smile sent a wave of heat between my legs.

"Blindfold. Put it on. It's a surprise."

Now, one thing he didn't know about me—I hated surprises. Especially the blindfolded kind.

"Do I have to?" I brought the fabric to my nose, giving it a cautious sniff just to make sure it was clean. He'd pulled it from the depths of somewhere, and nut sweat wasn't on my list of smells today.

"Yeah." He nodded with boyish enthusiasm. "Please."

Well… when he asked that nicely, I couldn't refuse.

With his help, I secured the cover over my eyes, and we eventually set off. Our security detail trailing behind.

Every sound was sharper without sight. Snow crunched beneath the tyres, metal chains grinding through the slush with every turn. Frost snapped at the windshield like it wanted in.

My anxiety ticked higher. The fabric itched at my brows and tickled the bridge of my nose.

"Where are we going?" I asked, peeling it up for a sneaky glance.

He nudged my hand away gently. "Keep it on, Chloe. You'll see in a minute." He eased it back down.

I slumped into the seat. Darkness again—just a sliver of light peeking through the edge.

"Can you turn the heat up a little?" I asked, blindly reaching for the console buttons.

A heard a soft click.

"Sure. Seventy degrees?"

I tilted my head left, then right, giving it my deepest consideration. "Hmm... let's do seventy-one."

He huffed, that quiet kind of exhale that always meant he was shaking his head. Well, if he didn't end this torture soon, I'd be the one shaking mine. And probably a whole lot more.

I toyed with my wedding ring, spinning it idly on my finger—my fallback when raising my toe failed to settle my nerves.

"So, is it a good surprise or...?" I giggled, hoping he'd cave.

He turned up the music from our shared playlist. One of our favourites: 50 Cent.

"I ain't tellin' you shit."

While I sang along to an old classic, Romeo just listened. I heard the steady rhythm of his finger tapping the steering wheel. Tension eased a little.

When the last note faded, I traced the seat's stitching like braille, counting the threads like seconds, hoping it might make time pass quicker.

My chest fluttered as another wave of adrenaline spiked. "Can I guess what the surprise is?"

The hairs on my arms tingled. I could've sworn he'd touched me. I flinched.

He chuckled—playful.

"You can guess," he said, lowering the volume. "But I still ain't tellin' you."

Hmm. I had a few ideas about what I hoped it might be...

"Is it a hot air balloon ride?"

"No."

"A helicopter ride?"

"No."

"A plane—?"

"No! What is it with you and bein' in the fuckin' sky all of a sudden?"

The darkness only seemed to darken. I twirled my thumbs in my lap, thoughts circling the same theme. Truth was, I'd been waiting for him to bring up the topic of our honeymoon—or lack of one. Maybe I was hoping he was finally whisking me away.

Actually, not maybe. Definitely.

I raised a hand to my eyes again.

"Leave it on, Chloe. Don't ruin this."

Like a sulky child, I dropped my hand, shoving it between my closed thighs alongside the other. My eyes darted side to side, searching for any scrap of light I might cling to.

"You know, it's kinda hard to talk to you when I can't see you."

The car slowed to a crawl.

Traffic lights?

"Pfft. Yeah, right. You sure as hell don't seem to be havin' a problem to me."

Even without seeing him, I knew he was smiling.

If I angled just right, I could make out a speck of colour in the gap between the fabric and my nose. Focusing on it helped lower my heart rate—just a little.

"Romeo, let's be real. If I didn't talk, there'd be no talking."

He didn't respond right away, but I wasn't about to let the opportunity slide.

"So, anyway," I pushed on, "I just thought maybe we were going to the airport… since we still haven't had our honeymoon."

Silence. Only the engine's roar as we picked up speed again.

Had he fallen asleep at the wheel? Had a seizure? Ejected himself through the sunroof?

"Hello? Did you hear me?" I waved my arm blindly until it landed on his rigid thigh.

He sighed. Nails against scalp, he was tugging on his hair.

"I guess with all the shit we've had goin' on, it slipped my mind."

Hmm.

Burglaries, infidelity, and DNA tests were bound to take his focus…

"It's okay." I smiled in what I hoped was his direction. "Can we look at some options this weekend?"

His finger tapped again. This time distracted.

"Sure."

Yes!

Elated heat bloomed in my cheeks, lifting my mood.

"So, how much longer?" I gripped my seatbelt, restless.

But he didn't answer.

The silence stretched. Now it was becoming irritating.

"Romeo, I asked how long?"

Still nothing.

My pulse kicked up a notch, imagination working overtime. I threw up the blindfold, heart thudding now, to find him watching the rear-view mirror.

"What's wrong?" I ripped it fully off, tightening my hold on the seatbelt as the air turned thick.

His Adam's apple bobbed.

"Nothin'," he muttered, facing forward again. Fingers digging into the leather like he was cutting off the car's blood supply.

A second later, the centre console lit up.

Romeo pushed the gas, the car lurching forward—our backs pressed into the seats.

Incoming Call: Tommy

"Boss," Tommy's voice snapped through the speaker. "We got a ghost."

Romeo's eyes locked on the mirror again.

"Black Dodge?"

A crackle of white noise.

"Yes, Boss."

His leg bounced softly. Thinking. Then his eyes narrowed, flicking to my stomach. "What crew do we got on board?"

"Five men, Boss."

Romeo hovered his thumb over the end-call button.

"Handle it." He cut the line.

Instinctively, I cradled my bump.

The beautifully scenic view as we tore down the freeway felt completely at odds with the pressure building inside the car.

"What's going on?" I asked, peering over my shoulder. The SUV was no longer directly behind us.

Romeo stayed silent. Jaw tight.

I kept my eyes locked on the threat. "Romeo, please. I'm freaking out!"

He blinked slowly. Took a deep inhale. Shoulders eased.

"It's Christmas Day, and I'm tryin' to surprise you." His tone stayed calm. "We ain't doin' this now."

Whether it was Christmas Day, Sunday, or somebody's bloody bar mitzvah, he was always going to find an excuse to keep things from me.

"Constantly keeping secrets makes it worse, Romeo. Please. I need to know if we're in danger."

He held out his pinkie finger.

I didn't take it.

"Chloe, please. I'm beggin' you to drop it."

His finger twitched. Waiting.

"Why can't you just tell me?"

Distressed, though trying to hide it, he cast me a sideways glance.

"You've proved every single fuckin' time that you can't handle this shit. You're pregnant. Let me deal with it."

My throat tightened.

After everything we'd been through, I wanted a normal Christmas just as much as he did.

I sighed, shoulders slumping in surrender. We weren't arguing anymore, but this wasn't done either.

"I want to talk about this later, okay?" I hovered my little finger beside his.

He didn't hesitate—just hooked his pinkie around mine and gave it a gentle squeeze. "Deal."

Fifteen minutes later, he turned down a familiar narrow dirt track, the car tilting on its suspension as it navigated the uneven terrain, pulling up outside a little stone structure nestled beneath a canopy of tall oak trees—Nonna's cottage.

"Welcome back, Queen."

The car rolled to a stop, and he cut the engine.

His forced smile said it all. He was trying his absolute best not to let the ghost ruin things. But it lingered, thick and quiet between us.

The clock on the dash flicked a digit. We sat in silence, waiting impatiently for the crew.

Snowfall had long since settled. Not a flake nor a flurry. Just stillness, with the odd bristle of leaves shaking off the cold.

I was desperate to push him further on what had just happened, but I guess now wasn't really the time.

Not a minute too soon, the distant hum of engines grew louder. Headlights pierced the fog, dipping and rising along the path we'd just taken. Tyres carved fresh lines through untouched snow, the crunch echoing around us. Shadows emerged as our security team rolled in, slowing to a stop right beside us.

Wasting no time, Romeo pulled up the hood of his jacket, bracing against the cold. Soft, dark curls fell over his forehead as he threw open the driver's door and came around the hood to my side.

He opened the passenger door, frost seeping in around us as he offered me his hand.

Our eyes met.

"Forget all that shit, yeah?" His breath bloomed between us, hanging like mist before vanishing. The hood shaded his face, but I still saw the sharp set of his jaw. The swell in his pupils was menacing. If you didn't know him.

I nodded. "I'll try."

His skin—warm, almost too warm against the winter air—enveloped mine as I placed my hand in his.

He helped me out, and I drank in the view ahead, deliberately ignoring the Giannetti S.W.A.T. team sweeping the area behind us.

The exterior of the property had been completely renovated. Gorgeous. Simply beautiful.

Once weather-worn walls now gleamed in a crisp whitewash, fresh and timeless. Even the maintenance had been meticulously carried out.

Guttering fixed, weeds removed, not a cobweb in sight. A striking red front door with a gold knocker completed the storybook aesthetic—the perfect biscuit-tin cottage.

"Wow," I whispered, taking it all in.

My mind flitted back to the first time I'd seen it. Now, it looked exactly as I'd imagined it would after receiving some much-needed love and care.

"If you like this," he said, looking up at it with me, "wait until you see inside."

We stood side by side on the new porch. Solid beneath our feet. Not a creak or a moan to be heard.

Our crew, deep in their security sweep, flickered like ghosts of a different kind around the perimeter.

Romeo paused a beat, composing himself, eyes fixed on the door. Then pulled a single key from his pocket and turned it in the lock.

The newly restored wooden door clicked open smoothly, revealing a beautiful transformation inside.

Solid wood floors, now varnished in a warm light oak, stretched from front to back. Modern fixtures and fittings blended seamlessly with its rustic charm.

The cottage was small, but what it lacked in size, it made up for in character. It reminded me of the history-soaked homes back in England.

"Just... wow," I said again, completely awestruck. "Romeo, I love it."

A gentle nudge in my lower back encouraged me further into the room.

The scent of fresh pine from a small, beautifully decorated Christmas tree stirred something in me. Like maybe, just maybe, the Christmas spirit wasn't completely lost. A veil of fairy lights hummed softly around the room in long drapes, complementing the refurbished fireplace—already prepared, with fresh logs ready to light. Brand new leather. New wood. Heavy, fancy curtains tied back like a statement. The warmth inside wrapped around me like a gift all of its own.

He lowered his hood, and the smell of his cologne hit me all over again.

"Take a look upstairs," he whispered against my cheek, hand steady at my back as he guided me toward the railing.

Even the staircase had been replaced with solid oak—no expense spared.

"Upstairs?" I stared up the narrow steps, pulse ticking as I imagined what was waiting for me.

"Yeah. Go on." His lips curved into the crook of my neck. His enthusiasm was palpable, radiating off him in waves.

The anticipation between us was intoxicating, intensifying with every stride. The first step melted into the second, my knees growing weaker as excitement bloomed. His body, right behind mine, pressed close—cocooning me, holding me in a moment that felt just for us.

When we reached the top, he extended his arm across my chest. My breath hitched. The cocoon hardened a little.

"Hold up. Let me go first." He brushed past me, stepping ahead to open the master bedroom door.

His fingers pressed against it, then he turned, eyes sparkling.

"Aight, this is our first Christmas. I wanted to make it special. Ready?"

I chewed my lip, then nodded.

He pushed the door. It swung fluidly with a whisper over the carpet, revealing a beautifully refurbished bedroom covered in a sea of red rose petals.

Sweetness clung to the air. New furniture met old wooden beams in a perfect display of quiet harmony.

My hand flew to my mouth, speechless.

A four-poster bed dominated the room, with a dressed window just behind the headboard, letting in enough light that filtered through the forest canopy.

The wind tapped gently at the glass, ice collecting on the pane—but the room was too warm, too filled with love, to let winter in.

He pointed toward the floral display. "These are from our garden. I know they mean a lot to you."

I slouched in the doorway, taking it all in.

How on earth had Romeo pulled this off? Or, more to the point—who had helped him?

"This…" I cleared my throat. "This is so thoughtful."

That's when I noticed it. A rectangular, gift-wrapped box placed neatly in the centre of the bed.

Romeo caught my eye as I spotted it. He folded his arms around me, resting his chin on top of my head.

"Go on. Open it." He encouraged me forward until my knees met the frame.

Rolling up the sleeves of my sweater, I crawled onto the bed. The mattress dipped softly beneath my knees, its plushness pulling me deeper as I aimed for feline elegance—but landed somewhere closer to warthog.

For some reason, my hand trembled as I reached for the box. Sitting cross-legged amidst the new sheets, I held it in both hands. It weighed almost nothing, and yet everything.

I took a breath, casting a glance at Romeo before peeling back the wrapping cautiously.

"Come on, Queen. Shit." He shifted nearby, unzipping his jacket fully open.

With my thumb and forefinger, I lifted the lid.

My jaw dropped.

Inside the smooth-hinged box sat a platinum bracelet lined with high-carat diamonds.

Speechless, in awe, I ran my fingers over the polished line of precious stones. Lifting the delicate metal to the light, I tilted it just enough to let the diamonds catch and scatter their radiance across the room.

"It's beautiful, Romeo. Thank you."

It was a wild coincidence that both brothers had picked the same Christmas gift. Was it wrong of me to wonder if my bracelet cost more than fourteen grand? Probably. But with the sheer brilliance of the stones embedded in mine, there was no doubt—I had to be the winner.

His fingers unclenched, falling to his sides, relief softening his smile as he stepped closer.

My husband, my child's father, had really done this for me. For us.

I handed the delicate chain to my king. "Here. Help me put it on."

Romeo took it carefully, the fragility of it at odds with his masculine fingers as he handled it as delicately as he could. Then he fastened it securely around my wrist.

I rotated my arm, admiring it from every angle. It might've been too soon to dig for the value, but I couldn't help myself.

"I wonder how much this arm is worth?"

Had to be at least five figures—hell, maybe even six.

I was already stacking quite the collection: my wedding band, my engagement ring, his grandmother's diamond—one that stayed firmly on my finger, much to his mother's revulsion.

Romeo's gaze lingered on my hand, his grin laced with adoration. He shrugged off his jacket, tossing it onto the accent chair in the corner.

"Priceless," he murmured, pressing a slow, reverent kiss to my knuckles.

While he played it frustratingly coy about the value of my newest treasure, I lay back against the pillow and let the atmosphere settle over me like a blanket.

"This cottage is amazing, Romeo. I love it."

His eyes flitted to my stomach again. "I love *you*."

Those three words leaving his lips washed over my entire body like sunlight breaking through a storm.

Unable to contain my emotions, I leapt up and wrapped my arms around his neck, my legs around his waist, pulling his nose between my cleavage.

That frosty air kept tapping, but there was no place for cold in here.

"I love you, too," I whispered into his hair. Coconut, honey, heaven nestled in his roots.

He squeezed me a little closer. The air shifted, intensified. Heat bloomed against my stomach as he hardened.

"Hold up," he said, voice muffled against my flushed skin. The warmth of his breath feathered over my chest.

He held me at arm's length. "Before you get my dick solid, I have somethin' else to show you."

He set me down gently, just enough to not ruin the moment. Keeping the contact, he gripped my hand, guiding me across the small hallway to the only other bedroom opposite.

The door glided open, revealing its new identity.

A nursery.

Snow framed the small window like a picture. Elegant yet cosy, the room had been dressed in neutral tones of cream and warm brown. It was refined, timeless—exactly to my taste.

My hands clutched at the flutter in my chest, my breath catching in my throat. "This is—"

His body instantly grew rigid. The sizzling connection between us shorted.

"It's what?" His shoulders rose, fingers gripping the doorframe. "You don't like it?"

Gobsmacked. I glared at him. "Are you crazy? I absolutely love it."

Crossing the room, my feet lost in the thick plushness of the new carpet, I reached for the blanket hanging artfully over the side of the sleigh-style crib. Soft as a whisper, it beckoned me. I leaned down, rubbing my cheek against the fur fabric, revelling in the warmth and comfort it provided.

His grip released, and he strode toward me. "You love it, yeah?"

He came up behind me, snaking his arms around my waist, cradling my bump and pulling me back into his chest.

"We don't have to stay here full-time if you don't want," he murmured, lips grazing my ear. "But when shit gets heavy at home, we can escape here."

I exhaled, eyes closing, leaning back against him. His hands over my stomach, stroking the skin where our baby lay, brought so much love into my heart I could barely take it.

My hands found his.

"I like that idea, Romeo. I really like that idea a lot."

For a long moment, we just stood there—wrapped up in the gravity of what this place meant. His breath in my hair. The feeling of his body entwined with mine while we stood in a room that would soon hold the greatest gift we could share.

He kissed my crown, sending a tingle racing along my spine.

"Now I'm gonna bury my dick inside your sweet pussy on our new bed."

Like the flip of a switch, there he was. His voice was a gravelly growl—dark, urgent—as he gripped my hand and led me out of the nursery, guiding me back toward the master bedroom with determined strides.

The moment we crossed the threshold, he dropped onto the mattress, stripping out of his sweats in one smooth motion.

I devoured the sight of him.

Red rose petals, unsettled by his movement, fluttered to the ground in slow, graceful spirals, framing his naked, perfectly sculpted body. The juxtaposition was mouth-watering.

I bit my lip, drinking in every inch of him. He was perfect.

"Show me those titties, Mrs Giannetti," he purred, stroking himself. His dilated pupils locked onto mine—dark with pure, unfiltered hunger.

With a seductive smile, I sauntered toward him, peeling off my clothes one piece at a time. I tugged the sweater over my head, letting it drop to the floor in a soft heap. Then, reaching behind my back, I unclasped my bra. My breasts spilled free in a gentle bounce—giving him exactly the show he'd asked for.

His ravenous eyes drank me in.

"You're so sexy." He continued to run his hand over his cock. "But that pregnant stomach makes me even harder for you."

Really?

My brows knitted together as I held my bump in both hands.

"You really like it?"

His jaw tensed.

"Just knowin' you're carryin' my son has me worshippin' you, Chloe. I love you more than life."

A soft, needy moan slipped from me at the weight of his words. No time was wasted. I peeled down my sweatpants and underwear, then climbed over him. Parting my thighs, I let his thick length press against my already throbbing clit.

The warmth from the radiator wrapped around us like a shield, guarding against a winter we weren't yet used to.

"You want me to put it in?" I murmured, catching my lip between my teeth.

His cock flinched.

"Yes, baby." His hands caressed my thighs. "Choke it with that sweet pussy."

Gripping him firmly, I guided the swollen head to my slick entrance and eased him in.

He gasped sharply as I took the first inch. His hands seized my arse, fingers digging deep as I rode him with reckless passion—just the way we both liked it.

Rose petals rustled beneath us. That sweetness lingered in the air, caught in the static between us.

Beat after beat, I moved. Just us in a world we'd made. The bed frame creaked beneath the rhythm. Sweat slicked my back. His hands glided over my shoulder blades.

"Is it safe for me to come inside you now?" His voice was tight. Hooded eyes locked on mine. His grip trembled, every muscle straining as he fought to hold back.

My mind flicked to last night's unrestrained fucking.

He hadn't asked then...

His cock swelled even more, the groan rumbling in his chest deep enough to rattle my rib cage.

Fuck—

My stomach clenched. Eyes fluttered shut, lost in the feel of him. Nothing mattered now.

"That's it... Grip my dick, you sexy slut... Shit." His eyes closed too. He buried himself deeper.

My thighs ached as I ground my hips. Calves burning from holding the rhythm, the pressure, the high.

"Can I come for you, Queen? Let me give it to you."

My pulse thundered. The air was thick, suffocating with lust. His hands slid to my waist, holding tight, keeping the tempo at a pace he could control.

I couldn't think—only feel. My mind clouded with ecstasy.

"Yes," I panted. "I want all of you inside me."

My body clenched around him. My breath hitched.

"I got so much nut for you, baby. My Queen. You get my dick so fuckin' hard."

My hips thrust deeper still, matching his tension.

"I feel it, Romeo. Oh God, I feel it—"

Oh. Oh, shit—

He pulled my chest to his, taking my nipple into his mouth. The bite of his lips sent me hurtling over the edge.

"Oh, fuck!" I cried, fingers fisting the bedsheets.

A bloom of heat exploded inside me like a splash into a lagoon. My orgasm shattered through me, clenching in pulsing waves, gripping his cock like a vice.

Our eyes locked. His locked tighter.

Both of us were drunk on the high, on the power, on the storm of euphoria crashing through our bodies.

And then—he followed.

A groan. A deep, final thrust.

His lips pressed against mine as his release flooded into me, warmth blooming throughout my entire core.

His face buried in the nape of my neck.

"My wife," he panted. "Fuck, I love you."

Our connection. Our promise. Finally healing. Finally holding. After everything—the lies, the chaos, the fear—we were still here. Still choosing each other.

"I love you too, Romeo. So much."

◆ ◆ ◆

The wind howled somewhere beyond the forest, distant and mournful like a lone wolf retreating.

Beyond the cottage window, footsteps from our crew cracked through the banks of snow, breaking the silence as Romeo and I basked in the afterglow of our lovemaking.

"Do you wanna go back home now?" he asked, fingers tangled in my hair, lazily twirling a strand as I lay sprawled across his chest in the warmth of our new bed.

For the first time in a long while, I felt safe. The air had begun to settle. Snow was starting to thaw—like the lingering doubt we'd both carried, now laid quietly to rest.

Still, the glance at his phone said it all. He was ready to go home, to face the ghost. Like a modern-day Scrooge, we were being haunted by our own Ghost of Christmas Present.

I lifted my head and pressed a kiss into the soft tuft of chest hair beneath my lips. A little salty from sweat. Still a trace of his cologne, not yet stolen by tobacco.

"Just a bit longer, please?"

He coaxed me back down, his warmth beneath my cheek cradling me like a lullaby. Reaching for the rumpled sheets at the foot of the bed, he tugged them over me, tucking them up to my chin—sealing in the comfort.

"Whatever you want, baby." He held me close.

Secure in his arms, I closed my eyes, listening to the steady rhythm of his heart, pretending, just for a moment, that everything beyond this room could wait. A peaceful stillness grew between us. A rare, comfortable kind.

After a while, my stomach let out a loud, protesting grumble.

"You hungry?" Romeo stretched his arms above his head, biceps flexing with lazy ease. "Want me to fix you somethin'?"

Instantly, I thought of the time he'd made me breakfast in bed.

Hmm.

"You're going to make me something to eat?"

He rolled his shoulders back, looking mildly affronted. "Yeah. I am."

Hurting his feelings, especially after everything he'd done, was the last thing I wanted. But his cooking still needed a little... work.

"Have we even got food in?" I asked, hoping it might be a lifeline.

It wasn't.

"Mm-hm. Had Mrs Knowles run to the store last night."

He leapt off the bed with way too much enthusiasm, clearly proud of whatever plan he already had in motion.

"Wait here." He strutted across the room, gloriously naked. That thick, long cock swayed side to side as he moved.

"Cooking in the nude, Mr Giannetti?" My brow arched.

Much to my dismay, he tugged on his sweats and pulled a crumpled T-shirt over his head.

"You wish." He flashed a grin, adjusting his watch. "I keep tellin' you—you can't get enough."

I peeled the sheet down slowly, just enough to tease the curve of my breasts, stopping just shy of exposing my nipples. His hand dropped to his crotch. He licked his lips, eyes dark with hunger.

With a playful giggle, I yanked the sheet right back up again.

Romeo blinked like a trance had lifted. "Fuck, you're too damn sexy. I'm only leavin' this room 'cause my son needs feedin'. Best believe those fine-ass titties would be in my mouth right now."

God, I loved teasing him, reminding him he couldn't get enough of me either.

"I'll be waiting." I bit my bottom lip, letting it slip slowly through my teeth.

His eyes darted between me and the door, then he practically sprinted out, bare feet slapping down the polished oak stairs, two at a time, landing with a satisfying thud at the bottom.

Silence settled around me.

The forest slept beyond the windows. No birds. No cars. Not a sound for miles.

I stretched beneath the sheets, the dull ache between my thighs reminding me how quickly we'd begun to heal.

As our relationship evolved, I'd grown content. Happy, even. A twenty-one-year-old wife to a gangster who lived life in the fast lane. Together, we were unstoppable. Without each other, we were nothing.

I laid my head on his pillow, breathing him in. His scent clung to the cotton like it couldn't let him go.

I knew how that felt.

The man I loved was downstairs—right beneath the floorboards—cooking, caring for his family.

My eyelids grew heavy, eventually fluttering closed.

"Queen," Romeo called from the kitchen below, his voice drifting up the stairs, snapping my eyes open. "It's ready."

I braced myself for whatever culinary masterpiece—or disaster—he'd produced. As long as it wasn't burnt, I could work with it.

By the time I reached the bottom step, the aroma hit me head-on.

"Ooh, smells... pretty good," I said, taking my seat at the small dining table in the modernised kitchenette. The table was set atop a cute, chequered country-cottage cloth, cutlery neatly arranged. I had to admit—I was impressed.

"What has sir cooked, then?" I sniffed the air. "Smells kinda eggy?"

"Check that shit out." He placed the plate in front of me with a proud smirk.

I picked up my knife and fork.

He'd played it safe—scrambled egg on toast. No signs of burnt edges. I smiled, genuinely appreciative, as my stomach grumbled. The knob of butter melting into the toast's cracks had my tastebuds tingling as my knife sliced the triangle in half.

"Is Tim teaching you how to cook, too? This toast is perfect." The satisfying crunch as I took my first bite really hit the spot.

"Pfft, woman, please. I can cook the basics."

Using a way-too-large ladle, he brought the still-spitting pan over to the table and scooped himself a portion of scrambled eggs fit to feed a family of four, tapping every last morsel off the spoon onto his plate.

I eyed his mountain. "Jeez, you'll get egg-bound eating all that."

Giggling at the thought, I took another crunchy bite of toast, humming in appreciation as I swallowed it down.

His knees skimmed mine under the table as he shifted, brow furrowing as he loaded in the first mouthful. "What the fuck does that mean?" He tore into his slice of toast, then gulped down a slurp of coffee.

I blinked at him, wiping my mouth with the napkin that matched the place settings. "You've never heard that saying before?"

The pan still hissed behind him as the oil cooled.

He shook his head, shovelling another heaped spoonful into his mouth. "You speak a different language with that British talk," he mumbled, waving his fork at me.

"Coming from an Italian?" I scoffed, scooping up a delicate forkful myself, shaking my head at the irony.

He wiped his mouth with the back of his hand.

"Mangia le tue uova prima di me."

My head dropped to my hand with a dreamy sigh at the glorious sound of his native language. Surely that had to have been something romantic. Maybe he'd just confessed his undying devotion—or that he was going to climb the tallest mountain and scream my name from the snowy peak while ripping off his vest. Earth. Wind. Flames engulfing the moment he proclaimed his life for me.

"What did you say?" My eyes softened as I peered into his.

He swallowed. "Eat your eggs, or I will."

The earth, wind and fire vanished—as did my appetite.

Before I could react, he stabbed his fork into my pile, stealing another helping.

"Oi!" I swatted his arm. "I was hoping you'd said something romantic."

I really needed to learn Italian if I had any chance of keeping up with his quick wit. God, what I wouldn't give to see his face if I threw something offensive at him in his native tongue—something definitely about his mother.

"Will you teach our son Italian?"

His thumb became an extra utensil as he scooped up the last of his eggs.

"Of course I will."

"You'll have to teach me too. I can't have you talking behind my back."

He stilled, setting his fork down on the table.

"Ti amo troppo, piccola."

I rolled my eyes. "Let me guess... 'Can I have a slice of your toast?'"

He chuckled, lifting his mug. Steam curled beneath his chin.

"No." He shook his head. "I said I couldn't talk behind your back because I love you too much, baby."

My cheeks warmed. Now he was being cute.

I toyed with my food, dragging my fork through the egg, carving out a crater. "I still have a present for you, waiting under the tree back home."

The soft twinkle of fairy lights and the gentle crackle of the log fire were truly beautiful, but they didn't compare to what was waiting for us back home.

"I got another present?" His eyes lit up.

There it was—that rare glimpse of the little boy inside him.

Suddenly, I was impatient to get back to reality. To us. No half-naked distractions I'd somehow grown fond of.

Romeo mirrored my thoughts, clearing his plate like a man on a mission.

"You finished with that?" His eyes flicked to my almost-empty dish.

Just half a slice of toast and a small mound of egg remained.

"Yes, thanks." I handed it over. "But before we leave, let's talk."

He froze. Plates in hand, he drew a long breath, eyes closing like a waiter with a sudden urge to speak to Jesus.

Whatever mantra he muttered must've worked—because when he opened them again, he looked calmer.

Calmer-ish.

His jaw ticked. Teeth gritted.

"Talk. About. What?"

He tossed the plates into the sink. The clatter of utensils against ceramic bit through the air.

"Ha! You know exactly what."

Woodsmoke curled from the stove. The fridge hummed. Silence settled like a third party at the table.

"Chloe, please. I don't wanna fight. Not on Christmas."

"Who said anything about fighting?" I raised my hands. "Just talking."

He raked his fingers through his curls. "Fine."

I sat back in my seat, arms folded. "Who was the ghost this time?"

He shoved the final scrap of toast from my plate into his mouth, chewing slowly, like it might buy him time.

"Saxon, again," he mumbled. "No big deal."

Fractured light spilled through the trees, cutting across the chequered tablecloth. A thin strip of sunlight divided fact from fiction.

I pinched the bridge of my nose. Suddenly, breakfast didn't feel so fulfilling.

"If you say 'no big deal' one more time, I'll show you what I call a *really* big deal."

He smirked, his gaze dropping to my cleavage.

"Do you mean fuckin'? 'Cause you ain't gotta ask me twice."

The outline of his semi-hard cock told me all I needed to know.

"Are you crazy? Why the hell would I be talking about sex right now?"

He poured another cup of coffee—black, strong, not for the weak-hearted.

"No fuckin' clue. You're always talkin' in riddles."

Shaking my head, I stood. The scrape of the chair cut through the silence, dragging the mood down with it. I stepped in close, gripping the front of his T-shirt in my fist.

"I can handle it. Tell me."

The sight of me yanking the shirt of a man a foot taller might've been funny under different circumstances.

He looked down at my balled fist and arched a brow.

I let go.

The fabric stayed creased in the centre of his chest—a reminder that I wasn't playing games.

"Aight, fine!" He exhaled, tossing the mug onto the counter, careless enough to spill it. "Remember the night of our weddin' party?"

The music. The laughter. The brothers hugging it out. The glow of it all still lived at the forefront of my mind.

I scoffed. "Of course I do."

He opened the fridge like the next sentence might be hiding inside. Pulled out a gallon of milk. Flicked off the lid.

"Saxon showed up." He glugged a whole pint like it might wash away the memory.

My mouth fell open. "Saxon did!? When!?"

My heart spiked. The image of him—that man—uninvited, unwelcome—sent a chill through me.

Romeo wiped the milk from his lips, another heavy sigh curling from his chest.

"Remember you were givin' me some sweet head? Best head I ever got."

The vivid picture he painted made me smile, despite the confusion.

"What on earth does your dick have to do with this?"

He always found a way to include it somehow...

The fire popped and crackled. Heat pressed in from all sides, suddenly stifling.

"Remember Tommy interrupted? Said the delivery guy needed payin'? That he'd only deal with me?"

A sick feeling uncoiled in my gut. "Yeah…"

Everything about that night flooded back. The G-Wagon. Nonna's ring. Our promise.

"Custom G-Wagon lands and the bill ain't already paid? That was code from Tommy—so you wouldn't freak out. Saxon showed up."

I gawked at him. My whole body lost its strength, gravity dragging my limbs as I slumped into the couch.

"Oh my God. I can't believe you didn't tell me. What did he want?"

The cottage felt half its size. Its thick stone walls pressing inward like the closing jaws of a tomb.

"That prick's been tryin' to land my ass in jail since Tat died. Still scrappin' around for anythin' to put me away. He didn't manage it that night, and he won't now. As long as we've got the best security detail money can buy, we're good. I ain't worried. Okay?"

I hadn't heard a word past jail.

Saxon was after Romeo's blood—which meant mine, too.

"But what did he say to you?"

Restless leg syndrome might as well have been Romeo's spirit animal. Even standing still, he couldn't stop moving. His foot bounced, fingers drumming out a jittery rhythm on the counter.

"Just empty threats. No big deal."

Ugh.

Talking to Romeo about serious matters was the most frustrating experience of my life. I stared into the embers floating through the flames, praying they might set me free.

"Can't we do him for harassment?"

"Chloe. I ain't no fuckin' rat."

He wasn't wrong.

I'd more accurately describe him as a low-down, dirty dog with a humping problem.

Frustrated enough to hurl something at him—with not a single piece of ammo in sight—I gave him my best lip-pursing glare.

"So we sit back and do nothing?"

Romeo huffed. Reaching into his pocket, he pulled out a fresh pack of smokes. The soft crinkle of foil as he peeled it back set my teeth on edge.

"Cops think they're smart. Saxon knows about my empire—he just can't prove shit. So now he reckons he's gonna catch me slingin', like I'm some punk bitch pushin' meth on a street corner? He don't have the first fuckin' clue. We got nothin' to worry about."

Hmm.

That street corner dig cut deeper than he even realised. To think I used to be a working girl, lingering around the very kind of men he just described, made my stomach twist.

I shoved the memory back into the box labelled: HELL NO—and slammed the lid shut.

"So what's the plan?" I asked, rolling my shoulders like I was about to personally handle his business. My sleeves hitched. My jaw set.

"What's that phrase you Brits use?" he said, tone casual. "Suck my dick and you'll see the nut?"

I froze. Blinked.

"...Excuse me?" A smirk curled at my lips before laughter burst from my throat. "Do you mean suck it and see?"

He nodded, completely serious. "That's what I said."

I kept chuckling, shaking my head at his impressive ability to break my mood—even when I was trying so hard to stay mad.

"So… you don't have a plan at all, then?"

"Sure I do." He leaned back like it was obvious. "But killin' a cop takes a lot of prep work."

◆ ◆ ◆

The tyres crunched over snow-covered gravel as we pulled into the driveway later that afternoon. The sun hung low in the sky, all golden promises of warmth—but it missed the mark entirely.

I'd been desperate to get home. But now that we were here, unease tightened in my gut. It wasn't just the conversation with Romeo, or Saxon's looming threats. It was the emptiness. The stillness.

The estate felt deserted. The trees stood quiet. The air, unmoving, hung heavy in a way that made it harder to breathe.

Only a couple of men milled about, fussing over King's ridiculous fleet of cars. Polished metal gleamed beneath the pale winter sun—too weak to melt the frost, but strong enough to catch the chrome. Everything was immaculate, despite the biting cold.

Romeo turned off the engine—the high-powered rumble faded into silence—then tapped my shoulder.

"You daydreamin' about my dick?"

Huh—

"Chloe?"

I blinked, snapping back to reality. "Yeah?"

"We're home," he said, watching me closely, trying to piece together what had stolen my attention.

I hadn't even realised how hard I'd been staring out the window, lost in my own head.

My eyes drifted across the rows of high-end cars.

"Do you need all of these?" I started counting, my brow arching as the number climbed. "You've got twenty. Doesn't it just make you more of a target?"

He smirked. "Twenty-four."

I rolled my eyes. Pedantic.

"No, I don't need 'em. But that don't change the fact I want 'em. And there ain't no punk ass out there that's gonna stop me doin' what the fuck I want."

I lingered on the view of our home. The house stood tall against the fading sky, grand and silent.

With the girls gone, the atmosphere had changed.

Too still. Too quiet. Far too exposed.

"I know Saxon's after you," I murmured, still scanning the grounds like I might spot him lurking in the shadows. "But let's not forget he threatened me, too. Do you think… I could end up in jail?"

Romeo's jaw ticked.

"Chloe, hear me when I say—that ain't gonna happen." His voice turned to steel. "The way I operate, everythin' revolves around keepin' you and my boy safe."

He hooked a finger beneath my chin, gently tilting my face toward his. The blue in his eyes caught the last of the light—a glint so bright it could burn.

"Like I keep sayin'. The less you know, the better. Maybe now you'll listen and stop askin' fuckin' questions. Yeah? It's only to protect you."

I nodded, though part of me still itched for the truth.

He leaned in to kiss me. The charge between us sizzled. His lips brushed mine, fingers skating over my cheek. My eyes fluttered shut. The hum between us smouldered.

Then—his phone buzzed twice in the cupholder.

My ears pricked, honing in on the sound. The heat between us fizzled like a hornet caught in a jar.

A voice note. On Christmas Day?

We both reached for it at the same time.

I won.

The screen glowed hot. My eyes burned as they landed on the sender's name.

He had a voice message, alright.

From none other than her.

Harper.

Actually—several.

Romeo unbuckled his seatbelt. The metallic click landed sharp, like the cock of his gun.

"Who is it?" he asked casually.

One of his crew circled a cloth over the hood of his car. I watched him through the windshield as he leaned in, close enough to listen.

"Small Tits," I snapped, fingers curling around the phone, ready to launch it through the glass.

Romeo's nose scrunched as he leaned over for a better look. "Who?"

Next thing I knew, Snake appeared with a bucket of soapy water, scrubbing at some imaginary mark in the paintwork like it couldn't wait.

I lowered my voice. "Your ex-girlfriend. Harper."

"Oh." He chuckled, reaching for the phone like it was no big deal.

Why was he laughing? This was not a laughing matter.

I held it tight to my chest, ready to fight. "What's so funny, Romeo?"

His expression shifted when he saw I wasn't in on the joke.

"Just you callin' her Small Tits. I found it funny, is all."

I still wasn't amused.

My thumb scrolled through his inbox. Message after message.

"Well. Small Tits has been busy, hasn't she?"

The sun broke through the windshield like a taunt. Romeo pulled down the visor, casting a shadow over his mood. The cabin fell quiet.

He ran a finger over the carbon fibre like he expected to find settled dust. There was none.

"Yeah. She wants her old job back." He shrugged.

Old job back, indeed…

A sharp jab of my pointer finger hit play on the most recent note. I held the phone between us. A shared experience.

"Romey, baby," she cooed, voice dripping in sleaze. "Call me. Mamma misses her Pookie."

My eyes snapped to his. Alarm spread across his face.

"No, Romeo." I snarled, jabbing the pause button. "She wants *you* back."

He reached for the phone again. But I was ready—yanking it away, skimming through her pitiful messages, my grip tightening with every desperate word.

"She ain't ever called me fuckin' Pookie before, I swear!" Romeo shifted in his seat. He threw his hands up like I'd drawn a gun on him.

And honestly? I was in two minds about whether I should strike. Maybe I wouldn't use a weapon, but I sure as shit fired him a look of disgust.

"Why did it sound like she was fingering herself?"

His lip twitched, smirking again.

I wasn't backing down.

"Have you had phone sex with her before?"

Of course he had. But I wanted to hear it from the horse's mouth.

His usual tell—one finger lifted, scratching the tip of his nose. "No."

"Liar!" I yelled, far too dramatically.

Both men, polishing the hood, lifted their heads in unison. They scattered the second Romeo gave them the glare. One went left, the other right.

"Relax, Chloe. None of this shit matters. She never had me in the first place."

I eyed him with suspicion. The twitch at his temple. The glisten in his eye. Should I have been mad? Had he actually done anything wrong this time?

In a bid to calm myself, I double-checked his role in all this, scrolling through the voice notes. Each one a cringe-fest of unreciprocated thirst.

"She loves to call herself Mamma, doesn't she?" I sneered, pausing over another nauseating soundbite. "How old is she?"

All he could offer was a simple look. Clueless.

Eventually, he gave a half-arsed shrug. "I never thought to ask."

"Well, you asked me—more than once."

His eyes tracked down my face, straight to my cleavage.

"With those perfect tits and that tight little pussy, I knew you were young. I wasn't tryin' to catch a case. She's clearly older than me. No reason to ask. I didn't care."

The thought amused me. Their first time together. Her ill-fitting negligee. Narrow hips. Long toes curled like a witch's talons. His disappointment.

"So she has small, saggy boobs, then?" I sniggered.

He sighed, scratching his stubble like he'd mistaken the question for permission to search his memory bank. "I don't remember."

My eyes narrowed. Fist clenched.

"Wait—" He raised his hands again. "I mean, yeah. Sure. Real saggy," he added, flashing that cheeky grin that always chipped away at my resolve.

I let that one slide.

My grip on the phone softened—only to tighten again as the next question left my lips.

"Did you ever call her Mamma when you slept with her? Don't lie."

He cupped his bulge. "Hand on my dick. Never."

For once, it seemed like he was innocent. He hadn't replied to her. Not even once. And that was a pleasant surprise. Coupled with the fact their situationship felt very one-sided these days, I figured I could let it go.

A deep breath in. A slow breath out through my nose. I bit back my temper as I handed the phone to him with a tight smile. His gaze lingered on the lock screen image of our baby's scan. Mine did too.

But just as he pulled the phone his way, I didn't let go.

"Did you change that photo of Harper in your contacts?" I asked, voice light. Almost breezy—like a seaside stroll with an axe-wielding maniac on the loose.

His expression blanked. "Err... no. I forgot." His eyes darted, calculating his escape.

Still, it was Christmas Day...

I lifted my chin. "Do that now, please."

The twitch in my eyelid said it all. This wasn't a request—and the longer he hesitated, the greater the punishment.

After a beat, he held it out to me instead. "Nah, you do it."

"Good idea." I snatched it with pleasure, opening Google to search for the perfect image.

Eventually, I found it.

A large, round hog, rolling gleefully in mud—clinging to its hide like mascara streaks on her cheeks when he ignored the latest cry for attention. I could've gone for a piglet, but no. Harper needed the full farmyard experience.

With a satisfied smirk, I saved it as her contact photo and handed the phone back with self-satisfaction glowing on my face.

"Happy now?" He shoved it in his pocket.

I gripped the door handle, tugging it open. "Very."

My restored mood only deepened as we stepped into the mansion's living room, the soft glow of our first Christmas tree casting a golden hue across the space.

The homely scent of pine and fresh bark lingered in the air as I strolled further in, Romeo hot on my heels.

How had I let petty grievances distract me from what today really was?

Crouching down, the soft jingle of ornaments clattered as I reached under the tree for the final wrapped gift, winking at me beneath the fairy lights.

Butterflies stirred in my stomach as I adjusted the bow—just right—then handed it to him. The air shifted, charged with anticipation.

His brow creased as he took it. And I couldn't help but wonder when he'd last been given a real gift. Something that wasn't a porn mag or a box of sex toys? Judging by the impatience on his face, it had been years.

Typical Romeo—with a smile playing at the corners of his lips, he tore into the wrapping with more force than finesse, shredding through the layers. The sharp rustle of paper filled the quiet until the final piece dropped away, revealing a grey Nike shoebox.

His eyes flicked to mine before he slowly lifted the lid.

I studied his eyes, nose, mouth, and throat, searching for any sign of what he was thinking.

His lips parted. "Woah," he breathed, his chest lifting. "Size thirteen?" He checked the tongue.

I smirked and nodded slowly.

A grin spread across his face as he pulled out one of the custom-made Air Force Ones—classic white, just like the pair he'd worn at our wedding. Only these were laced with flecks of real gold leaf. Painted drips melted delicately from the Nike tick. On the heel, embroidered in tiny gold letters, were all our most significant dates. His thumb lingered on the stitching, feeling the memory sewn into every thread. He turned the shoe over in his hands, eyes locked on the detail. His mouth hung open slightly, his throat bobbing as he tried to speak.

We had a habit of leaving each other speechless. Still—the suspense was killing me.

I brushed his arm, pulling him back to me. "So? Do you like them?"

He couldn't take his eyes off the shoes, even tracing the design on the sole.

He nodded. "These are tight. Thank you."

His voice came out rougher than usual. He let out a long breath, still running his fingers over the craftsmanship.

"No one's ever bought me somethin' that means somethin' before. The photo frame yesterday, and these today—"

I leaned in and pressed a soft kiss to his cheek. The prickle of his stubble warmed beneath my lips, blood rushing to the surface, making it all the more real.

"You're welcome, baby."

A door swung open beyond the living room. Muffled footsteps approached. The scent of sugar cookies seeped into the space just as a throat cleared at the doorway.

"Sir, dinner will be served at 4:30 PM."

Chef stood awkwardly in the entrance, dressed in crisp whites, the tip of his tall hat bent slightly under the frame. He rocked on his heels, fingers working a cloth between them. I recognised that look—he had a difficult boss to please.

Romeo barely acknowledged him. His focus stayed locked on me.

"Hmm… two hours don't give us much time to fuck," he said, a wicked glint in his eye as he carefully set the shoebox down. My chest fluttered.

Before I could respond, he yanked me into him, lips crashing to mine. A proper kiss. Heated. Raw. Leaving no doubt about what he wanted. Breathless, drawn into the pull between us, I deepened the kiss further.

"Two hours is more than enough," I teased against his lips. "You could get a couple of rounds in, easy."

I scraped my fingers through his hair.

"Oh yeah?" He swatted my arse.

The sharp sting bit into my skin in all the right ways. I yelped—half anticipating it, half revelling in it.

Unspoken promises hung thick between us. Gift wrap crinkled underfoot as Romeo scooped me into a bridal carry and strode towards the stairs. Held in his arms, pressed to his chest, I melted into him. Safe. Wanted. I was home.

The gloss in his eyes. The grip of his hands around my body. The promise in every step. Like a sponge, I absorbed everything he had to give.

But by the second stair, his hold loosened. His breath caught by the third. His throat bobbed by the fifth.

We made it a third of the way up before I couldn't watch him struggle any longer.

"Right, that's it. Put me down. Now." I wriggled free from his arms.

He didn't fight me. Chest heaving, face flushed with effort, he set me down with a wince—like his back had just given out.

"Don't start, woman." He grimaced, clutching his spine like a pensioner.

I plonked myself in the middle of the staircase, knees tucked as close to my chest as my pregnancy would allow. My fingers dug into my shins as I hugged myself tight.

"Don't start what, exactly?"

He sat beside me, one hand gripping the banister.

Together, we stared at the short distance we'd managed.

"Don't start kickin' off 'cause you think you're fat again."

My throat pinched. Tears pricked behind my eyes.

"I don't think it, I know it. Look at you—you can barely breathe after that!"

He exhaled sharply, jaw flexing. Then, without a word, he pushed to his feet and walked straight past me.

A stiff breeze left in his wake.

No glance back. No reassurance.

What the—

My eyes widened as he disappeared onto the landing and into our bedroom. Frustration bubbled. My fists clenched so tight my nails nearly broke skin.

He'd left me. When I felt at my worst.

A flutter landed in my stomach. My baby. My everything. I cradled the bump protectively, shielding him with both hands. It wasn't just about me anymore. When he left me, he left our son, too. We didn't deserve this. The man we both relied on—walking away just like that.

A rocket of rage launched me to my feet.

The polished wood of the banister slipped through my fingers as I tore up the stairs after him. One stomp at a time.

By the time I reached the bedroom, he was sitting on the bed, scrolling casually through his phone like nothing had happened.

I forced the door open wider with theatrical spite.

The room was dim, a pale wash of snowy light creeping through the curtains. I flicked on the overhead lights, flooding the room with cold, unforgiving brightness. Not a chance I was letting him hide in the shadows.

He glanced up briefly—then went straight back to his phone.

"Don't leave me when I'm upset! What the hell is wrong with you!?"

He barely moved. Still scrolling.

"T says I gotta be less reactive. If I feel myself gettin' pissed, I gotta walk away."

Hands on hips, I stared him down. One more scroll and I'd turn lethal.

"Tim told you to abandon your pregnant wife when she's heartbroken?"

He huffed, rolled his eyes, and tossed the phone aside, dragging both hands down his face.

"Chloe, you make it sound like I left you in the middle of the fuckin' desert."

I closed the closet door I'd left ajar earlier, my finger lingering on the handle—like shutting it somehow sealed off the ache in my chest.

"You may as well have."

Romeo reached into his sweats pocket, pulled out a sleeve of nicotine gum, and unwrapped the cellophane with infuriating calm. He popped two in his mouth and chewed slowly. Calculated. Eyes dark. Head tilted like he was biting back the urge to retaliate.

The heat of our mingling breaths—our hands all over each other just minutes ago—now felt like a distant memory.

"Stop bein' a little bitch," he muttered, gum rolling lazily. "Just come here and sit on this." He grabbed his crotch. "It'll make you feel better."

His cock twitched. The outline beneath the fabric thickened.

I froze, mid-breath. In that moment, I was no better than a crying child suddenly offered ice cream.

Crocodile tears wiped. Lips licked. Mood forgotten.

I tried so hard to hold the cards between us, but sometimes I just couldn't resist him—and it terrified me.

Since the DNA results came back, since I knew the baby I was carrying belonged to him, our sexual appetite had ignited like wildfire. Looking back, it was hard to believe there was ever a time I wasn't in the mood. Had the paternity question mark always been lurking in the background, quietly killing my desire to connect with him?

I didn't have time to analyse the psychology. That was Harper's job. I stalked toward him, eyes locked on the handsome, cocky bastard, and climbed onto his lap.

Arms open, waiting for me to land, he gripped my hips as I straddled him. I kissed him—the real kind. Tongue sliding into his mouth, revelling in how he always let me take the lead… before snatching control right back. His lips trailed to my neck. Heat met skin. Our spark ignited all over again.

"Fuck, Chloe," he breathed at the nape.

But just as my hands slipped beneath his shirt, a timid knock echoed from the door—three quiet rasps.

We ignored it.

Romeo groaned in my ear. "Don't stop."

His hold on me tightened.

His breath fanned hotter across my collarbone. "Touch my dick."

He guided my hand into the waistband of his sweats.

The door creaked open anyway.

"Boss—"

Romeo didn't even look up. "What!?"

His hand over mine, he wrapped my fingers around his cock, stroking himself through my grip.

Tommy hesitated, both military boots shifting heavily on the threshold.

"We got Harper out front. She said she won't leave unless she sees you."

I froze.

A cool gust from the open door cut through the warmth like Harper herself had brought a storm.

My hand slipped from his waistband like ice. Every inch of my libido drowned in a bucket of cold water. My heartbeat thumped like a drum in my ears. What the fuck was she doing here? Wasn't it bad enough she'd messaged him? Now she had to show up in person, on Christmas Day, to rub my nose in it?

Romeo's frown deepened. His thoughts mirrored mine.

"Tommy, brother—it's Christmas Day, and I'm tryin' to fuck my wife. Tell her to step."

He leaned in to kiss me again, but I pulled back, pressing a finger to his lips.

Tommy cleared his throat.

The soft click of his holstered gun as he clutched the handle offered him moral support.

"I'm sorry, Boss. She's… insistent."

Romeo tensed beneath me. Teeth gritted.

"Fuck!"

With a frustrated growl, he lifted me off his lap, shoved his dick back into his pants, and stormed toward the door.

Halfway there, he paused. Fingers curled around the door handle; he looked back at me.

My face stayed still. But inside? I was screaming.

He raked a hand through his hair. "You comin' with me?"

Hmm.

Now that was a good question. One that I took my sweet time answering.

Tommy rubbed the back of his neck.

Romeo's hand twitched at his waistband, adjusting the evidence of our interrupted intimacy.

"Um, no, thanks." I inspected my neglected nails. "I'll leave Mamma and Pookie to have their moment."

I folded my arms tight across my chest. I'd unloaded the first clip. Now it was his turn.

Did he take the bait… or do the right thing?

"Come on, Chloe, give me a break!" The sharpness in his voice made me flinch.

I watched him close.

His eyes narrowed. Pecs twitching like he was trying not to throw hands.

"Please?" he added, jaw ticking like a countdown to destruction.

Please? He said it.

My arms fell away. The internal screams ran quiet.

Now I was smiling. Winning.

And before I even registered the decision, I was already following him down the stairs.

The front door stood wide open. I wasn't quite ready for the blast of ice that rolled through the hall the second my feet hit the bottom step.

Romeo was already launching himself at the threat. The crunch of gravel underfoot rang loud as he stepped outside. Hoodie tucked behind the grip of the gun at his hip. He pulled up his hood—shadows cutting across each hard line of his face.

"What the fuck do you want?" he yelled the moment he caught sight of her.

The snowy backdrop—picturesque in all its purity—framed Harper in a way her body didn't deserve. Like a cougar rising from the ashes of his past mistakes, she stood just shy of our door in a skintight black PVC catsuit and red heels, a single sheet of paper clutched in her manicured hand.

Snake's muscular arm barred her from getting any closer. His face was unreadable, but beneath it, the same anger simmered.

The heat of the house warmed my back. The snow's chill prickled my front. I was stuck between two worlds—the past pressing against my chest like a dead weight, and the future inviting me to stay warm inside.

She smirked the second her greedy eyes landed on my husband. "There you are, Romey! You really think you can just dispose of me because your little whore tells you to?"

Air rushed from my lungs at the blow I hadn't braced for. Romeo yanked my arm, pulling me out into the open and into his chest. Finally. The reassurance I'd always wanted—right here. Mine.

"I got rid of you because we're done. This ain't got nothin' to do with Chloe."

I realised then it wasn't just the frost that made the air bite. It was her. The chill in her aura seeped deeper than the snow ever could, mocking me in my own home like she had every right. My nipples stiffened as the cold bled through my sweater. I hated that she made me feel this exposed. But with Romeo behind me, she'd never pierce deeper than the surface.

She huffed and slapped Snake's arm. The paper in her hand crackled like fire. He lowered it without resistance, giving us all a full, unobstructed view. Enemies, clear as day.

Her eyes snapped to mine. "Ahh, there she is. The preschooler in question," she sneered, scanning me from head to toe. "Gosh, you ought to get your thyroid checked. There's a heck of a lot of weight in your face."

My hand tensed against Romeo's stomach, balling the fabric of his hoodie in my grip. Resentment surged—but I kept my mouth shut. Harper was smarter than most. She could outmanoeuvre me in a war of words.

So, I waited.

"Keep your shit comments about my wife to yourself," Romeo snapped. "She won. Get over it."

Triumph rang in my smirk—loud and clear, like church bells.

Harper ignored him, stamping a heel into the snow with a dramatic pout. "Come on, Romey. How can we be over after everything I've done for you?"

She lifted the paper again. It fluttered in the breeze like a warning flag.

"You're talkin' bullshit," Romeo cut in. "There ain't been a relationship in years. I'm about to be a dad. There's no time for this shit. I got nothin' else to say to you."

He fished a cigarette from his pocket, perched it between his lips, and lit it without missing a beat.

Harper took a step forward, straight into the first plume of smoke.

"You'll change your mind when you see this." She slapped the paper against his chest. "That, my dear Romey, is all of your assets, sitting in offshore accounts I placed there for you."

Romeo took the page with zero urgency, inhaled deeply, then blew a thick coil of smoke into her face.

The crisp scent of snow and hot cigarette smoke curled in my nostrils, a warning that something bigger was about to ignite.

With a flick of his wrist, he shoved the paper back against her chest, holding it there with one finger.

"Take it."

Huh?

Was he serious?

Harper's jaw dropped. "Excuse me?"

My reaction mirrored hers.

A gust swept through. The trees shivered.

He was giving her all of his money?

"You heard me," he said. "Take the money. If that's what it takes to get you out of my life."

Harper laughed—sharp, stunned. "Are you on drugs again? This is ten million dollars we're talking about here!"

She waved the paper harder, like the movement might force the number to sink in.

Romeo smiled. Calm, cocky.

"I know." He smirked. "I can read."

His thumb brushed slow against my wrist, anchoring me.

Ooh. That was good.

Her face darkened. This was new information to her. That's why she kept sending voice notes. That's why she was here now. He hadn't told her. I should've felt elated knowing he hadn't spoken to her in so long. Instead, something inside me tightened.

"Um, Romeo? Can I have a word?" I stepped backwards.

He handed Snake his smouldering cigarette and followed without hesitation. Both of us taking the final step up into the safety of the mansion.

Harper stayed rooted to the spot, Tommy and Snake still blocking her path.

Cloaked in the shadows of his hood, Romeo looked like the devil's spawn. I tugged it down, dragging the devilment with it. There he was—black eyes now blue beneath the wall lights. A smile I barely saw beneath his makeshift cloak now, plain as day.

I peered over his shoulder, eyes fixed on my target.

"You're really gonna let her walk away with all that money?"

He shrugged casually, tucking his hands in his waistband—gangster style.

"What choice do I got?"

Harper leaned into the barricade, muttering something to the men, refusing to let her through.

"You could at least play her. Steal it back, then cut her loose."

He cracked his knuckles—still scarred. But that never stopped him.

"I'm tired of bullshit and games. All I want is my son here. And for us to move on." He pressed a hand to my stomach.

My chest ached as my heart absorbed his love. His face said it all. He was done.

My shoulders softened. Fighting fists eased. "Oh. I see."

What else could I say?

After a beat, his signature smirk returned. "Besides—ten mil is pocket change compared to what I actually got."

Ahh. That was more like it.

The air shifted. The house sighed in relief.

My lips twitched, remembering Romeo was never stupid when it came to money. If anything, I'd always underestimated him. And just like I had a habit of doing that, it seemed Harper did, too.

"I'm waiting, Romey!" she shouted from outside—her voice echoing against the stillness. "Is it her, or me, and ten million dollars?"

Romeo turned on his heel, took three long strides toward her—each one marking the end—and, without hesitation, plucked the cigarette from Snake's hand.

He flicked it in her face. The embers sparked off her skin like cutting wire on a rope bridge.

"I want you out of my life for good," he snapped. "You were nothin' to me, just a cheap fuck. Call my wife whatever you want if it helps you sleep at night, but you don't compare to her. Take the money and fuck off outta here."

I leaned against the door like it was my armour. "Yeah. What he said."

Romeo barely spared her another glance.

"Come on, Chloe." He took my hand. "We got business to attend to."

Harper's shrill voice chased us as Tommy shut the door in her face.

"You'll regret this, Romero! You just watch—you'll regret it!"

Her fists pounded on the wood, but her voice dissolved into background noise.

The mouth-watering hit of roasted rosemary potatoes and buttery goodness swept in from the kitchen as Romeo pushed open the door. The sights and sounds of such homely comfort stood in stark contrast to the war we'd just won.

Adrenaline drained from my system, warmth taking its place. He pulled out my chair at the island and motioned for me to sit. My heart settled into a softer rhythm.

I did as he asked, but not without shooting him a glare.

"Ten million dollars is pocket change to you?"

Chef continued cooking up a storm, completely unfazed by the chaos that had just unfolded. Boiling pans. Hot ovens firing on all cylinders. Gas rings on the hob, burning bright blue flame.

I swiped a roasted carrot from the warming plate, its sweet glaze coating my fingers. As I took a bite, Romeo leaned in and bit the other end.

"I got more than one accountant." He tapped the side of his nose with a playful wink.

My eyes narrowed in amusement. "So you are smarter than I thought?"

He dropped into the seat beside me, smirking.

"I didn't get to where I am now from luck and fuckin' whores." He stole a carrot for himself from the plate, holding it between his teeth.

I watched him—cocky and calm, chewing on a carrot like he hadn't just given up ten million for us.

My chest squeezed. He really loved me.

This time, I took the whole thing from his lips—perched like the cigarette he never got to finish. I bit down. The crunch satisfied something deeper than hunger.

"Amen to that, Pookie." I giggled, resting a hand on my bump. "Merry Christmas… to us."

CHAPTER 4

Days had passed since we learned the truth about our baby's paternity, and another since discovering Dan had sabotaged the medical records.

The reminder of that betrayal remained etched into Romeo's knuckle like one of his tattoos. Another chapter in the history of their broken brotherhood. But with Tim's help, he'd found a way to forgive.

After all, Romeo had won. He had the prize. A son.

I clutched my steaming mug of coffee to my chest as I pulled open the bedroom curtains. A spectacular panoramic view of our estate stretched before me—one that never failed to take my breath away.

The unexpected snowfall had since thawed. A streak of warmth from the dull sun broke through the glass, soft but fleeting. California was in for one of its harshest winters yet.

Outside, our fully reassembled crew moved like headless chickens—darting across the lot, scrambling to keep the grounds immaculate, the cars pristine, and the perimeter locked down.

I sipped and watched.

Frost still clung to the tips of the short blades of grass. Windshields stayed fogged. Christmas was in the rear-view, but I held onto the memories of that day with every breath I had, gripping it until my fingers practically bled.

I took another sip, my breath steaming up the glass in a coffee-heated sigh as the world ticked on by.

Today was unusual for us in more ways than one. Not only had we received an invitation, which was rare enough on its own, but it came from Mother Giannetti—summoning us to her traditional Italian New Year's celebration. 3:00 PM sharp.

I padded over to the bedroom mirror in one of Romeo's oversized T-shirts and a pair of his sweats. After giving myself the once-over, it was clear—this was going to be stressful.

The closet doors hung open. My coffee mug sat abandoned on the nightstand, steam fading. I'd barely scratched the surface of outfit options when my mood turned. The chill beneath the floorboards seeped through the carpet fibres, icing my bare feet and feeding the anxiety already bubbling beneath my skin.

"I'm feeling really worried about this," I muttered, watching Romeo in the reflection as he tossed back another whiskey.

He mirrored my nerves, but hid behind his addictions.

"You got nothin' to worry about, Chloe," he said smoothly, swirling the amber liquor in his tumbler like it wasn't his fourth or maybe even his fifth of the day.

"Well, you would say that. You're already drunk." I huffed, yanking open the next closet doors and snapping on the light, launching into the impossible task of finding an outfit that actually made me feel good.

He gripped the bottle's neck and gave it a lazy wave.

"Pfft. Give me a break." The liquor sloshed as he dropped onto the bed. "I already proved I can drink a whole bottle of this shit."

Typical. His solution to everything: liquor and denial.

"Being an alcoholic isn't something to be proud of, you know?" The words came out sharper than I intended.

Luckily, he let it slide—refusing to rise to the bait. A rare act of mercy that saved us both from me crying and him sleeping on the couch.

Meanwhile, I backed myself into a corner, overthinking every detail, fully aware of what we were walking into. A dinner with his entire Italian family? More like a nightmare.

I'd already learned at his cousin's engagement party that the Giannettis operated like a village of their own. This wasn't just a meal. This was a reckoning.

"Dan is going, right?" I aimed for casual—but it landed stiff.

The second his name left my mouth, the room seemed to contract, like I should've known better.

"Yeah?" Romeo's grip wavered, the rim of his glass clanking against his teeth. "Why the fuck do you care?"

That was a question I hadn't even asked myself yet. Maybe because I'd seen Dan at the jewellery store? Maybe I wanted to test that spark of jealousy—the one I'd hoped would disappear with the DNA result—had well and truly gone for good?

But Romeo didn't need a window into that tangled web of emotion...

Deflection, of course, would always be my way of handling awkward questions.

I plucked a black, full-length maternity dress from the rack—soft fabric, a belt cinched at the middle—and held it up against me.

"Since your mother already hates me, what the hell should I wear? This?"

Romeo smirked, setting his glass down on the nightstand beside my now tepid coffee, and pushed off the bed.

"Trust me, Chloe. Now she knows you're givin' her a grandson. She loves you."

I shot him a doubtful look before stepping into the dress, already resigned to the fact it didn't even fit me.

Fifteen try-ons later, time was creeping up on us. My toes curled as anticipation lingered. I twirled in front of him, the soft cotton of my pale blue dress hugging my curves just right, the neckline dipping low enough to stay tasteful—yet alluring enough to keep Romeo's eyes locked on me.

"Well? What do you think?" My teeth found my lip with a painful pinch.

While I'd been fussing over sophistication, Romeo, of course, had insisted on wearing a tracksuit. But we'd compromised. The dollar-sign necklace stayed in the jewellery box—a small victory. And since he'd slipped on the sneakers that I bought him for Christmas, I let the rest slide.

His slow, heated once-over sent a shiver down my spine. Hooded eyes, glassy from one too many whiskeys, glinted with ill intent.

"Sexy as hell," he said, licking his lips.

Straight to the point. That was all I was getting. The tension in my body slumped.

I rolled my eyes. "Really? You said that for the last fourteen outfits."

He reached for my hips, pulling me flush against him. The chill from outside never stayed cold when I was in Romeo's arms. His thumbs brushed over the fabric as he tilted my chin, exposing my neck.

"Really," he confirmed, his lips grazing the nape—lingering just long enough to set my skin ablaze. "You got my dick hard again."

The heat of his pulse, the slight flinch of his cock, made light work of exposing his true feelings for my body.

I sighed, stepping back and smoothing a hand over my bump, creating just enough distance before he tried—yet again—to bend me over the mattress. There wasn't time for that right now.

"Anything gets you hard. But I guarantee I'll get at least one bitchy comment from your mother before the afternoon's over."

He reached into the front pocket of his jacket and pulled out a pair of Ray-Bans.

"And if she does," he said, opening the dark-rimmed frames and slipping them on, "I'll handle it."

Sunglasses in winter were never my go-to. Romeo would argue until he was blue in the face that they discouraged the paps from following our every move. Those intimate shots always earned them big bucks. But this was deeper. A shield of his own to hide whatever was brewing beneath the surface.

His mother and his brother in one room? That alone was enough to fill his tumbler to overflowing.

"Okay, fine." I softened at his glimpse of vulnerability. "But if she comes for me, you better have my back."

"I got your back," he murmured, squeezing my arse before trailing a finger down my cleavage. "And your front." He lifted the glasses, his eyes cutting into mine with promise. "These titties got me all kinds of fucked up."

◆ ◆ ◆

"I need a shit. I can't do this," I blurted, fanning my face in blind panic as our SUV rolled up Mother Giannetti's long, sweeping driveway.

The tyres skidded to a halt, brakes squealing in protest, like even the car didn't want to be here.

As rich as her sons, the house was intimidatingly grand. A stone fortress at least twice the length of our mansion. Manicured lawns. An imposing fountain rising from the centre of a private lake. A Bentley. A Rolls-Royce. Stables in the distance, horses snorting and whinnying.

This was easily the most impressive property I'd ever seen. The kind of wealth Romeo's family possessed… I couldn't even begin to comprehend.

A staff member in smart overalls and a cap strolled past with a sweeping brush, collecting fallen leaves with militant precision.

Snake rolled down his window. "Parking?"

The man didn't even pause. "Mrs Giannetti doesn't want SUVs on the front. Park behind the garages." He doubled his sweeping pace, like the conversation had cost him precious seconds.

My eyes darted between Romeo and the door. My fingernails found their way between my teeth.

Winter air crept in through Snake's cracked window. Freezing, I hunched into my coat, heart pounding. A nervous sweat prickled across my forehead as I panted through the rising dread.

"I don't think I can do this." I shot him a look.

Romeo unclicked his seatbelt with a sharp snap and peered over his sunglasses—giving me the same look he wore right before I passed out in the panic room.

I was stressing him out.

The window rolled up. The car parked. Engine faded.

Romeo gripped the headrest and exhaled. "Aight, listen, Chloe. Since that last bullshit with Saxon, security's tight. Just do as you're told, got it?"

Snake added his two cents by sliding a round into his gun with a clean, metallic click. Tommy adjusted his vest with that same quiet efficiency—

like he'd already heard it all before.

I nodded my agreement. I had no choice.

The SUV door slid open. A metal on metal grind carrying its own kind of intimidation. Romeo stepped out first, me in the middle, and Tommy at the rear in what they liked to call the sandwich manoeuvre. The safest way to move from point A to B. Meanwhile, Snake stayed in the vehicle. Weapons loaded. Eyes sharp.

The sky was sunless, casting a bone-deep cold across the grounds. I took a shallow breath, steadying myself.

The front door stood wide open at the end of a polished stone path that stretched out like a runway. An invitation that felt more than a silent dare than a welcome.

Rose bushes. Sculpted laurels. Picture-perfect landscaping designed to put visitors at ease. Too bad I knew the owner better.

A tuxedoed butler waited on the threshold, white cloth draped over one arm like a scene from a mafia film.

"Mr Giannetti," he greeted with a nod, stepping aside to let us into a marble-lined foyer built to impress and silence in equal measure.

A gust of cold air followed us in, rustling the chandelier high above. The crystal strands chimed gently, scattering fractured rainbows across freshly painted cream-coloured walls. The scent of wood polish and lemon wax lingered—followed by the warm tang of tomato sauce floating in from the kitchen.

Tommy peeled off and took his post in the far corner, one hand resting near his holster, keeping up the illusion of normality.

"Is Tommy following us everywhere now?" I murmured, watching him scan the space like a sniper.

Romeo adjusted the Glock tucked into his waistband. "For the last time, yes."

I narrowed my eyes at his snappy tone, but let it go. We had a five-foot-tall, bigger problem on our hands right around the next corner.

From behind the kitchen door came a voice.

"*Oh, Romero, sei tu?*"

Angela Giannetti. Loud and commanding. Her tone echoed through the house like a gong.

Romeo adjusted his shades. His armour.

"Speak English, Mother, or we're leavin'," he hollered back, his voice booming just as loud, just as sharp.

The kitchen door swung open, revealing my mother-in-law in all her matriarchal glory. Her signature dark curls were pinned into a classic updo. A smear of tomato sauce marked her otherwise immaculate apron as she wiped her hands on a clean kitchen cloth. Of course, she was the one doing the cooking. I don't know why I expected her to hire help. Italian women were built different.

"Don't speak to me in such ways, Romero Luca." Her glare could strip paint. "I won't have your bad behaviour in my house."

His jaw ticked. Shoulders squared. The tension radiated off him the moment their eyes met.

I reached for his chest. My palm found his heartbeat—fast, tight. The effect of our connection was instant. His gaze dropped to mine, and the storm receded just enough to breathe through.

"Romero," she snapped, "take those silly glasses off in my house. There is no time for nonsense inside my walls. Do you understand this?"

He peered down at me again.

I gave him a single nod. The kind that begged for calm.

With a tight sigh, he snapped the sunglasses off and slid them into his jacket pocket. Behind the dark lenses, his eyes still burned—too bright to be dulled by her venom.

She raised her chin. "Better. We have manners in this house. You know this."

Romeo rocked on his heels.

Angela looked me up and down like a fattened cow at slaughter.

"Hello again, young lady." Her lips pursed so tightly she could've shot peas through a pipe.

"Um... hi." I lifted a hesitant hand, smile just as stiff.

Not that it mattered. Smiling clearly wasn't on Angela's agenda. She flicked her wrist at Romeo and turned on her heel, tapping those kitten heels like a weapon as she marched toward the kitchen.

"Go sit at the table. Your brother will be here soon."

Romeo chose his seat at the beautifully laid table, which stretched almost the entire length of the room. Each footstep he took across the stone floor reverberated like we were dining in a cathedral rather than his family home.

Herbs and garlic—tastebud-tingling aromas—coiled through the air like temptation itself, winding around us with invisible promise. A banquet so lavish, it felt less like a celebratory dinner and more like a last supper.

Above us, an even grander chandelier commanded the space, its glow catching the gleam of candelabras, fine bone china, and polished silverware—every detail oozed extravagance. Safe to say, there wasn't a throne in sight for him to claim, nor a single stripper to assist with digestion.

Hopefully, he brought antacids...

A waiter finished lighting the candles the moment we arrived, gave a small bow, and retreated to the wings with a wind-swept flourish. An older gentleman adjusted the chairs with precise care, then fussed with the window drapes just enough to allow the maximum amount of natural light without creating a glare off the silverware.

Aside from the staff and their final preparations, I was relieved to be the first to arrive. We had the space to ourselves—for me to acclimatise before the rest of the family made their entrance.

"Your mother despises me," I muttered, dragging the legs back on my chosen chair. "She barely said a word to me."

He shook his head as he dropped into his seat. "Trust me, that's a good thing." He stopped mid-thought and frowned at me. "What are you doin' all the way down there?"

I peered over my shoulder in case I'd missed something. "What do you mean? I thought Italians had to sit as far away from each other as possible."

A chuckle rippled through his shoulders, bouncing off the walls like a sinister haunting.

But I wasn't laughing. Today meant something to me. I was really trying to be the woman his family expected.

His smile faded. The final note of his laughter vanished into the far corner of the room.

"We do that at our own table, Chloe. Not here."

My fingernails dug into the tablecloth, shifting the whole thing towards me an inch. Candle flame flickered. China clinked.

"So, where exactly do you want me to sit at your mother's table? Outside?"

The waiter descended on the table in an instant, fixing the chaos I'd created—straight-faced, a slight flush to his cheeks.

Mother Giannetti ran a very tight ship.

Romeo let out a breath and surrendered with a shrug. "Chloe… just bring your ass over here."

He pulled out the chair beside him and gave the back a firm tap. The white-knuckling around the chair's edge said everything about how hard he was restraining himself.

I rose, swept my dress of creases. The hollow ring of my heels resounded sharper than my husband's as I crossed the floor, clashing with the soft drawl of an operatic piece humming from the ceiling speakers.

I did as I was told and slipped into the seat next to him as if he hadn't just insulted me.

He unzipped his jacket, legs spread, one arm draped lazily over the back of my chair.

"How am I supposed to be an Italian wife if you're not teaching me properly?" I muttered, tucking myself too far under the table. The second scratch of the legs along the stone sent the wait staff into a frenzy.

A new member of the team floated in and had just adorned his silver tray when Romeo beckoned him over with a single click of his fingers.

"If I wanted an Italian wife, I wouldn't have married a British slut with a tight pussy." He winked, snapping his fingers a second time.

His backhanded compliment had me smirking. He always knew exactly how to draw a smile out of me. Shaking my head at his ego, I let my gaze wander, hoping a little grounding might settle my nerves.

Server number two pulled out a bottle of wax polish, giving the sideboard one final sheen with a satisfying squeak. Citrus clung to the air, the atmosphere too perfect to be natural.

Server number four, or maybe five, fussed over the place setting at the head of the table. The soft clinks of cutlery being laid and relaid set my teeth on edge.

A young woman with a feather duster flicked her wrist over everything, even the frames of fine artwork lining the walls. But the art wasn't just decoration. It was a statement. Every piece screamed wealth and deep-rooted Italian tradition, a stark contrast to the man beside me, who was anything but conventional.

"I thought your mom might have some photos of you guys?" I asked, focusing on a particular painting of a wilted flower. Had to be worth thousands, but nothing about it said family.

He scoffed into his drink. "That ain't her style."

I smoothed out the one solitary wrinkle in the table linen.

"Even so, she's close with your sister, right? You wouldn't know it from the way she decorates the place."

Romeo glanced around like he was seeing the room properly for the first time. He raised his glass for another sip, then shrugged.

That's when it hit me. His sister.

"Is Natalia coming to this meal?"

A clatter of pans from the kitchen scattered my thoughts like marbles down a staircase. My eyes drifted back to the wilted flower. Suddenly, it felt personal. I hadn't even considered having to deal with *her*. That would ruin the whole experience and then some.

Fingers tightening around the glass. He shook his head, tousling his black curls. He lifted the tumbler from the table, leaving behind a ring of condensation.

"She spends the holidays at her boyfriend's place, which suits me just fine. Her and my mother together? No fuckin' thanks."

My heart ached for the most sensitive man I knew. Hard as steel on the outside—but underneath, wounds he rarely let anyone see. Scars carved by the two evils that were his mother and sister.

"I'm pretty sure you and your mom don't get on because you're so alike."

His features hardened. He hitched both sleeves, then took his final sip; more like a gulp.

"Don't say shit like that again, Chloe. I mean it."

Jeez. Okay...

Tapping my fingers against my thighs, I searched for a safer topic. "Why are we so early, anyway?" I watched as he clicked his fingers at the server for a refill.

"Security reasons." He held out his glass. "No big deal."

I opened my mouth to pry further, but he placed his long index finger against his lips. A silent warning.

My eyes narrowed, lips pursed. I'd show him no big deal in a minute—with my fist and a well-aimed uppercut.

One by one, the horde of Giannettis trickled into the dining room. Uncles, aunties, cousins galore.

The low hum of chatter offered a brief distraction, easing the tension his mother had draped over our shoulders the moment we walked through the door.

Chandelier crystals chimed in time with the classical music floating through the airwaves—an atmosphere tailored for America's top-tier elite. And here I was, somehow, seated right in the middle of it all.

For now, at least, the spotlight had shifted away from me and onto Amara—Romeo's cousin's wife—as she animatedly recounted the time she was heckled on stage after butchering a performance at the local theatre. We all understood why the crowd booed her. She, however, remained blissfully in denial.

With every new arrival and each swing of the dining-room door, the scent of rich, slow-cooked sauces drifted in from the parlour. A promise that, if nothing else, the food would be spectacular.

"Angela is a fantastic cook," said an older woman I didn't recognise, catching my eye from across the table. She'd been polishing her own set of silverware on Angela's pressed napkin for the last couple of minutes.

I nodded with a tight smile. "I imagine she is."

Her husband had been waiting for a way in to the conversation. He'd clocked my cleavage the second he took his seat opposite me.

"I'm Uncle Giuseppe, and this is Aunt Concetta," he said with a wink—and another not-so-subtle peek.

Unsure of his intentions, I glanced at Romeo, who was already watching. A soft tick in his jaw. Not enough to cause concern, but close.

"Nice to meet you. I'm Chloe."

Giuseppe placed his champagne flute down and extended his hand. "Ahh, Chloe. You're with Daniele, right?"

Oh, for God's sake.

That wilted flower painting may as well have shrivelled.

Romeo slammed his glass onto the table, whiskey sloshing violently across the linen in a pale flood.

The concerto playing overhead reached a violent swell—crashing in perfect sync with his threatening tone.

"*Parla di nuovo con mia moglie e ti faccio ingoiare la pistola!*" he barked, one hand twitching by his holstered gun.

My eyes darted between both men.

The room stilled. A handful of guests watched the drama unfold with the same poised detachment as the professional fold of Angela's swan napkins.

"Okay, Romero, relax. No need to start threatening people with guns," Giuseppe muttered, shrinking back slightly. He brought his glass to his mouth, fingers trembling. "I could've sworn that's who Daniele said he was dating—but clearly, I was mistaken."

Flustered, Aunt Concetta fussed over his lapel, smoothing it down in silence—pointedly avoiding our direction.

Hopefully, this wasn't the start of things to come…

The entrance flung wide, a gust of wind sending another delicate tinkle through the chandelier's crystals. Two or three couples I didn't recognise filtered in. Romeo nodded at one of the men, ignored the other.

I hadn't even realised I'd been waiting for him until Dan strolled in last. Fresh suit. Patent leather brogues. A plus one draped elegantly on his arm.

Heat flushed my cheeks. A pulse tapped at my temples. I shot Romeo a wide-eyed look. "Britney was invited!?"

She'd barely stepped foot inside our house since leaving on Christmas Eve, and now here she was, fully integrated into my husband's family, like she wasn't one of King's whores.

Well, Dan still hadn't asked her to move in. Which meant, technically, she was still mine. And I had a right to know where she was, and whether or not she was invited to my in-laws' damn supper.

Romeo's default response to everything lately seemed to be a shrug into his whiskey, and this was no exception. As if this was the first time he was hearing about it, too. He couldn't have cared less if he tried.

The crowd roused at their entrance. One or two guests greeted Dan with familiar phrases in Italian. He nodded back as the pair strolled arm-in-arm toward our end of the table.

But he didn't matter right now. How the hell had I not known Britney was coming until the moment she walked in? Fuming didn't even cut it.

Unfazed, ditsy Britney—dressed in a champagne-coloured gown that hugged her petite frame and showcased every curve—slid into the seat beside me. Her smile beamed, bright and unwavering, as she tucked a napkin into her lap.

The glint of her fourteen-thousand-dollar bracelet hanging loosely from her delicate wrist caught my eye instantly.

"Hey, bestie," she chirped, her sugary tone skipping straight through the hum of the now-dense crowd. At least thirty guests were seated around the grand table.

Her perfume didn't sit so well with me now—more like it launched a full-scale assault on my nostrils. My thighs clamped shut. A twitch threatened my eyelid.

"Hey yourself." I twisted my wrist just enough to catch the overhead light on my own bracelet, making sure she saw every last cut of my diamonds. "You never told me you were coming?"

Her pouty lips thinned. Now she understood the frost in my tone.

Toying with the solid gold napkin ring, she avoided eye contact.

"I'm sorry, Chloe. Honestly, I wasn't sure if you guys were invited. I didn't want to cause any trouble."

The fact that Britney had received an invitation before Romeo said everything about this family.

My thighs relaxed slightly. The twitch in my eyelid eased. Maybe she wasn't being so thoughtless after all.

"It's fine," I replied, adjusting my bracelet again, subtle as a billboard. "So… how was Christmas with Dan?"

The silky cling of her dress brushed against her soft skin as she shifted closer.

"Ooh, I love this," she gasped, catching my wrist in her delicate hands. Her admiration was almost childlike. "Was it a present?"

I glanced at Romeo, who was watching his brother. Dan, it seemed, was deep in conversation with a waiter about the wine list.

"Mm-hm." I nodded into my glass. "Romeo bought it for me."

She fluttered her lashes in Dan's direction.

"How totally weird! Dan bought me a bracelet, too." She held her arm out for me to admire. "Look."

My hands made a theatrical appearance against my open mouth.

"He did not! Oh wow, I didn't even notice your beautiful bracelet." The lie slid off my tongue like the silk over her cleavage. "It's stunning. Sure looks expensive."

Britney blushed. "Lala and Sophie reckon it's worth thirty to forty thousand, but I'm not sure."

I smiled inwardly and took a sip of my water.

"I'm sure it was even more."

Just then, Dan hitched his trousers and claimed his seat. Dark olive suit, crisp white shirt open at the collar. Effortlessly polished. He unbuttoned his jacket and lowered himself gracefully into the empty chair beside Romeo.

"Hey folks," he said, raising a polite hand to the entire table.

That Tom Ford cologne—so rich, so Dan—sliced through Angela's kitchen aromas and hit the back of my throat like a welcome treat.

Guests offered nods. Raised their glasses. Dan was a favourite.

Weirdly, the brothers looked right at home beside each other. And it wasn't just me who noticed. Britney had a spare seat beside her, yet Dan had chosen Romeo instead.

Her bracelet suddenly didn't sparkle quite as bright anymore.

"Daniele," Romeo acknowledged with a curt nod.

"Hey, Romero." Dan's easy smile softened the tension still lingering in the air between them.

For the first time since I'd known them, they actually looked like brothers again.

The first course had been served—homemade gnocchi swimming in butter and sage. Sure, I was hungry, and I cleaned the plate, but it settled in my stomach like a brick. I wasn't sure what I needed more, an antacid or the number of one of Romeo's strippers.

Conversation buzzed around the table, louder still, when Romeo and Dan launched into a discussion I wasn't invited to join. I leaned in, head propped in hand, listening out for anything I could grab onto. Business was mentioned. Nods exchanged. But with so many voices weaving around us, it was almost impossible to piece together what they were actually saying.

A burst of laughter from the far end of the room swallowed Romeo's next sentence entirely.

"What are you boys talking about?" I asked, eyeing his next refill as it landed in front of him.

He slid the glass off the tray, straight to his lips.

"I've got a business deal for Daniele," he said, eyes on the liquor. "Just ironin' out the details."

A business deal? So that was why he'd accepted his mother's invitation so easily. It all made sense now—why he and Dan had buried the hatchet so fast.

There was only one way I was getting the details. Romeo was trilingual—sex being his most fluent language.

"So, what's the deal?" I folded over the table, a deliberate spill of cleavage, lashes fluttering.

Britney mirrored my curiosity with a subtle lean of her own.

Romeo's gaze dropped to my breasts as I rested my heavy assets on the linen, casually strategic. His eyes lingered, locked in, just long enough to tell me exactly where his head had gone.

My hand found my neck, fingers drifting down to my collarbone, then lower, teasing the swell peeking from my dress. I dipped one finger beneath the fabric, revealing just a little more.

Romeo took a dry swallow. "I've got an opportunity I want handled before my son is born," he said. "Daniele's gonna help make that happen."

A server swept away his empty glass, replacing it with a fresh one, while another poured Dan an expensive red into the polished bowl of a crystal goblet.

"Okay..." I said, cautiously glancing at Britney—who looked just as intrigued. If both brothers were involved, it had to be big. "What opportunity?"

Romeo threw the entire glass back in one hit. "Abroad. Maldives. That's all you need to know."

Dan, in contrast, took his time. A slow swirl disturbed the wine's surface. He inhaled its scent, then sipped—controlled, unreadable. No reaction. No explanation. Media-trained arsehole. No matter how hard I tried to catch his eye, he barely looked at me since the moment he walked in.

Images of sun, sea, and salt-slicked skin sparked an idea. Sun lotion glistening on my thighs. Vitamin D in my bloodstream—and in my husband's swim shorts. The possibilities were endless.

"I'm coming too," I declared with confidence.

A server passed by with palate cleansers for the pleased crowd. Another laugh. A clink of a refill. Our conversation dissolved into the buzz.

"Pfft. No, you ain't," Romeo said, drawing a line with his finger into the tablecloth, like he was raising his shield.

I folded my arms, wrist angled just right for the chandelier light to catch on my bracelet—refracting straight into his eye. I left it there.

"You literally said we could start looking for a honeymoon. If you've got business in the Maldives, we'll turn it into our vacation."

He squinted against the assault, leaning back in his chair. "That's gonna take a lot of extra security, Chloe."

We both glanced at Tommy—locked and loaded, blending in behind the wait staff like part of the furniture.

"And leaving me home without you, wouldn't?"

Romeo threw Dan a look, but Dan stayed perfectly still. Silent.

I was onto something—and he knew it.

My finger found the crease of my cleavage. A slow slither down revealed another inch of skin.

"Aight, fine." Romeo raised both hands in surrender. "But you better fuckin' behave yourself."

A surge of satisfaction rushed through me like I'd just closed the biggest deal of my career. That same hand found his thigh. His cock was hard.

"Britney comes too," I added, grinning, brushing the sensitive tip just enough to make him flinch.

Yeah, I was pushing my luck. But that never stopped me before.

Romeo's arousal hadn't quite clouded all of his judgement. "This ain't a fuckin' joke, Chloe. This is business."

I arched my back slightly, breasts on full display. "What do you say, Brit?" I asked, ignoring him entirely.

She hesitated, her eyes flicking to Romeo for permission before turning back to me.

He rolled his eyes, relenting.

Her smile matched mine. "Oh my God, I'd love to!"

The unexpected third course, some kind of sausage dish, possibly with lentils, slid down my gullet like a flaming lump hammer. I shifted in my seat, easing the chair back an inch to make room for my ever-growing stomach.

Despite its grandeur, the room had grown humid—steaming plates, a freshly boiled coffee pot, the weight of too many bodies breathing the same air. I fanned my face, trying to calm the rising heat in my cheeks, a flush that didn't seem to afflict anyone else—least of all Romeo.

I had no idea how he managed it. He'd devoured his entire portion before scraping my leftovers onto his plate and polishing those off too.

Dan, of course, in all his quiet refinement, took his time. A chew. A dab of his napkin. A measured sip of wine. Brothers with not a single trait in common, yet somehow exactly the same.

And then there was the beautiful girl beside me. That sweet perfume still drifted, kissing my cheek with every word. Britney had been blabbing for five minutes straight about her period—when it was due, when it wasn't.

Honestly? Normally, I'd hear her out, offer advice, but I was too invested in my husband's conversation. Fact was, we'd get in the car after this, I'd ask what they talked about, and he'd keep three-quarters of the details to himself.

"What do you think, Chloe? Tampon or moon cup?" she asked, tapping me on the shoulder.

"That's nice, Brit," I replied, just as Romeo murmured something about a speedboat.

Footsteps echoed just beyond the room for the fourth time. Conversations dipped to a hum. Nausea rose with each step as a cluster of waiters emerged again. My stomach couldn't take much more of this.

An operatic piece rained down from the ceiling as cloches were lifted, unveiling dessert in all its sweetness. A thick, creamy tiramisù, homemade and plated like a work of art.

But it wasn't until another wave of servers followed with trays of filled champagne flutes that the room truly came alive.

Spoons lifted. Noises of appreciation rang out. The *oohs* and *ahhs* sat as heavy as the next mouthful would in my gullet.

From her place at the head of the table, Angela's voice sliced through the flow of discussion—leaving only Romeo's husky tones lingering, unbothered. He wasn't about to cut his conversation with Dan short for anyone. Least of all her.

She rose.

Even the music quietened.

"Before we take the first bite of our closing course, I would like to thank each of you for coming to my New Year's celebration. My husband would have been so happy to see... most of you." Her gaze locked on Romeo.

He didn't miss a beat, leaning in closer to Dan, murmuring something about a drop ship.

A few relatives raised their glasses in appeasement.

She offered a gracious nod.

"Gorgeous meal, Angela," Uncle Giuseppe murmured, dabbing his mouth with a napkin.

Re-taking her seat, she coiffed her curls.

"You are most welcome. My son Daniele helped prepare the dessert with his beautiful partner, Britney."

My shoulders inched up toward my ears as the room turned syrupy with fond smiles for the prettiest girl at the table.

Images flickered through my mind—flour on their noses, giggles wrapped in the golden haze of dessert-making love—only deepening my hatred for this entire meal.

Dan broke from Romeo just long enough to address the room.

"It was nothing, honestly," he said, nodding politely, voice smooth as silk.

"Just like your mamma, fantastic in the kitchen," an aunt chimed in, scooping her first bite. "When's your baby due, Daniele?"

Not this again.

A chill skimmed across the backs of my heels as the weight of the question settled like a storm cloud.

"No, Aunt Rosetta," Dan replied, casting a cautious glance at both of us. "Romero and his wife are expecting."

The glint in Romeo's eye sparked the fuse.

The topic of our child rattled down the table and landed square in Angela's lap. Her spoon froze, half-buried in her tiramisù. Then it clattered to the plate. She shoved it aside.

"My first grandchild, born without legitimacy, to a non-Italiano mother. I've had hot sweats every night since learning of this tragedy."

Prosecco fizzed in half-raised glasses. Bodies shifted, every one of them drawn to the scent of scandal. The weight of every stare pinned me in place as Angela's disapproval spread like a stain. I knew Romeo had been wrong. She hadn't changed. She was still ready to humiliate me.

Funny, really, that she backed Britney—an American hooker who didn't even like pizza.

Aunt Rosetta jumped in too fast. "Don't worry, Angela. Cousin Fabio's child was born to an American mother—he turned out okay. Road sweeper. Works real hard for his family."

Angela flung an arm across her forehead in full melodramatic despair, dabbing her brow with a handkerchief.

"I can't bear it. Headache pills. Now." She snapped her fingers at the butler like we were extras in a bloody soap opera.

I turned to Romeo, hopeful, expectant, only to find him still locked in quiet conversation with Dan, nodding along like none of this was happening.

So much for having my back...

Angela shot to her feet. "Enough of this too-much-speaking at my table, Romero! *Auguri di buon anno.*"

Her gaze swept the room, landing hard on my husband.

"Pass me the Prosecco." She clicked her fingers at him.

Spoons froze mid-air. Conversations halted. All eyes turned to him on craned necks.

Romeo blinked—slowly, unmoved.

He threw back the last drop of whiskey and resumed talking to Dan like she hadn't spoken at all.

Then, before any of us could react, something shot across the room, caught the light as it surfed through the air, and struck Dan square in the forehead with a solid clunk.

"Ahh, Mamma," he groaned, rubbing the spot.

The object dropped to the table—her dessert spoon.

"*Scusa, amore.* That was meant for your brother."

Without hesitation, she grabbed a butter knife and hurled it just as fast.

Gasps rang out from nearby guests. I flinched as the air shifted sharply around me.

Romeo's chair scraped loud against the floor as he stood fast, echoing its own threat.

His hand shot up, catching the blade in mid-air. His fist clenched around it hard enough to bend.

From the corner, Tommy flinched—his hand closing instinctively around the handle of his gun.

"You wanna try that again, Mother?" Romeo's voice landed like a leathal gunshot.

Angela's waiting hand received the pills she'd demanded. She popped them with a flick of her chin, swallowing them dry.

"Sit your *culo* down, boy," she sneered. "You never could behave. Your father would be so disappointed."

As Romeo and Angela squared off, all eyes locked on them—forgetting the injured party just a couple of seats away.

Dan rose unsteadily, pressing a hand to his forehead, where a thin line of blood slipped down his temple. A single drop landed on the pressed tablecloth, marking the end of whatever good mood had remained.

Angela flung a two-handed Italian gesture his way, eyes blazing. "You see what trouble you bring to this house, Romero? Your brother is bleeding because of you!"

Not a single guest dared speak.

Dan excused himself quietly while Romeo fidgeted, unzipping his jacket. A reckless part of me braced for the flash of his gun—but instead, he reached for a cigarette from his half-crushed carton.

Angela shook her head in theatrical despair.

"I'm sorry to you all that my son struggles with normal behaviour. He has been a curse on this family since the day he was born."

Romeo laughed—low and indulgent—through the cigarette perched between his teeth. Without a word, he reached for one of his mother's candlesticks and lit the end.

A slow plume of smoke curled through the room, dancing down the table, twitching Angela's nostrils. The sheer disrespect turned her puce with rage. She slammed her palms down. Cutlery jumped. Candle flames wavered. Even the chandelier seemed to lean away, bracing for the next blow.

"It's no wonder your sister didn't want to come once she heard you'd be here. Lighting that thing at my table? Take that nonsense outside. Now!"

The humidity seemed to chill in an instant, like someone had opened a window.

He held the cigarette between finger and thumb, cheeks hollowing as he took a long drag.

"I'll do better than that, Mother." Smoke trickled from the corners of his mouth. "We're leavin'."

With deliberate ease, he extended his hand to me. Ash spilled in a quiet flurry, searing into the already-tainted cloth like a final insult.

My bump scraped the edge of the table as he pulled me to my feet, leading me through the dining room, unhurried.

Chairs creaked. Bodies shifted. Eyes widened on stalks—every guest hungry for one last glimpse.

Angela's voice cracked like a whip behind us.

"You'll have your father turning in his grave with the way you behave, Romero!"

He stopped at the threshold. Tobacco and liquor trailing behind us like loyal followers.

His shoulders rose with a long, slow inhale. Then he turned to face her.

"Keep talkin', Mother." He blew the smoke in her direction. "That fuckin' mouth of yours is why you won't have grandkids at this table."

A collective gasp sucked the oxygen from the room. Every guest sat frozen, eyes pinging between them.

Angela raised her glass to her lips, knuckles whitening around the stem. She didn't retaliate. She didn't scream. Didn't even throw another utensil. She simply exhaled through her nose—slow, controlled. And in her eyes, a flicker of devilment rose. She was on the flip side of Romeo's sinister coin.

The cold snap of air as we left Angela's mansion caught me off guard, snatching at my lungs.

My dress flared as Romeo slammed the front door shut behind him—full Italian theatrics bringing a fresh draft at lightning speed.

Tommy took the lead in military formation, boots trudging over tarmac. Well rehearsed. Always prepared.

Romeo pressed against my back, keeping me sandwiched in the middle as they escorted us to the first SUV in a row of three, idling a few yards away.

With the flat of his heated palm, Romeo guided me in with a firm press to my arse, then slid in beside me just as the door clunked shut, sealing out the frost that had already clawed its way in.

He sat there all windswept and handsome. Angled nose. Perfect lips. Like he was the Archangel Gabriel himself.

Well, I had news for him. A little short of breath in the rush to leave, I shot him a look. "Guess who's mad at you?"

All he had to offer was a cautious glare, tugging his seatbelt across his chest with enough force to tear it clean from the frame.

He was taking too long to answer.

"Me!" I shoved him. "That's who. You said you'd stick up for me, but you were too busy talking to Dan. Your mom embarrassed me in front of your whole family."

The cigarette was long gone, but the threat of it still lingered at the tip of his tongue.

"Nah," he sneered at the mere mention of her. "She embarrassed herself."

I turned my knees away from him—my own little act of war. Aiming straight at the fans working overtime to break the ice we'd brought in with us.

Peering out the window, I caught sight of my bedraggled reflection. Wounded. Intimidated. The old Chloe shone through.

"So that's your defence, is it?" I blinked back the unexpected surge of emotion.

Romeo double-tapped the headrest.

Tommy nodded.

The SUV's engine rumbled beneath us as we tore out of the driveway, past the open gates, back onto neutral ground—faster than my overfilled stomach was ready for.

The instant we hit the main road, his shoulders slumped. Both hands dragged down his face.

"Aight, I admit I wasn't payin' attention. Had a lot to get through with Daniele, and time wasn't exactly on our side."

With narrowed eyes, I locked onto him. The shadows flickering over his features told a story his mouth wasn't ready to share.

Murmurs passed between the men up front. Eyes on the rear-view. Snake's finger pushed against his earpiece as they plotted the safest route home.

My stomach tightened with the stress of it all.

"You know, none of it made sense this morning when you said we were going to your mom's." I tapped my temple. "But now I've figured it out."

Romeo removed his Glock from his waistband—the snap of elastic against his skin sharp in the quiet—then let it drop with a metallic slap onto his thigh.

"What you on about, woman?" he asked, feigning innocence, finger hovering closer to the trigger.

My eyes trailed up his leg and to his face. He didn't scare me anymore. That gun was there solely to protect his ego.

"I had a feeling there was more to it when you said yes to her party."

He shrugged, playing it cool, but the smirk tugging at his lips told me everything I needed to know.

"You went there purely for business, didn't you?"

He patted the side of his nose and cracked open the window, letting in another sweep of icy air. The muffled sounds of the city swelled as he invited the outside in—fumes, fog, and dampness clinging to our hair and the fibres of our clothes.

I pulled my jacket tighter. "The deal's the only reason you forgave Dan for messing with the hospital records, isn't it?"

He nodded, eyes closed, face angled to the breeze, the wind whipping his dark curls.

As the SUV picked up speed down the freeway, tension began to simmer. Romeo rolled the window back up, drowning out the sirens, horns, and the chaos of LA. He settled into his seat—cheeks flushed, but visibly more at ease.

What he didn't realise was that he was about to become an unwilling participant in a game I liked to call *Question Time.*

"So. Details." I arched a brow, fingers twitching in anticipation of his resistance.

He made a half-hearted attempt at muttering something under his breath before thinking better of it. Instead, he popped out three nicotine gum pellets and shoved them into his mouth, one after the other.

"Chloe, don't start." He chomped down furiously.

The gun sat there in his lap, all innocent—its barrel catching flashes of streetlight like it was mocking me. Still, I wasn't scared. I grew taller in my seat.

"I'll start all I bloody well like. You dragged me there under false pretences. Details. Now."

He closed his eyes and pinched the bridge of his nose.

"Per l'amor di Dio."

So it seemed that mutter had now manifested into real words. Brave? Or stupid?

"Strike one, Giannetti." I kicked him in the shin.

He grunted.

"Don't you dare disrespect me with words I don't understand."

His lips flattened as he rubbed his leg.

"Sorry," he muttered. Just quiet enough that his men couldn't hear.

A crackle of white noise came through the car's speakers. Snake turned it down. Their business—not ours. Security had gotten real tight. So tense it was bursting at the seams.

I needed answers.

"Sorry enough to tell me what's going on?"

Tension sizzled between us as my intoxicated husband searched for the words I was waiting to hear. He couldn't blame the booze—not when he'd bragged that a full bottle wouldn't even touch him.

"Aight, fine." He shoved the gun back into his waistband, like he didn't trust himself not to use it.

"I'm tryin' to move away from English. This new contact will make me just as much money."

While I understood his reasoning for cutting ties with Benny English, it felt like he was leaping out of the frying pan and straight into the fire.

My curled fingers relaxed a little. "Why the Maldives, of all places?"

He pulled out his phone, the blue light catching the pinch in his brow as he searched for something. Then he handed it over. A map. An entire area outlined with facts and figures. Research.

I looked up at him. "What's this?"

"Rich tourists want a sniff of decent product. Easy sell—and even easier to get the locals workin' for me cheap. Once we're established, we use their docks to export. All planned out."

I chewed on his words—slow, careful—and handed the phone back.

"Okay... and your brother fits into this how?"

Romeo cracked his knuckles, stretching out his legs with a sigh. "I'm gonna need a lot of transportation with the plans I got."

I raised my hand. "I have another question."

He didn't say yes. He didn't say no. So of course, I carried on.

"You've got so much money, right? So why not just buy your own trucks? Surely we don't need Dan?"

That same glint of devilment that had flickered in Angela's eyes now danced in his. A sheen. A quiet promise of determination.

"Takes out half the risk when you involve someone else," he said, smirking. "Down to the cops to prove who put the drugs there. Him or me."

So much thought went into his operations. Where his upbringing had failed him, he'd more than compensated—building his empire from scratch, brick by thought out brick.

I loved that about him. My husband wasn't just a man—he was a calculated storm dressed like a gangster.

I held up my hand again. "Wait. One more question."

It was moments like this I knew he loved me. I could push him right to the edge of his sanity, and he'd still choose not to let me go.

He ran his hands along his thighs. Any faster and he'd light a fire. "I don't know how you manage to get shit outta me every single fuckin' time." The corner of his mouth twitched.

"Last question," he warned. "And it better involve your pussy wrapped around my dick."

The car slowed. Tommy took a familiar corner sharp enough to lean us all to the right. We were close to home. Question Time was nearing its commercial break.

I inhaled deep enough to reel the question off in one breath. "Why, if your mom hates you so much, does she keep inviting you to parties and forcing you and Dan to speak to each other? Our wedding, for example—it was her who brought you back together. Why?"

Streetlights cast warmth over the cool cut of his features.

"Simple." He rubbed his fingers together. "Money."

"Money? What do you mean?"

As we pushed seventy, flickering lights turned to strobes.

He reached into his pocket and pulled out his last sleeve of gum—empty. His reflexes kicked in, crushing the packet. A perfect symbol for his feelings about his mother. Frustration bubbled. He leaned forward, elbows on his knees, rubbing his eyes in slow, agitated circles.

"She had a stake in my legit company."

A horn blared up ahead. Then another. Brakes squealed, followed by a metal-bending smack. Another LA crash by the sound of it.

No time to waste. Tommy handled the backstreets like a native. We leaned left around the next bend. I only had maybe four or five minutes left.

"You went into business with your mom?"

A breeze slipped through the cracked window up front, lifting my hair off my shoulders. Romeo and his mother. Business partners? I couldn't wrap my head around it.

"Had to. She gave me a start-up loan—banks wouldn't touch me."

"So what's that got to do with her wanting you and Dan to play happy families?"

He didn't answer at first. Blue and red lights flashed through the cabin. All of our eyes focused out the window as we rolled past the head-on collision.

I poked his shoulder.

"Money," he said again—so flippant, like it was obvious.

A pair of taillights flickered through the windshield, casting blood-tinted flashes across his profile.

I frowned. "I don't get it."

I hated how hard he made it. Communication had always been our weakness, especially when he refused to engage.

He sighed, slumping back in his seat, one hand gripping the car's handrail.

"When Dan pisses me off, I pull the plug on our deal. The whores keep money comin' in, so I can hold out longer than he can."

I placed my hand on his thigh. The effect was instant. Tension eased—just enough space to breathe. Weakening him at the right moment would buy me the time I needed to dig deeper.

"So when you and Dan weren't speaking… she lost out too?"

He nodded. "Exactly. That fuckin' palace she's got don't pay for itself."

I shifted in my seat, unsettled. The only reason she ever got involved wasn't to protect her sons' best interests. It was her own.

"She's also part of Dan's business, then?"

"My dad might've left the business to him, but she made sure to take some back. And of course, Daniele let her—on account of him bein' a pussy bitch an' all."

He didn't blink. Just stared out the window like he wanted out. His family had always caused him no end of pain. That much was obvious. My heart ached. Romeo's inner child needed more than a hug. He needed someone who truly loved him.

"I'm sorry you never got the mom you deserved."

Instantly, the glisten in his eyes hardened to stone. He sat up straight, flicking the end of his nose. Sunglasses back on.

"Pfft. I don't care. Me and her never had a relationship to begin with."

"When you said she *had* a stake... she doesn't anymore?"

He shook his head with a sly smile.

"I bought her out. As you can tell, she's real happy about it."

The car juddered over the final stretch of uneven road.

Time was running out. I unzipped my jacket, trailing a finger in a rush around my exposed cleavage.

His eyes locked onto his target.

"One last, last question?" My thumb grazed the thread of my bra. So close—nearly exposing myself to him.

He fidgeted. Interested. Listening.

I fluttered my lashes, sneaking a glance at his dick. One I had no intention of playing with, but he didn't need to know that.

His eyes followed mine, and he adjusted himself with a smirk. "Go on."

My hand left my chest and settled between my parted legs.

"If your mom no longer gets an income from you, why'd she bother inviting you to her New Year's meal?"

I skated my fingertips along my inner thigh, then slipped them just beneath the hem of my dress. Just enough to create the illusion. Keeping his focus. Keeping him compliant.

"I told her she'd get a cut of this deal with Daniele if she convinced him to go through with it. I needed a secure place to meet him—somewhere she'd already put the legwork in. Made my life easier."

I hiked my dress another inch.

He adjusted his cock.

I had him. Right where I wanted him.

"So where does that leave the deal now that you and her have fallen out?"

His eyes hooded the moment my unzipped jacket let the cold bite at my nipples. They were as hard as he was.

"Business is business," he mumbled. "What happened back there affects nothin'."

His voice was flat, but something behind his eyes faltered. If this was just business, why did he look like it had cost him more than he could afford?

A flash of lights and camera shutters clicked at the gates as Tommy made the final turn into our driveway. I adjusted my dress back over my knees and pulled my jacket closed. Just like that, the conversation was over.

I smiled sweetly. "Thanks for filling me in."

The fog of his arousal lifted the second my body turned cold. And while a conversation that deep should've brought us closer, I couldn't help but worry that he'd forever associate me with the exposure of his rawest emotions. Like I was the one who caused him all that pain.

We both retreated—him to his phone, me to mine.

The silence said everything we didn't.

We waited another twenty minutes while security ran their perimeter checks.

The SUV door slid open. Floodlights from the house spilled into the cabin, snapping me out of my trance. I'd somehow lost track of time, hypnotised by soap-cutting TikToks.

"All clear, boss," Snake said, a waft of cigarette smoke drifting in with him, one finger pressed to his earpiece.

Romeo stepped out first—quieter than usual. I followed, battling the breeze as it clawed at my dress.

A soft beam of headlights swept across the driveway, settling like a spotlight at my feet as a cab pulled in through the gates. I'd recognise that blonde hair anywhere. Britney.

The car rolled to a stop beside me, the driver tipping his cap like he knew me. Holding myself close, I strolled to the passenger side. Wind howled across the grounds, the bushes and trees hissing in protest.

"You alright, Brit?"

She swung out one long leg, then the other. Took a clumsy step. Closed the car door—slightly off-kilter. Her ankle buckled as she fought against her heels on the loose gravel. Flustered from the alcohol, she swept her hair from her eyes.

"Dan needed to go to the hospital for a stitch, so I figured I best come home. Things got a little crazy when you left." She hiccupped.

That news didn't come as a shock to me.

I wrapped an arm around her shoulder. "Come with me. I'll make you a strong coffee to sober you up, then you can tell me *all* about it."

◆ ◆ ◆

Romeo had just finished a workout, part of Tim's latest attempt to clear his head after the disastrous family meal.

Damp and delicious, he flicked off the bathroom light and strolled into the bedroom, where Brit and I had been hanging out for the last couple of hours. Fresh from the shower, steam still clung to his skin, a towel slung low on his hips. Droplets of water trailed down his chest, catching in the ridges of his abs.

But for the first time since I'd known him, his gun was tucked into the fold of his towel—a sobering reminder that even here, in our own home, we weren't safe.

"You took that gun in the shower with you?" I asked, concern slipping through.

Thoughts of the burglary pulled my gaze toward the closet. The panic room.

He played with his curls in the mirror, flexing slightly—giving us both quite the show.

"Obviously. I ain't havin' Tommy in there lookin' at my dick."

Britney brought her fingers to her lips and chuckled, which for some reason irritated me. I was the only one allowed to find him funny.

"Anyway." I shot her a sideways glance. "You won't believe what your mom said after we left. Britney's just been filling me in on all the juicy gossip."

He sprayed cologne over his neck and chest—my favourite—smoked leather and crisp bergamot.

"She's still here?" His tone cut clean through the conversation as he swept his gaze over us—cross-legged on the bed, still deep in discussion.

I barely had time to respond before Britney's eyes flicked downward, cheeks flushing as he caught her staring at his bulge.

Uncrossing my legs, I fluffed the pillow with both fists, trying to dispel my irritation before it took hold.

"Put some clothes on, Romeo," I snapped. "We can all see your dick through that towel."

A glint of excitement darkened his eyes as he strolled towards the bed. The brush of cotton against his damp skin whispered through the air. He leaned in, pressing a slow, teasing kiss against the nape of my neck. My skin lit up. A line of heat beneath his tongue drew straight between my legs.

"Don't play. You love seein' my dick," he murmured, his soft lips brushing my skin, luring me in.

I sniggered, pushing against his firm, wet chest. That cologne only aided his advances. My legs begged to open.

"Stop. Not while we've got company, Romeo."

His tongue flicked out to taste the shell of my ear, teeth grazing my lobe before trailing down to my collarbone, searching for the spot that would make me surrender.

"Come on, baby." His fingers skimmed the waistband of my sweats. "Let her watch."

His hand slipped beneath my sweater, cupping my breast, his palm warm and possessive. He kneaded the soft flesh as his kisses found my mouth—deep and slow—his tongue sliding against mine with practised precision.

My confidence wrestled with paranoia. I stiffened beneath his touch, the battle raging internally. I didn't want to shut him down in front of Britney, but pregnant me hadn't felt sexy in a long time. Would she think I looked grotesque with my weight gain and swollen ankles? Could she even stomach the sight of my husband having sex with a whale?

Britney rose awkwardly from the foot of the bed. Now sober, she cleared her throat and shuffled to the other side of the room. Delicate feet brushing through the deep carpet pile—just a whisper beneath the unfolding chaos.

I barely had time to process it before Romeo's eyes met mine. Pupils blown wide, breath hitched. He eased me back onto the mattress, deepening the kiss as his hand slid between my thighs. He pushed my bottoms down to my ankles, stripped my panties from my hips, dragging the fabric past my knees with slow, deliberate intent.

"So fuckin' sexy," he groaned, slipping a finger inside me.

His touch lit me up. The crooked, back-and-forth motion sent a sharp ache of need curling deep in my belly. I was already soaking wet for him.

He withdrew his fingers, bringing them to his lips before reaching for his towel.

My breath caught when he drew the Glock from his waist and set it on the pillow beside me—barrel aligned with the window, his paranoia never far behind. He often acted like he didn't listen, but clearly, my comment about letting his firearm hit the ground had finally sunk in.

"I'm gonna take you in front of your friend." His voice thickened, fingers hooking into the edge of his towel. "You good with that?"

With a slow, sexy drop, it hit the floor in a heap. His cock stood hard and heavy.

"Answer me, Chloe." He ran his hand over himself. His shaft flinched with need.

If I could rewind time and consider this moment again, would I have stopped him? Probably not. It had been so long since we'd had an audience, I'd forgotten how much it heightened everything.

The muted chatter of a TV drifted from the hallway, mingling with the soft flick of a switch on the landing. Never alone. And now, with Britney here—not even in our bedroom.

I swallowed hard. "Yes, Romeo. I want you."

The sheets rustled softly. Then his body pressed against mine—and just like that, he was inside me.

Thick. Hot. Stretching me open.

My pussy clenched around him, slick and eager, pulling him deeper with every breath.

"My dick needs you, you little slut." His voice was rough.

His hips rolled in slow, punishing thrusts that had me gasping. He found my G-spot with every stroke, teasing me, wrecking me.

The Christmas lights still strung around the window tapped gently against the glass, the cold sweep of night brushing the house like our bodies were against each other.

"Fuck me," I whispered, nails digging into his shoulders. "I need you."

His stubble dragged over the rise of my breast like sandpaper. I knew exactly why he was this turned on. Stress made him crave me. Reclaim me. Brand me. And I wasn't about to argue. My flesh throbbed around him, blood rushing to every nerve ending as he buried himself to the hilt, making me take all of him. The wet slap of skin on skin thickened the air with each thrust.

"Fuck… shit," he moaned.

His rhythm slowed—dragging out every pulse—making sure I felt him everywhere.

He tilted my chin up, lips grazing mine.

"You like that, don't you, Queen?"

I moaned, eyes fluttering shut, hips rising to meet the next thrust. "Take me, please."

Shame tangled with pride, weaving a web of conflict as I felt Britney's eyes on us. Thrilling. Unnerving. Wrong and right, all at once.

Impatient for release, I braced my feet against his hips, trying to push him deeper, desperate for every inch.

"I'm gonna take all of you, Chloe. My wife."

Oh God—I was so close.

My fingers clawed the pillow, thighs trembling as I hovered on the edge. Exhibitionism burned through me like a flame. I wanted Britney to see. To watch him lose control for me.

"Don't stop, Romeo. Oh God. Don't stop!"

His movement faltered.

"Shit. I'm gonna nut, baby. I'm so close." His thrusts dragged in slower. Deeper.

"Oh—" Heat exploded inside me. My muscles clamped around him, aching and tight. "I'm coming!"

Britney gasped.

My orgasm tore through me, wildfire in my veins, every nerve alight. The hot rush of his release triggered another ripple—dizzying. Raw. Consuming.

The gun slipped off the pillow, landing on the floor with a dull thud—lost in the heat of everything. Ironic, really. He'd tried to keep it safe, yet somehow, it ended up right where it belonged.

Romeo barely caught his breath before his gaze flicked toward the door.

"Leave," he ordered Britney.

The tilt of his shoulders revealed the red trails I'd raked down his back. My thighs were still locked around him, squeezing.

"Don't forget your manners," I teased, fingers tracing his stubble.

"Fuck manners. I need to take you again."

The door echoed shut.

Cold air met hot as our mingled breath fanned our chests. The air shifted. Playfulness faded, replaced with something darker. Hotter.

That TV show down the hall laughed quieter.

Our smiles disappeared. Lust surged.

A silent understanding crackled like a fuse between us.

"You want me again?" I murmured into his mouth.

My pussy ached in the wake of where he'd just been. My flesh was still swollen, but ready for more.

The question melted into a kiss as he slid back inside.

Our combined slickness made the glide effortless. Each deep stroke lit something primal inside me. I opened for him. Took every inch. Every starving beat. My breasts ached—nipples hard beneath his tongue. He flicked and teased them in rhythm with his thrusts, each motion driving deeper.

I arched into him, needing more.

"I want you to come for me again, Romeo." I threaded my fingers through his damp curls, guiding his mouth to mine. "Take me."

His breath hitched. His rhythm faltered—just for a second. Then he drove further. Taking what he needed.

I wanted all of him. And he needed every piece of me.

◆ ◆ ◆

I caught up with Britney a little while later, after our abrupt dismissal of her from the bedroom. She was in the gym, perched on one of the top-of-the-range exercise bikes, deep in conversation with Lala. Sweat poured off her, dragging the alcohol out with it as her calves flexed in rhythm—smooth, controlled, up and down with each turn of the pedals.

The moment she spotted me, her lips curled into a knowing smile. Their conversation stopped in its tracks.

Heat crept up my neck, flushing my cheeks. In just my sweats and a lopsided bun perched on the side of my head, it didn't take a genius to figure out what I'd just been up to…

"Listen, Brit, sorry about before—"

She stopped pedalling instantly, pressing the off switch on her progress.

"Hey, don't be. It was hot," she said sweetly, grabbing the towel draped over the seat of the next bike to dab the moisture from her brow.

Lala, one of the more switched-on working girls, wasted no time making it her business to get the gossip.

"Ooh, why? What happened, you guys?" She leaned in, settling on the handlebars like it was story time.

Britney giggled in that playful way I loved.

"Chloe and Daddy got it on."

I shifted like a flashlight had landed on me.

Lala looked between us with a frown. "And? Don't they always?"

Britney scraped her thick hair off her neck, tying it into a ponytail. She fanned her face, unsure whether it was from the workout or the memory.

"Well, this time was different… because I watched."

Lala let out a low, husky laugh. A signature from one too many cigarettes. "Damn, that is hot. Can I watch next time, Mrs G?"

I took a step back, throwing up my hands.

"Let's not get carried away, ladies. There won't be a next time."

The ceiling fan chopped at the stale air like it was slicing through the unfinished business between me and Britney.

I shot her a pointed look.

"Brit, when you're done, find me in the kitchen. We need to finish our earlier conversation."

"Sure thing." She nodded, switching the machine back on. "I'm almost done here."

The murmur of voices picked up behind me the second I left the gym.

I waddled into the kitchen, the dark of night warmed only by the afterglow of Christmas lights we still hadn't had the heart to take down.

A handful of girls were gathered at the dinner table, their low chatter humming through the room—until I walked in. Then, silence. A running theme.

"Don't mind me, just getting a cup of coffee," I said, keeping my tone light. I wasn't about to adopt Romeo's brand of intimidation. I poured right to the brim. Splash of whole milk. "What's the gossip, anyway?"

Glances were exchanged—subtle signals over who'd be brave enough to speak.

Finally, Sophie placed her head in her hands. "I had a close call last night. My client refused to use a condom."

One of the girls at the island was filing her nails, foot propped on the next seat. I gave her a look. Her foot dropped.

Bringing the mug to my lips, I perched on the stool.

"And how did you handle that?" Impatient, I gripped the handle tighter.

She hesitated. "Err, well… I needed the cash, so I did what I had to."

My heart sank. Lips pressed into a thin line. After everything, they still weren't getting it.

"Sophie, I care more about your health than I do about the money. Don't let that happen again—and get your arse to the doctor for a check-up. Now." I checked my watch. "Well, tomorrow morning."

A bright smile spread across her face, like the command was a gift rather than a consequence.

"Yes, ma'am. Will do."

The stomp of big-footed confidence rolled through the room before he did.

"S'up, bitches." Romeo sauntered into the kitchen, bringing the room to a complete standstill.

He reached for the coffee pot, but one of the whores was already pouring it for him. Yes, he was drop-dead gorgeous, but seeing the effect he had on other women only stoked the fire further. Excitement bubbled. Breathing stilled.

My lower lip caught between my teeth. Out of all of these women... he chose me.

As expected, he made a beeline for me, one hand settling possessively on my lower back as he pressed a lingering kiss to my lips. Cologne, sex, and the mint of his gum circled the room like a perimeter fence.

When he pulled away, he squeezed my rear.

"So, how's business, sexy?"

Sophie took that as her moment. Her chance to shine.

"Actually, Daddy, I was just telling Chloe—"

Romeo's head snapped in her direction, instantly cutting her off.

"Y'all need to get outta the habit of callin' me, Daddy. That's reserved for my son. Got it?"

Her hand flattened against her chest. She stalled.

"Sorry, Daddy—I mean, King."

But he was already over it. His mouth found my neck again, like he hadn't already had his fill.

A shift in the room's energy made my skin prickle. Britney hobbled into the kitchen, flushed and sweaty from her workout—and suddenly, every set of eyes locked onto her.

I flitted between the girls. Their expressions. Their lifted shoulders. Why was everyone staring?

I clapped my hands—firm and sharp. A command.

"Right, back to work, ladies."

As the crowd dispersed, I kept my eyes locked on Britney. She flicked her ponytail like a defence mechanism. She felt it, too.

I gave her a reassuring smile.

"Grab a shower and meet me in my bedroom." My tone left no room for argument.

Then I turned to Romeo. "You too. We need to discuss what your mom said."

Romeo followed me up to the bedroom with a keen look on his face. His intentions made clear when he swatted my arse for a second time on the way up.

I paused on the landing, hand poised on the door handle. "Park that idea."

A soft patter of bare feet echoed down the hall. Giggles trailed behind before a door closed somewhere. Whoever she was, she distracted him just long enough to tick my jaw.

"What you on about?" he asked, feigning innocence. His hand in his pocket made an obvious adjustment to his erection.

With an eye roll, I nudged the door open with my hip, flicked on the light, and peeled off my sneakers, tossing them by the closet.

"You think I'm stupid? Britney's joining us, and now you can't leave me alone. If I said yes to a threesome, would you?"

My lungs still hadn't recovered from the stairs. Suddenly, I was too hot. The sweater came off next, landing near the hamper.

He kicked off his sneakers, too. His expression shifted as he sat on the edge of the bed, contemplating the question a little too seriously for my liking.

The look on his face boiled my blood.

"The fact you had to think about it tells me all I need to know!" I picked up my shoe and lobbed it across the room. The whistle it made wasn't far off from his mother's ammo at the dinner table.

Of course, he caught it.

His shoulders shook as laughter rolled out—especially when I picked up the other and chucked that at him for good measure.

Another one-handed catch with the same smug ease.

"What is it with women throwin' shit at me?"

I folded my arms. "You bloody would have a threesome, wouldn't you?"

He dropped my chosen weapons by his feet, then tapped his chin with a smirk.

My face fell. This wasn't a joke anymore. He was about to hurt my feelings.

He sighed. "No, Chloe, I wouldn't. I mean, I'd tell the boys I did—but I'm over all that shit."

Relief came in a fleeting wave.

Did I believe him?

I supposed I'd have to. Unless I wanted to test the theory. Which I didn't.

A soft knock interrupted the moment. Four pink nails curled around the doorframe. Britney's voice followed, hesitant. "Guys, can I come in?"

Romeo hopped up and made his way to the drinks cabinet. "Yeah. I don't got all day!"

I shot him a glare just as the sweetest girl I knew stepped through the doorway—straight from the shower, smelling like she'd dropped out of heaven.

He brought the glass to his lips, clarity seeming to come with every swallow.

My brow arched higher.

With a dramatic shoulder roll, he reset, correcting himself.

"I mean, I don't got all day… please." His lips twitched.

Britney crept in, wide-eyed and cautious, hovering by the closet like the panic room might call her name.

The black of night cast a ghostly shimmer over the trees outside, their shadows cloaked in cold. It added a sinister tint to a room already thick with my jealousy.

I stalked to the window, suddenly concerned the paps might hold on to that threesome story and run with it. I pulled the drapes closed, sealing us in. Warm air from the vents fluttered the fabric as I set them just right. No gaps at the edges. No gossip.

"You're an arse sometimes, Romeo."

He pointed his glass at me, tongue sliding over his lower lip. "Speakin' of *arse*—I ain't had a taste of yours in a while."

That's when I turned to the laundry pile, re-folding towels like I hadn't heard a word. If he thought he was about to eat my arse in front of Britney, he had another thing coming. It was always the same with Romeo. Give him an inch, and he'd take a bloody mile.

"So anyway," I said on the final fold, steering things back on track. "First off, Britney—are the other girls giving you a hard time?"

Britney shuffled near the door. "Err, no. Everything's fine."

I watched her closely. She played with her ponytail, toying with the ends. Nervous.

I took my place on the bed, patting the space beside me.

"I just sensed a weird shift when you walked into the kitchen earlier. But if you say it's fine, that's good enough for me."

Romeo checked his watch, already pouring another drink.

"I ain't got time for fuckin' girl shit, Chloe. If it ain't about ass, what did you bring me up here for?"

Britney eased onto the bed beside me. Our arms brushed. Almost too close for comfort.

"I brought you here because I wanted to tell you what your mother said."

He tutted, strolling to the nightstand. The drawer dragged open. He pulled out a fresh pack of cigarettes.

"I don't give a shit what my mom said," he muttered, gripping one between his teeth.

Britney and I exchanged a glance.

"You don't?" I tilted my head. "Why?"

Forgetting that Britney would always see him as a threat, she shifted uneasily when he huffed.

"Erm, shall I give you two a minute?" She played with her hair again.

I placed a hand on her arm. "No. It's fine."

Romeo flicked his lighter open with a metallic click. The flame cast a fleeting glow across his brooding face.

He inhaled deeply, cracking his neck like he was trying to shake something loose. He snapped the lid closed.

"I ain't got time to entertain her bullshit. And I ain't got time for this."

I leaned back against the pillows, crossing one ankle over the other— slowly, with attitude.

"Well, you better. She told everyone at the dinner table that you were a drug dealer and I was a prostitute."

Another cigarette left the pack. This one tucked behind his ear. What was this—a game of how many orifices he could plug at once?

"I don't know what you want me to say to that, Chloe."

Suddenly, he looked disappointed. Almost sad.

My shoulders softened. "Can you give us some privacy, please, Brit?"

She darted on the last word.

The door closed softly. The atmosphere shifted with it.

"What?" Romeo asked, tension rising as he caught my sorry smile.

"Your mom really gets under your skin, huh?"

He stepped back like I was the threat.

"Told you from the start—she's a bitch. Ain't nothin' new."

My Romeo was disappearing before my eyes, replaced by the wounded boy his mother had failed again and again.

But I knew how to bring him back.

A wicked grin tugged at my lips. I ran my tongue along the bottom one.

"I believe someone was in the mood for arse today?" I fluttered my lashes, watching the flicker of heat return to his gaze. "Would sir still like some now?"

His eyelids drooped. Jaw flexed. That step back became one forward. Then another. Now we were speaking the same language.

"Shit, I'm rock hard already. Get your hand round it. Feel how fuckin' solid I am for you."

A rush of heat surged through me when his hand wrapped around mine, completing the connection.

I licked my lips. "Come on, baby. Come taste me."

With his fingers still locked around mine, I tugged him toward me, stopping only when his shins met the bed frame.

His hands landed on my shoulders, turning me to face away from him.

Warm breath ghosted my ear as he rumbled in his best British accent, "Bend over. Show me that tight little *arse*."

The terrible impression never failed to make me laugh—but not this time. This time, it was a command.

My body obeyed without hesitation.

The drapes twitched as the heat crackled.

I bent over the bed, arching my back just enough for my cheeks to part, offering him a perfect view of everything he craved.

The fabric beneath my palms bunched as I steadied myself, the cool cotton a contrast to the heat spreading through me.

He moaned. Deep. Hot.

"So fuckin' beautiful. Sexy little slut."

His fingers traced over my sensitive skin, tingling a path down the crease before spreading me wider—exposing the tight, puckered opening he was hungry to reacquaint himself with. The warmth of his hands against my bare skin sent a jolt up my spine. Anticipation flared. My lips parted. Breath caught.

"Touch me, Romeo." I squirmed.

He didn't just touch my body—he silenced my doubts, one kiss at a time. The moment his lips touched my skin, a shiver rolled through me—tiny hairs rising beneath the heat of his tongue. A slow, deliberate lick traced over my entrance, wet warmth spreading in a bead of ecstasy. He worked me open with soft, filthy precision, slicking me, preparing me for more. His hands gripped the backs of my thighs, holding me in place as his mouth worshipped me—equal parts reverence and surrender.

"Shit, I wanna come in your ass so bad," he rasped. "Can I?"

The obscene pressure of his tongue clashed with the tenderness of his lips. Gentle one moment, devastating the next.

My toes curled. Fists coiling tight.

That he even asked sent a fresh wave of hunger ripping through me. Romeo never just took anymore—he adored. He devoured. He made me feel like a goddess.

"Yes, Romeo. I want it."

My moans mingled with the rustle of sheets and the wet, decadent sounds of him tasting me.

"You don't gotta tell me twice." His breath hitched, deep and guttural. "Get ready, baby. This is gonna be a lot of nut."

But he didn't rush. He kissed. Tasted. Teased—until I was trembling, the unbearable heat at my core leaving me desperate and raw.

The room thickened with sweat, sex, and his cologne—a warm, spicy musk that clung to my skin like a second layer I didn't want to wash away.

And then it came. The slow push. A filthy, perfect stretch that sent a shiver up my spine.

"Fuck—" My body clamped around him. My breath hitched.

He rocked us gently, the bed frame moaning with us. A third party to the rhythm we made.

His hand slid up my neck, finding my roots. With a sharp tug, he pulled the hair tie loose. My strands tumbled down in soft waves, brushing the goosebumps he'd raised along my skin.

With one hand against my breasts, he guided me back to his chest. Just enough pressure. Not too much.

"You like this?" he whispered.

Speechless, I nodded.

"Let me hear you." He thrust deeper.

The light dimmed behind my closed lids.

Breath laboured.

Heartbeat skipping.

Echoes blurred with my pulse, a distant drumroll to the ache building inside me.

"Oh my God, Romeo. Shit. I'm coming. Oh God. Please."

My elbows buckled. Face-first into the mattress.

"That's it, Queen. Feel me inside you." His rhythm turned savage. "I love you, Chloe Giannetti. Shit—I'm coming for you too. You feel it?"

The faint trace of liquor laced his breath when he growled into my neck. A sharp slap of his palm cracked across my arse, tearing a scream from my throat. The sting lit me up, pleasure detonating through me, amplifying the spasms already ripping me apart.

"Yes! Oh God, Romeo. I feel it!"

His grip tightened over my breasts as he collapsed against my shoulder as he surrendered to release. In that moment, I wasn't just his wife. I was his obsession. His escape. The place he poured every dark, broken part of himself.

For a while, we just lay there, hearts pounding in sync, bodies completely spent.

His cheeks were flushed. Chest rising and falling in even breaths.

"All I gotta say to that is—holy fuckin' shit."

I giggled, curling into him, resting my head against his chest. "That was… amazing."

He lifted my hand to his mouth, kissing each fingertip one by one. "Amazin', yeah? I like the sound of that."

◆ ◆ ◆

"Shit, Romeo, what time is it?"

The room had gone dark. Stillness throughout the house. Not a sound beyond the bedroom. We must've fallen asleep.

I nudged his chest, then shoved him. "Romeo!"

He groaned, barely cracking an eye. "Hmm? What'd you say?"

"We fell asleep. What time is it?"

He sat up and stretched those thick, defined muscles.

"8:35 PM. Why, what's the deal?"

I threw off the covers. The cool post-sex air drifted across my naked body. My nipples instantly tightened.

"Fuck! I've got an audition at nine. I need to shower—shit!"

Romeo flicked on the light, blinking against the sudden glare as he watched me scramble for my clothes.

His face twisted in mild disgust. "Why do you need to shower?"

I rolled my eyes, sniffing the armpits of my sweater.

"Because if I don't, your come will be dripping out of my arse the entire time. That's why."

He shrugged. "What's the issue?"

I stomped toward the bathroom, muttering under my breath.

"You do you, Queen," he called after me. "Who is she anyway?"

The hum of the waterfall shower made conversation harder. I poked my head around the doorframe, frowning.

"Who's who?"

He strolled over, catching a glimpse of cleavage. His finger ran down the centre. "The whore you're auditionin'."

"Oh! Jamie, something. Why?"

He followed like a puppy, eyes glued to my body as I stepped beneath the steam. It coiled around my legs like a soothing invitation, cleansing every pore.

Adjusting his semi, he licked his lips. "Can I watch?"

I turned away playfully, covering my breasts. "You already are, cowboy."

His fingers twitched. "You know what I mean."

"You want to watch the audition?" I laughed, shaking my head as I poured a long stream of honey cream wash into my palm.

"Sure. But there won't be any sex."

Silence.

I glanced back to find him pouting.

"Oh," he said flatly.

He was always sexy. Rarely cute. Until now.

I giggled. "Are you on new meds or something? Your dick's in overdrive."

He shrugged, placing his toothbrush back in the holder—the one he'd abandoned on the counter this morning.

The fogged mirror barely showed his features. But he didn't need to explain. I already knew. Since the DNA results came through, Romeo had found himself again. I hadn't realised how unsure of himself he'd been—until that confirmation landed.

The faucet squeaked as I turned off the shower. Water traced the curves of my body as I reached for a plush towel and stalked past my agitated husband—ignoring the restless energy bouncing off him.

Now... what the hell was I supposed to wear?

◆ ◆ ◆

"Romeo, she'll be here any minute." I clicked off my phone screen. "Are you not going to change?"

He pushed off the sofa and looked down at his vest, grey shorts, pulled-up socks, and sliders. That ridiculous dollar-sign chain? Pretty sure he'd only thrown it on to wind me up.

"What the fuck are you on about? I look fly." He lifted the pendant, flashing it under the ceiling light like a personal beacon.

I mean, he wasn't wrong. My husband could wear a bin bag and still look mouth-watering. But these days, I liked to run my business with a hint of professionalism—and his outfit was giving anything but.

"Maybe some jeans and a polo shirt?"

His lip curled before he could stop it. He adjusted the chain, brushing off the insult like lint.

"I'm gonna pretend I didn't hear that. T says I can do that if I don't have a word for how I feel."

My petulance melted. These new, endearing little quirks got me every time.

I rose onto my tiptoes and kissed him softly. Hooking my fingers around the pendant, I tugged him closer and smirked into his mouth. "Tim needs a pay rise."

His hands settled at my waist.

I brushed a loose curl from his forehead. "I'm glad you've got someone you connect with."

"Yeah," he said quietly.

His eyes fluttered shut as I cradled his face, pressing a wet kiss to his cheek—loaded with love.

"You're turning into a real softie, Romero Giannetti."

His eyes snapped open. The glisten in those ocean-blues darkened. His hands dropped.

"You said you wouldn't bring up what happened the other day. You promised." His tone turned steel.

Here I was, trying to be nice—and he thought I meant that. His performance issue the night we got our baby's DNA results.

"What? No!" I pulled him close again. "That's not what I meant at all. I just... I don't want you to lose your edge. That's what sets you and your brother apart."

His jaw flexed. A vein ticked at his temple.

"Wait. You think I'm tryin' to be like Daniele?"

Shit. Now I'd really offended him.

My fingers closed around his wrists, tightening instinctively. Grounding him.

"Maybe subconsciously, you think that because he and I had a thing… if you took on some of his qualities, I wouldn't bolt again."

He yanked free. Reached into the waistband of his shorts. Pulled out his gun.

"That's real smart, comin' from a whore," he muttered, raising the weapon straight ahead like he was picturing Dan at the other end of it.

The cold press of the barrel against my palm made it real when I eased it down. That word stung more than he'd ever understand. But this time, I got it.

"I know why you just said that. So I'll let it slide. I'm sorry I offended you. I love you, Romeo."

He thought I was shaming him—when, really, I just didn't want him to forget who he was. Not for me. Not for anyone.

His small smile tugged at something raw in my chest. He tucked the gun back into his waistband.

"I love you too."

A throat cleared in the doorway—Tommy.

"Sorry to interrupt, Boss. Audition's here."

I smoothed the creases in my maternity dress—the one I'd thrown on last minute. "Ahh, perfect timing. Let her in, please."

A confident stride hit the carpet. Then another. But when two became four, my eyes locked on our unexpected guest, and her plus one.

The floorboards creaked louder. The silhouettes grew faces.

Romeo was too busy peering down the V of my dress to notice. But the second he caught the shift in my posture, he turned—expression instantly hardening.

Faster than I could react, he reached for his holstered gun again and raised it. The platinum dollar-sign swung against his chest, throwing reflections like flashbulbs. Thumb twitching over the safety. Tension burning off him like heat.

"What the fuck is a dude doin' in my livin' room?" he snarled, trigger finger itching—ready to fire.

The man and woman standing before us looked just as alarmed as I felt. Her step faltered.

"Um, Jamie?" I asked, eyes flicking between the strangers.

The woman stepped forward with a hesitant wave.

"Hi. I'm Jamie." Her delicate hand brushed the man's chest. "And this is Harry."

A sleek black bob framed her symmetrical face, while his blond curls screamed '90s boy band. Mismatched on the surface—but something in their chemistry moved N-Sync.

"I'll say it again," Romeo growled, grip firm on the gun. "Why is there a man in my house?"

The temperature dropped to sub-zero. Outside, snow might've been thawing. But in here? It was fucking Antarctica.

"For God's sake, Romeo, put the gun down!"

He clicked off the safety. Just to make a point.

"Chloe. This is my house. You don't get to tell me when I use my piece."

I flashed the couple an apologetic smile, then ran my tongue over my teeth. Stepped into his space. Pressed a finger to his chest and lowered my voice. "Strike two."

A tense beat passed.

Metal clinked as he adjusted his grip. My touch stayed firm, digging just enough to hold him steady. He flitted a glance at my stomach, then finally holstered the weapon. His posture stayed rigid, coiled tight.

But this… was progress.

Jamie's bob curved neatly against her jaw. The light kissed the sharp angles of her cheekbones. There was something about her—her presence, her smile.

"Sorry about him. He's not feeling well." I lowered myself onto the couch, legs crossed. "Anyway, a couple? What's the story with you two?"

Jamie lifted her chin, confidence settling over her petite frame. Despite her pale colouring, she carried herself with purpose.

"Harry and I have been doing couples sex work for a while now. We figured with your celeb status and protection, we could earn way more."

I nodded, filing it away as a solid prospect.

Beckoning my simmering husband, I shifted the cushion off the seat beside me. "Romeo, come here for a sec."

He hesitated, still eyeing Harry like he might throw a stealth punch, then dropped down beside me.

I leaned into his ear. "I really like this idea. We could make good money from a duo."

Romeo's nostrils flared. "Queen. Hear me good. We ain't havin' a dude livin' in this house. I mean it with all of my dick and balls. Got it?"

Fair. The territorial streak came with the vows. And I had no plans to move them in. This was strictly business, not a sleepover.

"I agree. They won't be moving in."

He slouched back, pulled a gum packet from his pocket, and popped two pieces into his mouth.

"Sure." He chewed with his mouth open, gaze locked on Harry like he was daring him to blink. The crossfire of stares sparked with dominance and control.

The couple stood close to one another, like herded sheep waiting on command. Directly beneath the ceiling light, their shadows stretched across the carpet—long, expectant. Almost theatrical.

"Right then," I said, giving Jamie a nod. "Show us what you've got."

To my surprise, Harry stepped forward first. Confidence blooming, he moved to the centre of the room like it was second nature. He undressed without fuss. Jeans, shirt, socks, boxers. All stripped with easy rhythm.

Jamie followed, hips swaying with smooth precision. Her tease was slow, unhurried. Professional.

Naked and waiting, Harry's erection stood proud. Decent length. Solid girth. Confidently displayed. I let my gaze linger, mildly impressed.

Jamie's petite frame was well-proportioned. Her breasts—natural, perfectly shaped—rose and fell with each measured breath. The whole performance was fluid, elegant. Practised.

From the corner of my eye, I caught Romeo watching them, oddly unbothered by the naked man in our living room. Then again, when it came to sex, Romeo had a one-track mind. And right now, it was locked on her tits.

The pair didn't waste a second. They moved like clockwork—his palms kneading her breasts, her hand stroking his cock with finesse. Whether they were seasoned performers or just real lovers didn't matter. The chemistry was there.

Romeo's hand landed on my knee. His fingers trailed upward—slow, electric. They slipped beneath the hem of my dress, brushing against my heat.

He leaned in, voice low against the shell of my ear.

"You like girls. Why don't you get her over here to lick your pussy?"

Hmm.

Jamie flashed me a look as Harry nibbled her neck.

A bloom of heat flared in my core, but simmered just as fast. I pressed my thighs together. My body couldn't take another orgasm.

Romeo's fingers slipped beneath my panties. "Do you like girls more than you like me?"

His thumb caught the pulse of my clit. My breath hitched.

Thoughts spiralled—how could he even think that?

"No." I shook my head, breathless. "I only want you."

His pupils dilated. A growl vibrated deep in his chest—possessive and primal.

"My queen," he murmured, his breath hot against my neck. "I'm gonna show you I ain't lost no edge. Let me worship your body while you watch them fuck. You're gonna come in my mouth. And I'm gonna taste you."

Oh, God.

When he spoke to me like that, when he needed me to show him the truth. My fingers gripped the arms of the sofa as Romeo sank between my legs, his hands parting my thighs with devotion. The walls seemed to swell, the room closing in as the tip of his nose brushed the flesh beneath my dress.

Across the room, Harry's mouth worshipped Jamie's body—his tongue tracing the curve of her breast before trailing lower.

Determined to keep my eyes open, I focused on Jamie's reactions. The way her chest rose, her spine arched into his touch. I mirrored her, absorbing every ounce of pleasure Romeo gave me.

He spread my folds with gentle fingers, pressing featherlight kisses to my swollen clit before pushing back the hood with his thumb, exposing the most sensitive part of me.

My eyes widened. "Oh, fuck."

My head tipped back as heat flared from my core. His tongue worked in slow, sexy flicks—teasing, tormenting, consuming. He licked from my clit to my arse and back again. I could barely breathe.

A faint moan from across the room edged me closer.

"Watch them fuck, Queen," he whispered against my soaked flesh. "Feel my kisses on your tight pussy."

I writhed—

"Oh, shit, Romeo."

The lights flickered. The room tilted. That strip of hallway light pressing under the door felt like a spectator.

Romeo slid a finger inside me, stroking my inner walls with devotion. Every pass sent sparks spiralling through me, coaxing exactly what he craved.

All too soon, my body surrendered, releasing a hot rush of ecstasy onto his waiting tongue.

"There she goes. My little squirter." He groaned. "You taste so fuckin' good, Chloe. Give me more. King's thirsty. Come on, baby."

My fingers flexed, nails digging into the sofa's fabric. Another wave of pleasure surged out of me. He lapped it up greedily, not wasting a drop.

"Shit, Romeo…" My hips bucked. Legs trembling, thighs quaking. The pressure built, unbearable.

His finger plunged deep one final time—his mouth sealed over my clit and sucked hard.

Stars exploded behind my eyelids.

"Ahh. Holy fuck! I'm coming, Romeo. I'm coming for you."

The last thing I remembered was the climax detonating through my body, the world spinning wildly out of reach.

When my eyes fluttered open, the room was colder. Darker. Just me, my husband, and the warm glow of a single lamp.

I blinked through the haze, my forehead damp with sweat, my stomach curling with nausea.

I placed a hand on his chest. His heartbeat, steady beneath my palm. "Where did they go?"

The rough pad of his finger brushed a loose strand of hair behind my ear. "You passed out, so I hired them and told them to step."

I sat up, eyes darting as memory replayed. Her breasts, their tangled limbs. Heat that swallowed the room.

"I passed out?"

"Not gonna lie, that's a first for me." A devilish smirk tugged at his lips. "Is it weird that I came in my shorts?"

A snort escaped before I could stop it. Only he could make me laugh at a time like this.

"You didn't! Show me."

Pride glinted in his eyes as he hooked a thumb into his waistband, peeling it back just enough to reveal a decently sized release soaking into the fabric.

"My skills got you so good, your body just shut down. Sexy as hell."

If I ever thought Romeo and I had issues, moments like this proved we did. Was it normal to black out after an orgasm? Probably not. Something to bring up at my next OBGYN appointment.

But would I shatter his confidence?

Absolutely not.

Safe in the knowledge that he wanted me—whether I was conscious or not—I knew we were on the right track.

Gone were the days I needed constant reassurance. If anything, it was the other way around now.

The moon smiled at us through the long stretch of window, a cool white glow bathing us in quiet intimacy.

Between Romeo backing down in the heat of the moment and trusting my judgement with that couple, we hadn't just turned a page—we'd rewritten a whole damn chapter.

We'd grown so much in so little time. The world was ours for the taking. And that moon? He made me feel like it already belonged to me.

I rested my head on Romeo's chest.
He exhaled. Instantly, he relaxed.
Safe in each other's arms.
Always.

CHAPTER 5

A sliver of light peeked through the edge of the curtains, waking me a little earlier than I'd have liked.

When I say I was awake; I wasn't, really. That half-conscious kind of slumber where dreams still feel real. Right now, it was me and Romeo holding our baby boy. Log fire. Candlelight. Safe and secure without a single worry.

A soft, rhythmic movement elsewhere in the house crept into the dream. Footsteps on the stairs, maybe? But in paradise, that noise was just the bartender breaking ice for my first piña colada. The log fire had become the heat of the sun as we strolled hand in hand along the beach.

I'd just taken my first sip when the bedroom door breezed open, sending freshly burned tobacco drifting my way. My eyes fluttered open. The drink vanished with every blink. The soft golden glow faded to the cold light of day.

There he was. Romeo.

Too early for anyone to be this alert, let alone him—but he moved with purpose, glistening with sweat. Tim had clearly worked him hard this morning.

He scrubbed his damp hair with a towel. "Oh, you're awake. How you feelin', sexy?"

The wide-open door let morning light spill across the room.

I stretched, a yawn rippling through my limbs.

"I'm okay. Still a little nauseous after blacking out last night, but overall, pretty good."

Head still buried in the pillow, I pulled it closer. Somehow, it felt softer than usual. My eyelids drooped again. The bartender was back, ready to take my next order.

That's when a little snort cut the dream short for a second time. Eyes open, I caught Romeo stifling a laugh, then flexing his biceps in the mirror like he hadn't just tripped my internal alarm.

"What are you giggling about?"

That towel became an accessory around his neck, like a boxer at the ring of the bell. The twitching lips and flared nostrils told quite the tale.

He turned, flexing again. This time giving me the full show. Abs, pecs, biceps, hell—even triceps.

"These are bigger, right?" He flexed his pecs for emphasis.

Wincing from a pinch in my back, I sat up, narrowing my eyes. "Don't change the subject. You only giggle like a girl when you're up to something."

His eyes lit up, a telltale spark of mischief firing to life.

He perched on the edge of the bed, back angled like he was bracing for impact. "Aight, listen. I know you said not to, but… I told Tommy about what happened."

No. He. Did. Not.

As if on cue, the front door swung open downstairs. A snap of wind rushed up the stairs and slammed our bedroom door shut. I couldn't have timed it better myself.

The air stilled. Just the sound of my pulse now. My palm smacked my forehead, already picturing the two of them whispering like schoolboys, passing notes at the back of the class.

"You told Tommy I blacked out when you went down on me? Why the hell would you do that?"

He adjusted the semi bursting at the seams of his shorts. I didn't give him the satisfaction of looking.

"I'm sorry, baby, but a man can't not tell a story like that. If you thought they respected me before—you should see them now."

I groaned, flopping back into the mattress, sinking into the sheets like I could claw my way back into that dream.

"You're an arsehole. I'm genuinely mad about this."

Romeo slid in beside me, fingers lazily trailing along my arm, igniting just enough exposed skin to soften the edge of my irritation.

"You can't be mad at somethin' so sexy." He kissed my shoulder. "Wanna do it again?"

My nostrils flared as he inched closer.

"Oh God, Romeo—you stink!" I pinched my nose. "Please go and shower. I'm not kidding."

He backed off with a huff. A beat passed. Then he shoved off the bed and stalked toward the bathroom, the towel now dragging behind him across the floor. One final glance over his shoulder—then he slammed the door hard enough to make the echo circle the room twice.

Truth was, this wasn't really about his smell. My defences were up because my insensitive husband wasn't taking my blackout-prone condition seriously enough. I was scared. And instead of supporting me, he was milking it—feeding an ego already bloated enough to burst.

My freshly washed husband emerged from the humidity of the bathroom, coconut and bergamot clinging to his damp skin. A towel sat low on his hips, framing the abs he worked so hard to maintain. He was—chef's kiss—perfect.

Shower steam curled around his feet like a message as he stalked past me. Still pissed, he huffed, tucked his gun into the towel's fold and tore through the clothes rail, yanking shirts out only to shove them back again.

"What's the issue, Romeo?"

He pulled out a plain black T-shirt, gave it a once-over, then snapped it back onto the hanger with a sharp flick of his wrist.

"Nothin'."

Hmm.

I threw back the covers, the warmth beneath the sheets replaced by my husband's cold mood. Planting my feet onto the thick, soft carpet did nothing to warm my toes.

"Tell me, or I'm coming over there."

His broad back tensed. Muscles shifted beneath olive skin, the red marks I'd left down his spine now fading like last night's intimate memory.

He finally turned to face me.

"Twenty fuckin' nine years I been alive. Not once did anybody say I stink. You told me I do—more than once."

Shit.

I blinked.

I hadn't expected it to have bothered him so much.

"When you say offensive shit like that to me, I gotta work real hard not to act up. And it takes a lot outta me. But it feels like you don't give a fuck about how hard I'm workin' on myself."

Ahh, this was Tim's bloody influence. If anything, the man was getting *too* good at his job—and now I had no easy way out. Romeo had me cornered with a level of emotional self-awareness I wasn't remotely prepared to handle.

With no better option, I deployed the only tactic that ever worked Avoidance through seduction.

I stepped in behind him. His skin was a tropical paradise, the coconut practically cracking its shell and pouring its scent all over us.

The edge of his damp towel brushed my thighs as I wrapped my arms around his waist. Our eyes met in the mirror. His dick hardened instantly beneath the thick cotton, straining like it begged for my touch. His back was warm and damp against my cheek as I kissed one shoulder blade, then the other. My hands came around his torso, fingers gliding over his chest, grazing a nipple until it stiffened beneath my touch.

He held my gaze, unwavering, as I traced a slow line to the edge of his towel—stopping just shy of his favourite toy.

"I'm sorry I upset you, Romeo."

He moved fast, flipping our positions until my back was pressed to his chest. His hands landed firmly on my waist, radiating heat.

"You're a bitch sometimes, Mrs Giannetti," he murmured, kissing the nape of my neck before burying his nose in my hair and breathing me in.

We stared at each other in the mirror, neither of us blinking. Then something shifted. His hands still cradled my waist—just as a nudge came from deep within. A tiny kick.

"Did you feel that?" I asked, bringing my hand over the top of his. His fingers flinched.

"Did the boy just kick me?" Romeo's voice lit up.

I smiled. "I think he did."

"Or maybe he punched me." He raised his fists in front of us, sparring with the air, making the right sounds.

I giggled. "You're an ass-hat."

He jabbed the air again, full of boyish pride. "He might be a boxer. That'd be cool, right?"

I hadn't really pictured the baby beyond the newborn phase yet, but clearly, Romeo had.

We grinned at each other in the mirror. A little fogged from his heat, but the glow on our faces shone right through.

Argument resolved.

"You've had a haircut?" I turned in his arms, brushing the freshly cropped curls. "Looks like someone took my softie comment to heart."

His hands stayed on my waist. Another kick. Another smile.

"Yeah. The wife said I'd turned into a pussy bitch. Figured the hair needed sharpenin' up."

I took his head in my hands, bringing him down for a closer look. He folded over without hesitation.

"Hm. It's a little short." I inspected. "I won't be able to play with your curls now."

His spine instantly straightened. Teeth clenched.

My hands dropped to my sides.

He leaned into the mirror again and scrubbed the top of his head. His coils still sprang—just no longer floppy.

"Too short?" he said, almost to himself.

I'd hurt his feelings again...

The towel slipped an inch. He caught it.

"One of these days, you'll look at me and say, 'Damn, Romeo, you look so fuckin' sexy I need to finger myself.'"

Stifling a giggle was impossible around him.

"In your mind, that's what I'd say, is it?"

"Well, I'm always tuggin' my dick over you. Only fair."

Taking inspiration from him, I opened my closet door. "Anyway, less of the romance. I didn't realise the time. I need to get ready."

Romeo slammed his hand against the wood, closing it with a deliberate thud. A barricade over my independence.

His tall frame loomed like a storm cloud, blotting out the light bleeding through the drapes.

"Why?" His tone turned clipped. Eyes narrowed. "You ain't goin' anywhere."

He stood firm, broad, and immovable. A human brick wall.

Hands on my hips, I hit him with the arched-brow glare.

"I already told you last week. I'm giving Britney a driving lesson today."

His palm stayed pressed to the door like he might shove straight through it.

"Are you for real? You ain't a good enough driver to teach someone else."

Air rushed out of me at the unexpected jab.

"Excuse me?"

Okay, fine—he wasn't wrong. But I wasn't going down without a fight.

Maybe I'd take up boxing myself. Gloves on. This was a battle for the belt.

"Chloe. If you'd told me you were givin' one of the sluts a lesson, I'd have said no. That ain't happenin'."

To prove my point that I was in charge of my own damn destiny, I jabbed him in the ribs with my elbow.

He grunted, low and unamused, loosening his grip on the closet. I reopened the doors and pulled out one of my looser-fitting dresses.

"Yes, it is happening—because I already promised her. We'll use my old Mini. It's not a big deal."

I threw him a smug look. His own words coming back to haunt him.

His hand, still cradling the invisible wound, caught my arm. His breathing hitched. A crack in the control.

"You're pregnant, Chloe. Not happenin'."

We stared each other down. Tension rose between us like lava beneath a volcano—pressurised, inevitable.

And this time, frustratingly, he wasn't backing down.

"Fine!" I snapped. "Leave. I don't want you watching me get changed."

"Oh yeah?" He scoffed, straightening to full height. "You think you're the boss now, huh? You know I let you win, right?"

He stepped closer. Irrevocable. His voice dropped to a dark tease. Heated fingers curled lightly around my throat.

"I'm the man of this house—and it's my right to see you naked. So get your fuckin' robe off and show me your tits."

He tugged the belt.

My lips thinned. Overconfident prick.

But who was I kidding?

I loved how he lusted after my body.

◆ ◆ ◆

"Ready? Turn on the engine. Black button. Right there." I jabbed the console.

Doors locked. Seatbelts on. The Mini Cooper, abandoned at the far side of the lot, had something to prove—that she still had my back.

I peered over my shoulder through the rear window, checking we hadn't been spotted. It had been ages since I'd last sat in this car. The scent of stale air freshener lingered, and my ratty old purse still waited on the back seat. The memories it carried were ones I'd rather leave buried.

Britney reluctantly pushed the button. The heater groaned to life, coughing through months of disuse. She sat pale as a sheet, gripping the steering wheel like her life depended on it.

"Chloe, I'm really not sure about this."

A crew member popped up from behind one of Romeo's cars at the sound of the ignition. We had seconds to move.

"Stop stressing. I'll handle Romeo. Foot down. Now!"

The Mini sputtered to life. Reluctant but loyal.

That same guy shielded his eyes from the winter sun, rounding the hood for a closer look. My heart kicked into gear. Any second now, he'd reach for his earpiece.

"Okay. Let's get out of here."

Britney hit the gas a little too hard. The Mini lurched forward, then slammed to a stop. We both rocked in our seats. I braced against the dash, instinct kicking in.

Hmm.

Maybe Romeo had a point. Still—I needed this. Just a little time out of the house. A break from the isolation.

"Try again. Let's go," I urged, checking the rear-view. Another valet had joined the first. Two men. Arms folded. Watching.

"Are we being followed?" Britney asked as we bunny-hopped onto the street.

We passed the paparazzi at the gate, who barely glanced up, probably assuming we were just another pair of forgettable whores.

Once we hit the open road, I finally leaned back in my seat.

"No. Romeo's with Tim in the gym. Again. Snake's out picking up his new car. Tommy went to the bathroom five minutes ago—he takes at least ten."

A nervous giggle escaped her lips. "How do you even know that?"

I tapped my nose. "Not my first time escaping."

We cruised down a palm-tree-lined road. The fronds swayed above rooftops, still dusted with the last of the season's snow. I zipped my coat a little higher—trying to keep the anxiety out and the heat in.

Half a mile in, and she was getting the hang of it. Her steering grew steadier with each turn. And, surprisingly, I wasn't a half-bad teacher.

"Okay, take this right turn here," I said, relaxed, tapping my fingers to the soft thrum of my old hooker playlist.

The road ahead was calm. Picture-perfect lawns. Wide, empty streets. Ideal for parking manoeuvres.

Unfortunately, that's when I realised Britney didn't know her left from her right. She took the turn full throttle.

My eyes widened. Time slowed.

A car swerved. Horns blared. The Mini jumped the kerb, all four tyres skidding—and slammed into a fire hydrant.

The crunch of metal tore through the silence. The hood popped with a hiss of steam, fogging the windscreen. Glass shattered, sparkling across Britney's lap. The front end crumpled around the impact.

My seatbelt yanked tight across my chest, searing into my collarbone. My heart thundered in my throat.

"Chloe," Britney whispered, trembling. "Oh my God, I think I hit something."

The engine groaned like it was dying. The blinker still clicked—like it had no idea what had just happened.

"You think!?" I gasped, forcing air into my lungs.

Thankfully, she hadn't been speeding. Aside from the shards of glass, she looked okay.

But me? I patted myself down. Head, fine. Legs, fine. No blood. No sharp pain. My hands found my bump.

A little kick. Thank God.

Relief flooded me. All I wanted right now was to hold my baby.

Then came the sound. Like a thunderclap from the sky. The hydrant erupted. Water burst high, drenching the car in a torrential downpour. It hammered the roof like war drums.

I turned to Britney. "Are you okay?"

Too calm. Too quiet. No response. Just shallow breaths and a wide-eyed stare as the wipers squeaked uselessly across cracked glass.

"Britney?"

She blinked, sucking in a breath like it was her first. "I can't breathe. I'm—I'm so sorry, Chloe."

My fists unfurled. "Shh. It's all right. We're fine."

Then I saw it. Red and blue lights flashing in the side mirror.

Shit. A police car and a fucking fire truck.

"The cops!" Britney squeaked. "Is now a good time to tell you I don't have a driver's permit?"

A sliver of glass slipped from the frame and landed in the footwell with a final clink. My heart stalled. Mouth dropped open. The crack of my arse started sweating.

Oh shit.

I unzipped my coat, heat crawling up the back of my neck.

Her pale knuckles clenched the wheel. Lipstick smudged across her cheek. Panic everywhere I looked.

A cop strode toward us. Long-legged, thumb hooked into his belt, gun visible from all angles. His walk screamed authority.

I straightened in my seat. Composed myself. Smoothed down my hair like it was nothing more than a scuffed rim.

A fake smile stretched from ear to ear.

Just act natural.

Then came the tap on my window.

My stomach clenched into a tight fist.

"Everything all right in there, ma'am?" The young male officer hollered over the roar of water, cupping his hand to his brow as he peered inside. "You've been in an accident."

My stomach clenched into a tight fist. I rolled down the window. Water sprayed inside, mingling with the scent of scorched rubber and regret. A fire crew of four honed in on the hydrant.

This was turning into a spectacle.

"We're fine, Officer. No problems here. No problems at all." I raised my thumb, just to seal the deal.

He stepped out of the blast zone, removed his soaking cap, and tucked it under one arm. Fire-red hair. Pale blue eyes. His gaze flicked from Britney to me.

"Who owns this vehicle?" His voice rang loud and clear.

I lifted a shaky hand. "That would be me."

He nodded, reaching for his notepad and licking the tip of his pencil—just as the firefighters shut off the hydrant with a wrench. The last drop slapped the tarmac, then silence. A final sigh from the car's engine rattled to a stop.

The cop nodded at the rescue team, then stepped closer.

"Can I take your name?"

That question always provoked mixed reactions.

I hesitated. He probably wasn't a fan of my husband…

"Chloe Giannetti," I said, steadying my voice with a confidence I didn't feel.

The firefighters began inspecting the car, preparing to secure it. Pointing at the hood. Scratching their chins.

The cop's pencil froze. So did all of my reflexes.

Britney's hand crept into mine, clammy and cold.

"Chloe, I'm freaking out," she choked out.

I ignored her, eyes locked on the officer. Waiting for the fallout.

"You related to Romero Giannetti?" he asked, one brow arched, his stance shifting.

I giggled nervously, tucking a strand of hair shakily behind my ear. "That depends on whether you like him or not."

Just as it seemed I might talk my way out of this, the screech of tyres rang out, urgent and sharp, stopping right behind us. The sound prickled up my spine.

"Oh, fuck." I turned to Britney. "It's Romeo."

"Chloe!?" His voice boomed through the chaos, footsteps thunderous behind it. "Where's my wife?"

Shirtless. Breathless. His glistening torso flexed as he gripped the window frame, scanning my body. Heat radiated off him in waves.

"Are you okay?" he panted.

Eyes wide, I shook my head.

"She doesn't have a fucking permit," I hissed.

Romeo froze. His jaw ticked. Posture shifted completely.

"I'll handle this, Officer," he said coolly, leaning against the car—completely blocking the cop's view of us. The chill in the air clung to his damp skin, raising every hair over his body.

Tommy attacked from the rear, backing the fire crew away from the vehicle like it was no longer their concern.

The cop stiffened as the fire truck pulled away, replaced by Tommy and Snake closing in—silent, armed, unreadable.

He looked left, then right, clocking the men boxing him in. His walkie-talkie crackled. Tommy reached over and silenced it.

"You still takin' bribes?" Romeo asked, pulling out his wallet.

The cop nodded, holding out his hand.

Romeo peeled off the hundreds, rolling the bills into his palm. "Here. Five hundred. Same as last time."

"You'll get this car towed within the hour?" the cop asked, rifling through the notes and slipping the rest into his pocket.

Romeo nodded, holding his stare—reading him like prey. "You got your money, now leave," he commanded.

He stepped forward, arms out, just wide enough to make the officer flinch. The cop didn't argue. He slapped his cap back on and practically sprinted to his car.

As the patrol vehicle disappeared down the road, I sank into my seat. Heart hammering. Throat tightening.

Romeo yanked open the door, releasing it from the crumpled frame.

"Is my son okay?" His tone was ice.

My breath caught.

"Yes. So am I," I murmured, cradling my bump.

Did he not care if I was okay?

Without another word, he took my forearm and pulled me from the Mini, steering me toward the waiting SUV. Its door was already open—like a deadly invitation. The sharp dig of his fingers cut like glass, digging deeper the further we walked.

My knees buckled. I stumbled, ankles threatening to give way as he dragged me forward.

Clutching the SUV door, I glanced back. Britney clung to Snake in a clumsy embrace, weeping.

"Get in." He nudged my back.

Reluctantly, I stepped inside. Romeo took the seat beside me, energy coiled tight.

The SUV door slid shut behind us like a bite, snapping shut and swallowing the light.

I hesitated, trying to gauge his mood.

"Are you so mad at me you ripped your shirt off?" My voice barely carried.

Please laugh.

He glanced down at his bare chest, pecs flexing.

"I was liftin' weights when Tommy told me you'd run. No time to put a shirt on."

I pressed a hand to his chest. His heart still hammering. But his lip curled as he looked me over, more irritation than affection.

"You better not have hurt yourself, Chloe, or I'll be fuckin' pissed."

Sinister Romeo. Fully reloaded.

My hand dropped into my lap.

"I'm fine. Not even a scratch."

He placed a hand on my stomach. A second passed like an hour, waiting for confirmation. Then—finally—a little kick.

"I'm takin' you for a check-up," he said. "Then I'll deal with this fuckin' mess."

◆ ◆ ◆

"Are you not going to talk to me for the rest of the day, then?" I asked again, peering over at the pouting driver of a very fast sports car. The leather seat groaned as I shifted, its cold surface sticking to my thighs.

Romeo and I had been travelling in silence for five minutes, ever since we'd left Arnold's office. The engine's power vibrated through the soles of my shoes as he weaved through traffic at his own speed.

"No," he snapped.

Cars blurred past, matching the mess of thoughts tumbling through my head.

"Fine! I didn't want to talk to you, anyway!" I folded my arms and turned to face the window.

Shame simmered beneath my ribs, no matter how stubbornly I stuck to my guns. But if he wanted to be horrible, then so would I. I studied my fingernails like the cuticles held secrets. Romeo could sulk all he wanted. I wasn't bothered in the slightest… Except I was.

Eventually, the devil himself couldn't take the heat of his own creation any longer. His voice sliced through the quiet.

"You know what pisses me off the most about you?"

The blow landed in my chest. I blinked away the assault.

"Wow. Go on, let it all out." I toyed with my bracelet.

"I told you not to go out with that whore. You're carryin' our baby, but for some reason, you're too selfish to give a shit. It's times like this I look at you and think—I married a girl, not a woman."

Did I just hear that right? Did he seriously use those words? Weren't those the exact words his mother spat when she tried to tear me down?

Arsehole.

Insanity rose like a tide. I'd lost myself the moment he called me selfish.

"Let me out of this car. Now. Let me out!" I screamed, yanking at the handle—thankfully locked. I wanted to vomit. And kill him. In that order.

He flexed his fingers, caught between grabbing me or gripping the wheel tighter.

"I ain't lettin' you out here. You're comin' home. And you'll stay there until the baby's born."

The seatbelt across my chest felt more like a restraint than a safety net. The car seemed to roar louder, shoving me deeper into my seat. Keeping me there. Holding me tighter.

Until the baby's born? Was he planning to kick me out after that?

I stared at him. Rage and malice tangled like live wires inside me. One spark away from explosion.

"What is this? Kidnap?"

The car felt like a confession booth. Every word echoed louder than it should.

"Well, you're the one actin' like a kid, so I guess it is."

I don't know what possessed me, but before I could stop myself, my clenched fist struck the side of his chiselled face.

Shit.

Heat bloomed in my knuckles. His cheek flared red. One eye watered from the unexpected blow. But he didn't speak. Didn't move.

Silence reigned the whole way back to the mansion.

Flashbulbs popped at the gate. With his sunglasses on, we rolled in like it was just another Tuesday.

Romeo parked at the entrance but left the engine running. He slid his shades onto his head, pulled down the sun visor and checked his reflection in the mirror, angling to inspect the damage. I watched every second.

Carefully, I reached for the door handle—but he knew. He blocked me before I could move.

"No. I ain't lettin' you out, so you can run back to my brother. We ain't doin' that shit anymore."

Caught red-handed, I knotted my fingers in my lap and pressed my lips into a tight line.

"After what you said? I've got nothing to say to you, Romeo."

He turned in his seat, draping one arm along my headrest. "No problem, Queen—'cause I got plenty."

The SUV rolled up beside us, their doors flinging open like a tactical unit. It wouldn't be long now until we got the all clear to go inside.

"Go on then, smart-arse. What have you got to say to me?"

My heart skipped a beat. Divorce. Or murder. Both felt equally plausible.

He unbuckled his seatbelt, raking a hand through the curls that no longer bounced.

"Chloe Giannetti, I fuckin' love you with everythin' I got. I never loved anyone 'til I met you."

He placed a hand over my bump. My stomach coiled tighter.

"We got a baby comin', and we've done good sortin' our shit out. 'Til now—"

My shoulders sagged. That wasn't what I expected at all. I thought there'd be an axe. Maybe a few warning shots from his favourite gun. But no. He chose love over violence.

"I'm sorry, Romeo." My lip trembled. Guilt pressed against my chest. I flashed back to the Mini in pieces. His face when he arrived.

He reached for me. I flinched, but he ignored it—tucking a strand of hair behind my ear.

"You're bored at home, yeah? That's why you took Britney out?"

My shoulders sagged. Just like that, we understood each other.

I smiled faintly, pulling at the edge of my coat. "How did you know?"

"I called T on the way to rescue your slippery ass. Talked it over. He gave me advice. But when I saw the state of the car, I lost it. The thought of seein' you and my son dead made me wanna shoot myself." He swallowed hard, rubbing the back of his neck.

"I'm sorry, Romeo. I am."

Tommy gave the nod for clearance, but Romeo didn't move.

"You put me in that position for a reason. I figured, with security so tight, you feel trapped."

I looked down at my lap. "When you put it like that… I guess that does make me a child, huh?"

He brushed my arm. Our eyes met.

"Nah," he murmured. "I'm sorry I said that, Chloe."

His hand slid onto my thigh, squeezing the thickest part with a possessive calm.

"So… are we friends again?" I fluttered my lashes.

He chuckled. "You seen this fuckin' bruise? Should I be friends with you after that?"

I nodded, hopeful.

"I have an idea," he said, cutting the engine.

"You do? What sort of idea?"

"I got some business to attend to later. I figured I'd let you come with me."

◆ ◆ ◆

"Aight, we're leavin' now, Chloe. I ain't gonna tell you again!" Romeo's voice bellowed from the bottom of the stairs like a foghorn.

Typical. Always rushing me.

I'd spent the last hour getting ready for my first-ever time attending business with him. Dressed in black sweats and white sneakers, I looked casual, but sharp. The only thing I hadn't decided on was the sunglasses.

"Chloe!" His exasperation echoed through the house like a warning shot.

One final tug on my ponytail locked everything in place. I snatched up my purse, slung it across my body, and left the sunglasses behind. He was throwing enough shade for the both of us.

When I climbed into the back of the SUV, Romeo was already waiting. A fresh cigarette butt still smouldered in the gravel, smoke curling through the cracked window. His eyes dropped to my stomach.

"Don't lie to me. Are you sure you're alright for this?"

I sighed, shooting him a glare. "Arnold said I'm completely fine. Don't take this away from me. I'm actually excited."

He reached down by his feet and picked something up wrapped in cloth. Probably the same scrap of fabric that moonlighted as a blindfold.

"You won't need it, but here. Hold this."

He peeled it open. Gun oil and fabric softener rose into the air—followed by a glint of metal.

A small silver handgun.

Instinct kicked in before logic. I took it without thinking. The weight dragged my hand down, heavier than expected, for something that size. "Wait, why the hell have you given me a gun?"

The chassis shuddered over uneven ground as we pulled off the estate. That's when I noticed the crucifix shifting against his chest.

My eyes narrowed. "Am I missing something?"

I craned my neck, glancing out the tinted window, scanning the blur of the horizon for answers. The insulated hush inside the cab was broken only by the rattle of the suspension and the creak of leather.

"Romeo, why are you wearing that necklace?"

He traced the cross with his thumb before lifting it. "Just for show. In case the paparazzi catch a glimpse. Don't worry. I ain't takin' you anywhere dangerous."

My grip around the gun tightened before my brain caught up. "So the gun's just for show too? Should I point it at their cameras if they get too close?" I teased, waving it a little too freely.

Tommy's eyes flicked to the rear-view mirror. His shoulders tensed.

"Put that fuckin' gun down, woman," Romeo snapped. "Jesus Christ, it's loaded."

Sheepishly, I placed it on the seat beside me—barrel pointed at him, just in case.

"On second thoughts, give it here," he muttered, sweeping it back up and slipping it into his inside jacket pocket.

The SUV jolted over a pothole as we merged onto the freeway. The baby lashed out with a sharp kick, and I winced, pressing a hand to my ribs.

"What's wrong?" he asked, eyes darting between my face and my bump. His hand hovered near his seatbelt like that would help.

"Nothing. He just nudged my ribs. I'm fine." I breathed through it, and Romeo slouched back in his seat.

The radio crackled to life. Some guy reading out rigid coordinates. Tommy and Snake nodded at each other.

"Where on earth are we going?" I asked, staring through the windshield at the green road signs pointing every which way. We could've been headed to Canada for all I knew.

"My club," he said, casually checking the rounds in his favourite gun.

His club? If I'd known that, I wouldn't have even bothered.

My lip curled. Defences rose. So this was it—he'd brought me along for a whore night.

"You've got business to attend to at your club?" I asked flatly, inching away from him.

Now would've been a great time to fish out my designer frames and hide the jealousy flashing in my eyes.

"Yeah. Figured you could help me out."

Oh, how generous. I could help him out, could I?

The mood curdled faster than he could count money. I stared at him, trying to figure out what game he was playing. Sat there, all handsome, fresh cologne, neat haircut—like he was out to impress?

Was this my punishment for the Mini? Surely there were better ways to express your feelings than casually pimping out your pregnant wife to LA's biggest sleazebags.

The SUV pulled up outside a building so familiar, yet somehow… unrecognisable. The neon sign still glowed and hummed, casting flickering shadows across the moonlit street.

Easy Access.

And tonight, for some reason, it actually lived up to the name. From the outside, the place looked derelict. Tumbleweed quiet. Not a sound from within. No crowd in sight. The air of the building clung to my skin like the memory of that first night.

I glanced at Romeo as he fished a key from his pocket and unlocked the main door.

"The crew already swept the area. We're good," he muttered, taking my hand as he shouldered it open with a shove. The door groaned on a hinge, rusted from neglect, echoing into the darkness as we stepped into the foyer.

Dark. Damp. Dust particles suspended in time. A faint trace of sweat and booze still lingered beneath the sharp bite of mildew. It was nothing like I remembered.

"What the hell happened here?" I asked, stepping cautiously into the gloom.

He flicked a switch. The LEDs sputtered to life, casting a sterile glare over the once-packed dance floor. The same space Hanna and I once… never mind.

Romeo released the safety on his gun, keeping it low by his thigh as we moved toward the centre of the room.

I half-expected music to erupt from the walls, like the building remembered us. But there was only the sound of our footsteps.

"She's been closed a couple months now," he said, a little disheartened. The room felt enormous now that it was empty.

"Why did you close it?"

He exhaled, brushing a finger over a cobwebbed barstool propped against the counter. "Had no choice. Drug raid."

My lips tightened as the realisation hit. A full-blown police raid. And I was only finding out now?

"I would ask why you didn't tell me, but there's no point, is there?"

He ignored that, pulling me into his body. Just the two of us, standing in the heart of his empire. It was almost romantic—if not for the gun pressing into the small of my back.

"You stood in this exact spot the first time I saw you," he murmured into my hair. Our bodies began to sway, like we were dancing to a ballad no one else could hear.

I tilted my head, meeting his gaze. "I can't believe you remember that."

The heat from his erection pressed between us. Welcome warmth in the cold shell of the building.

"I wanted you the moment I saw you."

His free hand cupped my chin, tilting my lips to his. His mouth covered mine, tongue sliding against mine, kissing me like he meant it. Like this time, we'd get it right.

When I broke away, I traced my fingers along his jaw.

"Why are we here, Romeo?"

There had to be more to this than nostalgia.

"I wanna get this place back on its feet." His voice flickered with excitement. "Figured since the whores are yours now, that makes you my business partner. So I need your input."

My eyes shimmered beneath the raw overhead lights. Me? His business partner? He wanted my opinion?

My nails scraped lightly through his curls as I pulled him back in for another kiss. But just as things started heating up, he backed off.

"Listen, Chloe, I wanna fuck you *real* bad." His eyes swept the room, dust sheets hanging like ghosts in the corners. "Just not here."

"Oh." I folded my arms. "Since when did you gain self-control?"

"It ain't like that, and you know it. Security's tight. I need to keep my eyes open. Your pussy drugs me. I can't risk that here."

I wasn't too offended. Especially not when he was handing me a stake in his business. I pushed against his chest and stepped back, but he followed immediately, closing the space again.

"Don't walk away from me, Chloe. You can see my fuckin' hard-on." He caught my hand and pressed it against him. "You know how difficult this is for me. I'm thinkin' of your safety."

He'd dodged a fallout by the skin of his teeth—mostly because I was too excited to explore.

"So, if you don't want to have sex with me, can I at least have a look around?" Sarcasm dripped from my tongue as I wandered toward the bar, picturing that cute bartender with the cheeky smile, polishing his glasses, waiting for my order.

I unhooked a barstool that had been left face down on the counter. The same stool, with its same dodgy leg, tilted beneath me as I sat, giving me a clear view of the dance floor. If I looked hard enough, I could almost see Hanna and Hulk across the room. Frozen in time. Ghosts of the past.

"Sure. We'll take a look." He pulled the dust cover off the beer pumps before lifting an open bottle of whiskey, inspecting the label. "I'll get my designer in. We'll make your ideas happen."

My fingers paused mid-stroke along the dusty bar top, leaving a faint smear across my fingertip.

I turned in my seat to face him. "Designer?"

Suspicion edged my tone—but I wasn't jealous. Not yet.

"Yeah, you know. She redesigned the apartment, the cottage... pretty sure she had a hand in the mansion at some point."

She.

My teeth clamped down on my tongue.

"Mm-hm," I replied, clipped and cool, with a tight nod.

The scent of stale beer and sweet mixers clung to my skin like this was the real thing. God, what I wouldn't give for a shot of the good stuff right about now.

"What?" He set the bourbon bottle down the moment he clocked the shift in my mood.

"How many times have you slept with her?"

"Ah-hah!" He lit up like a kid in a spelling bee. His sudden enthusiasm nearly knocked me off the stool. "Tim already told me how to handle this."

He straightened, eyes fixed somewhere beyond me like he was reading from an invisible script. One hand tucked behind his back, chest puffed like he was about to recite the national anthem.

"I had sex with her one time. Three years ago. It was bad, and I do not wish to engage in fuckin' her again."

His jaw flexed, like he was bracing for the slap that never came.

A reluctant smile curled my lips, spreading when he winked.

I snorted. "Tim gave you those exact words, huh?"

He shrugged. "I couldn't remember 'em word for word. But somethin' along those lines."

I'd made it my business not to pry into his sessions with Tim, but on this occasion, I couldn't resist.

"Why were you talking to Tim about your old conquests, anyway?"

"Sometimes we practise..." He pressed two fingers to his temples, summoning the word. "Oh yeah—conflict resolution."

The surrealism of standing inside this grimy old club while my husband used terms like conflict resolution sent my head spinning. My smile didn't quite reach my eyes until the humour settled between us.

A flicker from the faulty neon sign outside pulsed through the window like a heartbeat, bathing the dance floor in a wash of colour—bright enough to lift my mood.

"Come on then, Pookie," I sighed. "Give me the grand tour."

He reached for my hand, helping me to my feet—but arched a brow on the way up.

Mine shot higher in response.

"Figured since you were practising conflict resolution, I'd remind you of another one of your exes."

"I see what you did there, Mrs Giannetti." He paused at the door, amusement tugging at the corner of his mouth.

"Tommy, do a full security sweep and take inventory of stock. Chloe, follow me."

Back in the foyer by the front door, Romeo paused at the base of the stairs. Wind pushed against the main door left ajar, nudging it like an inquisitive hand.

"You remember it's just the VIP lounge up there, right? Lotta steps—if you're sure you can make it."

For a second, I forgot I was pregnant. I opened my mouth, ready to give him an earful.

He leaned away, hands raised. "Hey, relax. Don't need another black eye. You were in a car crash this mornin'. I didn't want you bustin' my balls, callin' me insensitive."

I gave him a puzzled look, eyeing the stairs like they were mocking me. "Why would I do that?"

"Oh, Romeo," he drawled in his best impression of my voice, "'You insensitive arsehole, makin' me—a sexy British slut—walk up these fuckin' steps after I had an accident this mornin'.'"

Inside, I was giggling, but I wasn't about to stroke this man's ego more than necessary.

I raised a finger. "One, I don't talk like that. And two, you still can't say 'arsehole' properly."

I fought back a smile.

Reluctantly, we took the flight. One step creaked after the next. A strange sensation crept over me as I watched him ahead—yet in my mind, Hanna's perfect figure swayed in front of me. She'd climbed these same stairs once, desperate for his attention. And for a moment, the past and present blurred.

By the time we reached the glass double doors, my throat burned.

He paused, hand on the handle. "Holy shit, Chloe, you're bright fuckin' red."

Leaning forward, I braced my hands on my knees, dragging in deep breaths. Pregnant or not, those stairs were brutal.

He held the doors open, and I strolled in first. The view from up here was just as I remembered. Only now it carried a lifeless twist. Still air bristled as I stepped through the veil of dust.

His Majesty's throne sat beneath a draped sheet, waiting. Romeo whipped it off with a flourish, dust motes swirling through the stale air. He gestured for me to sit.

I adjusted my rear, hands curling around the velvet arms. Very comfy, indeed. From my new regal perch, I replayed our first meeting from his point of view. God, he really thought he was something—getting head from one of his whores while trying to intimidate me.

How things had changed.

Cigars. Alcohol. Sex. The scent lingered like a stain that would never lift. Sweat trapped in the velvet. A reminder that my husband's life didn't start at *I do*.

I clicked my fingers, dust settling around me like a crown. "Oi, Pookie, fetch me a couple of strippers. I need help to digest my meal." I flashed him a grin.

"Very funny, Mrs Giannetti," he smirked, leaning back against the balcony railing.

Even he couldn't argue. It was a solid bit from any angle.

No matter Romeo's past, the space itself was fantastic. I wrapped my fingers around the gilded arms of the throne, eyes sweeping the room, already buzzing with ideas.

"Maybe I'll make this my VIP lounge," I mused, casting him a look as he surveyed the dance floor below.

"Yeah?" he asked over his shoulder, playing along.

I nodded, serious. "Couple of male strippers right here. What d'you think?"

"Alright, enough." He turned to face me, one foot resting against the wall. "I was a prick, okay? You don't need to remind me."

My smile faded. I hadn't meant to hit a nerve. I'd forgotten how sensitive he could be. Without hesitation, I parked my jealousy.

"Is that all there is up here?" I asked, glancing around. "What's that other door off the hall?"

He narrowed his eyes like he needed the reminder.

"Office," he said, like it wasn't a joke.

I leapt from the chair with the grace of a full-term pregnant panther. "You have an office?"

I had to see this. Neatly stacked invoices? A photocopier of his own? A cheque book?

He strolled after me, swinging the dustsheet like a lasso.

"Obviously I didn't use it. Not my style. Maybe you could?"

I shoved the door open and flicked the switch. Light flickered to life with a welcoming hum, like the place was begging me to give it a shot.

A desk. A chair. A small window overlooking the world below. The single filing cabinet in the corner made me giggle.

He came up behind me. "You can do somethin' with this room if you want."

I leaned back into him with a sigh, his whole body enveloping mine—warmth in the draft. My strength, when my spine felt like it was giving out.

"God, the ideas I have. I can't wait."

He kissed my neck. "Come on. Let's check on Tommy and that inventory."

With the upstairs layout cemented in my mind, we made our way back down the stairwell. The walls slanted steeply on either side, like the building itself was stirring awake to welcome us home.

Romeo leaned out of the entrance door, giving Snake a quick nod from the SUV.

"Wait." I halted. "We have another room?" I nudged my chin at a black-painted door that blended so seamlessly with the décor it was practically invisible—unless you knew it was there.

"Of course. In there's the strip club."

Figures. I'd always wondered why the club's logo was a silhouette of a woman with her legs open. *Easy Access*, indeed.

He rifled through his crowded key ring, selected one, and jammed it into the lock. The door groaned open on stiff hinges.

He flicked the light switch up and down a few times, but nothing happened.

A chill snuck in, sliding across my skin and raising goosebumps. I huddled myself.

"It's cold in here." My breath fogged in front of my words. The room's damp, gritty presence felt like it hadn't breathed in months.

Like the chivalrous man he was trying hard to be, he slid off his expensive designer jacket and draped it over my shoulders, swallowing me almost whole. His scent enveloped me—cigarettes and that cologne. I pulled it closer, breathing him in.

"Thank you," I said, offering a shy smile. "Imagine you offering me your jacket the last time we were here."

He flicked a second switch. Still nothing.

"Pfft, what d'you mean? I'm a sharin' kinda guy," he scoffed. "They call me Generous Giannetti."

"Jeez, all these nicknames you have—"

He cut me off with a raised hand. "Don't bring up Pookie again. That's all I ask."

My mouth clamped shut. But my stare? That upgraded to a full-blown, narrow-eyed smirk.

He shot me a side glance before striding off, pretending to test the fire door. A firm tug on the bar and a solid shoulder nudge confirmed it was secure—but I knew the truth. He needed distance. Just a few feet between us before his temper sparked.

"It's good. Secure," he called. "Come on in."

A new layer of stench hit me the second I stepped inside.

"Oh, God—do you smell that?" I winced, taking another unnecessary sniff. "It's like unwashed dick and arse in here."

He looked confused, took a sniff of the air. "I can't smell anythin'?"

I rolled my eyes. "If you smoked less, maybe you'd pick up on the dick cheese and butt crack."

Out of habit, he reached for his jacket pocket—only to remember it wasn't on him. He played it off with a casual rake through his curls.

"I ain't got a fuckin' clue what you're on about, woman. Smokin' ain't got shit to do with smellin'."

He paused, eyes dipping between my legs, tongue grazing his bottom lip. "I can smell your tight little pussy just fine."

A flicker from the strip lights above. Then a hum. After some fiddling with the fuse board, the room finally lit up. Almost as if the bulbs knew the place was done, they worked just enough to shed light on the matter—not enough to bring the corners into view.

Hmm. The place needed work.

Old flyers peeled from the walls. Stains from too many left spillages blotched the floor. A lipstick phone number scrawled on a napkin just sat there, abandoned.

This place was better suited for storage.

Sure, turning it into a strip club made sense—more revenue for my girls. But I wouldn't let them work in here. Not like this.

I approached the pole with a frown, inspecting its grubby, tarnished surface. I dared to touch it. Sticky beneath my fingers.

"When was the last time this thing got cleaned?"

He crouched by the electrics, acting like he was qualified. "How the fuck should I know?" he shrugged.

Of course. This man only cared about two things: his dick and his money.

By the time he joined me, his arm draped casually around my shoulders, he'd finally tucked his gun into his waistband—an act that eased something inside me.

"You know how we ain't at home?" he murmured into my hair.

His cryptic tone made my shoulders tense.

I glanced left. Then right. "Um… yeah?"

"Can I grab a quick smoke?"

Of course. If he wasn't trying to fuck me, he was fantasising about his next cigarette.

I sidestepped away from him. "Go on, then. I guess."

He stared at me expectantly.

"What?" I snapped. A little too sharp. "I'm not bloody lighting it up for you as well."

If I had to question why my tone was laced with so much bite, it probably stemmed from a deeper fear. If it ever came down to a life-or-death choice—would he pick me, or his fucking cigarettes?

He smiled. "My smokes are in my jacket."

Oh.

Begrudgingly, I reached into the pocket—only to jerk my hand back with a horrified yelp.

"Eww, what the hell!"

A stringy glob of chewed nicotine gum clung to my finger like a parasite.

Romeo found it hilarious. Proper belly laugh and everything. But the second I flicked my wrist and the gum shot off my hand, landing in his hair, his smirk vanished.

He blinked.

The moment hung there. Suspended.

The air stagnated as we both waited for his reaction.

Eyes squeezed shut, he took a deep breath and reached for his hair. "Not cool, Chloe. Not cool at all."

Unable to contain my giggle, I tossed him his half-smoked carton. He caught it mid-air.

"Do I got a wedge of fuckin' gum in my hair?" He was already fussing over his pride and joy.

"Come here, let me see." I tugged his head down toward me. A little tangled—nothing dramatic.

"Ooh… you might need to lose a couple of curls," I teased.

"What!?" His voice cracked under the strain of panic. "I ain't havin' no fuckin' bald patch!"

"Relax. It's not a big deal." I winked.

I could see now why he used that phrase so often. It fit most situations perfectly.

If Romeo had been an animal in a past life, he'd have been a bear. A grizzly one. He growled, grumbled, then muttered something incoherent under his breath.

There was only one way to get him back under control.

"Anyway, grumpy arse—wanna hear my thoughts on this place?" I asked, pressing into his chest. A little spill of cleavage never did anybody any harm.

Distraction technique: successful.

His hands left his hair and wrapped around my waist.

I edged closer, my fingers hovering near his cock.

He swallowed. Breath held, lips parted. "Of course I do."

My palm settled on his chest. "Clean it up. Strip room becomes storage. The dance floor next door—a mixture of both rooms. This place has great potential."

Broken glass crunched underfoot as he shifted. It had been a while since I'd paid him a genuine compliment—and it showed.

"Like I said, I want you to make it yours. I'll set up a meetin' with the designer."

Despite the idea of yet another woman in his life, I figured the threat to our marriage was minimal. If he wasn't hiding her from me, then he probably wasn't still screwing her.

"So, how long are we closed for?" I pulled open an old box, kicked that napkin toward the trash, gave the room one last once-over.

"Permanently." He picked up the same napkin, balled it, and sank it into the bin, first time.

My face said it all.

"We reopen with a new licence in your name," he clarified. "Fresh start. You can rename it whatever you want."

He shrugged, as if this, like everything else, was no big deal.

Suddenly, the room seemed bigger. The whole damn place felt like a monster.

"Holy shit. That's a big responsibility, Romeo." I hugged his jacket closer around me.

"My wife is a scary woman." His eyes widened at the thought. "She can handle it."

While I appreciated the vote of confidence, this wasn't something I could take on alone.

A faint drip from an unseen leak echoed into a puddle somewhere beyond the light. More work to be done—we'd barely scratched the surface.

Romeo checked the diamond-encrusted watch on his wrist. The glint caught the light, scattering it like broken promises across the walls.

"Aight, it's gettin' late. Let's grab Tommy. We'll come back after the business trip to go through shit properly."

He nudged me toward the door. I stopped him in his tracks.

"You mean our honeymoon?" I cocked my hip, serving up enough sass to make his eyes water and his balls shrivel.

"Chloe… d'you know what? Sure. The honeymoon." He gave me another playful shove. "Come on, let's step."

Tommy was exactly where we'd left him, perched at the bar with a pen in hand, scrawling on a scrap of paper, no doubt reminiscing about a time when he was free to do whatever the hell he wanted. Since I'd known him, he hadn't taken a single day off.

"How many bottles of decent whiskey we got, brother?" Romeo asked, strolling toward him with a lazy swagger.

Tommy ran his finger down the handwritten list.

"Eight, Boss."

Romeo reached around the bar and scooped up a bottle by the neck. "Make that seven." He began unscrewing the lid.

I leaned on the bar, looking at him through my lashes. "Surely that can wait until we're home, Romeo?"

His lips thinned. He cast a fleeting glance at Tommy, who kept his eyes on the paper. To my surprise, Romeo did as he was told—screwing the cap back on firmly.

"Aight, let's go," he muttered, checking his gun before tossing the dust sheet back over the bar—just as an ominous sound outside pricked Tommy's ears.

The sheet seemed to pause mid-air when a flash of light streaked past the window.

"Boss, we got movement." Tommy armed his weapon, lifting it in a steady grip, his aim locked straight ahead.

With lightning-fast reflexes, Romeo vaulted over the counter and positioned himself in front of me, gun raised in the same direction.

"No word from Snake?" His voice was rough with adrenaline.

Tommy tapped his earpiece—but there wasn't time to answer.

The door brushed open. Pitch black outside. No light followed the intruder.

I gripped Romeo's T-shirt, burying my face into the warmth of his back. His heartbeat thudded like a drum—but it didn't race. He was the calmest I'd ever seen him.

"Romero Giannetti," a familiar voice called into the room, followed by the slow, deliberate thump of boots on hardwood.

"Saxon?" Romeo's tone bristled, eyes locked on the shadow

approaching. Harsh light fractured across the man's face, slicing it into strange angles.

Romeo adjusted his stance, planting both feet.

A chill trailed in through the open door, catching the edge of the dust sheet and brushing cold against my ankles.

"Had a bit of trouble with your boy out front. Took a bullet," Saxon said, racking the slide of his gun with a slow, deliberate click. He unscrewed the silencer and shoved it into his pocket.

My lungs collapsed.

Snake was hit?

Romeo puffed out his chest, broadening his shoulders. "This is private property. Leave."

But Saxon wasn't like the last cop. He didn't flinch. Didn't back off. Just kept coming—cool as ever.

"Get your guy to wait outside. We need to talk," he said, strolling into the centre of the room. He marched across the dance floor like no one had a weapon pointed at him.

Romeo's fingers tightened around the grip of his gun.

"Fuck you. I ain't doin' shit."

I tried to match his breathing, but my heart pounded. A juddering breath in. A shaking breath out.

"Hold on a minute," Saxon said, his gaze dropping to my hands curled at Romeo's waist. He leaned to the side, spotting me behind him.

A slow smirk lit up his face. "Looks like I hit the jackpot. Romero Giannetti and his little wifey, Chloe."

Romeo tensed. Every muscle coiled—ready to snap.

Tommy stayed frozen. Gun raised, eyes locked.

One wrong twitch and this whole room would become a blood-bath.

Saxon stepped out of the shadows and into full view, moving like he had all the time in the world. He reached the bar, lifted the cover, and let out a low whistle.

"Real shame this place got shut down, Romero. Real shame."

Romeo adjusted his stance, subtly shifting me further behind him.

"We all know you were behind it, Saxon."

Saxon pointed at himself. "Me? Never. Although it's about time that you got what's coming to you. Wouldn't you say, Romero? Or do you prefer *Romeo*?"

The room held its breath.

He wasn't lurking in his car anymore. He was here. Inside. Armed. And he knew too much.

Had he killed Snake?

Was he here to finish the job?

"You're wondering why I'm here?" he said, answering the question none of us dared speak aloud. "I'll tell you."

He stepped forward slowly, an untied bootlace dragging behind him. His gun hung loosely at his side. The four of us stood locked in place, tension thick enough to choke on.

His voice dropped to a menacing rumble.

"Tonight is the night Tatiana can finally rest in peace."

Romeo's arm shifted behind him. A silent check that I was still there, tucked safely against the warmth of his back. His jaw clenched. He didn't budge.

"Why are you so fuckin' hung up on Tat?" He snarled. "She was my girlfriend—fuck all to do with you."

Shaking his head, Saxon replaced the already loaded magazine in his Glock.

"That's where you're wrong, Romero. Tatiana was everything to me. She was carrying my baby."

Romeo stilled. His breath hitched, so subtle most wouldn't have noticed, but I did.

The gasp that escaped my lips came out raw. Every breath scraped down my throat like sandpaper. My hands trembled, but the sensation felt far away—like they belonged to someone else.

In that moment, everything clicked.

That was why Saxon locked me in a cell with Frankie-Jo. Why he'd warned me. Why, when that failed, he'd threatened me. The mystery car. The prickling at the back of my neck. The unshakable sense of being watched.

Saxon had turned our lives upside down—and now I understood why. Romeo hadn't just ended one future. He'd ended Saxon's, too.

A tense, suffocating silence settled between us.

Romeo's grip flexed around his gun, lowering it slightly.

"The fuck did you just say?" His voice remained eerily calm. The kind of calm that came right before a catastrophic storm.

Saxon's eyes darkened.

"You heard me. That baby was mine."

"So it was you she was fuckin' behind my back?" Romeo's voice wavered—just for a beat. "You she was feedin' information to?"

"She wanted to bring you down as much as I did," Saxon sneered. "I wanted your ass in jail from the start. Got close a couple times. But the day you took her from me—you took my life. We were gonna be a family."

Without hesitation, Saxon raised his gun, levelling it at Romeo's forehead.

"This moment right here? I've been waiting for it."

"What now? You gonna kill me, Saxon?"

"No, Romero." He shook his head slowly, dragging his tongue across his teeth. "Death's too easy. You're gonna rot in a cell for the rest of your life. I know a couple of people inside who'll make sure of that."

His smirk returned—sharp enough to slice steel.

"Wonder who'll raise your son when you're both behind bars?"

Saxon was baiting him. Pushing for a reaction. Trying to justify pulling the trigger.

"Fuck you. Chloe ain't involved in this!"

"Funny, that. She's standin' right here." He cocked his head. "Looks pretty involved to me." His grin widened. "It's over, Romero."

Romeo stepped us back. "Ain't nothin' over until I say it is."

Saxon reached into his pocket—movements slow, deliberate. "I think I'll be the judge of that."

He tossed something in the air and caught it again.

"Right here," he said, catching it with ease, "is enough cocaine to see you both locked up for a long, long time. Real shame I just so happened to stop by after hearin' a disturbance… only to find you distributin' product in high quantities."

His grin deepened. "Real shame."

Romeo shot Tommy a look. His fingers twitched near his hip. "That ain't gonna stick and you fuckin' know it."

"Both of your prints all over the goods?" Saxon chuckled. "You underestimate my power. It's all part of the plan."

Romeo's chest expanded—his breath steady but loaded.

"Aight. Here's the deal. Let Chloe go, and you can take me in. I won't put up a fight."

"What!?" I gasped. "Romeo, no!"

Saxon rubbed his chin, dragging it out with a show of fake contemplation. "You know what? I like that idea."

His eyes gleamed beneath the spotlights. "Your wife and your brother raisin' your son." He laughed. "Must be tough, huh? When she keeps runnin' back to him?"

Romeo didn't flinch. Somehow, against every instinct, he held back. He turned to me, his touch soft as he pressed a kiss to my forehead. Eyes closed, he poured everything into that connection.

"I love you, Chloe. You and my son—more than anythin'," he whispered, just for me. "I promised you wouldn't go to jail. Go with him. Trust me. I got the best attorney. I'll figure this out."

My grip tightened on his arm, adrenaline flooding my system. But the look in his eyes told me—there was no other way.

"Please, Romeo. Don't make me do this."

My knees buckled as I stepped away, already aching to be back in his arms. Every step felt like the last walk of a death row inmate.

Saxon's caramel eyes sparked with glee the moment I came to stand beside him.

"You've made my day, Romero. Tat's death will finally get the punishment it deserves."

He unhooked a pair of cuffs from his belt. "Once he's in custody, you're free to go. This was never really about you, Chloe. You've had your life tarnished by enough men like him. Like I told you at the courthouse. I couldn't save Tat, but I can save you."

I nodded, mute. My throat sealed shut.

Should I beg? Offer myself instead?

"We'll take this nice and easy, Romero. No sudden movements. Both of you—drop your guns and kick them towards me."

Romeo and Tommy complied. The metallic scrape of barrels across the floor sent a cold spike of dread up my spine.

Unarmed. Defenceless.

I pulled Romeo's jacket tighter around me.

That's when I felt it. The weight of the gun in his pocket.

My breath hitched.

He was unarmed. But I wasn't.

My heart pounded, fast and loud.

De-dum. De-dum. De-dum.

If he went to jail, my life was over.

I couldn't raise a child alone.

What was I willing to become to protect him?

Sweat slicked my palms. My thoughts fractured. It was like I'd become a passenger inside my own skin.

I reached into the pocket. Fingers curled around cold steel.

The silhouette of a man in front of me. His back an open target. Right between the shoulder blades? Or left—towards his heart?

Romeo's focus was fixed completely on Saxon. Tommy on Romeo.

This was my choice. My decision.

And with my eyes wide open.

I pulled the trigger.

"Chloe!"

A voice echoed through my mind. Familiar, yet distant.

"Chloe!"

There it was again—pulling me from the static. The ringing in my ears dulled, receding into the background.

I blinked. My vision sharpened until Romeo's face came into focus, framed by shadows and fear. His hands gripped my shoulders, shaking me firmly.

"Baby," he said, eyes locked on mine. "You with me?"

"What… happened?" My voice rasped like gravel.

I peered around his frame—my breath hitching.

Tommy was crouched beside a body.

Saxon.

"You killed him." Romeo's voice was low, urgent. "We gotta move. Now."

◆ ◆ ◆

"Thank fuck—she's awake," Romeo muttered, crouched beside me in the back of the SUV. His ocean-blue eyes flashed darker with every passing streetlight, the tension in his jaw set deep.

I groaned, rubbing my temples as a headache pulsed behind my eyes. "What the hell happened?"

"You passed out," he said, placing the flat of his hand on my forehead.

Before I could respond, nausea surged through me. I lurched forward, vomiting into the footwell with a violent splatter.

◆ ◆ ◆

I blinked again.

Big window. Curtains drawn. Beside lamp on.

Our bedroom.

Familiar sheets. Familiar scent.

I reached out. Romeo's side of the bed—empty.

Panic gripped my chest in an instant.

"Romeo?" I bolted upright. "Romeo!?"

The door flew open.

He strode in, phone wedged between his shoulder and ear.

"Aight, she's conscious," he said, ending the call. The phone landed on the bed with a thud. "Jesus fuckin' Christ, Chloe." He raked a hand through his hair, exhaling hard. "You good?"

I swallowed down the nausea climbing my throat.

"Did I really kill Saxon?" My voice cracked, the aftertaste of bile still clinging to my tongue.

A sob tore from me, raw and uncontrollable. My stomach twisted. Had I ruined everything?

"Yes, baby. You killed him." He dropped beside me, pulling me tight against his chest. "You're fuckin' incredible."

My tears stilled mid-stream. I blinked. "I am?"

"If it weren't for you, I'd be in jail for the rest of my life."

Another wave hit.

I sprinted to the bathroom and collapsed over the toilet, retching violently. The cold porcelain pressed against my knees. The air stank of stomach acid and fear.

Romeo followed without hesitation, kneeling beside me—one hand rubbing my back, the other sweeping my hair away.

"I got you, Queen. I got you."

The toilet rim cut into my forearms. I heaved again.

My head snapped up as a new fear sliced through the fog. "What about Snake? Oh my God. Did Saxon kill him?"

Romeo's hand moved in slow, grounding circles across my spine. "Took a slug, but no big deal. He was wearin' a vest."

Relief and dizziness collided. My grip loosened on the bowl. I didn't have the strength to lecture him about bulletproof vests—but I prayed he'd learned something from it.

"So... everyone survived. Except Saxon?"

He pulled me into his arms again and kissed my vomit-slick lips like they were the finest liquor. I wasn't sure if the pounding I felt was his heartbeat or mine—but it was the only thing keeping me tethered.

"You saved me the day I met you," he whispered. "And you've been savin' me ever since."

He pressed his body to mine, letting me feel the full weight of his arousal.

His breath hit my neck, hot, hungry, unashamed. His lips dragged across my collarbone toward my mouth.

My breath caught. "What are we doing about Saxon?"

"Don't worry about a thing," he murmured. "Tommy's handlin' him as we speak."

CHAPTER 6

"*Breaking news: L.A.P.D. Detective Carl Saxon's body has been found at a salvage yard in downtown LA. Sources tell JDG News his death is being treated as suspicious, but no further details have been released at this time.*"

Reaching for the remote, Romeo switched off the TV. A flicker of blue light cast one final blur before plunging the room into a dark, eerie silence.

We hadn't even bothered to open the curtains this morning. Not that paparazzi had ever managed to get a shot through our bedroom window —but today, it felt like all eyes were on us.

Him in sweats. Me in a dress I'd thrown on. Dark circles beneath both our eyes. We'd spent the last few hours perched on the edge of the bed, eyes glued to the screen, waiting for confirmation that Tommy had handled our situation.

The stale scent of last night's whiskey and cigarette smoke clung to Romeo's hair, lingering in the air like guilt. He'd tried to mask it with cologne earlier, but all he'd created was a blend of then and now.

My throat felt dry.

I glanced at the glass of water still sitting on the nightstand—bubbles suspended in the stillness. But for reasons I couldn't explain, I denied myself the relief of taking a sip.

The mattress shifted as he got up. He pinched my chin, tilting my face up to meet his gaze. Even in the muted light, the spark in his ocean-blues met the haunted haze of my blueish-grey.

"We don't talk about this again. Got it?"

The rasp in his voice carried unrest. That tick in his jaw held back a dozen unsaid things.

I nodded. There was no need to argue. The look in his eyes made it clear. This wasn't a suggestion. This was our survival.

Neither of us knew exactly how Tommy had handled Saxon's body. As always, the less we knew, the better.

It struck me then: Romeo rarely dealt with body disposal himself. The logic was smart. If he were ever cross-examined, he couldn't lie about what he genuinely didn't know.

Still, something didn't sit right. Dumping Saxon at a scrapyard? Right there for anyone to find? It felt off. Too exposed. Rushed, even. And Tommy wasn't sloppy. Not usually.

I swallowed hard, fingers trembling as I rubbed my damp palms across my bare thighs, just beneath the hem of my dress.

Still too early for movement—no cars beyond the glass, no creaks in the floorboards, no footsteps down the hall.

Just us.

He flicked on the bathroom light. A wash of warm glow and homely scent spilled across the carpet—stopping just shy of my feet, like I didn't deserve the comfort.

"Why a scrapyard?" I muttered, mostly to myself.

Romeo stalked back in, armed with hair gel.

The extractor fan hummed behind him. A dull drone that merged with the static in my head. He stilled in front of the mirror, fixing his curls. His expression darkened in an instant.

"How the fuck did you mess up the first thing outta your mouth?" His voice cracked like a whip. "I said, we don't talk about this."

Frustration gripped the air between us—for different reasons. He wanted to forget. I didn't.

"Okay, fine." I tugged the hitched dress down over my thighs, trying to cover the bare skin that suddenly felt too vulnerable.

Tension was high. And in our marriage, that only meant one thing: Plenty of arguing.

I'd be lying if I said I wasn't torn about what I'd done. I didn't regret saving him from a life sentence. But it meant more blood on my hands.

And Saxon's revelation—that Tatiana was carrying his baby—brought a strange, unsettling relief I hadn't been ready for. That chapter was now closed. If there was grief in her loss, it wasn't mine to carry.

For once, my conscience was clear.

And if anything good came from this, it was the certainty that I wouldn't make the same mistakes she did. My baby would survive this world I'd fallen into. I'd make damn sure of it.

The right moment to ask Romeo how he felt hadn't come. At one point, he thought her baby might've been his. And that was a big deal. So I wouldn't shy away from the conversation when the time came. I needed to know we were on the same page.

Sensing my retreat, Romeo closed in and cupped my shoulders, his blown pupils locking onto mine.

The sour warmth of whiskey and mint clung to his breath—heavy with things left unsaid.

"From this moment on, we don't look back. You hear me, Chloe?" He gave me a gentle shake. Just enough to rattle me.

I nodded, eyes falling to my open palms. My fingers stayed steady. Proof my body hadn't caught up with the chaos.

"Let me hear you."

"Yes," I croaked.

He searched my face, looking for reassurance. Compliance, even. Then he stepped back with a single nod.

"Aight, good. 'Cause we got a flight to catch."

◆ ◆ ◆

The morning sun had broken through cloud cover, streaking pale light across the walls. The window was cracked open just an inch—enough to let the stale weight pressing on us breathe a little. It helped me pretend, if only for a moment, that we were just going on vacation.

"Pass me that sunscreen, Romeo." I held out my hand, fingers twitching with impatience.

He rummaged behind him and lobbed a bottle my way. It flew through the air with just the right amount of force for an easy catch.

I knew instantly, just by the weight in my palm, it wasn't what I'd asked for. Raspberry flavoured. Latex safe. Convenient sports cap for easy application.

"This is lube, ass-hat." I shot him a playful scowl and hurled it back with more force than necessary.

He caught it like an American football and chuckled. Rare for him, and honestly? Worth it. Romeo didn't laugh-laugh often, which made it all the more of a treat when he did. This time, he looked proud of himself.

"Stick it in the case, anyway." He adjusted his crotch. "Ain't never too wet." He tossed it back over.

Mildly offended, I zipped it into the side pocket of his carry-on. "You think we need lube?"

I almost blamed his foreplay just to avoid the finger being pointed at me.

Outside, muted laughter drifted in from the workshop. The sounds of prep beginning for our long trip ahead.

Were they laughing at me?

He unscrewed the lid of his deodorant and rolled on a generous helping in wide, circular motions.

"Who said anythin' about you?" he muttered. "Chafes like fuck if you jerk it too much with no lube."

The hand action wasn't necessary.

I blinked, watching him sniff his armpits like there was someone else in the room who cared. He'd applied so much, I could smell the overcompensation from here.

"The fact that you're pre-planning to masturbate so much on this trip that you need lube is offensive."

He shut the conversation down without hesitation. Scooping the actual sunscreen off the nightstand, he passed it to me. But when he saw where it was heading, he tutted.

"Chloe, I already said, I don't need that shit."

I rolled my eyes and tucked the bottle neatly inside his case, rolled into a pair of his boxers for safekeeping.

"Who knew oiling up your dick was more important than protecting your skin? I don't know what you think your heritage is, Romeo, but you'll burn to a crisp. The sun hits different on vacation. You wanna look like an old leather handbag?"

He stalked to the closet and disappeared into the panic room. I heard the twist of the safe's hidden knob and the heavy swing of metal.

"What you on about, woman? 'Different sun'? Pfft. You ain't got a clue."

He stepped back through the wardrobe like the lion or the witch, clutching a thick bundle of cash and flipping through it with practised ease.

"I got proper Italian skin. Smooth as fuck."

I wasn't about to tell him that lately, I'd clocked a few fine lines creeping across his forehead. That revelation could wait.

"Boss, can we come in?" Tommy hovered at the doorway, already in full S.W.A.T. gear, one hand resting on his holstered gun. The anxious look on his face told its own story.

Romeo had spent the last ten minutes wrestling with my suitcase, and he still couldn't get it zipped.

"S'up, brother?" He wiped his brow, where, disappointingly, not a single curl had flopped out of place. "You got too much shit in this case, Chloe."

Tommy checked his watch. "If you're gonna make the flight, we need to leave now."

Everything about his posture screamed tension. Whether from what had just happened or what lay ahead, I couldn't tell. But the man looked like he was running on two hours of sleep and a whole pot of coffee.

Beyond our bedroom, an engine coughed into motion. One door opened. Another slammed. Music from the last drive was still playing, until someone turned it down, fast.

Today was the day I'd been waiting for since our wedding. Only, like everything in our world, it came with a plot twist.

In the wake of Saxon's death, Romeo had brought our flight forward. If the heat caught up with us before takeoff, his biggest drug deal to date would be dead in the water.

I wasn't complaining. If anything, it made the trip feel like a real escape. We'd go on ahead, get some much-needed alone time. Dan and Britney would join us later, when the brothers needed to handle business.

It was all figured out right down to the last detail.

Romeo eyed me. That's when I realised—so was Tommy.

"Stop fuckin' daydreamin', Chloe, and shift your ass."

"Wait, I thought we were doing a quick call with Nelly first?" I raised my phone. The same one I'd been clutching since I woke up. Fully charged. Ready for her pep talk.

Booking a last-minute session before our rescheduled flight had definitely raised her suspicions. But she didn't say a word.

Romeo snatched it from my hand and shoved it into my carry-on, yanking the zip shut with unnecessary force.

"Clearly, we've got no time. And besides, she already told us this was a really fuckin' bad idea."

Hmm. Fair.

Our last session with Nelly hadn't gone to plan. She'd made it clear she was uneasy about Dan and Britney coming along on 'vacation'. Concerned that bringing the one person I struggled to stay away from might undo the fragile progress Romeo and I had made.

Still, she'd given us tools. Triggers to watch for. Ways to stop our fights from spiralling. One last call this morning was going to solidify it all. Apparently not anymore.

I wasn't even sure we'd make it to the airport—let alone survive the trip. And remembering her advice in the heat of a fight? Not a bloody chance.

Romeo shoved my suitcase and carry-on toward the door, stacking them beside his with a solid thud.

"You heard him, Chloe. We need to leave. Get your ass to the car."

I looked at the pile of unpacked things still on the bed.

"But—"

He raised a hand, opening the door wider. "No buts. Car. Now."

"Fine!"

I grabbed my jacket off the back of the door and stormed out, leaving them to deal with the luggage.

By the time I climbed into the SUV, Snake was already waiting in the driver's seat, engine running, sunglasses on, cool as a cucumber. The familiar scent of polished leather boots and hair wax never failed to bring a strange sense of comfort. Without a word, he adjusted his glasses and gave me a slow, steady nod through the rear-view mirror.

I was under strict instructions not to mention Saxon around him—never mind ask about his fractured rib. The curiosity burned inside me. Who knew you could still end up injured wearing a bulletproof vest? Apparently, I was the only one who hadn't received that memo. Not that it had slowed him down. After getting the all-clear from Arnold to resume his duties, only this morning, Snake—like the rest of the crew—was tough as old boots. Or, in his case, highly polished, perfectly laced military boots.

If anyone could take a hit and keep moving, it was him.

While I had my own opinions about Arnold and his questionable moral compass, I couldn't deny the convenience of having him around. Before, I was naïve to this world. But now, I understood it.

I was so sidetracked by thoughts of last night; I didn't even notice we had a passenger up front with Snake.

His frame shifted in his seat. Black hair, shaved tight to his scalp. A glint of a whistle chain around his neck.

Tim—Romeo's life coach.

"Oh. Hi Tim. I wasn't expecting to see you."

His hand wrapped around the chair's shoulder as he turned to face me.

"Mrs Giannetti, you're glowing." Morning light slipped through the windshield, catching the gleam in his warm brown eyes as he offered a polite smile. "I'm just here to give Romero some last-minute guidance before your vacation. I know he's a little on edge about you joining him and his brother on their business trip."

Oh.

So the 'we don't have time' rule didn't apply to Romeo. I should've stood my ground and made that call to Nelly. Why the hell did I fold so easily? Maybe I was overtired…

Although bringing Tim along felt like a step too far. A phone call was one thing. But an in-person emergency session? A little extreme—especially considering Romeo had told me more than once that he wasn't even bothered.

Why hadn't he just said he was struggling with this trip as much as I was? If he'd been honest, at least we'd have had something in common.

The SUV door slid open, and Mr Secrets and Lies climbed in with a sigh, trailing the lingering scent of a freshly smoked cigarette. Crew fell into formation behind him, loading our suitcases into the trunk.

"That was fuckin' hard work, but I think we got everythin'."

"Oh. Hello," I muttered, lifting my chin and turning my knees away from him.

Romeo reached for my face, gently tugging my chin toward him. "What's wrong with you?"

The leather that had been temperature controlled moments ago now stuck to my thighs amidst the growing heat of my agitation. I gave him the once-over before dignifying him with a response.

"You never said you were having panic attacks over our honeymoon. Am I that awful to spend time with? Is it because I've put on weight?"

Romeo's seatbelt slid into place with a smooth click. "Airport, Snake. Don't wanna be late."

Silence descended. The kind that left the road beneath us shouting obnoxiously loud over the quiet hum of the radio.

The tight grip my arms held across my body loosened as I waited for his retaliation. It never came.

He caught me watching him from the corner of his eye, but quickly turned back to the road—like something far more fascinating was happening beyond the windshield.

"Why are you ignoring me, Romeo?"

His cheek twitched with a tight smirk. "I'm not. Just not gettin' involved in your bullshit."

What!?

We passed under the overhead sign for the airport. Snake changed lanes. Tim's eyes flicked to us in the rear-view, watching like he'd already begun planning the outcome of this moment.

My pulse drummed faster with every exit we passed.

"Excuse me? How is me feeling humiliated on my honeymoon bullshit?"

Romeo's leg jiggled. That familiar rustle of fabric gave Tim his cue to turn down the music and swivel around in his seat.

"Hey, guys. Let's play a quick game."

My upper lip curled. A game?

We didn't have time for that. Not when I was bleeding out from my emotional wounds.

Tim kept his gaze locked on Romeo. "Tell your wife three things you're excited for on this vacation."

Romeo cracked his knuckles, fidgeting in his seat. "Come on, T, you know I hate this girl shit."

Tim, it seemed, was a silent assassin. He didn't have to say anything else—Romeo caved all on his own.

"Fine!" He ran an exasperated hand through his freshly washed curls, the movement stirring the air with a mix of woody cologne and coconut shampoo.

"I guess I'm lookin' forward to seein' your naked titties, my dick in your mouth slidin' it all the way in, and my nut down your ass crack."

Tim shook his head slowly, silently admonishing.

In response, Romeo's second leg joined the first, creating a rustling Mexican wave with an Italian flair—a sensory overload of restless energy.

He rolled his eyes skyward.

"Aight, fine." He relented with a sigh. "I'm lookin' forward to spendin' some quality time makin' love, eatin' good food, and havin' some fun. Like, activities or whatever."

My jaw dropped. I looked at Tim, who was smiling at Romeo. His uncharacteristically heartfelt words had rendered me speechless. And earned Tim that pay rise.

Romeo studied my face, scanning for a reaction. His gaze flitted to my mouth, searching for even the smallest hint of a smile. A sign we were friends again.

I scooted closer, heated skin peeling off the leather, and pressed my lips to his—soft, plump, still tasting faintly of smoke. Our mouths intertwined, and I poured my love into him—my tongue moving in slow, sensual circles, curling around his with deliberate tenderness.

When I broke away, I grinned. "That was very romantic, Romeo."

The hardening of his features melted away. He winked and pulled me against his chest, his warmth seeping into me as he pressed a final kiss to the top of my head.

I hadn't had my turn at our impromptu challenge yet, but it seemed game time was over as Tim settled back into his seat, his focus returning to the road ahead. Music cranked up a notch. Calm restored.

We'd been in the car for what felt like an hour already. A knot of anxious excitement twisted in my belly, too loud to ignore. Romeo wasn't talking, and I was bored.

The blinker clicked off. Another queue of traffic.

"How long until we get there?" I asked, scanning the three men for signs of life.

My feet tapped. Toes curled. The A/C did nothing but chill my sandalled feet. I needed a distraction: from Saxon, the flight, Dan and Britney, and the looming drug deal.

How the hell Romeo sat there, just watching the world pass him by. I'd never understand.

He peered out the window, eyes narrowing as he did a quick mental calculation based on the bumper-to-bumper crawl.

"Twenty. Maybe twenty-five if traffic keeps up."

Car horns blared. Sirens screamed as an ambulance sliced through the gridlock.

Welcome to LA.

"Perfect." I smiled. "Hand me my carry-on."

He tugged at his seatbelt like it had just grown too tight.

"No." His clipped tone landed like a slap. Jaw tight. Body rigid.

Snake's aviators caught the sunlight, his expression unreadable when he took a glance.

What the hell was ass-hat's problem?

From the front, Tim glanced back, as cheerful as ever.

"Hey, Romero. What's the stage before conflict resolution?"

Romeo groaned, dropping his head into his hand.

"Conflict... prevention," Tim answered himself.

Romeo exhaled sharply. "Aight, whatever."

He leaned down, yanked the case from the footwell, and dumped it onto the seat between us.

The heat trapped in the leather bloomed. Or maybe that was just him—nearing explosion.

Tim nodded in approval and turned back around.

Romeo scowled. "We don't got time for fuckin' around. What do you want that for now?"

"Just a final check-in with the girls." I unzipped the bag. "With how quick the renovations are moving, I told them to send me their thoughts. I want to make sure that they're on board."

The club's reopening was just weeks away. Every trace of Saxon had already been erased—like he'd never set foot inside. The cleanup, disguised as an earlier than planned remodel, had started almost as soon as his body hit the floor. Now, it was a shell waiting for my mark.

But one thing the designer couldn't help me with was my girls. I needed women I could trust to solidify my place in a man's world. To prove I was different. That I could be trusted to lead them the right way.

That was my intention when I messaged them this morning. Naively, I'd expected more optimism. These girls had been burned one too many times. My husband's clubs included. I was determined to prove this time was different. Romeo trusted me. Now, I needed their trust.

"You're stressin' way too much," he muttered, agitated. "If they don't want in, there'll be plenty more bitches who do."

I wanted to tell him it wasn't just the lack of enthusiasm that had me spiralling. It was something deeper.

What happened on that dancefloor—should've rattled me more. The old me would've crumbled. But now? I was ready to sink my teeth into this project. Make it my own. And that was scary.

Even though a loud bang earlier had made me flinch, Romeo was right. With every trigger pulled, it got easier.

I checked my phone. Every messaging app.

Still nothing.

Hmm.

"Okay, Boss," Snake called, as we rolled to a smooth stop in a private section of the airport. The hum of the engine faded, replaced by the dull roar of jet engines overhead.

He adjusted his earpiece. "We got Tommy waiting to execute the SM."

The flash of yellow runway markings blurred in the distance, distorted by heat rising off the tarmac. It seemed the freak LA winter snow had died with Saxon. Even the weather had moved on fast.

Not being fluent in tactical slang made it hard to follow their conversations, but I knew that one—SM. Sandwich Manoeuvre.

"The paps have been handled?" Romeo asked, already reaching into his jacket.

A half-empty Coke bottle fizzed in its holder. Snake reached for it without looking.

"Yep. Tommy paid them off." He unscrewed the cap and took a sip. "Confirmed. No one's on site."

"Good." Romeo nodded, slipping our passports back into his inner pocket.

Then, lower: "Aight, take this."

Like a king passing down his sword, he handed over his most sacred possession—his gun. The cold weight shifted into Snake's palm, but Romeo's fingers lingered, reluctant, like he might change his mind. He breathed in deep. Then let it go.

Tim leaned back subtly in his seat, clearly uninterested in firearms.

"Ready?" Romeo's eyes locked onto mine like it was now or never.

I swallowed dry. And nodded.

"Hold up, Romero." Tim's voice cut in. Calm but firm. "Remember what we spoke about?"

Romeo's jaw ticked. His hand twitching on the car's handle.

"Most important thing," Tim reminded gently. "If it gets heated, think about your words before you say them. Call me if you need me. Good luck. Enjoy."

Being new to all this, I had no idea VIP treatment started as early as the parking lot. The moment Tommy stepped out and opened the door, the quiet efficiency of it all hit me.

I hooked my arm through Romeo's as we made our way toward the check-in desk. The VIP section was eerily calm.

No crowds, no queues. Just staff in sharp suits gliding like clockwork across gleaming polished floors. Soft ambient music floated above the click of designer suitcase wheels, a soundtrack tailored for the elite.

"Good morning, sir," a stunning brunette purred from behind a waist-high counter.

Cherry-red lips curled into a well-rehearsed smile. "I've been expecting you. Please follow me to our executive suite. Your flight is scheduled to depart on time in just under an hour."

It had been Romeo's idea to fly commercial—an irrational fear that private jets were more likely to crash. It surprised me. Not just because of how disgustingly rich he was or how much he loathed the public, but because it reminded me, there were still things beyond even his control.

Miss Heels-Legs-Tits-and-Ass led the way with a sashay so deliberate it deserved its own spotlight. The back seam of her vintage-style stockings curved up toned calves beneath a long-line skirt, her stride flexing with dancer-like precision.

Instinctively, I glanced at Romeo.

Of course, he'd noticed. He always did. The man never missed a chance to use the gift of sight, or seize an opportunity to get a hard-on.

The melodic slap of her heels softened as she stopped outside a private cubicle. One perfectly arched finger curling around the black-lined curtain.

"This is your private booth," she cooed, sweeping it aside with a practised flourish. "Please make yourselves comfortable. I'll return shortly with refreshments."

Speakers of our own whispered a slow jazz number through hidden grilles in the ceiling, welcoming us into the dim, climate-controlled calm. Two reclining chairs. A small round table with a box of tissues perched on top. A wall-mounted flatscreen TV, already on the sports channel.

The tissues said it all. This was where powerful men came to handle business of their own...

Grateful for the break, I collapsed into the leather chair with a sigh, legs stretching out. The air-con wrapped around my skin like silk. Warm enough to soften the upholstery beneath me. Cool enough to keep sweat at bay. I shimmied down into it, completely content.

Romeo lingered in the doorway, bag still in hand.

My skin prickled—his gaze locked on me. Watching.

I cracked open one heavy eyelid. "What?"

"Nothin'. You just look really pregnant all of a sudden."

Both eyes snapped open. I tugged the ruffled fabric of my dress lower. "Are you calling me fat? This is exactly why you're an arsehole."

His eyes lingered on my stomach, and suddenly it felt heavier.

"Stop looking at me like that!" I flicked my wrist.

He growled, frustrated, and dropped into the recliner beside me. "That ain't what I meant. I looked at you and thought… this is the last trip we'll take before we're parents."

The throb of revenge in my fingers eased.

Oh.

Well. I guessed that changed things.

Before I could even think of apologising, Miss World returned, gliding in on a cloud of expensive perfume, this time accompanied by a suited older man wearing a bow tie.

"Here we are, sir, miss." She bent forward to set down our drinks. Her fragrance hit with an exorbitant, alcohol-heavy sting, the kind that lingered for days.

"Two glasses of orange juice and a tumbler of our finest whiskey. Anything else?" She straightened in front of Romeo's reclined seat, legs subtly parted. Probably no panties.

He didn't flinch. Didn't even glance.

I knew better than to think he hadn't noticed. But he gave her nothing at all to work with.

Progress.

He threw back the whiskey in one gulp, then remembered his manners. "No. Thanks."

The glass remained in his hand, melting ice swirling slow.

As she vanished behind the curtain, the suited man stepped forward, sliding on a pair of pristine white gloves.

"Would sir like me to take your cases and stow them on the plane ahead of your arrival?" His fingers hovered near the handle.

Romeo slammed the glass onto the table. The crack of crystal made me jolt.

"No fuckin' chance," he snapped. "I've got boxers in there. I know what you people are like. I'll open it at the other end with no fuckin' underwear left."

The man's eyes widened—comically so.

"I can assure you, sir—"

"I said no!"

He offered a stiff nod and backed away, nearly tripping over his own feet as he yanked the curtain closed behind him, dragging his disappointment along the rail with him.

Romeo didn't even blink. Just slouched back in his chair, ankle crossed over his knee, eyes dragging over me like I was the main event.

Slut number two pattered in with my husband's refill—unprompted. Napkin beneath glass, she handed it over with a practised curtsy and vanished just as fast.

"Can I help you with something, Romeo?" I giggled, kicking the air in a loose swipe at his shin.

He continued to sip while he watched me.

"Strike one, Mrs Giannetti." He smirked into his drink.

I huffed, playful. "Who said you could use that threat against me?"

Muffled airport announcements floated through the silence. We both paused—just in case. Then it faded.

I aimed again, but this time, he was ready. He leaned down, caught hold of my foot, and raised a brow.

"I believe that was strike two."

He swirled his whiskey, watching me over the rim as he took a slow sip. The ice clinked as he swallowed.

My grin faltered. The now all-too-familiar sting settled behind my eyes like pins and needles.

"What?" he asked, letting my foot fall gently.

I hesitated. "I feel a little guilty that I'm having a nice time."

His glass scraped across the table, sharp enough to knock the tissue box to the floor.

"You better not be talkin' about Saxon again." He adjusted his watch, then checked the time. "How can you feel guilty when you weren't involved? Someone else pulled the trigger. Not you. Got it?"

I pressed a hand to my chest, drew in a breath, and let his words settle before I nodded.

"If you ain't careful," he warned, voice softening, "you'll get a strike three."

I leaned in with a smile. "Yeah? And what happens when I hit strike three?"

Rubbing his chin in mock seriousness, he stretched his arms across the back of the seat. All confidence.

"Three is oral sex."

Hmm.

My legs parted slightly without permission.

I flicked a glance toward his crotch. "Oral for you or me?"

He pushed up from the chair and dropped to his knees, dragging my dress higher—inch by inch—until cool air kissed my thighs.

He kissed my skin. "You."

My weak attempt to resist was met with fire. The second his hands touched my knee, my body betrayed me. Only my panties were left between us, thin, damp, and utterly useless against the heat of his mouth.

"Come on, Romeo. I know you want me blacking out again, but not right before a long flight."

A cool breeze whispered from the vent above, brushing my exposed skin as he pushed my dress higher.

He didn't hear a word.

The moment his lips found my flesh, the world dropped away. The tip of his tongue traced a slow line along the crease, pausing at the soaked fabric. He inhaled deeply, then kissed the cotton like it was sacred.

"Let me do it again, Chloe." His voice vibrated against me. "Come on."

My pulse throbbed at the base of my neck.

I squirmed. "I haven't even reached strike three yet."

My thighs fell wider on their own. A bead of sweat slipped between my breasts, hot and raw. I nudged his shoulder. Futile.

"Rule change," he said, lifting his gaze. "Strike three is you not lettin' me love you."

The flame flickered, almost dying out. I rolled my eyes, muscles instantly tensing. It was clear now this wasn't about love—it was about proving himself to his crew. About showing off the one skill he thought could level everything.

Before I could even get a word out, he was there—lips dragging up my inner thigh, unhurried and knowing. Then he hooked a finger around the edge of my panties and pulled them aside, exposing me to the air—and to him.

My body wilted. Fingers buried in his hair, I surrendered. The velvet heat of his tongue slicked over my entrance. His breath stirred something primal.

"Romeo," I groaned, shifting as the recliner swallowed me deeper. "Take me. Please."

He lifted his head, letting the damp fabric snap back into place. His eyes, darker now, locked onto mine.

"You want my dick, yeah?" He smirked. "I fuckin' love you, Chloe."

A booming voice burst through the speaker: *"Final call for passengers travelling on Flight 314 to Malé, Maldives. Please proceed to Gate B18 immediately for boarding."*

The fog lifted. Eyes wide, I snapped my legs shut like a trap.

"Romeo, that's us!"

His hand slid beneath his waistband—already hard, already waiting. "Just gimme a minute. I'll nut in five seconds. Watch."

The squeak of suitcase wheels and the shuffle of footsteps beyond our curtain sent a jolt of panic through me.

"No!" I shoved his chest. "We'll finish this on the plane. Help me up."

His frustrated scowl twisted into a satisfied grin.

"Fuck yeah, we will."

The moment we stepped onto the plane, a soft burst of filtered air washed over me, reaffirming my title as Queen. Not just at the mansion, but wherever my husband took me.

Plush carpet cushioned the soles of my strappy sandals as I made my way down the aisle—each step a quiet reminder that I wasn't just any passenger anymore.

First class stretched ahead, a cocoon of climate-controlled luxury that erased the last traces of outside's unexpected humidity. Exactly what I needed.

A sharply dressed stewardess in a fitted waistcoat over a crisp white blouse greeted us by our seats with a polished smile.

"Welcome aboard, Mr and Mrs Giannetti," she said, without even asking our names—something I still wasn't used to. "I'll be back in a moment to get you settled in."

Grateful, I sank into the window seat with a soft hum, one hand instinctively cradling my bump. My OBGYN had cleared me to fly until next month, making this my last window for a proper getaway. Yet, despite Romeo's constant reassurances, I couldn't shake the feeling that this trip was a mistake—especially now, considering everything we were leaving behind.

Romeo slumped into the seat beside me, his broad frame visibly out of sync with the confines of the luxury pod. The playful man from the lounge had vanished, replaced by someone distant and restless.

"You look worried. What's wrong?" I asked, already feeding off his energy like an addict chasing a high.

He breathed out hard through his nose, tension rippling along his jaw. "Just need to get today out the way. Things'll settle once our crew land tomorrow."

Hmm.

I'd known postponing their flight to handle loose ends would bite us in the arse. And the guilt only deepened knowing it was me who'd forced the plan to change. Forced them to stay behind and clean up the mess.

"Well, I did say maybe we should cancel—"

Static crackled faintly from the intercom before a cheery, confident voice filled the cabin.

"Good morning, ladies and gentlemen. This is your captain speaking, welcoming you aboard Qatar Airways Flight 314 from Los Angeles to Malé, with a scheduled layover in Doha.

Our journey today will cover just under 9,800 miles in total, starting with a 15-hour, 45-minute flight to Doha, followed by a second leg of just under 5 hours to Malé.

For those of you tracking the time difference, Doha is 10 hours ahead of Los Angeles, and Malé is 11 hours ahead. So although we're leaving at 10:00 AM local time today, you'll be arriving in the Maldives around 7:15 PM tomorrow evening, local time.

Refreshments will begin shortly after takeoff, followed by meal service throughout the flight. For those in our premium cabins, please make yourself comfortable. Our crew will be with you shortly to introduce your suite and amenities. Enjoy the journey."

Romeo pointed to the ceiling speaker.

"You heard him. Best thing for us right now is to get ten thousand miles out of California."

From that, I could only assume one thing. The cops were sniffing around. If they weren't already, they would be soon. Saxon had made Romeo a target. And now that the detective was dead, a whole army of colleagues would be ready to avenge him.

"Any updates from home?" I tried to sound casual, though the tightness in my voice betrayed me.

He fiddled with his seatbelt, tugging the strap to stretch it over his lap. "They're still cleanin' up. Hold on—wait." He raised a finger. "Did you hear that?"

I sat up taller, glancing over the rows ahead. The steady hum of the jet engines filled the cabin. A murmur of passengers. The weighty thunk of overhead bins closing.

"Huh? I didn't hear anything—"

Then came the sound.

A slow, deliberate fart rippled into the sanitised leather, followed by a childish giggle.

Anger flared inside me, a coil of rage leaving my body like steam from a cracked pipe. Right then, I wanted to ram the in-flight safety card straight down his smug throat.

"If you think that's gonna stop me asking questions, you're dead wrong." I pinched my nose shut, bracing for the inevitable stench.

Despite everything going to plan so far, Romeo was clearly on edge. No crew. No weapon. Not even a cigarette between his teeth. He was unarmed. Vulnerable. And he hated it.

I took a cautious sniff—narrowly dodging the worst of it—then exhaled and reclined my seat, shifting in search of relief for my aching back. The flight hadn't even taken off, and already, I wanted it to be over.

"Me again," our hostess chirped as she reappeared, sashaying toward us with a blanket draped over her arm. "Here's your complimentary—Oh my!"

She faltered mid-step, hand flying to her chest, nose wrinkling as her polite smile crumpled.

"I do apologise for that questionable aroma, sir. Perhaps another passenger is unwell. Would you like me to relocate you both to the other side of the aircraft?"

Romeo bit the inside of his cheek, barely holding back a grin.

"Nah," he said, fighting laughter. "A whiskey will see me right for the inconvenience."

She adjusted the blind on the seat in front and composed herself. "I'm sorry, sir, we're about to take off. But once the captain gives the all-clear, I'll be right on it."

With a polite pivot at the waist, she headed to the front of the plane to begin the in-flight safety demonstration.

I rested a hand on Romeo's jiggling thigh, trying to still his restless energy. "I don't think you need any more liquor."

His eyes flashed with something too complex—too dangerous—to be unleashed in the confines of an aircraft.

Taking the hint, I zipped my lips with two fingers and mimed locking them shut. Message received. None of my business. Until *I* said otherwise.

Seatbelts fastened as the light flicked on overhead, we prepared to begin our journey to indulgence. As the engines roared and the plane began to taxi, I leaned into Romeo's ear.

"You nervous, Romeo?" I teased, trailing my fingers beneath the longer-than-usual stubble on his chin.

A pretty hostess gestured toward both exits while her colleague held up the well-worn demo life vest and oxygen mask combo.

The plane juddered. Overhead lockers clattered with the weight of shifting luggage. A bing bong echoed—cabin crew only.

He frowned. "No. Why would I be?"

"You just seem tense."

His balled fists loosened, only to disappear into his sweats.

"That's 'cause the nut from earlier's still at the end of my dick, waitin' to fire."

I saw it—the tip of his blushed-pink cock peeking from his waistband. Unbelievable.

My eyes fluttered closed as I shook my head. This man, closer to thirty than twenty, still acted like a horny teenager.

"I thought those pills from Tim were supposed to help with this issue?"

"Chloe." His fingers curled around the armrests. "There's somethin' wrong with the world if a man can't get a nut when he wants. I ain't takin' pills to stop my dick workin'. End of."

Here we went again. Circling the drain of Romeo's sex addiction. The one he refused to acknowledge.

I didn't have the strength to argue, so I turned to the window, watching the runway blur into streaks of light. Even my reflection looked more emotionally present than he did.

We'd only been airborne ten minutes when the seatbelt light switched off. Romeo sprang from his seat and bolted for the bathroom like a man escaping a hostage situation. Judging by the urgency, that fart from earlier had been a warning shot—and the war had just begun. Whatever part of his breakfast caused the rebellion, it clearly wasn't planning to stay.

"Ma'am? Can I offer you a warm towel and a glass of juice?"

I startled, eyes snapping open to find a male flight attendant beside me, tray in hand. The scent of freshly brewed coffee drifted up from the pot like a whispered promise.

"Oh, um… could I have coffee instead, please?"

He smiled like I'd just made his day.

"Certainly." He poured with slow precision, filling the mug with steaming black comfort.

"Hey, my guy. I'll grab one too," came a voice from across the aisle.

I peered around Jeeves.

Athletic build. Late thirties. Kind eyes. Sculpted jaw, dusted with stubble. No ring.

"Hi, beautiful," he said—a velvety rasp beneath the boldness. Paired with a shy wave, it caught me off guard.

The air-con seemed to crank up a notch, a cold stream angled straight at my chest. Goosebumps swept across my skin.

I swallowed. "Um, hi."

He leaned closer, resting one arm on the headrest in front. A whiff of woody cologne drifted my way. Expensive. Clean. Masculine. "I'm Elijah."

"Chloe." I smiled, tight-lipped, unsure why my heart had picked this exact moment to flutter.

He took a sip of coffee, then slid into the empty seat beside him, leaning closer across the aisle.

"So… you come here often?" he joked, flashing straight, perfect American teeth.

There was something effortlessly charming about him. I found myself smiling back.

He inched even closer, like he couldn't help himself. One foot now closer to my seat than his.

My wedding ring dug into my skin, suddenly too tight under the cabin pressure. That was when my sanity clicked back into place.

"I'm actually on my honeymoon." I lifted my hand, flashing the glittering stack of diamonds.

His sneaker tucked back under the seat in front of him.

"Say no more." He held up a thumb, grinning. "Though I swear I've seen you before. Have we met?"

Shit.

He'd probably seen me in a tabloid. But I wasn't about to confirm anything that might spook him.

"No. I don't think so. I've got a good memory. I'd definitely remember you."

Why did I say that?

His smile broadened—but in an instant, his eyes widened. The shift was sudden. Alert.

The engines rumbled as the plane jolted through a pocket of air. Before I could react, he lunged. Like a cheetah.

My breath caught in my throat as his body crashed into mine, hot and fast, pressing me deep into my seat. The scent of his skin and his aftershave, everything, flooded my senses. I forgot how to breathe.

A thud against his back snapped me out of it. A bag from the overhead locker had come loose during the turbulence and whizzed past my face, smacking him square in the spine.

He grunted from the impact. The case thumped to the floor, vibrations rippling through our feet.

Elijah had just saved me.

Panting, he hovered inches from my face. Mouth too close. The warmth of his coffee-laced breath ghosted over my lips.

"Th-thank you," I murmured, dazed.

Another inch and we'd have kissed.

A ripple of gasps from the rows behind shattered the moment. And just like that—like he'd been summoned by a curse—Romeo appeared. Out of nowhere.

His hand clamped around Elijah's neck, yanking him back with a snarl. Fist cocked. Ready to destroy.

My skin prickled. Adrenaline surged.

"What the fuck are you doin' on top of my wife? A man can't even take a shit without some punk bitch tryin' to make a move!" Romeo's teeth clenched like he'd rip flesh from bone.

Elijah raised both hands, eyes squeezed shut, bracing for impact. "I wasn't doing anything, I swear!"

Muscle against muscle. Elijah's sweet nature had become his weakness.

"Romeo, relax. Please. He just saved me. The bag nearly took my head off." I pointed to Romeo's own holdall. The one he hadn't secured properly in the overhead locker.

I tugged his arm. His pulse throbbed beneath my fingers, but the iron in his grip slowly softened. Still, his glare stayed locked on Elijah.

My hand slid to his chest. My wedding band pressed against the heartbeat beneath it.

After a long beat, he let go.

"She's married," he said—too calm. "To me." He jabbed himself in the chest like he was stamping a final full stop on the sentence.

Elijah's wide-eyed terror said it all. The bead of sweat trickling down his temple sealed it. He knew exactly who my husband was. There weren't many people unfamiliar with Romero Giannetti's capabilities.

"No sweat, my guy," Elijah mumbled. "I just reacted when I saw it falling."

The cabin seemed to shrink as the two of them filled the aisle, thick with masculine tension. The space turned claustrophobic. A brick wall of pressure settled over my chest.

I snaked my arms around Romeo's waist, grounding him. "Let it go, baby. Please."

Across the rows, passengers craned their necks. Staff flitted nervously between seats, doing their best to keep order.

At my touch, the tension bled from his shoulders. Romeo sank into the chair beside me, fingers tightening around the whiskey he hadn't yet touched.

Across the aisle, Elijah straightened his polo collar and dropped back into his seat without a word.

This was going to be a long flight.

I folded my arms and gave Romeo a pointed side-eye. The awareness of being watched from all directions crept under my skin, drawing my posture straighter.

"What?" he asked, genuinely confused. He took a swig of whiskey, swirling it like mouthwash.

My knees bumped the pod walls as I shifted against the tight discomfort.

"You overreact to everything. I just hope you washed your hands before storming out of the bathroom to strangle someone."

Feeling brave, I uncurled his fingers and sniffed. Lemon handwash. Clean and fresh amidst the shit storm at 30,000 feet.

Romeo was gearing up for a comeback—until we were rudely interrupted.

"Hey, Romero. Remember me?" A flight attendant with honey-blonde hair, pouty pink lips, and curves like a pin-up leaned into Romeo's space. Her blouse was popped open just enough to serve cleavage on a platter.

Romeo recoiled instantly, shifting closer to me.

"No." He looked her up and down. "Should I?"

She huffed, hand to her chest like a pearl-clutching housewife. "We've slept together. Twice. Don't tell me you've forgotten Paris."

His thigh muscles locked. So did mine.

"I don't know what you're talkin' about. I don't know you."

Lowering her voice, she came closer still. Any more and she'd be an accessory to his outfit. "I tried to arrange another meet-up with Tatiana, but she never replied."

He adjusted, casting me a glance.

"That's 'cause she's dead. Now leave." His voice turned blade-sharp.

Just when I thought we'd closed the chapter on Romeo's past, it crawled out from under the seat in front. Had she not mentioned Tat, I might've believed him.

I sat there like a spare part, watching them both, trying to gauge whether she was good in bed—and if he'd enjoyed it.

Jealousy twisted in my gut like barbed wire.

"No way," she gasped, dripping faux sympathy. "Tat died? Shit. I'm so sorry."

Another pocket of turbulence nudged the cabin. No one else flinched. Just me.

Romeo scrubbed a hand over his head, then rubbed his eyes. A low growl brewed in his chest. Detonation in five… four…three…

"Look, I'm gonna ask real nice—fuck off and don't come near me again."

Her slutty aura snapped shut around her like a clam.

"Ew." She jerked back. "If you're gonna talk to me like that, I certainly won't be having sex with you again."

I cleared my throat into my fist and rose slightly, just enough to command attention. "Lady, this is awkward for me. I'm his pregnant wife, and this is the first I'm hearing of your time together. Would you mind giving us some privacy?"

Our rising voices pulled curious gazes once more. The soft engine hum became background to the unfolding soap opera.

A male flight attendant, polished and professional, arrived just in time to usher her away with a tight smile, like closing curtains on the final act. She resisted a little, protesting just enough to feed her ego. Then she was gone.

The whole damn cabin released a breath.

I faced him. Arms folded like a barrier.

"You know, Romeo, I was going to have a supportive conversation with you at some point about your ex. But I've decided not to waste my breath."

He had the audacity to frown. "What do you mean?"

My eyes trailed over him like something stuck to my shoe. "Obviously,

I'm referring to Tatiana's baby not being yours."

His jaw twitched—only slightly. But I saw it.

He crossed his arms, mirroring me, even though the pod barely allowed it.

"There ain't no need to talk about that."

While I didn't agree, bigger questions were clawing their way forward.

"So you took Tatiana and that slut to Paris, huh?"

He bit his lower lip, searching for a version of the truth that might sting less.

"Honestly, Chloe. I don't know what to say. I had no fuckin' clue she'd be workin' this flight."

"How many vacations did you and Tat take?" My insides clenched. "Bearing in mind, I had to beg for this honeymoon."

He looked at his fingers—actually looked—like he was counting.

Any more than one trip, and he was done for.

His knee started to bounce. "Two. Paris and Brazil."

My mouth opened, then just hung there. Stunned.

"You're disgusting. Do you know that?"

I slammed the privacy button with a shaking finger and watched the partition begin to rise.

In a battle of wills, he pressed his button too, and the divider ground to a halt. Frantic jabbing wouldn't bring it back, no matter how fast or hard I pressed.

"You're makin' it seem like I took her on romantic getaways. I went there to fuck women. Foursomes, fivesomes—whatever. Tat may as well not have been there. And that woman just now? I ain't lyin' when I say I don't remember her."

My pulse thudded through my still-pressed finger. "You're telling me you went abroad solely to sleep with women?"

The forehead vein was back with a vengeance, throbbing beneath the surface of his glistening olive skin.

Poor Pookie was stressed.

"I used to like travellin' to places where women hadn't heard of me. Fuckin' them just 'cause they wanted to. Not 'cause of who I was." He exhaled, shaking his head. "Lookin' back on it... I don't get why I felt I had to do that."

The aircraft vibrated through our bodies. An in-flight message about the sea we were flying over got completely lost between our shared vulnerabilities.

My shoulders softened as I collapsed into my seat. I knew exactly why he did that. We were two peas in a broken pod. Reassurance was our glue. The only way we knew how to hold the shattered pieces together.

"It's obvious, Romeo. You thought women only slept with you for the status."

The tropical scent from deep in his curls drifted into the charged air between us as he swept a hand through his hair.

"That makes me sound like a pussy."

I laid my hand over the soft rise of his chest, feeling the beat of him through cotton.

"No, Romeo. That makes you a real-life person with feelings."

Our eyes locked, and our souls reconnected. No matter how broken we were, we never gave up on each other.

I scooted closer to him, dropping my voice to a whisper. "Recline your chair."

He obeyed, and I pulled the complimentary blanket over both of us. It floated through the air and settled in our laps with promise.

My hand slid across his stomach, rubbing his dick through the fabric of his sweats, teasing him slow.

Beneath the blanket, I slipped my hand inside, cupping his cool testicles gently. It didn't take long. He began to grow—hard and eager beneath my touch.

"Shall I make you come?" I kept up the slow, seductive rhythm, massaging the tightening leather of his sack.

He kissed me, his hand cradling the back of my head. For once, no trace of tobacco lingered between us.

I shifted my hand, stroking him—long, firm motions from root to tip. Stroke after stroke, the way he liked it.

Rock solid. Straining against my grip.

He was ready for me.

"I can't wait to have this baby so you can give me another," I murmured, making sure he heard every word. "God, I love you, Romeo."

His hand slipped beneath the V of my dress, cupping my breast through my bra. His fingers brushed over my nipple—just enough to make it pucker for him.

"Chloe... Fuck."

"Come for me, baby."

His eyes clamped shut. A moment later, he erupted, hot and heavy, soaking the waistband and spilling across his stomach. I didn't let go until his chest stopped heaving.

Lifting my hand discreetly, I slid a semen-laced finger between my lips, tasting him.

A blissfully unaware hostess bustled past, juggling orders. I caught her arm to get her attention.

She snapped her head toward me, sharp-eyed. "Meals are on the way. Five minutes."

"Hot towel, please."

Her posture eased. "Certainly, ma'am." She handed one over with silver tongs.

I rolled it between my palms, letting the warmth seep in, soothing the ache from my earlier clenched fists.

Once she moved on, I ducked beneath the blanket to clean him, wiping him gently.

Right now, I just wanted to take care of him. To worship him the way no one ever had. Not even his mother.

The blue of his irises had almost vanished. His pupils so wide they eclipsed the rest.

"Do you wanna fuck in the bathroom?" he panted, cupping my breast again, greedy and unashamed.

I looked at him over the top of the glasses I wasn't wearing.

"One—you just came. Two—I won't fit in there on my own, never mind the two of us. Three—no."

He chuckled, utterly content. "You know me, Queen. I got plenty left to share."

I glanced around the cabin. A few passengers were still watching, headphones on, movie screens playing silently, eyes lingering like they hadn't blinked in minutes.

"You know everyone can hear us, right?"

Romeo followed my gaze, locking eyes with the nearest couple. They looked away instantly.

"Do I look like I give a shit what people think?"

His honesty made me snigger.

"Everyone knows who you are, Romeo. You should care. Whatever happens on this plane will be in a gossip magazine by Monday—including an exposé starring that flight attendant. Title: Romero Giannetti's Dick in Paris."

He adjusted his semi, still throbbing in his sweats.

"Bullshit lies get printed about me all the time. Don't bother me one bit. If I wanna fuck my wife, I'll do it. Simple."

I raised a brow. He needed bringing down a peg or two—especially after having the audacity to get mad at Elijah, only for one of his ex-lovers to show up like a punchline.

"Don't you mean, if you want to fuck your wife, you'll ask nicely and respect her wishes?"

Romeo side-eyed me, then leaned in to kiss my neck.

"That's what I said."

Hmm.

The scent of over-cooked meat drifted through the cabin as the meal trolleys made their slow journey down the aisle.

First stop: Romero Giannetti.

"Here we are, sir." The latest attendant practically folded herself in half over him, desperation dripping as thick as the peppercorn sauce on his plate. "Perfectly cooked to your specification. Medium rare. Exclusively for you."

His tray clicked into place—steak topped with a fried egg, fries drowning in sauce.

He'd already tucked a napkin into the neck of his T-shirt like a king preparing to feast. Cutlery poised. Lips licked.

The only thing missing was his strippers.

I arched a brow as he stabbed into the meat with a plastic fork, tearing into it like a savage.

Steak juice dribbled into the folds of his napkin, the royal bib doing its best.

"I would've thought you'd go for lasagne?"

He huffed through a mouthful. "No chance. American lasagne is an insult to my people."

With that nugget of culinary wisdom, I took a disheartened bite of my cheese sandwich—only to realise, too late, it wasn't dairy free.

◆ ◆ ◆

"Look at that view!" I perched on the edge of the bed, legs dangling, gaze locked on the breathtaking panorama framed by the open double doors of our suite.

The sun kissed the ocean's surface, sending ripples of light dancing across the bedroom walls. A warm breeze drifted in, carrying the faint scent of salt and tropical blooms brushing my cheeks, leaving my skin cool and tingling.

Aquamarine blue was my favourite colour, stretching endlessly before me in a body of water I'd always dreamt of swimming in. And now it was real. A dream I shared with the most attractive man on the planet. Part of me wanted to rip my clothes off and dive straight in, completely naked, as I padded toward the private deck, drawn by the crisp evening air. But a bigger part of me was too self-conscious to expose myself like that.

Instead, I lingered by the doors, letting the breeze toy with the sheer white curtains, making them sway like the tide they mimicked.

"This place is something, isn't it, Romeo?"

In awe of our surroundings, I took in the suite—minimal, sophisticated, designed for the absurdly wealthy. A grand four-poster bed dominated the room, draped in voile curtains that billowed with the breath of air. Pristine white cotton sheets lay in wait, an open invitation. The private bathroom was discreetly hidden away, but nothing compared to the real showstopper—our exclusive ocean access.

"I'm gonna fuck you in that later," Romeo said, nodding toward the sea as he passed.

Waves crashed in the distance, mingling with the lazy rustle of palm leaves, a rhythm as intoxicating as the scent of jasmine and warm stone.

He poured himself a glass of complimentary whiskey from the cabinet and downed it in one. The clink of his diamond wedding band against the glass made my smile twitch.

"The table's booked for 9:00 PM. Do you wanna see my dick now or later?" he added, pouring another.

I tapped a finger on my lips, playfully weighing up his offer.

"I was actually just thinking how amazing it would've been to make a baby here."

Romeo stepped in beside me. The heat from his body bled through my thin dress as he laid a palm across my bump—possessive, protective.

"I'll bring you back here to make the next one," he murmured into my hair.

I looked up at him, smile spreading, chest fluttering.

"You will?"

"Yeah," he said, his voice as smooth as the liquor still warm on his breath.

I traced his wrist with my fingertips, pressing his hand more firmly to my belly. "I like the sound of that."

◆ ◆ ◆

That same evening, fighting off jetlag, we made our way to dinner at one of the island's exclusive restaurants.

Sandals in hand, I waddled along the sandy path, slightly breathless, my swollen feet protesting with every grainy crunch beneath my toes, clinging to the soles like sequins.

Romeo's hand stayed firmly entwined with mine, his thumb tracing slow circles in silent encouragement.

Lost in thought, I smiled when he lifted my hand and kissed the back of it.

"I love you, Mrs Giannetti."

I stopped in my tracks. Turning to face him, my feet sinking into the uneven ground, I studied him.

"I love you too, Romeo. So much."

He tucked a stray strand of windswept hair behind my ear, his touch lingering.

"What happened earlier on the plane… all that talk about women, Tat, Paris—it made me realise how much things have changed. For the better."

I was glad he'd acknowledged it. I'd be lying if I said I hadn't worried he might grow bored one day. Miss the freedom to sleep with whoever he pleased.

"I thought the same," I said softly. "You're a completely different man."

He held my gaze. "Do I make you happy, Chloe?"

A breeze rippled through my dress. My breath caught.

I nodded. "You do. So much." Then, quieter, "Do I make you happy?"

His thumb skimmed across my knuckles before he lifted them to his lips again. "I don't got words for how much."

At the beachside restaurant, Romeo pulled out my chair but didn't attempt to tuck me in. My precious cargo jutted too far for that now.

Over the horizon, the sky deepened to coral as lanterns flickered to life around the coastal retreat.

Beneath the striped canopy shielding us from the not-quite-set sun, maracas, ukuleles, and soft saxophones blended in cheerful harmony.

The scent of grilled seafood danced on the salty breeze. Ice clinked in nearby glasses, making my tastebuds tingle and my stomach growl.

Or maybe it was that cheese sandwich from earlier…

Romeo, like a meerkat, stretched his neck to scan the place—visibly on edge. More than once, his hand hovered near his waistband, instinctively reaching for a gun that wasn't there.

"Everything okay?" I asked, watching tension ripple through his shoulders.

After a moment, he slouched back with a rigid nod. "Been a long time since I had to watch my own back."

Our waitress arrived quickly. Native, but trying hard not to sound it—tiny shorts and a barely-there bikini top suggesting she offered blow jobs on the side.

My gut twisted. Whether it was jealousy or nausea, I couldn't tell, but the stomach growl ramped up to a full-on gurgle. She was perfect for him, and that thought alone sent trapped gas rising like it wanted out of my body.

"What would sir like?" she purred, fluttering her lashes and arching her back just enough to make her arse jiggle.

"Whiskey on the rocks. Double. And a decent pack of smokes."

She tossed her hair over her shoulder, releasing the scent of sun-kissed skin and sea salt.

"Mm-hm, sure," she said, syrup-sweet. "And for you?"

She looked at me like something she'd stepped in wearing open-toe sandals.

I clenched my cheeks. This fart was about to do me dirty.

"Sparkling water," I muttered, sucking it all the way in.

"Okay. Whiskey, cigarettes, and a water. Anything else?" Her nails dragged down his shoulder, practically inhaling the cologne I'd bought him.

"Maybe you should get yourself a glass of water," I said sweetly. "You seem parched enough to thirst after my husband right in front of me."

She pulled back with a huff, hand planting on one hip. "Sorry. I don't know what you mean."

I narrowed my eyes at Romeo. He hadn't intervened—too busy ogling my cleavage. The moment our eyes met, I gave him a sharp kick under the table. He jerked, banging his knee and rattling the condiments.

"We ain't decided on food yet. Hurry up with that whiskey. Bring a lighter too."

I crossed one leg over the other, then switched. A bead of sweat clung to my brow. A third gurgle landed. The fourth straight after.

"I'll be right back." She strutted off, hair swinging with every exaggerated step, the ends skimming her exposed lower back.

The soft glow of the lanterns danced like fireflies across the tablecloth. Platters of oysters, rare meats, and bright fruit floated past, briefly distracting me from the chaos brewing in my stomach. Trying to focus on anything else, I tracked the servers weaving between tables—willing myself to think about *anything* other than unclenching my arsehole—until I was forced to meet Romeo's stare.

He was watching me. Brow low. Eyes sharp.

"What now?" he asked, cautious.

The sea breeze cooled the back of my neck, but it didn't come close to putting out the burn of my jealousy—or the silent threat brewing beneath the tablecloth. Still, I wasn't about to give him the satisfaction of knowing what I had going on down there.

"You know exactly what!" I folded my arms in a huff. "That slut practically had her pussy lips in your mouth."

Yes, it was childish. But I couldn't help it. Not when I felt this self-conscious in my own skin. Just because I'd decided not to let the fivesomes he'd taken part in ruin our trip didn't mean I hadn't thought about them every damn second since.

His lips flattened as he leaned back on two legs of the chair with forced ease. "Don't start, woman. I mean it."

But the steady jiggle of his foot gave him away. He was simmering.

"Why don't you pop one of her tits into your mouth when she comes back?"

A glint flickered in his eyes. Elbows on the table he folded forward, he dragged his tongue across his lower lip.

"No thanks. But I'll have one of yours again." His gaze dipped to my breasts. "If I suck your tight little nipples just right, they reward me with a drop of that milk you're makin'. Like a taste of heaven."

Heat surged into my cheeks. I giggled. Relaxed my thighs—and everything else a little too much.

"So you still find me attractive, then?"

Why was I asking that now? Ah, because I loved ruining the moment. Not that it mattered anymore. What I'd been desperately trying to prevent just happened. A puff of air escaped, silent but hot and deadly. An air biscuit lifted beneath my dress like a rising green smog.

Any second now, the breeze would carry it to him—gift-wrapped.

The spark between us dimmed. He slouched back, putting distance between us. "What's with the dumb questions? You know you're sexy as fuck."

He hadn't smelt it yet. Time to play it cool.

Of course, I deployed the failsafe. Deflection.

I gestured toward the waitress, letting my insecurities leak through the cracks. *Ironic.*

"She's got the body I used to have."

His shoulders tensed. He gripped the edge of the table.

"I don't know how many times you need tellin', Chloe."

My thumbs circled in my lap, caught in silent turmoil.

"A few more, obviously."

The truth was, I needed to know he still saw me that way. It would break me if he didn't.

"You won't believe me, but I find you sexier now than I did before you were pregnant."

He leaned in again, voice low, beckoning me closer across the table. "When I think about you... you're pregnant and ridin' my dick. Gives me a boner every time."

My pulse twitched. My guard lifted—just a little.

Did I believe him? I had to. Still, it scared me. What if I never got my body back?

Just then, Miss I'm-Gonna-Steal-Your-Man returned, all urgent and breathless.

That's when Romeo's nose wrinkled.

Shit.

"Here you are, sir. Double whiskey and a pack of our finest cigarettes." She practically smothered him with her tits as she handed over the lighter.

I shot up, knocking the table with my bump. Whiskey sloshed across the wood in a shallow puddle.

"How desperate do you have to be?" I snapped, fists braced against the tabletop.

Her nostrils flared. Her whole demeanour changed. Another curl of wind flicked the edge of her apron. She sniffed, then lifted her finger to her nose.

Romeo raised his glass in a toast. "Yeah, that's right—I farted. Sniff it real good." He winked at me, eyes glinting as he took the final gulp of his drink.

The waitress glanced between us, visibly assaulted by the smell, clearly struggling to comprehend how a man that attractive could be responsible.

With a tight smile, she took a cautious step back. Her clit must've shrivelled on the spot. She turned on her heel and stomped off through the sand, just as the next salsa tune kicked in.

I peeled my attention away from her and back to Romeo. He still hadn't taken his eyes off me.

Was he tipsy enough from the jet lag and whiskey to believe he'd actually done it? Good. I wasn't about to implicate myself.

"What is it about you?" I asked, narrowing my eyes—changing the subject without saying it.

"What you on about now, Chloe?" he muttered, frowning at the off-brand cigarette carton.

With the first cig of the night between his lips, he struck the lighter. The flame flared, casting shifting shadows across his brooding face. A gust of wind blew it out. He had to spark it again.

"You know exactly what I'm on about. Women are always trying to fuck you. It's annoying."

He inhaled. Cheeks hollowed. Smoke spiralled from the corners of his mouth. A fleeting calm settled over him.

"Shame my wife ain't one of 'em." He dragged the ashtray closer.

"Haha. Very funny."

Still smirking, he stood, cigarette clenched between his teeth, and tossed a crisp note onto the table.

"Come on, Mrs Giannetti. Let's get outta here. Pretty sure you need a shit... We'll get room service."

The walk back was slow. By the time we reached our suite, the lanterns had melted into a warm amber glow against the deepening sky.

We headed straight to the private deck, drawn to the water we'd been craving since we arrived. The moon shimmered across the surface, casting silvery ripples that lapped at the deck's edge.

I dipped a toe in first. Warm, like a bath. Just as calming. Island music floated from the restaurant behind us, faint but familiar. Wherever we went, it felt like we'd stepped into another world.

"How's your stomach now?" Romeo's voice cut through the soft hum of life beyond our sanctuary.

I glanced up. He smirked.

My submerged toe turned into two whole feet, like that might somehow stop the blush creeping up my cheeks.

"I don't know what you're talking about. My stomach's just fine."

His brow lifted. "Yeah?"

The ocean gave a lazy lap against the shore, like even it was judging.

"If you're referring to that smell in the restaurant. That was the slut waitress. Not me."

A gull squawked overhead—probably laughing.

He stooped and pressed a kiss to the top of my head.

"Yeah. I know, Queen. I know."

The warmth of his touch washed over me, soft as the ocean drift. The reverence. The reassurance. It was all I needed.

"Thanks for taking the blame. I appreciated it."

"Figured I should pay Arnold a visit when we get back... reckon I might have a problem after I dropped that one." He rubbed his stomach in slow circles, chuckling like it really was his problem.

I sighed, leaning back on my elbows.

Why did I eat that damn sandwich?

Romeo kicked off his sneakers, the ones I'd given him for Christmas, and stripped without hesitation.

Confident. Unbothered. Gloriously naked.

From behind, he was all sculpted dominance—broad shoulders

tapering to a lean waist, his peachy bottom was toned and curved in the most obscene way. A living masterpiece.

"You don't have a back tattoo?" I asked, letting my calves slice through the gentle waves. The breeze cooled my earlier sun-kissed skin.

He turned. The front view was even better. His cock hung thick and heavy, slightly raised at the root.

"You want me to get one?"

"Absolutely. I love your tattoos. Come here. Let me see what you've got. We'll look at some inspo later."

He swaggered closer, flexing just for show.

Smoke clung to his skin, synthetic and sharp, completely unlike his usual scent back home. I let my fingers drift over the tattoos that curled up his arms and across his chest and neck. My hand slowed at the old scar on his abdomen—the stab wound we never spoke about. Then paused again at a patch of dense ink. Newer. Darker. At odds with the rest.

"What happened here?" I asked, narrowing my eyes.

His pecs flinched. He scratched the tip of his nose.

"Don't recall."

My fingers stiffened. "Why are you lying? What is it?"

He looked up at the stars—scattered across the sky like dust.

"Can we talk about this after we fuck? I've been lookin' forward to this moment all day."

That was his best joke yet.

My hands dropped from his body.

"Tell. Me. Now." My heart ticked faster.

"Fuck! Why is there always somethin' with you?" He groaned in frustration. "It's a cover-up. Of Tat's name. There. You happy now?"

My fists clenched at my sides. And for reasons I couldn't explain, tears rushed in.

Romeo's tone softened in an instant. He scratched the top of his head, torn between guilt and regret.

"Don't cry, Chloe. I'm sorry I snapped."

My shoulders shook with sobs.

Saxon. Tatiana. The air hostess. The waitress. And now this?

He eased down beside me, feet dipping into the water beside mine.

"Baby, I'm sorry. This is our honeymoon. I don't want anythin' to come between us."

I looked at him through blurry lashes. And slowly, we both smiled.

It still hurt, knowing Tatiana had meant that much. But the tattoo was gone. He'd chosen to remove it. Not me. His decision.

"I love you, Chloe."

My breath hitched one final time as I drew in a steadying breath. "I love you too."

Waves lapped the edge of the deck. An invitation too tempting to ignore.

He nodded, sharing the moment with quiet certainty. Then, from his seat beside me, he dove in—smooth, effortless, his technique sharpened from swimming lessons with Harper.

"Join me," he called, floating on his back beneath the moonlight. Flecks of glitter danced across his wet hair.

This was the part I'd been dreading.

Wiping my nose on the back of my hand, I battled to my feet and began to undress—self-conscious of my pregnant body in more ways than one. No matter how often he told me I was sexy, I never quite believed him.

My clothes fell into a crumpled heap. Stepping out of the safety of fabric, I padded barefoot to the edge of the deck and eased into the water using the ladder.

Before I was fully submerged, he swam close, his hand trailing over the curve of my rear.

"I love seein' you naked," he murmured.

He pulled me into him, my legs wrapping around his waist as we floated together, gloriously naked beneath the stars.

Like a puzzle piece sliding into place, his erection slipped inside me with ease. We fit. Always had. Two halves made to match.

"So beautiful. My sexy wife," he whispered, his breath brushing my ear as our bodies stayed afloat, powered by his slow, confident strokes.

I huffed. Even now, the insecurities clung like shadows.

His hands roamed the length of me, guiding my movement. But just as

I began to lose myself in the rhythm, he stopped. Slipped right out of me.

The shift jolted me back.

"You don't believe me, but I'm gonna prove it to you. I want you to watch me come just from lookin' at your sexy body. Get out." His voice was thick with lust.

Okay...

We sat naked and dripping wet on the deck, just above the glistening surface.

Moonlight washed our skin.

"Face me. Play with your sexy tits. Watch me nut for you, Chloe. I'm so fuckin' hard already. Look."

Veins rippled along his shaft, the flushed head swollen and twitching with need.

I listened. My hands slid over the weight of my swollen breasts—sensitive, tingling.

I watched his every flinch.

He barely touched himself. Didn't have to. The fire in his gaze devoured me whole.

"Play with your clit. Love your body the way I do."

I hesitated. "Romeo—"

"Come on, baby. My nut's waitin' on you lovin' yourself. Show me."

The second my fingers grazed my thigh, he groaned—low and raw.

I slid one finger inside, biting my lip as a moan slipped free.

That's all it took.

With one firm stroke, his orgasm tore through him. Thick, hot streams painted his abs in ribbons.

His jaw clenched, muscles flexing with each pulse. He stroked himself through the final wave, milking every drop as his breath came in ragged gasps.

Watching him unravel just from looking at me sparked something feral in my chest.

His ocean-blue eyes met mine.

A lazy smirk curled his mouth. "Now I'm gonna lick your pussy 'til you come."

His cock twitched, still half-hard, a milky bead lingering at the tip as he leaned between my legs, easing me back on my elbows.

Like a cat to cream, he devoured me.

I swelled for him instantly.

When he slid a finger inside and found the spot, he knew better than anyone. I broke. Completely.

The orgasm I'd been dreading. The one I feared would cause me to black out—hit like a wave. Violent. Convulsive. Endless.

"Fuck!" I gasped, as he drank every shudder from my body, relentless in his worship of me.

We lay naked and spent on the deck, stargazing through wisps of drifting cloud.

"Believe me now?" he mumbled into my hair.

"Mm-hm," I managed, voice soft and used up.

"I won't hear nothin' else on it. You're the sexiest little slut I ever saw. Got it?"

A smile tugged at my lips. "Mm-hm."

He rolled into me, cupping the back of my head with one hand, the tip of his nose brushing up the length of mine.

"*Mio per sempre*. Mine forever."

CHAPTER 7

"Yeah, just findin' it real hard," Romeo muttered into his phone, unaware I was awake.

One hand propped him up at the open doors as the rhythmic lull of waves rolled through the suite, a soothing contrast to the tension in his voice.

His side profile, bathed in the hazy gold of dawn, looked far away. Adrift in thoughts he hadn't shared with me.

After a beat, he nodded. "Aight, bye."

Someone was feeling secretive. And I wasn't about to let it slide.

The moment he caught my beady eyes watching from the comfort of our luxurious bed, his shoulders dipped. His expression hardened as he stepped back inside.

"Oh. You're awake," he mumbled.

That was all he had to say?

I shifted, propping myself on my elbows. "I'm sorry, Romeo. Does me being awake bother you?"

He snatched his diamond watch from the table, clipped it on with a sharp click, and shot me an unamused glare. His silence only made me dig deeper.

"So, who were you on the phone with?"

Beneath the sheets, my fists clenched. There was a very short list of safe answers.

The double doors swung shut behind him with a sigh, like they already knew where this was headed.

"T," he mumbled, adjusting the oversized dial just right.

Tim. Okay. I could live with that. The tension coiled in my chest began to unwind. My fingers slowly unfurled.

Still, something didn't sit right.

With a sigh and a roll, I turned my back on him and hugged my pillow.

"You know I hate when you give me one-word answers."

The mattress dipped behind me. Freshly smoked tobacco curled around my shoulder just before his lips pressed to my skin—soft, warm, lingering.

Goosebumps sparked in his wake. Anticipation pulled tight across my body. The remnants of last night still clung to my skin, mingling with the salty ocean air drifting through the open windows, thickening the space between us as his arm looped around my bare waist.

I already knew what he wanted.

His fingertips found my chin, guiding me gently to face him.

"Come here, sexy," he whispered against my lips.

Whatever irritation had been building inside me melted the moment his tongue found mine.

"Take the bedsheet off you, Queen. I wanna see your beautiful body."

I didn't usually take orders from my husband—but this was an exception. I kicked the covers down, exposing the damp warmth of my shape. Urgency twisted the fabric between my feet.

His eyes drank me in, lingering on my breasts, then the swell of my pregnancy. He hardened instantly. Not just aroused. In awe.

Our tongues tangled again as I lay naked beneath him, the smoky trace of last night's whiskey dancing between us. His need to connect ignited every nerve in my body.

I tugged at the hem of his T-shirt, craving the heat beneath. In one smooth motion, he crossed his arms over his chest and peeled it away —slow, teasing—before tossing it aside to reveal a sculpted masterpiece. The kind that made my pulse spike.

Kneeling above me, he hooked his thumbs into the waistband of his shorts and shoved them down to his knees. His cock sprang free. Thick. Solid. Perfect.

With a low groan, he gripped the base.

"When I grab my dick like this, I always think of your sexy body."

I parted my lips to reply, but only a breathy sigh escaped.

"Spit on it, Queen, so I can stroke it for you."

He dragged his hand along the engorged length, gliding up to the tip before pressing the crown through the tight circle of his fingers.

I did as he said.

Wet bubbles coated the head, slicking down the shaft. The squelch of his pleasure made my thighs clench.

"You see what you do to me, Mrs Giannetti?" he rasped, eyes hooded. "I need to bury my dick inside your sweet pussy."

I cupped the cool weight of his testicles, rolling them gently, syncing with the rhythm of his strokes.

"Shall I touch myself for you, Romeo?"

He stilled. Knuckles white. Pupils blown. Owned by the image he saw in his head.

All mine.

"Part those pussy lips, you little slut," he growled. "Show me what you've got."

No sooner had I made my move—trailing my fingers down the length of my body—than his strokes quickened, the slick sound of spit thinning under the pace of his fist.

I circled the pad of my fingertip over my clit, slow and deliberate, matching his rhythm. Every pulse, every breath between us, tightened with need.

"You wanna feel me inside you?" His voice dropped, thick and earthy.

I caught my lip between my teeth and nodded.

"Let me hear you, Chloe."

Heat built beneath my hand, but I didn't rush it.

"Yes," I whispered, eyes flicking between his ocean stare and the twitch of his cock.

"Good girl," he growled. "Now watch it slide in."

He lined up against my entrance, teasing the tip, lingering at the edge —before sinking deep. All the way.

My head rolled back into the pillow, breath shattering as he filled me, stretching me to the limit.

"Look at me while I make love to you." That voice was rough, commanding. Impossible to ignore.

My eyes instantly opened, locking on his. Wide, unwavering. Letting him take me exactly how he wanted.

The scent of sweat, sex and sea air enveloped us. His body moved over mine like a building storm—unstoppable. I dug my nails down his back, lips grazing the rough warmth of his chest.

"Do you remember who you belong to?" His words vibrated against my ear, raising the hairs along my skin.

I wrapped my legs around his waist, pulling him in—deeper, tighter, completely.

"Yes," I gasped. "Of course I do."

He didn't stop. Didn't waver. Each thrust hit its mark, sharp and brutal, like he needed to drive it into my soul.

"Tell me who owns you."

His hips rolled again, deeper still. My back arched as he hit the spot that shattered my thoughts.

"Tell me—"

"You, Romeo. Oh God… it's always been you."

A twitch deep inside told me he was right there, teetering on the edge.

With a ragged moan, he pulled out, bracing one hand against the headboard. His chest heaved. Eyes burned. The tip of his cock twitched—red-hot and pulsing.

The first slap of semen hit my chest, so hot it almost burned. The second landed hotter still.

By the third, my face took the hit. Like flicking paint off a brush, each splatter found its own chaotic pattern.

My eyes screwed shut as I took the hit.

One breath. Two. His orgasm hit hard.

Again. And again.

The swollen air stilled. Did the storm usually calm before or after the damage? Because right now, the tornado had hushed—just after ripping the roof off.

He collapsed beside me, stealing breath like he'd earned it.

Mine. His. All of it.

That's when the fury hit.

I wiped the come off my face and flicked it straight at his chest.

"What the fuck was that!?" My voice shot up several octaves as I shoved him with both hands, blinking through the mess now clinging to my lashes. "I literally have your come in my eye!"

He blinked, dazed.

I smacked his chest. It didn't make a difference. The man didn't even flinch.

I hated when he gave me one-word answers. But this? This was worse.

Everything I'd buried—Saxon, Tatiana, the sluts on the plane—had manifested itself as a final mockery, splattered white across my cheeks.

Swinging my legs over the bed, I slapped my bare feet onto the cool floor. Without a word, I stormed for the ocean doors. Ten steps. That's all I needed.

The sheer curtains tangled around my body as I pushed through, yanking them aside so hard I nearly tore the rail from the ceiling.

I didn't stop. I walked right off the edge of the deck. Straight into the ocean. The water swallowed me whole, sealing over my head as I sank deeper.

For a moment, I allowed myself to float, suspended and weightless beneath the surface. Letting the salt sting my eyes. The cold burn my skin. The water wash away every trace of him.

Of course, I was a little heavier than my anger had accounted for, and it took more effort than expected to float back up.

By the time my head broke through, Romeo had already dived in. He scooped me into his arms, pulling me against his chest, holding me steady as my breathing evened out. My nostrils burned. Throat raw as I coughed up the water, I'd somehow managed to inhale.

Nothing but the rustle of palm leaves and the distant hum of holidaymakers' laughter disturbed the brooding silence.

When our eyes met, he crashed his lips against mine—like his life depended on it. A taste of desperation I'd never tasted from him before.

"Do you love me, Chloe?" he breathed against my mouth, dragging me closer, clutching me like he couldn't bear the space between us.

His hand curled around the back of my neck. His tongue pressed between my lips again. The crack in his voice. The tremble in his grip.

I broke away first.

"Of course I love you, Romeo. Why are you asking that?"

His words caught in his throat, like his heart had split in two. He swallowed hard, tucking a soaked strand of hair behind my ear, freeing it from where it clung to my cheek.

"I need to know that when my brother arrives today..." His voice splintered. "That you love me more than you love him."

The weight of his words crept into my shoulders.

Suddenly, it was hard to breathe.

A wave crashed behind us like cymbals. Leaves shuddered like they shared his fear.

"Romeo..." My chin tightened. "I love you more than anything. I promise you. I won't mess this up."

With my legs wrapped tight around his waist, he swam us back to the ladder, lifting me up first.

The water landed like rainfall before I did. I flopped onto the wooden deck, the heated grain biting at my thighs. Legs slung over the edge, toes kissing their reflection on the surface.

Every sinew of his body flexed as he hoisted himself up beside me—shorts clinging low to his hips, no ladder required. Tension lingered in his movements, like it had nowhere else to be.

I hesitated.

He tousled the water from his curls, muscles flexing, body folding into itself.

I nudged against him gently.

"Was that call to Tim earlier... about me?"

His pecs twitched.

Droplets shimmered on his chest, catching the light as they slid through the grooves of muscle.

He nodded.

Shaking my head, I huffed.

"He advised you to come on my face?" My lashes fluttered—softening the dig.

Romeo huffed too, leaning back on his hands.

His abs glistened, the sun casting a spotlight across his sculpted perfection.

"He told me to talk to you. But I figured that wouldn't work, so I went with what I knew."

Had I expected Romeo to struggle with this vacation?

Absolutely.

Conversations with Nelly echoed in my mind, the kind where I'd pictured this exact moment. And Romeo's lukewarm contribution during those sessions had already raised red flags.

He'd kept relatively level-headed until now, but knowing Dan and Britney were due to arrive in the next couple of hours... It had started eating away at him. More than he'd expected.

"Hand on my heart, I don't have feelings for Dan anymore. Okay?"

He didn't face me. Still staring at the ocean. But he glanced sideways, just once. "Do you swear?"

I held my pinkie between us.

"I swear it's always been you."

He linked his with mine. A tighter curl than usual.

Promise sealed.

◆ ◆ ◆

I peered at my Casio wristwatch as we waited at the small wooden dock for Dan and Britney's boat transfer to arrive.

Hot and humid, hair stuck in wet strands to my neck. I was thankful for the ever-present sea breeze.

"What time are they due in, Romeo?" I swiped the sweat off the backs of my knees.

"Noon."

There he was with the one-word answers again. His clipped tone matched the rigidity in his stance, his hands firmly planted inside the front of his sweatpants. The tight set of his jaw, the way his eyes narrowed against the glare bouncing off the white sand, could've been mistaken for aggression—but I knew better.

"Did you take your mood pill at eleven-thirty?" I caught a bead of sweat trickling down his temple.

"No."

Figures. Maybe that was his issue?

Since we'd landed, he'd made it obvious how eager he was to get his business venture underway. I could only hope the stress he was putting himself under now was solely down to the meeting with their contact—and not about me and Dan.

"Why didn't you take it, Romeo?"

I'd seen it countless times: Tim cautioning him not to skip his pills. The ones that, for the most part, did a good job of keeping his outbursts in check.

He shot me a look before shrugging his shoulders.

Okay, buddy...

I eyed his choice of outfit under the blistering midday sun—a full tracksuit, sneakers, and a thick chain. Not exactly what I would've chosen for him. Maybe that was adding to his agitation?

"You look a little sweaty." I swiped another droplet of salty heat from his forehead. "Do you want to change before they get here?"

"No."

Fine. If he wanted to put on what he considered a masculine display in front of his brother—Mr I Don't Feel the Heat, Nor Do I Need My Pills—that was his choice.

"FYI, your nose is burnt," I sneered, figuring that if he wouldn't talk to me amicably, then a little dig at his appearance might get his tongue moving. "Told you sunscreen was important."

He rubbed the tip of his nose, wincing when the friction hit the delicate skin.

"Pfft," he muttered under his breath, shifting his weight, sneakers practically melting into the hot wood.

A compact speedboat appeared on the horizon, bobbing gracefully along the water at a brisk pace. It announced itself with the distant hum of its petrol-fuelled engine.

I rose onto my tiptoes, shielding my eyes from the bright light. "Is that them?"

He adjusted from one foot to the other. "Looks like it."

I peered back at my perspiring husband.

"Wow, I got three words from you that time. What's the problem? I thought we already fixed the issue this morning?"

He pulled out his burner phone, the glint of sun blinding off the screen, and after a scroll or two, shoved it back into his tracksuit pocket with a pensive look.

"Waitin' on a reply from our guy."

If he'd told me once, he'd told me a thousand times to keep my nose out of his business. But honestly, I just couldn't help myself.

"Why? What did you ask him?"

Lifting his chin, he peered into the distance, suddenly very interested in a brewing storm cloud hovering on the horizon.

"I asked him if he's got any tips on how to make a woman stop talkin'."

Ahh. Comedian Romeo was out to play—not that it was a problem for me. I could handle it. I had no issue matching his passive-aggressive banter with my own devilish streak whenever I put my mind to it.

"Haha. Not funny." I glanced beyond Romeo's shoulder, expecting to see our full security detail. The usual handful of men normally stood twelve feet away. Only Snake hovered in close proximity.

My brows pinched. "Where's Tommy, anyway?"

While we didn't need security, tailing our every move on the island—Romeo wasn't exactly a celebrity here—we still had to be cautious. Just in case.

"He's handlin' somethin'. Issues at the airport. Stop gettin' in my shit, Chloe. Your boyfriend's about to arrive."

I crossed my arms, bracing against the tension, and glared at him. Even his forehead vein was out.

"You did not just say that to me. After what you did this morning? I probably have an eye infection."

No matter how many times he tried to deny it, I bloody well knew it was still bothering him.

If Tim had been here, he would've steered Romeo in the right direction. I'd definitely noticed a decline in his behaviour since we arrived—without his life coach to keep him in check.

He raised his hands to me, finally regaining some self-control. "My bad. Come here."

Pulling me into an embrace, he pressed a kiss to the top of my head, his minty breath a quiet reminder that, in this moment, he was stone-cold sober.

Truth be told, I hadn't really believed that Romeo claiming my body this morning would miraculously fix the past. Far too much had happened for old wounds to heal that quickly. And with the weight of one of the biggest business deals of his career pressing down on him, the thought of all of us spending an extended period of time together was more than my husband could stomach.

See, at the time, the lure of drug money and my breasts spilling out onto his mother's perfectly presented dining table had clouded his judgement when he agreed to let me tag along.

But now that we were here, in the moment, I knew he was having second thoughts.

The boat finally reached the shore, docking just ahead of us as the captain's mate prepared for the passengers to disembark. The churn of the motor faded into the lapping tide as the boat slowed.

I spotted Britney and Dan before they saw us.

Britney, of course, looked effortlessly stunning in a fitted pale yellow sundress, sunglasses perched on her nose, and wedged sandals that elongated her already perfect frame. The stiff ocean breeze toyed with her hair, strands licking at her face as the steady tide rolled against the shore.

Unsurprisingly, Dan looked as handsome as ever in a light cotton shirt, unbuttoned at the collar, a pair of linen shorts, and black leather Hermès sandals. I smiled, appreciating his appropriate dress sense. I couldn't get Romeo in a pair of sandals if my life depended on it.

As I watched Dan help Britney off the boat, his chocolate curls whipping in the wind, I felt a strange flicker of something deep in my chest—something that filled me with dread.

I still fancied him.

Britney nudged Dan, pointing our way.

"Hey, you guys!" I called out, waving a little too enthusiastically. Anything to distract me from myself. "Over here!"

This was either going to go really well or be the biggest catastrophe the island had ever seen. There was no in-between.

Each minute that passed as they strode towards us left my pulse thumping that bit harder, as if the wound was reopening.

When they reached us, Dan nodded curtly, wheeling their small luggage bags behind him.

Another gust blew. Now close, the crisp scent of his Tom Ford cologne drifted over me—familiar, nostalgic, and impossible to ignore. As the wind ruffled his hair, my eyes caught on a fresh scar, a small pink indentation beneath his curls. A lasting reminder of how their mother conducted herself at the dinner table.

"Romero." He extended his hand for a firm, businesslike handshake.

"Daniele." Romeo offered an equally rigid hand.

To my surprise, they went in for the shake first—then a brotherly hug took over. The back-patting between them quickly escalated into a silent competition of who could hit harder. The hollow slaps against their broad backs created a near-melodic rhythm against the bustling backdrop of new arrivals to the island.

Watching them, it was almost easy to forget that Romeo had only made peace with his brother for the sake of the deal. Dan seemed genuinely happy. Blissfully unaware of his brother's true intentions.

Britney and I exchanged amused smiles at their embrace.

"I'm so glad to see you." I beamed at her. "Good flight?"

She nodded, pulling me closer. The all-too-comforting aroma of warm vanilla tingled my senses.

"It was great. This place is amazing!"

When the boys broke apart, Dan's eyes met mine. Heat rose in my cheeks before I could stop it when his emerald green irises shone like precious stone.

"Chloe." He offered his hand. A softer approach, just for me. A single beat of hesitation stretched like an hour as I stared at his proffered hand. I already knew it would feel velvety against my skin, gentle and assured.

My mind was made up for me when the three of them stared me down, waiting for my reaction to his manicured olive branch.

Not wanting to sour the mood before we'd even given this a chance, I offered a cautious handshake—barely letting our skin touch. The heat of his palm enveloped mine, his fingers gently closing around my skin.

Anticipation loomed.

The island's chatter simmered. Wind stilled.

But nothing happened.

Not a single spark flew between us.

Was he anticipating the electricity too? The flood of emotion that hadn't materialised in the way we were used to?

His lips thinned—answering that question for me.

Romeo's clenched teeth eased. Hands back in his pockets like the gesture alone had been enough to say everything.

Turning my attention swiftly to Britney, I took her hand in mine. "Welcome to paradise. Come on, guys, let's show you your place."

I glided through their one-bed, one-bath suite next door to ours with the confidence of a seasoned realtor.

"Your private bathroom is through that door over there. The closet's just here. And if you're hoping to watch TV… you can't—unless you're into foreign films with no subtitles." I giggled, perching on the edge of their beautifully made king-sized bed, where a swan-folded towel sat proudly at the foot.

Dan dropped his case on the floor, sending a ripple through the room, and wandered over to the double doors that led out to the ocean. An identical view to ours.

He seemed lost in thought, something playing on his mind. If I had to hazard a guess, it was the upcoming meeting with the Maldivian drug lord. Talk about being thrown in at the deep end. Romeo was certainly feeling the pressure. Dan must've been, too.

Lost, for just a moment, in Dan's world, I turned my focus back to my husband—only to find him already watching me from a short distance away. Hands still in his pockets. Ticking jaw.

He had definitely caught me looking at his brother.

Shit.

Playing it casual, I winked, a small smile teasing my lips—my usual tactic. But the look he gave me in return needed no explanation.

He was annoyed.

"Aight, brother," Romeo announced, pushing himself off the wall he'd been propped up against. "Meetin' with the crew in an hour. Get changed and come next door to our place in fifteen. We got some preparin' to do."

The tension building inside Romeo transferred through our interlaced fingers as we made our way back to our suite.

"Are you sure you're alright, Romeo? I feel like you wish I wasn't here."

Kicking his feet along the sandy walkway, he stared at the ground ahead.

"It's weird for me," he said quietly. "Knowin' my brother fucked my wife is not somethin' I ever thought I'd have to think about."

He fished in his pocket for the key, stepping inside first. Unzipping his jacket, he tossed it onto the bed.

As soon as the door clicked shut behind me, I sighed in relief. Kicking off my sandals, I massaged the balls of my feet, savouring the cool kiss of natural wood beneath my soles.

"Let's not forget here, Romeo, that I could say the same for you and Britney. When I left to live with Dan, she fell in love with you."

The rubber-tipped stopper squeaked in protest as Romeo eased the glass lid from the crystal decanter and poured himself a neat whiskey.

He took a gulp before setting the glass down on the table. "Me and her. That was different."

I padded barefoot towards him, clocking his first pour. Any more than five measures of whiskey in the next hour and he was having it.

"Please. How are you and Britney any different?"

Hitching his sweatpants, he knelt on the ground and flipped open the lid of his suitcase. He refused to unpack it, just in case a quick getaway was needed. He rummaged through the contents, searching for something.

I watched him closely—utterly fascinated.

Elbow-deep in the contents, he pulled out a sock, sniffed it, then stuffed it back.

"It's different, 'cause you loved limp dick and kept runnin' back to him. She might've caught feels for me, but I never loved her."

Oh.

What the hell was I supposed to say to that?

My hesitation prompted him to peer up at me from his crouched position, looking smug as he waited for my response.

I sighed in defeat and sank to the floor beside him, crossing my legs, studying him.

With a knowing smirk—because, of course, he was right—he finally pulled out what he'd been searching for. A wooden box housing his most prized possession. His crucifix.

He secured it around his neck, the weight settling heavily against his chest, positioning it perfectly at the centre. A little more himself now that he wore his armour. He offered me his hand, pulling me to my feet.

Nose to nose, the fresh scent of liquor laced each steady breath he took. "I won that one, Queen."

The playful shift in his mood made me smile.

"I already told you before. I didn't love Dan." My voice cracked, emotion swelling in my throat before I could push it down.

"Yeah, you did," he said with a matter-of-fact shrug. "But you don't anymore, so I'm cool with it. Plus, I know for a fact his dick is smaller than mine."

Hmm.

Tangled images of the brothers with tape measures didn't quite add up.

I peeled myself out of his hold, curiosity getting the better of me. It was no secret I had firsthand knowledge that he was, in fact, correct—but how the hell did he know that?

"Wait… how do you know?" I asked, grinning at the thought of the brothers having an impromptu dick-measuring contest.

The smirk on his face thinned into a tight line, and suddenly, my initial thought felt way off track.

He flicked the lamp on. Shadows crossed his face.

"Don't matter." Then flicked it off again. "Anyway, you want a snack from the bar before the meetin' starts? I'll grab it for you."

He stepped sideways, attempting to brush past me, but I caught hold of his wrist in a firm grip.

There was a woman involved.

"Hold on a minute. How do you know Dan's dick is smaller than yours?"

An uncomfortably long pause followed. Long enough to confirm what I already knew.

My fingertips pressing deeper into his flesh.

Eventually, he cracked.

"Aight, fine! Britney told me, okay? Drop it, please."

Britney?

As he stomped back towards his amber-coloured comfort blanket nestled atop the table, I folded my arms—strategically enough to boost my cleavage.

"Britney? Why the fuck did you get her involved?"

He reached into his pocket, retrieving his cigarettes.

A full glass of whiskey and a smoke? Pookie was really feeling the pressure.

"If your wife can't keep off another man's junk—there's usually a reason. I needed to know his ain't bigger."

With the ample size of Romeo's dick an ever-present nuisance in our relationship, I struggled to believe he thought anyone's—let alone Dan's—could compete.

"And you didn't believe me because…?"

He huffed. No eye contact.

"I needed to hear it from someone who was too scared to lie to me."

No matter what he said, I couldn't shake the fact he'd been in secret talks with Britney about something so personal.

"Just when I thought we'd moved past the issue of other women, here we are. And on our honeymoon, too. Wonderful. Absolutely fucking marvellous."

Taking a sip, he let the liquor bite, savouring the burn as it rolled down his throat.

"Chloe, come on. It ain't a big deal."

"Oh, of course it isn't!" I flailed my arms in exasperation. "Well, sorry to tell you this, *buddy*—but she was lying to you!"

I turned on my heels, pushing open the balcony doors. Fresh air met the heat of my cheeks, my heart thudding as a foul mood wrapped around me like a rain cloud.

What I wouldn't have given for a speedboat to appear from nowhere and rescue me from the man who couldn't keep other women out of his life.

The warmth of Romeo's breath ghosted over my neck before he spoke. "See, at one time, I would've lost my shit over a comment like that. But now I know you said it 'cause you're hurtin'—her bein' your best friend an' all. Well, guess what? I'm hurtin', too—'cause of what you did with Daniele."

My skin prickled when his plush lips grazed the nape of my neck, sending a shiver right through me.

I faced him, drawn in by how much sense his words suddenly made.

Emboldened, he continued.

"Fact is, Chloe, you shouldn't even be here. I've had to work real hard to make this happen for you. Even before all that Saxon shit. I think I already proved those bitches mean nothin' to me. But have you given me reassurance you won't run off with my brother again? No, you ain't."

Every inch he drew me closer felt like the weight of his worries pressed my back against the railing.

"Well, I mean—"

He put his finger to my lips. "Shut up, woman. I'm talkin' now."

Liquor in one hand. His fingers tightened around my waist before trailing down to my arse, anchoring me against him.

"Did I agree to let you come just to keep you happy? Yeah, I did. Are you suckin' my dick to thank me? Well, it sure as shit don't look like it!"

For the second time in five minutes, my husband left me speechless—and with Tim's influence, I doubted it'd be the last. There wasn't a single word I could say. He was one hundred percent right.

My bottom lip quivered as my emotions began to stabilise.

"So, you asked Britney to measure Dan's dick. That's it?"

His shoulders eased at the calm in my voice, one hand raking lazily through my tangled strands.

"Yes."

"And you didn't show her yours?"

His focus snapped away from the contents of his glass.

"Fuck no."

Times like this served as a reminder of just how much damage we'd done to each other.

I truly thought he'd believed me that day—when he'd worked himself into a full-blown tizzy after the tape measure didn't confirm what he'd convinced himself.

And there it was again. That word that plagued us both.

Reassurance.

"Okay. I guess that's alright, then."

Was I being truthful? That I was actually okay with it?

I think so.

Britney measured Dan's dick? Pfft. So what?

As long as she kept the hell away from Romeo's... that was all that mattered.

The unrelenting sun beat down. I took his free hand, drawing him back inside—away from the scalp-burning blaze, only to be met with the humidity of the suite. The ceiling fan churned a breeze overhead, struggling to make a dent.

Walking him backwards until his calves bumped the bedpost, I pressed calculated kisses to the tips of his fingers, looking up at him through my lashes. My way of showing I understood. My attempt to move past it.

"You abused Britney's feelings for you by asking her to do that. Don't do anything like that again. Got it?"

When I reached his pinkie, I took the whole length into my mouth and gave it a slow, gentle suck.

His whole body softened. He smirked as he set his glass down. Gripping my wrist, he pulled me into him, guiding my lips to his. He kissed me—lingering, slow—his tongue trailing toward the nape of my neck.

"Got it," he murmured, warm against my skin.

Somehow, we'd dodged an argument. No therapists required.

Not a cloud in the sky. Sunlight spilled through the window, catching the diamonds on his necklace and refracting a streak of brilliance. I took the crucifix between my fingers. Its cold weight never failed to surprise me.

"I love this. Such a beautiful, timeless piece," I sniggered, flipping it over to reveal the identical other side.

He already knew my real thoughts about his jewellery collection.

Catching onto my sarcasm, he played along. "I brought a matching bracelet, too. Hold on."

Intrigued, I followed lazily behind him.

Arm buried in his luggage again, he rummaged deeper.

"Hold on. Can't find shit in this fuckin' thing—"

Then he froze. His whole face turned to stone.

At first, I thought his worst fear had come true. That airport staff had finally stolen his underwear.

"What's wrong, Romeo?"

In silent explanation, he slowly withdrew his arm—caked from forearm to fingers in thick, bright white goo.

Lightly fragranced. Cooling for sensitive skin.

Sunscreen.

"What the fuck!?" he snapped, flicking his wrist. A splatter of white slung across the wooden floorboards, painting an abstract streak like modern art.

Peeling open a pair of his best underwear, he found the culprit. A leaking bottle of sunscreen. Lid popped. Contents oozing.

Trying to keep it playful, I giggled. "Gosh, what happened there?"

He shot me a glare, then tossed the rest of his case around, holding a few shirts up to the light, scrutinising each one.

"You're fuckin' lucky it didn't leak anywhere else. If it got on my tracksuits… you don't even wanna know what would've happened."

We both knew he was all talk.

"While you've got it all over you, why don't you pop a little on your nose?" I stifled a smile, teetering on the edge of laughter.

He gave me *the* look.

"Great fuckin' idea," he muttered, stalking toward the en suite. "Just the image I'm goin' for. Turn up to a deal with a bright white fuckin' nose, smellin' like a girl."

He reappeared with a freshly laundered towel, wiping himself down with full Italian theatrics. Still pushing back.

I shifted my approach.

"I'm just trying to look after you," I said, pouting, wishing he was more receptive to my need to take control.

"I know." He was calmer now, looping the towel around my neck and gently drawing me in. "But real men don't need lookin' after. That's my job—to take care of you."

He trailed the tips of his fingers along my jaw, a smirk playing on his lips before he pressed a soft kiss to the corner of my mouth. My tongue darted out, tasting the spiciness of his skin, tinged with lingering smoke and heat.

An idea struck.

Biting my lip, I smiled with intention.

"Do you wanna have sex before Dan and Britney arrive?"

I was pretty sure I could lather his whole body in suncream the second I climbed on top of him.

Sometimes the issue didn't even need to be that deep. But if I wanted something from Romeo, I had to get it. Give him an inch, he'd take a country mile.

No sooner had the words left my lips than the towel hit the floor. His way of evidencing lust. Dropping his guard.

Gripping the waistband of his tracksuit pants, he shoved them down. Now bare from the waist down, his cock stood heavy with arousal.

He checked his watch. "Yes, I fuckin' do, you sexy slut. We got three minutes before they get here."

A cotton-candy-pink cloud drifted in front of the sun. A fleeting dimness that broke the island heat, letting the moment simmer slow and sultry.

As if fate was playing tricks of its own, a knock at the door shattered the spell after barely fifteen seconds.

We both snapped back to reality.

"Come in," I called, amusement flickering in my eyes as Romeo yanked his pants back up, muttering curses while tucking his erection into his waistband. His hard-on would have to wait.

Dan and Britney strolled in, arm in arm. Their relaxed smiles didn't match the gauntlet hanging in the air.

The first thing I noticed was a thick streak of sunscreen smeared across Dan's cheekbones, nose, and forehead—glaring against his olive-toned tan like war paint.

Romeo clocked it, too. His nostrils flared.

"Oh, looky here." I turned to Romeo. "I see you're taking care of your skin, Dan?"

Britney ran a manicured finger across Dan's cheek, rubbing in the cream a little more thoroughly, then laid a splayed hand on his chest.

"You betcha," Dan said with quiet confidence. "Giannettis burn like you would not believe."

Cocking my hip, I folded my arms and gave Romeo's already pink-tinged features a slow once-over. I arched a brow, waiting for him to connect the dots.

Romeo smirked. "You're forgettin' one thing, Chloe," he said smoothly.

"Oh yeah? What's that?"

"He's a girl."

Dan, seemingly oblivious to the jab, let go of Britney's arm and stepped further into the room—only to skid slightly on the slick floor. He caught himself just in time, eyes darting downward.

"Oh God," he whined. "That better not be what it looks like." He lifted his shoe, inspecting the sole.

Earlier distractions had left us sidetracked. The flicks of sunscreen from Romeo's suitcase still streaked the floor in pearly white splashes.

Dan grimaced. "Surely you didn't—"

Romeo raised his chin and stood taller. "Empty my sack on the floor? No, brother, I didn't." He gripped himself. "Savin' that for the wife later."

Dan's shoulders dropped. He swiped a hand across his forehead in relief. "Thank God."

He stepped around the mess, coming a little closer to me than Britney. Romeo exhaled sharply, checked his watch, then shifted gears.

"Aight. Enough about my ball sack. First order of business." He began circling Dan like a predator. "Get that fuckin' suit off. This ain't a joke."

All eyes landed on Dan—his perfectly tailored grey two-piece and pristine black leather sandals were at complete odds with the mission ahead.

"What do you mean, Romero?" He tugged at his lapels. "This is how you command respect. Dress to impress, not distract."

It sounded like something their mother would say. But Romeo wasn't buying it. He'd been eyeing Dan's footwear since the moment he stepped through the door.

"I don't know who the fuck told you a suit and grandma sandals were fly, but they lied. Jesus himself wouldn't be seen dead in those."

He unzipped his suitcase, flung back the lid, and dug through the contents—pulling out the pair of soaked boxers first. With zero hesitation, he tossed them to the floor with a wet slap.

Dan recoiled. "Oh my God." He sucked in a sharp breath, flinging an arm protectively across Britney's chest and forcing them both back a step.

Romeo's confusion lasted half a second until he clocked the milky white stains and caught on to Dan's misinterpretation. A wicked smirk crept across his face.

"That, right there, is real men's underwear, Daniele. Don't forget it." He yanked out a black velour tracksuit and flung it at him. "Put this on. You best be wearin' boxers. If not, you can borrow those."

I concealed my laugh as best I could.

Dan caught the expensive designer bottoms, holding them like a biohazard. "You want me to wear these?"

"Look, brother. You're makin' it real obvious this is your first deal. We don't got time to argue. Put it on. Now."

There wasn't a word to describe how I felt watching Dan shrug off his satin-lined jacket and lay it neatly across the bed. The same cologne from the dock drifted toward me again, freshly reapplied. He smelled mouth-watering—like a platter of sliced citrus fruits.

He peeled off his shirt, revealing a sculpted torso. More defined than the last time I'd seen him. Olive-toned skin, lean muscle, cut abs. He'd been putting in work.

I didn't realise I was gawking until Romeo hooked an arm around me, pulling me tight against the solid strength of his body.

"Your eyes belong to me. You wanna see a real man? Look this way," he murmured into my ear.

The heat between us crackled. His earthy, woody scent mixed with Dan's citrus undertones—a heady cocktail of testosterone and tension.

"Tell every fuckin' body in this room who your pussy belongs to," he ordered.

The shift was clear. Pinched brows, that hard angle to his jaw. Eyes burning. Romeo wasn't just my husband anymore.

He was becoming King.

My breath hitched. His ocean-blue eyes had darkened to midnight. The sound of his voice made something inside me bow to him.

"It belongs to you, Romeo."

His gaze dipped to my cleavage.

"You're damn fuckin' right, you little slut. Show 'em. Kiss me."

A soft breeze lifted the hem of my dress as I rose onto my tiptoes, wrapped my arms around his neck, and pulled his lips to mine. Our tongues tangled, our love transferring between us in a language only we understood. No doubt about it. I loved Romeo with my whole heart.

Still... something about Dan wearing my husband's tracksuit confused the hell out of me.

By the time we pulled apart, Dan had finished changing. Matching jacket. Matching pants. Plain muscle-fit tee underneath. He stood stiff, like the coat hanger was still inside.

"This stinks of cigarette smoke," he muttered, lifting the sleeve to his nose. "This is not the impression I want to give our client."

A flicker of something crossed Romeo's face—but King shut it down instantly.

"That's what a man's supposed to smell like, Daniele. You wouldn't know. Get used to it."

Dan twisted at the waist, checking himself from every angle.

"I look absolutely ridiculous," he mumbled.

But the truth? He looked just like his brother. Rugged. Delicious. Absolutely mouth-watering. Chocolate curls and green eyes were the only real differences now... well, that and maybe a couple of inches.

The jewellery box snapped shut.

"Here. Put this on too." Romeo handed him the garish dollar-sign chain like a proud father passing down a family heirloom.

Britney and I exchanged a look. She fancied my husband—no doubt about it. Well, now there were two of him.

"Okay, I'm ready," Dan said, adjusting the chain.

Tracksuit. *Check.*

Flashy jewellery. *Check.*

Suitable footwear?

Still no.

Even Romeo's demeanour softened as he cracked a smile at the finished look. "Take those fuckin' sandals off, Daniele. Mom might think you're the second comin', but let me tell you right now—you ain't. A suit's one thing, but my best tracksuit with that shit on your feet? What the fuck."

Dan glanced down at himself. "I can't help that my feet are sweating,

Romero. It's a hundred degrees out."

Through the window, sunlight beamed in shimmering waves. Distant thunder clapped—dry, low, and meaningless. Not a drop of rain in sight. The same kind of storm that was now brewing inside our suite. The threat of relief had passed. But in here, it poured with restless energy.

Romeo rummaged through his bottomless suitcase of props and finally tossed a pair of sneakers at him. "Here. Try these on."

No surprise—they were at least a size too big. Probably two. Which meant we were down to the last resort: Dan's own sneakers. Pure white Ralph Laurens, neatly laced. Not exactly fly, but they'd have to do.

Romeo gave him a final once-over, resting a crooked finger against his lips before shaking his head. "Brother, you look like a cop."

Dan exhaled, fingers brushing the fresh scar on his forehead. His expression mirrored the rest of us—tense, unsure.

"This was never part of the plan, Romero. I'm really uncomfortable about this."

Romeo prowled the suite like a predator, each step slow and measured, heels striking the floor with deliberate rhythm. Whiskey glass in hand, he took a long sip.

"How the fuck was I supposed to know you'd show up completely unprepared?" he snapped. "Own it."

Rigid and bewildered, Dan stood there adjusting the heavy chain around his neck like it weighed a tonne.

Another dry rumble of thunder. Still no rain.

Dan rolled his eyes. "Own what, exactly? I don't operate my business like you do."

Romeo handed me his glass. The liquor's heat curled in my throat as I caught its scent.

"First off," he said, voice sharp enough to silence the room, "stand like your dick's too big for your drawers. Roll your shoulders. Loosen up."

Dan tilted his head left, then right, before executing the most uncomfortable shoulder roll I'd ever seen.

Romeo groaned. "No. Like this."

Feet shoulder-width apart, one hand stuffed casually down the front of his tracksuit bottoms, gripping himself—just like that, Romeo became who he really was. A natural gangster.

Dan recoiled. "I'm not doing that! I didn't study business at Harvard just to end up dressed like this. And I'm not about to fondle myself in front of everyone."

Suppressing my laugh was becoming impossible. He might've looked like Romeo, but he never let us forget he was nothing like him.

"Lose the posh talk," Romeo said flatly. "You get in front of this guy talkin' about business school. You're dead before we sit down."

Dan's frustration was mounting. "How else do you expect me to speak? I wish you'd given me more insight before I agreed to this."

"Repeat after me," Romeo said, gesturing. "'Aight, slut. Show me some titties.'"

Dan grimaced so hard I thought it might stick. "Romero, I cannot and will not say that. 'Aight' and 'titties,' etcetera—those aren't words I can just toss out and sound believable."

Romeo shut his eyes. Took a long breath. On the surface, he looked like he was drowning. I just hoped he'd found a way to kick back to the surface.

"Whatever. I'll do most of the fuckin' talkin'. Just don't fuck this up. I didn't bust my ass gettin' us in the room with this guy for you to blow it."

Dan's stance relaxed slightly. "It's not like I won't try, Romero. But this is a lot."

Romeo glanced at the time, then at the door, then back at his brother.

"Aight. Second order of business. When was the last time you snorted a line, Daniele?"

He swept the whiskey bottle aside and wiped the tabletop clean with his sleeve.

Dan stiffened, inching backwards. One hand gripped the zip of his jacket, fingers toying with it like a nervous tick.

"You already know the answer to that. Never."

"Thought so." Romeo reached into his pocket and pulled out a small silver packet. "Come here and make a line."

Dan didn't move.

Britney and I exchanged a look.

Romeo dragged the table a foot closer.

After a long pause, Dan took a cautious step forward, each movement tight with reluctance.

Romeo handed him the packet. "Here."

Dan held it between two fingers, raising it to eye level. "What is this?" He gave it a shake, upper lip curling.

Standing there in Romeo's tracksuit with a dollar-sign chain slung around his neck, asking what's in the bag was the final puzzle piece in an already surreal picture.

He looked the part. But he didn't act it.

"Sugar," Romeo huffed. "What the fuck do you think? Best cocaine on the market. You should already know this—you've moved my shit around the States long enough."

This was the first time I'd ever seen Romeo handle anything drug-related. And the shift in him was instant. His arrogant confidence was razor-sharp. Like this world was second nature.

Dan hesitated again, still holding the packet like it might explode.

Romeo jabbed a finger at the table. "Come on, limp dick. Line it up."

Dan sighed. Peeled open the packet. Then poured out the entire contents.

"Not all of it! God damn it!"

Dan flinched.

"How the fuck are you gonna get the leftovers back in the bag?" Romeo barked. "Each gram's worth two hundred fuckin' dollars!"

Dan cast a fleeting glance at his audience—me and Britney. Neither of us had looked away from the unfolding disaster. My thighs sweated in sympathy. My heart ached a little at Dan's purity in Romeo's imperfect world.

After what looked like a silent war behind his eyes, he finally shrugged. "I don't know how to get it back in the bag, Romero. Clearly, I'm not as skilled at this as you."

The ceiling fan hummed overhead, loud but useless. The harder it worked, the less it seemed to do. I wafted my cheeks with both hands.

Britney fidgeted helplessly.

Romeo muttered under his breath, rolling up his sleeves like he was prepping for open-heart repairs.

"You got a hundred-dollar bill on you?" he asked, holding out his hand, fingers twitching with impatience.

Dan dry-swallowed. He reached into his suit jacket draped over the bed, flipped through his wallet, and handed over a crisp note. Its dry texture crackled in the exchange—like the desert storm brewing between them.

Without missing a beat, Romeo rolled it into a tight tube and held it out.

"Here. Snort the coke through this."

Dan's face twisted in disgust. He stumbled back, hands raised. "I'm not doing drugs, Romero. No way. You never said I'd need to do this."

Even from across the room, Romeo's intensity pressed down like a vice. His jaw flexed, muscle twitching just beneath the skin. His restraint was threadbare.

"Do it. Now."

Dan pressed his fingertips hard against his temples, eyes locked on the pristine white line laid out in front of him. The silence stretched, tension fraying at the edges.

Then Romeo changed tactics. His voice softening, coaxing like he was speaking to a child.

"All you gotta do is close your other nostril and sniff up. Simple."

Dan's mouth drew tight.

"Simple for you, maybe. I didn't sign up for any of this."

That was it.

In a flash, Romeo fisted Dan's jacket and yanked him nose-to-nose.

"Take this fuckin' serious, Daniele. We'll only survive this if we do it right. Get your fuckin' nose along that fuckin' snow. Now!"

I sucked air through my teeth, wincing at the clench in Romeo's other fist. This was hard to watch. Harder than I was prepared for.

"Romeo, please." I broke from the background, stepped forward on my toes, palm pressing to his chest. His heart pounded beneath it—fast, hard, and unforgiving.

But he didn't soften. His shoulders stayed stiff.

"Keep out of this, Chloe," he snapped, cold and detached.

Then he swerved away from my touch—out of reach, out of range. He wasn't just pushing me away. He was locking me out.

King was here now. Romeo... completely gone.

Dan's fists curled at his sides as he loomed over the table. Neither he nor King backed down. The silence between them sizzled—thick, volatile, waiting to explode.

Finally, Dan exhaled. Leaned down.

Paused.

King's eyes glinted. "Go on, brother. It's the best shit there is."

Dan's fingers flexed near his nose. Then—

He snorted the line.

King clapped him on the back like it was some kind of warped celebration.

Dan jerked upright, breath caught in his throat as the burn hit. His fingers hovered near his face, torn between soothing the sting or letting it ride. He blinked rapidly, Adam's apple bobbing as he swallowed hard.

"*Oddio*," he muttered hoarsely, the Italian brittle in his throat. His pupils dilated. Jaw clenched. The hit was fast and unforgiving.

Britney crossed the room, movements feline. She slipped an arm around his shoulder and eased him into the chair. Concern drew fine lines across her pretty features—one brow lifted, the other furrowed.

She looked just as worried as I felt.

The suite door burst open, slamming into the wall.

If the air hadn't been so stale, it might've brought a gust. Instead, it delivered a wall of thick, suffocating heat.

Tommy stood in the doorway, Snake a step behind, both of them stone-faced.

"What?" King barked, his posture snapping upright.

Whatever he saw in Tommy's face hit him like a punch to the gut.

"Boss..." Tommy hesitated, swiping the sweat from his bald head before glancing at Snake. "Everything that could've gone wrong... it fucking has."

King didn't flinch. Just flicked his wrist toward me.

"Chloe, go for a swim."

I did the opposite. Feet rooted to the floor.

"No chance. I'm staying right here."

I shoved the whiskey glass into his chest. He took it.

Then I crossed the room and sat on the bed, legs crossed, hands folded over my knee—settling in.

"Okay, Tommy. What's the problem?" I asked, like I held the solution.

Tommy looked to King, but he offered nothing—just a long pull of whiskey and a stare colder than steel.

Snake stepped forward. Combat boots thudding against the varnished floor.

"We lost all our men at the airport. Cops saw us coming."

"Fuck!" King roared, glass clinking dangerously in his grip. The whiskey glass, half full and half weapon, glinted like a threat. "How?"

Tommy swallowed.

Snake answered.

"Sniffer dogs," he said tightly. "Only crew we've got left are me and him. We need to abort. Now."

King sprang into action, pacing the room as he dragged a hand down his face in frustration. "Johnny, Trevor, Mike—all of 'em?"

Tommy did his best to avoid eye contact. "We'll know more when we get home. But yeah, looks like they'll all get slapped with attempted drug smuggling."

Snake nodded grimly. "What do you say, Boss? Pull the plug?"

King stopped dead. Grabbed his crotch and gave it a sharp tug. "The only thing I'm pullin' is my fuckin' dick! Bailin' on this deal ain't an option—and you fuckin' know it!"

Dan blinked slowly, still swaying slightly in the chair.

"Wait… what's going on?" His voice cracked, a half-choked chuckle escaping. But there was nothing funny about this. "What does all of this mean, Romero?"

With glassy eyes, he looked between King and Tommy, searching for reassurance he already knew wasn't coming.

"Six crew down," King snapped. "Just these two pricks left for security." He threw a look at Tommy and Snake, both of whom bristled.

Dan pushed to his feet, catching himself on the edge of the table. "So… we back out?" His voice was shallow, every word like sludge.

King yanked open the decanter lid.

"No fuckin' way!" he barked, pouring himself a double and downing it in one hit. He slammed the glass onto the table. "Grow a fuckin' spine. All of you."

The room fell into heavy silence. Only the soft rumble of waves rolled in from outside. I gripped the bedsheets, palms slick with sweat. A plan so meticulous, so carefully laid, was crumbling in real time.

King's voice sliced through the quiet.

"Aight, listen up. This is the play." He took three long strides, positioning himself at the centre of the room. The fan above gave him everything it had, but his black curls stayed rigid—like his jaw. "Tommy and Snake stay here with the women. Me and Daniele handle the deal."

Tommy stiffened, hand resting on his empty holster. "No way, Boss. That's suicide."

"It's suicide if we bail!" King shot back. "No other choice."

I raised my hand. He was already pouring again. The whiskey curled into the glass like poison.

"What, Chloe?" His eyes bored into me, wild and wide.

He was past the five-drink limit I'd begged him to respect. But now wasn't the time to argue.

I kept my tone even. "Me and Britney will be fine here while you go with Tommy and Snake. Won't we, Brit?"

King cackled, a jagged, unhinged sound, before zeroing in on me with eyes glazed in fury.

"No fuckin' chance."

Sometimes it felt like he said no just for the hell of it.

I recoiled, hands raised. "Okay, jeez. I was just trying to help."

He shoved the small table toward the centre and eyed the crew. "Stack it up. How much product do we got?"

Tommy sighed, placing a small black bag onto the glass top.

King stared at it. Waiting.

Then reality landed.

"What the fuck is this—half a brick?" He snatched it up, pinched it between his fingers, and slammed it back down.

"We lost all the product with the crew. That's all I had on me, Boss."

With a roar, King gripped the edge of the table and flipped it. The whiskey glass crashed to the floor, shattering. The bag of cocaine sailed after it.

"This changes everythin'. Fuck!"

I had questions, but the storm rolling off him froze them in my throat. He was spiralling—and it was terrifying.

"Boss," Tommy said cautiously, "if we're not bailing, the only way this works is if the women come with us. Can't risk sending you and your brother out with half a key and no cover. Can't leave them behind either."

Silence again. Not a breath.

The storm clouds refused to spill, but a stiff breeze finally skimmed off the ocean, drifting through the balcony doors. The sheer curtains danced, and somewhere in the distance, restaurant music floated in on salt air.

A plan was forming.

King raised a finger. All breath held. Then, he nodded—slowly, like a man pleased with his own genius.

"I have a play. Since we gotta take 'em anyway… Britney'll make up for the missin' product—"

Dan stumbled over his own feet. Britney's hand flew to her mouth. I frowned.

"Hold on." I stepped in. "What do you mean, make up for it?"

He gave me a look of pure impatience. Like I should've already known.

"Standard protocol. If you've got a wife, you offer her up to compensate. Shows respect. We already prepped for this with English. We can do it again."

I swallowed hard.

So that's what he meant by 'prep'? His dick buried inside Britney's pussy?

I scanned his face, desperate to read something. Anything. But his pages were wiped blank. Not even a glossary left.

"I thought English requested your 'wife' to close the deal, not open it?"

"Yeah, he did." He sneered, like I'd offended him. "English was different. I underestimated his power in Europe. Did what I had to do."

My stomach dropped.

So this was happening again. Britney, my best friend, his new temporary wife?

Was this standard protocol… or payback for Dan?

"Excuse me?" I rasped. My mouth was desert-dry. Even the empty glass on the nightstand wouldn't save me now.

King stared. "What now, Chloe?"

"Where does that leave me?" I glanced around the room, hoping someone—anyone—might back me.

But no one looked my way. All eyes were on him.

"It leaves you standin' at the fuckin' back. I don't wanna hear a word from you. Got it?"

If I'd had the nerve, I'd have kicked him in the shin. But the man in front of me wasn't Romeo. And I didn't trust what King might do next.

Tears pricked the backs of my eyes just as Tommy caught the shift in my expression.

"Maybe your job'll be to keep an eye on Dan while Boss handles business?" His gaze flicked to the far side of the room.

Dan had wandered into the corner, fumbling with the zipper on his jacket. He had no idea where he was, let alone what he was meant to be doing.

I bit down on my lip, catching Snake's attention. These days, he could read me like a book.

"Don't worry about Britney," he said evenly. "She's an experienced decoy. This guy will be easier to please than English. It's how the game works. We fucked it by not having enough product. This makes it right."

"Enough!" King roared, snatching a second liquor glass from the minibar tray and hurling it across the room.

It smashed against the wall with a splintering clash. Loud, violent, and utterly unceremonious.

A shatter of shards at the centre of the room. Another by the wall. His shows of emotion were becoming dangerous to us all.

The already strained tension snapped taut. King dragged a hand through his tight curls, like he was trying to reboot himself.

"Aight, everyone just calm the fuck down!" he snapped at the room. But the command was clearly for himself.

"We have a plan," he continued, his tone levelling out. "Our guy gets a small sample of the good shit. Britney finalises. We shake on it and pray he doesn't clock how light we've travelled. Guns are a last resort. Got it? Weapons guy'll be here soon."

Murmurs of agreement rippled through the room—until I raised my hand.

Silence dropped like a blade.

"Yes, Chloe?" King said through gritted teeth, a pulse throbbing in his throat.

I narrowed my eyes. "Why the hell do you need a gun if you're doing business?"

He scoffed. "Just 'cause a man says he wants a deal don't mean he won't change his fuckin' mind. Gotta be ready. Tommy, give Chloe your shell."

Shell?

Now wasn't the time for crafting nautical necklaces on the beach.

Tommy tore the Velcro from his bulletproof vest. The rip sliced through the room like a weapon. He handed it over. I took it begrudgingly.

"Doesn't Tommy need this?" I asked, pulling it over my head. "We don't have another one?"

He shook his head. "That's it. Snake's still injured, so he keeps his."

I wanted to scream. Romeo still hadn't learned a damn thing about safety. Why the hell hadn't he brought the vest I gave him?

I strapped it around myself, ignoring the damp warmth left behind by Tommy's body and the masculine scent that clung to it. Sweat was already slicking my skin. The vest only suffocated me more.

Then I glanced at Britney. Her wide-eyed, knee-knocking terror was palpable. But she knew better than to argue.

"Britney needs a vest too," I said, watching Romeo's tongue roll over his teeth.

"Oh yeah?" he huffed. "She gonna fuck him real good in Kevlar? Give me a break, Chloe."

The salt in the air clung dry to my lips. They cracked as I snapped. "Don't speak to me like that. You just announced Britney as your new wife. Show some fucking compassion for the woman who got there first."

He turned. Crucifix swinging. Muscles coiling tight.

Then—without warning—he drove his clenched fist into the wall. It smashed clean through the drywall, his knuckles tearing it open like paper. Dust rained to the floor. His breathing turned ragged. No one moved. No one spoke.

Flexing his hand, he shook it off like it was nothing. Even though the red, raw skin told another story.

"If you'd stayed out of it," he muttered, voice lethal, "Britney wouldn't fuckin' be here. Now you deal with the consequences. I don't want another word. Got it?"

The glint of the crucifix around his neck caught the light—diamonds sparkling like a fresh warning. I still waited for the day I'd get to shove the pointy end right up his arse.

I hated King. Loathed him. Detested him.

Romeo was buried so far beneath the surface, I could barely remember what he looked like.

King pulled Britney to his side, curling a hand around her waist with possessive ease. Fingers dug into her skin just enough to claim.

"Get into character," he said, shaking himself off. "Remember how we did it last time?"

She nodded. "Yes, King."

She slid into place like it was muscle memory.

I watched her, silently begging her to look at me.

Eventually, she did. Her eyes lifted. Apologetic. Doe-eyed. Brimming with anguish. My heart swelled. She didn't want this either.

Tears threatened. I blinked them away. I had to stay strong. For the baby. For myself. I couldn't fall apart.

King glanced at me, face hard.

"Don't fuckin' cry, Chloe. This is survival. We all better get used to dyin' bein' on the table. I'm tryin' to stop that."

And like a switch, the room shifted. Expressions hardened. The humidity dropped like we'd all accepted our fate.

Everyone fell into line.

Britney's posture morphed. She leaned into him, shoulders square, head high—confidence I'd never seen in her before. And just like that, I knew how far it had gone between them last time. While I'd been trying to build something real with Dan, they'd been mastering their act. She'd fallen for him. Maybe he had too.

"Chloe," King said, holding out his hand. "Take your rings off."

I raised my trembling fingers. "My rings?"

He nodded, fingers curling. "Give 'em to Britney."

I snatched my hands close to my chest.

"You want me to give her my wedding ring? Are you insane?"

Tommy checked his watch, wiped sweat from his brow.

"Boss, weapons guy's five minutes out."

King strode towards me. Dampness glistened along his hairline. He didn't ask. Didn't check in. Didn't flinch.

He grabbed my hand and ripped the rings off, scraping them over my knuckle like he had every right.

Should I have been grateful he left Nonna's ring? Or insulted that he thought I'd still want to wear it after this?

Without a word, Britney slipped my rings onto her finger. It felt like a warped wedding ceremony—right in the middle of my worst nightmare. Like the first time we got married. Grotesque in its absurdity.

"Wow. That was beautiful," I said dryly, offering a slow clap. "What now? Does Dan get down on one knee and propose to me?"

I glanced over my shoulder and instantly regretted it.

Dan's jaw clenched, eyes vacant, as he dragged a shaky hand across the back of his neck.

What the hell was King thinking? Forcing him to take hard drugs before the biggest meeting of his life?

Or was that the point?

Had it all been intentional? Ten steps ahead, like always. Cripple Dan just enough… knowing I'd want to retaliate?

"Am I the only one really upset here, Romeo? Because it fucking feels like it!"

He adjusted his waistband with a sneer.

"Trust me, Chloe. Ain't nobody more fuckin' upset about this than me."

Every eye in the room locked on the bed, on the neat row of guns laid out like party favours for a mob boss funeral.

The sharp tang of well-used metal clung to the air, heavy with the scent of war on the horizon.

For the first time, King let me in. Not just into the room—but into the fold. Whether he liked it or not, I was finally part of something he'd spent our entire relationship trying to shield me from. If I was going to survive in his world, I had to see it for what it was.

A shifty-looking local man—reeking of seawater and fresh fish, decked in a floral shirt and thong sandals—fidgeted as he guided King through the display.

"HK MP5," he said. "Perfect accuracy. Suppressor compatible."

King raised the weapon, sighted an invisible target, and gave a single nod. "I'll take it."

"Excellent choice." The sleazy fisherman grinned, already reaching for the next one. "Uzi. Highly lethal. Easy to conceal."

Tommy stepped forward. "We'll take two. Wrap it up—we've got business."

We waited on the heated dock. Dan's clammy fingers tangled with mine as I steered his wrecked body towards the boat.

Just seeing King with Britney made something ignite in my gut—hot and wrong and almost convincing me I belonged with Dan. But this time,

I knew better. I knew this wasn't real. This was to protect me. Our son. To fix a mess I'd helped create. But holding onto that thought was like gripping smoke.

Like a scene scripted by him, for him, King placed a hand on Britney's arse and helped her into the rocking boat. They settled together on the bench at the front—like some fantasy couple.

Dan climbed in behind them, slumping into the rear seat, eyes fluttering shut, head lolling like his neck couldn't hold the weight. I took the spot beside him. Babysitting duty.

We'd been given one instruction: speak only if spoken to.

No problem. Dan couldn't speak. His pupils were blown, his gaze glassy. Reality was already slipping through the fingers he couldn't stop fidgeting.

The boat barely skimmed the surface before we arrived at the neighbouring island. A tropical postcard hiding something darker beneath.

Palm trees leaned low over the shore, their fronds rustling in the breeze. It should've been beautiful. Instead, my stomach coiled.

Eight barefoot men stood in the glare of the unshaded beach, machine guns slung across their chests.

Expressionless. Unmoving. Watching our every move.

And there I was. Neck sweat. Crack sweat. Throat dry.

This wasn't a meeting. This was a day trip to meet the devil.

My heart climbed into my throat. My palms turned slick. Suddenly, this was real. Dangerously real.

I glanced at Dan, desperate for some flicker of presence.

Nothing. He was long gone.

While the captain negotiated with the men, King turned to me.

"Whatever happens here..." His voice dropped. "Chloe, I fuckin' love you. I'm doin' this to protect you."

That was the last glimpse I got of Romeo.

He slid on his sunglasses, took Britney's hand, and stepped off the boat. The shift in weight tilted us violently, the water churning beneath

—along with my gut.

Dan clocked the scene. His brother holding hands with his girlfriend, history repeating itself all over again.

"S'up, Romero," one of the men called, offering an aggressive nod.

King leaned in for a man-shake. "Bodu Manik, ready for us?" His voice came calm. Steady. That version of King—the one that radiated control—could command fear even from strangers with assault rifles. He didn't flinch. Even when he knew he had nothing of value to offer their boss.

The man slung his gun behind him. "Follow me."

They led us through a back entrance. A couple of guys playing cards at a leaning table barely looked up.

Through a battered doorway, we entered what looked like an abandoned tackle shop. The sour stench of bait and ocean rot clung to every surface.

Dan had unzipped his jacket, standing a little straighter now. I guided him down a narrow corridor, its walls streaked with mould and decay.

At the far end, a door stood ajar. A thin wash of light spilled through the crack, illuminating our path to whatever lay ahead.

Island percussion thumped faintly inside—tropical drums somehow twisted into something menacing.

"Romero, my good friend. Come in, come in." The voice was deep. Brassy. Too eager.

A guard stood across the doorway, holding a gun. His eyes skimmed over each of us with thinly veiled contempt. King stepped up, almost chest to chest. The man shifted aside.

Inside was no office. No boardroom. It was a closet at best—humid, dark, thick with the cloying stink of cannabis, mildew, and baby oil.

King paused in the doorway, removed his sunglasses, and handed them to Britney. She tucked them neatly into her purse. He'd never asked me to do that. And somehow, in that moment, it stung worse than anything else.

In stark contrast to the fish-stinking henchman outside, the shirtless man who welcomed us was young, muscular, and heavily tattooed. A spark in his brown eyes hinted there was more to him than violence.

Like any self-respecting drug lord, he wore a thick, 24-carat gold medallion encrusted with diamonds, resting proudly against his chest. He had an image to uphold—confirmed the moment two bikini-clad women drifted in behind us, sliding into place on either side of him like it was just another day at the office. He reached for a retro boombox and dialled the music down.

Our party of six stood in silence before his throne-like chair, the humidity settling over our skin like wet gauze. A wide table sat between us. It felt less like furniture, more like a boundary. A small ceiling fan whirred above, blades flickering shadows across his face like smoke signals from hell.

"You've come a little light, my friend?" Bodu Manik asked, lifting a smouldering Cuban cigar from the ashtray. As he inhaled, his tattooed biceps flexed, dark ink shifting with the movement.

King didn't flinch. "Figured I didn't need soldiers. We're not at war, are we, brother?"

Smoke curled around Bodu's head. He held the stare, eyes narrowed through the haze. "Depends if I like what you gotta say."

The words dropped like a quiet detonation. My breath caught. My fists clenched. Even Tommy's chest paused, stalled mid-rise.

Then Bodu burst into a rasping laugh—loud, jarring, theatrical. The heat still sizzled like meat on a skillet, but the chill lingered.

"Anyway." He grinned around the cigar, arms stretching behind his head. "Let's get into business."

While King and Bodu slid into negotiation mode, the rest of us lingered by the door. I stood behind Tommy, heart hammering beneath the suffocating press of my bulletproof vest. The weight of it made it even harder to breathe through the thick air.

"Queen. Come here," King ordered.

My toes twitched inside my sandals, ready to obey. Then Tommy's arm extended in front of me, a silent block.

My baby jolted inside me in protest. I pressed my hand to my stomach beneath the vest, anchoring myself with the movement.

Britney didn't hesitate. Her sheer dress whispered as she moved forward, each step graceful and deliberate. She slid into position beside him like she belonged there. Like he belonged to her.

"Come sit with me, baby," King said, giving her the look that once melted me on sight.

She obeyed, settling close. He kissed the rings on her finger, draped his arm over her shoulder, and grazed the swell of her breast—marking her like his.

"Sexy woman, Romero," Bodu hummed, eyes trailing slowly over her curves. "Sweet pussy?"

Britney laid a hand on King's thigh. He kissed her temple, pulling her tighter.

"The sweetest," he murmured, tongue sweeping his lower lip as he parted her thighs. Subtle but clear.

Bodu's eyes narrowed on her.

"First we talk business," he said, barely containing his excitement. "Then I sample product. Yes?"

The fan's low swish did nothing to ease the heat.

King gave a single nod, cool as ever.

Gunfire cracked somewhere in the distance. A flock of birds exploded skyward, fleeing a chaos we had no way out of now.

I longed for Romeo's arms. For safety. Reassurance. But all I had was Tommy—his damp arm brushing mine, a silent shield between me and the threat.

"I have another business partner to meet, no? Is he joining us today?" Bodu asked, nodding toward us.

At his cue, the dancers unscrewed a bottle of baby oil and began massaging each other—slow, sensual, hypnotic.

"Yes, Bodu," King replied, lounging like a king himself. "Daniele." He gave our group a look.

Something shifted in Dan. Whether it was the remnants of cocaine or some last flicker of pride, he squared his shoulders and stepped forward.

"Aight," Dan said, halting in front of the table, hand jammed into his waistband. "Could do with some titties right about now."

Silence.

We all held our breath.

Bodu watched him for too long. Then tapped his ash again.

"You never said your brother was slow, Romero."

King's glare could've shattered steel.

Dan yanked his hand out, fists clenched awkwardly at his sides.

"He ain't slow. Just took a hit of the good shit. He's comin' down."

Bodu grunted, stubbing out the cigar and pushing the ashtray aside. "Good. I don't do business with the inbred."

The dancers moved closer, gliding hands over oiled breasts. Panties slipped down slick thighs.

My own legs didn't need oil. Sweat already tracked the backs of them all the way to my toes.

I looked to King.

He didn't look back.

Was ignoring me easier? Or had he already chosen Britney?

"Brothers," Bodu said, fingers steepled. "Tell me—what's your offer?"

King leaned forward, elbows on knees, his smirk slow and dangerous.

"You're a big name. I like your style. I'm expandin'. And you're the guy. We tap your network, grow the empire. I supply the product. My brother handles the import. All we need is your approval—and a handful of your crew."

Bodu nodded once. "My cut?"

"Thirty percent of the profits. And as much product as you want."

Bodu shot up from his chair, the sudden movement jolting my nerves. A startled squeak escaped before I could stop it.

Was he about to reject King's offer?

Towering over the room—easily as tall as King—Bodu gripped his cigar between his teeth and snapped his fingers. One of the dancers stepped in, reigniting the glowing tip with a gun-shaped lighter. It clicked off when the ember caught.

Bodu took a slow drag, exhaled through his nose, and filled the air with a foggy plume that hovered thick and unmoving.

"I like the idea," he said with a nod. "Now, I need a taste."

Tommy moved forward without hesitation. The moment his warmth left my side, a chill swept in—leaving me exposed.

He handed over the small bag. "This is some of the best cocaine you'll ever come across. Pure. Uncut. Perfect."

Bodu rolled the bag in his palm, studying it.

"Should I be offended by this?" His voice gave nothing away.

He opened a drawer, retrieved a set of scales, and dropped the product onto the plate. "Half a kilo?"

King rolled up his sleeves. "No offence intended, brother. Ran into a problem at the airport. But that won't be an issue once we move through the waters. As a show of good faith, my wife's here to help set things right."

Bodu scanned the room. His eyes locked onto mine now that Tommy was no longer shielding me. The glint in his gaze drank me in. My calves tensed, ready to bolt.

"What about her?" he asked, eyes flicking between me and Britney.

King didn't flinch. Didn't even look at me. Just flicked his wrist in my direction.

"That slut's used goods. Pregnant." The mock disgust in his voice was so convincing it nearly fooled me, too.

Bodu grinned and rubbed his hands together.

"She got milk in those breasts yet? It's been too long since I tasted God's best creation."

A flicker of something sharp passed behind King's eyes. Gone as quick as it came. He leaned back, voice steady as he draped his arm along the back of his chair.

Unzipping Britney's dress, the fabric slipped off her shoulders, exposing the curve of her breasts.

"Queen, give Bodu Manik some respect."

His hand slid into her bra, pushing the lace down until her cleavage spilled over.

Then he nudged her to stand, guiding her with a hand on her lower back.

She didn't hesitate. Nipples out, face composed.

That, more than anything, shocked me. What was it about my husband that gave her so much confidence? Like she fed off him. A leech on his skin.

With practised grace, she circled the table and dropped to her knees. As Britney took Bodu's cock into her mouth, the dancers massaged oil into his shoulders like it was just another Thursday.

It wasn't the act that stunned me. It was her self-assurance. For a second, I questioned everything I thought I knew about her. Where was the meek, insecure girl who'd crumbled at that client's house and left me to finish the job?

King laid out a line of coke, rolled a bill, and offered it to Bodu.

Dan hovered behind me, shifting awkwardly—coming back to himself just enough to clock what was happening, but not enough to process it. Twitchy fingers. Blown pupils. He was the round in the barrel. The trigger pull that never fired.

Bodu looked at the bill and pushed it back to King.

"Do the honours, my friend. It's not that I don't trust you... you understand?"

Now it made sense.

This was why King had Dan take the drugs earlier. He'd known Bodu would want a demonstration.

King finally looked at me—a fleeting glance. Then he pressed the bill to his nose and inhaled the line in one clean hit.

No hesitation. All performance.

His head snapped back. Eyes squeezed shut. Jaw tight as he rode out the rush. It had been years since he'd touched hard drugs—something he'd once sworn he'd never do again. Watching him now, so controlled, so calculated, unnerved me.

Was this a one-off necessity? Or was he toeing a line we couldn't afford to cross? Not with our son on the way.

Bodu prepared a fresh line, sweeping it clean with a credit card. "Your brother's turn."

He tapped the table, impatient now.

King didn't speak. Just looked at Dan.

That was all it took. Dan stumbled forward, swaying like the floor wasn't stable. For a second, I thought he'd collapse into the table. But somehow, he made it. Bent low. Inhaled the whole line.

Bodu chuckled in approval, then leaned down and took one for himself, snorting up the remnants clinging to his nose as he sat back with a contented sigh.

The room fell quiet. Just Britney's wet sucking. Her shallow breathing. The scent of sex and drugs colliding in the humid air.

Bodu sat back, grinning as he rode the high.

"Good product like this..." He sniffed again. "Makes me hungry for pussy."

King nodded in agreement, keeping the act alive.

The bill lay limp beside the powder like a spent weapon.

Bodu sat up taller. Inspired. "I'm gonna take your wife right here." He yanked Britney up from her knees. Her lips were swollen. Her face flushed.

Without warning, he lifted her dress and bent her over the table. King watched, eyes blown wide, fingers twitching open and closed like he wasn't in his body. His face was unreadable, but the tension in his jaw said everything.

This was the cost. The price of survival.

Britney clutched the edge of the table, her body trembling as Bodu fucked her with the mindless rhythm of a man used to taking anything he desired. Until he looked up—past Dan's shoulder. Right at me. Right into my eyes.

My breath caught.

The sweat trickling down my back slid under the waistband of my panties.

Still, I didn't move. His stare held me.

"You know, Romero, your wife's got a nice pussy." He pulled out, groaning with satisfaction as he adjusted himself. "But I can't help but wonder what *she* feels like."

King's lips parted. His body stiffened. The drugs clouded his expression, but his fists gave him away.

Then Bodu curled his finger at me.

My heart slammed into my throat.

King shot to his feet, stumbling enough to catch the table with one hand.

"You sure you don't wanna finish with my girl?" he said, voice casual, calculated. "Look at her sexy ass, spread over your table."

He slapped Britney's arse, parted her cheeks, and offered her like she was nothing more than a gift. "Look at that perfect asshole. Take it. It's yours."

But Bodu didn't flinch. His gaze never left mine.

He lifted one hand and pointed—right at me.

"You. Come."

The tatty old shutters down the corridor slammed closed, like the storm outside was chasing us down. A bead curtain rustled over the doorframe, rattling softly in the breeze.

Tommy stepped aside, reluctantly giving me space.

Each step I took over the hollow, uneven floorboards pulled me closer to a place none of us had prepared for. This man might've been attractive, but I was never supposed to be part of the exchange.

I looked to King. His gaze flicked to my stomach, then dropped to the floor.

We were outnumbered. Out of options.

"There's something about this one, Romero," Bodu mused, dragging his eyes over me like I already belonged to him. "Got a hard-on just looking at her. I reckon you married the wrong slut."

That old stench of cigar I'd grown to hate on King was back—hot and sour on Bodu's breath as I drew closer.

He licked his lips and took my hand. The heat of his skin soaked into the cold of mine. I stiffened. My pulse slammed.

He guided me to the table and tore open the Velcro straps on my vest.

"They got you strapped in tight, huh, beautiful?" he murmured, eyes drinking in every inch of me.

The vest hit the floor with a thud. Not just the weight, but the heat of it lifted. For a moment, I could breathe.

That's when Romeo cracked.

"Blow job only with this whore," he snapped, voice sharp and raw. His eyes hit my stomach again, then locked on Bodu's with pure steel.

Bodu's brow lifted.

Then he slammed his fist on the table.

Thud. Thud. Thud.

The weighing scales and ashtray jolted forward, vibrations rattling up my spine.

"You telling me what to do, Romero?"

That was the cue.

The door burst open. Eight of Bodu's men stormed in, rifles raised.

King didn't move.

Bodu reached beneath the table and pulled out a gun. Aimed it. Steady. Right at my husband.

"No one tells me what to do. I thought you understood that, Romero?"

Click. The safety released.

King's fingers twitched. He squared his shoulders, chest puffed in defiance.

No one was dying tonight. Not if I could help it. If Romeo had become King, then just for now. I was Jasmin. I would save him. And remind him I was more than Britney ever could be.

Jasmin slid over me like silk. A second skin. I locked eyes with my target, licked my lips, softened my gaze, and wrapped my hand over his, lowering the gun—a move I was already close to perfecting. The cold metal tingled against my fingertips. A sharp reminder of just how dangerous this had become.

"My name's Jasmin," I whispered. "And I love sucking big… thick… cock. Let me show you a good time?"

Bodu smirked. Nodded.

He dropped the gun. Its metallic edge caught the light, bright against the dimness of the room.

A cheeky hair flick. Shoulders back. I slipped off the table and dropped to my knees—owning the moment before it could own me.

I glanced up at King.

His jaw swung loose. Muscles coiled. Even high, he knew exactly what I was doing.

I licked my lips. Took all of him in.

Britney's scent clung to his skin: warm vanilla, slick baby oil, something sweeter underneath. A faint lipstick smudge marked the base of his cock, tangled in dark curls.

If she could do this, so could I.

I swallowed him to the root. Deep. Right to the back of my throat.

King's thighs tensed. His lips parted. Breathing hard—like it was his dick inside my mouth instead.

"Holy shit, you suck good," Bodu groaned, breath catching.

He raked a hand through my hair, gripping tight as his hips rolled. Slow. Deep. I kept the pressure just right. Matched his rhythm. Let him fuck my mouth until the pace faltered. Then stopped completely.

Just like the rest of them... he came quick.

I swallowed before I could think. Bitter. Sharp. Coating the back of my throat in a thick burst, I wanted to forget.

Bodu exhaled, palms flat on the table, catching his breath. When he finally looked up, he extended a hand across the table to King.

"We got ourselves a deal."

◆ ◆ ◆

We'd been back in our honeymoon suite for forty minutes. In that time, Romeo had said maybe two words to me. Neither of them kind.

Dan was too high to string a sentence together, so he'd been escorted to his room to sleep it off. Hopefully, by tomorrow, today would feel like a distant memory. Britney had been all too happy to take care of him.

Romeo, on the other hand—despite snorting cocaine for the first time in years—still had plenty of stamina left to be furious with me. Seated face to face on the patio furniture, he barely cast me a sideways glance.

The sticky hum of insects around us became my only source of comfort amidst the brooding silence.

I caved first. "How are you mad at me, Romeo? I had no choice!"

He ignored me completely. Stubbed out his cigarette in the ashtray like he was snuffing me out with it. Then he shot up, stripped off his clothes. The thick humidity amplified his comedown as he stalked into the suite and threw himself onto the bed like he could fall asleep instantly.

The soft pat of my feet turned into an emotionally exhausted thud when I reached his side of the bed.

"Oi, dickwad." I shoved him in the back. Solid muscle flinched, but he barely moved. "Talk to me. Please."

After a long minute of ocean-filled silence, he turned to face me—pulling me down beside him effortlessly.

"I've been doin' drug deals for ten years. Not once did anythin' go sideways until I met you."

His body heat burned—drug-induced, hotter than hell.

"Okay..." I shrugged. "Where are you going with this?"

"You know why this deal didn't go to plan?" He lay on his back, arm thrown over his eyes. "You. That's why."

I huffed and shifted so our legs no longer touched. "How the hell is this my fault?"

"First, you bamboozled me with those fuckin' tits, so I said yes to you comin'—even though the timin' had been worked out to the second. Then you shot a fuckin' cop, which meant our security had to travel separately. We were fucked before we even started."

His words stung like a wasp.

"I killed Saxon to save you from jail."

He sat up, legs slung off the bed, back to me.

"I only took you to that club 'cause you were bored and actin' up. Everythin' that's happened since you got in that car with Britney, behind my back, is on you."

When he said it like that...

The sting gave way to something heavier. Guilt.

"I'm sorry, Romeo."

"Pfft. No, you ain't." He sneered, dragging the sheet over his naked body. "How am I supposed to feel knowin' another man nutted in your mouth?"

The tension rippled through his back, every muscle clenched tight.

I pinched the bridge of my nose, inhaling a slow, steady breath. "You're making it sound like I wanted this."

"You fuckin' did." He snapped his head towards me. "I knew as soon as he saw you, he'd want to fuck you. Every fuckin' prick out there does."

"Romeo, please."

I leaned in to kiss him, desperate to calm the storm raging inside him, but he shoved me away with his palm against my forehead.

"No. He came in your mouth. No fuckin' way."

I dropped back onto my heels, stunned.

"What, you're not going to kiss me again? Grow up."

His jaw ticked. Rage humming beneath his skin. Then, with a low growl, he launched off the bed and stormed into the bathroom, slamming the door behind him.

I sat back, watching a foreign TV channel without subtitles—some old guy in a rocking chair playing guitar, laugh track rolling, for God knows what reason.

Meanwhile, Romeo licked his wounds in the en suite. The extractor fan hummed steadily, the only reminder I wasn't completely alone.

There was no denying what happened back there wasn't what either of us wanted. But if that was the price for walking out alive, I'd pay it again, and deep down, I knew he would've let me.

Eventually, he stomped back into the room and flung his phone onto the bed with dramatic Italian flair.

"Aight. Talked it through with T. I guess I'm sorry," he muttered, eyes locked on the sun sinking behind the pink-stained horizon. A warm wash of colour cut across his face, melting some of the ice from his defence.

My breath left in a slow, steady stream.

Thank fuck for Tim.

"What the hell did you tell him?"

There wasn't exactly a sugar-coated version of what happened.

"I told him you sucked another man's dick when the drug deal went south." He shrugged like it was no big deal.

Wow.

"Tim really does know it all, huh?"

Romeo prowled across the bed and pulled me into him, tipping my chin until our eyes met.

He exhaled slowly, eyelids falling shut as his lips brushed mine—tentative at first. But then our connection took over. Tongues met. And just like that, we erased the thing we both wished had never happened.

Our honeymoon hadn't played out the way I'd imagined. Not even close. But if we didn't give up on each other... we could survive anything.

CHAPTER 8

The intensity of the morning sun, peeking over the horizon and kissing every surface of the suite, woke me earlier than I would've liked.

Blinking awake, I stretched my arms overhead as a yawn took hold, my mind already drifting back to the events I was trying so hard to forget.

The fishing tackle shop. The rusty brine stench mixed with suffocating heat. Drugs. Fear. Bodu Manik.

Yesterday had, without question, been the most overwhelming experience of my life. Had I said that before? Probably. But the deeper I sank into Romero Giannetti's world, the more consuming it became.

Romeo couldn't deny it. Me being on this island had never been part of the original plan, but my unforeseen involvement in that deal was the reason we were still here.

Alive.

The fact remained: this vacation, chaotic as it had been, had worked in our favour. Not only had Romeo's deal gone through, but it had also given us a way to escape the fallout back home with Detective Saxon. A chance to heal. Fast, maybe too fast—but still, a chance.

And after some space to reflect, I'd come to a sobering realisation that problems didn't always find me. I was becoming part of the problem.

The spot beside me in our feather-soft super king bed was empty. I'd grown used to waking alone, so used to it, in fact, that panic no longer crept in when Romeo wasn't there. Still, it didn't stop me pouting as I absently toyed with my rings, now firmly back where they belonged.

My quiet was interrupted by the soft click of the bathroom door. A plume of fragrant steam drifted into the room as my husband slouched out—feet dragging, eyes heavy, groggy and sleep-deprived. He wore nothing but a pair of shorts slung low around his hips, water droplets clinging to the ridges of his torso in a soft, glistening sheen.

I sat up to get a better look. The usual sparkle in his eyes had dulled.

"You don't look very well," I said cautiously.

The tropical scent of his shower gel lingered in the air as he raised both arms and dragged his hands down his face.

"I ain't had a comedown in a long-ass time." He scrubbed at his skin again. "Had a shower, but still feel like shit."

He flopped onto the bed, draping an arm over his eyes. The warmth in the room had already begun drying him off.

With my middle finger, I lightly traced a heart shape around his nipple, keeping up the rhythm until his areola tightened.

"Romeo?"

He sighed. "Mmm?"

"Do I need to worry you'll go back on cocaine?"

He shifted his arm just enough to find me. "Why the fuck would you ask me that?"

I kept my eyes on my hand, still tracing the shape against his skin, hoping to disarm him.

"Because it looked like you enjoyed it."

His breath caught. Then he exhaled sharply through his nose—a telltale sign. He sat up, scratching the back of his neck, leaving a faint red streak on already sunburnt skin.

"Yesterday was one of the worst days of my life," he muttered.

I wrapped myself around him, kissed his shoulder blade. The tone of his voice, the weight behind the words, tightened something in my chest.

"Because of me?"

He huffed and glanced over his shoulder at me. "Yes, Chloe. Because of you. Guess that's why men like me don't have families. A wife and kids just makes everythin' harder."

The ache in my chest settled deep. My chin tightened. The faint sting of sunburn where my legs dragged across the sheets met its match in my heart.

"Are you saying you don't want to be with me anymore?"

His brows pinched—exasperated. Then he got up without a word, striding toward the doors. He flung them open with a sharp shove, letting the salt-laced wind flood the room. Waves rolled. Music drifted in from somewhere outside.

The sheer curtains over the bedframe caught the breeze, billowing like they were reacting to the tension. Under any other circumstance, it might've felt cleansing.

I waited, breath held, but the answer never came.

Anxiety surged. I tore away the bedsheet and crossed the room, my naked, pregnant body fully exposed to the ocean air. All my self-consciousness dissolved in the face of something worse—being abandoned.

Thighs tense, shoulders tight, he sank into a wooden deck chair with a freshly lit cigarette in hand, eyes locked on the lagoon. When he saw me, his jaw clenched.

"Put a robe on, Chloe," he murmured—voice thick with smoke. "I already had to deal with another man's dick in your mouth. If anyone sees you naked today, it'll finish me off."

I cocked my hip, arms crossed.

"You don't get to walk away from me when I ask a serious question."

He squinted into the sunlight, taking another slow drag.

"You don't get it, do you?"

I looked behind me, confused. Just turquoise water and stillness for miles. "Get what?"

He looked me over, his gaze stalling on the rise of my stomach. "It blows my mind that you don't see it."

My arms folded tighter over my exposed skin.

"See what?" I whispered, already bracing. If he brought up my weight, I might as well throw myself off the fucking deck.

"The effect you have on men. Hell, even women." He flicked ash into the tray—its embers floated on the wind like my sanity. "My dick gets so hard it hurts just lookin' at you. I want you that bad. From the second I saw you in my club, I had to have you. And it ain't just me, is it?"

Was that a rhetorical question? The look in his eyes told me he wasn't done.

"It isn't?" I asked, hesitantly shifting my weight from one foot to the other.

"My brother felt it the moment he laid his limp-dick eyes on you. Bodu Manik couldn't keep his fuckin' hands to himself, either."

Heat bloomed in my cheeks at the passion behind his words, but it felt like the uneasy calm before a world war.

"I'm nothing special," I mumbled, digging my heel into the coolness of the shaded wooden deck.

He stubbed out the half-smoked cigarette, shaking his head. "If I had to choose between you and my lifestyle, I'd choose you. Every time. I don't get why you always need reassurance, Chloe. Do you not see how fuckin' obsessed I am with you?"

A flock of gulls fanned past, honking like they didn't believe him. I wasn't sure I did either.

If I'd been honest, I would've told him—obsession never lasted. One day, he'd wake up and see an older woman he didn't want anymore. That thought terrified me. Right now, I was young. Less street-smart. Was that part of the appeal?

The ache in my chest felt like a brick swinging in the bow of my sternum. It wouldn't be long before the rope snapped. But if I voiced that fear, I was sure I'd manifest it.

I took a deep breath. Shoulders rising, falling. Trying to claw back control.

"So... you're not back on cocaine, then?" I smirked, letting the shift in topic land with playful defiance.

He shook his head and beckoned me into his lap. I hovered—until he parted his thighs and yanked me down, forcing all my weight onto him. One hand cupped my breast, squeezing until a droplet of colostrum beaded to the surface. He leaned in and sucked, biting just enough to taste it.

"I quit drugs for a reason," he murmured, licking the sweetness from his lips. "Made me more of a prick than I already was."

The moisture he left behind caught the breeze, heightening the tightening of my nipple. How he took from my body in a way I desperately wanted to give was a power move I struggled to match.

"Holy shit," I giggled, watching him savour the moment. "Didn't think that was possible."

His fingers twitched at my waist, holding me tighter. "You don't know the half of it."

And something told me I didn't want to.

The stubbed-out butt smouldered a little longer, tainting the air with a thickness so familiar now, it was almost more comforting than clean air.

"You're the sexiest woman I've ever met. Don't think I ain't thought about what you gave up when you shot Saxon. I ain't stopped thinkin' about it since we got here."

I settled against his chest. His arm curled around me, both protective and possessive.

"Weird you say that, because I was just thinking about him, too." I laid my head on his flexed pec, letting the steady rhythm of his heartbeat anchor me. "What are we even going home to? Cops crawling all over the place?"

He stiffened. "Swim?"

Then smacked the curve of my arse—a silent cue to stand. He hoisted me off his lap. The heat of his body vanished, replaced by sun-warmed wood and an ocean bite that prickled my skin.

"You know I use that technique too, right?" I arched a brow. "Avoidance? Therapists hate it."

His lips twitched. "You're smarter than you think, Mrs Giannetti."

My thoughts stalled along with the air. What did he mean by that? Did I come across like I wasn't smart?

Suddenly, Bodu Manik's comment about Dan echoed back. Slow was one thing Dan definitely wasn't.

"Have you checked on your brother yet?"

He'd already dipped a foot in the water, but snatched it back like it burned. "I take it back about you bein' smart. Why the fuck do you care?"

Hmm. Good question. Maybe it was just courtesy, after someone's first drug experience.

I wrapped the woven blanket from the lounger around me. Still warm from the sun, it wrapped me like an emotional buffer.

"Before I say more—did you take your pill this morning?"

A whisper of air sifted through the fabric, useless, like I wasn't even wearing it. The gloss of his curls lifted in that same breeze, brushing across his forehead.

"Yeah. Why?" His tone was laced with suspicion.

"Just checking who I'm speaking to..." I paused, meeting his gaze. "King or Romeo?"

He tilted his head, fingers grazing my jaw, igniting my skin.

"Maybe I should ask you the same thing... Jasmin?"

A bloom of heat stirred in my belly. Maybe I hadn't quite boxed her away completely.

My eyes drifted down to his shorts—the outline of what was mine pressing through the fabric.

His earlier arousal hadn't faded.

"Stop lookin' at my dick like that," he said, fabric stretching as he cupped himself—barely contained in his palm.

My cheeks flushed as I giggled. "Like what?"

I bit my bottom lip, letting it slowly slide free.

He stepped back, lifting a hand between us like a shield. "Nah. I saw that look in your eyes yesterday. That's Jasmin."

Feeling playful, I prowled a step forward. Hips swaying. Eyes low beneath fluttering lashes. Letting the weight of the moment settle between us. Maybe this would help us move past Manik.

"Stop, Chloe." His tone hit like a slap to the face.

The island stilled. Its gust dropped to the ground like a fallen kite.

Instantly, I froze.

Brick by brick, the wall over my heart dropped into place.

"Stop what?"

He raked a hand through his curls. Blowing out through pursed lips, he sent my confidence into a downward spiral.

I gripped the blanket tighter. "What the hell is your problem, Romeo?"

He didn't answer. Just fumbled in his pocket and pulled out his pack of smokes.

"I don't know," he muttered, toying with the lid—snapping it open and shut like it echoed his reluctance to speak.

"Looks to me like you feel about Jasmin the same way I feel about King. And let me tell you. I do *not* like King."

He finally plucked out a cigarette and perched it between his lips.

"I am King," he mumbled around the filter, shielding the flame as he lit the tip. His cheeks hollowed—like the space growing between us.

My grip loosened. The blanket slipped off my shoulders. "No, you're not. I'm in love with Romeo, not King. The arrogant, terrifying son of a bitch you were yesterday? That wasn't my husband."

He took another drag, eyes locked on the horizon. As if the answers might appear behind the drifting cotton clouds.

"All I know, Chloe, is I don't wanna see that side of you again. That's how I'm gettin' past the fact you sucked another man's dick. It wasn't my wife—it was Jasmin."

This man's audacity knew no bounds. Caught in a loop of his own making.

I hugged the blanket around me like armour, sucking air through my teeth as I tried to regain control.

"Um, are you conveniently forgetting two very important points here?"

Propping himself against the railing, he tapped ash over the edge and took another drag. "What are you talkin' about?" he muttered, blowing smoke that danced for him like one of his strippers.

"I'll tell you exactly what I'm talking about. One—" I raised a finger. "—you kissed Britney and groped her arse right in front of me, and I'm just supposed to be fine with it. Two—" I raised another. "—I sucked that man's dick to save your life. Are you lickin' my pussy to thank me? 'Cause it sure as shit don't look like it."

With dramatic flair, I spun on my heel, smirking. I'd just tossed the same grenade back at him. The one he'd pin-plucked and lobbed at me yesterday.

The hairs on the back of my neck rose as Romeo stalked up behind me, snaking his arms around my waist beneath the fabric.

"I see what you did there, Mrs Giannetti." His voice dropped—quieter now, like a white flag folded into words. "Aight… let's agree to keep King and Jasmin out of our marriage."

Since his time with Tim, and our joint sessions with Nelly, he'd started to understand himself, and the world around him, with more clarity. We both had.

I turned in his arms, pulling his lips to mine. "How about we keep them in our back pockets… just in case we need them? Not against each other, but for anyone who tries us."

"Fuck." His breath fanned warm with tobacco against my sun-kissed neck. "You just got my dick hard again."

◆ ◆ ◆

Catching the paper straw with my tongue, I took a sip of hand-squeezed lemonade. Ice clinked against the curvy, condensation-slicked glass. The perfect fusion of sugary sweetness and citrus tang sent a tingle along my jaw as I swallowed the thirst-quenching zing.

Keeping his promise, Romeo and I were practising the art of enjoying some much-needed alone time. The calm we'd found now stood in stark contrast to yesterday's chaos.

I slumped into the lounger, basking in the warmth on our private deck. Palm leaves rustled. The tide rolled gently. A lullaby of sound framed our idyllic escape.

Peeking over my sunglasses, I stole a glance at my husband. Apart from his swim shorts, he was completely exposed—olive-toned skin glistening under the sun's unrelenting gaze.

"You're quiet," I said, sliding my shades to the top of my head. The sun lotion snapped open with a soft pop. And just like that, his pectorals tensed.

Romeo, who'd lost sunglasses privileges after leaving them in Britney's purse, raised a hand to shield his eyes. "I'm just chillin'. We don't gotta talk twenty-four-seven, you know."

Well, that was rude.

"Funny, that," I muttered, working the cream into my thigh with unnecessary force. "Because we don't gotta have sex twenty-four-seven, either."

With a snap of flair, I slid my glasses back down and shut the lid. Laying flat, I let the cloudless, blue-skyed blaze draw me into a drowsy lull.

There was a huff. Then a growl. Then darkness. The light behind my lids vanished.

My eyes fluttered open to find Romeo crouched over me, the oaky, floral spice of Cognac on his breath brushing my lips. Heavenly.

"You fuckin' love talkin', don't you?" His tone carried a flicker of irritation, but the spark in his eyes was all passion.

I lifted my sunglasses and grinned. "Yes, I do, actually."

Satisfied I was no longer pissed, he scraped his chair across the deck and dropped it beside mine. "Shame I didn't fuckin' know this from the start. I'm just thinkin' about how I used to bury my dick in your sweet pussy, and you barely said two words to me. No questions, no arguin'. Bliss."

My foot shot toward his shin. He caught it mid-air, like always, with lightning reflexes. His fingers curled around my ankle like a bear trap.

"Strike one, Mrs Giannetti. I got bruises 'cause of you. Look at this shit."

He wasn't wrong. Three small bruises in varying shades lined his shinbone.

Oops.

I took another sip of lemonade, forcing him to match my pace. Setting the glass down, I dragged a finger through the condensation and slipped the dewy tip between my lips.

"I never used to talk to you, Romeo, because I was scared of you." I met his gaze. "Is that what you want in your marriage? A wife too afraid to speak?"

He blew out a ripple of air, lips puffed like a deflating balloon. "Even if I wanted you scared of me, I think we've both learned what you're capable of. I should be fuckin' terrified of you."

We sat with that truth.

I'd always seen Romeo as a calculated killer—ruthless, with a buried heart. But now, there was no denying I'd become something I never thought I would.

"Romeo?"

He tore his focus from the glittering refractions dancing along the water's edge. "Yeah?"

"Is it crazy that I can bury my feelings about killing people?"

Without a word, he reached for the crystal tumbler beside his chair and took a contemplative swig.

"You're no crazier than me, Queen." He shrugged. "I don't even think about it anymore."

My whole body sagged. That question had been sitting just behind my lips this whole time.

"I've killed people. Yet I can still look at myself in the mirror. That's not normal, is it?"

Romeo caught the shift in my voice, instantly recognising I needed reassurance.

"Nelly showed me your file. I know what you went through as a kid. Don't surprise me, you can hide your feelin's—just like that. Except when I've pissed you off. Then you got no problem lettin' *all* that shit out."

Our eyes met. I couldn't help but chuckle as his widened, clearly reliving one of my outbursts.

But Nelly flooded my thoughts in an instant.

"When did she show you my file?"

He paused, treading carefully, plucking an imaginary something from his liquor to avoid my stare. "She asked me to go to her office. The day after we talked about Daniele coming on vacation with us."

Well. That explained the quiet ride home from therapy.

I filed the moment under Benefit of the doubt. I'd challenge Nelly later.

"The fact we're carrying on as normal doesn't make us bad parents, does it?" I cradled my stomach. "I mean… we've both killed people. Does that mean there's somethin' wrong with us?"

He shook his head, almost violently. "Ain't nothin' wrong with us,

Queen. We're just cementin' our legacy."

Clutching his glass, he reclined, eyes tracing the endless sky. A faint smile tugged at his lips as he took a sip.

"Just think. Our son's gonna be the second most powerful man in America, right after his dad. Then, when I'm dead and buried, he'll take my spot. He'll make you the proudest mum. Just watch."

It always made me smile when he went out of his way to say mum instead of mom. The British accent never quite fit his mouth, but he tried—and I loved him for that.

Mirroring his ease, I leaned back too with my drink in hand, watching another flock of birds glide overhead, their wings slicing through the breeze. For them, escape looked simple. For us, not so much.

Even imagining having a son of my own, a boy who could command a room, gave me butterflies. The weight of the ever-growing power nestled in my palm was becoming harder to contain.

"Anyway, while you're finally talking to me, are you going to tell me what's bothering you?" I asked, hoping to catch him off guard now that he was thinking about our son. "You keep looking out to sea like you want to get lost out there."

The warm smile that had been softening his face vanished, replaced by a hardened frown. He let out a frustrated groan, slinging an arm over his eyes.

Never a good sign.

I set my empty glass down carefully, then folded into his personal space. The pinkness of his skin, sizzling under the searing heat, prompted me to take matters into my own hands.

"Does this have something to do with Tatiana's baby?" I squeezed a ketchup-sized helping of sunscreen onto his bare chest. The cool lotion melted like butter against his overheated skin, smearing beneath my fingers as I worked it in.

To my surprise, he didn't stop me, but he flinched. And I couldn't tell if it was the lotion or the question that made his jaw twitch.

Just as I reached for the bottle again, an intensely raw emotion rumbled through his chest in waves. He snatched it from my hand and hurled it across the deck. It skidded along the boards, teetering just shy of the edge—one final bounce away from splashing into the water.

"Don't ever bring that shit up again, woman. I mean it!"

I glared at him, forgetting he couldn't see my reaction, with sunglasses masking my eyes. But his outburst told me everything. He was trying to outrun something bigger than he could handle.

Tatiana had meant more to him than he would ever admit. And it hurt more than I could explain. But I wasn't going to let that grief consume him. I wouldn't let it distract him from the responsibility of the child I was carrying. So right then and there, I made a silent vow. I'd never bring it up again.

He took my silence for brooding.

"Look, Chloe." He shifted beside me. "I don't give a fuck about that Tat shit—"

Hmm.

"I can't explain it good, but my nuts tell me when trouble's brewin'. And my left nut's been tinglin' since last night."

My nostrils flared. A snort escaped. "Are you being serious?"

He looked back at the sky. Easier than making eye contact.

"Serious enough to have ordered a Glock. I know you said no guns outside that business deal, but I need somethin' I'm used to handlin'."

I extended an arm and poked his shoulder, forcing him to look at me. Slipping off my sunglasses completely, I hooked them inside my bikini bra.

"Are you worried about Bodu Manik? You shook hands on the deal. That's done, right?"

The glint in Romeo's eyes, that emotional glisten King could never replicate, shone almost as bright as the sun.

His fingers scratched through his chest hair.

"We got no men, no product, nothin'. We're sittin' ducks out here, and he knows it. The sooner we get back to America, the better."

There was an obvious solution, which only confirmed this wasn't as simple as it seemed.

"So why don't we book an early flight home?"

He huffed, scrubbing a hand over his head. Any more and he'd expose scalp.

"Saxon," he muttered. No explanation.

Frustrated, I slapped his sweat-slicked chest—harder than I meant to—leaving a white print amidst the red.

"I bloody knew you were keeping something from me! What's going on back home?"

His pecs twitched. Sitting up, he claimed higher ground.

"Nothin' we can't handle. But between here and home, we're better off waitin' it out 'til the heat dies down."

To settle my nerves, I grabbed my empty glass and sucked at the straw for the last drop of melted ice.

"So, what's the play?" I asked, slurping like my life depended on it—heart rate climbing in sync with my blood pressure.

In my head, blue lights flashed. Cold steel cuffs bit into my wrists. Miranda rights echoed in the background. One last look at my husband before they took me away.

"All we can do is keep our eyes open. Other than that, we enjoy the rest of this vacation until we get the all-clear."

The icy chill of my pale, anxious hands prickled my skin as I caressed my bump protectively.

"Who's going to give us the all-clear?"

"T. He's the only guy I trust—aside from the crew we got here."

Jeez. Who'd have thought my husband could form a tight bond with an English teacher turned therapist?

He unhooked the sunglasses from my bra and slipped them on with a sigh. "No more questions. Not for at least an hour. Got it?"

With a pinkie promise, we silently agreed to close the lid on the box labelled: HOW THE FUCK DO WE GET OUTTA THIS?

◆ ◆ ◆

After promising to enjoy the rest of our stay until it was safe to return home, we cooled off beneath the ceiling fan above the bed. Curtains billowed. Sheets rippled. Then came a confident knock at the door.

"Hello, sir. It is room service," the friendly waiter called through the gap.

Reclined against the pillow, Romeo wore nothing but a pair of shorts, one arm slung lazily behind his head as the fan stirred his curls. The rich scent of lotion and his heated, sun-drenched skin filled the room—heady, intoxicating, mouth-watering.

"Come in," he hollered, his voice a smooth, masculine rumble.

A key slid into the lock and Tommy emerged first, swinging the door open wide before stepping aside to let the server in. The trolley wheels clicked rhythmically across the hollow wooden boards, each rattle echoing through the quiet room.

"Here we are. Strawberry. Melon. Delicious fruits," the man said with a genuine smile, placing the handled tray neatly at the foot of the bed.

Instantly, my mouth watered at the sweet, tropical scent—the dewy freshness of sliced watermelon, pink juice seeping from its vibrant red flesh.

Two glasses of freshly squeezed lemonade sat side by side, pulp swirling beneath the surface, matching straws overhanging—kissing one another beneath the fan's breeze.

Romeo didn't flinch. Didn't even lift his head. One hand slipped into the pocket of his shorts, retrieving a rolled-up bill he handed over without a word. I could've sworn it was Dan's hundred-dollar note from yesterday.

"Too kind, sir." The server bowed, walking backwards with his trolley. "I come back later with more."

The clunk of the key turning in the lock was our cue to dive in. The satisfaction of my teeth sinking into the juicy flesh of the melon quenched my thirst instantly. Romeo took his time, plucking grapes from the stalk one by one, pressing them to his lips before sucking each into his mouth with slow, deliberate ease.

I lifted my glass and took a sip. He was watching me more than the food. Giving me *the* look.

Leaving Jasmin firmly in her box, I set my glass back on the tray and fluttered my lashes, walking my fingers along the length of his arm. The scent of aloe vera mingled with salty, sea-kissed skin had me wanting to take a bite right out of him.

He popped a whole chocolate-covered strawberry into his mouth, plucking off the green stem before tossing it aside. The satisfying crack of chocolate against soft, seeded fruit filled my mouth with saliva.

"Go on then," he sighed in mock exasperation, still chewing, eyes locked on me with a smirk. "You can't leave my dick alone for a minute."

We both shared a chuckle. Then came a delicate tap at the door. Still locked for security. The handle jiggled but didn't give.

I glanced at Romeo, who'd already kicked off his shorts.

"I'll get it, shall I?" I narrowed my eyes, catching him already fiddling with his erection.

We both knew who it was.

The door creaked open, revealing Britney—effortlessly beautiful in a sundress and sandals, her hair piled on top of her head in a thick, messy bun.

"Sorry to disturb you both," she said cautiously, her doe eyes widening. "But Dan's acting really weird. He hasn't spoken to me since last night."

Doing what I should've done already, I placed a hand on her delicate shoulder. "I was going to ask how you were feeling about what happened yesterday?"

Her eyelids flickered involuntarily before she offered a warm smile. "Did I do okay?"

That wasn't what I'd asked—but I got the sense that, just like me, she had a habit of not checking in with herself.

"You did great, Brit." I gave her shoulder a gentle squeeze. Just enough not to aggravate her sunburn.

She clapped her hands together in relief.

"And we're still besties?" Her sandals scuffed nervously on the floor, one toe curling over the other.

I smiled. "Always."

"Thank God." She twirled a loose tendril of her hair. "Can we all go out for drinks? See if it helps Dan's mood?"

Romeo had made a deliberate choice not to put his shorts back on.

He was making a point as he sauntered up behind me—dick swinging proudly, slapping with confidence against his thighs. Without a word, he splayed his hand across my stomach, planting a deliberate wet kiss at the nape of my neck.

I tilted my head to look up at him, the smile coming easily, whether I wanted it to or not. The heat of his erection pressed into the arch of my lower back, his body aligning with mine like a perfectly tailored suit.

"You're disgusting, you know that?" I said with a grin, my voice threaded with intimacy.

He wore his arousal like a challenge—daring me to deny him, daring Britney to look away. The sexual chemistry between us was undeniable. Thick in the air, almost tangible.

"I'm gonna fuck my wife first, then we'll head out," he said, voice low and full of promise as his greedy hands slid inside the parting of my robe, fondling my breasts with shameless intent. "She comes quick, so we won't be long."

Ha! Good one.

I wanted to interject—to inform Britney that, in fact, it was my husband who lacked stamina when we made love—but considering he'd only just started looking past what happened yesterday, I kept my lips sealed.

Britney's cheeks flushed a shade to match her glossy lips as her eyes darted anywhere but at Romeo's very present erection.

"Oh, err… okay." She shifted her weight, fingers fidgeting with a stray wisp of her hair.

"Besides," Romeo added with a smirk, "Daniele's a lightweight. Ain't gonna be much drinkin' goin' on."

His fingertips continued their slow exploration of my body, each brush sparking a pulse of electricity beneath my skin. The fragrance of sweet fruits clung to his breath as he leaned in, mouth ghosting behind my ear, inhaling the delicate scent of my skin.

Britney's breath caught, but that never dissuaded Romeo from doing exactly what he wanted. I knew he was getting off on the idea of us having an audience again.

I placed my hand on the door, closing it just slowly enough for Britney to get the hint.

"Give us ten minutes. We'll come for you when we're done."

"Ten minutes?" Romeo sneered. "She means an hour."

He grazed my neck, lips moving to my collarbone.

The latch clicked shut on civility—and opened something far more primal between us.

I turned, leaning my back against the closed door.

"An hour?" I chuckled, raising a questioning brow.

"If you want an hour, I'll give you an hour of my best moves." He took hold of his cock, stroking the solid length while his other hand pulled me closer.

"Romeo, I can make you come just by looking at you." I kissed the plushness of his soft lips. "What makes you think you can last that long?"

His cock flinched as his hand slid over the tip. "Because I ain't been tryin' not to. I can do it. Let me prove it to you."

He didn't wait for my answer. He took it upon himself to prove his stamina immediately.

◆ ◆ ◆

Dan and Britney strolled hand in hand through the heated sand, the salty breeze offering a touch of relief from the sun's relentlessness. Behind them, I trudged beside my smug, sexually satisfied husband as we made our way back to the same beachside restaurant Romeo and I had visited on our first night.

While Britney claimed Dan was acting completely out of character, he'd seemed almost like his usual self when we arrived to collect them from their suite.

Still, I had a feeling he was quietly wrestling with the aftermath of yesterday. An experience that went against everything he stood for. Drugs of any kind, let alone cocaine, had never been part of Dan's clean-living regime. And that, coupled with the knowledge his girlfriend had been intimate with another man right in front of him—while he was too powerless to stop it—was bound to keep him up at night.

The slow walk along the sandy path grew more exhausting with each step, not helped by the fact I hadn't yet recovered from Romeo's best moves back in the bedroom.

Thoughts of his lips trailing kisses up my inner thigh, his cock pulsing just from looking at me, made all our real-world issues melt into insignificance. Safe to say, my little hooker trick—clenching around his dick just right—was always a surefire way to finish him off. Never failed. The thought alone made me smile.

Romeo leaned into my ear like he already knew exactly what I was thinking. "Don't tell them I didn't last an hour. I mean it, Chloe."

With a playful nudge to his shoulder, I offered a silent promise. It was our little secret.

Salsa music blared from the beach hut speakers, pulsing through the humid air as we arrived at the seafood restaurant—one that conveniently catered to the more basic palate with a side of American-style burgers.

The hum of lively customers filled the space as we weaved through the occupied tables. No heads turned. No sideways glances. For once, we weren't the main event.

It was such a relaxing experience, being able to move freely around the island without a single 'fan' snapping photos or a pack of paparazzi trailing our every move. Actual freedom.

Of course, I'd forgotten all about Romeo's biggest supporter—until we were reminded of her. The same waitress from the other night was serving again, her familiar slutty demeanour and perfect, sweat-slicked skin as disarming as ever. Notepad in hand, pen perched behind her ear, her hips swung like they were on a loose hinge as she led us to our secluded corner.

Britney and I were the first to take our seats at the four-seater table, the large parasol above casting a welcome shadow that offered instant relief from the blistering sun.

I already knew my husband was sexy, but watching him close in behind me, I wasn't the only one who noticed. A quick glance over my shoulder revealed a few women at nearby tables stealing peeks, their open-mouthed expressions giving them away. They didn't know who he was, but the raw attraction was instant. And suddenly, I understood why he used to fly halfway around the world just to fuck women who didn't know his name.

My mood shifted the second I caught the server's vagina nearly prolapsing at the sight of him—reacquainting herself with every inch of his body as his muscles bunched, pulling out his chair.

It was a stark reminder. Romeo really was something special. But this time, of course, we had an extra Giannetti with us. The audible gasp she let slip when Dan took his seat brought the entire restaurant to a chew-stopping halt.

"A very good afternoon to you, sir," she purred, eyes locked on Dan as if Romeo no longer existed—a wise move on her part. Plucking the pen from behind her ear, she brought it to her lips and sucked the tip with a little too much enthusiasm.

Silently, I willed the little plastic stopper to dislodge and fly to the back of her throat. But I'd never been that lucky.

Romeo wasn't one to be overlooked. With a single raised finger, he reclaimed the spotlight.

"Double whiskey on the rocks for me. And an orange juice for my wife."

Was he jealous now that the attention had shifted? Hard to tell with the stern, pinched-brow expression he wore—though I suspected it had more to do with the fact he still hadn't gotten his sunglasses back from Britney.

Dan straightened in his seat, directing his full attention toward the waitress in the apron.

"Whiskey for me too. And whatever she's having." He gestured loosely toward my best friend.

I flicked a glance at Romeo, who was already looking at me. We both knew Dan wasn't a whiskey drinker, let alone a double helping.

"Err... I'll have a gin and tonic, please," Britney said timidly, adjusting the bun somehow still holding upright in the wind.

And there it was again. The complete switch in personality—from the woman who, under my husband's control, sucked dick like she craved it, to this delicate, well-mannered little mouse when she was with Dan. Whatever was going on with her, she needed to break out of the shell she was retreating into—because if she wanted Dan to respond, she had to meet him halfway.

I watched her as she smiled at Dan to get his attention. He was too busy adjusting the fold of his napkin.

Something about yesterday had thrown them completely off course. The spark between them had dulled, and the distance now sat heavy in the space between them, like a barricade. My incessant need for male reassurance would've liked to believe it had something to do with me, but the truth was, Dan had barely spared me a glance since he arrived.

Miss I-was-going-to-steal-your-man-but-now-I'm-stealing-hers sashayed back to the table with our drinks, balancing the tray with impressive speed. Glasses clinked as she slithered through the gathering mounds of sand along the deck—only a few strides away from us now.

Dan's leg fluttered softly under the table, almost melodic as it ruffled the tablecloth.

"Here we are." She stopped with a bounce in her stride that jiggled her breasts.

Please...

Snatching the tumbler from the tray, Romeo threw back his first double shot in one hit, not even flinching. He didn't give the burn a second to settle before snapping his fingers for another. Typical Romeo. This wasn't about the drink. It was about dominance. No one, especially not Dan, was going to outdrink the man at the head of the table.

While I slurped on my straw, cheeks sinking as the citrus sweetness cooled my throat, Dan raised his glass with quiet caution. His attempt to play it cool backfired when the liquor caught the back of his throat, triggering a cough that left his eyes watering. He tried to finesse it—like he was just clearing his throat—covering his mouth with a clenched fist. But the flush rising in his cheeks gave him away. Dan could pretend all he wanted, but he was never going to keep up with his big brother.

Romeo smiled, watching the spectacle with barely contained amusement.

"Hey, Daniele. Remember when we were kids and stole liquor from Dad's cabinet?" he asked, nearly giggling, the curve of his lips reaching almost to his eyes.

Dan cleared his throat a final time. "Yes, Romero. I do."

He didn't seem nearly as eager to continue, but I was desperate to know more.

My focus flicked between them like a spectator at a tennis match. "Come on then, what happened? Tell us." I leaned in.

Excitement bubbled in my stomach at the thought of finally getting a glimpse into their childhood.

Romeo, it seemed, had been waiting for this moment.

"Aight," he said, cupping his glass. "I can't remember how old we were… early high school, maybe. Dad took us on a fishin' weekend, but we had to come home early on account of Daniele's nightmares."

He side-eyed Dan, who was already turning purple—not just from the alcohol, but from sheer embarrassment.

"Romero, please. I was not having nightmares."

Romeo glanced at me, then across the table to Britney.

"I don't even need to say more on that. It's obvious—he was a kid who had nightmares."

"So… what happened?" I urged, watching as Romeo brought the tumbler back to his lips.

"Dad got one of his security team to bring us home. For some reason, Mom wasn't in. Her and Natalia were out."

Dan shifted in his seat, dragging a hand across his forehead to wipe his damp skin.

"They don't wanna hear this story, Romero," he muttered, leaning back with his arms folded.

"Pfft, the fuck they don't," Romeo said with a grin. "Anyway, the liquor cabinet was open. That never happened. I stole a bottle of his scotch, and we tried it." Laughter burst from his chest. He fell back into his seat, eyes closed as it took over him.

"Come on, I'm dying here!" I said, glancing at Britney, who was hanging on Romeo's every word.

"I shit in my bed, okay? Can we drop it, please?" Dan snapped, exasperation cutting through the laughter.

The muffled clatter of cutlery and conversation filled the silence. You could've heard a pin drop in front of us—though the other guests remained blissfully unaware.

Dan with a sassy attitude? Very unexpected.

"Holy shit," Romeo wheezed, breaking into a smoker's cough as he wiped a tear from the corner of his eye. The sheen in his gaze said it all. This story was one of his favourites.

"Mom grounded your ass for a week."

"Yes, Romero. I remember it like it was yesterday. Should we talk about the time you wound up in hospital on a drug overdose?"

The moment Dan snapped, the restaurant noise seemed to hush around us—like the earth paused mid-spin.

Suddenly, Romeo wasn't laughing. He straightened in his seat. "Nothin' to tell."

And just like that, it was Dan's turn to serve.

"Come on, Dan, share your story. I'd love to know." I beamed at the opportunity. I lived for moments like this—peeling back layers of my husband one story at a time.

Romeo lounged back, one ankle hooked over his knee, while Dan sat stiff, fingers white-knuckled around his glass.

"If I recall, you snorted cocaine off that woman's breasts and had a seizure, right?"

Romeo's head turned sharply.

"Daniele," he said pointedly, "if you're gonna tell a story, don't lie. Yes, I snorted coke off those titties. But seizure? Please. You know damn well that was Mom's attempt to embarrass me—nothin' more."

Dan's fingers tightened around the base of his glass, like it was the only thing grounding him.

"Perhaps you shouldn't have done it at the family party, then."

I gasped. "Wait. What? He did drugs in front of your family?"

This man had no shame.

Romeo sniggered into his glass. "Aunt Silvia sure had some fine ass titties for an old bitch."

"What!?" My jaw dropped. "Tell me you're joking, Romeo? Your aunt? Are you sick!?"

He chuckled again, though this time, a little less so.

"My uncle remarried. She wasn't blood."

Oh. My. God.

Maybe I'd changed my mind about wanting to know more about Romeo's past. Suddenly, I wished he'd been the one who shit himself.

"Speakin' of quality snow… how's the hangover, brother?" Romeo shot the question across the table with a smirk.

Dan set his glass down, pinching the bridge of his nose like the memory alone was painful.

"I don't feel right. Is it normal for the inside of my nose to hurt?"

I shot Romeo a look.

His smile curled around the rim of his glass as he took another slow sip of his second round of liquor.

He placed the glass down carefully.

"I hear that's a common problem… for girls," he mused, amusement dancing in his eyes.

Dan's lips thinned, irritation brimming—but true to form, he didn't take the bait. He wasn't one to make a scene, especially not in public.

I had half a mind to knock Romeo down a peg by announcing he hadn't lasted the full hour he so confidently bragged about, but I held my tongue. Constant fighting was starting to wear me down.

A few rounds later, all three of them had loosened up, making for a far more pleasant atmosphere.

Safe to say we parked story time in favour of more present matters. The past, it seemed, was best left in its box.

Britney, now sniggering into her fourth gin and tonic, had grown noticeably more tactile with Dan than I'd ever seen. Her hand drifted to his thigh more than once, her posture open… inviting. Credit where it was due: Dan's bedtime accident story hadn't put her off. I'd be lying if I said I hadn't pictured it once or twice. Not that I was counting.

Watching them felt like front-row seats at a zoo exhibit, studying an extinct species to see whether the male would accept the female's advances. But every time she made a move, he simply laughed. No spark, no glint, no heat. Nothing.

Romeo was his usual self, with the rare addition of a fixed grin. For the first time since we arrived, he looked genuinely relaxed—no doubt helped by the fact Tommy and Snake, fully armed, were stationed at the next table.

"Romero, did you speak to Mom yesterday?" Dan asked, nursing his third whiskey. A glass of water sat beside it, likely to tone things down.

Romeo leaned back. "Why the fuck would I speak to Mom?" His lip curled at the mere mention of her name.

The packet of cigarettes he'd carelessly tossed onto the table—his own makeshift centrepiece—was suddenly back in his grip. He plucked out his next victim.

Dan cast me a quick glance, then took another sip. The ice tapped faintly against the glass, barely wetting his lips.

"She just wanted to check how the flight was, and whatnot." He unfolded his napkin, wiping his hands like he was scrubbing off the lie.

Whatever look I wore must've mirrored my husband's. Romeo gave me a tight, stifled smile.

"I left preschool a long time ago, brother. So no, I ain't spoken to her. Next time that bitch calls, it'll be for a cut of the profit."

Britney's alcohol-infused giggling came to an abrupt halt. I found myself chewing my lip as the conversation took a nosedive. Brooding Romeo with a skin full of whiskey wasn't exactly my vibe.

A subtle sea breeze rolled through the open-air restaurant, laced with salt and chargrill. It carried Romeo's resentment straight out of the place.

Thankfully, the tension didn't linger when the mouthwatering scent of grilled meat drifted over as the server returned, four loaded plates balanced effortlessly in her arms—each one teasing us with its arrival.

Stacked burgers, each skewered with a cocktail stick to keep their towering form, and crispy fries dusted in seasoning. Just what I'd been craving.

"Here we are," she said, ponytail swishing as another gust of wind rolled through uninvited. The parasol lifted slightly before thudding softly back into place.

Dan was the only one who acknowledged her, offering a polite nod and a smile.

"This looks great. Thanks." He grabbed a couple of fries, dragging them through the sauce. "I brought it up because Natalia's pregnant."

Romeo's foot dropped off his knee.

"Holy shit," he muttered, tapping ash into the tray before blowing a slow curl of smoke in Dan's direction. "Didn't see that comin'. Who's the dad?"

Dan wafted the smoke away with a flick of his wrist. Mildly affronted, but true to form, he let it slide.

"Not her boyfriend, Enrico. Some American guy. Mom is real pissed."

Romeo let out a low whistle, grabbed his burger with both hands, and tore off a hearty bite.

"So, what's the plan?" he asked, mouth full, a smear of ketchup in the corners. "Pretend it never happened and marry her off to Enrico, anyway?"

Between the savage chewing and the half-smoked cigarette smouldering in the ashtray, keeping my opinions to myself was becoming a challenge.

Dan nodded, a flicker of amusement sparking behind his eyes as he dabbed his mouth with a napkin. "Pretty much."

A conga line of drunken tourists snaked past our table just as the music kicked up a gear. The atmosphere was electric—though you'd never know it by looking at the brothers. Having fun wasn't really their thing. They, like their mother, had their own way of doing things. And we all knew how Angela Giannetti operated.

I couldn't begin to imagine the scale of her fury when she got wind of Natalia's news. When her children failed to bring home a 'suitable' partner, she made damn sure everyone knew it. The fact she'd rather her grandchild live a lie than know the truth? That was a job for a therapist.

Romeo was down to his last two fries when I finally picked up my fork.

"Whoever it is has gotta be fuckin' stupid to shoot his load in her," he muttered, sucking ketchup from his fingers. "I feel bad for him."

He eased back in his seat, posture loosening as he slung an arm over the back of my chair. His whole energy shifted now that he'd eaten. He dragged me a little closer. The woody trace of his cologne drifted over me, comfortingly familiar.

Dan mirrored the move, leaning back, but kept Britney at bay. "I guess we'll meet him at the baby shower."

Britney leaned in, inserting herself into the conversation. The loose hang of her diamond bracelet scraped faintly against the table as she steepled her fingers.

"How come you haven't had one, Chloe? I love parties."

Truthfully, a baby shower was the last thing I wanted. With no real friends or family, it would've made for a pretty depressing celebration.

"Um… just didn't fancy it, I guess." I shrugged, pushing the last few fries around my plate.

It wasn't that I hadn't enjoyed our time together, just the four of us. But like my husband, any mention of his mother was a surefire way to sour my mood—unless the sentence started with: there's been an unfortunate accident.

An attractive male waiter approached—dark skin, wavy hair, and eyes full of charm. His walk had a spring in it, a tip to be earned. But the moment he reached our table, his focus locked on Britney like a magnet. His smile turned up a notch just for her.

"Can I get you a refill, ma'am?" he asked, caramel-toned eyes never leaving hers.

Romeo instinctively placed his hand over the top of my glass, answering the question before it could be asked.

"No, I'm good, thanks," Britney giggled, tucking her hair behind her ear.

"Sure thing. Anyone else need anything?" he asked, barely glancing at the rest of us before strolling off with the same swagger.

No sooner had he gone than Romeo reached for his glass and knocked back the last of his sixth neat whiskey. He reached for the cigarette propped on the ashtray. Brows raised. "Bro." He exhaled. "You gotta deal with that shit."

Dan blinked. "Deal with what?"

"That prick was all over your girl. If that were me..." Romeo's lips pressed into a tight line, his silence louder than any threat.

Dan didn't respond. Beside me, Britney's shoulders tensed. Her fingers drifted to the hem of her dress, fiddling with the fabric.

Hmm. Not good. Something was off. Dan had morphed into a walking red flag overnight.

I yawned—more openly than I meant to.

"Let's stroll along the beach before bed?" I offered, already reaching for my chair. "Romeo, help me up."

The walk had been just what the doctor ordered.

Britney and Dan wandered ahead, fingers entwined, while Romeo and I trailed behind at a slower pace—more suited to my heavily pregnant waddle.

The heat of the day had finally begun to retreat, the sun dipping behind a layer of cloud. A refreshing sea breeze kissed my skin, carrying the salty spray of the ocean—just enough to take the edge off the humidity.

"How are you, Mrs Giannetti?" Romeo asked, slurring the last syllable with a lazy grin.

"I'm fine, thanks. Are you drunk?"

"Nah," he replied, unconvincing, as he lost his footing in the soft sand.

I rolled my eyes, nudging my body into his. "Well, walk in a straight line, then. Please."

The further we walked, the stronger the wind became along the water's edge—not enough to whip my hair, just a gentle flutter that mirrored the slow roll of the tide creeping in. Romeo's curls, on the other hand, had taken it upon themselves to tousle in the gust. He looked utterly handsome—enough to give me butterflies.

Catching a glimpse of his profile, the way his brows furrowed in concentration just to stay upright, I smiled. He really was something else.

Still... if I could change just one thing about him, it would be that tattoo around his eye. Such a gorgeous man, yet I often fantasised about dabbing a little concealer over the lettering—just to take the edge off. Of course, even I didn't have the guts to bring that up. Maybe one day I'd colour-match his skin tone, hold the tube, trip ever-so-haphazardly, and 'accidentally' fall into his lap—concealer first—just so it happened to cover the whole thing perfectly.

"What?" he asked, catching me mid-stare.

"Oh, nothing." I smiled, swaying our interlaced fingers back and forth like a pendulum, soft and steady.

He gave me a look. One of those squinting, half-suspicious looks like he knew I was lying, but didn't feel like pressing. So I squeezed his hand a little tighter, silently thanking the universe for giving me this moment with him. Even when drunk, he still felt like home.

Up ahead, just ten steps between us, Dan stopped abruptly then dropped to one knee in front of Britney.

I froze. What the hell was he doing?

The silence hit like a punch. Only the distant thrum of restaurant music and the rhythmic crash of waves filled the space between us.

For one breathless second, I thought he was proposing—and from the way Britney's hands flew to her mouth, I knew she thought the same. But to both our disappointments, all Dan did was bend down and scoop up a pebble. He rolled it between his fingers like it meant something, then flicked it across the water. It skipped once. Twice. Three. Four times—before finally sinking.

Romeo let go of my hand. I didn't need to ask why. I could feel the shift in his energy. The unofficial competition had just begun.

He stooped low, selected a similar-sized stone, and launched it with precision.

One. Two. Three skips... then a plop.

I cocked my hip and folded my arms. We were about to be in for a long night.

"Romeo—"

"Shh, woman, I'm concentratin' here."

He crouched again, selecting his next piece of ammunition like it was life or death. This time, the stone barely made two skips before it sank.

Oof—

"Fuck! Wait, I got this." He wiped the whiskey-induced sheen from his brow with the back of his hand.

"Please, come on. You've had too much to drink, and it's throwing you off. Try again tomorrow?"

"No," he snapped. "Now."

Another stone. This one skipped four times before disappearing beneath the surface.

I glanced at my watch. All I wanted was to crawl into bed.

"Romeo, I'm tired. The baby's tired. Hurry up."

With a kiss to its smooth edge for good luck, he threw his final stone with a determined grunt—five clean skips before it plopped beneath the water.

A collective sigh of relief swept through us.

"Satisfied now?" I asked, hopeful.

Dan and Britney had wandered ahead, completely over it.

"Yeah," Romeo said, chest puffed out like he'd just saved the world. "We can leave now."

Romeo and I parted ways with the unhappy couple five minutes ago and made it back to our room, where he unlocked the door and held it open for me.

I stepped inside first, a playful smile tugging at my lips as I walked backwards, keeping my gaze locked on the glint in his ocean-blue eyes. Reaching for the thin fabric of his shirt, I was just about to pull him in for a kiss—

When the atmosphere instantly changed.

His expression shifted in a heartbeat, eyes widening with alarm. Before I could react, he grabbed me—yanking me back out of the suite with a force that sent my pulse into overdrive.

"Get out. Now. Go next door. Hurry," he hissed, his grip unrelenting as he steered me towards Dan and Britney's door.

"What? Romeo, what's going on?" Panic tightened in my chest.

He didn't answer. Just reached for the gun I'd explicitly told him not to bring to dinner.

My breath caught.

"Someone's been in here," he said, eyes locked on the darkened room beyond the doorway. "Go. I'll come get you later."

Still frozen, I barely had time to process what was happening before Tommy stormed past, weapon drawn.

Snake grabbed my arm, snapping me back to the present. "Move," he barked, dragging me across the sand-sprinkled deck into Dan and Britney's room.

The moment my feet crossed the threshold, he peeled away, disappearing to back up Romeo.

Adrenaline surged, knocking the strength from my knees, my legs moments from folding beneath me. The only sound in my ears was the frantic pounding of my heart.

I turned to face the room, spotting Dan by the open double doors to the balcony—dressed in a robe, a glass of red wine in one hand and his phone in the other. His brows lifted in confusion.

"Britney?" I called, my voice laced with panic.

"She's not here." He set the wine down and straightened, cinching the belt around his waist. "We had a bit of a fight. She went to get some air. What's going on, Chloe?"

I swallowed hard and sank onto the edge of their perfectly made bed, my hands trembling against my thighs.

"It looks like someone broke into our suite while we were out. Romeo told me to wait in here with you guys." I glanced around. "Although, if he knew it was just the two of us, I think he'd rather I got shot." A breathy, awkward laugh escaped as I ran my hand up and down the length of my arm, trying to soothe the rising panic.

Dan slipped his phone into his robe pocket and came to sit beside me. "Are you okay? I mean... you haven't been hurt or anything?" His eyes scanned me from head to toe, searching for any sign of injury.

"No, I'm fine. Thanks for asking." A blush crept up my cheeks, and I hated myself for it.

The thick night air pressed against my skin—heavy and sticky, like a film I couldn't wipe off.

He shifted a little closer. His knee brushed mine. Intentional or not, the contact sent a bolt of guilt through my chest. The crisp citrus of his cologne mingled with the warm, smoky notes of earlier whiskey, confusing my senses in the worst possible way.

"Is the pregnancy going well?" he asked, voice softer now.

I nodded hesitantly.

He wasn't Romeo. He wasn't my baby's father.

"Dan, look... I know I've just been forced in here uninvited, but I think we need to keep our distance."

He exhaled, raking a hand through his hair, the weight of restraint pulling at his shoulders. After a long beat, he reached for his wine glass again.

"I never stopped loving you, Chloe," he said quietly. "You'll always be my sunflower. But I'm trying. Really trying. To move on. It's just..." His voice faltered. "I don't think Britney is the one."

My thighs stuck uncomfortably to the edge of the bed, sweat cooling rapidly as the adrenaline petered out.

"But why, though?" I asked, calmer now. "She's gorgeous. Fun. Sweet. What's wrong with her?"

He shrugged, swirling the bowl of his glass by the stem.

"I realised yesterday... with that Manik guy." His eyes dropped to the wine as it moved in lazy circles. "I didn't feel anything when I saw Britney laid out on his table. No anger. No jealousy. Nothing."

He paused. Took a sip. "But when you dropped to your knees in front of him..."

A flicker of something unspoken passed through his eyes. He drew the folds of his robe tighter. "She's just... not you."

We sat in silence, our breathing in sync. In another life, under different circumstances, maybe I would've made a move. But right here, right now, I knew with absolute certainty—it was Romeo I wanted. The father of my son. The man I was destined to spend the rest of my life with.

Was I satisfied now that I knew Dan still had feelings for me? Absolutely. That was all I needed to finally close the book on us. It was done. My reassurance meter—restored. And the silence between us said the rest: There was no rekindling. No second chances.

The evening had fully settled. Lantern lights swayed in the wind, their glow spilling across the oak floor like lava.

Heavy footsteps thudded outside the door just seconds before it flew open. Romeo burst into the room, his face tight with distress. His eyes scanned the scene in a single sweep, a sharp crease forming between his brows.

Dan immediately shot up off the bed, coming to stand behind the frame—a barrier between him and his brother.

"Hold up. Where's the hoe?" Romeo asked, glancing behind the door.

I rolled my eyes. "You mean Britney? Her and Dan had an argument. We don't know where she is."

Romeo twitched the drapes.

My throat tightened as worry crept back in. "Is everything okay in our room? What happened?"

He still held the gun tightly in his grip as he stalked into the centre of Dan and Britney's suite.

"You mean you've been in here alone with him this whole time?"

"Yes," I said without hesitation, meeting his glare dead-on. "But I swear on our son's life that nothing happened. Now tell me what's going on next door!?"

His jaw flexed. A silent beat passed before he finally holstered the weapon into the waistband of his shorts—hand a little shaky, not from nerves, but from restrained fury. A gesture that spoke loud enough for next door to hear.

"Well, my suitcase has been emptied, and all my chains are gone. So… just jewellery. Oh, and two hundred grand." He shrugged. "Could've been worse."

I blinked. "Wait—you had all that money in your suitcase? Who does that?"

His hand found the grip of his gun again. "You know I always carry cash. It was two-fifty... until I bought the Glock."

"Hold on." I pinched the bridge of my nose. "That gun cost fifty thousand dollars?"

Dan tightened the loosening belt of his robe. "Should we be worried they'll come back?"

I internally rolled my eyes. *Come on, Dan, grow a pair.*

Our security team of two, headed up by Tommy, strolled into the room—turning the space into an impromptu briefing.

Tommy cleared his throat, one hand resting on his holstered weapon. "Perimeter's clear. You should be safe to go back now, Boss."

I walked to the door, peeking out, silently hoping to see Britney on her way back. Fog hung low and clinging, like damp cotton stretched between the palm trees. It muffled the world, shrinking our visibility to just a few metres.

Narrowing my eyes, I peered into the distance. The only silhouettes belonged to the swaying trees, their leaves rustling softly in the breeze. No sound of flip-flops slapping the uneven ground. No sign of her. Nothing.

"She's still not back." I chewed my lip, looking at Tommy. "Will one of you go and find her, please? I won't be happy until she's back safe. Tell them, Romeo."

Romeo, fully settled into his alpha role, didn't hesitate.

"Aight. Both of you. Go find her. I've got it here." He checked his gun one last time. "Come on, Chloe. Daniele can look after himself."

Back in our suite, I took a moment to feel the gravity of it all. The dim glow of bedside lamps spilled warm light across the dishevelled room, throwing long shadows over open drawers and twisted sheets. Drawers left ajar like a violation. The bedspread crumpled in ways we hadn't left it. The air still carried a faint, musty trace of whoever had been inside—a whiff of cologne that didn't belong to Romeo.

We sifted through what little remained of Romeo's ransacked suitcase. A couple of tracksuits, some underwear—nothing of real value, aside from what was missing.

"So they took your crucifix necklace, too?"

He rifled through the small pile one last time before letting out a long, frustrated breath.

"That's what I'm pissed about the most. That chain was my ride or die."

The smile behind that thought softened the blow.

"I mean, I'm not exactly disappointed." I giggled, hoping to lighten the mood.

He snapped the suitcase shut and held out his hand to help me to my feet. "Yeah, yeah. I know you don't like my shit."

The atmosphere shifted the moment my chest brushed his. A silent current passed between us—heavier than before.

"Romeo?"

He kissed the top of my head. "Yeah?"

"You know Dan and I—"

His body grew instantly rigid.

"Fuck." He flung himself onto the bed, dragging an arm over his face. "Let me guess, you played with his dick."

I crawled along the mattress and yanked his arm away, forcing him to look at me.

"No, you idiot. I was going to say that Dan and I have no chemistry whatsoever. It was awkward and, honestly? He's kinda lame."

That got his attention.

His eyes narrowed with intrigue before his grin stretched wide, cocky as ever.

"Lame, huh?" he said, propping himself up on his elbows like I'd just handed him the best news he'd heard all week.

I closed in on him, breathing in the heady scent of masculine sweat. Somehow, no matter the situation, he always smelt delicious.

"The way Dan freaked out over the intruder? I mean, come on. That's the woman's job, right? I love how you handle things. How you keep me safe. And more than anything, I love you."

He tapped the spot beside him, pulling back the sheet. "What can I say?

Only room for one real man on this island."

I slid into bed and relaxed into his hold as he wrapped an arm around my shoulder. His heart beat strong and steady against my cheek.

"Should we be worried about this?" I gestured toward his luggage. "What does your left nut have to say about it? Shall I ask him?"

Smirking, I pulled my hair back, lowered my head into his lap, and rested my ear against his crotch.

"He don't got good hearin', so you gotta get real close if you wanna ask him," Romeo said, smirking.

"Hey, Romeo's left nut, it's me. Chloe. Are you tingling, or are we safe?"

"Sorry, Queen, he still can't hear you. Gotta get him out, you know… skin to skin."

In a bid to show my husband some love and appreciation, I did as instructed—freeing his erection and testicles, an intoxicating combination when handled correctly.

Romeo cupped the back of my head with one large hand.

"In fact," he said with an uncontrolled wriggle, "put your mouth round the end of my dick and talk to him that way. He'll hear real good."

We both chuckled at our ridiculous game, but I wasn't about to stop now. Wrapping my fingers around his length like a microphone, I pressed my lips to the engorged tip.

"Hello, Romeo's nut. Can you hear me?"

The sound of his breath hitching, that sharp inhale through his teeth, was the most honest thing he'd given me all day.

I tilted my head, feigning seriousness, like I was waiting for a real answer.

Romeo's gaze darkened, his arousal spiking.

"He said if you suck it, he'll definitely let you know."

His shaft, warm and heavy in my palm, pulsed with anticipation—flesh betraying the humour in his voice.

Games aside, I took my time, savouring the way his body responded to me.

When an alpha male puts his life on the line, it's his wife's duty to give him what he craves. And in this moment, all he wanted was release.

I didn't stop. I didn't let up. I pushed him to the edge, held him there —and when he finally tipped over, he shuddered through it, spilling hot into my waiting mouth.

I swallowed, taking it all. Everything he had to give me. My way of showing him just how deeply I loved him.

Dan was a thing of the past. And right now, I was diving headfirst into the future.

CHAPTER 9

Relaxed and cosy, I woke to the rhythmic roll of waves against the shore and a warm breeze drifting through the open doors of our honeymoon suite, brushing softly over my bare legs. The curtains draped around the bed swayed gently, ebbing in time with the tide.

Propping myself up on my elbows, I squinted into the light and spotted the silhouettes of my husband and his brother before me, leaning over the balcony, staring out to sea.

Were they talking?

I rubbed my eyes and checked again. Sure enough, there they were. The sound of Romeo chuckling at something Dan said, paired with the subtle shift of Dan's shoulders as they shared a moment, warmed my heart. After all the damage they'd caused each other, they were finally beginning to repair the mess their father left behind.

Not wanting to miss the conversation, I swung out of bed, messy hair and all, and tugged on the T-shirt Romeo had left on the floor last night. Just long enough to cover my modesty.

I padded across the warm wooden floorboards towards the boys, who fell instantly silent.

"Don't stop on my account." I smiled, settling into the patio furniture beside them. The hem of Romeo's shirt clung to the tops of my thighs. Suddenly, I felt too exposed under Dan's gaze.

Romeo stubbed out his cigarette against the balcony railing, flicking the smouldering stub into the ocean before wafting the curling smoke away from me. A glint lit his eyes as he strolled over and tipped my chin up, guiding our lips to meet.

"Mornin', beautiful."

His breath carried that familiar blend of mint toothpaste and tobacco. My safe space.

I grinned, caught off guard by his unusually good mood.

"Morning yourself." I honed in on his red cheeks. "Did you put lotion on?"

The pink blush at the tip of his perfectly angular nose answered for him.

"You best believe I did," Dan cut in, already poised with the long-handled net as he fished Romeo's cigarette butt from the water. His eyes skimmed over me a little too casually, like he thought I wouldn't notice.

Romeo upped the arse-kissing. "More important than that. Guess how many push-ups I did this mornin'?"

Dan raised a brow.

I smiled, watching him flex his bulging biceps. "Go on, then. Tell us."

He flexed again, his T-shirt tugging across his chest. "Four thousand."

Dan blew air through puffed cheeks, muttering something under his breath. He wasn't the only one who didn't buy it.

The veins in Romeo's arms thickened as he kept up the show. Then something caught my eye.

"Hold on. What's that?" I leaned forward in my chair, honing in on a skin-toned patch stuck to his bicep. "Did you get a booboo?"

Romeo flexed his fingers, the patch wrinkling with the motion. He lifted his chin and slapped it like a badge of honour.

"Nicotine patch."

The smoke still curling from his lips made the gesture borderline comical.

Bemused, I glanced at Dan, who mirrored my expression.

"Um... you literally just smoked a cigarette?"

Romeo adjusted his stance, unbothered.

"Can't get any decent smokes on this island. T suggested it." He shrugged like it made perfect sense. By now, nothing about Romeo's logic surprised me.

Dan kept watching me from the side. Knowing he still had feelings left an awkward charge hanging in the air, but I was doing my best to ignore it.

I tugged the hem of Romeo's shirt a little lower. "Pretty sure he meant for you to actually start quitting. No?"

Romeo gave me an appalled look, holding the patch like I'd threatened to rip it off.

"Why the fuck would he mean that?"

Then, after a pause, his voice softened. "But I guess... since wearin' it, I have smoked less."

Now that was the kind of good news I was more than ready to hear.

"That's amazing, Romeo." I beamed, a flutter rising in my chest. "How many less?"

He tossed the numbers around before answering.

"Dependin' on how crazy you've been..." His lips twitched. "...on a chill mornin'? I'd have smoked, what—five by now?"

Five cigarettes in one morning? I'd spent so much time stressing over his drinking, I'd nearly forgotten how bad the smoking had gotten. Worse, maybe.

I poked my tongue into my cheek, eyes narrowing. "So, how many have you actually had?"

He dug into his pocket and flipped open the carton, counting under his breath.

"One, two... six—"

"Six!?" My eyes flew wide. "What the hell? That's more!"

He paused, doubling back. "No, wait," he muttered, recounting. "I meant four."

I didn't believe him. But honestly? I couldn't be arsed to argue.

Dan kept trying to catch my eye whenever Romeo wasn't looking. My bare thighs had always been his weakness.

Whoever said men in sandals were innocent had clearly never met Dan Giannetti. He was more underhanded than most. And if I wasn't careful, I'd land myself in trouble again.

"Anyway—" I cleared my throat, smoothing down my hair. "Hold up." I glanced around the deck. "Where's Britney?"

Dan's lips thinned as he returned the net to its wall hook. "Likely sleeping off a hangover."

He slid his hands into the pockets of his linen trousers, shifting his weight above a pair of white Hermès sandals.

I looked between them. "Did she say where she ran off to? I was up all night worrying about her disappearing like that."

Romeo arched a brow, clearly unconvinced by my inaccurate version of events, especially with the pillow-crease marks stamped across my cheek that betrayed the truth of a restful sleep.

Dan shrugged, his perfectly trimmed chocolate curls settling over one eye as the salty drift eased. "Haven't had a chance to ask her."

I didn't love how little effort he'd made with my best friend, but I understood. His feelings for her just didn't run deep enough. A shame, really.

Still, I couldn't pretend it didn't stir something—knowing that what he and I had shared had left enough of a mark that he'd never fully let go.

Did I feel the same? After everything… could a bond like that ever truly vanish?

The boys carried a shared energy that was slowly rubbing off on me, their renewed camaraderie shifting the mood. A flicker of excitement passed between them. They were finally making progress. Strengthening their bond could only bring good things—for the business, and for us.

I couldn't risk ruining that by telling Romeo the truth. Dan's confession would remain a secret. Locked away in the box labelled: NONE OF MY BUSINESS.

With the lid firmly closed, I smiled at them both.

"What?" Romeo asked, growing rigid in an instant.

The heat rising off the decking warmed my bare feet and travelled all the way to my chest.

"Nothing. I'm just glad to see you two getting along."

The tension in his jaw eased, a flicker of relief softening his expression as he gave his brother a nod.

Did I always put him on edge? Seemingly so.

Like a lightning bolt forking the ground, a sharp twinge shot up my spine.

"Ouch." I drew in a sharp breath, biting back the pain as my hands flew to my stomach.

Romeo was on me in an instant. "What's wrong?"

The faint scent of cigarettes clung to his fingers as he placed his hands over mine.

"I'm fine. Just the baby kicking," I said, shifting my position on the hard-backed chair. The frame creaked. I ignored it.

Another sharp thump from our son jolted his hand.

"You see that?" Romeo's eyes lit up. "Got some fuckin' kick on him already."

Our hands stayed entwined as another thump landed.

"He sure does." I giggled, watching his giddiness crank up a notch.

"Imagine that. I take him on my business deals, and if shit slides, he kung-fu's their sorry asses."

My smile faded. Just like that, he'd tipped over the edge into the land of ridiculousness.

I was seconds from calling him out when Dan stepped forward, cutting the joke short.

"Not long now, Chloe," he said, his tone softening with something close to nostalgia. "Romero said you were further along than we thought. Around seven months now, right?"

We? Our time together was clearly still on his mind.

"Honestly, I can't wait." I rubbed my back, though my smile didn't quite stretch.

Truth was, I was terrified of screwing it all up.

"Anyway." Romeo straightened, flexing his muscular back. "This talkin' between you two is makin' my dick soft."

His poetic way with words needed work, but moments like this reminded me he was trying. Dan had to see that, too.

An uncoordinated thud against the bedroom door snapped my attention back. Britney.

Someone had been drinking too much on this vacation—and for once, it wasn't me.

"Oh, look who it is!" I called, catching the warm vanilla notes drifting in on the breeze. "What were you thinking, going off on your own last night?"

She wrestled with the sheer drapes before stumbling out onto the deck, cheeks flushed, eyes glassy.

Her messy bun had completely given up, hanging limp to one side. Mascara streaks painted the truth. She'd been crying.

"Sorry, Chloe," she mumbled. "I won't do it again."

Dan rocked back on his heels, eyes scanning her dishevelled appearance. "A little more thought next time, Britney."

Jeez. He wasn't wrong… but if Romeo had spoken to me like that in front of everyone, I'd have laced up the gloves and thrown the first punch.

Trying to lighten the mood, I pushed myself up out of the chair—albeit with great difficulty and zero sex appeal.

All eyes landed on me.

"So… what's the plan for today, then?" I brushed myself down.

The boys exchanged a look, a flicker of excitement sparking between them.

"We've booked an activity for this afternoon," Dan said, practically bubbling with enthusiasm.

Romeo winked at me. It was the first time I'd seen him genuinely happy about something that didn't involve sex. Or did it? If he so much as hinted at a foursome, he was in for a rude awakening.

I frowned—first at Dan's chipper grin, then at Romeo, who immediately started fussing with his nicotine patch, pressing down the curling edge.

My lukewarm reception brought their shared enjoyment crashing down. Both wore matching, pensive expressions.

"You booked an activity without asking me?"

Their smiles faltered.

My foot tapped impatiently. "Well, what is it?"

The happy squeals of children playing on the beach echoed between us. Something told me their joy wasn't about to become mine.

Dan scuffed his sandals against the decking. Romeo fished into his pocket, a cigarette perched between his lips like a lifeline. Britney fussed with her hair, trying to tame the chaos. Was she in on it, too?

Heat shimmered off the wood. The soles of my feet burned. My toes flexed. Foot tapping quickened.

"Hurry up and tell me," I snapped. Irritation curled low in my stomach.

One more minute of stalling and that cigarette was going right up his arse—along with the crucifix.

What the hell were they up to?

Romeo took a drag and exhaled slow curls of smoke through his nostrils. "Aight, fine." He rubbed the back of his neck. "We hired pedal boats."

"Pedal boats?" I repeated flatly.

Very apt—for a gun-wielding drug lord with a nicotine patch and anger issues.

"I mean, we wanted to jet ski," he added quickly, "but figured it wouldn't be fair on you. You know, with you bein' pregnant."

Was he kidding me?

Dan adjusted his shirt collar. Britney toyed with her bracelet.

"Oh, how very considerate of you!" My heel struck the floor in protest, a sharp release of building tension. "You're making it sound like I'm spoiling your fun. Sorry for carrying your child!"

He flicked the lighter once. Then again. The third time, the flame caught, reigniting the fizzled tip.

Taking another drag, he exhaled. "Chloe. Did you hear a single word I just said, or are you makin' up shit that didn't happen?"

I narrowed my eyes, choosing my next move carefully.

"Because you're pregnant," he continued, more calmly, "we booked pedal boats instead. I'll do all the pedallin', and you can sit your pregnant ass down and watch me bust my balls."

I threw up my hands. "So now you're calling me overweight? What kind of honeymoon is this? I'd rather go home and face the cops than be treated like this."

Romeo glanced at Dan and Britney, who wisely stayed quiet.

"This is what fucks me up," he muttered, jabbing a finger at me. "You can't reason with her."

He looked at his brother. "You know what I mean. Pussy's magic—but the personality?" He gave a low whistle. "Could use a little work."

On today's episode of What Not to Say to Your Pregnant Wife...

"Hey, leave me out of this, Romero," Dan said, folding his arms and stepping back like he was dodging crossfire.

My fists clenched. Rage prickled beneath my skin. A shimmer of heat blurred the edge of the horizon. A shared blaze engulfed my heart.

After everything I'd done for him. Everything I'd been through. And he treats me like an inconvenience? Like I'm the problem?

"Can you two give me and my husband a moment, please?"

The slap of my foot on the ground as I stepped forward sent a ripple across the water beside us. If I'd been wearing long sleeves, I'd have rolled them *all* the way up.

Romeo backed off.

"Come on then, Romeo. Bring it. I'll kick your arse. Don't try me." I swung. The strain across my bump caught my breath faster than I expected.

Fortunately for him, I narrowly missed his chest. What started as mock outrage twisted into hormone-fuelled fistycuffs.

Romeo shuffled back, more amused than afraid, raising both hands in surrender. The kind of man who never backed down from a challenge—yet somehow, this time, he managed it with ease.

"Queen, I was messin' with you." He dodged another swing. "Chill out, please. It was a joke, okay?"

Fists still raised in front of my face, I sucked in air. More out of shape than I realised. Maybe a gun would've been better. Locked and loaded at his ballsack.

My heart thumped hard. Thoughts of getting him back in his sleep tonight calmed my pulse a little.

"Well, no one laughed. So I guess you're not funny."

He smirked, unfazed. "Boats booked for 12:45. You best go get your sexy ass ready."

◆ ◆ ◆

"Romeo, I'm not gonna say it again. Look at that boat, then look at me. There is no way I'm squeezing into that stupid little thing."

Overheated and mildly irked, my toes scraped across the molten sand —unshaded, unrelenting, blistering beneath the midday sun. A bead of sweat traced a slow path down my back, pooling at the base of my spine.

"Stop moanin' just for a minute, Chloe," Romeo grumbled. "We're stuck on this fuckin' island, and it's about time I had some fun."

Something in his tone stopped me cold. Fun, he says?

My fingers curled, nails biting into my palms. Fine. I'd show him fun.

All four of us stood at the glistening edge of calm water, eyeing the ridiculously compact pedalos my husband had apparently deemed a brilliant group activity. Sectioned off for exclusive access, we had the entire stretch of beach to ourselves—one of those rare moments when being married to a rich man came with obvious perks.

The sand, warm and silky between my toes, clung to my damp skin, while the salty wind tangled strands of hair around my face. The gentle slap of water against the boats' hulls fed a craving to submerge myself completely—just to cool off, physically and emotionally.

A young man with sun-bleached hair and a thick local accent approached, gesturing toward the boats.

"Sir, please take your seat in boat three," he said to Romeo with a polite nod. Then, turning to Dan, "And you, sir—boat six. I will assist the ladies."

Romeo and Dan, grinning like schoolboys, climbed into their respective pedal boats—completely unfazed by the minuscule size of the floating death traps.

Britney and I, however, didn't share their enthusiasm. Helplessly feminine, we hesitated in the shallows. The only upside being the tepid waves lapping at our ankles, soothing the dull ache in my bones.

The biggest downside to all of this? Romeo hadn't even thought to help me climb in. Noted.

The young man approached, offering his rough, sand-gritted hand.

"Ma'am, you go with him." He nodded toward Dan's boat.

I yanked my hand back. "Wait—no. My husband's in boat three."

Romeo's pedalo had already drifted further out, the lazy tide carrying him away like driftwood on the shoreline of life's regrets. His back was turned, completely oblivious—focus glued to the boat's controls. Not once did he glance over.

Did he even care what was happening with me? Obviously not. Too wrapped up in his own selfishness. Too eager to forget I was even here. I knew it from the beginning. He never wanted me on this trip.

The man shook his head. "No, ma'am. Not possible. Too much weight." He motioned to the swell of my stomach. "You go with smaller man."

As he tugged Dan's pedalo closer by its rope, Dan tried to act casual, but the glimmer of hope in his eyes gave him away.

"I don't mind, Chloe. You can share with me."

Hmm.

I cupped my hands around my mouth. "Romeo!? Romeo!?"

But the high winds swallowed my voice whole. And my husband? Well, he was already yards away, tongue caught between his teeth, flustered as he fumbled to gain control. No response.

What should I do?

Then. A light bulb moment.

If he was selfish enough to book this ridiculous little outing, knowing I'd hate it, and audacious enough to blame his lack of fun on me... then I could be selfish enough to climb into this damn boat with Dan—and make sure Romeo regretted it.

I exhaled sharply and turned to the young man. "Fine. Help me in."

No sooner had our boat slipped into open water, gliding effortlessly across the surface, than I heard the deep, rumbling bass of my husband's displeasure.

"What the fuck is Chloe doin', and why the fuck are you gettin' in my boat!?" he roared—at poor Britney, who looked like she'd rather be anywhere else.

I winced, realising I'd forgotten about Britney in all this. I just hoped he wouldn't make her cry again.

Meanwhile, Dan's legs were working overtime, pedalling like his life depended on it.

"Don't worry about Britney," he puffed, barely catching his breath. "She'll be fine. Anyway—look at that view. It's stunning."

He wasn't wrong. As we drifted further from shore, the rippling water lulled us toward what felt like the edge of the earth. The sky kissed the ocean, so close I could almost touch it, yet still impossibly far.

I glanced back, the pedalo tilting slightly with my weight shift, just in time to catch Romeo spinning in chaotic circles. For some reason, his boat refused to steer straight.

"I shouldn't be laughing," I said, biting my lip, "but I think their boat's broken. Why are they just spinning like that?"

Dan looked over his shoulder, smirking. "He's steering it like a car instead of the opposite. He'll figure it out, eventually."

Satisfied that Romeo was finally getting a taste of his own medicine, I sank back into my seat and let the view take me.

"You need help pedalling? You're looking kinda red," I teased, giggling as a bead of sweat rolled down Dan's temple.

"No way," he huffed. "You relax. I've got this."

Only then did I realise how tense I'd been since landing. There wasn't an ounce of fight left in me to argue. Dan told me to relax—and that's exactly what I intended to do.

Out here, Bodu Manik and his men couldn't touch me. Couldn't touch any of us. We were safe. That thought alone made my whole body melt into the curve of the plastic seat. With my back finally supported, I let the sun kiss the apples of my cheeks, its warmth luring me into a hazy, fleeting peace.

A sudden splash hit my face, jolting me from tranquillity.

What the—

My first thought was Dan's sweat, but that seemed more like something Romeo would do.

I wiped my cheek with the back of my hand. "Did you feel that?"

The cool droplets evaporated almost instantly, but the chill they left behind had me craving more.

Dan, however, wasn't even looking at me. His gaze was fixed on the rhythmic splash of turquoise water, eyes wide with childlike wonder.

"I'm pretty sure there's a dolphin circling our boat," he said, voice threaded with awe.

The fog of relaxation lifted instantly. I shot upright, peering over the front of the pedalo. And there it was—sleek, grey skin just beneath the surface. A bottlenose dolphin. Gliding effortlessly, it wove circles around us like it was playing.

So majestic. So breathtakingly beautiful.

"Wow, no way! It's a dolphin!" My voice brimmed with giddiness. I'd never seen anything so stunning in my life.

Dan leaned in. "I know, right? Amazing." His tone dropped to a reverent whisper.

Its fin sliced through the calm water, then vanished, only to launch skyward in a gleaming arc, sunlight kissing its soaked skin mid-air.

Instinctively, I reached out, fingers skimming the surface—then hesitated. "Do you think I can touch it?"

Dan stopped pedalling and let the boat drift. The mechanical churn gave way to a quiet stillness. He pulled out his phone from his pocket and started tapping.

"Hold on. Let me check." A frown landed. "Wait, damn. No service."

He lifted the phone high, squinting like the wind might carry a signal.

But I wasn't waiting. My fingers dipped into the salty coolness, and suddenly, I felt it. A smooth, rubbery texture brushed against my skin, sending a ripple up my arm.

"Oh my God. I just touched it!"

Dan leaned in, resting his arm across the back of my chair as he peered over the edge. "You did? What did it feel like?"

His closeness sent a tingle through my senses, but I brushed it off.

I rubbed my fingertips together, replaying the sensation. "Um... wet leather. Not what I expected." I laughed softly. "Wow. This is just—"

Then our eyes met.

Time hiccupped. The world blurred into nothing but the rhythm of our breath and the lull of the sea.

He was close. Too close. I could smell the citrusy trace of his cologne. So clean. So familiar.

Daniele Giannetti.

Just two people, adrift in the middle of nowhere, staring at each other like the past had never ended.

This was the part in the movie where the orchestra swelled. Where lips crashed. Where furniture toppled. And my mouth, traitorous and twitching, seemed to know the scene.

Stop.

A current pulsed between us, invisible but charged. The emerald in his eyes glittered with something unspoken. And then, just like that, reality slammed into me. I wasn't sharing this moment with my husband.

Dan's smile grew almost shy. Almost hopeful.

My pulse kicked. Panic surged. This was so fucking wrong. We were half a mile out. No signal. No Romeo.

A lump formed in my throat. My baby nudged against my ribs. I hooked my fingers around the back of the boat, scanning the water behind us.

"Dan… where are Romeo and Britney?"

He blinked, startled, then reached for my chin—drawing me towards him. Close enough to catch the sweet burn of spearmint gum on his breath.

"Romero had to go back. Something wrong with the steering." His eyes fluttered closed.

I recoiled like he'd scorched me. "So why the hell didn't you take us back!? He's probably losing his mind!"

Dan flinched, scrambling to explain. "You looked peaceful. And I figured… I didn't want to ruin it. Then the dolphin showed up…"

He forced a smile. I didn't return it.

My thighs snapped shut. "Get us back. Now."

He nodded, slamming his feet onto the pedals, pushing hard. Each rotation dragged us closer to shore.

The weight of silence sat between us like an anchor. Thick. Dragging. Impossible to ignore.

Flustered, he mumbled, "You just looked so calm. And I read pregnant women need peace. I wanted to give you that. I—I didn't mean—"

"Dan… just get us back."

As the beach came into view, Romeo emerged like a storm. Veins bulging. Fury rolling off him in literal waves.

He didn't shout. Didn't speak.

He just dived. Like an Olympian. A perfect, furious front crawl, slicing through the water with terrifying grace. A silent assassin. Probably a skill honed by a woman I refused to name.

He reached us fast. One final stroke, and he surfaced, wiping the water from his eyes with a growl.

"Where the fuck have you two been!?"

He smacked the bow of the pedalo, sending a jolt through the hull.

Water streamed from the coils of his hair, trailing down his jaw, dripping from the tip of his nose like rain from a gutter.

"Romeo, please." I folded my arms. "Stop acting insane and swim back."

But his ears were clearly on strike. With brute strength, he hauled himself partway onto the boat using just his arms—tilting it dangerously, water sloshing inside.

He fisted Dan's shirt. "If you don't bring this fuckin' boat back to shore, I'll kick your weak ass."

Dan didn't blink. His legs kicked into high gear, the pedals creaking under the force as Romeo dropped back into the sea with a heavy splash.

And just like that, it became a race.

Romeo, fuelled by rage, torpedoed toward shore with every stroke powerful and clean.

Dan pedalled hard against the wind and my weight, sweat glistening on his brow. But he didn't complain. He never made me feel like a burden.

By the time we made it back to shore, our overly friendly local guide —the one who'd facilitated this entire mess—was flapping his arms in a full-blown panic. Judging by his wide eyes and frantic gestures, Romeo had already threatened him.

"So sorry about this, ma'am. So sorry, sirs. I only charge you half price," he babbled, anchoring the pedalo against the dock with clumsy haste.

Romeo stood tall beside Britney, quiet, soaked and menacing. He'd been back on land a full minute longer than us. His silence still screamed louder than any threat.

The young man rushed toward me, eager to help me off the boat like his entire family's lives depended on it. I took his hand, stepping onto the sun-baked, pearlescent sand—

And froze.

My stomach flipped.

Silhouettes sharpened into focus.

Britney. My best friend.

Handing my husband a towel.

And him… he fucking took it.

Not only did he take it, he smiled. A warm, appreciative smile with that signature nod he reserved for people he liked.

What the—

He raked the towel through his hair, rubbing down his damp chest, muscles still twitching from exertion.

And suddenly I felt it.

I just knew.

Storming toward them through the loose footing, I stopped dead in front of him, fists bunched, ready to swing again.

Britney toyed with her wind-slicked hair, her gaze flitting anywhere but mine.

"Did you fuck her while I was gone?"

My voice was sharp. Throat so tight even an EpiPen wouldn't help.

Romeo froze mid-motion, towel slack in his hand. His eyes flicked between mine, calculating.

Then, slowly, he let the towel drop.

"Did you just ask if I fucked her?" A bitter laugh escaped as he jabbed a finger toward Britney, like she was a stray pube on a bar of soap.

"Yes," I snapped, baring my teeth. "You sure looked like a couple just then."

Romeo huffed through his nose and curled two fingers. "Daniele. Get your limp dick over here."

My pulse raced to match the spiral in my head.

Had they made love?

Did he come inside her?

Did he give her the orgasm his brother couldn't?

Dan trudged through the thick, dry sand and stopped beside me, close enough to feel the static rising off his skin.

His voice was cautious. "S'up, Romero?" His hands dipped into his pockets.

Romeo looked him over. "Don't play dumb, brother. Chloe's actin' up, which means she's guilty of somethin'. So what was it? Did you finger her? I know you didn't fuck on that small-ass boat, so come on—spit it. Did she suck your dick?"

We both gaped at him, mouths open in disbelief.

The tide crept up the beach, cool water kissing our feet like it was reclaiming what it owned.

Sweat tickled behind my knees. "What? No!" I fired back. "The only people fucking here are you two!"

Britney's eyes welled, but honestly, I wasn't sure I believed her.

She reached out. "Chloe, please. I would never—"

I stepped back. "Don't. I'm mad at both of you."

Romeo raked his hand through his soaked curls.

"Tell me how this is our fault," he snapped, "when you two were out on a romantic-ass boat ride with hand jobs and finger fuckin'?"

The wind howled through the dock. Boats knocked against one another. My dress kept riding up my thighs like it had a mind of its own. A storm wasn't just brewing between us now.

"That didn't happen!" I shouted.

"Well, it wouldn't be the first fuckin' time, would it, Chloe?" His voice dropped, low, dangerous.

He closed his eyes, muttering something under his breath. A curse, or a prayer?

Then he opened them. Locked on.

"Did you fuck? Yes or no."

Dan and I shook our heads in sync.

I brushed sand from my calves like I could scrub away temptation. Was it lying if we technically didn't do anything… but I'd almost wanted to?

"Aight. Neither did we."

And just like that, the four of us stood at a crossroads.

Option A: take the moral high road.

Option B: armour up and dive headfirst into battle.

Did I even have the energy for another war?

The boat guy hovered nearby, raking the sand, pretending not to listen.

"Okay, look," I sighed, sweeping my gaze across the group. "We're supposed to be making the most of this trip, right? Let's not let this ruin everything."

Romeo scooped the towel off the ground and slung it over his shoulders, flinging grains in every direction. The pulse in his temple finally calmed.

"Give me a break, Chloe. You were the one comin' at me."

A reluctant smirk tugged at my lips. "Truce?"

"Whatever, you crazy bitch." He spun on his heel. "Let's go."

◆ ◆ ◆

The ceiling fan whipped up a storm of its own. Cool air swirled over my sun-kissed skin as I smoothed after-sun lotion across my shoulders. Romeo's tan had gone beyond the burn. He was now a delicious golden brown. Which only fed his smug self-satisfaction.

We'd spent the rest of the afternoon pretending the morning had never happened. It was something we'd become surprisingly good at lately. And while Romeo's ability to move on so quickly should've been a relief, it only raised more questions.

Was he guilty as charged?

Britney herself had assured me nothing had happened—and really, she had to trust my word just as much as I did hers.

The four of us had landed right back where we'd been before: trust was all we had. And at this point, I'd do well to take it.

"What are you gonna wear?" I asked casually, lounging on the bed and flicking the lotion lid open and shut as I watched my husband get ready for our dinner with Dan and Brit.

Romeo stood wide-legged in front of the mirror, looking oddly naked without at least one garish piece of jewellery hanging from his neck. No glint against the sun. No clink of heavy metal. Just him.

He spritzed cologne across his neck and chest, enough to hit the back of my throat by the third spray. Delicious. Heaven wrapped in a leathery jacket of masculinity. My nostrils flared as the scent ignited my senses, making a direct beeline for my clit.

"I'll wear whatever you want me to?" he said, turning to me with narrowed eyes, like he thought it was a trick question.

I held up my hands in surrender. "No, no. Wear what you want. I was just asking."

I wasn't looking for a fight, but the way he answered made me realise just how much he'd matured and how hard he was really trying to make me happy.

He flicked his gaze back to the mirror, fixing his curls. "I was just gonna wear what I already had on."

Loose-fitted shorts. A simple T-shirt that framed his muscles, but not intentionally. Modestly fuckable.

My eyes dragged over him. I repositioned, fussing with the fabric of my dress caught in the bedsheets. "Okay, sure."

Arguing was pointless. Women would fuck him if he wore a paper bag.

He fidgeted with his watch clasp. "Do you want me to change?"

Did I? Or was I confident enough to believe my husband wasn't trying to impress that same waitress? I guess the answer would reveal itself soon enough.

"No, you look good. Good, like you're not trying—so that's fine with me." I gave him a wink, interlocking my hands behind my head as I drank in the view.

He moved to the foot of the bed, popped open his cigarette packet, and started counting.

I frowned. It was like watching a toddler line up his crayons. "How many have you got left?"

"Ten." He paused. "No, wait—nine."

My patience snapped like elastic. Even the fan couldn't cool the heat rising in my cheeks. "Wait… wasn't that a pack of twenty?"

"Yep." He closed the carton and tucked it back in his pocket.

"So, you've smoked eleven today?"

He shrugged. "Nothin' wrong with your math."

I hoisted myself off the bed, dizzy with haste, and stormed toward him, yanking up the sleeve of his shirt to reveal the curve of his perfectly sculpted bicep. "Why aren't you wearing a nicotine patch?"

Romeo barely spared me a glance as he adjusted his watch again. "When you had that nap earlier, I jerked off to pass the time, but my dick went soft before I finished. Figured it was the patch—so I threw 'em all out."

My eyes flicked to the nightstand. That fucking bottle of raspberry lube. Tipped over. Oozing from the nozzle in slow, sticky beats.

"Did you even research that theory before tossing them out? Have you asked Tim?"

The way he jerked off like it was no more serious than brushing his teeth infuriated me. Imagine if I chose to finger myself over sex with him? I'd never hear the end of it.

He smoothed his sleeve back into place like the conversation was over. Our eyes locked.

He eventually shook his head.

"Romeo, I'm honestly lost for words. Even if you did throw the patches out, I thought you were cutting down."

He shrugged again, casual as ever. "I have cut down. Normally, I'd have seen off twenty by now."

I sank back onto the bed. Suddenly, the whipped air felt too strong, coiling around me like I'd been swept up in a tornado. Accurate, really. Romeo was a fucking whirlwind of his own.

The truth was, he had more than one addiction. And I wasn't sure which should concern me most.

Sex. Drugs. Alcohol. Cigarettes.

Was there a single vice he wasn't battling? And beyond the usual habits... was he playing with himself more lately? Or was I reading too much into it?

He pressed his fists into the mattress, leaning over me. "Don't start a fight right before we leave just so you can justify tryin' to get Daniele to give you attention over the dinner table."

I eyed the lube bottle again. Mocking me. All fruity and silky. My husband's favourite combination.

"I'm not." My voice shot up several octaves.

Shit. Was he right?

I'd have to bring it up with Nelly in our next session. After all this time, it was becoming painfully clear—I was the one who hadn't made any real progress. And maybe what should concern me most wasn't just Romeo's addictions, but the way I kept pretending they weren't tangled up with mine.

Dan and Britney strolled into our suite without knocking. A bold move. At first, I thought they were crazy, risking walking in on something X-rated... then I remembered how pregnant I was. Even they knew it wasn't likely.

Still, was I fulfilling Romeo's needs? His earlier masturbation confession gnawed at my subconscious. Was I even close?

Britney, dressed in a breezy sundress with sunglasses perched on her head, gave effortless glam. Dan moseyed in with his hands in his pockets, handsome as ever—even if he looked slightly uncomfortable. On paper, they were the perfect couple. Reality, however, told a different story.

Dan propped himself against the wall, slipped off his sandal, and tapped out the loose grains of sand before sliding it back on—then settled into a casual pose. Top button of his linen shirt undone, a light smattering of chest hair on show. He lifted the curtain, peeking out at the view.

"Romeo, why don't you wear sandals like Dan?" I mused aloud. "Your feet stink in those sneakers."

A low, menacing grumble rumbled from the depths of my husband's soul. "You married a real man, Chloe. Get used to it."

To finalise his point, he tugged on the tongue of his sneaker with smug defiance, slapping the side like he was tapping that ass.

I'd be spraying something in those shoes later, that was for sure.

Dan, sensing another toxic plume of tension in the air, checked his Cartier. Thick stainless steel. Perfectly fitted to his wrist. The right balance of masculine and practical.

"Okay," he said, a hint of anxiety creeping into his voice. "Are we ready?"

I scooped up my purse and took a final glance in the mirror. Wrapped in a long-line maternity dress that skimmed to my ankles, I wasn't exactly competing with Britney in her thigh-high, summery number with spaghetti straps.

But if my husband had a problem with it, I'd give him a right hook followed by a swift knee to the crotch.

As had become tradition, the four of us took our usual seats at the beach hut restaurant—four chairs around a low table beneath a slouching parasol. It barely shielded us from the last of the golden heat as a breeze rolled in off the water, tugging at the corners of our napkins.

Tonight's setup was buffet-style. No table service. A perfect surprise.

With a round of drinks in hand, and mine as always, a freshly squeezed lemonade over ice, I skimmed the menu before sliding it back into the condiment stand with a sigh.

Nothing tickled my fancy. Not unless I suddenly developed a craving for the meat-eaters' banquet Romeo had already tucked his napkin in for.

"Just make me up a plate, please." I toyed with the salt shaker. "Not too much meat. I'm already constipated."

Romeo didn't even blink. Did that say something about our relationship? Oversharers—or unconditional lovers?

He leaned in, winding one arm around my waist. "You should'a said earlier. I know somethin' that'll work that shit right outta you."

"Oh God," Dan muttered into the rim of his Cognac, trying once again to keep pace with his brother.

Romeo enjoyed winding Dan up almost as much as he loved having sex with me.

I elbowed him in the ribs, a silent warning to stop while he still had a chance. To everyone's surprise, except mine, he actually obeyed.

Still… that seemingly playful comment had barbs beneath it. Was he getting bored of our vanilla sex?

I sipped my lemonade. Refreshing. Citrusy. Thirst-quenching. Exactly what I needed. The soft bass of island reggae drifted over the tables, blending with the low hum of conversation along the buffet line. Everything felt slower. Even the locals were fanning their faces. Maybe the sun had finally worn everyone out.

"Can you do me a plate too, please, Dan?" Britney added, her voice laced with a confidence she clearly wanted to match with mine.

He gave her a reluctant nod. I clocked it. Ignored it.

As the boys made their way to join the queue, Britney and I sank into quieter conversation.

Pretty and softly alluring, she rested her elbow on the table, chin in hand, looking at me with warm fondness. A salty snap curled through the restaurant, lifting damp strands of hair from her beautiful face.

"Thanks for inviting me on this trip, Chloe," she said, taming her wind-blown waves with her fingers. "Even if things with Dan aren't great, I'm still glad I got to spend proper time with you."

No matter how long Britney had been in the game, she still wore her heart on her sleeve. And I loved that about her.

"I'm glad you're here. I know you keep saying you're fine, but what happened with Bodu Manik…" I leaned in. "You're okay, right?"

She giggled like I was joking. "Chloe, I'm a sex worker. I might not be super good at it, but I know it's my job."

She shrugged, eyes drifting to the second most attractive man on the island, currently waiting in line. "My main worry right now is my relationship with him."

Hmm. We could all see why.

"Everything will work out with Dan." I watched as her gaze lingered on him. "I can feel it."

She fidgeted in her seat, straw between her lips. "I wish I had your confidence. Did he say anything when you two were out on the boat together?"

The bartender's hand slipped mid-shake. A glass shattered behind the bar. Gasps echoed—almost as loud as the one in my head.

Honesty is always the best policy. Unless it involves your best friend's boyfriend.

"Um. No, he didn't. We hardly spoke."

Liar.

We both turned as someone rushed past with a broom.

"Oh. Okay." Her face fell. "I kinda hoped you'd put in a good word for me."

Shit and fuck.

"Of course I did!" The words flew out too fast. "Didn't mention it 'cause I thought it was obvious. First thing I did."

And the award for Worst Liar in the World goes to… Chloe Giannetti.

"You did? That's awesome, Chloe. Thanks! What did you say?"

Crap.

I hooked my tongue around the straw and gave it a firm suck.

"Well. Let me tell you what I said." I sucked again, buying time. "I told him you're a stunning woman who deserves the best… and that he's lucky to have you."

"O.M.G. Really?" She beamed. "And what did he say?"

Ugh.

I was officially the worst best friend alive.

Liquid running low, I sucked once more—then let it fall back into the glass.

"He said he knows he's lucky…" I stirred with the straw. "Can't remember the rest. Sorry."

"Wow," she slumped back in her seat, smiling. "That really cheered me up."

A direction change was urgently needed. One more question and I'd be exposed.

I glanced toward the buffet, Romeo and Dan still only halfway down the line. The bar staff had calmed. The pace had reset. A guest wandered past with a plate piled high with meat, potatoes, and salad. My stomach growled.

"So, what's the latest with you and Dan?" I asked, nudging the last ice cube in slow circles.

Britney shrugged. "Well… we had sex this afternoon. First time in two weeks." No excitement. Just quiet resignation.

I hadn't realised things had gotten that bad.

I stopped stirring. Keeping my tone neutral, I took another sip. "Oh? How was it?"

My immediate thought? Guilt sex. The fallout from that near-kiss on the pedalo with me.

"It was… okay, I guess." She took a hearty gulp of her drink, some spilling at the corner of her mouth.

"Just okay after two weeks?"

"I know. Not a good sign, is it?" She swirled the last of her cocktail, condensation trailing down the glass like a slow drip of doubt. "How is sex with Romero these days?"

I shifted in my seat, the woven chair imprinting faint patterns on my thighs as I crossed one leg over the other.

That nagging thought returned. Romeo popping the cap on that lube and taking matters into his own hands. Literally. If he jerked off again tonight, my fears would be confirmed.

"Same as it always was, really. Aside from my pregnancy getting in the way."

Britney lowered her voice, leaning across the table. "Question. Do you always come?"

I glanced around. No prying ears. Just the roll of the waves and the glow of the setting sun.

My nails tapped against the glass in a rhythmic, tense pattern. A nervous drumline.

"Um… not always. Sometimes I like to give him a gift I don't expect repaid."

She sighed, tossed the coaster onto the table. "I haven't had an orgasm with Dan in at least a month."

I blinked. Unwanted flashbacks of me and Dan in bed shoved their way to the surface.

"Wait—what do you mean? He nuts and then bails?"

That didn't sound like the Dan I remembered. Back then, he'd been an excellent lover.

"Yeah. He finishes and then just sort of turns over."

That was unexpected.

I nudged the condiments back into line. A feeble attempt to organise my thoughts.

"Have you talked to him about it?"

"Nope." Her gaze dropped. "I'm scared to hear he's bored of me. And I know we said we wouldn't talk about it again, but…" She hesitated. "I know he still has feelings for you."

I snorted into my drink. "I don't think that's true, Brit."

But even as I said it, guilt swelled in my chest.

Why was I lying to her again?

Britney's eyes shimmered like glass, holding back tears she refused to let fall.

"I peeked at his phone while he was in the shower," she whispered. "There were loads of messages from women he works with. And…" Her voice dropped further. "A couple from a while ago. From someone called Sunflower. Do you know her? Whoever she is, he was definitely in love with her."

Oh, no.

There was no way I was admitting Sunflower was me. That must've been back when we lived together. Why the hell had Dan kept those messages?

A strange chill threaded through the ocean drift, like the sea itself had caught wind of our conversation.

Time to change the subject.

"Sorry, Brit. No idea…" I said breezily, waving it off. "So—Lala called me earlier."

Britney stabbed her cocktail umbrella into the ice. "Oh no. What's happened now?"

Another happy customer passed with a fruit platter. I tracked the movement until it disappeared. My mouth watered.

"Chloe?" Britney snapped her fingers.

I blinked. "Sorry. I'm starving. Where was I?"

She giggled in that way I adored. "You were telling me what happened with Lala."

"Right. Yeah." I edged my chair closer, voice low. "I had to sneak off to the bathroom to take the call. She was in a state. Apparently, a few of the girls have been misbehaving."

Britney's brows lifted. She leaned in, the warm scent of vanilla and booze drifting off her breath.

"I knew they'd do this," she muttered, full of second-hand irritation.

"Mm-hm. No security at the mansion. Just the valet team. Sounds like there's a lot of sex happening, and not much else."

Her expression twisted into scandalised amusement. Elbows propped on the table, she closed in like it was story time.

"So, what did you say?"

"Told Lala to pass on a clear message. I want a hundred grand on the table when I get home or they're all getting replaced."

Britney nodded slowly, gnawing on a fingernail. "What did Romero say about it?"

I huffed. "Are you kidding? He has no idea. So keep it to yourself. If he found out I wasn't doing a good job with the women, he'd take them back. None of us want that."

"Ooh. True. My lips are sealed." She lifted her glass, took a delicate sip, and set it down again—her fingers circling the base in slow, idle loops.

"Lala's sweet," she added quietly. "She'll be great when the club reopens."

I nodded, slurping the last drops of juice. "Have you thought any more about working there? Something more like a manager's role?"

She shook her head, golden waves shifting with the movement.

A shadow fell across our table—and a sultry voice interrupted the flow. "Evening, ladies."

A strawberry blonde appeared behind us, startling me.

Clad in a bikini top and short skirt, my first thought was that Romeo had ordered strippers to help digest his meal.

Her hands landed lightly on our shoulders, soft and deliberate. A subtle tingle climbed my spine.

"Um, hi?" I frowned, already wary of her overly familiar tone.

"Girls' holiday?" she asked, her glossy lips curling into a playful smirk.

From four tables away, Tommy stood, his hand instinctively going to his gun.

I raised mine discreetly, signalling him to stand down with a flick of my fingers.

Britney and I exchanged a glance.

"No," I replied flatly. "My husband and her boyfriend are right over there."

Romeo and Dan still had their backs to us, blissfully unaware.

"Ahh, okay." She nodded, grey eyes glittering. "Tell me—have you ever wondered how much your partner truly loves you?"

My stomach dipped.

Had she been listening?

"Did you know most infidelities happen on vacation?" she continued, voice as smooth as her skin. The scent of baby oil and bad decisions radiated off her.

Britney stiffened beside me.

"I offer a honey trap service," she said. "I can test your man's limits—see if he'd cheat if given the chance. If you're interested… contact me."

She slid a sleek black card across the table like a poker chip, then turned and walked off, hips swaying, scent trailing behind her.

The music felt louder. The air—thicker. Like the whole island had tilted on its axis.

"What the hell…" I muttered, picking up the card.

Gold-embossed italics gleamed in the fading sun:

Camilla Harrison

A number. An email. No title necessary.

Britney folded. Eyes wide. Breath hitched. "What do you think?"

What did *I* think?

I arched a brow. "Do you really want to do it?"

We both knew Dan needed testing. But was this the way?

She chewed her thumbnail. "Will you do it too?"

Hmm.

That wasn't a good idea. Was it?

I'd be lying if I said I hadn't thought about Romeo's little beach exchange with her at least once in the last half-hour. Add that to the fact he was masturbating more than usual… and yeah. The thought lingered like a warning siren.

If I wasn't meeting his needs, would he look elsewhere?

"I don't know about that," I said, glancing toward my husband. His broad back was still turned, two half-full plates in hand, waiting patiently in line.

"We're already on thin ice after what happened with Manik. And then this morning's disaster."

Britney clasped her hands together like a kid begging for sweets. "Please, Chloe? I don't want to do it alone."

Why was I even tempted? Why did my mouth water like I was starving for it?

Romeo was right about me. I needed help.

"Okay," I sighed, slumping back in my seat. "Wait 'til they're back at the table. We'll make an excuse to leave. Maybe you've come on your period and need to pop back to the suite?"

Britney's eyes lit up. "You're so smart, Chloe."

I wasn't sure that was something to be proud of.

"It has to be convincing, though," I warned. "Give it your best shot."

Another five minutes passed before our men returned, plates piled high with food that looked far from appetising. Too much meat, barely a hint of colour. The kind of meal that screamed gout.

I gave Britney a discreet nod.

"Ooh, ouch," she groaned, clutching her stomach like she'd been stabbed with a pair of safety scissors.

My chair legs shifted in the sand as I sprang up. "Oh my goodness, Britney, whatever is the matter?" I gasped, laying it on thick while side-eyeing Romeo for a reaction.

He barely looked up—too busy tearing into a greasy chunk of meat still clinging to the bone. Mildly interested, but mostly distracted.

"Ooh... ouchy," Britney repeated, rubbing her belly in slow, pitiful circles.

I threw Romeo a sharper glare. He was now picking at his teeth with his pinky.

"What?" he asked, sucking grease from his fingertip.

"Britney's clearly struggling here, Romeo. Are you not going to ask if she's okay?"

His nostrils flared as he gave me a look of utter disgust, then chomped another bite.

"I don't give a shit," he mumbled, mouth full. "That's Daniele's business."

Dan shrugged without looking up, calmly spooning plain rice into his mouth before patting the corners of his lips with a napkin like this was normal.

We needed one final act to seal it.

I eyeballed Britney, urging her silently to go big.

"Ouch! Ouch!" she yelped louder this time, then—just a shade too dramatically—toppled off her chair with a theatrical thud.

"Oh, my! Britney's just had a menstruating collapse! Did you see that!?" I gasped, arms flailing like I was reporting a murder.

Romeo flicked a shred of meat from his canine. Still unmoved. Not even a blink.

Britney, already halfway back into her seat, muttered, "It's fine, Dan. I'll help myself up."

I glared between them. "The lack of support you men are showing is disgusting," I hissed, and kicked Romeo under the table.

Instant regret. My sandalled foot throbbed from the impact. He didn't even flinch.

He ran his tongue along his teeth, then glanced at Dan, who simply shrugged, completely baffled by women's issues, fake or otherwise.

Perfect.

"Come on, Brit," I said, reaching for my purse. "These insensitive arseholes don't understand us."

Romeo shot to his feet like a bullet, yanked the napkin from his collar, and let it drop. "What the fuck are you doin'? Sit the fuck down."

Tommy flinched in the distance.

I tore my hand from his grip. "Britney's period has taken a bad turn. She needs one of her special pills from the apartment."

Grease shimmered on his lips like designer gloss.

He chewed another bite, muttering through it. "She can take Tommy with her. You ain't leavin'."

I didn't budge. Arms folded. Hip cocked. Holding my ground. "She needs support. But *you* wouldn't know anything about that."

With an exasperated sigh, he tossed the stripped bone onto his plate like a rock hurled at porcelain, then raised a hand to flag Tommy.

It took ten seconds.

"Yes, Boss?" Tommy said, sharp as ever.

"These two need to head back to the apartment. Full sweep first. Report back."

Tommy nodded and disappeared into the shadows.

Snake stayed planted. Watchful. Silent.

Safe to say, I was already back in my seat by the time Tommy reappeared fifteen minutes later. Britney had kept the cramps act going, but even she looked done with it.

"All clear, Boss," Tommy announced, sweat glinting off his bald head like he'd taken a quick dip on the way back.

Romeo gave a tight nod. "Aight. Tommy and Snake will shadow you. Be back in under ten."

I rolled my eyes. "Please. Britney will need at least thirty minutes to clean up. But you wouldn't know—on account of never bleeding out your dick once a month."

Romeo cut his eyes toward Dan.

Dan raised his hands like a hostage. "I'm staying out of this one."

"Be quick," Romeo grumbled. "I don't need to tell you why."

With Snake and Tommy posted outside, Britney and I perched side by side on the edge of the immaculate bed. A swan-shaped towel sat proudly at the foot, and two heart-shaped chocolates waited on the pillows like rewards we hadn't earned.

Housekeeping really was something else. The air inside felt too clean—like it didn't belong to the grime of our choices.

Face to face, we mirrored each other's posture. Legs crossed. Fingers restless.

"Should I just text the number?" I murmured, running the sleek black card between my fingers. "Or do you think I should call?"

Britney didn't answer fast enough.

I was already typing.

"Yeah, I think message," she said, barely above a whisper.

I hesitated. Then hit send.

<Me>

Hey. It's us from the bar. We're interested in your services.

<Camilla>

Excellent. Send me a photo of each of your men and their current location on the island.

I got up and paced the room, scrolling through my camera roll for a recent shot of the two of them together.

Ironically, the only one I had was from our wedding—taken just after the brothers had finally made peace.

I paused. Thumb hovering. Skin prickling.

Honey-trapping my husband with our wedding photo? Even for me, that was bleak. But I'd already crossed the line. Might as well take the damn photo with me.

A chill climbed up my arms as my thumb twitched over the send button. I swallowed hard.

"Okay, I've sent it." My voice cracked. "Why do I regret this already?"

My throat tightened. This could blow everything apart.

Britney was lost in her own mess. Rubbing the back of her neck. Rocking gently. Not even listening.

"I think Dan will cheat," she murmured, smoothing the pillow like it might fix something inside her.

I slapped my thighs and instantly regretted it as the sting of sunburn bloomed across my skin.

"I guess we'll find out soon enough."

I couldn't speak for Britney. But I already hated who I was becoming.

Twelve long minutes passed. Each second dragging like crawling over broken glass.

Then my phone buzzed.

<Camilla>

I have a video of each of your men. If you want to see them, PayPal transfer 1,000 US dollars each.

My heart stuttered.

I had the money, but only through Romeo's credit card.

Shit. This was a moral dilemma if ever there was one.

But then it hit me: If Romeo hadn't cheated, there wouldn't be a video to show. Right?

Fuck. Did he cheat?

Britney bit her lip, her expression wilting. "That's a lot of money, isn't it?"

My skin prickled. Images of Romeo doing all sorts at that bar flashed through my head—bending her over the buffet, screwing her on top of the bar. My knuckles whitened.

"I'll pay for both," I whispered, barely keeping my voice steady. "We need to know what's on those videos."

We waited.

My nails scratched absently over my wrist, each bite into skin making it feel more real. Britney rocked beside me, creating a slow, nauseating wave through the bed that pulled me along with it.

Then a thumbnail appeared. Romeo's face frozen mid-motion as the file began to download.

Phone resting in my lap, I fanned my face with both hands. My body had gone clammy, despite the breeze drifting through the room.

Did I even want to watch this?

With a deep breath, I tapped play.

"Hi, I'm Brianna," the honey trapper cooed, her voice sugar-slick as she approached my husband.

Romeo didn't even look up. He just flicked his hand in her direction, casually dismissive. "Not interested."

My heart thudded. The video quality was grainy, the dim lighting making it hard to see beyond the outline of Romeo and Dan, still eating at our table, mountainous plates in front of them.

"That's cool. Can I hang out?" Brianna purred, sliding into my empty seat beside him.

He had no clue he was staring straight into a hidden camera. Those eyes. So intensely terrifying when they weren't focused on me. "No. Leave. Please."

She placed a hand on his shoulder. "Ooh, I like a man who's hard to get."

My pulse hammered. A kick from my son punched me in the gut. Was he ashamed of me?

I held my breath, bracing for impact. My fists clenched the bedsheets, palms damp, heart stammering. Anxiety surged through every nerve like a live wire.

He knocked back a whiskey and raised the glass, signalling for another.

"I'm married." His wedding band glinted. "I ain't interested."

Brianna, bold as hell, leaned in, anyway—voice dripping with seduction.

She circled a finger along the tablecloth. "Since when did being married matter? I can give you what your wife can't. Anything your heart desires."

Romeo didn't flinch. Didn't look at her. Didn't even acknowledge her. He kept talking to Dan like she didn't exist.

The video cut off.

Another file began to download.

The thumbnail: Dan.

For the first time since this mess started, I took a breath. Process what I'd just seen.

My husband. Romero Giannetti. The man with a sex addiction who used to fuck women for a living. Didn't cheat.

He stayed faithful.

I swallowed past the knot, climbing my throat.

"You ready?" I croaked, glancing at Britney.

Her breathing was erratic. Teeth chattering like she was sitting in an igloo—despite the ninety-degree heat in the suite.

"I can't do it," she whispered, eyes wide. "You press play for me, Chloe."

She curled into my shoulder for support, fingernails chewed to the quick.

I hit play.

A different woman appeared on screen—another honey trapper on the prowl.

"What's your name? You look like a soldier with that physique," she purred.

Dan wiped his mouth with a napkin and took a slow sip of his piña colada, completely unfazed.

"Hi. I'm Dan."

She smiled. "Hey, Dan. I'm Jennifer. Can I buy you a drink?"

He pulled out his wallet. "Shouldn't I be asking you that?"

She reached for his arm, fingers grazing the muscle.

He smiled.

"If you don't mind, I'll have a Sex on the Beach." Her voice was breathy, more moan than speech.

His gaze locked onto hers. Then dropped straight to her cleavage.

"Do you wanna get out of here?" he asked, in a tone I didn't recognise.

The way he threw back his chair and downed the rest of his drink in one go—

That wasn't Dan. Not the Dan I knew.

She slipped her hand into his without hesitation.

And the video ended.

A veil of silence smothered the room.

Oh no.

No, no, no.

The wind whistling through the window frame sounded like a distress call.

"Oh, Britney, I'm so sorry. We shouldn't have done that—"

Before I could blink, the door to our suite slammed open. Romeo stumbled inside in an alcohol-fuelled flourish.

I clutched my chest, pulse leaping to my throat. Ears ringing, like my body was trying to drown out the panic.

"Oh, Romeo—it's you. Where's Dan?"

I already knew. I just needed to hear it from him.

Romeo, in all his terrible lying glory, rubbed the tip of his nose and took a lazy sidestep.

"He, err, wanted to stay out longer. But you were takin' too long and, err… I'm real tired."

He stretched theatrically, tossing in a fake yawn for good measure.

Britney burst into tears.

Without warning, she bolted. She knocked over a chair, scattered magazines, and nearly took the swan towel with her.

Romeo scowled and shut the door she'd left wide open.

"What the fuck's wrong with her?"

Shit.

Should I tell him? Or would that just prove what a terrible wife I was?

He took a stumbling step closer, letting me know he'd been drinking more than I liked. Strong liquor clung to his breath. Tobacco lingered at the edges of his lips.

"Chloe, I hate when I ask you a question and you don't answer. It gives me a bad feelin'—and I only get that feelin' when I'm about to get shot."

Maybe if he's drunk enough, he'll laugh. I sucked in a breath and hoped for the best.

"Fine. Um… we know Dan is cheating."

Romeo pulled out his cigarette pack and slid one between his teeth.

"How do you know that?"

Instinctively, I cradled my stomach.

"Don't get mad at me. It's not good for the baby."

His jaw flexed.

In the heat of the moment, he lit the cigarette inside the room, inhaling too sharply as he moved to the patio doors.

The smoke poured out of him when he snapped. "Don't you fuckin' dare use my son as a weapon. What did you do?"

I swallowed hard. My stomach cramped, dread cinching like a belt.

"We didn't plan any of it. I swear on our child's life."

The balcony doors yawned open behind him, flooding the room with cold wind. Curtains flapped like warning flags.

His shoulders tensed. His chest rose.

"Tell me. Now."

"Okay. So…" I wrapped the sheet tighter around me. Goosebumps lit up my arms like pinpricks of guilt. "When you went to get our food… a woman stopped by our table."

His cheeks hollowed as he sucked the cigarette. "And?"

Even from across the room, I saw the vein bulge in his forehead.

There was no easing into this.

"She said if we paid $1,000, she'd try to, you know… seduce you." I rushed it all out in one breath.

Romeo nearly bit down on the cigarette.

He spun on his heel, yanked the balcony doors wider still, and let them crash against the wall.

The air rushed in—cutting through the suite like a blade.

He snapped his head toward me, eyes ablaze.

"You paid a thousand dollars to a honey trapper? To try and catch me out on our honeymoon!?"

Now definitely wasn't the time to mention I'd covered Britney's bill too. His next credit card statement was going to be one hell of a conversation.

"Not really," I backtracked. "We just wanted to trap Dan. They haven't had sex in weeks, and he doesn't make her come."

For a fleeting moment, it worked—his irritation faltered, eyes flicking with curiosity. But it didn't last.

His chest puffed. "You're tellin' me that after everythin'... you still don't trust me?"

I finally lifted my gaze, meeting him through my lashes. The truth was, I wasn't even sure how I felt. Was I expecting him to fail the test?

My silence was all he needed. His nostrils flared. He shook his head slowly, heavily, disappointment thick in his eyes.

"I'm goin' outside to finish this smoke."

A distant motorboat buzzed like a fly. Somewhere, someone was having a good time. But thanks to me, that someone wasn't my husband.

By the time I reached him on the decking, he was already halfway down to the filter. I placed a hand on his chest, feeling the twitch of tension beneath his skin.

"I love you, Romeo."

The night air, lit only by moon and stars, cooled the fire between us instantly.

Sadness shadowed his features. He took a step back.

"No, you don't."

His words sliced deep.

My fingers curled over my chest, holding myself together. "Don't say that."

"I can't believe you did this to me." His voice had softened, but it carried more weight than any scream. "I don't know what else I need to do to prove myself to you."

I stepped closer. "I'm sorry, Romeo. I get it if you don't believe me, but we didn't plan any of this. I swear to you."

An eerie stillness settled between us. Waves lapped the shore. Palm leaves rustled in the breeze. But all I wanted—needed—was his voice, telling me we were okay.

Desperate, I did what I knew best. My fingers slid lower, reaching for the waistband of his shorts.

"No." He swatted my hand away.

I snatched it back like he'd scalded me. "What do you mean, no?"

He stubbed the cigarette into the ashtray, a final curl of smoke rising as he turned and walked inside. "I can't even look at you right now."

The curtains fluttered behind him, unsettled, just like us.

I stood there, raw and alone. Tears welled. Panic surged through me.

What the hell do I do now?

After several agonising seconds, searching for a miracle cure that didn't exist, I followed him in.

A little warmer in the suite, the humidity hit me as hard as his emotional brick wall.

To my surprise, he was already in bed. The covers pulled up to his neck like armour. I climbed in beside him, tentative. Even now, angry and guarded, he still smelled like comfort.

I reached for his arm, trying to guide it around me.

"Don't." His voice was flat. Distant. He yanked his arm away and rolled over, facing the wall.

I leaned over him, trying to read his face. The peak of his eye socket tattoo creased at the edge.

He was really mad.

"Please *don't give up on me*, Romeo. I can't handle it." A tear slipped down my cheek, landing warm against his shoulder.

"Shouldn't it be me fuckin' cryin'?" His voice cracked as he turned to face me.

"I'm so sorry, Romeo. Please believe me."

"I know you're young. I know you've been through shit. But you can't keep killin' me like this, Chloe."

I reached under the cover again, pleading with my touch.

"Let me make it up to you." My fingers brushed the length of his cock.

He caught my wrist. "No. We can't fix everythin' with sex."

A lump rose in my throat, thick and unrelenting.

"You don't find me attractive anymore, do you?"

His eyes snapped to mine, stunned. "This ain't got nothin' to do with that—and everythin' to do with you payin' someone to get me to cheat. With my own fuckin' money."

Hearing it out loud like that…

Jesus.

"Do you want a divorce?" My voice broke. The very word made my blood turn to ice.

He turned over fully. Eyes on mine.

"No." His jaw clenched. "But it don't change the fact that my chest hurts. It hurts so bad… I couldn't get a hard-on if I tried."

He dragged a hand down his face, tired and torn. "The last time I felt like this was… you know exactly when."

I swallowed, the guilt making it hard to breathe. I'd put him through so much.

"I love you, Romeo."

His eyes softened, just a fraction. But the weight in his voice didn't lift.

"I love you too, Chloe. I just wish it was enough."

CHAPTER 10

The next morning, I was awake early for a number of reasons, but mostly because yesterday still weighed heavy on my mind.

The sun had yet to rise; it was dark out, just a silvery hue of light shining through the sheer curtains.

Soft snores filtered from Romeo's nostrils as his chest rose and fell in rhythm with the world outside our suite, offering a sense of comfort I didn't deserve.

Our connection had always felt deeper than most, and true to form, Sleeping Beauty beside me stirred the moment he sensed my eyes were open.

I took the chance to catch him off guard.

"Morning, handsome."

He stretched his arms above his head. Yesterday's deodorant still clinging to the light smattering of underarm hair. A tropical paradise, all of my own.

"Hi," he murmured, scrubbing the top of his head, tousling his glossy black curls.

I walked my fingers through the hair on his chest and settled over his nipple.

"Are you still mad at me?"

He pretended to think it over, but the answer was already waiting on the tip of his tongue.

"Yep."

Okay. He wasn't being too aggressive about it.

Sensing him softening toward me, I smiled. He was playing along—ish.

"Out of ten… how mad?"

He stroked the longer-than-usual stubble on his chin, the rasp playing havoc with my senses.

"Hmm. Gotta be ten." His eyes shone with a flicker of playfulness.

I pressed soft kisses to his pectoral, watching the muscle twitch beneath my lips.

Then, lower still—tongue gliding across the velvet-soft skin of his hardened areola.

"Yikes, that's high." I grinned against his chest. "What were you last night?"

He breathed deep. "Shit, I dunno. At least two hundred."

Two hundred felt like a fair score for the way I'd behaved.

"So it's come down quite a bit, then?" I sniggered, catching my bottom lip between my teeth. "Does a ten mean you still don't wanna have sex with me?"

I trailed my foot up his outstretched leg toward the heat of his morning erection. Gently, I curled my toes around the thick weight of him, squeezing softly.

That move had never failed me.

Until now.

This moment carried a weight neither of us could ignore.

My grip loosened.

"Come on, Romeo. Take me. Please. I need us to be okay."

He looked at me, the base of his throat pulsing.

"Please?" I whispered, pulling the cover off me completely.

Without a word, he shifted his weight, tugging his boxers down with one hand and bracing himself above me with the other. His knee pressed between my thighs, parting them—a move I hadn't felt in a long time. Now, suddenly, it felt intrusive.

He pushed the head of his dick through my folds.

Neither of us was ready.

His shaft bowed with the pressure. I winced.

The abruptness stung. My sensitive flesh flared as he drove forward.

In search of anything familiar, I found nothing.

No stale tobacco on his breath. No sharp bite of whiskey.

Just clean air and cold distance.

A wolf in sheep's clothing.

And I'd let him in.

Sadness punched through my ribs as I let him take me the way he thought I deserved.

I stared into his eyes… but Romeo wasn't there.

No kisses. No tenderness.

Just rhythmless thrusts until he spilled inside me with a low, detached grunt.

That was it.

He rolled off without a word, breath heaving beside me, one arm slung over his eyes.

I didn't deserve that.

No one did.

Disgust churned in my gut like a bad dream. I cradled my stomach protectively, shielding my baby from the shame burning through my chest like heartburn.

I couldn't stay.

I moved fast, hauling myself out of bed, the mattress springs protesting.

Only one motive that drove me now was to leave him.

My feet hit the cold floorboards with purpose, the chill grounding me instantly.

"Chloe, where are you goin'?"

His voice cut through the fog, panic lacing every word as he shot upright. One leg off the bed—frozen like a deer in headlights.

I didn't answer. I didn't need to.

My middle finger said it all as I bolted, slamming the apartment door behind me.

Wrapped in nothing but a towelling robe, I fought the early morning wind, not yet warmed by the sun.

Clutching the fabric tight, I rushed to the door a few strides beyond ours. The grit of the sandy path bit into my bare feet. Almost as hard as my husband's actions.

"Britney! Let me in—quick!" I banged my fist against the door, breath sharp and fast, adrenaline surging.

Any second now, I expected him to charge after me, probably waving a gun.

The door creaked open, the hinge groaning loud enough to wake the neighbours.

There she was. Mascara-streaked cheeks. Tangled blonde hair. The prettiest girl I knew, now marred by sorrow.

My voice dropped. "Hey… can I come in?"

Tears slipped freely down my face. Salty echoes of heartache gathered at the corners of my mouth, aching to speak the pain I couldn't.

She nodded silently, stepping aside.

I rushed across the chilled floor on tiptoes. Tearing back the covers, I climbed into her bed and pulled them over me like armour. The muted lull of the same waves drifted beyond her doors—yet from this bed, they sounded unfamiliar.

Britney followed, curling in beside me.

"Did Dan not come home last night?" I asked, feeling the coldness of the unslept sheets beneath me.

She sighed, the sound catching in her throat.

"Nope. I've texted him," she said, clicking her phone screen, "but he hasn't replied."

Wiping her nose on her sleeve, she draped herself over me. No vanilla perfume—only stale tears and heartbreak.

I wrapped my arms around her.

"I'm so sorry, Brit." A sob escaped before I could catch it.

She pulled back slightly, concern softening her brows.

"Are you okay, Chloe?"

She brushed a tear from my cheek with her thumb, leaving a tingling trace behind.

Her question brought it all rushing back. His face, his actions, the hurt.

My chest tightened. "We, um… had a fight."

I guided her head against me, holding her close.

We sank into silence, breathing in each other's sorrow like secondhand smoke.

One thud along the deck outside became two, then more. The door burst open so hard the walls seemed to shake.

Romeo filled the frame. Chest heaving. Eyes wild. Possessed.

The morning sun rose behind him, casting a golden halo around his silhouette. His shadow stretched into the room like a threat. A demonic angel from my nightmares.

His mouth opened.

I was already done listening.

"Chloe—"

"Fuck off, Romeo. I'm not interested in what you have to say." I turned away.

The air changed. Thickened.

Footsteps moved fast, heavy. He was coming. Whether I wanted him to or not.

In one move, he scooped me up, locking me against his chest.

"Get off me!" I shrieked, thrashing wildly.

My heel cracked against the nightstand with a thud, tipping the lamp on its side. The ache in my foot barely registered.

Britney scrambled upright, sheets falling around her.

"Put me down, Romeo!"

He gripped me tighter. "Shut up, woman, you'll get me arrested!"

"Good!" I panted, breath ragged now. "It's what you deserve."

Why did I say that? No matter how I felt about what he'd just done, I would never wish that on him. On our family.

My body wilted. The fight drained from me instantly.

Fresh air brushed my cheeks when he stormed us outside. Slumped in his arms, I let him carry me back to our suite in silence. Only the sound of his laboured breath filled the quiet.

With care and unexpected tenderness, he set me down at the threshold of the room, my bare toes sinking into the hush of cold timber. Only now did my heel start to hurt.

He handled me like I was made of splintered ice on the lake of his sorrow, creaking beneath his feet.

He stepped in front of me, his hands finding mine. The heat in his palms lingered, but nothing about it was comforting.

The hush of the room crept in, like the tide swallowing the shore was eavesdropping on our conversation.

"Chloe, I—shit." He shifted his weight, discomfort in every movement, his guilt-ridden eyes unable to meet mine for long. "I shouldn't have done that. I'm sorry."

I tore my hands away and stepped back, one foot over the line as though it defined my safety.

Fresh tears burned down my cheeks, chilled by the draft seeping in through the open door.

"What you did... it was close to rape. And we both know I've had enough of that in my life!" My voice cracked as the words left my mouth, the fragile sting in my throat a reminder of how painful those words were to say—and to feel.

A hundred steps back. That's how far we'd fallen.

His lip curled, not in anger but in something else. Revulsion. With himself.

His hands fell to his waist. "Don't say that to me."

For the first time in a long time, I didn't feel safe with him.

Folding my arms, I grew taller as I adorned my shield.

"Well, that's how I feel."

He raked a hand through his curls, frustration clinging to every movement as he replayed the events that led us here.

"But you asked me to have sex with you?"

I shook my head slowly. "No. I wanted to make love. What I got was a quick fuck—for your pleasure, and no one else's."

"Shit," he muttered, shifting on the spot as if evading his own thoughts. "I'm sorry, Chloe. I was just so... mad."

The first light of dawn broke through the window, golden and forgiving, casting soft angles across his face. No longer a stranger—Romeo was still in there, somewhere beneath the surface of his self-doubt.

"Well, guess what, ass-hat? Now I'm mad, too."

I tightened the fold of my arms, a makeshift barrier he wasn't allowed to cross. The ache beneath my ribs made one thing painfully clear—

No matter how much he loved me, he had the power to hurt me more than anyone else.

His face softened, seeking an opportunity.

A cautious smile crept across his lips.

"Out of ten?"

I didn't move. Arms locked. Walls high.

"At least three hundred." The corners of my mouth twitched, betraying my true feelings.

The fight to hold back my smile slipped a little.

He whistled. "Shit, that's real high."

Stepping forward, he closed the distance I'd created and pulled me into his chest.

My stomach hit his body first—our son part of this, too. The moment the weakness of my body met the strength of his, I released a shaky exhale.

Romeo had always been my Achilles' heel, and just his presence alone was enough to chip away at my anger.

I let him touch me.

Then, all too soon, I wanted him to touch me.

The warmth of his plush lips pressed against the crown of my head as he inhaled the scent of my hair.

A gentle sigh left his nose, warming my scalp.

"Wanna make love?"

His erection, resting subtly against my stomach, conveyed his feelings better than words ever could.

He needed to connect. And truthfully... so did I.

"Um... no, thank you." I smiled sweetly.

Of course I did. But I wasn't letting him win just yet.

"Fair enough." His hand trailed slowly down the length of my back. Spine tingling. Emotionally charged.

I nestled into his heartbeat like it was the only thing steady in the world. As the rhythm quickened beneath my cheek, I leant back to study his face, trying to gauge what he was thinking.

The subtle flinch of his arm as it curled tighter around me felt like a quiet promise. He wasn't letting go. Not yet.

And now, it was clear. His actions today weren't about selfish stupidity. They were the overspill from my screw-up yesterday. I'd tried so hard not to fuck everything up with him. But somehow, I'd done exactly that.

I searched his expression for anger, for a hint of resentment in the line of his jaw or the tension in his brows. But instead, he gave me something I hadn't even realised I was craving.

Reassurance. That this wasn't goodbye. That we were still us.

"I'm more trouble than I'm worth, aren't I?" I said, a small smile playing on my lips, laced with the usual trace of vulnerability.

"You are trouble. No doubt." Romeo raised my chin with his thumb, brushing his lips against mine. "But you're worth it."

His hand slid around the back of my neck, thumb grazing along my jaw, sending a fresh wave of heat straight to my core.

The cool scent of mint from his nicotine gum lingered in my nose—a quiet sign he was trying.

Addictions had their place. But not here. Not in this moment.

The kiss that followed wasn't rushed—it was deliberate. A slow, hungry exploration.

His fingers tangled in my hair. Our breaths mingled. The press of his mouth deepened with quiet desperation, and the tension between us melted into something molten and familiar. The kind of kiss that didn't need words. The kind that only ever meant one thing.

He peeled the tie of my robe, letting the fabric fall from my naked body, his hands possessive as they mapped my curves.

"Lie down and let me show you how sorry I am."

Without hesitation, I complied. This was what I'd wanted in the first place.

He grasped my foot, brought it to his lips, and planted soft kisses along the arch, tingling a line straight through me, before taking my big toe into his mouth. His tongue swirled lazily, teasing—sending a delicious jolt of sensation straight between my legs.

A sinful smirk tugged at his lips as he trailed slow, lingering kisses up my calf, each one fanning the flames of deeper need.

By the time he reached his destination, I was already writhing beneath him.

He inhaled deeply against my inner thigh, the warmth of his breath setting fire to my heightened skin.

"Hmm. Someone's already been here this mornin'," he murmured, his voice a low vibration that sent a shockwave through me.

I bit my lip. "Yeah... he was such an arsehole."

"Oh yeah?"

His hand slid across my knee, snaking beneath to grip my rear with one hand while stroking his cock with the other.

His fingers explored with confidence, slipping beyond the curve to tease the crack, tracing the soft, puckered entrance of my hole.

"But was he sexy as hell?"

I tilted my head, pretending to think. "I mean... sure, if you're into arseholes."

His eyes darkened, jaw tightening, as the swollen heat of his cock pressed firmly against my slick entrance. The weight of him alone sent a shiver up my spine, anticipation pooling low in my belly.

"Oh, I am. Your *arse*hole is my favourite."

Everything about this moment coiled my spring of desire. His handsome face. His self-assured masculinity. Him.

He continued, "But this *arse*hole really wants to make you feel good. You okay with that?"

My breath caught.

The air between us hummed with tension.

The morning was breaking. Birds awakening.

Life opening its eyes beyond our room.

I nodded, unable to form words—desperate for the connection.

He dragged the engorged head along my folds, slow and careful, the tip slickening with each pass.

Parting me slightly, then pulling away.

Teasing. Torturing.

My body arched, pulse pounding, hips chasing him instinctively.

His pupils were blown wide, black with lust, his restraint hanging by a thread.

Then it snapped.

With one deep thrust, he filled me entirely, stretching me to the edge of breaking. A moan tore from his throat as he rocked into me—each stroke deliberately designed to leave an ache.

The sound of wet friction grew louder, more urgent, matched only by the ragged rhythm of our breath and the squeak of the mattress beneath us.

His hands caught my wrists, pinning them above my head. The pressure of his hold made my pulse thrum against his grip as his mouth hovered over mine, breath hot, sweet.

My tongue tingled against the salt of his skin as I kissed the hollow of his shoulder, the comfort of it colliding with something addictive.

He withdrew to the tip, making me gasp. His gaze flicked between my eyes, watching me fall apart beneath him, his voice thick and low.

"Tell you what…" he murmured, his cock twitching in his fist as he pulled away entirely,

"I'm gonna lick this tight little pussy…" He dragged two fingers through my wetness and sucked them clean. "…and while I do it, I'm gonna stroke my dick—just thinkin' about how fuckin' sweet you taste."

A wicked smirk played on his lips as he slid down my body, his hands gripping my thighs and spreading me wide for him.

The rough stubble of his cheeks against my heated flesh sent my senses into overdrive.

Then his tongue met my clit, and I almost shattered.

With expertise only held by a man like him, he licked and flicked my swollen, damp flesh, each rhythmic stroke teasing until my breath hitched. The wet, sticky sound of my arousal against his tongue was louder than it should've been, like my body was betraying my every secret.

It wasn't long before I was gasping for air, toes curling, heart hammering against my ribcage.

His jaw tightened.

"This greedy little cunt is so sweet. You wanna come for me, Queen?"

I nodded, thighs trembling, body wound so tight I thought I might snap.

Romeo sat back on his heels, gripping his cock at the base—thick, engorged, and leaking a heavy bead of pre-come.

"Play with your pussy. Let me watch you."

The demand sent a shiver through me.

My orgasm loomed dangerously close, but I wanted him to give me that pleasure, not my own hand.

Still, I indulged him.

My palm dragged over my breast, down the curve of my bump, fingers settling just above my pubic bone.

Poised, I traced slow, calculated circles over my swollen clit, mimicking the rhythm he'd set moments ago.

Romeo groaned, tilting his head back, eyes fluttering shut as he stroked himself—matching my pace.

When he looked at me again, hunger darkened his gaze. But he didn't let himself go.

Instead, he lowered his mouth between my thighs once more, flattening his tongue against me. I couldn't hear anything but the echo of my own gasps, the rising tide in my ears like a warning I was about to break.

Slow, lazy circles sent heat pooling in my belly, coaxing my climax to the surface.

I gasped as liquid pleasure shot from me, splashing against his waiting tongue. He groaned against my flesh, pressing one final kiss there, and my entire body convulsed—ears ringing from the force of release.

The tumbling of the ocean beyond our bubble poured back into the moment, its rhythm syncing with the rise and fall of our bodies.

When I came back to myself, Romeo lay beside me in quiet contemplation, his erection still thick and stiff against his stomach.

"Hey," I murmured, fingers skimming over his abs.

A lingering musk of sex and sweat filled the air—a sweet, perfectly salty mix.

He smirked, eyes glinting with satisfaction.

"So… was it good?" he asked, hopeful.

His chest rose slowly as he breathed through the tension, the sheen of exertion catching the light across his stomach.

"Mm-hm." I mirrored his grin, then glanced down at the evidence of his restraint. "Wait. Did you not come?"

His hands gripped the sheet tighter.

"Nah. I wanted to give you my love. This can wait."

The almost inaudible catch in his throat matched the hitch in mine.

I sat up, brow arching in confusion.

"Wait. You chose not to nut?"

His hands tucked behind his head, the picture of smug self-control. "Can't lie. It's the hardest thing I've ever done."

Something about the way his cock lay heavy against his stomach, thick and flushed and pulsing, had me licking my lips without thinking.

"Careful, Queen," he warned, voice tight with restraint. "It's one rub against the sheets from goin' off. I'm layin' real still here."

That only spurred me on.

He'd given me pleasure so selflessly—now I wanted to return the favour.

My fingers curled around his length, guiding the tip between my moistened lips.

I kissed the head first, slow and reverent, before taking him fully to the back of my throat.

Thick veins skimmed the swell of my lips as I pushed him all the way back.

The moment I did, he came with a ragged growl.

"Fuck." His hips thrust on their own. "That's it. Swallow it all, baby. Holy fuckin' shit."

His entire body tensed as he pulsed against my tongue, thick ropes of release spilling into my throat.

His large hand cradled the back of my head as I swallowed every drop, milking him until he had nothing left to give.

When I finally withdrew, I licked my lips, watching his chest rise and fall with heavy, satisfied breaths.

A wicked grin spread across his face.

"You're a sexy slut, Chloe Giannetti."

I kissed his soft lips, tasting the tang of my own arousal. I could smell myself on his breath, the scent musky and unmistakable. "Are we friends again?"

He swatted my arse. "Looks like it, don't it?"

◆ ◆ ◆

"Hurry up, woman. I got places to go and shit to do."

Romeo stood by the door of our suite, repeatedly checking his diamond-encrusted wristwatch. The metallic clink of the steel links, a warning shot of his growing impatience.

Face to face with the weathered wood of the bathroom stall, I relished the final trickle spiralling down the toilet bowl.

"I said give me a minute! Can't a girl pee in peace?"

His voice crept closer with every warning stride of his sneakers across the suite.

"Only if it's on my face. Now hurry your ass up!"

My bladder had officially become my worst enemy, dragging me to the bathroom every hour. I heaved myself upright, the weight of my pregnancy tugging at the chords of my spine.

Eventually, I reemerged, smoothing down the hem of my summer dress. A little sweaty for no reason whatsoever.

"Okay, I'm here. Where are we going?"

He patted the side of his nose with a grin, unusually playful considering the urgency in his tone a minute ago.

"You'll see. Come on."

With my hand locked firmly in his, we walked in sync toward the mystery location, drifts of sand creating a textured crunch beneath my sandals. Something about the energy in his stride sent butterflies flitting through my stomach.

After a short stroll beneath the palm trees folding in the breeze, he came up behind me and covered my eyes with his broad hands.

"No peekin'. I'll direct you."

Not a hint of tobacco laced his fingers. Had it really taken our argument for him to start tackling his addictions seriously?

Naturally, I placed my hands on top of his for balance.

"Don't let me fall, Romeo. I mean it."

He huffed against my ear. "As if I would. Now shut up and concentrate."

One step. Two. Three—

The surface beneath my feet shifted.

The ground no longer felt like gritty sand, but something smoother. Almost water-like.

"Are we at the beach?"

The encroaching sounds of rolling waves crashing against the shore were a dead giveaway, coupled with the freshness of the cooling spray as the air carried skin-quenching dew.

"Shh. No questions."

I tried prying his cologne-scented fingers from my face—the same scent he'd slapped onto his neck earlier now flooding my senses all over again.

"Romeo, I don't like this. I need to see where I'm going!"

"Be patient. We're here now." He peeled his hands away. "Open your eyes."

My lids flickered open—and my jaw slackened, shoulders slumping as my heart swelled.

Right in front of me, just beyond my strappy sandals, was a candlelit pathway. The heated wicks infused citronella into the air, battling the strength of the warm wind.

The handmade trail, curving in its haphazard nature, led to the small dock we were now all too familiar with—thanks to yesterday's disastrous excursion. But this time, a quaint wooden rowboat bobbed on the surface at the very end.

Palm fronds rustled gently behind us, while the boat's mooring ropes groaned softly, stretched tight with expectation. Painted in blue and white stripes, weathered in her long service, she waited patiently for us to embark.

I turned to Romeo, who smirked at my speechlessness.

"Did you set this up?"

He shrugged, casual as ever in moments like this.

"Figured since part of this trip was supposed to be our honeymoon, we should actually spend some time doin' somethin' before we leave tonight."

Leave? Tonight?

"Wait… it's safe for us to go home!?" The excitement in my voice surprised even me.

He nodded, a flicker of relief softening his features—clearly, he felt the same way.

I took a moment to scan our surroundings, soaking in the romantic scenery my husband had gone out of his way to organise.

Flickering candlelight reflected off the ocean, which seemed to calm in our presence. The sky, painted in rich hues of purple and gold, offered an enticing backdrop to his creation. The gentle lull of the waves invited us in, promising us a safe trip.

It was… perfect.

The dock creaked beneath my feet as our familiar local friend—the same guy from yesterday—stood at the boat's edge, gripping tightly to keep her from drifting away.

"Come on, Queen." Romeo took my hand, leading me forward. "Let me take you on a boat again. This time, without my brother."

A thought crossed my mind. An image too funny not to laugh at. A snort escaped. I stifled it with my fingers.

He turned back to look at me. "What the fuck you gigglin' at?"

I bit my lip. "Oh, nothing."

Romeo narrowed his eyes with mild annoyance. Clearly, he didn't like being left in the dark any more than I did.

"Nah, that ain't nothin'. Tell me."

I shook my head, shoulders trembling with restrained laughter.

"It's just—" I exhaled sharply through my nose. "I can't stop picturing you spinning in circles on that damn pedalo yesterday."

His expression darkened, but the twitch at the corner of his mouth betrayed him.

"You really gonna bring up my worst moment when I'm tryin' to start somethin' romantic with you?"

I wiped the corner of my eye, brushing away the tear my laughter had produced. "It wasn't your worst moment. Just... top three."

Romeo threw his leg over the side of the boat and dropped into his seat with a little too much enthusiasm, rocking the bow from side to side.

"Whoa, sir! Please be careful," our guide warned, grabbing for the rail. "Too much water in boat and she'll sink!"

But Romeo wasn't paying him any attention. His gaze was locked on my mouth, tracking every twitch as I fought—and failed—to stifle my laughter.

"You're still gigglin'," he muttered, adjusting his grip on the oars. "What's so funny about it?"

Lowering myself into the seat opposite him, the soft creak of the wood echoed beneath me. A hint of rope resin clung to the air as we drifted.

I caught the glint in his eyes and cracked a full smile. I couldn't hold it in any longer.

"I'm sorry, Romeo, but watching you spin in circles on that pedal boat was hilarious."

He grumbled under his breath, the sinew in his forearms tightening as his knuckles whitened around the oar handles.

"You know the steerin' cable was cut? Tommy reckons sabotage."

Just like that, it wasn't funny anymore.

The lightness in my chest shrivelled, replaced by a sinking pressure—like the tide dragging something precious from right under me. The gentle lap of water against the hull filled the sudden silence.

My amusement dropped, replaced by a hard thud of unease in my chest. "Wait. Are you serious?"

"Accordin' to him, yeah. Said it looked tampered with." He shrugged, too casually for my liking. "But I figured it was nothin' to sweat about. If you're tryin' to kill someone, there's way better ways than that."

Oh, no.

My stomach twisted, the memory of yesterday's laughter curdling into something far more sinister.

"I'm glad I only just found this out now, as we're leaving tonight. God... I would've worried the whole time."

He nodded. "Why do you think I didn't tell you?"

A thoughtful quiet stretched between us, heavy with the weight of what might've happened, had the sabotage gone as planned. The ocean felt unnervingly still, as though it, too, were reflecting.

Romeo picked up the pace, slicing through the water with strong, deliberate strokes. Each rotation pulled us farther from shore, the oars dipping and lifting with rhythmic precision.

I stared out at the horizon. The sky bled streaks of burnt orange and lilac, the ocean reflecting back the twilight like melted glass.

"Such a beautiful view, isn't it?"

His brows pinched. "Yeah. It is," he said with sarcasm. "Missed out last time on account of someone tryin' to kill me."

My head snapped in his direction, eyes narrowing.

"Don't talk about that now—especially not while we're in the middle of the ocean!"

He slowed his rhythm, glancing over my shoulder.

"Chloe. We can still see our guy smilin' and wavin' at us. We're a few hundred yards out, if that."

I ignored his petulance and sighed, dreamily trailing my fingers across the water's crystal-clear surface. It shimmered like a mirror.

"God, I love it out here. I wonder if we'll see a dolphin again—"

Oops. Shit. I didn't mean to say that.

Fuck, fuck, fuck.

His oars stilled. The boat swayed in place. The slosh of water went quiet. The creak of damp wood filled the sudden stillness.

"A dolphin?"

"Um…" I tucked a wind-swept strand of hair behind my ear, stomach lurching at the reminder that we were very much away from the safety of land.

"Yeah…"

"So while I was back on that fuckin' beach, you were out here gettin' fingered by my brother while watchin' dolphins. How fuckin' romantic."

I glared at him, exasperated. He was practically leaning over the side to get away from me.

"Romeo, you already know there was no fingering going on!"

"Hmm." He kept his eyes on the horizon. "That's what they all say."

I smacked his thigh, slick and tense from rowing.

"Anyway, isn't this supposed to be a romantic boat ride? You're ruining it!"

The wind kicked up, swirling across the surface. His curls bounced over his forehead, retreating with the breeze.

The hairs on my arms lifted. Suddenly, I was as cold as the atmosphere my husband was creating.

"Jeez, this is the first time I've wished I had a jacket on this island." I rubbed my arms.

He didn't miss a beat, grabbing the oars again and rowing faster—like he was racing Dan all over again.

"Do you want my vest?"

I frowned, trying to work out if he was serious. I pinched the damp fabric between my fingers, brushing his skin.

"Is this a thermal vest?"

His muscles bunched with each pull. Veins throbbed down his forearms. He flicked me a glance. "Err, no. Why?"

I rolled my eyes, letting the cotton fall back onto his shoulder.

"Because I'm trying to understand how you think a sweaty vest is going to keep me warm."

For the second time, he stopped rowing. This time, clearly over it.

"Whatever. We're at the right spot now."

My eyes darted side to side. "Huh?"

I scanned the view. Nothing but open sea. A single buoy bobbed lazily in the distance.

"What do you mean?"

Romeo rose slowly, feet shoulder-width apart, careful not to rock the boat. The soaked wood groaned beneath him.

Then, from his waistband, he pulled out a gun.

The gun.

My stomach flipped.

Wait—what is this?

Was he going to kill me? Had the honey trap incident fucked him up that badly?

Had he brought me out here to kill us both?

Romeo and Juliet style?

My hands shot up instinctively. Panic scorched my windpipe. "Oh my God, what are you doing!?"

My skin prickled. Salty ocean spray chilled the heat in my cheeks. My hand found my baby, instinctively guarding him.

His brows furrowed as he followed my gaze to the weapon.

"What the fuck is wrong with you, Chloe? You think I'm gonna shoot you?"

The knot in my chest loosened.

"Well, you dragged me out to sea, got mad at me, and now you've pulled a gun!"

Even the wind seemed to still. The boat rocked gently beneath us. Nature, too, held its breath.

A low chuckle rumbled from his chest. "I guess when you put it like that…"

He wiped the Glock down with his vest—handle, barrel, trigger—then tossed it into the ocean.

Plop. A ring of ripples shimmered outward, vanishing fast, like it never existed. The surface swallowed it whole.

Silence followed.

"I just needed to get rid of it. Can't take that on the flight home, Queen."

Appalled, I leaned over the edge. The rim of the boat dug into my knees, stopping me from tipping any further.

"You just threw fifty grand into the ocean? Are you mad?"

He smiled faintly, indifferent. "Mad enough to have married you, yeah."

I huffed, looking away, unimpressed. "Hilarious."

The lull returned. Water lapped gently, rocking us softly—like the world just wanted us to stop fighting and rest.

"Wait. You brought me out here just to get rid of that gun? You used me as a cover?"

He shrugged, unapologetic.

And just like that, it clicked.

The candlelit pathway. The fake urgency. The doting show in front of the boat guy.

All a performance.

My voice rose, disbelief rising with it. "So the whole romantic gesture was just a fucking act?"

He didn't flinch. "Would've looked real suspicious if I went out alone."

I turned away from him. Knees. Shoulders. The whole lot. Seething. My thoughts flicked back to the last time I was out here... with Dan. I half-expected to see his reflection in the water's sheen as I peered over the edge again.

But the man staring back wasn't Dan.

It was Romeo.

My husband. The man who bent the world to his will. Even the sea. It moved for him. Reacted to him. Worshipped him.

Dan had given me peace. Reflection. Romeo? He stirred the elements. Woke them. Commanded them. The waves slapped harder against the sides of the boat, splashing onto my thighs like the ocean itself was taking his side.

Dan suddenly seemed like the safer option. But safer didn't always mean better. I knew that.

Didn't I?

It was hard to remember how he'd treated Britney when he'd always been so gentle with me. Something my husband could learn from.

I swiped the water off my thighs. "Take me back. Now, you arsehole!"

He exhaled like I'd asked for the moon, then repositioned himself at the oars. "Sure."

What I wanted then was an apology. A shift in mood. A glimmer of softness.

But nothing with Romeo was ever that clear-cut.

We hadn't spoken a word since Romeo's little revelation, but as we neared land, the same dock worker waving cheerfully, I knew we needed to talk.

"Why did you think it was okay to use me like that? I'm about to be the mother of your child."

Romeo kept his focus on rowing, his smoker's lungs working overtime to maintain speed and rhythm.

"Funny you ask, 'cause I was wonderin' why you thought it was okay to try and trap me. I'm about to be the father of your child."

We glared at one another, neither backing down.

Our friend at the dock grabbed the side of the boat and dragged us in.

"Ahh, welcome back! Did madam and sir have a wonderful time?"

Neither of us answered. Our shared frustration had climbed to the top of the list.

Romeo climbed out first, athletic enough to sway the boat gently, his feet landing with a splash and a thump on the shore. Then, almost begrudgingly, he turned and offered me his hand.

"Come on, woman. I don't got all day."

I shot him a look but took the familiar heat of his coarse palm, letting him help me onto the crisp warmth of the sand before pulling away almost immediately.

The faint shuffle of his sneakers through the sandy decking created a soft, percussive rhythm—echoing the tension still hanging between us.

Romeo finally spoke.

"I met fire with fire. I'm sorry," he mumbled.

The island listened—only a whisper in the wind rustling the leaves.

I waited for more.

But that was it. The apology I wanted, just not quite the delivery I'd hoped for.

Did I even have a right to feel this hurt when I'd betrayed his trust so much deeper? Or was now the perfect time to call a truce?

I took a cleansing breath, exhaling the weight of my emotional back catalogue through my nostrils.

"I'm sorry too."

Leaning against the closed apartment door, he reached for my hand. He kissed my wedding band like it still meant something. Then pulled me in—his dewy lips brushing mine.

"Let's pack our shit and go home."

◆ ◆ ◆

The four of us sat in silence inside our private booth in the airport VIP lounge, waiting for our flight.

Nothing about the island remained. The air was clinical—cleaning products and artificial sweetness masked the life we'd just left behind. And honestly? I almost missed the sunscreen argument, if only for the delicious smell of heated lotion on Romeo's sunburned skin.

Two chairs faced two. Britney and I sat side by side, as far from Dan as the booth would allow. Neither of us had spoken a word to him since his night with the honey trapper. Girl code came first—even before my tangled history with him. And I hadn't exactly been subtle about it. A few side-eyes had made my position clear.

Britney twirled her hair, staring at the man she loved. The man who didn't love her back.

I wanted to reassure her. To tell her Dan would come around. But the more I watched him not give a shit, the less hope I had—and the tighter my fists curled.

Romeo tried to catch my eye more than once. I refused to look. We'd made peace, technically, but my anger toward Dan had started to bleed into how I felt about my husband. Especially after the boat ride. Maybe it wasn't fair. But pregnancy made me raw. And if Romeo wanted things back on track, he'd have to try harder.

"Chloe, come sit over here with me." His voice cut across the lounge, low and commanding. He dragged a chair out beside him, the legs screeching like cat claws on tile. A smirk ghosted his mouth—already trying to move past our latest squabble. But he knew better than to expect me to make it easy.

I gripped the armrests of my chair. "No thanks. I'm sitting with Britney. She needs my support right now."

I threw a pointed look at Dan, who still wouldn't meet my eyes. Typical.

Romeo frowned. "What about the flight?"

I let the question hang. "You sit with *him*. I'll sit with Britney."

His nostrils flared. Then his fist slammed the table. The crumpled tissue box toppled over with a soft, defeated crash.

"No."

Dan folded his arms. Britney flinched. I didn't.

"Yes," I shot back, crossing one leg over the other.

The air con kicked in with a low hum, reacting to the rising heat. A distant tannoy announced final calls.

Romeo's glare sliced the space between us. "I said. No."

I rolled my eyes, letting it land for Britney's benefit. I had to win this—for her. To show her that if she took up my offer, I'd protect her at the club. If I could handle Romeo, I could handle anything.

"Why do you even care?" I tugged the hem of my dress lower. Too much thigh gave too much of me away. And right now, he didn't deserve it.

His jaw ticked. He dropped an elbow to his knee, leaning in, voice a husky rasp.

"Because I ain't stopped thinkin' about when you played with my dick under that blanket. You best believe I'm waitin' on part two."

My eyes darted to the outline in his shorts—slightly thicker down the thigh. My mouth betrayed me, filling with saliva like I was about to suck the world's last ice lolly.

Of course, that was the reason. Not because he missed me. Not because I gave him strength. Nope. Dick overruled head. Every. Damn. Time.

Dan clocked the shift in Romeo's shorts and dragged his chair further away with a loud scrape.

Britney's gaze flicked toward me.

"Will you be okay sitting next to Dan, Brit?" I asked, trying to keep girl code intact.

Dan was still well within earshot. I didn't care. Not anymore.

She glanced at her fingers, knotted tightly in her lap.

"Err, I suppose."

This was going to be another long flight.

"My VIP guests, right this way!" a beautiful young woman called across the gate area.

The sea of passengers parted. Romeo took the lead, gripping my hand. Always warm. Always possessive. A cocoon of heat wrapping me in our complicated tether.

At the plane entrance, the flight attendant beamed.

"Mr and Mrs Giannetti, welcome back! Please, take your seats." She gestured toward the very front.

Swirls of rose and soapy amber clung to the air like a perfumed wall. Custom-made for the airline's elite.

I offered a polite smile and slid into the window seat—same as last time. Romeo dropped beside me with no regard for space whatsoever.

I scowled, yanking the trapped hem of my dress from under his thigh. "Can you be more careful, please?"

He eyed the rise and fall of my chest, clocking how hard I was breathing. "What did I do now? We've been on this fuckin' plane for ten seconds."

Yet somehow, he'd already pissed me off.

The plane rumbled beneath our feet. Passengers settled in. This wasn't the time for another fight. Not with a connecting flight still ahead.

Despite everything—the botched deal, the robbery, Dan—I was sorry to leave the Maldives. Chaos aside, I'd needed the distance. The space to breathe.

If the cops came for me now, I'd be ready.

Who shot Saxon? Wasn't me.

When we stepped back onto American soil, I'd have my wits about me.

Britney and Dan passed by, taking their seats directly in front. Not ideal. But at least I could keep an eye on her.

I leaned into Romeo, watching the chocolate swirl of Dan's hair settle ahead of us.

"I cannot believe your brother went off with that woman," I whispered, like I was spilling tea at a gossip circle.

Romeo's eyes were shut, faking sleep.

"You women can be… persuasive."

Oh.

I jabbed him in the chest. His lids fluttered open.

"You felt tempted, Romeo?"

Did I even want to know?

He shifted toward me. The seat squeaked in protest.

"You want me to answer honestly?"

I clicked the air con button, desperate for cold. Nothing.

Oh God.

His eyes shimmered with something unreadable. My stomach tied itself in knots.

"Yes," I said, clutching my seatbelt. "Honestly. Were you tempted?"

My breath stalled. I waited.

If he said yes, I wouldn't be held responsible for what happened next.

The cabin noise swelled. Passenger voices blared like sirens. I wanted to stand up and scream: Shush! My marriage is on the line!

He studied me—eyes tracing from mine to my mouth.

Then he smiled. Shy. Boyish.

"No, I wasn't. Not even close. I used to crave women in my bed. One, then the next. But it's always been different with you."

He rewarded me with a cautious, yet handsome, smile.

I loved listening to him when he shared his vulnerable side unprompted. My tightly bunched shoulders loosened, as relaxed as a cat sunbathing in a window.

I fixed my hair. Reset myself.

"Well, I'm glad you feel that way." I smiled brightly, kissed his cheek, then nestled into his shoulder. Firm, muscular—sturdy enough to serve as a pillow. Not my first choice, but it would do.

We'd been airborne about twenty minutes when the seatbelt light finally dimmed. Romeo unlatched his belt and stood like he had somewhere urgent to be.

Feeling devilish, I couldn't resist.

"What's wrong? Do you need a poo again?" I giggled into my fingers.

He glanced over his shoulder, scanning for eavesdroppers.

"I told you. I don't poo, I shit. And when I do, it breaks the bowl. I'm a real man. Men like Daniele drop little rabbit pebbles. Your man blocks the drains."

He always had to one-up me—and this time, he won.

Dan turned in his seat, fingers gripping the headrest as he peered over with a grimace. The leather creaked. A faint trace of citrus cologne and sour tension clung to the air between us.

He didn't need to say a word. He wasn't amused.

Romeo chuckled, pleased with himself.

"Sorry, Daniele. Just sayin' it how it is. Anyway, I don't need a shit. I'm gonna speak to Tommy real quick."

As he adjusted the waistband of his shorts, the outline of his dick shifted visibly. Sometimes I genuinely wondered if it needed to be that big.

Penis aside, I was relieved our security team was flying back with us, even if it was only two of them. Romeo would be rebuilding the crew soon. I trusted him with that.

I caught his wrist. "What do you need to speak to Tommy about?"

Romeo wiggled a finger in front of my face. No tobacco residue—just nervous energy.

"None of your business. Just work shit. I'll be right back."

While he disappeared into coach to deal with whatever secrets I wasn't allowed to know, I leaned forward to check on the tension-filled couple in front of us. The recycled air had turned sickly, thick with unspoken hurt.

I just hoped she was okay.

"You alright, Brit?" I poked my head through the gap between the seats.

Soft, rosy lips curved as she leaned through the space, too.

"I'm okay, Chloe." She booped my nose. "Are you?"

"Yeah, I'm fine. I'd ask if someone else was, but… we're not talking to him, are we?"

Dan took Britney's space between the seats, his nose nearly brushing mine. Too close.

His breath smelled like melted chocolate and hazelnut whip—my favourite. Warm. Stupidly disarming.

"I'm fine, thanks, Chloe. I've already apologised to Britney. We're grabbing coffee when we get back."

I huffed.

"Because coffee cures everything," I muttered.

He smiled like he couldn't help himself.

"It sure does in my book."

Shit. He wasn't supposed to hear that.

The hairs on my neck bristled. Even the engine's hum seemed to falter. A subtle drop in pressure triggered turbulence. The cabin lights flickered.

And then—there he was.

"Oh, look," Romeo said, voice low and thunderous. "I'm gone five seconds, and she's already suckin' Daniele's limp dick. I don't know why I'm surprised."

My gaze snapped to his. I tried to see past the fury.

"Romeo, what are you talking about?"

"Forget it. I'm back now, so you can put your pussy back in your drawers."

"Mr Giannetti," the flight attendant cooed—sugar-sweet and reeking of Chanel No. 5. She leaned in close, lips glossy, inches from his cheek. "Meal service will be arriving shortly."

He nodded, brushing himself off. Like he'd won.

I narrowed my eyes.

"Did you ask her when the meal was coming while you were supposed to be with Tommy? What else have you been doing?"

He slouched into his seat with even less care than before.

"Look, you asked me to cut down on smokin'. I've only had three today. I needed to keep busy. So unless you wanna fuck, stop your whinin'."

Wow.

He was on one today.

A waft of overcooked meat and stale veg rolled down the aisle as servers emerged from behind the curtain, trays in hand, cloches steaming.

Miss Hourglass Body didn't hesitate. She made a beeline for Romeo. Her blouse gaped so wide a nipple might've grazed his fork. If she wanted him that badly, she could have him. He was a pain in the arse on a good day.

She handed me my tray as an afterthought. Tight-lipped. All business.

Hmm.

With nothing better to do, I peeled back the cloche. The flimsy plastic stuck to my fingers. Steam hit like a biohazard warning, unveiling something that barely resembled food.

Ugh.

What the hell was this?

Romeo did the same. His plate held a brown, lumpy heap that smelled vaguely sour.

"What the fuck is this shit?" he growled, snapping the lid shut.

The plastic fork bent beneath his grip. One more second and it'd snap.

"Not what you ordered?" I asked, dry as dust.

"No, it ain't! Oi—you—come here." He beckoned with two fingers toward Miss Lip Gloss, who looked like she'd reapplied just for him.

She brushed a hand over his arm. "Mr Giannetti, is everything alright?"

I was sure she'd spritzed on more Chanel, too.

He reopened the cloche. "I always get steak. Sunnyside egg. Fries. What the fuck is this?"

She winced. "That's ragu, sir."

He stabbed it with his fork and let the slop slide off.

"Rag—who? Where's my order?"

Another flight attendant joined her, clearly backup.

"Apologies, sir. There's more than one Giannetti on board. It appears your meal was given to the gentleman in front of you."

"Oh, hell no." Romeo shoved the tray away. "Daniele, give me my fuckin' steak. Now!"

But Dan didn't move. His head slumped.

Romeo stilled.

"Daniele?" he said again, quieter. He nudged his brother's shoulder.

No response.

Romeo's entire body changed. He shot to his feet. Britney stood too.

The cabin stilled. Even the wind beyond the windows halted its cheerful whistle. Waitstaff froze. Plates hung mid-air. Passengers stared.

Romeo's face drained of colour.

"Is there a doctor on board? Someone help my brother!"

He shoved past the hostess, knuckles whitening against the seatbacks.

Dan groaned faintly. "Ugh… I don't feel… well."

My heart slammed against my ribs. I couldn't move.

What the hell was happening?

Romeo's voice sliced through the stunned quiet.

"Doctor! Now!"

From the back of the aircraft, a man emerged. Business suit. Round glasses. Leather briefcase. The kind of man who'd been training his whole life for this exact moment.

"I'm a doctor. What's the problem?"

Romeo's chest heaved, rising and falling in erratic bursts. But his face remained like stone.

"My brother. He's sick."

Moments like this, seeing Romeo concerned about someone other than himself, were rare. But this wasn't just concern. This was business and family rolled into one.

A woman from the first aid team clutched a medical kit to her chest, eyes flitting between us like a cornered animal.

"Do we need to inform the captain?" she stuttered.

Dan shook his head. "No, no. I'm alright. Really."

He raised a trembling hand, a shiver running through his arm. His fingers twitched like live wires.

"I think we should?" said another.

"Please don't. I don't want to delay the flight for Chloe. She's heavily pregnant. I'll be fine..."

The woman looked at Romeo like she knew him. She probably did. He gave a single, sharp nod—enough for her.

No more questions. She backed off, allowing the Giannetti way to play out.

The doctor crouched beside Dan with clinical precision, calm and composed like we were the ones overreacting.

It was hard to hear much over the engine hum, the murmurs of curious passengers, and the occasional chime from a captain blissfully unaware of the chaos in his cabin.

I studied Romeo. His focus was absolute. The tension carved into his forehead eased—just slightly—as he watched the doctor work.

Eventually, the doctor straightened and addressed Romeo directly.

"Now, I don't want to cause panic..." He hesitated.

Romeo raised a brow.

"Without proper testing, I can't be certain." The doctor stepped closer, lowering his voice. "But between you and me. It looks like poisoning. There's an injection site on the meat." He leaned in further, practically breathing Romeo's air. "We won't know for sure without lab work, but look—right here."

Romeo lifted the plate, inspecting. His jaw flexed, the muscle twitching beneath his stubble.

"It's a good thing your brother eats slow," the doctor continued. "The effects kicked in before he could finish."

"Aight. Give it here." Romeo unfolded a napkin, carefully wrapping a slice of the tampered beef.

He scanned the cabin. The man across the aisle was staring openly. No shame.

"Mind your business," Romeo snapped.

Then, with care, he slipped the evidence into the inner pocket of his jacket, still draped over the seatback like a sleeping bodyguard.

The cabin buzzed with static energy. The kind that preceded a storm.

"So what now, Doc?" Romeo asked, running a hand through his curls.

The doctor glanced at Dan, pressing a palm to his forehead.

After a long pause, he nodded.

"If it were up to me, I'd say land the plane and get him treatment immediately. But he's refusing. Plenty of fluids and rest, and he should be stable until you land. Get him to a hospital the moment you touch down."

Romeo collapsed into the seat beside me, his body heavy with tension. It pulsed off him in waves.

I stared at him, shaken.

"That meal was yours, Romeo."

He sighed, dragging his hands down his face until they clung to his jaw. "Yeah. I know."

Tears stung my eyes. "I'm terrified someone's trying to kill you. Your jewellery was stolen. The pedalo. And now this?"

He sniffed hard, flicking the end of his nose in that cocky, gangster way he always did.

"You best know if I'd eaten that steak, it wouldn't've touched me. You see how men who poo react versus men who shit?" He smirked.

Only my husband could make jokes at a time like this.

"Romero, I have a bad stomach. I'm not deaf!" Dan called out.

Romeo ignored him.

I shook my head, needing to ground him.

"No, Romeo. You're wrong. It would've been worse for you. You heard the doctor. Dan was saved because he eats slowly. Have you seen the way you eat? You're like a wild animal."

"A wild animal with a massive dick." He grabbed his crotch—of course he did.

And somehow, God help me. Even in the middle of this chaos, his dick had started to rise from the root.

I swatted his chest. "This is not the time for jokes. I'm worried sick."

Romeo's humour might've been his shield, but I was the one absorbing all the hits.

"Relax, Chloe. Ain't no one gonna finish me."

His arrogance would be the death of him.

The pretty attendant swept past like nothing had happened, handing out in-flight snack vouchers as if the show must go on. No one—not even Dan—knew this was sabotage. And with the way Romeo worked, I knew he planned to keep it that way.

"Are you going to tell Dan the truth?"

He pressed a finger to his lips and shot a sharp glance at the back of Dan's seat.

"No. Shh."

A thought struck. I picked up the discarded menu, flipping the page.

"I know for a fact steak isn't normally on the menu. Who arranged that for you?"

His tongue skimmed his teeth, a smirk pulling at his mouth.

"The airline knows who I am. I ask, they deliver."

He shrugged like that, explained everything.

I clenched my jaw. We had bigger problems than his ego.

"So someone knew you'd be on this flight. They knew what you'd eat—and they sabotaged it. But who? Bodu Manik?"

He exhaled hard through his nose.

"Fuck knows. But it ain't for you to worry about. Tommy'll handle it."

◆ ◆ ◆

I must've dozed off, because the next thing I knew, Romeo was nudging me awake, his voice low against my ear, coaxing.

"Seatbelt, Queen. We're landin'."

Blinking through the fog of sleep, I sat up as he reached over and clicked it into place for me.

"Hi," I croaked.

He huffed, gesturing to his shoulder. "Look at this shit. You drooled all over me."

Despite the complaint, a smile threatened, but I knew him well enough to tell he wasn't best pleased. The shirt was custom-made designer.

I eyed the soggy patch and wiped the corners of my mouth.

"Oopsie." I giggled.

Ahead, Britney's soft laugh floated back, followed by the subtle shuffle of Dan's sandalled foot slipping into the aisle. A quiet reminder that he was still here. That he'd really been poisoned…

"Is Dan okay? Have you checked on him?"

Romeo tensed, his fingers curling around the headrest. "He's fine. Britney's lookin' after him."

Well. If a near-death experience wasn't enough to call it water under the bridge, I didn't know what was.

I stretched, yawning, arms raised above my head. My limbs still felt suspiciously heavy—like sleep hadn't quite let go yet. My mouth was dry. A faint buzz tingled beneath my skin.

"Jeez, I can't believe I fell asleep at a time… like… this—"

My heart stopped.

Reality struck like a bolt of lightning. My mind flickered back to the panic room.

"Wait a minute!"

The cabin tilted on its descent, air pressure shifting. I latched onto the armrests, pulse thudding in my ears. Eyes locked on Romeo as he scratched the tip of his nose. Too casual. Too telling.

"You did not sedate me!?"

A dull hum crawled beneath my skin. Familiar. Unmistakable. I knew that medicated lull.

"I needed to do it," he said. "The doc gave me a lil somethin' to slip in your drink. We both agreed the stress might put our son at risk."

"No, ass-hat," I hissed, practically panting. "You need to stop drugging me!"

He thinned his lips—more sorry I'd figured it out than sorry he'd done it.

"Let's be real, Chloe. With how anxious you get, it was best for everyone the lights went out."

For a second, I decoded that to mean: more time for him to flirt with the flight attendant. Because let's face it—my stress levels were just as high during that drug deal as they were watching Dan nearly die.

But was even Romeo that sick in the head?

"Does Tommy know what happened?"

The sorry-not-sorry look vanished. He sneered. "Why would Tommy give a fuck if I slipped you a pill?"

"No, you moron! I mean about Dan getting—" I craned my neck toward the seat in front of us. "You know... P.O.I.S—"

"Aight, Chloe. Shut up!" His eyes bore into mine.

His request for silence lasted... all of a second.

"You best keep me in the loop on this, Romeo. I mean it."

He gave a curt nod, usually his way of saying hell no.

An awkward silence floated between us.

"So... what've you been doing while I was knocked unconscious against my will?" I smiled tightly.

While I was appalled, I was also—grudgingly—grateful for the break from my own head.

Romeo smirked, gripping the crotch of his shorts.

"Jerked it a couple times."

I gasped. "No! You didn't?"

He chuckled. "Nah. I didn't. I stayed still, 'cause my pregnant wife was sleepin' so peacefully on my shoulder, and I didn't wanna wake her."

My heart softened. Just a little.

"I guess that's sweet, Mr Giannetti."

His expression shifted. More genuine now.

"The more you slept, the less you panicked. The safer you and my son were. I don't regret it."

That made me pause. In a twisted sort of way... he was right. And that was the hardest truth to swallow.

❖ ❖ ❖

The SUV ride from the airport was quiet. Reflective.

The night sky felt too dark—no moon, no stars. Just flickers of streetlight ghosting across the tinted glass.

Romeo stared straight ahead. Jaw tight. Shoulders high.

He looked how I felt.

What were we coming home to?

Would I finally feel safe now that Saxon was gone? Or was someone else already waiting in the wings?

My hands curled protectively around my stomach. No matter what happened, I'd keep my baby safe.

Romeo tapped his thigh. Steady. Measured. Deliberate. The glint of his wedding ring caught the light, and I wondered if he'd use that same hand to kill whoever sent the message.

He might've brushed off the flight incident, but sedation or not—we both knew. We were never truly free.

At least Dan was no longer our problem. Tommy had it arranged—he and Britney went straight to the hospital the moment we landed. The fact that Dan could walk reassured us all. Whatever this was, it wasn't meant to kill.

Romeo was right.

First, the stolen jewellery.

Then, the sabotaged pedalo.

Now, poison—just enough to rattle us.

It was a message.

But what the hell was it trying to say?

The more I thought about Dan's silence, choosing not to cause an emergency landing, the more my resentment softened. Maybe, deep down, he wasn't all bad. I'd check in on him at some point. But I wouldn't be stupid about it.

The SUV's blinker clicked off as we turned into the driveway.

The tyres crunched loud over gravel—announcing our return. Just one slumbering paparazzo, camera slumped against the wall.

Tommy was already there, opening Romeo's door and handing him his favourite Glock like it was a handshake.

The LA night air hit me full force. Dry. Heavy. Almost too still. Like time itself had stalled, just waiting for us to come home.

The mansion loomed tall and silent.

No cops. No handcuffs. No chaos.

Romeo tucked the gun into his waistband and exhaled, like he'd finally clicked back into himself.

He turned to me, a glint in his eye.

"You ready?"

I took his hand. Frowned. "Ready? For what?"

"Debrief."

CHAPTER 11

"Alrighty, Mrs Giannetti. Now we're back to the fabric of the building. We can do whatever your heart desires." Lucy, our interior designer, grinned—her eyes sparkling with excitement.

Buxom and apple-shaped, with breasts that led the way, she strolled into the soul of the club. The light tap of her heels against the bare concrete echoed through the expanse. The slit in her calf-length skirt revealed just enough to show the soft friction of her thighs.

With a notepad hugged to her ample chest and the tip of her personalised pen poised against her lips, she swivelled, ready for my inspiration.

"I've thought of nothing but this place," I said, following the path her footprints had carved through the settled dust.

The once stagnant air that hadn't moved since the club's closure, thick with old perfume and the ghost of sweat, had since lost its identity.

Now, with chalky walls exposed and concrete floors stained by grease and rubber, the place was barely recognisable. Tools and machinery lay piled in the corners, remnants of the contractors' work.

Strange to think it had been a couple of months since I'd last stepped foot inside. The club's original, lively atmosphere was still etched into my memory: dancing with Hanna, the thumping music vibrating through our chests, our friendship. But she wasn't someone I could think about for long without a lump catching in my throat.

I positioned myself where the central dancefloor used to be—where Saxon was last seen alive. Now stripped away. Gone. Just like him. As planned, no traces of his DNA remained. No incriminating evidence. Nothing.

Safe to say when we landed back on U.S. soil, it wasn't long before the cops showed up in a bid to seek justice for one of their own.

But true to my word—I was ready.

And guess what? They weren't.

I'd told myself so convincingly, thanks to Romeo's encouragement, that someone else pulled the trigger that night. I believed it. So much so, the cops did, too.

Of course, they didn't really suspect me, anyway. Romeo was at the top of their list, but the conviction in my voice was enough to steer them clear of both of us.

I'd finally figured out my place in my husband's world. And we were thriving.

With a new air of confidence, I turned my attention to the only window wall in the room, strolling past Lucy, who watched me attentively. The chilly breeze of the dormant space threaded through my hoop earrings as I moved toward the glass.

"Ooh, I can smell inspiration cooking, Mrs Giannetti," she said, her pen poised above the page with an edge of excitement.

Using both hands, I tugged down the old drapes—the last remnants of the club's former life. The fabric slid free like butter in a hot skillet, offering no resistance. They crumpled to the floor like theatre curtains on closing night. Final. Resigned. A chapter ending in a book no one cared to reread.

Exactly what the room had needed.

Dust plumed on impact, swirling in the sunlight like a phoenix rising from the ashes. The particles danced, catching the light before settling on the concrete like snowfall in summer.

Golden rays poured through, warming the cool bite in the air. I caught a glimpse of my reflection—and expected to see Chloe. But the woman looking back at me? She was all Jasmin.

Sure, Romeo and I had agreed she was staying in her box. But here—in my club, surrounded by people taking orders from me? She was ready. Proverbial gun: locked and loaded.

"So, no drapes?" Lucy asked, slightly confused by where I was going with this. She stepped beside me, our reflections now layered—hers seeing something entirely different.

Oaky-suede, floral undertones and a trace of leather curled through the disturbed air. That was something I loved about Lucy. Her scent. Men's cologne sometimes worked on a woman. On her, it absolutely did.

The first time we'd met, I asked her straight up if her one time with my husband was something she wanted to revisit. I soon came to learn that her experience with him reinforced her curiosity in women. But I wasn't going to tell him that.

As she stood close, shoulders brushing, it gave me nothing but reassurance. She was on my team.

Don't get me wrong. I didn't have a thing for her. Not even close. It was more a sense of relief that, while she'd been in my husband's life for a long time, there was absolutely nothing between them.

I turned on my heel, seeing the space in a whole new light.

"I have to remind myself this is still going to be a nightclub, so we'll need something for privacy. But crushed red velvet is not my style. Modern. Airy. Homely, even. That's what we need here."

A quiet dig at my husband's taste wasn't unjust. The place had once resembled something straight out of Hugh Hefner's mansion.

Lucy, always one to nod in agreement, made notes.

While she scribbled down my thoughts, the man himself strolled into the room, Tommy in tow.

Two sets of footsteps became three when Snake completed the military lineup. A sandwich manoeuvre—without me, the filling.

Absent of a heart I'd yet to revive, the building remained lifeless, and with that came an almost frosty edge to the air. The A/C hadn't worked in months, but that didn't matter. Cold was never a problem for Romeo, strolling in wearing a muscle vest and shorts. The only hint of the chill was his hardened nipples.

I couldn't feel his magnetic pull from so far away—but my skin tingled in anticipation.

"Aight boys, perimeter check and report," he ordered. His eyes swept the room, momentarily puzzled why there was so much natural light pouring in.

Tommy and Snake didn't hesitate, making an immediate about-turn.

I waited a moment, clenching my tongue between my teeth in the hopes that Romeo would leave, too.

He didn't.

"Can I help you with something?" I asked curtly. It came out more aggressive than intended, but he knew I didn't want his involvement.

He shoved one hand down the front of his shorts, adjusting himself. No fucks given.

"Security handled for openin' night. A team of eight. Should be enough."

One thing I appreciated about Romeo was how seriously he took my safety. Last thing I wanted was to get bogged down interviewing sweaty, balding men with massive egos and poor hygiene—when I could be unleashing my creativity on a project as important as this.

"Oh, okay. So we aren't using any of the new crew from home?"

Distracted, he picked up a claw hammer from the pile and started swinging it around like a nunchuck. Bruce Lee style.

"I want you safe wherever you go." He took another swing, whooshing through the air. "Two teams. One here. One at home."

Not a single familiar face remained at the mansion, since the entire crew had been wiped out at the airport. Tommy and Snake were the last men standing from the original team. Not to mention we were down to a handful of girls after we got back from the honeymoon to find an orgy in my living room.

"Thanks for sorting it, Romeo." I smiled warmly, but that smile cooled as he kept coming.

Hammer still in hand, he tapped the metal head against the unfinished wall. Plaster crumbled. Dust billowed. A mess hit the floor.

He looked down at the debris by his feet, seemingly satisfied, then swung the hammer up to rest on his shoulder. Sauntering across the room with that same sexy confidence that always caused a distraction, he began to whistle—like he'd just clocked off after a hard day's work.

None of us wanted him here, but that never stopped him. While his puckered lips played their tuneful tune, I was already planning his punishment.

"Um... what the hell are you doing?" I frowned, flicking my wrist dismissively. "Can you not go and play somewhere else, please? I'm a little busy here."

Romeo's hearing aid must've been on charge because no sooner had he entered the room than he was right by my side, soft, warm lips at my temple.

"I wanna see what you got so far." He trailed his lips down the side of my face. The fine hairs on my skin tingled as he moved lower, coming to rest at the nape of my neck.

It's amazing how much difference the wearer of a cologne can make to the experience. I'd go as far as to say Romeo and our designer were wearing a similar note—rich and musky, probably sandalwood or tobacco flower with a touch of leather—but on him, the coil of desire tightening between my thighs was impossible to ignore.

And for some reason, watching him grip a manly tool like it belonged there only piqued my interest further.

Lucy, only too happy to share our ideas, trotted the length of the room toward the area we were calling the stage.

Up a level on a newly built platform along the back wall, it would be a safer place for the girls to dance on their poles. Customers' hands well and truly kept to themselves.

"Four poles?" she asked, her steps hollowing as she ascended the two-step platform. The brush of her hand along the stainless steel handrail was rough—yet somehow silky smooth.

"Yes." I nodded, a crooked finger to my lips in thought. "And another in the private booths."

Taking three assured strides, the muted clack of her heels across the timber frame came to a halt. She placed a sticky note on the ground, marking the pole's approximate location, then took another three strides to do the same again. Her tailored suit jacket tugged slightly at the seam as she bent forward.

"If I order the poles today, they should be here next week," she mused aloud.

"I could've built that stage," Romeo muttered, slapping the flat of his palm with the hammer—loading it for another pointless swing.

Lucy continued. Focused. Unbothered.

But it wasn't long before a tattooed hand flailed in front of my face, gesticulating his point further.

"Close 'em together more and you could get another pole in that space. More pussy, more money," he added, rubbing his fingers together like he was counting invisible bills.

Neither of us listened.

Before rising back to full height, Lucy smoothed the last sticky note with a circular stroke of her fingertips. A quiet message meant just for me: my opinion mattered most.

"It's aight. Don't take my word on it," Romeo mumbled. "Not like I ain't been doin' this shit the last ten years."

The hammer was out again—tapping the timber, causing yet another distraction.

I placed my hand over his, halting him.

"Stop." My glare didn't waver. "Right now."

His pectorals twitched, sinews tightening with restraint, but he didn't retaliate. Not yet.

"Mrs G," one of the building crew hollered from across the room, just visible behind the doorframe. His voice travelled through the space, landing neatly between us—a welcome interruption. "We've got a steel going in next door. Just letting you know to expect some noise."

He was kitted out in the full works. Bright yellow hard hat, dirty overalls, boots thick with plaster dust. His skin was streaked with soot and charcoal smudges, evidence of the graft going into these renovations. I hadn't caught his name yet, but I was fairly sure he was the one running the show.

"No need," Romeo said, lifting the hammer like it proved something. "I'll fuckin' do it. Gimme ten minutes. I'll be there."

The builder looked immediately alarmed—distressed, even.

I had no choice but to step in. If Romeo got involved in something he clearly wasn't qualified for, and an altercation unfolded, the risk of him reaching for his gun wasn't just likely. It was inevitable. And if that happened, my club was in jeopardy.

"It's alright, you carry on," I called across the room. Taking Romeo gently by the waist, I turned him to face me. "My husband is needed elsewhere."

Hard hat tipped, steel-toe cap boots turned. He was gone in a flash.

"I fuckin' knew you were after my dick," Romeo said smugly, looking down at my hands on his hips. "Felt it soon as you saw me with this."

He tried to twirl the hammer's claw around his finger, but fumbled—catching it mid-air like a toddler who'd stolen a kitchen knife. One thing my husband wasn't… was a handyman.

Trying to ignore the fly in the ointment, I focused on Lucy's crowded file of fabric swatches.

Romeo, now bored, had moved on to a new toy—fiddling with something vaguely gun-shaped. Garish colours with a long nose and a metal tip. A drill, maybe?

Hunched forward, back to me, he was definitely up to something down the front of his shorts that I was trying my best to ignore.

Then, perfectly timed with the quieting of the workers around us, he snapped around on his heel, rubber soles grating against the powdery floor. With a poorly executed crossover move, he whipped out his gun and the drill from his waistband like he was in a two-gun shootout.

"Freeze, bitches!" he announced, best L.A.P.D. cop-show voice on full blast, pointing the drill like a weapon.

The real gun rested on his thigh as he pulled the trigger on the drill, revving it like a car engine. Three sharp bursts in my direction—close enough that I could smell the warm gear oil.

Lucy let out a whisper of a giggle. Shoulders dancing, fingertips to her mouth.

I shook my head, amused, but not enough to let him steal the spotlight.

"The more we pretend he isn't here," I murmured, pointing vaguely at a swatch like I was choosing it, "the sooner he'll get tired."

She nodded, lips twitching as she did her best not to laugh again, shifting her focus to the fabric under my finger.

Ramping it up a notch, it only took ten seconds before the dry scrape of churning wood set my teeth on edge. Romeo—starved of attention—had begun drilling into the base frame of the stage, bringing with it a storm cloud of plaster from the freshly skimmed wall, and a loud crack as more peeled away like banana skin.

"Jesus Christ, Romeo! What the hell are you doing!?"

Pulling the trigger again, he grinned.

"Makin' some adjustments to this shit. Whoever did it don't know shit about carpentry. They used to call me Jesus's dad at school, on account of me knowin' exactly what I'm doin'."

At this point, my temples needed a massage.

In his element, I watched in disbelief as he undid all the contractors' hard work from yesterday.

"Funny that, Joseph." Arms folded, I looked him up and down. "Because you're holding that drill the wrong way round."

He wasn't. But unskilled as I was, he still took the time to check.

Giving us both a well-earned break, I tasked Romeo with checking the fire door—because I'd heard a noise…

"I've known Romero a long time. Never have I seen him so happy. Playful. It's lovely to see." Lucy smiled at me, flipping my bad mood toward him on its head.

Romeo? Happy? He certainly did seem full of beans today.

"The baby is almost due," I offered. "Maybe the excitement's getting to him?"

Like a T-Rex in Jurassic Park, his thunderous, self-assured steps in my direction rippled water in a nearby glass.

"Door is secure, ma'am," he reported, chest puffed, waistband adjusted as he scanned the room for more imaginary threats.

Lucy had just shown me two types of silk for the private room bedsheets when—uninvited—Romeo leaned in. His tool-stained fingers reached for the fabric.

That's when I lost it completely.

I swatted his hand. Not playfully.

"Is there something you want?" I snapped, hip cocked, fist loaded.

Excited for his son or not, if he butted in again, I wouldn't be able to stop myself. I knew he was desperate to be involved, but I'd made it clear his masculine, outdated ideas weren't welcome.

He plucked an imaginary piece of lint from my shoulder and blew it off his fingertips. If I didn't know better, I'd say he was intimidated.

"Just wonderin' if you were keepin' the sports lounge," he murmured, eyes avoiding mine.

Hmm. That was a fun little discovery—stumbling across the concealed door at the back of the VIP lounge upstairs.

"Romeo, please." I rolled my eyes. "Sports? More like the bouncing titties lounge."

Who would've thought men's obsession with breasts could be so extreme they'd actually pay to masturbate over girls jumping rope and using pogo sticks in the nude?

Of course, the only remaining evidence in the now-abandoned room was a pile of gym equipment dumped in the corner. And without even needing to ask, Romeo very kindly explained their use—with a little more excitement than I would've liked.

Simple-minded, the lot of them. My husband included. Hell, he was the damn founder of the club.

He raised his hands, eyebrows to match.

"Just sayin', Queen. That room alone pulled in ten grand a night."

Indeed… I'd pay ten grand right now to shut him up. But since he found the credit card bill with two transactions to the honey trapper, he'd disabled my access indefinitely.

"This club is going to be a classy place, Romeo. Quality girls offering quality services will attract only the best clients."

He wasn't one for hiding emotions, and this was no exception.

"Oh," he said flatly.

The disappointment curled in the air and rested on the tip of my tongue. But I swallowed it with an unspoken, satisfied ahh.

"Anyway, leave me with Lucy for the next hour. We've got a lot to do today. Remember?"

He shoved his hands in his pockets.

"Yeah, I remember," he mumbled, like a kid being told what time to come in for supper.

"Go on, tell me."

This was the kind of test he usually failed, and it always ended in a fallout.

Resting back against the wall, foot propped, he toyed with his lighter—rolling it through his fingers.

"We got whores auditionin' for a spot on the poles. Then we got a session with Nelly. And err… then it's… oh yeah, baby shoppin'."

He smiled triumphantly.

Holy shit.

The smile twitching at the corners of my mouth turned into a full-blown grin. Things were really changing around here, and I fucking loved it.

"Well remembered. Did you also remember to ask Tommy to check on Britney's whereabouts? I still haven't heard from her since we landed, and I'm getting a little worried."

He scratched the tip of his nose. Then an itch to his earlobe.

"Yeah. He's workin' on it."

Lying son of a—

As if summoned, the door opened, bringing with it the obnoxious sound of drilling and banging, and the sharp scent of tree sap from freshly planed wood.

"Oh look. Here he is. I'll ask Tommy myself."

Lifting my chin, I swivelled, locking eyes with a man I now considered a friend.

"Do we need to file a missing persons on Britney?"

Tommy had an excellent poker face, but I was attuned to his micro-expressions. The widening of his eyes lasted a nanosecond, but it was there.

"No, Boss. She's been found safe and well. After her and Dan split, she left town. Nothing more to tell."

Would she really up and leave me like that, after everything we'd been through, without saying a word? A slug to the gut would've been easier to deal with than my best friend vanishing like that.

Romeo sensed my retreat. His hands found my shoulders with just enough grip—an anchor catching me before I could drift out to sea completely.

"Hey, don't sweat it, Chloe. You got a baby due any day and a club to open. Deal with your shit, then we'll deal with her. Got it?"

That was exactly what I needed to hear. He was right. I was already burning the wick at both ends.

"Err, Boss." Tommy cleared his throat, pulling me from my spiral. His voice carried with enough weight, even the walls leaned in to listen. "I came in to say the first whore is here for an audition. Waiting up in VIP."

I blinked. Slow. Steady. Letting the moment click back into place.

"Excellent." I beamed, fixing my hair. "We'll be right there."

I left Lucy to come up with ideas for dressing the windows while Romeo followed me to the staircase that led up to VIP.

"Why the hell did we decide to audition up there again?" I asked, peering up the flight like it was Mount Kilimanjaro.

With little urgency to strip away the fixtures and fittings in this part of the building, the scent of spilt beer, stale smoke, and a hint of sex still clung to the carpet. Placing my foot on the bottom step only disturbed the aroma further.

Romeo huffed, like he'd been waiting for this moment.

"We? This was all you, Queen. No fuckin' clue what goes on in your head sometimes. Come on, I'll help you."

The smirk on his face said it all: I'd made my own bed, and now I had to climb it.

I made my entrance, finally reacquainting with a room I'd waited far too long to reclaim. Dimmed lights caught the fringe of the velvet curtains, pooling warmth across the gold inlays of the walls.

An overwhelming sense of royalty surged through my veins. All that was missing were a jewelled crown and a corgi as I took my seat in what was once my husband's throne, still planted dead centre in the VIP lounge.

Almost as though it had been waiting for me. The comfort, the homeliness, the righteousness—it flooded my senses, seeping straight through to my core. This little velvety number understood who her new master was. Me.

Romeo, a little lost in his own world, dragged a stool from the far corner, the legs scraping along the carpet as he came to sit beside me. A minty hue of nicotine gum wafted my way as the little pellet tumbled around his mouth.

Was he anxious? Nothing about this arrangement was the norm for him. But credit where due—he was sticking to his word. Letting me have my moment.

Tommy waited patiently for my cue. Any minute now, I'd give him the nod.

But not just yet. I needed to feel the tatty carpet beneath my feet, the way it now belonged to me.

The air was mine.

The space was mine.

The smell… hmm. Maybe not the smell.

Romeo could have that.

Sex, drugs, alcohol, and cigarettes would most certainly be replaced with florals and freshness. Maybe an air purifier or two…

The nod came before I'd consciously acknowledged it.

Show time.

Tommy opened the glass double doors wide, allowing entry to a petite, dark-haired woman with thick curves and even denser confidence. A bralette top, schoolgirl skirt, with knee-high socks, and hooker heels were her offering.

I was instantly interested.

The sashay in her walk as she made a beeline for the space in front of me whispered of experience—like she'd walked this runway a thousand times before.

Gripping the throne's arms, I stood instantly. And when I say instantly,

I mean like instant coffee: after the long boil of the kettle, followed by the slow pour into the mug. Yes, Romeo helped hoist me to my feet. But besides that—I made my point effectively.

She looked at me. Dark eyes, almost black under the dimmed lighting, with thick eyeliner that didn't do her features justice. Her silhouette stretched long across the deep ruby-red carpet, shadows exaggerating her legs, her curves—like she'd already learned how to weaponise her image.

She was trying to intimidate me. But that wasn't going to happen. Not in my club.

"Name?" I asked, my tone guarded, and for a calculated reason.

"Diamond Daisy, ma'am," she said, voice more melodic than I'd expected based on her entry. "Or Double D's, for short."

I huffed, hands on hips. The pet name matched her ample breasts, and I knew Romeo had already added her to his sports lounge list of maybes.

"One thing you need to learn very quickly, Miss Daisy…" I paused, letting the silence press against her. "…is that this club is mine. I will be your boss."

I let that sit, like sand running through the timer. One grain after the next, each a measure of my wearing patience.

Tilting my head, I pointed vaguely in Romeo's direction. "And this guy right here? My husband. Nothing to you. Got it?"

As if summoned, Romeo rose from his stool, adjusting the waistband of his shorts—revealing not only his imposing height, his beautifully sculpted body, and his ample bulge, but something even more disarming.

His gun.

And just like that… it gave me an idea.

Flashing him a warm smile, I made a calculated attempt to lure him into my trap. Snaking my hand from his chest southward, the waistband of his shorts shifted beneath my tease, his muscles tightening in anticipation. His cock swelled gently against the seam, no doubt expecting I was about to suggest a threesome.

Instead, I curled my fingers around the skin-warmed metal handle of his gun. Not a drill this time. Most certainly the real thing.

His breath caught—just a flicker—but it was all I needed.

He wasn't in control anymore.

I was.

Taking my seat without an ounce of hesitation, I rested my arm along the throne's edge, the barrel of the gun pointing her way. And just like that, she stood taller. More serious.

Now I understood. Now it all made sense.

"Okay, first thing—I already have a team of girls. All I'm looking for is one or two sprinkles for my fairy cakes. Tell me, are you a sprinkle?"

Romeo released a soft chuckle.

Instantly, the barrel swung in his direction.

"What!?" I hissed under my breath.

He placed his hand over mine, steadying it and guiding the aim back toward our guest.

Leaning closer, his lips brushed my ear. "I was just thinkin' how different we handle shit. Sprinkles… was funny is all."

I let out a forced laugh for Double D's benefit, then gave him a sly dig in the ribs.

"You'll be waiting outside if you mock me again."

"Sheesh," he grumbled, rubbing the invisible wound. "You got real mean these last few weeks."

He reached for his neck out of habit, searching for the heavy platinum chain that wasn't there, courtesy of the thief back in the Maldives. His hand dropped, settling into a restless fidget.

"As I was saying…" I refocused on her. "Are you my sprinkle? Or are you more of an egg, flour, sugar, etc.?"

Romeo gave me a puzzled look. But that was only because he wanted her to get her tits out already.

I needed more than that. I needed to know if she could offer my clients something worth paying for.

"I can be your sprinkle, ma'am," she said, her gaze flicking to the weapon every few seconds.

"Tell me—what's your background? Sex worker? Stripper?" I kept just enough grip on the handle to let Romeo know he dared not try to take it back. I meant business.

Still a little restless in my peripherals, I cast him a sharp glance, expecting resistance. But instead, his expression was warm, almost inspired.

Which only spurred me on.

"Well, ma'am," she replied with a stutter. Someone had just lost a few kilos of confidence. "I used to work the poles here—a few years back."

Hmm. Interesting.

"Did you fuck this one?" I asked Romeo, nodding toward her.

He seemed more focused on the twitch of my fingers wrapped around his firearm than on the girl in front of us.

"Huh?" he said, brows pulling together.

"Did you, Romero Giannetti, fuck her—Dangerous Dan?"

We both cracked a smile at the impromptu dig. She didn't really deserve it... but I was having too much fun.

"I ain't gonna lie. I don't recall... ma'am," he said, playing along.

I turned back to our auditionee. Brow arched, I crossed one leg carefully over the other. The fine grit of stubble rasped as calf met shin—less silk, more sandpaper. A not-so-subtle reminder that my last shave was a distant memory.

"Well? Did you sleep with him?"

Her eyes dropped to the floor, fingers fidgeting, unsure where to land.

"No, ma'am."

Did I believe her? I mean, let's face it. He'd probably slept with the throne my arse was currently nestled into.

But did I care? Not really.

"Alright, Daisy." I adjusted my position so the dim overhead lighting hit the cold metal of the gun. "Show me what you've got."

She strode toward us, heels digging into the carpet, curving softly toward Romeo.

"Woah, woah. Hold on a minute! What are you doing?" I raised my hand like I could shove her back with an invisible force alone.

"I was... going to give your husband... a lap dance?" Her eyes darted between us, searching for approval.

Romeo leaned in again, this time with the courtesy of letting me lead.

"She's here for club work, Chloe. Poles, laps—that's the deal. This ain't like an audition back home."

Shit.

"I wondered why you'd got yourself all cosy next to me. Hoping for a lap dance, were you? Dream on, ass-hat."

His smirk was all the confirmation I needed.

I hated to admit it, but he was right. She'd come here for reasons beyond what I was used to. And while the poles hadn't even been ordered yet, someone's lap would have to do.

"Tommy!" I yelled—loud enough to carry.

The glass door swung open almost instantly. Firearm drawn, he entered with slow, calculated steps. Eyes wide, adjusting to the shift in lighting.

"Boss?"

Without needing to speak, a skill Romeo had mastered, he raised a hand and silently commanded Tommy to lower his weapon.

"Tommy," I said sharply, clicking my fingers. "We need to borrow you. Take a seat on Romeo's stool."

For some reason, Romeo took offence.

"Get your own goddamn seat." He pointed at the stacked stools by the railing.

Tommy blinked slowly, like a stunned owl—each lid operating on a different timer. Conflicted and confused, he unhooked the tangled legs of one stool and did as instructed.

Seated centrally now, legs parted, Tommy perched awkwardly as Diamond Daisy placed her feet shoulder-width apart in front of him. Breasts jutted forward, back arched.

Settling in for the show, the only thing Romeo and I were missing was a bowl of buttery popcorn.

"Who's been a bad, bad boy?" she purred, her voice curling around the room like smoke. It licked its way along my thighs, let alone Tommy's.

I shot Romeo a look. If his cock was hard, my fist would be hitting his nose. Fortunately, his gaze was locked on me.

Hmm. Good choice.

Double D's, true to her name and nature, teased her audience with a cheeky button pop of her skirt, revealing a glimpse of her completely bald pussy.

Tommy seemed a fan. I'd never seen him so... still.

One hooker heel lifted and settled in the gap between his open thighs, resting on the edge of the seat. Her bare toes didn't quite touch his cock—but almost.

It felt all kinds of wrong seeing our most respected security guy sitting there with a full-blown hard-on. But it was the first time in a long time he looked like he was enjoying himself.

Miss Daisy wasn't done. With a flawless head roll, her long brown locks whipped into a full 360 before settling to frame her face. A coy lip bite preceded a spin-slut-drop combo that had me checking Romeo's face again.

Safe to say, my husband wasn't risking anything. His focus stayed squarely on my cleavage the entire time.

Good boy.

By the time I refocused, she'd removed her skirt and was face to face with Tommy—riding his thigh in nothing but a thong and bra. Her lips hovered near his, close enough to tease, never quite making contact.

My lip caught between my teeth. Watching her move filled me with a rush of excitement for the club's future. More women like her, and I'd be up there with the best female club owners in the country.

As the possibilities flooded in, my whole body relaxed: shoulders, thighs, even my fingers sinking into the chair like it was made of jelly.

But just as she hit her rhythm, Romeo cut in, halting her mid-motion.

"Aight, that'll do, Titties. I don't want my best security gettin' his nut on the job."

Slumped in my seat, I straightened my spine. Snapping back to reality, I cleared my throat, mind instantly made up.

"You're hired," I said—only then realising I'd completely let go of the gun.

Daisy dressed quickly and bowed to her master.

Me.

"I need a dancer who's happy to take it all the way—if the client pays the right price. You'll have top-tier medical insurance, regular health screenings, security on standby, flexible shifts, and a 60/40 profit split. Look after me, Daisy, and I'll look after you." My words hit harder than the building work echoing around us.

Her eyes glistened. "Perfect," she said, bowing again. This time with her eyes fixed on my trigger finger.

"I want you here for opening night. You'll get the full details in a text. Any questions?"

"No, ma'am."

"Great. You can leave now."

I let the moment settle, giving the testosterone time to drop and the erections time to soften.

Tommy followed her out—almost sprinting. He didn't speak. Just adjusted his belt and disappeared down the stairs like his life depended on it. The rattle of the glass as the doors shut said more about the effectiveness of the gun in my hands than anything else.

Then I turned to him.

Romeo.

"All right. Show me your dick," I said, voice clipped, eyes menacing. My loosening fingers tightened again, grip re-finding the trigger.

Of course, he didn't hesitate.

Ugh. Hard. As expected.

"Listen, Chloe." He shifted on his stool. "Before you start thinkin' this woody's got somethin' to do with her—it ain't. My dick got hard the minute you pulled my gun out."

His eyes lowered, not to the weapon but to the way I held it. Like it had belonged to me all along.

Unspoken, he dropped to his knees in front of me, hitching the hem of my dress up my thighs—igniting my skin like flames dancing on an oiled surface.

Well. If this wasn't a complete image swap...

The VIP lounge had a new star of the show. Its predecessor

relinquishing control like he'd been waiting for this moment.

Peeling down my panties—first to my knees, then to my ankles—he ran the tip of his nose along my inner thigh. His breath warmed the skin just above my clit. A single exhale that made my thighs twitch.

"I love this sweet pussy," he murmured.

The low rumble of his voice vibrated through my skin, sparking a ripple of tension that made my legs twitch. "Give her a gun, and she's soakin' wet."

A sensual overload. My body writhed beneath the weight of his words. My finger on the trigger shifted slightly. Romeo knew all too well the level of control it took to hold a gun at a moment like this.

It reminded me of that time on his couch, giving him head with the same gun pointed straight at me. Now, a mirror image.

He placed his hand over mine, taking possession slowly—a silent trade between power and pleasure. With the weapon tucked securely back into his waistband, his shoulders finally relaxed. And that's when he really let loose on me.

My legs still twitched. Ears still rang. As my husband retook his seat beside me. A sheen of my orgasm glistening on his lips.

"FYI," he said, voice rough from exertion, "I nutted on the carpet by your feet. Tellin' you so you don't go off on me if it got on the bottom of your shoe."

That, amongst other reasons, was why this club had way too much earthy masculinity seeping from its pores. It was a damn good job the carpet was being replaced, or I'd have been pissed.

Tommy slipped into the room discreetly. The timing made it obvious he knew exactly what we'd just been doing.

"Okay, Boss. Last auditionee for today. You ready?"

He stood off to the side, hands braced at the arch of his spine. No hint of what happened in here earlier remained on his face. Professionally wiped clean.

I held my hand out to Romeo, who watched me closely.

"Give me that gun back, please."

But when he didn't jump to it right away, I locked eyes with him. "Romeo, what the hell is that face you're pulling? If you farted, I want you out—right now."

He chuckled, flashing the full gleam of his American smile. The eye tattoo creased slightly as his eyes sparkled.

"I was just smellin' your sweet pussy in my moustache."

He sniffed again. Deliberate. Filthy. Unapologetic.

I paused. Watching him. So in his element—curling his upper lip under his nostrils, taking in my scent like it was oxygen.

Would I ever extend the same courtesy to him?

Not in a million years.

"While you're sniffing your top lip, give me that gun."

The roll of his lip snapped back into place.

"Hell no." He grasped the protruding handle like it was surgically attached to him. Post-nut clarity apparently gave him the misinformed right to an opinion.

"That was a one-time deal. Don't get me wrong, it was hot as fuck. But it's back where it belongs."

Our eyes danced, reading each other in silence. Testing the limits. Holding our breath.

Then he broke the tension with another slow sniff of his moustache. Of course he did.

Each time he sniffed, I swore I could feel it—like he was inhaling me all over again. A move like that was only ever going to make me crack, and he knew it.

"Okay, whatever." I sighed, pretending to be annoyed. Forcing myself not to smile. "What happened to that pistol you bought me last year? I wasn't ready then. I am now."

His grasp loosened, and his smile widened.

"Fuck… Sayin' shit like that got me hard again."

A little irritated that he still wasn't taking me seriously, I reached for the handle, but his lightning-fast reflexes clamped my wrist in a vice grip. He shook his head and gently placed my hand in my lap. The static of our electrically charged connection remained, even though he wasn't giving in to my demand.

"I'll sort you a piece, Queen, don't you worry. Let's get this last one over with so we can go home and make love properly."

His hopes were high, clearly. And while making love was nowhere near the top of my list today, I'd let him fantasise. If anything, it would keep him quiet.

We heard them before we saw them, more than one set of footsteps approaching from the stairwell. Two figures finally emerged from the dim corner by the double doors.

A hush seemed to fall as they stepped in—like the room itself questioned their intentions.

"Oh…hey." My gaze flicked between the man and the woman. "I haven't seen you two since we first met. Romeo, do you remember Jamie and her husband, Harry, from their audition?"

Romeo's smirk was instantaneous.

"Sure I remember. 'Cause that was when you—"

My fingers curled around the velvet arm of the throne.

"Right. Enough talking from my husband." I shot him a glare, then offered the couple a tight, businesslike smile. "He's still not feeling well. So—what can we do for you? You're here to audition for my club?"

I prayed Romeo had let go of the memory of what had happened during their audition. His exhausting obsession with making me black out from orgasm had grown old fast. Was that the only reason he'd gone down on me earlier?

Jamie, dressed sharply in a tailored pantsuit and kitten heels, handed her black Birkin 35 to her husband—hooking the handle over his outstretched finger like she was passing him a leash.

A his-and-hers cologne lingered between them, something classic yet cutthroat.. They smelled like a boardroom meeting I'd accidentally walked into. And I sure as hell wasn't the one chairing it.

Something told me this visit had nothing to do with her wanting a spot on my poles.

"We have a business proposition for you, Mrs Giannetti," Jamie said, voice smooth as polished glass. "If you're interested, of course."

Her approach dripped with confidence. The kind that dared you to underestimate her. This wasn't part of anyone's plan, and instantly, Romeo was suspicious. I wasn't far behind.

He stood slowly, stool legs groaning beneath him. The freshly holstered weapon at his waistband caught the light—saying plenty without a word.

We locked eyes on the couple.

Romeo spoke first. "First off, it ain't *she*—it's *we*. If you've got business, it's mine too."

Jamie glanced at Harry, one final sip of courage, then launched into her pitch.

"Our biggest client has made an offer. One I don't think you can refuse."

It wasn't just me drawn in by her tone. Even Romeo, usually impossible to impress, had stilled—drawn to the certainty behind her words.

I cocked my head, finger brushing my lips. Intrigued, but cautious. "Okay. But first, what's in it for you?"

"If I can make this work," Jamie said, hands clasped, practically buzzing, "I'll be paid a price of my own."

Romeo didn't sit. The sheer weight of his silence dwarfed them both. "What does he want with my wife, then?"

Her lips curved. Too pleased with herself.

"This is where it gets really exciting. Our client knows all about you, Chloe. Wants to work with you. Thinks the two of you could make a lot of money together." She let the idea hang. "Before I say anything more… he wants to meet."

I glanced up at Romeo, who hadn't taken his eyes off the couple. "He wants to meet me?"

Jamie nodded like she was offering the crown jewels. "Of course, there'll be a scene of his choosing. A show of respect—"

Romeo's arms flailed like a wildfire had just broken loose inside his shorts. "Fuck no!" His hand found his gun.

I grabbed his wrist, glaring. "Why aren't you even thinking about this?"

He didn't answer, just pointed at my bump without touching it. "Did you forget you're about to fuckin' pop? Ain't no man puttin' his dick anywhere near you. You think I'm gonna let you do a scene? Pfft. Give me a break."

Now would've been the perfect time to kick him in the shin and straight out of the damn room.

The silence that followed swallowed everything.

No one moved. No one dared.

Just the drill's vibration through the walls.

The lights flickered.

Then quiet.

Eventually, Romeo broke it. "If that's all you had to offer, we're out. Now leave."

Pig-headed idiot.

As they turned to go, I rose with more conviction. Romeo's eyes locked on me. I brushed down my dress, smiling just enough to distract him.

"Jamie's tampon string was showing. Girl code. You stay here or she'll get super embarrassed. I'll be right back."

That'd keep him away long enough. The level of clueless it took to fall for that excuse was honestly impressive. A tampon string—in a pantsuit? And yet he lapped it up.

"Wait up," I called, catching Jamie at the top of the stairs. She flinched, then relaxed when our eyes met.

A contractor adjusting a light fitting quietly made himself scarce. Everyone here knew I was the boss. But did Jamie's client believe it too?

"So, he wants to work with me, huh?" For some reason, the idea gave me butterflies.

Her sleek bob shimmered in the artificial light. "Yes, of course. You're big news, Mrs Giannetti."

While America might've known me as the wife of a famous gangster... had my status really risen beyond the club?

Harry remained quiet, Jamie's bag in hand, like he knew his place.

Shame Romeo wasn't as well trained.

"I'm working hard to get this place off the ground. Would your client be interested in this area of business?"

Footsteps echoed in the distance—Romeo.

Jamie glanced past me and nodded quickly, tucking her hair behind her ears.

"I'm interested," I whispered. Hairs prickled on my arms. "Not right now, but I won't be pregnant forever. We'll talk again, okay?"

Jamie nodded. Harry gave a tight smile. I hated letting them walk away, especially with opportunity still warm on the table.

His mouth-watering scent hit just before he did. Romeo barged into our little impromptu meeting, his scowl deep enough to hollow out the drywall.

I leaned against the wall, casual. "So Jamie. As I was saying…"

He zeroed in on me.

I nearly tripped over my words under his glare. "…Don't be embarrassed about what happened earlier."

Jamie blinked like I'd grown a second head.

I jabbed Romeo's ribs. "You weren't offended by Jamie's period-related issue, were you?"

As the only one in on it, I widened my eyes—daring him to follow through. He reached for the heavy chain that still wasn't there, then scratched his head instead.

"I don't give a shit, Chloe. I wanna go eat." His hand found his stomach like he hadn't just devoured a buffet breakfast.

Even they knew better than to cross a hungry Italian.

They left fast, maybe too fast for the stairs. Black bob and blond curls vanished, taking my chances of making it big along with them.

I swivelled, jaw clenched. "Call yourself a businessman? We could've commanded anything we wanted in that deal."

He shook his head, retreating out of the light. "Once a whore, always a whore."

What the—

I yanked on his shoulder, dragging him back into it. "Excuse me,

Romeo. Do you have a problem?"

He flailed. *Extra Italian.*

"This club means a lot to me. I'm not going to shy away from opportunities."

Scraping his fingers through his hair—coils stretching, snapping—he gave me a look of pure disappointment.

"Puttin' yourself on the table makes you look desperate."

The same contractor reappeared, tools in hand, then backed off again under the weight of Romeo's glare.

"Well, from what I learned with Bodu Manik, I could get what I want without doing a scene. I'd get a fake husband—like you did with Britney—"

His hand slapped across my mouth. Firm. Final.

"I don't wanna hear any more bullshit. Fake husband? As if."

Funny how when he shined, I had to applaud. But the second I reached for the spotlight, he wanted to cut the power.

It was then I realised I wasn't being smart. I had to speak to him in his favourite language—the only one he respected.

My brow softened. Eyes sparkled.

I peeled his hand away. He let me.

"So, are we not friends now?" I peeked up at him through my lashes, swaying my dress from side to side like bait.

That alone must've released my scent—he sniffed his top lip again, eyes flashing with wicked promise.

Bingo.

Trailing my fingers down his front, I skimmed hot, ripped skin. Drawstring undone. Access granted. I reached past his semi-erect cock, straight to his balls.

His thighs tensed. One arm caught the doorframe.

"I know what you're doin', Chloe." His breath hitched.

My fingers rolled his balls gently, coaxing a twitch from his cock.

"Yeah? What's that?" I asked.

"You're playin' with my nuts to make me forget what just happened. I'm still mad you wanna fuck other men. Especially while you're carryin' my son."

His erection betrayed him.

Eventually, he gave in.

"If you're gonna play with somethin'... make it my dick. If you give me a good nut, I might forgive you."

He raised a finger. "Might."

I licked my upper lip, slow and teasing. "So... sir wants a Chloe Special?"

"Make it the Supreme Chloe Special. On account of me bein' supremely mad."

I grinned against his chest. "I'll see what I can do."

◆ ◆ ◆

"You two look tanned and rested," Nelly mused, settling behind her imposing walnut desk like she'd never left it.

At this point, we were practically part of the furniture—and likely her most complicated clients.

Nothing had changed since our last visit. Fresh linen scent. Fixed furniture. A ticking wall clock marking time with soft authority. Even the temperature felt curated. I had a feeling the familiarity was intentional. This woman was a professional.

I raised my hand, forgetting I wasn't in preschool. Something I did more often than I cared to admit.

"Yes, Chloe?" she said warmly, opening a drawer and pulling out a fresh A4 notepad—like she already knew we'd fill it.

"There's something I'd like to speak to you about first, please."

She took a two-handed sip from her mug, then set it down carefully on a coaster. "I wholeheartedly encourage patient-led sessions. Absolutely, Chloe. Go right ahead."

My heel bounced restlessly. I'd rehearsed this already.

"Romeo... I mean, Romero told me what you did."

She cast a knowing glance his way, then turned back to me. Steepling her fingers beneath her chin, she offered a patient smile. "Please. Share."

She eased back into her chair. An open invitation.

"Well. You showed him my file. I want to know why you did that behind my back."

Just picturing the two of them alone—sharing space without me—felt impossible. And yet, it had happened.

"Mm-hm. That's right. To give your husband an unfiltered view of your past." She didn't blink. "You were about to be in a different country. Pregnant. Alone. Spending time with another man who's done more harm than good to your relationship. I did what I felt was right."

She took another sip, licking the foam from her lip like this wasn't the confrontation I'd been mentally rehearsing for weeks. "And the fact you're both sitting here now tells me it was the right choice."

Romeo stayed silent. Thighs spread wide, reaching again for the chain that wasn't there.

The clock ticked louder, like it was mocking us.

"Was there a further question on the subject, Chloe?"

My thumbs rolled over each other—any faster, and I'd start a fire in my lap. This was it. The question that trumped the rest.

"Did you sleep together?"

Usually, when I asked something that insane, people would laugh. Rushed to defend themselves. Anything. But Nelly just leaned forward, elbows resting on the desk, and looked me dead in the eye.

"What do you think happened, Chloe?"

Tick. Tock. That damn clock listened in.

And there it was. My mind began crafting scenes I didn't want to imagine. Clothes on the floor. Whispered confessions. Him needing comfort… her offering it. His cock in her hand. Her breasts in his. The stale scent of sex sticking to my nostrils.

I recoiled as my thoughts dragged me somewhere false—but visceral. I wiped the damp from my forehead.

"The rational part of me thinks that would never happen. But… I guess I struggle to ignore the little voice in the back of my mind."

She nodded, like she'd expected it. Then took pen to paper.

"Let's say we indulge that voice for a moment. What is it saying?"

I hesitated. The backs of my knees prickled with sweat. Then I pushed through the foolishness.

"I guess it's saying… that Romeo bent you over the desk. That he didn't use protection. Maybe even got you pregnant…"

The words sounded ridiculous out loud—but in my head, they felt terrifyingly real.

She stood slowly, gliding a hand across the desk as she came to sit directly in front of me. Romeo ceased to exist in her periphery.

"Do you know what that little voice is, Chloe?"

I shook my head, instinctively reaching for Romeo's hand. He offered it —steady, warm—just enough to keep me grounded.

"That voice," she said gently, placing her hand on my knee, "is the result of past trauma. A coping mechanism you developed to offer reassurance, even when the truth isn't clear. One of your diagnoses is OCD with generalised anxiety and catastrophic thoughts."

My calf muscles softened beneath her touch.

"So what tends to happen," she continued, "is it becomes pre-emptive. Your mind creates false scenarios to protect you from future hurt. Would you agree?"

I shrugged. But deep down, it clicked.

"I guess," I whispered.

I'd rehearsed this confrontation so many times. In my mind, she waved a pregnancy test in my face. Maybe laughed about it with my husband. But this? Calm, rational clarity?

I wasn't prepared.

Nelly, ever perceptive, conducted the room like a symphony. One breath from her, and the silence shifted in harmony.

"So tell me… how was the holiday? Sorry—vacation. Too British for my own good sometimes."

She smiled, her gaze falling to my bump.

"Chloe, I must say, you're glowing. Nearly full term, right?"

I placed both hands protectively over my stomach.

"Just a couple of weeks to go."

Romeo, more at ease with the shift in tone, rested his hand over mine —his thumb brushing slow lines into the fabric of my dress. I loved it when he did that.

Safe to say, the Chloe Special he'd received an hour ago had made us friends again… and then some.

I laced my fingers through his, tracing the warm wedding band on his ring finger. A reminder: he was mine. I was his.

"We've been doing well. The honeymoon was amazing."

I smiled at the memories. Sun. Sea. Sand. Bliss.

Nelly returned to her seat, flipping the first page of her pad and turning to a fresh sheet. I imagined it joining a thick file somewhere. Each page stamped with a red X. Impossible to cure patient.

"Excellent. And how are you feeling, Romero?"

"Err, yeah. Fine." He shifted, ankle over knee, defensively. "Until my wife hired a honey trapper to try to catch me cheatin'."

Even the clock hands seemed to recoil—curling back like they couldn't bear to witness what came next.

Mouth open, throat dry. My whole arm took over, open palm whipping through the air to swat his firm chest.

"You said you wouldn't say anything!"

Nelly glanced from me to Romeo, then back again. Her expression shifted. Subtle, but unmistakable. Not furious. Worse. Disappointed.

"Is this true, Chloe?"

Fuck—

My body nearly folded in on itself.

"Yes," I mumbled—barely louder than a field mouse's squeak. My lips trembled. The sting of tears gathered fast.

Nelly sighed, scribbling something onto her well-thumbed notepad. "I see."

She pushed her fingers beneath the rims of her glasses, rubbing her eye sockets in slow, circular motions. The frames bobbing with the weight of her thoughts. Then, with a softness that made it land harder, she blinked slowly at me.

"Do you know why you hired a honey trapper, Chloe?"

The reaction came before the thought. I shook my head, eyes fixed on the carpet. Was it normal for the pattern to blur like that? My vision swam, everything else fading as I tried to stay present.

Nelly stood again, perching on the desk between us. The scent of clean linen and calm authority anchored me.

"Do you know what I think?" she mused. "I think you've convinced yourself there's no such thing as a healthy relationship. So, you push your husband away whenever the opportunity presents itself."

The room fell silent. Only the clock dared to continue—its tick now applauding her insight.

"What happened to you as a child paved the way for how you connect with men. You don't trust Romero's actions. You doubt his feelings. And that—" her hand gestured gently, "—is part of the emotional wound we're working so hard to heal."

My eyes dropped to my hand, the glint of my engagement ring catching the light. I turned it slowly, searching for comfort in its sparkle.

"He wouldn't sleep with me after he found out about the honey trapper," I murmured.

"That, just then, was avoidance," Nelly said gently but firmly. "But since we're letting this session be patient-led—Romero, what's your response to Chloe's claim of a lack of intimacy? Or should we call it what it is... a lack of reassurance?"

Romeo couldn't help himself. The leg-jiggle-fabric-rustle combo said it all.

"Bear in mind," he said, leaning forward with both hands rubbing together like he was cold, "she paid for it using my credit card. Do you see what I gotta put up with?"

Nelly's lips thinned. "I see. Let me ask you this, Chloe. Would you want to be intimate with someone who betrayed you? Regardless of the reason?"

Hmm.

Would I?

A yes or no question. But the answer refused to surface.

I glanced sideways. He was watching. Waiting.

I shifted in my seat. "We always have sex after one of us messes up."

Nelly propped her chin on her interlaced fingers, bracing herself against the storm of our dysfunction.

"Romero... I think Chloe's asking for reassurance now."

He leaned forward again, dragging his palms over his thighs. "I love my wife. But when she pulls dumb shit like this. It makes me not like her. I wanted to walk away that night."

My lips parted. My heart cracked open. The ringing in my ears felt like death.

"You did?" My fingers curled around the collar of my dress, clutching it like it was the only thing holding me together.

"Just when I thought we were good," he said, voice tight, "you did something else."

He wouldn't look at me. Eyes fixed on the filing cabinet. The bin. The curled edge of the rug.

Nelly raised her hands, gently steering us back from the edge. "Okay, guys... let's bring this down a notch. The last thing I want is a pregnant woman crying in my office."

She swivelled toward Romeo. "How do you feel now, Romero?"

He shrugged. Held his tension for a beat. Then let it out with a long breath. "I love her. That's all I know."

Nelly adjusted her glasses, sliding them back up the bridge of her nose. "And that's all we can hope for right now."

With a light sweep across the desk, she recalibrated the room. "Let's pivot. Based on how this session began, I'd like to explore the past a little. A toe-dip into the lagoon of Chloe's life, if you'll indulge me. It might feel like a step back, but I promise, it's how we measure growth."

She turned to me. "That okay, Chloe?"

"Um... sure."

I bit the inside of my cheek until the coppery sting warned I'd drawn blood. I could've protested. Should've defended myself. But with each session, I was learning something hard to swallow—I didn't understand half as much as I thought I did.

"So, when we first met," Nelly said, scanning her notes, "one of Romero's main triggers in this relationship was his brother—who you were previously involved with, Chloe. Is that still a problem after the holiday?"

I shook my head, thoughts already drifting.

Dan.

The drugs.

Bodu Manik.

The boat.

His confession.

His sacrifice on the plane…

"They actually got on really well while we were away."

Nelly leaned back, satisfied, but not done.

"Well, that's a good start," she said, flipping to a clean page.

The soft rustle of paper confirmed what we all knew. There were still plenty of stones left unturned.

"Chloe, your biggest issue with Romero was the way he intimidated you and sought revenge through other women?"

I looked at him. "I suppose we're both guilty of that."

Our eyes met—his ocean blue, mine muted grey. A flicker of a smile passed between us. Fleeting. Fragile.

Nelly pushed her glasses into her hair and scraped it back from her face.

"Accepting accountability. That's progress, Chloe."

She shifted in her seat, voice softer now—acknowledging the storm we'd just weathered.

"Let's go even further back. You've both endured significant hardship. Romero, with a lack of family support… Chloe…" She trailed off. She didn't need to finish. "Do you feel like that's had an impact on your marriage?"

My brows pulled together. "I don't know. Has it?"

She gave a single assured nod. "Yes. I think so."

Romeo shifted in his chair, restless. Guard rising.

Here we go.

Both legs started to bounce—just slightly. Like rocking a baby. Soothing it. Lulling it back to sleep.

But I noticed. One jiggle at a time. He was getting ready to bolt.

Nelly remained composed, her voice a calm thread through the tension. "Now's the time to embrace the past. Begin the work of repair."

Romeo slid a hand inside his jacket, pulling out his cigarette pack. He flipped the lid and stuck one between his teeth.

"I ain't forgivin' my mother for landin' my ass in jail as a kid—if that's where you're headin' again," he muttered around the filter.

The familiar scent of tobacco in a storm brought comfort, even to me these days.

I reached out, gently curling my fingers around his.

"Please. Don't leave."

But he rose partway from his chair.

"These fuckin' therapists cause half the fuckin' problem," he snapped —razor-sharp. "She's just thinkin' of ways to make more money."

The cigarette bent under his grip, seconds from snapping. He shoved off the chair, its legs skidding over the rug and scratching fresh marks into the varnish beneath.

He was leaving. Again.

My whole body tensed.

"You said you wouldn't do this to me." My voice cracked. My worst fear unfolding before me.

But then he turned. His hand came up, tilting my chin with the same fingers that moments ago had pulsed with fury.

He looked into me—deep. "I ain't leavin' you. I'll see you in the car."

And just like that, he was gone. Not before cutting Nelly with a sharp look, then shutting the door behind him—not quite a slam, but enough to rattle the air. His steps rang loud and clear until they melted into nothing.

A cloak of emotion settled over the room. Heavy. Stifling.

The second hand on the wall clock ticked louder now—less a measure of time, more a countdown of my loneliness.

I cradled my bump and forced a weak laugh. "Um... I think bringing up his mother was too soon."

Nelly slid her glasses back into place with calm precision. Her voice, cool and deliberate. "Romero creates drama when he's confronted with something he doesn't want to feel. It's deflection. An exit strategy."

She tapped her pen on the pad, slow and steady. "We seek validation from the ones who hurt us most."

Her words echoed in the silence, each one landing like a truth I hadn't asked for, but couldn't ignore.

I narrowed my eyes, knees turning away from her.

"You're not gonna ask me to forgive my stepfather, are you? That's not why you shared my file with Romeo?"

She gave a warm smile. Patient. Gentle. But something flickered behind it.

Plucking a fresh pen from her desk tidy, she scribbled in a different colour. I craned my neck, squinting, but the words blurred. Even at twenty-one, my eyes weren't what they were back when I could read a therapist's notes from across the room.

"I'm not saying forgive him," she said. "But maybe… write him a letter. One we don't send. Ask your unanswered questions. Begin closing a door you've been peeking through your whole life."

Her words stuck like a sucked lollipop pressed against skin. Too raw to peel away. Too uncomfortable to leave untouched.

I traced slow circles over my bump. A little foot popped against my palm, like I'd somehow tickled his toes.

"My body's already under enough stress. Maybe after the baby's born."

She clicked her pen twice. That sharp, metallic snap slicing through the quiet.

"I agree," she said with a nod. "Let's revisit it next time."

She studied me closely, her gaze steady. "Before you go… have you spoken to your foster father, Bob?"

My breath caught.

Of all the people.

Truth was, I'd thought about him every day since the wedding. But fear always froze my hand before I could reach for the phone.

"I've thought about it," I said softly. Not ready to admit how much.

The silence from him had haunted me. So loud it screamed.

Had the cancer already won? Or was there still enough fight left in him for one last goodbye?

She arched a brow. "Enough to make the first move?"

Footsteps echoed outside the door. For a second, I thought Romeo had come back to stand beside me.

But the sound faded. A door down the corridor opened and closed. Not ours.

"Um… no. I haven't." I swallowed the lump rising in my throat.

She gave a short nod. "We'll end the session here. I'll see you both soon."

I didn't need telling twice. I reached for my purse, clutching it against my belly like armour—as if I could protect the baby from what it might cost me to open that old wound again.

"I hate it when you leave me." I opened the car door and tossed my purse into his lap. A dramatic gesture to match the way I felt. Like lobbing a freshly pulled grenade into enemy territory.

I sat, waiting for the detonation.

Never one to say the right thing, Romeo scooped it up and flung it into the back seat like it hadn't cost him eight grand at that overpriced boutique.

"And I hate when she gets on my dick about my mom," he muttered, flicking his half-smoked cigarette through the open window.

The butt spiralled out, ash trailing like the remnants of his temper. He waved the smoke away from me with the back of his hand, like that made it all okay.

I buckled my seatbelt. "Just talk about how you feel next time, instead of leaving. You might actually learn something about yourself."

I watched him as he drove, eyes flicking to the pressure around his jaw, waiting for it to soften.

The sports car's engine filled the silence with an aggressive rumble. A growl that perfectly matched the tension lingering between us.

What was he thinking? God, I wished I had a tapped line straight into his brain. But even if I did… would I want to hear the truth?

"Well, what do you want?" he asked as the car rolled to a stop.

The window slid down, and the smell of fast food curled into the cab, coating the air like a greasy blanket.

I blinked, caught off guard. Lost in my catastrophising, I hadn't even noticed we'd pulled into the McDonald's drive-thru.

The speaker crackled. "Good afternoon, welcome to McDonald's. What can I get started for ya?"

Romeo leaned out the window, then glanced back at me, waiting. But the surprise of it all—and the pressure to decide—left me flustered and pink-cheeked.

"Um. Um." My thighs stuck to the leather.

His tattoo flexed across the back of his hand with each clench around the wheel.

"Aight, give me the double cheeseburger with large fries and a Coke," he said, snapping open the glovebox for his overstuffed wallet. His thumb skimmed beneath the hem of my dress, sending a pulse of heat spiralling up my spine—completely unhelpful for decision-making.

I still hadn't made up my mind.

He cast me a knowing look. "Make that twice," he said, then pulled forward.

Ugh. The last thing I wanted was a double bloody burger. But after that therapy session, this was not the time to test his patience.

"Oh my God, Amy, look! It's Chloe and Romero Giannetti!" The once faceless voice now had a body—peaked cap, polo shirt, and a spotty grin. He cupped his headset mic, voice rising as he summoned a crowd.

Romeo didn't flinch. Handing over cash, he signed napkins shoved at him by overexcited co-workers.

A manager leaned out next, ponytail swinging, badge clipped to her blouse. Her bracelet tapped against the paintwork—a small sound that set Romeo's leg bouncing again.

"Can I just say, Chloe… you're my idol. I love you."

Her voice cracked with excitement, like I was someone worth noticing.

Romeo looked at me. I looked at him.

"Um... thanks," I said, cringing at my own awkwardness. This wasn't my comfort zone, being the one people admired.

"Here you go, sir." The boy handed over the bag, which landed heavily in my lap with a thud.

Romeo started the engine and hit the gas harder than necessary. The car revved, roaring like a beast, drawing squeals from our makeshift audience.

Should I have been less annoyed? Maybe. But sometimes I didn't know how to respond to the version of him that performed for everyone but me.

The heat from the food soaked into my thighs, radiating through my bump and giving the baby something to wriggle against. The greasy scent clung to the air con vents, doing nothing to erase the bitterness that still hung between us.

Romeo pulled into a lay-by. No paparazzi. No screaming fans. He grabbed the bag and tore into his fries—fistfuls at a time.

In the rear-view, headlights flared. Tommy, Snake and some new guy. Their SUV idled with a soft purr behind us.

Normally, he'd be the one to speak first. But this time, silence stretched.

Alone with my thoughts, Nelly's words wouldn't stop echoing. Bob was one thing. But the letter... it clung like static I couldn't shake.

Romeo glanced at me, reading my quiet. The cologne he'd sprayed this morning was now buried beneath stale fries and lingering frustration.

He bit into his burger—its contents spilling out from the sides.

"So, what'd the old bag say when I left?" he asked, mouth full. His tongue darted out, wiping ketchup from the corner of his lips.

I shrank into the seat, wishing the leather would swallow me whole. My stomach tightened like a steel band.

"She wants me to write a letter. To my stepdad."

His jaw stopped mid-chew. A storm igniting behind his eyes.

The bag crinkled in his grip. "We ain't fuckin' goin' back there again." He slurped his Coke like it could drown her words. "She's a fuckin' psycho."

I exhaled, pinching the bridge of my nose. My palm settled protectively over my bump. "She might be right."

"Right, my fuckin' ass." Another slurp. Ice rattled in his death grip on the cup.

Done pretending to eat, I shoved my food back in the bag.

He dipped a few fries into ketchup and jabbed them at me like a warning. "I'll die before that happens. He'll die before that happens. I ain't havin' it. Just knowin' what he did to you—fuck!"

His rage erupted. He gripped the wheel hard enough for it to creak, the car jerking in protest.

I reached out, resting my hand on his bouncing leg.

"Forget it. I'm not even thinking about it until after the baby's born. Come on. Hurry up and eat. The baby store closes in an hour."

Crying babies and the sweet sting of talcum powder overwhelmed my senses as Romeo and I stepped into the mother and baby store. The last few shoppers were being ushered out through the rear, making way for our private shopping experience.

The A/C was cranked high for the comfort of expectant mothers. We stood there, skin prickling, completely lost. High shelves loomed around us like a first-time parent's nightmare—stacked with diapers, wipes, and bottle sets. Too many options. No clue where to start.

Outside, a restless crowd gathered. Fists thudded against the locked glass, muffled voices swelling with frustration—like a hive of bees riled into motion.

Inside, the silence felt surreal. Just us, alone in a space usually drowned in crying, tantrums, and chaotic sprints down the pacifier aisle.

Romeo shifted beside me. The soft pop of his knuckles was the only sign of his restlessness. He didn't belong here, not really. Too big, too solid, too much for a world this soft.

Trish, the store manager, jogged towards us after closing the rear door, her mom sneakers squeaking on the over-polished floor. Ready to cash in. Her grin was that of a woman who'd just hit the retail jackpot.

My headache, brewing since therapy, now pulsed behind my eyes as she led us through the store. Aisle after aisle of brightly coloured packaging surrounded us—foreign objects with names I couldn't pronounce stared back like I was already failing motherhood.

But one thing I could say for sure was that Romeo had never stepped foot in a place like this before. Which meant, for once, he hadn't slept with a single member of staff.

"Best shit only for my son," he told the young clerk, who was dragging a cart behind us.

"Romeo!" I hissed, nudging his ribs. "Don't swear in here."

He blinked at me like I'd overreacted. Maybe I had. But I wasn't having him swearing around the baby once he was born. No chance.

Our first stop: the clothing aisle. Tiny cardigans. Palm-sized trainers. Rompers so small they looked made for dolls. My chest tightened.

"You're having a boy, right?" Trish asked, pulling out a baby blue all-in-one. Tiny ducks and lambs were crocheted into the cotton.

"A boy, yeah." I rubbed the fabric against my cheek. The softness nearly undid me. I sniffed and blinked fast. Soon I'd meet him.

"Ain't no son of mine wearin' that," Romeo cut in. "Where's the thick jewellery? Fire tracksuit? Goose-feather jacket? High tops?"

Trish blinked. Her assistant blinked. I sighed.

"We'll take this whole rail, please," I said, grabbing vests, T-shirts, and soft trousers.

Romeo picked up a small brown leather jacket, inspected it, then returned it to the rack. "You got any kids' guns?"

All three of us turned to stare at him.

The hum of the A/C filled the jaw-dropping silence.

He raised his hands. "Fake, obviously. I ain't slow."

"You will be in a minute if you keep embarrassing me," I muttered, going for another rib shot. He dodged it, crouching to inspect a sun hat with a dinosaur motif.

"What the fuck is this?" He held it on the tip of one finger.

I snatched it and smacked him on the head. His curls bounced, the scent of his coconut shampoo rising between us—softening my annoyance, but only slightly.

"Stop swearing." I cracked a smile for the staff. "And keep your stupid opinions to yourself."

Outside, the thudding intensified. The pressure in the air swelled, like impatience was seeping through the walls and into my skin.

"So," Trish said, recovering her nerve, "have you thought about an all-in-one system?"

She led us to a wall of prams—some chunky and off-road ready, others sleek and impractical.

I stared blankly.

Romeo shrugged.

"Um… we'll go with whatever you recommend," I said, feeling wildly unqualified. Little did she know we'd spent the past few months running drugs, dodging bullets, and renovating a strip club—not researching bloody pushchairs.

Romeo lifted one with ease, inspecting the tiny wheels. "What are these? Two-inch tyres? Nah. Gimme somethin' with eighteen-inch spinners, run-flats, sound system. Whatever. I'll pay."

"Romeo, it's a pram, not a car," I hissed.

He glared at Trish, who was now visibly shaken, her clipboard trembling in her grip.

"Sorry, sir," she stammered. "That's all it comes with. But I can show you this." She gestured to a vintage-style pram: charcoal grey with white spoke wheels. Classy. Elegant. I loved it instantly.

"That's women's shit." He pushed it away from him like it offended him.

"Strike one, Giannetti. Swear again and you're out."

Trish and her assistant froze.

He rolled his eyes. "Whatever. But I ain't bein' papped pushin' a girl's God damn pram."

That froze me to the spot.

"Wait. You want to push the pram?"

He huffed and grabbed the handles, testing the push like it was a Rolls-Royce. "Are you crazy, woman? 'Course I want to."

That hit differently. A part of me relaxed. The other part bristled with fear. If I let myself believe he was all in—what would happen if he got bored? If he walked away?

Just as we reached the checkout, chaos erupted at the doors.

Raised voices. A loud slam.

Romeo's body snapped to alert. He didn't speak, but I stepped behind him, anyway.

Tommy stood at the left, Snake on the right. Both suddenly still.

The crowd parted slightly… and there she was.

A slim woman, expression wild, tore off her shirt. The screech of skin against glass scraped at my ears, nipples flattening like suction cups as her breasts smeared against the pane, fogging slightly from the heat of her body.

"Let me have your baby, Romero!" Her voice was muted by the thick glass, but somehow still echoed around the four walls of the baby store.

Of course, she caught his attention. Hell, she caught mine.

What I didn't appreciate was the little smile he gave her. That cocky nod—like she'd complimented his shoes, not offered to bear his fucking child.

My whole body clenched. That right there was the signing of his own death warrant.

The trunk of the SUV was already piled high—strollers, prams, cots—everything we needed to start our new chapter. But as I slammed the door shut, I couldn't help but wonder how long it'd be before I used that trunk for my husband's body bag instead.

Crowd control had become a safety issue the longer we'd browsed the store. Tommy decided the sports car would be used as a decoy while we slipped out quietly in the back of the SUV. In silence.

Me—brooding over Romeo's behaviour.

Him—blissfully unaware.

"I'm lookin' forward to makin' love when we get home," he said, testing the waters.

"Oh, so the woman flashing her tits at you got you going, did she?"

"Aaahh." He dragged the sound out, the bulb just flicking on. "So that's why you're mad. I kept thinkin'—surely it ain't 'cause I said shit a couple times. But then I figured… with you, it could be anythin'."

The cold blast from the air vents grazed my ankles, doing nothing to cool the burn behind my eyes.

"For your information, ass-hat," I said, folding my arms, "giving a thirsty fan the nod of approval was, firstly, incredibly disrespectful. And secondly—it'll encourage other thirsty bitches to keep doing that every single time we go out."

His hand tapped against his thigh, casual and rhythmic, perfectly in time with the song on the radio, as if I hadn't just spoken.

It seemed every time I tried to express myself to him, he shut down. Stopped listening completely. I knew because his eyes always gave him away—glazing over, drifting lazily to my breasts.

Streetlights streaked past in hues of gold, painting ribbons across the SUV's dark interior. Each flicker across the glass marked another day ending. A step closer to meeting our baby.

He finally pulled his gaze from the window and sighed. "I get why you're mad."

Pausing, he rubbed his hands together, warming them against the chilled air.

Then, with a grin, he sniffed his upper lip and licked it slowly. "Let me give you a Romeo Special to make it up to you."

He never could wrap his head around the fact that, while he could be manipulated through his cock, my clit didn't hold the same power over me.

"No, thank you." I tugged my jacket tighter around me.

Giving up quicker than I expected, he slapped his thighs with a loud smack. That must've stung.

"Looks like I ain't gettin' that love-makin' you promised, am I?"

Ha!

"Stop calling it love-making when it has nothing to do with love. You just want to blow your load inside me. Where's the love in that?"

Caught off guard by the venom in my tone, he glanced at his watch like he was praying it might beam him the hell out of the SUV.

"What the fuck is wrong with you, Chloe? Last couple weeks, you been nothin' but... a bitch. Yeah, that's right. I said it."

If I was honest with him, I might've said, Yes—I am a little stressed. I've got a baby due any minute, a club to open, a best friend to find. Don't even get me started on Bob, my stepfather issues, and everything in between.

Was I taking on too much?

Was I strong enough to keep going like this?

"I'm tryin' real hard to show you how much I love you, Chloe. You got your ways of needin' it—I got mine. I figured you liked makin' love. Sorry, I got it wrong."

The air curdled. Sadness crept in.

He was right.

I was a bitch.

My lungs emptied. Every part of me weakened.

The leather smacked cold against my back as I slumped into the seat. It was like a bucket of water had been dumped over my head—snapping me into clarity.

Romeo, the most feared man in America, was seeking reassurance... from me?

Right now, he needed love in the way he understood it. And of course, I could give him that.

I unbuckled my seatbelt and scooted over, undoing his as I went. My thighs peeled from the seat with a sticky snap.

With all the grace a full-term pregnancy allowed, I straddled his lap—with his help—settling into place.

His eyes stayed on mine. No smile. Just something raw and steady.

The burn in my legs reminded me the baby was nearly here. The pressure at the seam of his shorts told me he'd been ready the whole time.

He raised me just enough to guide me down—filling me completely. His arms locked around me, holding me in place.

Every muscle flexed, taking on the full weight of my heavy load. No matter how hard I tried, I could barely move off his lap.

"This is too hard for you. I can tell," he murmured, lips brushing my neck. "I appreciate you wantin' to give me somethin', but I don't want you strugglin' like this."

Still inside me, he cradled me closer. His tobacco-tinged breath warmed my cheek. Comforting in its familiarity—despite everything.

He brushed the hair off my face. "I love you, Chloe. More than I can tell you."

Tears pricked the corners of my eyes. That paper-cut kind of sting, impossible to ignore.

How did we always manage to fight to the death... only to wave the white flag right before pulling the final trigger?

I collapsed into his neck, the warmth of his skin wrapping around me like a blanket of security.

"I love you too, Romeo. So much it scares me."

CHAPTER 12

"Hello?" I answered the unknown caller ID.

Eight in the morning, birds singing and the sun barely awake. It had better be worth it.

Crossing the bedroom carpet, I winced with each step. Too heavy these days for the balls of my feet not to ache. I made it across the room without alerting Tommy—who was most definitely waiting in the hallway.

I flicked on the light. The bathroom door clicked gently into its frame behind me. Lowering myself onto the closed toilet lid, I flinched as the cold porcelain bit into my thighs. A wake-up call I wasn't quite ready for.

"Mrs Giannetti, it's me. Jamie." She paused just long enough for me to put two and two together. I didn't remember ever giving her my number.

Luckily for both of us, Romeo was still with Tim. He'd be another half hour, at least. I was alone. But that didn't mean I wanted to talk to her for long.

"What can I do for you, Jamie?" My voice echoed off the tiles, already laced with caution. No matter how soft the whisper, it felt like I was speaking into a megaphone.

"I know you said we should talk after the baby's born, but my client wants to put an offer on the table. Can we meet to discuss? I figured you wouldn't want your husband in on this."

Hmm. She wasn't wrong. Romeo had made it very clear I was to stay away from Jamie, and whoever she represented.

At the mention of the baby, a phantom ache tugged at my lower back. He shifted inside me, just enough to remind me where my focus should be.

I didn't answer right away, but my silence must've sounded like a maybe.

"This client, Mrs Giannetti, is someone you should give a chance. I promise you won't regret it."

I tapped my bare toes against the cold tile, trying to jolt myself fully awake. Her words sharpened in my ears.

This guy really, really wanted me.

"Okay," I said, stroking the curve of my belly, feeling the swell of my son beneath my fingertips. "Meet me at the club this afternoon. Fire escape. Four o'clock. I've got a meeting with my designer, anyway. We'll work around that."

A floorboard creaked out in the hallway. My hand stilled.

"Perfect," she said, her smile audible. "You won't regret it."

◆ ◆ ◆

"Aight, close your eyes," Romeo said, a boyish flicker of excitement lighting up his face from across the breakfast table.

No strippers in sight. Promising start.

He'd been in a good mood all morning since his session with Tim. I still didn't ask what they got up to. I didn't need to.

He dropped his fork carelessly, the scrape against the china too loud, then pushed back his throne. Its heavy, dominant weight growled across the marble as he came around behind me, covering my eyes with both hands.

"Why?" I laughed mid-chew, trying to peel his fingers away while swallowing down a bite of toast that refused to go quietly.

The scent of freshly cooked bacon clung to his skin, layered with the harshness of his morning cigarette.

Smoky bacon. He smelled delicious.

The room fell still. Silence crept in on tiptoes, curling around me. Even the last few whores still living with us, sat stiff at the table, didn't make a sound. No chewing. No swallowing. Just held breath. The only intruder was the distant hiss of the coffee machine.

Knowing all eyes were on me wrapped around my body like clingfilm

—tight at the throat, choking me without touch. Would this surprise warm my heart... or tear it out in front of everyone?

Behind me, a door creaked. Featherlight steps crossed the floor, stopping at my side.

My senses went haywire. I could've sworn someone touched me. My skin prickled. The hovering became unbearable.

I swallowed dry. My eyes twitched behind his palms, darting into the darkness as if it could offer answers. My hands reached forward into the void, searching for something to anchor me.

Finally, Romeo's hands slipped away, leaving my skin cold in their absence. Light flooded back behind my lids, but I wasn't quite ready.

"Open your eyes then," he said, voice soft and laced with warmth.

I blinked up at him. He stood there grinning. A box in hand.

"For you," he said, a flicker of vulnerability behind the smile as he thrust it forward.

Matte black. Satin bow. Déjà vu hit instantly.

"Is this what I think it is?" I asked, tucking my bottom lip between my teeth as I eased up one corner of the lid.

My fingers trembled slightly, like they could already feel the power inside.

He didn't answer. Just watched, dragging his thumb along his jaw, grazing the fresh stubble. He felt it too.

The kitchen drew a breath along with us. Chair legs shifted. Someone sniffed. Chef hovered mid-stir over his bubbling pans. Even the security staff leaned in.

This wasn't just a gift. This was something deeper. Something sacred.

"Come on, Chloe, shit!" he snapped, patience thinning. His fingers flexed like he might open it himself.

I lifted the lid.

There she was.

Nestled in silk. Sleek. Black. Powerful.

My very own gun.

He reached in, handling it with the tenderness of someone cradling a hatchling.

"Look right here." He tilted the barrel toward the light.

One word was etched along the side. A word with more meaning than any bouquet or box of chocolates ever could:

Queen.

He placed it in my hand.

"I got matchin' on mine, too. Here. Check it out." He pulled the weathered Glock from the waistband of his shorts.

King.

Two matching guns for two people too tangled to untwine.

One word was all it took to breathe power into my lungs. This man kept giving me more than I probably deserved.

He holstered his and cupped my hand—steadying the weight of the one resting in mine, sharing half the load.

"You're ready for this, right?" he asked, eyes scanning my face.

I shifted. Took the full weight back. Raised it. Closed one eye. Looked down the barrel.

Shoulders down. Breath steady. Stance firm.

I was ready.

"Thank you, Romeo. I love it."

◆ ◆ ◆

Later that morning, lying on the bed, my head hit the fresh pillow and I could've fallen asleep instantly—like the twelve hours I'd had last night still weren't enough.

The housekeeper kept our bedroom so perfectly unlived-in that the scent of Summer Breeze fabric softener seemed to renew itself daily. Crisp linen. My favourite smell in the world.

"What time you goin' to the club today?" Romeo asked from the drinks cabinet, toying with the neck of one bottle before picking up another.

"I'm meeting Lucy at three-ish. Why? You're not coming, are you?"

Shit. Too obvious.

Did he notice?

He popped the cork on one of his aged whiskeys, pouring from a height into a crystal tumbler. Potent enough, I could smell it from across the room.

The glug as it hit the glass mirrored the gulp of apprehension in my chest—because if he flipped the script and came to the club, I'd be in a heap of trouble when Jamie showed up.

Peering over his shoulder, he cast me a glance. "Just wonderin'. Tommy's takin' you. I got a meetin' with Manik."

Phew.

He seemed too distracted to clock the subtle urgency in my tone. Sure, Tommy would be tricky to shake once Jamie arrived, but it wouldn't be the first time I'd pulled it off.

In a bid to steer the conversation elsewhere, I propped myself up on the pillow, narrowing my eyes slightly as I watched him. "Did you find out yet who was behind the poisoning? It wasn't him, was it?"

He scratched the tip of his nose, then lazily raked a hand along his jaw. "Pretty sure it ain't Manik. Earnin' decent money with him right now." He paused. "Anyway, you look sexy."

Deflection at its finest.

I looked like a whale stranded on a beach. But I, too, was a master at changing the subject.

All the baby gear we'd bought last week, still in boxes, was piled high by the closet. A reminder the baby was coming any day now. And an even bigger reminder that we weren't even close to ready.

"Did you call me up here to sort that lot out?" I nodded toward the tower of cardboard, the smell of chemically compressed paper already ruining the calm I was trying to curate in what was meant to be my sanctuary.

Romeo swirled the whiskey in his glass, then took a slow sip. His eyes didn't leave mine.

"Nah. Somethin' bigger than that." He winked.

Instantly, I perked up. "Wait. You've planned something more exciting than building our son's crib?"

Breathy. A little anxious, my mind wandered.

Maybe a choir of angelic voices would serenade me.

Wildflowers cascading from the ceiling.

Or a baby shower I said I didn't want…

A familiar hollow knock, Tommy's signature two-beat rhythm, preceded the slow creak of the bedroom door.

My heartbeat thudded harder. Lips parted. Air kissed the tip of my tongue. Who—or what—was this extra surprise?

A single leather oxford stepped onto the carpet first, the hem of a tailored trouser lifting with the motion. Then the rest of him followed, crisp and composed, briefcase in hand.

A man. Suited. Sharp. Someone I didn't recognise. The gleam on his patent leather shoes suggested success.

His frame filled the doorway with quiet confidence, like this wasn't the first time he'd stood in our home. A waft of Mrs Knowles' cleaning products coiled in behind him as she fussed on the landing.

"Who the hell is this?" I asked, a flicker of disappointment slipping into my voice before I could stop it. The fantasy of sentimental baby gifts dissolved instantly.

"Jewellery guy," Romeo said, excitement thick in his tone. "Nate, meet my wife, Chloe."

I shot off the bed with a solid thump—letting our guest know that while I wasn't light on my feet, I was still spicy.

"Are you kidding me? Jewellery is more important than building the crib?!"

Nate, clearly startled by my welcome, took a cautious step back, like I was a rabid dog snapping at a frayed leash.

"Don't start, woman," Romeo groaned, rolling his eyes. "Just come see. You'll like it, trust me."

Realising I wasn't getting a party, I tucked my tail and leaned into the moment. If I kicked off now, he'd be glued to my side all afternoon trying for makeup sex I really didn't want.

After a shaky start, Nate stepped in and heaved the large case onto the foot of the bed. A quiet grunt escaping him as he let go.

Romeo and I flanked him, silent and alert, watching as he flicked open the gold latches—each click a precise promise—and lifted the lid.

Two silver boxes. One larger than the other.

"Ready?" Nate asked, his accent more New York than LA. He reached for the bigger box, cradling it against his chest before lifting the lid toward us.

Inside, resting on a bed of black velvet, was a diamond-encrusted crucifix. Bigger. Flashier. A glistening upgrade from its predecessor.

Romeo's whole body softened. His smile morphed into a grin.

"Ooh shit. Real nice," he said in the same tone he used when he looked between my legs.

He unhooked the crucifix from its housing and moved toward the mirror. With practised ease, it was around his neck in seconds. But the man staring back in the reflection wasn't the same one who'd reached into that box.

Before, he was Romeo.

Now, he was King.

His eyes sharpened, hard and fire-like, as he turned back to me, pecs twitching and biceps somehow looking even bigger.

"What you sayin'?" He swiped the point of his nose gangster style.

But if King had been let out for air—then so had Jasmin.

I took the weight of the diamond cross in my hand. It filled my palm, stretching the length of my fingers.

Cold. Electric. Alive with promise.

I peered up at him through my lashes. He knew the look.

"I like," I murmured, tugging on it, bringing him closer, just enough heat to raise the temperature.

King, never one to miss an opening, slid his hands around my waist, pulling me close enough to taste the liquor on his breath.

"Aight. Your turn." He spun me to face Nate.

The warmth of his body trailed down my spine as I waited.

Nate opened the second box. No squeak—just the hiss of a hinge oiled in wealth.

Nestled in black velvet: a fine chain, a diamond pendant—glinting like a secret. A crucifix of my very own.

Nate closed his briefcase with a click. "White diamonds, precision-cut. The centre stone alone weighs two carats. Only the best for the best."

This wasn't just a symbol of faith. It was power.

Every facet caught the light with cold intent, echoing the sharp gleam of Romeo's chain. Fine platinum links framed the cross in a delicate, feminine silhouette—but the weight told a different story.

His was heavier. Harsher. A weapon.

Mine—sleeker. Designed to be worn like armour.

I flinched at the chill as Romeo fastened it around my neck. Then I took hold of the cross. No taller than an inch. No wider than my finger. It wasn't heavy. But it meant everything.

My own gun. My own crucifix.

"Wear this every day." Romeo took the cross between his fingers. "It's your protection against everythin'. Long as you've got this on, you've got God's arms around you. Got it?"

I clutched it like pearls. In a strange way, it gave me an extra ounce of strength—and a full measure of courage.

"I was mad at first," I said, fingers closing around it, feeling its force. "But now... I actually love it."

My pulse fluttered as my eyes trailed down his face. I kissed his lips, soft, plush, familiar.

Our necklaces met with a clink.

Metal against metal.

King and Jasmin locked in place.

He wrapped me in his arms. Tight. Relentless.

And in that moment, the deeper I dove into Romeo's world, the clearer his reasoning became.

We'd ruined each other in a way so potent.

Together, we had the power to live forever.

◆ ◆ ◆

It had only been four days since my last visit to the club, but from what Lucy said on the phone last night, things were moving fast enough for final approval on fixtures and fittings.

Tommy, as planned, was my driver today and my shadow while Romeo handled business that apparently didn't concern me. Grateful as I was to have my husband out of the way, I couldn't help but wonder what he was really up to in that so-called remote board meeting with Manik.

My fingers drifted to my neck, toying with the cross he'd given me. A symbol of unspoken reassurance. Smooth to the touch, the diamonds offered a strange sense of calm—completely at odds with the stupid idea I was about to follow through with.

Meeting Jamie behind Romeo's back had felt like the right thing to do this morning. Now... well, I wasn't the type to back out last minute.

"New guy, what's your name again?" I asked the rigid man sitting in the front passenger seat beside Tommy.

Traffic was heavy—as always in LA, no matter the hour. Horns blared. Sirens screamed. We rolled to a stop in the middle of the highway, boxed in on all sides.

He turned. Rich, warm brown eyes met mine.

"González, ma'am," he said, voice edged with a nervous wobble that made me question why he'd been chosen at all. Nothing about him had the time-served assurance of the original crew, but I guess they all started somewhere.

"Can I have my gun now, please?" I asked sweetly, hand out, fingers curled.

Tommy piped up before González had the chance to move. "I'm sorry, Boss, but I don't trust you with a Glock in the back of my car. When we arrive, I'll sort it, okay?"

Hmm. Seemed I was the boss until it wasn't convenient.

Truth was, ever since I'd asked Romeo to source me a gun, I'd had a vision in mind. When he handed it over like a righteous sword at the breakfast table, it hadn't exactly lived up to it. I'd pictured a short barrel. A palm-sized, pearlescent handle. Something feminine. Refined. An ally if I needed one—not a stranger I had to reacquaint myself with before pulling the trigger.

But Romeo hadn't thought about the firearm's new owner when he picked out an identical Glock to match his own.

I wanted to hold it. Become friends with it, even. Get comfortable with the weapon I'd handled so easily at the club.

Jasmin might be ready to fire at a moment's notice—Chloe needed to warm up to the idea first. Maybe that's what Tommy sensed when he took it from me as I stepped into the back of his BMW.

I shifted in my seat, sticking to the leather like it was summer, even though we'd barely hit spring. I was restless—first, to see the club and its progress. Second, to figure out what the hell Jamie's client wanted with me.

Too warm one minute, too cold the next. I fiddled with the A/C until the balance felt right. Then, a minute later, I was too hot again.

My stomach tightened and released in short bursts—sharp enough to steal my breath. Between baby kicks, backache, and anxiety, I was starting to realise the wick I'd been burning at both ends was nearly gone. The two flames were getting dangerously close to meeting in the middle.

Still uncomfortable, I cracked the window for air.

Bad idea.

The sour bite of exhaust fumes curled up my nose, coating my tongue with that heated, metallic tang only LA traffic could deliver.

My stomach gurgled, and the baby kicked again—a quiet hello. Or maybe a warning. Either way, he was packing his little suitcase, ready to meet the world any day now.

Was I excited? Absolutely.

Terrified? You bet your arse.

But with how attentive Romeo had been lately, I had nothing to fear but fear itself.

Peering out the window, I watched as the silhouette of the building came into view. An abandoned crane hung limply outside the club's entrance. Clocked off for the day. Not a single construction worker in sight.

It was quiet, but the kind of quiet filled with anticipation, the anticipation of life just beyond its doors.

Tommy's armour-plated BMW came to a rolling stop outside. Engine off, the hum of the city wrapped around us like it knew I was here.

While the building's footprint remained unchanged, its exterior had evolved. Blacks, reds, and golds replaced with neutrals. Neon signs gone.

Red rope lanes were now a thing of the past. It was still a strip club—but now, it was by appointment only. And women were very much welcome as customers, not just workers.

"Gonzo, sandwich. Got it?" Tommy barked at his new recruit. Unclipping his seatbelt, he slid the magazine into his gun with a sharp metallic snap.

I assumed he meant the manoeuvre, not a quick snack. But the way González glanced back—lights on, nobody home—made my stomach tighten all over again.

Out in the open air and wedged between two bodies, I caught the familiar scent of Tommy behind me and something completely alien up front. I stayed in line. A little armpit. A touch of car wax. He was nothing like what I'd grown used to since becoming a permanent fixture in Romeo's world.

Still, we made it inside with little resistance—aside from González's wrong turn, like he was headed for the building next door. All in all, I'd rate him a 3 out of 10. Plenty of room for improvement.

No sooner had we landed in the foyer than Lucy's eyes lit up at the sight of me.

In the corner by the door stood a mountain of discarded furniture and old knick-knacks. Among the broken light fittings, worn fabrics, and splintered wood, the throne from the VIP lounge sat proudly—its rich red velvet entirely at odds with the junk surrounding it.

"Don't throw that out," I said, pointing. "Can you get it delivered home? I want it at my dining table."

Inspired, I was already picturing a his-and-hers moment. One throne at each end.

Lucy, practically part of the furniture herself, scribbled something onto her pad. "I sourced that throne from the Kingdom of Naples. I'm glad it's finding a new purpose."

Of course she did. Nothing Lucy said surprised me anymore. Romeo probably paid six figures for it, too.

"If there's anything else completely over-the-top and expensive, let me know before it goes. I might want it." I winked.

Another scribble. Then a final full stop.

"Okay, Mrs G," she said. "I cannot wait a second longer. Follow me."

She gave nothing away.

As she turned, her oaky, leather-floral cologne drifted behind her, flaring my nostrils. She was always on my team.

Opening the door, a couple of tentative steps were all it took—then my breath vanished.

Soft uplighting along the baseboards gave the room a faint glow, like it was expecting me. A welcome home from a cherished friend.

The elevated stage, my well-thought-out addition and new focal point, stood proudly at the rear. Four gleaming poles spaced evenly apart. Spotlights poised above them, ready to showcase the beautiful bodies of the women who'd soon claim them. And for the first time, I saw it not as a work site, but as my future. Once my husband's. Now something of my own.

I, Chloe Giannetti, had become someone who had something to offer the world.

My sneakers squeaked across the freshly varnished oak floor as I strode forward—an army captain leading the way for her future troops. And in the very near future, this place would be teeming with clients and workers alike. A safe haven. A place for women to earn good money—without a single hair harmed on their pretty heads.

Lazy Boy chairs now stood where the dance floor used to be, one for each customer, angled towards the stage, ready for armchair comfort while they watched my girls move.

A freshly stocked bar glimmered in one corner, the low hum of refrigeration units not yet drowned out by loud music.

Opposite sat a plush group seating area, inviting conversation, seduction, or both.

The room held the warm scent of new upholstery and the sharp undertone of fresh paint. Exactly how I'd envisioned it.

"I have two surprises for you." Lucy trotted towards the window, a temporary veil thrown over it. "Now this was your husband's idea; I just made it happen."

Hearing of Romeo's secret involvement last minute—especially in such an important part of the design—wasn't ideal, but there wasn't room to ruin the vibe now.

Her hand gripped the veil, poised and ready.

I cradled my stomach.

"Okay, show me." I inwardly crossed my fingers.

The fabric floated to the ground in a feather-soft whisper.

And there it was. The only window in the room. Once forgotten behind heavy red velvet curtains, she now welcomed daylight through stained-glass panes. Obscured from the outside, but something so beautiful for those within.

I hadn't quite figured it out at first, but the man and woman etched into the glazed tapestry were a depiction of me and Romeo—face to face, each holding the other's tipped crown from falling.

By day, the space was bathed in a soft kaleidoscope of colour—light through the crown catching on my diamond crucifix like a private spotlight. My quiet link to the soul of this place.

By night, I already knew it would become something sacred.

"Do you like?" she asked, taking a step back.

I brushed my fingers over the smooth glass, rainbows of light bathing my skin. "Romeo really thought of this?" I turned, expectant.

"Well... he said something along the lines of you bent over. Him from behind. But I knew this is what he *really* meant."

I snorted. Of course, that's what he meant.

"Come, come, I'm not finished with surprises." Lucy beckoned, rushing as best she could in heels toward a temporary table in the centre of the room. She tapped confidently across the newly laid wood—no longer stirring dust clouds with every step. The space was almost ready.

Something caught my eye. Large. Flat. Draped in hessian cloth.

"Ooh, what's this?" I asked, stealing a peek underneath. My fingertips caught against the rough weave, almost sparking with sensation.

The ache in my back swelled like my pregnancy had finally tipped into too much. Gripping the edge of the table for relief, I leaned forward and glanced at Lucy with a smile.

"Your brand new door sign." She beamed. "New logo. New name."

She bounced where she stood, her bra barely containing her excitement. "You ready to see it?"

My hands hovered mid-air.

"I'm ready," I said, floating somewhere between reality and a dream. "You take off the cover."

She peeled back the cloth, tossing it to the floor.

There it was: *Jasmin's.*

Coloured light from our window spilled across the table, illuminating the sign like it had been waiting for this moment. Waiting for me.

The logo remained a silhouette of a woman—curvy, unapologetic, black against a white backdrop. But now, she held a red rose in her hand.

A dedication to the woman I couldn't save.

A promise to the women I would.

The longer I stared at that rose, its crimson petals dripping in both blood and love, the closer I felt to Alice. If she were here, she'd wrap her arms around me. Proud of what I'd become. And even though she wasn't, every woman who walked through that door would carry my protection. Always.

The silhouette was me.

The rose was every girl I'd hold in my hands.

This club meant everything. And this… this was just the beginning.

"So?" Lucy asked, still bouncing. "What do you think of the new sign?"

"You've nailed it. The window… this… I absolutely love it."

We sat together on the edge of the stage, our legs swinging side by side as we soaked it all in. I'd signed off every detail. Final choices made. Fabric fresh. Glasses polished. We were ready.

"What time is it?" I asked, a sudden jolt of nerves fluttering in my stomach. My visitor was due at four.

Lucy tapped her phone awake. The screen lit up—a photo of her with a sleek black cat in her arms. Its yellow eyes stared back at me. Unsettling. Like it knew something I didn't.

"3:45," she said, slipping it back into her purse.

Shit.

Tommy loomed in the far corner, not quite in earshot. His new recruit hovered close by, still stiff as a board, looking like he'd bitten off more than he could chew with this role.

I leaned into Lucy. "I can trust you, right? I know you worked for Romeo first, but..."

Her gaze flicked to Tommy. Even from here, the gleam of his holstered weapon caught the light—loud in its silence.

"Sure you can trust me," she whispered, her smile immediate. Soft. Reassuring.

Outside, horns blared in the distance—life continuing. My visitor soon to arrive.

The quiet between us was fragile as I chose my words carefully.

"My husband doesn't want me meeting a potential client." I edged even closer. "I've kept him busy so I can meet her here."

Our legs swung in sync. A silent pact.

"Okay." She nodded. "What do you need from me?"

I'd been building to this all day.

"Create a distraction out front. Just for five or ten minutes. I'll pop the fire door, let her in, and be done before Tommy realises."

Her smile curled into something wicked. Maybe she didn't fully understand Romeo's capacity for destruction. But she was game.

"No problem, Mrs G. I have an idea."

She slipped off the stage. Her feet landed with a clap that echoed like a starter's pistol. Her chin dipped with the movement, but her curves never missed a beat.

I watched as she jogged toward Tommy—who instinctively rested his hand on his gun. A couple of hushed words passed between them... then she left.

Hmm.

Sliding my bag across the stage, I popped the gold clasp and lifted the flap.

There it was. The gun Tommy didn't think I was ready for. But I'd show him.

I brushed my fingers over the weapon, nestled tight in its place. I wouldn't need it—not for Jamie. But just knowing it was here gave me the edge.

Headlights flickered through the stained-glass window—blue, green, gold—shining through our shared image, painting the walls before they vanished again.

Lucy's car. It was leaving.

So she wasn't going to help me? After everything?

Had I really misread her that badly?

Red light flashed through. A squeal of brakes. Then came the crash. An almighty collision. Metal on metal. Car alarms erupted in chorus. Amber lights pulsed through the glass like sirens.

Tommy pressed a finger to his earpiece.

"Boss, wait right here," he called. "Lucy's crashed into my fucking BMW! González—eyes on this room."

He bolted.

Wow. A full-blown crash?

That was… dedication.

I took my shot. Sliding off the stage, my back flared with pain as the baby shifted heavy beneath my ribs. But his weight was mine. Ours. Until he was ready to make me his mother.

He—and every woman I'd sworn to protect—were the reasons this place had to work. Nothing was going to stop me now.

González, about as useful as a chocolate fire guard, stood there watching as I made a beeline for the fire escape.

I slammed a shoulder into the quick-release bar.

It budged, stiff, but not quite enough. I forced it again—no time to waste.

The door flew open. A blast of wind smacked me in the face. My eyes snapped shut, stinging.

When I opened my eyes again, my stomach dropped and breath caught in my throat. I stumbled forward, unsteady.

A dark silhouette filled the doorway, cloaked entirely in black—heavy fabric swallowing every inch of skin, a jacket zipped tight, and a ski mask hiding all but two wide, unblinking eyes, pupils dilated like voids swallowing the light. The gloved hands hung loosely, fingers curling slowly into clenched fists.

I gripped the cross hanging around my neck, but it felt like a last, useless hope. I was alone in this.

"Please." I raised a trembling hand and stepped back.

Something moved behind me. A faint squeak of rubber against concrete echoed in the heavy silence. A subtle shift in the air brushed past my skin. The hairs on the back of my neck prickled.

Then darkness swallowed me whole. The rough fabric pressed tightly over my head, damp and grimy against my skin, sticky with sweat and something sour beneath it, trapping me in suffocating blackness.

Each sharp inhale pressed the fabric against my lips; every breath out pulled it away, a cruel rhythm I couldn't escape, starving me of the fresh air I so desperately needed.

My life moved in slow motion as the darkness carried me forward. Panic, sheer paralysing terror, froze me. I couldn't move a muscle.

I always thought that in a moment like this, I'd scream. But my vocal cords stayed silent—my cry ran dry.

My ears filled with a sharp, piercing squeal that sliced through the silence. Deafening.

Then it faded.

Replaced by the pounding rhythm of my heartbeat at the base of my throat. Almost spilling from my mouth, my only plea for help, one only I could hear.

Whispers closed in around me. Footsteps like an army.

Light shifted at the edges of the fabric. Then everything stilled. Slowly, my hearing sharpened.

A car door opened.

I was lifted off the ground and shoved inside, landing hard on cold leather. The door slammed shut behind me.

But I wasn't alone. I felt the stranger. A presence right beside me. Heavy. Watching.

My stomach clenched and released. Tight as a vice, then soft as a feather. I winced. Not that it mattered. With my face hidden, my weakness was mine alone.

Then hands found mine. Firm. Steady. The heat of skin beneath thick gloves burned through the fabric, anchoring me in place. I struggled, but the grip was unyielding.

An engine rumbled to life. It vibrated beneath my seat—my only thread to reality.

The car moved. A slow roll at first. Then faster.

Where were they taking me? What did they want from me?

A voice ahead of me pierced the darkness.

"You scared?" His tone was harsh. Rough. Like sandpaper dragged over skin.

Another twist in my stomach—deeper this time. Harder.

I sucked in air, unable to hide the strain.

Fingers clenched tighter around my wrists as I fought back.

"Yes, I'm scared," I said quickly, desperately. "Please. Let… me… ouch!"

The word caught in my throat as pain bloomed, sharp and hot, across my belly. A serrated pressure, like a knife sliding beneath my skin.

"You better be scared." The voice mumbled. "If you don't do as you're told. It won't end good for you."

My stomach clenched again. Speckles of light flooded the darkness.

"Please don't hurt me. My husband… he has money—"

Then, as if things couldn't get worse, a sudden gush spilled from my body, like a water balloon bursting with a pinprick. I fought to hold it in, drawing my legs tightly together to slow the relentless flow.

Panic prickled at my skin. My waters had broken. My baby was coming.

"Fuck!" The earthy, masculine voice cursed beside me.

Wait.

My breath hitched. My thighs parted instantly, muscles relaxing with the familiarity.

I knew that voice.

The hold on my wrists vanished. The cover was ripped from my head, flooding my vision with blinding light.

I blinked furiously, eyes adjusting, only to find the figure still masked, still dressed in black.

But those eyes gave him away.

Piercing blue. Wide. Terrified.

"Romeo!?" I gasped, reaching a shaky hand for the ski mask and tearing it from his face.

Pain ripped through me. Sharp as shrapnel.

"Ahhh! Shit! Ouch!" I whimpered.

Our knees touched. I flinched against the connection.

"Is the baby comin'?" he choked, his tousled curls as wild as the moment he'd orchestrated.

A plate of armour seemed to harden over my stomach—then disappeared again as the contraction eased.

My vision sharpened. My mind caught up.

Tommy was driving. A new recruit I didn't recognise sat beside him, a piece of paper in hand. Were those lines he was reading? Like a script from some low-budget movie?

I blinked. Shocked. Confused.

Romeo's hand reached for mine. I pulled back.

He was behind this? My husband was my captor?

"What the fuck is wrong with you!?" Without thinking, I swung. My fist connected with his jaw.

The pain in my knuckles was nothing compared to the fire ripping through my abdomen.

His head jolted. He didn't block it. Didn't flinch. He looked stunned. Shaken. Like he'd only just realised what he'd done.

A red mark bloomed across his jaw.

"I... I just wanted to teach you a lesson," he stammered. "For goin' behind my back."

Pain eased off. Clarity sharpened.

"You kidnapped me to teach me a lesson!?"

He dragged his hands through his hair like he was clawing at his own thoughts.

"Your phone's tapped," he said finally. "I heard you on the phone with that bitch, plottin' to meet. I had to teach you that without me, you ain't safe."

A stab in my stomach flared again.

"I don't need you," I hissed, teeth clenched so tight I could feel my molars crack.

"Oh yeah? Where's your gun? The one you begged me for?" His eyes weren't cruel. They were desperate.

Desperate to keep me safe. Desperate to keep me.

It hit me then.

My bag was still on the stage.

My Glock…

Shit.

He had somehow become the nest. And I, the chick trying to break free. Was he right? Were my wings not strong enough to fly?

"You had Tommy in on this, too?" I panted through the pain.

The air turned poisonous.

Romeo was my husband. My protector. My best friend—turned enemy in an instant.

"Chloe…" He dragged his hands down his face. "You think I'm fuckin' dumb or some shit? I know everythin' about everythin'. I knew about your plan the second you did."

He leaned in, eyes bloodshot, breathing heavy. "What happened today? All of it. Planned by me to show you that you ain't as ready as you think."

Here we were again. At the same impasse, we always seemed to find ourselves. I'd gone behind his back. He'd sought revenge—wrapped in bloodstained gift wrap, tied with the excuse of protecting me.

A poorly concealed attempt to make this about my safety.

We were both in the wrong.

My stomach hardened again—tighter this time. A thread of pain wove through my entire core, pulling everything taut.

"Hospital, Tommy. Now!" Romeo barked, his voice cracking on the edge of panic. "My son is comin'!"

By the time we reached the hospital, I was howling in agony.

"Breathe, baby," Romeo urged, trailing behind the wheelchair as a friendly nurse wheeled me through the labour ward and opened the door to my private suite.

We hadn't said a word about the 'kidnap' since my waters broke, but it clawed at the back of my mind all the same.

My skin was slick with sweat despite the A/C working overtime. This was it. My son, my baby boy, was ready to meet me. And I was so ready to meet him too.

A doctor floated in moments later, composed and efficient, the door clicking shut behind her with quiet finality. The chaotic hum of the hospital dulled to silence.

Now it was just us.

Dressed in a long white coat and wearing a calm smile, she was the only one in the room who wasn't rattled.

"Hi, guys. I'm Doctor Peterson, but with the amount of money you're paying me, just call me Sophie." She smirked, snapping on a pair of blue latex gloves. "I'm just going to examine you. Try to relax if you can."

I lay back against the bed, unsure of what to expect. The crispness of the sheets mixed with the bite of hospital-grade detergent grounded me. I was here. This was happening.

Romeo's cold hand locked with mine. Steady, but tense. His other hand curled into a fist at his side—ready to fight the pain for me if he could. His jaw locked tight. His eyes never left Sophie as she rested her hands on my propped-up knees and gently coaxed them wider.

Then, without warning, she inserted what felt like her entire hand inside me.

The fluorescent lights above buzzed faintly, a sound I hadn't noticed until everything else went still.

What was she doing? Was everything okay?

Her expression shifted—concentration giving way to calm preparation. "Oh, wow. This baby is impatient. They'll be here very soon! You're already nine centimetres dilated."

She carefully withdrew her hand, tossing the gloves into the trash.

My body slackened. I exhaled as my legs dropped back onto the hard, slab-like mattress.

Ah, shit. Another contraction.

Eyes screwed shut, my body turned against me. My back arched, hips lifting as the pain ripped through. I didn't know whether to scream, cry, or laugh—but somehow, I was doing all three.

Romeo's upper lip curled. "Is this normal, Doc? All this pain she's in?"

Wait. What was that?

"I need the bathroom!" I cried, shooting upright. "Ouch! Oh fuck. Shit."

Sweat beaded in the hollows of my knees, slicking the backs of my thighs against the crinkled sheets.

Back between my legs, Sophie adjusted her glasses.

"Focus on your breathing. Loosen your shoulders, Chloe," she said gently, squeezing my calf. "The fullness you're feeling in your rectum is the baby's head in the birth canal. You're very close."

Romeo stood by my head. Ironic, really. He looked more uncomfortable in a delivery room than he ever had murdering someone in cold blood.

Sophie leaned in for a closer look. Relaxed. Focused.

"Okay, keep calm. Let's do this. Dad, do you want to hold Mom's hand?"

A nauseating wave of pain clenched my stomach.

"Ahh! Shit! I can't do this." Cheeks puffed with breath, I panted through the agony.

"Push now, Chloe—on this contraction, push!"

Chin tucked to my chest, I gave it everything.

Eyes shut, it was just me and my body. A resounding thud repeated in my ears as my heart took the brunt.

A gasp in. A scream out. Seconds stretched into hours. My knees knocked. My ankles threatened to give out.

"It's burning!" I cried. "I can't do this. Please. Fuck! Why is it burning!?"

"Holy shit," Romeo muttered, shifting on his feet, wiping his forehead with the back of his hand.

Sophie pressed her palms to my thighs—grounding me. Steadying me.

"Chloe, look at your baby being born. Open your eyes. Watch this magical moment."

No sound remained. No machines. No voices.

Just breath.

Just me.

Just this.

My eyelids flickered open—just in time to see a piece of my soul leave my body.

The slick stretch of pressure as he crowned was like fire meeting silk. First, dark curls. A perfectly round head. Then plump shoulders, a chubby body, arms and legs with tiny fingers and toes.

I clutched my necklace—my strength. My protector.

I was giving birth to the life I'd longed for.

And just like that. We were two.

Me and my baby. Together at last.

A flood of emotion washed through me as I stared at my entire world cradled in the doctor's hands. So small. So real.

Was I dreaming?

Had I really just given birth?

"It's definitely a boy," Sophie said gently, her sandals squeaking faintly as she stepped closer and laid him on my chest with care.

The warmth of his skin met mine. Damp yet sticky. Velvety soft. A connection so immediate, so overwhelming, I wasn't sure I could breathe through it.

It felt like a piece of me had been taken away—only to be returned seconds later.

He was here.

A hush settled over the room.

A stranger in my arms. Yet somehow, I knew him.

My creation. My masterpiece.

His round, warm-toned face, cherub-like, with a perfect little nose and rose-red cheeks, looked up at me like he recognised me.

I kissed the soft curls on his head—the same dark waves he shared with his father. His scent was intoxicating. That newborn smell. Not bottled like cologne. Not artificial. Just... him.

He smelled like me. But also like his father.

Something inside me clicked into place. I wanted to give him everything. I needed to love him with everything I had.

I was a mother now. And Romeo… he was a father.

We did it. We made it this far.

Our little bundle began to cry and instinctively, I pulled him closer, cradling him to my chest.

"Shh… it's okay, baby. Mummy loves you. Shh…"

Did he love me yet, the way I already loved him?

Could I be everything he needed?

I looked up at Romeo.

He stood over us, towering but stripped of menace. Arms stiff. Eyes wide. A ghost of a smile on his lips—gentle and stunned, pride glistening in his lashes. A single tear pooled in the corner of his eye. He wiped it fast.

Doctor Sophie waved a pair of scissors in his direction, snipping the air with a playful grin.

"Do you want to cut the cord, Daddy?"

He cleared his throat, wiping his eyes again with a sniff. "Yeah," he croaked. "Of course."

"Oh! You're a lefty. Hold on—I'll grab the special scissors," she said, turning to the sterile tray.

My finger paused on the baby's cheek. My head snapped up. "Wait… you're left-handed?"

How the hell didn't I know that?

Something so small, so seemingly insignificant, felt massive in that moment. A new discovery about the man I thought I knew inside out.

"You best believe it. Only real men are left-handed," Romeo said with a shrug full of bravado.

"You're not wrong," Sophie added. "I did a paper on it in uni once. Left-handed men in battle had the advantage—attacking from the opposite angle. What was once considered a weakness turned out to be a strength. It even helped keep the population growing."

The room paused, sharing a glance—caught in her unexpected tangent. Romeo stood there, the only one dripping with smug self-satisfaction. I didn't think she fancied him, but she sure as hell knew how to stroke his already inflated ego.

While he fumbled through the simple task, tongue caught between his teeth like he was defusing a bomb, he finally made the cut. The first snip needed a second, but the smile that followed was worth its weight in gold.

Doctor Sophie reached for her clipboard, picking up a pen and a name tag.

"Right then." She smiled. "Do we have a name for this beautiful little boy?"

Romeo handed the scissors to her assistant and ran his fingertips gently through our son's hair, who lay peacefully against my chest.

"Romero Luca Giannetti the Fourth," he announced, pride thick in the Italian lilt he saved for moments like this.

Sophie's mouth dropped slightly. "My goodness. What a powerful name. Giannetti—is that Italian?" She frowned, already struggling with the spelling.

Romeo took the pen from her gloved hand. "Here, let me do it."

Watching him write our son's name on the ID tag with such care. The feeling was indescribable. A sense of calm after the most intense storm settled around us, warm and weightless.

Time reset—machines softly beeping, the whir of monitors slipping back into awareness. Like someone had plugged my world back into the wall.

My life was restarting in a way I never thought possible.

This time, I'd write the script myself.

This time, I'd control my own destiny.

The love pouring out of me wrapped around my son like a second skin. Our souls already tangled together.

I kissed the top of his head again. That smell, that warmth... him. Love at first breath. Love at first everything.

Doctor Sophie stepped closer, hands reaching gently toward me. "Let me just take him a moment—he needs to be weighed."

No. He's mine.

My brows pulled tight as I cocooned him protectively against me, a primal vulnerability flaring just beneath the surface. I wasn't ready to let go. Not yet.

She offered a soft smile, patient and reassuring, then gently scooped him up with the confidence of someone who did this every day.

"We'll be right back, Mommy." She rocked him lightly. "Little Romero," she whispered, bouncing him just enough to soothe his cries. "All these dark curls. He looks just like his daddy."

She placed him on the scale.

Each second my arms lay empty, the rhythm of my heart grew louder, pounding through the hospital monitors like a silent scream. I needed him back.

Helpless, I waited. Heart so full. Soul beginning to crack.

How could I love another human being this much when I'd only just met him?

Did I love Romeo like this?

I wasn't sure I did.

"Wow! Nine pounds, four ounces," she said, exchanging a glance with her assistant. "He's a big boy."

She wrapped him snug in a soft blue cotton blanket and finally placed him back on my chest—right where he belonged.

I shifted slightly, propping myself up with a wince. A dull tug pulled between my legs, a raw reminder of where he'd just come from. "He felt every ounce of that on the way out, too."

She tucked her pen into her top pocket. "Don't worry. You didn't tear. Just a little swelling." She paused, tilting her head. "Do you need a hand with breastfeeding?"

I glanced at Romeo, who suddenly looked very interested.

"Um… I think so."

She nodded, calm and efficient.

"Sometimes the breast needs a little massage to get the milk flowing."

Without warning, she reached into my gown and scooped out my breast in one smooth, professional motion.

Romeo's eyes widened like it was Christmas morning and Santa had done good this year.

It didn't take long—under her firm, clinical pressure, a warmth built behind my nipple. Tingling. Strange. I felt it before I saw it. A single trickle of pale yellow milk beaded on the surface.

She seemed pleased. "Okay. Let's position baby."

Like father, like son—my baby boy latched on immediately and suckled, releasing light whimpers of pleasure through his tiny button nose.

The sensation was indescribable. Incredible... yet completely overwhelming. My breast, once a source of pleasure, had become something sacred. Something I could barely comprehend.

Romeo stood stock-still in stunned silence. The quietest I'd ever seen him. His eyes stayed locked on us, wide with wonder.

"I'll leave you alone for a while," Doctor Sophie said gently. "See you in a couple of hours."

When Romeo's gaze finally met mine, I smiled through the euphoric haze. "You ready to hold your son?"

He nodded slowly, a flicker of uncertainty creasing the lines in his otherwise unreadable face.

"Take off your 'kidnapping shirt'," I teased.

It was almost comical to think that just hours ago, he'd bundled me into the back of a van to 'teach me a lesson.'

Now, here he was—bare-chested, sheepish, silent.

A man undone.

Without a word, he did as he was told. Tentatively, he perched beside me on the bed, and I guided our baby into his arms. Skin to skin, Romeo inhaled the moment. Breathless.

"Thank you," he whispered. "For blessin' me with a boy."

He kissed the top of Romero's head, eyes closed, breathing him in like it might save him. "I love you so much, Chloe."

I absorbed the vision in front of me—every detail, every word.

"I love you too, Romeo. I love you both... so much."

The universe shrank in that moment, tightening into a quiet, perfect bubble like we were the only three people alive.

We basked in the quiet, soaking it in. Each of us tethered to this tiny human we'd waited so long to meet. So small in Romeo's arms. So fragile. And yet, somehow, this child, his son, had become his power source. I could already see it—their future colliding like atoms in a nuclear blast the world wasn't ready for.

I stifled a yawn into my fingers. "Should we talk about what happened earlier?"

Now wasn't the time for confrontation, yet the unanswered questions waited too loudly to ignore.

He kept his eyes on Junior. His only reaction was the slow knit of his brows. "What's there to talk about?"

Junior's peaceful breathing filled the space. So innocent, so unaware of what his father was capable of.

Did he really need it spelled out?

"Tell me exactly how you knew I'd arranged to meet Jamie at the club."

He kissed the tip of his son's nose, breathing him in. Calming him. Soothing him. Choosing his baby over the conversation. On any other day, this would've been a minefield—loud, volatile, brimming with raised voices and raw emotion. But the newborn scent lingered like a hush, wrapping the room in peace.

"First off," he said without looking up, "I ain't dumb. You chasin' Jamie down in VIP over some bullshit tampon string in a pair of pants? That got me suspicious real quick."

He gave a slight shake of his head, almost amused. "I was waitin' for it to happen. Came sooner than I expected, but kept me light on my feet."

Jeez. I already knew I'd underestimated him—but this? This was next level. What else had he let me get away with?

Stunned into humbled silence, I waited.

"Since the honey trapper," he went on, "I put a mirror tap on your cell. I see it all, Queen."

His eyes met mine, clear, cutting, ocean blue. "The girl-on-girl porn tab you open sometimes… lookin' at Daniele's profile on Instagram… the message you typed to him and deleted before you hit send."

He tilted his head slightly. No judgement. Just fact. "You name it. I've seen it."

Oh my God.

I had messaged Dan to ask if he was okay after the poisoning, only to change my mind and delete the evidence.

The heart monitor still taped to my chest picked up pace. No amount of nose-breathing could calm it. If the look on my face didn't give me away, the monitor sure as hell did.

"So you knew before you gave me the gun this morning?"

I reached for the cross nestled in my cleavage. I took hold. Took cover.

He nodded, casual as ever. Still too absorbed in the bundle in his arms to fully acknowledge me.

"But if you knew," I pressed, "why were you in such a good mood? Excited, even, to give it to me?"

He smirked, flicking a glance my way.

"I kinda wanted you to try and shoot me durin' the kidnap. The idea got my dick real hard."

My mouth opened, but no words came out.

He watched me expectantly, like he was waiting for a reaction. Like I might giggle and pencil it in my diary for next week. A part two?

"So you heard me on the phone and what, got the entire crew to stage a hostage situation to prove a point? Even Lucy?"

He gave one slow, assured nod. "Even Lucy."

Shit. No wonder it had all worked in my favour. It had seemed too easy.

The claustrophobic calm of the hospital room closed in—quiet, sterile, suddenly thick with the weight of what might have happened.

"But what if I had shot you? Killed you even?"

That, apparently, was the funniest thing I'd ever said. He chuckled low and controlled, just enough to soothe the baby, not disturb him.

"I've seen you shoot a gun enough times to know the signs. I can tell exactly when you're 'bout to pull the trigger. I was ready for it. But you proved me right, anyway. You ain't ready for a gun."

I couldn't argue with that logic. Maybe I wasn't as ready as I thought, but a smirk tugged at my lips as the first image flashed through my mind when the blindfold came off.

"You know what you're not ready for?" I nudged him teasingly. "Writing scripts. You told him what to say, right?"

He huffed, replaying the scene with a dry chuckle. "That was just the openin'. Didn't even get the chance to get down to the good part."

My smile faltered. Something told me I didn't want to know what else he'd had in mind.

"The fact you went to the effort to use a new crew member, so I didn't recognise his voice, shows how much effort you put into your plans."

His eyes held a mix of amusement and disbelief. "But with you, there's always somethin' that goes wrong." His voice softened. "Didn't think this little guy would be on his mum's side, busting his ass out of his nine-month jail sentence early."

Exhaustion weighed down my limbs; I fought off the yawn clawing up my throat, the cool evening air slipping in through the cracked window brushing against my skin.

"He just wanted to meet his daddy already."

Romeo smiled gently, pressing a tender kiss to Junior's forehead, then both cheeks, his warmth wrapping around us like a protective blanket.

"Forget that now. We both learned somethin' from it." He looked at me, his eyes steady and warm. His hand slid down to squeeze my thigh—gentle, grounding. "Go to sleep, Queen. I got this."

I shook my head, eyes heavy, lids fluttering. "Put him in his crib for a bit and sleep with me. I need you beside me."

No matter how reckless his plan had been, no matter how stupid, he wanted to prove how wrong I was in the only way he knew.

The thought of him knowing I'd gone behind his back again dragged those words back into my mind—the ones he said in therapy. Could he really walk away from me now? Or did this just show me how much he truly couldn't give up on me? On us.

"Nah. I don't need sleep." He adjusted Romero gently in his arms, rocking slightly like it was second nature.

But I saw it. The heaviness behind his eyes. The tightness in his shoulders. The telltale twitch of his fingers against our son's blanket. He needed sleep. He just didn't want to leave himself vulnerable. Not again.

"Besides, you did all the hard work. Credit where it's due, woman. Seein' the boy's head come outta you like that… made me feel kinda sick."

That was a memory I had no interest in reliving.

I rolled my eyes, catching the look on his face—clearly, he was reliving it, too.

"Oi! I told you not to look!"

He let out a low chuckle. The usual tension gone from his body.

I yawned again as I lay back, ready to surrender to the most welcome sleep of my life. But just before my eyes fluttered shut, the same thought whispered through the fog.

I reached for my crucifix. I understood now what the symbol meant to him. A connection to something higher. A trust that, somehow, everything would be okay.

"Don't give up on me, Romeo."

He looked at me. His gaze serious.

"After the gift you just gave me?" He reached for my hand, linking our fingers together. "I'll be by your side until the day I die."

My cheeks flushed. "Or until I do something silly again?"

He smirked. "Even then. It's me and you. Always."

◆ ◆ ◆

My feet shifted over the rough-textured sheets when I woke a few hours later, back a little stiff, breasts swollen and heavy.

My baby slept peacefully in his crib, and my husband snored softly in the hospital recliner—head tilted back, mouth wide open.

I reached over and nudged his shin gently with my foot. He snorted awake, eyes flying open with a jolt. His head whipped around, blinking like he'd forgotten where he was.

"Hey, Daddy," I whispered, smiling shyly.

He stood slowly, shoulder popping as he stretched the creak from his joints. The soft rustle of his shirt rising over his abs broke the quiet.

He stepped toward the crib and leaned over it. His eyes softened instantly. "I woke up thinkin' it was all a dream. Got me real worried."

He reached inside and brushed his fingertips over Junior's soft skin.

"Hey, Son," he said gently. "It's your daddy."

The metal bedframe creaked beneath me as I crept forward beneath the covers, aching just as much in my body as I was to be close to him. I touched his forearm—the soft hairs against the heat of his skin grounding me. Usually, those arms were wrapped around me during intimacy. Now they guarded his heir.

"Romeo, talk a little softer. Don't wake him."

He nodded, lowering his voice to a whisper. "Do you think he likes me yet?"

The sun dipped low through the blinds, casting a golden haze across Romeo's face. An almost angelic image to match the sincerity of his question.

"Of course he does. Babies are born loving their parents."

Romeo frowned, thoughts drifting. "Yeah? I didn't love mine."

The weight of his reply landed between us like a rainy day.

"You did… until they let you down. We won't make the same mistakes our parents did."

He turned to me, eyes burning. Not just with emotion, but with want. His fingers curled around the crib rail like he was holding on for dear life.

"Can we do it again—?"

The door swung open with a hiss, letting in a rush of clinical air thick with antiseptic, and the distant screams of women reaching the crowning point of labour.

"Hi folks!" An unfamiliar nurse bustled in, all cheer and bounce, oblivious to the moment she'd crashed.

"Just here to check on Mommy and Baby," she chirped, rubbing her hands together above the crib. "Let's warm these hands up first, shall we, baby Romero?"

Carefully, she scooped Junior out and lowered him onto the changing mat. I held my breath until he was safely placed.

He stirred, a little puff of air escaping his lips as he grimaced. Tiny fists balled. Arms flailed. Legs tucked up tight—gearing for a cry.

As soon as his voice broke the surface, my body responded. My nipples hardened. Milk surged. That primal ache returned—ready, at a moment's notice, to keep him alive.

Romeo stood close, radiating hostility at the intrusion.

He tapped her shoulder. "You'll know the answer to this, nurse. When can we try for another baby?"

Her smile vanished like someone had flipped a personality switch. She snapped open the poppers on the baby's sleep suit.

"Your wife's been through quite an experience, Mr Giannetti. She needs time to heal."

His fists clenched, thumb wrapped tight across his fingers. The tension from earlier—the kidnapping, the secrets—still clung to him. Hidden just beneath the surface.

"I know. I was there. But that don't answer my question."

She bit her tongue and continued with the nappy change. A wipe of his bottom. The rustle of a packet. Junior whimpered. Then sobbed. Then settled again under her careful hands.

"Six months. Minimum. Even that's too soon."

"Bullshit," he growled. "Would it hurt her if she got pregnant in a few weeks?"

Watching another woman fight my corner restored something in me. The nurse wasn't impressed. I wasn't either, but strangely, I wasn't completely opposed to the idea.

Her cheeks flushed. Irritation radiated off her like heat from a boiling kettle. He had that effect on people. The line between love and exasperation was always wafer thin with Romeo.

"Mr Giannetti," she said, tight-lipped, placing Junior firmly back in the crib. "That is an unrealistic expectation. I strongly advise against it."

She turned to me with a softer smile and reached forward. A wave of cool, lemon-tinged sanitiser lifted from her scrubs as she brushed my forehead gently. "I'll be back shortly to check your blood pressure."

Her eyes met his as she left—with noticeably less bounce than when she arrived.

"She was a bitch," he said a little too loudly as the door closed behind her.

I sighed, rubbing at my heavy eyelids. This was a conversation that required energy I didn't have.

"Help me up, Romeo. I need to pee."

That wicked glint returned to his eye. The thought of impregnating me again had already stirred the beast in his kidnapper trousers. Seeing me on the toilet might just finish him off.

"Oh yeah? Need some help with that?"

I hobbled successfully to the bathroom door and paused in the frame, raising a brow.

"Behave, or I'll get that nurse back in here to kick you out."

He leaned back against the bedframe, smirking. "Leave the door open so I can at least watch."

He adjusted himself, eyes pinned to my body like he was hunting his next meal.

"You're a pervert, Giannetti." I giggled, shaking my head.

Reassurance, it seemed, came in many forms.

I didn't even need to ask if we were okay. After everything… I knew we were better than ever.

Sitting on the cold toilet rim wasn't quite the experience I'd imagined. With no hospital bag amid the urgency of our arrival, the balls of my bare feet pressed against icy porcelain, adding another layer of discomfort to my already overloaded body. It felt like a battle to keep my internal organs in while trying to let anything else out.

Clench. Release. A coordination game I hadn't trained for.

From the other room, Romeo's voice floated in. "Are we callin' him Junior, then?"

I flinched.

The flow had just started—then stopped immediately.

I grabbed the handrail. "Hold on. I'm trying to concentrate here."

I returned, walking tenderly with a dull ache low in my belly. Everything from the neck down felt like it wanted out of me. The blinds were closed, wall lights dimmed. The room's warmth wrapped around me like a thick blanket.

Romeo looked up. "So, we callin' him Junior?"

I glanced at our sleeping bundle. Gorgeous. Perfect in every way.

"Yeah. I think so." I tucked the blanket around his little body tighter. "Don't you?"

The baby let out a little snuffle. A contented sound.

I sat beside Romeo, easing an arm around his shoulder, fingers toying with his earlobe.

"I mean, Romero is your name. It'd get confusing."

He didn't answer straight away—just gazed into the crib, then slowly leaned forward and rested his chin on the edge.

"But you call me Romeo," he said, pouting like a child with a dropped ice cream cone.

I kissed his temple, smiling at the softness in him. The forehead vein was nowhere to be seen. For now.

"You want to call him Romero, huh?"

He nodded—full grin, all teeth. A man who'd just been handed the universe.

"Okay then," I said softly. "That's what we'll call him."

◆ ◆ ◆

After a quick shower and another nap, I was finally starting to feel a little more human—especially now that Tommy had stopped by with supplies, including my hospital bag.

The soft glow of streetlights spilled through the slatted blinds, lining the walls in golden stripes.

Our first day with our baby was nearly over.

I might've felt more like myself again, but my milk had other ideas. It soaked clean through my freshly worn pyjamas and refused to let up. Not even for a second.

Romeo smirked from across the room, eyes locked on my chest. "I don't know why, but seein' your titties like that turns me on. Like, I ain't kiddin'. I'm hard."

He stalked over, cocky and playful, and hooked a confident finger inside the neckline of my top, popping the first button.

"You're so fuckin' sexy."

The swell of my engorged breasts was too much for either of us to ignore.

"Behave," I warned, swatting him as I fought a laugh. "Pass me some nipple pads from my hospital bag."

His face screwed up like I'd just bitten a lemon and spat the juice in his mouth. "Nipple what?"

"Nipple pads." I smirked. "I think there might be a cream in there, too."

That got his attention.

With all the enthusiasm of someone hunting for treasure they didn't know existed, he unzipped the holdall, peered inside at the mountain of creams, baby gear, and maternity chaos—then gave up entirely.

"There's too much shit in here. You look." Too impatient to work for his reward. He shoved it at me.

While I rummaged through the organised mess, most of it picked out under Trish's expert guidance, Romeo perched on the edge of the bed, tracking my every move.

Correction: tracking my boobs. His tongue swept across his bottom lip like he hadn't eaten in days.

"Can I try it?"

I glanced down, following his eyeline.

"My milk?" I asked, popping the next button without thinking. "Yeah. I guess."

His grin bloomed like someone had handed him a triple scoop of redemption.

"Can I try now? Kinda thirsty over here." The excitement in his eyes radiated.

"Not now, Romeo." I refastened the buttons, already picturing the horror on Doctor Sophie's face if she walked in and found me nursing my husband instead of our newborn. "Let's save that for when we get home."

He placed a warm hand on my thigh, stroking gently. His touch reverent, eyes dark with want. The heat I thought had been extinguished during birth reignited in a single stroke.

"Chloe?" he murmured, voice low and loaded.

"Yes, Romeo?" I squirmed.

"I really wanna try for another baby soon. Do you?"

The thought made my whole body flutter. Whether it was hormones or the idea of another tie binding us for life, it gave me butterflies.

"Of course I do. But not just yet. "My vagina really hurts, and your dick is way too big."

He looked half smug, half sympathetic. A dangerous mix that always worked in his favour.

Then—a knock landed at the door. Harsh. Rushed.

Followed by the muffled voice of a nurse, sounding a little frantic.

"I'm sorry, ma'am," she called. "They're not accepting visitors right now—"

"Romero, *dove sei!?*" A woman's voice echoed down the corridor. Italian. Familiar.

Too familiar.

Oh no. This could only mean one thing.

His fucking mother was here.

I snapped my head toward Romeo, eyes wide with panic, only to find him just as horrified as I was.

I clutched the bed sheets, raising them higher over my chest. My only protection against a woman who could've been so much more to me.

"Please move from this door, nurse. I am his mother, and I have a right to see my grandchild!" Her voice bounced down the hallway like a curse.

A silent standoff played out on the other side of the wall—soft breaths, brushing fabric, tension radiating through the wood.

The baby stirred in his crib, already sensing emotions building around him.

"Ma'am, they do not want to be disturbed," Tommy said. Flat. Authoritative. Unfazed. I already knew he had his hand on his gun.

It was like birdsong and rainbows in our world one minute—flames and burning buildings the next.

Romeo muttered something under his breath, too low to catch, then stormed across the room, yanked the door open, and faced the chaos head-on.

"*Non sei il benvenuto. Partire.*"

Wait—what did he just say?

Was he leaving… or telling her to leave?

The answer came fast.

She slapped him across the face. Italian style—with all the drama of a TV series finale.

"How dare you, Romero Luca! You cannot stop me from seeing my grandchild!"

He didn't flinch, but the slap landed hard. His cheek reddened instantly. Between my sock to the jaw and his mother's handiwork, Romeo was fast becoming a martyr to his own behaviour.

Arms folded across his chest, he stood tall in the doorway—his entire body a blockade.

"I don't want you here, Mother. Leave."

I knew this moment had been coming since her New Year's dinner. I'd seen the shift in him then—when she humiliated him in front of everyone. He'd said it plain; his children would never sit at her table. Business partners were one thing. This was something else entirely.

As only a crazed mother could, she shoved past him and stormed to the crib. Junior had been sleeping—peaceful, perfect—before her intrusion. That didn't stop her. She scooped him up like she had any right, unsettling him instantly.

My stomach flipped. Panic crashed through me like a wave.

The air shattered around me. Vulnerable in my post-partum state, I hated how scared I felt, helpless.

"Please put him down! Romeo, do something!"

I angled my body toward the crib like a shield, arms wrapped tightly across my chest.

Romeo's chest heaved. His pulse pounded visibly in his neck, the throb at his temple a silent warning.

"Mother," he growled. "Do as you're fuckin' told and put my son down. Now."

His voice sliced through the room. Even the hustle and bustle down the corridors seemed to pause.

Junior's tiny fists curled tighter, twitching. If I didn't know better, I'd swear he was bracing to face her, too.

Mother Giannetti must've inherited her son's hearing loss. She didn't listen.

"*Oh, mio dio,*" she muttered, slinging Junior over her shoulder like a handbag. She patted his back with entitlement. "This boy needs feeding."

Then her eyes found me.

"Are you incapable of producing milk, child?"

Junior whimpered. My blood boiled—like the milk spilling from my breasts. The word child tipped it over.

Romeo stepped between us. His voice dropped, lethal in its restraint. "Stop callin' my wife a fuckin' child. She's the mother of your grandson."

He hadn't had a cigarette in hours. Anyone could see the twitch in his jaw. The strain in his shoulders. He was hanging on by a thread.

She scoffed and finally handed Junior over into his outstretched arms.

Her perfume lingered, thick and outdated. Like mildew. It clung to the air like poison—like she stank of all the damage she refused to acknowledge.

"That baby is cursed, Romero. Can you not see?" she sneered. "Half American, ugh! You should've had a baby with a beautiful Italian woman."

Romeo said nothing.

He placed the baby down gently.

Then, with a look of unflinching resolve, he grabbed her arm, rough and unforgiving, and dragged her across the room.

The sharp slap of her closed-toe kitten heels echoed against the polished floor.

I couldn't wait for her goodbye.

Without another word, he threw open the door, shoved her through it, and slammed it so hard the frame rattled.

Sighing heavily, Romeo ran a hand through his hair—fingers dragging not so much with frustration, but the kind of fatigue only his mother could draw out of him.

"I'm sorry about that," he muttered, cracking his knuckles one after another. Resetting himself.

I dragged the covers higher. "That can't happen again, Romeo."

Before he could reply, the door creaked open a second time.

"Yo, Boss," Tommy called, voice cautious.

Romeo spun on his heel—quick as ever. He might've been resetting, but he was always ready.

"What now?" he barked, too loud, then winced, eyes darting to the crib, hoping he hadn't woken the baby.

I hadn't even realised I was still white-knuckling the bedsheets.

Tommy stepped inside, a little sheepish. The shine of his polished boots caught the light, but far from inviting. Military posture. Clean lines. But the energy in the room had him stepping lighter than usual.

"After what happened at the club? I guess I felt somewhat responsible," he said, one boot half-turned, chin dipping in submission. "Ain't my place, I know, but I wanted to apologise to Chloe."

Romeo crossed the room in long strides. T-Rex was back—rippling the water in the glass beside the bed.

He cracked the window. A snap of cold air bristled through as he exhaled a slow, burning drag into the night. Smoke curled and twisted, carried off by the breeze—particles scattering like sparks from a firework. The cigarette burned fast between his fingers. His nerves clung to the fix.

"Is that all?" Romeo asked, gaze pinned to the quiet world outside. Birds retreating. Traffic fading. The chaos of his mother shrinking into memory.

Tommy and I shared a silent, knowing look. Romeo felt guilty, but he'd never admit it. Not out loud. Who did that sound like?

Tommy placed both hands on the small of his back, spine straightening, as he smiled. "Congratulations, Boss."

Romeo flicked the cigarette out the window and snapped it shut, sealing the outside world off again. The scent of tobacco followed him.

He gave a curt nod, then glanced at me like he was checking I was still here. "Thanks, brother."

Junior had been napping on Romeo's bare chest for the past hour

—peaceful and content. His little legs curled beneath him, a tiny fist gripping a tuft of his daddy's chest hair. Father and son. Breath rising and falling in perfect sync. One day, I had no doubt they'd be a force to be reckoned with.

Stretching my arms above my head after my latest power nap, I smiled. This room was starting to feel like home. A quiet, sacred space. Just for the three of us—made even more secure by the rain tapping softly against the window, streaking the glass in a comforting rhythm.

I grinned at the vision of the two of them. "Do you want to change his diaper?"

"Sure," Romeo said without hesitation, cupping Junior's head in one hand and his bottom in the other. He rose from the chair like a pro.

It still surprised me how instinctively hands-on he was. He hadn't lied when he said he wanted to be a father. There was something rooted in him, deep and paternal, and if he kept this up, I wouldn't hesitate to try for another baby.

With the care of someone handling a china doll, he breezed past me. Not a trace of smoke on his fingers—I'd made sure he washed his hands first.

He placed Junior gently on the changing mat, always supporting his little head. Romeo's hands were big and broad, made for power, but somehow they moved around his son like they'd been made for this too.

He loomed over the baby, eyes scanning his setup. "Aight, cool. What do I do now?"

It was dark outside. The only light in the room came from the monitors—silent and dim—casting a soft blue glow across the walls. Women in the next rooms sleeping. The world beyond ours tucking itself in for the night. I felt just as settled.

"The fresh diapers and wipes are in the bag."

I watched with amusement as he armed himself like he was about to perform surgery.

He peeled back the Velcro straps with caution, then opened the diaper. Paused. Eyes narrowing.

I froze. "What's wrong?"

His brows pinched. "Dang, son… you got a tiny pee-pee." He turned to me, genuinely concerned. "Is it supposed to be that small?"

His reaction made me snort. "Yes, it's absolutely supposed to be that small. Imagine if it wasn't?"

But before I could finish laughing, Romeo suddenly weaved left and right like he was dodging bullets.

"Aah, shit—he's pissin'! It's goin' everywhere! What do I do!? Help me!"

He squinted one eye shut as Junior's stream shot past his shoulder.

My stomach cramped as I collapsed into a belly laugh.

Romeo flailed like he was defusing a bomb, hands everywhere, Junior mid-arc like a garden sprinkler that wouldn't shut off.

"God, Romeo." I wiped a tear from my eye. "You can make me laugh without even trying."

I held my stomach as the giggles consumed me again. My post-birth abs were barely functioning, but the sight of Romeo in meltdown mode only made it worse.

"Damn it, I'm covered in piss! Look at this shit!" He stared down at his soaked T-shirt in disbelief. "Don't just laugh at me, woman. Come help me!"

I lay back down, propping the back of my head with interlocked fingers. "The damage is already done. Just get him changed first—then go wipe yourself down."

Romeo re-emerged from the bathroom a short while later, clicking off the light behind him, bringing the room back into a soft, comforting darkness.

He strode in, rubbing at his shirt with a damp bit of toilet paper that crumbled with every swipe—leaving a trail of white lint across the fabric.

"Look at this," he grumbled. "Five hundred bucks down the drain."

At this point, he probably wished he'd kept his 'kidnappers' shirt on.

I raised a brow. "Still want another baby?"

Before he could answer, Doctor Sophie entered without waiting for permission.

"Hi, Mr and Mrs Giannetti," she beamed, clipboard in hand. She tugged the light cord, and the room awoke in an instant. My eyes flew to Junior's crib as he stirred.

"Congratulations again. He's beautiful. The nurses say he's the most gorgeous newborn they've ever seen."

Romeo and I shared a smile. They weren't wrong. He was the image of his father.

Sophie dragged her pen down her notes. Two or three pages in, and she was done.

"I think you're just about ready to go home in the next hour. Baby's feeding well, and your stats are stable, so we've no reason to keep you."

Then she cocked her head. "How is it, you know... down below?"

My lips thinned. I was suddenly conscious of the throb again. "Um. Very sore."

"You'll likely have some discomfort in that area for a week or so. All normal—especially with how big he was." She turned to Romeo. "What are you, six-three? Six-four?"

His back straightened.

"Somethin' like that," he said, a little pride in his tone.

"I reckon your son will hit that—maybe even taller."

Just picturing the two of them out in the world one day, chasing it all down together...

The possibilities were endless.

She smiled. "How are you feeling, Daddy?"

He shrugged, still trying to wipe the bits of tissue off his ruined shirt. "Sweet. We wanna try for another baby as soon as possible. When's that?"

The hum of the overhead lights buzzed louder. Spotlight fully on the man who never did know when to quit.

Sophie glanced at me with a raised brow, her voice turning gentle. "Err... that really depends on how quickly your wife heals. And, of course, if she feels ready."

She rested a warm hand on my shoulder. Firm. Grounding. She knew exactly who Romeo was. "The ball's in your court, Chloe."

Was it too soon to think about another baby? Probably.

Did I care what people thought? Not in the slightest.

I used to think the love I had for my husband was infinite.
But then I gave birth to his son.
Now?
Well… it was immeasurable.

CHAPTER 13

Our first night as new parents didn't exactly go how either of us would've liked.

Junior kept us awake for most of it, crying, fussing, and not doing much sleeping.

The air clung with stale, milky vomit, refusing to let us forget that a missed sick patch was lurking somewhere, just waiting for one of us to lie in it.

It was still early. Even with the curtains drawn, I knew the sun hadn't risen yet. The air was thick, warm, and far too quiet, apart from the rasp of Romeo's snoring and the soft croak of grasshoppers beyond the glass.

The world hadn't yet woken, but with a newborn, our days were only going to get longer. And while I never expected having a baby to be a walk in the park, I couldn't help but wonder if I'd underestimated just how hard it was really going to be.

Groggy and bewildered, stomach aching, womb throbbing in ways I hadn't prepared for, I peered across our super king-sized bed at Romeo.

Flat on his back, one arm slung over his stomach, he breathed a little too loudly for my liking, chest rising and falling in a steady rhythm.

Those glossy black curls—thankfully passed down to his son—fell ever so innocently across his forehead. Bless him. He looked like he'd gone twelve rounds in a boxing ring, and lost.

Rocking the baby gently, I listened to the soft snuffles from his tiny nostrils as his lips closed around me. The feel of his mouth on my skin, tugging at the sensitive flesh, gave new meaning to the word mother. No words could capture the sensation—the bond created by breastfeeding was unlike anything else. I was his life source, strengthening and nourishing him with everything he needed to survive.

Romeo's eyelids reluctantly peeled open. Just halfway.

"Morning, Sunshine," I murmured, brushing a coil of hair from his eye.

"Hmm?" Still adrift in a sleepy haze, he turned to face me. His unwashed body, manly, earthy, sexy as hell, wrapped around me like a safe haven.

As he pulled the covers with him, the sheets shifted beneath me, tacky and too warm from the baby sweats no one had warned me about.

Despite the bags under his eyes and the stubble shadowing his jaw, a weary smile stretched across his face the moment our eyes met—reaffirming just how ridiculously handsome he was.

Tiredness didn't dull his vigilance. His gaze dipped to my exposed breasts.

"Looks like my son's gettin' a snack." His hand slid onto my thigh—too tired to flirt properly, but giving it his best shot, anyway. "Can his daddy get some of that, too?"

I shook my head with a knowing smile.

Give in now and he'd milk me dry.

With a gentle dab to Junior's mouth, I wiped him clean of his feed, then carefully shifted him onto my shoulder and began rubbing his tiny back, praying for a burp. The soft cotton of his little dinosaur sleepsuit brushed against my skin as I worked the air bubbles free.

Romeo had made it very clear his son wasn't wearing anything of the sort until he saw him in it and caved immediately. Neither of our hearts could have been any fuller.

He huffed dramatically and flung the covers over his head.

"A man can't even get a sip of the good stuff," he grumbled.

Ignoring him, I kissed the soft spot at Junior's crown, inhaling the sweet warmth of his skin. A faint smile ghosted across the baby's lips, and instantly, my heart swelled.

His tiny hand had found a loose strand of my hair. It felt like another thread binding us together—small, but unbreakable. He was holding onto me in the only way he could.

"Your daddy is a pain in Mummy's bottom," I whispered into his dark baby curls.

The covers peeled back slowly, like a tiger stalking prey.

Romeo peeked out, eyes alight, smirking.

"Did you say bottom?" He licked his lips.

"Oh, please relax," I sneered, still patting Junior's back like a drum with paper-thin skin. "Can I not say the word bottom now without you getting a hard-on?"

He sighed, exasperated, amused, and suddenly playful.

When his dick was awake, so was he.

"The next baby ain't gonna make itself, Queen."

He rolled his hips, practically dry-humping the bedding like that alone would get me going. It didn't.

My hand stilled. I gave him a look.

"I hate to break it to you, Romeo, but you don't make a baby that way."

I snorted and shook my head.

He looked like Magic Mike. All he was missing was the baby oil.

"And anyway, after last night, you're really telling me you still want another? Neither of us got any sleep!"

He sat up, scratched his head, disturbing the bounce in his coiled strands, and leant into his armpits, sniffing deeply.

"Yeah, I do want another baby." He sniffed again. "You ready now?"

Brow raised, I glared at him through my lashes.

"Not with those musty armpits, no."

His earthy musk told a tale of unsettled dreams.

He met my stare, raising both brows.

We'd been together long enough to recognise when one of us said something out of character. And if I was honest, which I wasn't about to be, his armpits had nothing to do with it.

This was about me and my post-birth insecurities.

Him seeing me naked like this? No thanks.

Suspicious, he honed in. Heat radiating from his torso, transferring from his skin to mine.

Our connection sizzled the moment sparks flew, but the invisible wall of my self-doubt stood between us. A fragile armour against his charms.

The sharp tip of his nose grazed behind my ear, followed by a soft kiss at the nape of my neck.

"Don't play. You love my smell," he murmured.

"I do..." I smiled into his hair. "...after a shower."

Despite the teasing, I did love his scent. Virile. Masculine. Never crossing the line into body odour. But I wasn't about to tell him that. No chance. It was way too soon to stroke that ego when mine was practically non-existent.

He narrowed his eyes, burrowing those ocean blues into mine.

"This right here—" He jabbed a finger into the mattress. "—is a man's bed. And it smells how God intended. You want fuckin' flowers? You need a girl's bed. I'm sure Daniele's preppin' his for you right now. Fuckin' pillow sprays, heated fuckin' blankets, flippin' a coin over who gets to wear the sexy underwear."

Amused more than offended, I shifted Junior onto my other shoulder to soothe the fuss he was gearing up to make. His little legs curled to his chest, soft whimpers puffing from his tiny nose—reminding us we weren't the only ones in the room anymore.

"Feel better now you've got that off your chest?" I teased.

He smirked, nostrils flaring as the coiled tension finally released. "Yeah, actually. I do."

I lifted the corner of the sheet, letting it fall right out of my grasp. "So... God intended the bed to smell like pits and ass, did he?" I added with a sarcastic nod.

See, I knew how to push his buttons to cause a distraction. And he always fell for it. Always.

Romeo bolted upright, eyes sharpening with a glare full of offence. His muscles bunched beneath his skin. He could've torn the bed linen in half if he wanted to.

"I'll tell you somethin', woman." He drew the cover up his body defensively. "Not once did a woman ever complain about my smell. Not once. Then you come along and it's fuckin' constant. 'Oh Romeo, take a shower after you've farted. Oh Romeo, wash your hands after a smoke.'"

He puffed out his chest proudly. "You should enjoy my farts. Full of fuckin' goodness."

All this drama was over nothing, but he was giving me his best performance.

I blinked slowly, waiting for his next move.

He zeroed in, his mouth inches from mine. My morning breath never did seem to bother him.

"Anyway," he said with a hint of a smile. "What you sayin' about some sugar?"

Like a brick wall rising in front of my eyes, he was the guy with the lump hammer, always ready to break through.

"Not today, no." I pushed against his chest, but he didn't budge. "Let's take a nap while the baby's sleeping."

His lips cracked a smile, a soft sigh escaping as he cast a longing glance at the son he'd always wanted. Still nestled in my arms, Junior yawned softly.

Romeo cupped the back of the baby's head in his large palm—like a marble resting in a catcher's mitt—and the tension visibly drained from his body. His hand lingered there, thumb stroking gently, as if memorising the shape of his future.

Then he closed in and pressed a soft kiss to Junior's forehead, a simple gesture packed with the kind of devotion most men could only dream of. He was naturally a fantastic father.

"Yes, ma'am," he said, his voice softening. "But I gotta take a leak first."

He threw off the sheets, then plodded into the bathroom one lethargic step at a time—scratching his naked arse as he went.

The light flicked on behind him, casting a warm glow across the bedroom carpet. Dust drifted through the beam, catching on the air like flecks of gold.

I called after him, "Wait for your dick to go down before you pee, or you'll get it everywhere!"

A moment passed before he peered around the doorframe, gripping the wood like he might snap it in half.

Tall, dark, and stupidly handsome. Black curls unstyled. Tattoos stretched across his body, each one telling a story of its own. Eyes narrowing, he glared.

"You're actin' like you do the fuckin' cleanin'!" He snapped at me like I was pecking through his patience. "My dick's always hard. You know this. Try ridin' it a bit more and it might soften up."

Before I could even roll my eyes, a knock at the bedroom door cut through his moot point.

"What!?" he barked—then immediately winced, glancing at the baby with regret.

"Can we come in, Boss?" Tommy called from the other side, easing the door open an inch.

The toilet flushed, and Romeo stormed out of the bathroom, pulling on last night's discarded T-shirt and shorts from the bedroom floor.

"Nah, wait there. She got her tits out," he said, tugging on the shorts first. His dick was still semi, but he wasn't about to let that stop him. "I'll come outside. I need a smoke anyway."

But I didn't want him to leave. Not yet.

"No, don't go. We're done now. Look, I've put them away."

I adjusted my nightie and settled Junior into his crib.

The wood creaked softly as I leaned over, ribs still sore, stretched, healing. The snuffling sounds he made as he drifted into a milk coma comforted me as much as they did him.

Romeo gave the go-ahead with a single nod.

It was Tommy who stepped into the room first, followed by Snake, who lingered near the bed. Each wearing a small, respectful smile.

Military through and through. Clean-cut, straight-backed, but they smelled outdoorsy, like they'd just come off night patrol. Faint traces of night air and sweat clung to them like proof of their loyalty.

Almost as proud as new parents themselves, they looked on with quiet awe. "What do we call him, Boss?" Snake asked, a hint of honour in his voice.

"Junior," Romeo said, like he'd already moved past our conversation at the hospital. No big announcement. No lingering pause. Just that one word, and everything shifted. Like the name had been waiting on the tip of his tongue.

He eyed the pair of them. "Anyway. Did my delivery come through yet?"

Tommy smiled and pulled a small delivery bag from his back pocket, handing it straight to Romeo.

Tearing into the plastic with his teeth, Romeo dug inside the package. All three men waited for the contents to emerge.

"What is it, you guys?" I asked, playing it coy—but secretly, I was hoping Romeo had bought something for me. Anything, really. Just a token to show his appreciation.

I sat up on my knees, edging as close to the moment as I could.

LA stirred beyond the drapes, the first birdsong of the morning calling for his mate, like even the wildlife expected Romeo to deliver something heartfelt.

"Ready?" Romeo grinned.

We waited.

Hand lifting from the depths of the bag, Romeo clutched something that made my heart skip a beat.

"Ready," I said, a plume of anxious excitement blooming in my stomach.

This must be something really—

Oh.

Three seconds. That's all it took to realise this wasn't a gift for me. And another couple to confirm my husband was still just as much of an idiot as he was before our son was born.

"What the hell is that?" I asked, craning my neck over the bassinet, following his hands as they disappeared inside.

As carefully as if he were handling a baby chick, nestled in Romeo's palm was a tiny, perfectly crafted toy gun—like he'd stolen it from an action figure. Black. Glock-shaped.

I don't need to say any more…

The men waited with bated breath, leaning over the crib like the three wise men as Romeo hovered the toy against Junior's hand.

And when his little fingers curled around the handle, they shook hands like it was a mafia meeting and the new recruit had just been handed his first weapon's licence.

"He was made for this life. I can feel it," Romeo said, receiving pats on the back from his two best friends. "Look at him throwin' it around like that. Couple years and he'll be emptyin' a full clip like a pro."

The room quietened as they all looked at my son like he was the next chapter—the heir to the king's throne. I could see it on their faces, already imagining the years to come when Junior would be the one barking orders.

"What do you think, Queen? You see how he's aimin' it like that?"

I pretended to care, just to save face. Watching my son involuntarily flail his little arm around, clutching a plastic gun, felt like something out of a parody. But the way Romeo looked at me, all wholesome and excited, swept me up in his buzz.

"Looks great." My smile barely touched my lips.

I folded up the idea of a new piece of jewellery and posted it into the box labelled: LOOK PAST IT. FOR NOW.

He cupped my shoulder, pulling me in for a kiss on the temple. Happy as Larry. As unaware as ever.

The world beyond our bedroom had awoken, a low hum settling in the distance. Car horns. The familiar crunch of loose gravel turning at the gates of our property as the paparazzi arrived, waiting for their first shot of the day. Now the baby was here, we were even bigger news than before.

"Anyway, brother," Romeo said, bringing the three of them back down to earth. Angling his body away from me, he got my attention immediately. "That two-point perimeter check come back clean?"

Tommy shifted his weight, knuckles whitening around the edge of the cot. "Still workin' on it, Boss. Report due at eighteen hundred."

My ears pricked. Romeo had this way of speaking when he was being secretive—like talking through a window. Slow. Over-articulated. Each word carefully deliberate. His tone triggered something, like we were back in the Maldives, still tiptoeing around danger.

"You're talking in code like I don't know what's going on," I said, slipping into my bad-ass tone reserved for times like this. "Has this got something to do with what happened in the Maldives? The pedal boat?

The poisoning?"

Romeo laughed, but I had no idea why. He ran a hand down his jaw, eyes flicking to the window like someone might be listening. "Your job is to keep my son alive. My job is to keep you alive. You see what I'm sayin'?"

Almost connected—but not quite. The more his father acted up, the more wriggly Junior became.

"Not really, no." I rocked the crib side to side.

Romeo propped his foot on the bed and leaned into it, elbow on his knee like he was posing for a mob boss portrait.

"I'll break it down for you real simple." He flicked his lighter open. The flame dancing between his fingers. "I'm goin' for a smoke. While I'm gone, you'll get your tits out and feed my boy. Then, when I come back, you will have saved some for me. Got it?"

The room took a collective sigh. A gust of wind tapped against the window, like it was hoping to push open the curtains for a peek at my reaction.

But I was smarter than my husband realised. With a calculated smirk, I nodded slowly. My agreement was completely deliberate.

I had no doubt in my mind I'd get the information from him. And when eighteen hundred rolled around? I'd be the first to know what the hell was going on.

Romeo's phone vibrated on the bedside table, skipping across the glass top like it had somewhere to be—threatening to take a dive at any second.

Half whispering, half yelling, I covered the baby's ears. "Romeo, you've got a text."

The faucet squeaked shut, and a few moments later, he padded in with a towel slung low around his waist. A billow of steam drifted from the bathroom, following behind him like hordes of women did whenever we went out in public.

Beads of water dripped from the ends of his curls, trailing over the ink on his shoulders and chest—tracing his body the same way my fingernails did when we made love.

My attraction to him was almost too much to bear sometimes.

"Aww, look, Romero," I cooed to Junior. "Your daddy learned how to use a towel properly."

Romeo tightened the fabric around his hips with a smirk. "Don't want my son gettin' a glimpse of my dick."

My joker husband. He always made me laugh without even trying.

He picked up his phone, all casual, completely at ease. Until a beat later, when his smile morphed into a flatlining scowl. His thumb hovered over the screen like he wanted to crush it.

"What's wrong, Romeo?" Reading his face, I'd already narrowed it down to a few options.

"My fuckin' mother wants to come see Romero again."

Oh.

His mother wasn't in my top three of likely contestants.

I peered down at my son. Love at first sight, every time I saw him. His chubby cheeks. His soft breaths whispering to me. So small. So safe right beside me.

"Just make an excuse until our next therapy session. Nelly can tell us the best way to handle it."

He nodded, more agreeable these days than not.

Our progress under our therapist's guidance, coupled with Romeo's one-on-one sessions with Tim, was exactly what we needed to survive our marriage. To rebuild from the wreckage into something stronger than before.

His eyes narrowed as he continued reading.

"Did your mother send you a whole novel to read?" I chuckled. "You're taking a while."

It was safe to tease his reading these days. Tim said he'd hit high school grade already.

Romeo glanced up from his screen, distracted. "Hmm? Oh. I was readin' somethin' else. Got a text from Daniele askin' to see his nephew."

Wait. Dan had messaged…

The sounds all around me stilled. A sudden release of butterflies in my stomach crawled upward, tightening my throat with their frantic wings. Unexpected yet perfectly timed, this was my chance to fix things. To reassure Romeo that the message he saw—the one I never actually sent to Dan—meant nothing. Just a check-in. That was all.

That was definitely all it was…

I pulled a convincing grimace. Tongue first, then a lip curl.

"Ugh, not Dan," I said like he'd give me cooties. "He's not still sick from the poisoning, is he?"

That was convincing enough…

Rumour had it he'd made a mess of his underwear on that long flight home, but as Romeo wasn't exactly a trusted source, I'd taken the news with a pinch of salt.

Romeo smirked at the thought, like it was a fond memory. "Dunno. Ain't spoken to him since. He's been out of hospital a while now, so I doubt it."

I studied his face, watching the tension settle into his jaw.

"I don't care if he comes." I lied. "Do you want him to?"

He ran his tongue across his teeth, mulling it over. "Shit, why not? T told me I gotta handle shit like this head-on. If I don't let him come over, you'll probably go behind my back and see him, anyway."

The smile I tried to suppress twitched at the corners of my mouth. I forced a frown to hide it.

"I don't want to see him." I lied again. "But I admire your patience and understanding on it."

A soft flush rose in his cheeks. "He's comin' over in the next hour."

Shit. An hour? No time like the present.

I eased myself out of bed, the tug in my stomach reminding me how fresh everything still was.

Junior, sensing my departure, began to stir—so I scooped him up and passed him straight into Romeo's waiting arms. He looked impossibly small against his father's chest.

Romeo settled him against his shoulder, resting his cheek on the tiny rise of his son's body. His eyes slipped shut for a beat. A man finally at ease.

No sooner had I stepped foot on solid ground than Romeo's eyes shot open. "Don't go puttin' on somethin' sexy for his benefit."

I turned on my heel, hands on hips to mask the internal thoughts he seemed able to hear. The floor creaked—like the mansion was groaning in anticipation of a fallout.

"I take back what I just said about admiring you."

Romeo didn't rise to it. He stayed focused on Junior, voice soft and low. His thumb stroked the baby's tiny foot, those little toes rolling between his fingers.

"Your mummy's a little slut sometimes, Romero. But when you're big, you can help me keep her in check."

While I appreciated his use of the word 'mummy', the rest of the sentence needed work.

"Excuse me! Talking softly doesn't mean you can say whatever the hell you want to him!"

He continued, brushing Junior's tiny fingertips across his lips. "What a handsome little guy. Just like his daddy."

I stifled a laugh. Once I'd pressed the self-destruct button on our relationship, there was never any going back.

"Little, huh?" I goaded, keeping Romeo at arm's length—mainly so he didn't press for intimacy again and see the body I wasn't ready to share.

He stopped dead and looked me square in the eye. Unflinching. Like he already knew I was playing one of my games.

"Queen, come on. Small dick jokes don't land on a man like me. We both know what I can do with a semi."

And while he wasn't wrong, this was no time to over-inflate the man's ego to bursting point.

I hobbled over to the closet, swinging it open with a mission. I needed to look effortlessly beautiful—for no reason at all.

"Hmm. Well, you won't be unleashing that thing on me anytime soon," I said in a smarmy tone, enough to bring his peg down a notch.

He came up behind me, the heat of his erection pressing into my back.

"I'm dyin' here, Chloe. I can't take much more."

Pfft. Please.

I flicked through hangers with purpose.

Not that dress.

Definitely not those jeans.

That one made my arms look fat.

"Did you hear me, woman?"

I spun around and wagged a finger in his face. "Go fuck one of the whores, then!"

Just when I thought he'd grown up. His lack of empathy hit a nerve. How dare he push for sex the day after I gave birth?

Sure, I wanted to. But my body wasn't ready. Not yet.

He scoffed. "As if I'm 'boutta do that."

I closed my eyes and took a deep breath, shoulders rising, lungs aching. There wasn't enough energy in my body to fight properly.

"Give me a break, Romeo. I had your child yesterday. There's something wrong with you."

Not only was I deprived of a gift—he was really starting to push my buttons.

After a minute or two, he exhaled slowly, chest expanding as he inhaled, then deflating as he released it.

"I'm sorry, Queen. I know I'm bein' a dick… but I can't describe how much I love you—and how much I want to get you pregnant again."

Uninterested in his excuses, I held a dress against my body and studied my reflection, fatigue settling over me like a weighted blanket. My arms drooped. Eyes ringed in pink.

Angling towards the mirror, I scrutinised every inch of myself. The softness of my stomach hidden beneath my nightie, the stretch marks along my exposed thighs, the new terrain of motherhood etched into my skin.

"Are you sure this isn't about re-staking your claim on me just before Dan gets here?"

He stared into the distance, eyes unfocused. Like a man in the desert spotting an ocean—unsure if it was real or just another cruel mirage.

"Nah," he said, voice flat. "I just need a nut."

Junior twitched in his arms, chasing dreams in his sleep.

We paused mid-breath. Romeo's grip tightened slightly, holding our son closer, as if bracing against the stillness.

"He better sleep more tonight." I dusted off a pair of comfy sneakers from the top shelf, the soles landing gently on the carpet.

"If he don't, I'll just pull your tit out and stick it in his mouth." He smirked. "Then I'll take a suck myself."

I turned over my shoulder, eyeing him with a tired smile and an exasperated head shake. "You're a pervert, Giannetti."

◆ ◆ ◆

We relaxed in the living room, watching the big-screen TV like any normal couple while we waited for Romeo's brother to arrive. I'd be lying if I said there wasn't a layer of anticipation in the air. Neither of us acknowledged it, but it was there.

Junior, in his bassinet beside us within arm's reach, slept soundly after his latest feed. I prayed to God he stayed that way.

Still, I found myself checking on him every few minutes, just to soothe my irrational fears. All I needed to ease the new worries of motherhood was to watch his tiny chest rise and fall. And when it did, I could breathe again.

I leaned in, resting my chin on the side of the crib. Just watching him. In his own little cocoon, the scent of newborn warmth clung to the surface of his blanket, disturbed only when I reached in and gently touched him—just to remind myself he was real.

Freshly washed from his first bath, dark hair dusted the top of his head, one soft coil resting against his forehead like a kiss from heaven. His lips suckled on themselves, a quiet motion that soothed him until his next feed. Those chubby fingers, still curled into tiny fists, weren't quite ready to unfold and feel the world just yet.

How did we make something so beautiful?

I loved him. Eternally.

In a bid to be discreet, I flicked my wrist to check the time. My stomach twisted when I realised Dan was due any minute.

Romeo didn't notice my anxious clock-watching—or at least pretended not to. His glazed-over eyes stayed fixed on the TV, but the soft jiggle of his knee was a dead giveaway that his thoughts were racing too.

"How's my son?" His voice cut through the moment, low and serrated, like a knife through chilled butter.

He trailed his fingers down my back, hand coming to rest around my waist, anchoring us together in the midst of this latest challenge.

"He's still sleeping," I said with a cathartic exhale. "Isn't he just incredible?"

With barely any effort, he drew me closer. Skin brushed skin. Side by side. His breath fanned warm against my neck as he pressed a kiss behind my ear.

"I can't wait to put another baby inside you," he murmured.

He splayed his hand across my stomach, still swollen from birth. Nothing like it used to be.

There was comfort in his closeness, but beneath the surface, that worry stirred again—that when he finally saw my naked body, he wouldn't find me attractive anymore.

A knock at the living room door interrupted the thought, snapping the moment clean in two.

Dan pushed a foot through the gap, Italian-polished leather gleaming under the soft light filtering through the window. I already knew he'd be wearing a perfectly tailored suit. Of course he would.

"Safe for me to come in?" he asked carefully, like he was assuming one of us might be naked.

"Come in," Romeo said, his voice carrying an edge sharp enough to match the room's vibration. He muted the audience laughter from the sitcom, silencing the whole house with a single, deliberate click.

Placing the remote back on the arm of the sofa, he settled into a pose that was anything but casual, one leg resting over the opposite knee, arms stretched wide across the back of the couch. Dressed in a T-shirt and sweats, Romeo was never one to compete with the enemy.

Their eyes met, but no words were needed. The message was clear: the wife, the baby, the family were his—a vision Dan could only ever dream of. And while I wouldn't say the better man won, I was glad it was Romeo sitting beside me.

Dan sailed into the room like a ship on her maiden voyage, braving uncertain waters with a mission he looked to have rehearsed in his mind a thousand times.

A crinkle of cellophane brushed the wall as he entered, revealing a large, over-the-top bouquet of flowers. A ruby-red bow tied it all together—the perfect accessory to a thoughtful gesture. His grip was firm, knuckles pale against the stems, like this really meant something to him.

I sat there with a small smile, warmth rising to my cheeks, knowing they were meant for me, yet careful not to assume.

Thankfully, Dan, the smart man that he was, hadn't brought tall-stemmed sunflowers. Wouldn't have taken Inspector Romeo Giannetti long to piece that little mystery together.

Just remembering the time I was hiding in Dan's hallway closet while Romeo smashed my vase of sunflowers against the wall, sent a wave of nausea rolling through me. Times had changed—but at the same token, they hadn't.

Dan wandered over, the fine craftsmanship of his formal shoes scuffing softly against the carpet. Anticipation crackled in the air with each step he took. His green eyes, beneath a tousle of chocolate curls, honed in on his target. Me.

Without a word, just a warmth in his shy smile, he handed the flowers over.

Speechless, I accepted them.

The heated air beside me shifted.

Romeo's hand, resting along the back of the couch, flinched against the nape of my neck. Alerted, the hairs on my scalp prickled. An irrational fear that he might use that hand to strangle me swelled in my chest, forcing me to think on my feet.

Carefully, like the flowers belonged to someone else, I placed the bouquet on the coffee table without missing a beat.

Almost impossible to ignore, I could feel the tension radiating off Romeo's body as he watched my every move like a hawk poised above its prey.

Although even he, in the midst of quiet fury, couldn't deny they were stunning. A mix of lilies and chrysanthemums.

So thoughtful. Elegantly beautiful. The kind of bouquet that said: I still know what you like. And that was the thing about Dan. He just knew how to make me feel... cherished.

"Thanks, Dan," I said a little awkwardly, like meeting up for coffee with an old acquaintance. "You really didn't have to."

What I actually meant was: You *shouldn't* have to. Wasn't it my husband's job to lavish me with gifts after birthing his son?

"It's nothing, really." Dan reached into the inside pocket of his jacket and placed a small container beside the flowers. Wooden lid. A red bow, pressed flat on top. "A little of my famous nut butter if you fancy a snack later."

He tapped the lid, smug with the kind of confidence that came from knowing his homemade treat always hit the spot.

Hmm.

Did he remember our inside joke? Peanut Dan?

Romeo eyed the container like it had insulted his bloodline. The same tight-lipped glare his mother wore when she wanted the whole room to know she was offended.

The longer he stared, the more his emotions tangled—until the mask slipped. He gripped the TV remote like it was the firearm I'd asked him to leave at the door with Tommy.

"Hold the fuck on. Am I missin' somethin' here? Nut what?" His tone dropped the room's temperature by five degrees. "You rubbed one out and what—thought it'd be a real nice gift for my wife? I always knew there was somethin' wrong with you, Daniele."

"No, no..." Dan held up a hand, stepping back as Romeo's grip tightened.

The remote—suddenly just as threatening as a gun.

"It's just Peanut Dan. My own recipe peanut butter. That's all."

I smiled inwardly. He did remember.

Romeo let the words sink in.

Then, after a beat, his grip loosened, and a slow, mocking smirk spread across his face.

He shot me a look. "Peanut fuckin' Dan? I knew his dick was limp. No wonder you came home to the only real man you ever had."

Dan rocked back on his heels, taking the first shot fired. But, of course, he was in no position to retaliate.

The tension between them snapped taut, like an elastic band on a slingshot. One breath, and it would all go flying.

Romeo, trying not to react to the obvious connection between me and his brother, looked like a man with ants under his skin.

See, the big difference this time compared to the vacation we'd all just been on was the absence of one person.

Britney.

My best friend. Hell, my only friend.

She'd been the closest thing I had to a sister.

Now? It was like she'd never existed at all.

But truth be told, a part of me wondered if I was the reason she left. Because she knew, as well as we all did, that Dan still had feelings for me.

A heat bloomed low in my belly. Like a power surge strong enough to light the city. Because with Britney gone, the cord on my backup parachute wouldn't fail if my marriage ever did.

Reassurance wasn't just a comfort. It was my lifeline. Proof that men, not just my husband, still saw me as something more than a hooker. And whatever this was with Dan? It could give me that.

There was no denying I missed her. As a four-piece, we worked. Britney plugged the holes Romeo left when work came first. Dan stitched the wounds Romeo opened when he hurt me.

But what mattered now? I needed confirmation that my theory was true. Although I had to keep my emotions in check, those same emotions spilling out with every breath I took.

I clutched the hem of my dress, twisting the fabric until a loose thread tugged free. It curled around my finger like it was trying to escape—same as the question burning on my tongue.

My lungs held still. Slingshot drawn. Waiting for the right moment.

"Peanut fuckin' Dan," Romeo repeated, twisting in his seat, unravelled from the inside out.

His voice yanked me from my spiral.

He was still here. Right beside me.

When our eyes met, his hand landed on my thigh—firm, possessive. His thumb flexed once. Anchoring me like I might slip away.

A silent reminder of where I belonged.

I glanced down. His wedding ring caught the light, flashing its promise across the room we were all pretending wasn't on fire.

Junior stirred in the bassinet. A soft breath fluttered from his nose, like a wake-up call I didn't know I needed.

I was his mother. Romeo, his father.

Whatever this moment was becoming—I couldn't let it rewrite that.

My instinct pulled me toward the crib. Junior's fingers curled around mine, warm and weightless. The kind of trust I hadn't earned today.

Clarity poured through me. Strong. Undeniable.

I smiled, now knowing what I had to do. I had to end this back and forth in my mind and close the door. Give my husband the same reassurance I always craved.

Why was I focusing on my backup when the main event was sitting right next to me?

Time to look after what mattered. Everything else could wait.

"I never did like peanut butter anyway," I said, lips tugging just enough to silence the storm inside him.

To remind him I hadn't forgotten who I'd chosen.

It worked.

Romeo's shoulders dropped.

That crooked smile, the one he reserved for victories, spread across his face. And just like that, the fuse fizzled out.

Sure, Romeo didn't really know what I liked. Dan had taken the time to learn my cravings. That's why he'd held a place in my heart all this time. But my marriage? It ran deeper than a bloody sandwich spread... Right?

Dan stepped forward, hands tucked behind his back as he peered into the crib.

His suit jacket sculpted his frame like it had been built around him. And that cologne—citrus and musk—coiled through the air, sharp and dangerous.

It reached me like it always had. In his bed. On our dinner dates. In every memory, I hadn't quite erased. He'd always been that for me. A comfort blanket I never found time to pack away.

"What on earth…" Dan muttered, lifting the plastic toy gun like it might detonate. "Not sure this is the safest thing for a newborn. Was it even ethically sourced?"

He sniffed it, nose wrinkling.

Romeo sucked his teeth.

We both watched as Dan pulled a pressed silk handkerchief from his pocket and wiped the toy down like the moment needed more theatre.

"Gettin' the boy used to handlin' business properly," Romeo muttered, fists clenching. "Put it back in the fuckin' crib."

Dan obeyed, slow and careful, then dusted off his jacket like none of it had touched him.

"When he starts exploring, that'll be the first thing lodged in his throat," he mumbled.

"It'll be lodged in your fuckin' throat in a minute if you don't mind your business! We know what the fuck we're doin', Daniele."

Their eyes locked. Oil and water. They never did quite mix.

"Understood." Dan sighed, tone softening as he turned back to the crib. "Any postpartum issues, Chloe?"

The shift caught me off guard. He was talking to me, but through the baby.

Whether it was the pregnancy hormones, Romeo not buying me a push present, or just everything piling on—I couldn't bring myself to shove that damn comfort blanket in the hamper. And those flowers, sitting right there. Beautifully thought out. Each stem picked with meaning. I wanted to bury my face in the bouquet and breathe in his thoughtfulness. Let it settle somewhere deep, where the ache lived.

"Chloe?" Dan arched a brow, pulling me back. He always knew when my mind wandered.

I glanced at Romeo, who looked genuinely lost.

"Oh… um, just a couple things." My eyes dropped to the gleam on Dan's shoes. "Nothing major."

Dan stayed focused on Junior. "Loads of advice in that guide I mentioned—managing milk flow, recovery timing, etcetera."

Instinctively, I folded my arms across my chest. Milk flow was a dangerous topic. And Dan knew exactly what he was doing, bamboozling Romeo with terminology he wouldn't understand.

"Great, I'll take a look." I smiled, tight. "Thanks."

Dan nodded, gaze softening.

"Hi, nephew." He let Junior grip his finger. His whole face lit up—like fairy lights flickering to life. "I'm your uncle Dan. *Benvenuto al mondo.*"

I frowned. Dan could always read me like a book.

"Sorry. It just means welcome to the world," he translated.

I bit the inside of my cheek, frustration prickling beneath the surface. The pleasantries felt hollow. My own feelings—messier still.

"Thanks. I'm trying to pick up the bits I hear. But Italian is hard."

Romeo barged into the moment. He squeezed my shoulder, pulling me closer in what was meant to be reassurance—but his need to urinate on the moment won. "Don't sweat it. I'll teach you."

Dan undid the top button on his jacket and dropped into the far chair, putting a deliberate distance between us.

"You're smart, Chloe. A few sessions with a real instructor, you'll pick it up in no time. I'll arrange something if you like."

"She don't need no lessons," Romeo cut in again, jabbing a thumb at himself. "I already said that I'll do it."

The offers, both sweet in their own way, meant nothing now.

I didn't need a tutor. I needed the truth.

Did Britney leave because of me?

Only one man in the room could give me that answer.

I let the silence stretch, biding my time. Waiting for the right moment—a moment where I could ask the question without my body betraying the reaction. If I was right, I'd need to keep my shit together. Romeo knew me too well.

Dan's eyes met mine from across the room. His pupils widened just as my breath caught.

That obnoxious gleam of sunlight bounced off Dan's Cartier. A glint.

A dare. A push for me to do it. Now was my moment—before Romeo clocked the shift in my posture.

"So, tell me, Dan…" I crossed my legs, wincing at the ache still blooming between my thighs. "What happened with you and Britney?"

The room stilled. Dan's shoulders dropped. Romeo stiffened beside me. Even Junior stirred—his tiny fist flicking against the blanket like he could feel it coming.

Dan ran a hand through his chocolate curls. A move so like Romeo's, but quieter. Tamer.

This was where he filled in the gaps. Where he reminded me he'd always be around. Just in case I needed him.

If Romeo dipped. Got bored. Detested my post-birth body—I wouldn't have to do this alone.

Dan checked the time. Shifted on the spot.

"It wasn't planned," he said carefully. "But I've found myself in a new relationship. Britney, unfortunately, walked in on us."

Like a slow-motion punch to the stomach. Spit flying. Skin rising off bone. I blinked as the ringing in my ears swelled, deafening, then faded to nothing.

The words stung like acid in my eyes. Like fire in my throat. Like lava across my feet.

Dan in a new relationship?

Their breakup had nothing to do with me?

I'd never been successful in articulating my true feelings—not even to a therapist. But the ultimate level of pain always triggered the same reaction in me.

The whole damn thing went right in the fucking box.

This one labelled: HELL NO.

My body jolted like a surge of pain flexed every muscle. I felt it in my toes, right through to my fingertips.

Then came the quiet. The peace, once the lid slammed shut—sealed, not to be lifted again.

"What the fuck is wrong with you?" Romeo leaned away from me, his eyes narrowed, wary.

Huh?

I blinked again, the fog in my head starting to clear.

Dan's brows were drawn. Romeo's jaw ticked.

"What do you mean?" I asked, brushing myself down—trying to reset.

"What do I mean?" Romeo scoffed. "You were literally shakin' in your fuckin' seat." He shifted another inch away, like I might explode.

That's when a bead of sweat slid right down the crack of my arse.

I gulped, adrenaline-fuelled fingers swiping a strand of hair off my face. Deflection time. It was the only way through this.

I turned to Romeo. "First off, it's cold in here, okay? I'll be damned if I can't shake a little in my own living room."

He didn't buy it. Not with the sprinkler hissing over the lawn. Not with the heat rising in waves off the patio.

His lip curled.

"Second," I dug deeper. "You knew he cheated on Brit, didn't you? Why didn't you tell me? I could have supported her."

He ran a hand through his hair—the same move as his brother. But this one wore the ring.

That got him.

"'Cause you were about to drop our son, and I didn't wanna stress you. And honestly? I'm sick of you meddlin' in other people's business. He fucked another bitch. They broke up. Big fuckin' deal."

The words hit harder than Dan's silence.

I stood too fast. Light burst behind my eyes.

I grabbed the chair's arm, swaying—everything tilting for a beat too long.

The irony wasn't lost on me. Romeo claimed he was protecting me from stress, yet had no issue bundling me into the back of an SUV to teach me a lesson.

"The issue here, ass-hat," I said through gritted teeth, "is that my best friend is gone. And no one had the balls to tell me the real reason why!"

But what I really meant was—the issue here? Dan was in a new relationship. He'd moved on. Reassurance gone.

I turned to Dan, glaring.

Hurting my best friend was one thing. But showing up with his fancy flowers, waving our connection in my face while fucking someone else?

"I hope you're pleased with yourself." I laced my fingers together to stop them trembling. "Who is she, then? I hope she's worth it."

"Shh." Romeo lifted a finger to his lips. "You'll wake the baby. And it ain't none of our fuckin' business."

Anger prickled beneath my skin. I peered into the crib. Little toes twitched under the cotton blanket, his eyes screwed shut, clinging desperately to sleep while tension buzzed in the air like static.

A tear slipped off my cheek and landed in the basket.

"Chloe, why the fuck are you cryin'?" Romeo reached for the TV remote again.

Looks like it was my turn to get both batteries.

My lip trembled, clenched tight between my teeth. "I'm not crying, thank you very much. For your information, I have allergies."

The silence that followed left a mark. Teeth still locked. Chest rising and falling under the weight of words I couldn't say.

Eventually, I sank into the chair. The cushion swallowed me whole, heat and rage thudding inside my ribcage. My husband would be getting all of it later for keeping this from me.

Dan brought nothing to the table. Not a condolence. Not an excuse. Not even a word. But the look he gave me, the 'I'm so sorry' eyes, spoke louder than anything his mouth could manage.

The tightness in my jaw began to loosen. I exhaled.

We locked eyes.

His glistened first. Maybe he did still want me.

That thought cracked something open.

Had his confession in the Maldives been bullshit? Or was I right all along? Same pattern. Same setup. Moving on to someone else—but never really letting go of me.

Even now, after I'd given birth to his nephew, there was still something electric between us. Something we were both refusing to let die.

Maybe, just maybe…

"Anyway, enough about me," Dan said, voice awkward, peeling off his jacket like a peace offering. He draped it over the chair, trying to reset the tone.

But Romeo was never one to play nice.

"What you in that fuckin' suit for anyway, Daniele?" he snapped, redirecting the heat like Dan's outfit had been the issue all along.

Dan adjusted his tie, keeping his cool. "Ahh, this old thing? Just got out of a meeting with my accountant."

Romeo let out a dry laugh. "Don't fuckin' surprise me one bit that you put on a suit to please her."

A new piece of information slid into my lap.

Her?

None of my business but mine all the same.

"Erm, yeah," Dan said, clearing his throat. "She said the deal with our overseas Maldivian friend is going very well indeed."

Romeo gave a slow nod. "Yeah. Real nice. Ordered another Lambo to celebrate. Matte black. Sick as fuck."

Dan relaxed back, ankle hooked over his knee. As soon as cars came up, it was like watching a reunion.

"Yeah? Did you go for the Revuelto?"

Romeo huffed. "Fuck off. As if I'd buy a hybrid. You still drivin' that shit Mercedes?" He let go of the TV remote like the tension had finally deflated.

Dan smirked, offended but too polite to make a scene. "You'll be pleased to know I upgraded. AMG S63."

Stealing focus from me and my newborn to chat cars? Not today.

"I don't like cars," I muttered.

Both heads swivelled. Practically the same DNA. Same expression. Like I wasn't even meant to be involved in this part.

"You don't gotta tell me, Queen." Romeo side-eyed me and leaned towards his brother. "That fuckin' G-Wagon I bought her? Drove it once. Six hundred grand down the drain."

Dan nodded like it made sense. Like he knew me. Then he winked. Subtle. Intentional.

That wink was my confirmation.

He still cared.

I slouched back in my seat, watching. Listening.

"Mom bought one last week," Dan said, "but I think she paid three or four hundred."

Romeo clicked his tongue. "That reminds me. You ain't told her how well it's goin', have you? She don't need no more fuckin' cash than I already gave her."

The sun slipped through a cloud and spotlighted Dan like it had something to say.

His eyes flicked sideways. "Err... course not."

Busted.

He'd most definitely shown her his bank statement.

"Keep your fuckin' trap shut," Romeo warned. "We're about to make six figures a month. Each. You want her old ass takin' the cream off the top?"

My brain stuttered. Six figures? A month? Each?

So it couldn't have been Manik behind the poisoning. Romeo had money rolling in.

Then who the hell was it?

Dan, meanwhile, looked like he hadn't lost a wink of sleep. All suit and shine—like the idea he'd been poisoned hadn't even crossed his mind.

"What did they say at the hospital then, Dan?" I asked casually, though I felt anything but. I crossed my legs the other way, mirroring his posture. Pain radiated through me. My son had come from there just yesterday.

Dan glanced at Romeo, clearly thrown.

"Grumbling appendix," he said, like it was an achievement. "Didn't rupture, so I avoided surgery. Guess I'm one of the lucky ones."

Now... that was either the truth, or someone had spun him a complete lie.

Romeo. I could feel his fingerprints all over it.

Drawing in a long, measured breath, I glanced his way. He looked... irked. Either because Dan was here, or because I might just expose one of his little shenanigans.

"Gosh, Dan. That must've been rough," I said, tone laced with edge as I looked directly at Romeo. "But I'm glad you're all fixed up now."

Romeo shot up from the chair, then realised he had nowhere to go.

We were caught in a push-pull.

When I stayed quiet, the brothers thrived. The moment I spoke to Dan, the atmosphere nosedived. All the work we'd done on vacation—unthreading, stitch by stitch.

Like a chessboard. Everyone waiting on the next move that might end it all. And while I held the queen in my hand, warming in my palm, I hadn't checkmated my king.

I reached for Romeo's arm, hot to the touch, power humming beneath the surface. Recognising I might be the problem here… that was progress, right?

His shoulders softened instantly.

"You boys can go out for an hour if you like? I'll be okay if you want to talk business."

The softness vanished.

"No," he snapped, dropping beside me again.

The absence of tobacco as I breathed in his leathery cologne was a welcome change. Fresh fragrance clung to his shirt like a whisper begging me to peel it off him.

"Okay, sheesh. I was just trying to be nice."

He huffed. "No. You were tryin' to start some shit."

I rolled my eyes and slid from the seat. Lifting Junior from his crib, I cradled him carefully, not wanting to wake him.

He wasn't due a feed yet, but he made an excellent shield now that I'd been caught red-handed.

Dan hesitated, then stepped forward.

"May I have a hold?" he asked softly, hands hovering mid-air. A quiver of vulnerability.

It was a bold move. Surprised all of us.

I flicked a glance behind me, checking Romeo wasn't foaming at the mouth.

"Um, sure," I said, stepping tentatively into Dan's space.

I hadn't been here in a long time.

The closer I moved toward him, crossing that invisible line, the louder the birdsong outside became.

Like nature was calling to me. Like the grass really might be greener on the other side.

It was… confusing.

Then Dan's skin brushed mine during the handover.

My nostrils flared. A rush of old memories. Old heat.

Something primal that scared me.

His scent mingled with minty breath and honey cream body wash, tingling my senses in a way they hadn't in a while.

Wait… wasn't that the same body wash I used?

Our eyes met—green to bluish-grey—as I made the careful pass of my precious load. Junior needed a 180-degree turn to get into Dan's arms safely. An awkward giggle slipped between us during the unpractised shuffle.

"Oops—hold on, got him, thanks," Dan said with a hint of a smile.

"Wait, I just realised. You're right-handed," I said, adjusting Junior into his hold. "With Romeo, it's easy. I just pass him straight over."

At the sound of his name, Romeo stood. Hands shoved deep into his pockets like he was physically restraining himself from interrupting this tender exchange.

Dan chuckled. "Glad it's finally coming in useful to you, Romero. Remember that time Dad took us fishing on Castaic Lake?"

Romeo glanced into the distance, searching for the memory—but too many ghosts got in the way.

"Wait, I haven't heard this story." I beamed.

I loved hearing about their childhoods.

Dan smiled. Romeo didn't stop him.

"Dad had this thing… weird, really. Refused to let Romero cast off left-handed." He chuckled again. "When that fish hook caught Dad's ear? One of my favourite memories."

Romeo huffed, nudging at the carpet with his shoe.

"That son of a bitch always gave me a hard time." He raised his right hand, palm up, like he was reading something written in the lines.

"Still can't do shit with this hand, no matter how hard he forced it."

They shared a nostalgic smirk.

Dan spoke first. "D'you know, it wasn't until second grade I realised your real name wasn't actually Southpaw? Even I remember all those boxing sessions."

"Fuck yeah. Forgot he used to call me that." Romeo's smile faltered. "Pretty sure it was when I broke my wrist he stopped talkin' to me completely."

Dan's expression softened. His glance toward me said what he didn't voice.

"Romero was lined up as a pro boxer. Until he got injured during a warm-up fight."

The humour drained from Romeo's face. The smile vanished as the memories caught up. He flexed his fingers like he could still feel the pain.

I watched in quiet awe, learning something new about the man I thought I knew completely.

Our eyes met. "I can't believe I didn't know this about you."

The room fell silent.

"All in the past," Dan interrupted quietly. "Dad would've been proud to meet this little guy."

He brushed Junior's cheek with his thumb. So natural. So at ease. And for a split second, outside Romeo's bubble and inside Dan's, it almost, very nearly, felt like he was the father.

Junior squirmed. His lips tightened. His eyebrows creased—but he didn't cry.

An out-of-body experience unfolded.

An uncle meeting his nephew. In a twisted tangle of reconciled hearts.

Once, he had loved my son like his own. This man had sung to my baby in the womb. And now... here they were. Meeting at last.

The birdsong outside swelled. A moment like a clash of cymbals and a lulling of violins—nature itself celebrating something quietly monumental. A missing puzzle piece had been found. One I hadn't even realised was missing.

"I need a photo. Romeo, go stand beside Dan." I reached for my phone on the couch.

The camera was already open before he had the chance to object.

Buzzing with adrenaline, my hands shook. Of course they both looked at me like I was crazy.

"Come on, hurry up. I want a photo of the three of you."

Whether I'd caught him off guard or he was just trying to keep the peace, I was surprised when Romeo obeyed. He moved beside his brother, standing three inches taller.

Neither stepped into the other's space. Two men. Two worlds. Each allowing the other to cross enemy lines. Just for this moment.

"Smile." I held the phone landscape, framing every inch of them.

Romeo's smile came first, disarmingly handsome. His face, so painfully kissable, eased into it with natural confidence. Hands still in his pockets. Inked arms stealing the frame. His eyes met mine with that usual intensity. But he didn't need to look at me like that. I was a moth to his flame, always.

After a beat, Dan followed suit. His smile mirrored Romeo's in shape, but not in meaning. Something quieter beneath it. A different kind of ache.

It reminded me of the framed photo in Dan's office: two boys holding a fish they'd caught together. A shared result. Only this time, it wasn't a fish. Romeo was letting Dan hold his son. Letting him feel the weight of his achievements.

I tapped the screen. Once. Twice. Again. Again.

Capturing the moment before it could slip away. And with those Giannetti genes, it wasn't a difficult task.

"Okay. Perfect." I grinned, already wondering if it would be overstepping to set it as my lock screen.

Footsteps approached from the hallway. Muted voices. A conversation that cut the charge.

The door cracked.

"Boss?" Snake entered cautiously, cutting in. "Can I have a word?"

Romeo's smile soured. "S'up?"

Did he already know?

"Just the, err, situation, Boss. Need to run something by you. In private."

We all exchanged looks while Romeo decided. Stay and keep an eye on us... or leave and handle business?

He paused in the centre of the room, chest puffed, glaring at his brother still holding the baby. The atmosphere thickened like treacle. He checked his watch. His phone. Even the scene out of the window, searching for the right choice.

Eventually, he ran both hands down his face. "I'll be gone five minutes, max. Can I trust you, Chloe?"

Snake cleared his throat. Shifted. This was urgent.

"Boss. I need to speak to you. Now."

"Aight, I'm comin'."

Romeo's gaze flicked back to me. "Chloe, you better keep that cunt to yourself."

He didn't flinch. Eyes locked. Then a flick downward. And back again. "Got it?"

I nodded, giving him a small, controlled smile. "Got it."

Was I truthful? Almost certain I was. Whether Dan still loved me or not only mattered to cure my sickness—my need to feel wanted. I had no intention of following through...

But seeing Dan hold my baby had left a sweetness on my tongue I couldn't help but taste.

Romeo's sneakers thudded heavy against the carpet as he steamed toward me like a train off the tracks.

Anticipation curled in my gut. My fingers slackened. The phone slipped from my hand and hit the floor with a thump.

He tilted me back, carrying my weight with ease. One hand cupped the back of my head, just like he did with his son. A tenderness pulled straight from the pit of his soul. That's when his mouth found mine.

The brush of his soft lips like he was drawing breath from me. Like I was his life source. Then his tongue entered—forcefully intentional. A move to mark territory. Proof of his dominance. I was his possession.

Curling his fingers in my hair, he gripped just hard enough to prove his point.

"I love you, Chloe," he said, pressing his forehead to mine. A little clammy, he was fighting demons from all sides. *"Ti amo."*

I closed my eyes and shared the air as he exhaled. Nothing compared to the tangle of his breath with mine.

"I love you, too."

The door whispered closed, but didn't quite meet the latch.

Green eyes sparkled across the room. The air stayed thick. Suddenly awkward.

"So," Dan said, fidgeting his weight on the spot.

Those flapping butterfly wings in my stomach stilled. The melodic atmosphere took a nosedive. No longer birdsong and symphonies, something was missing.

Was I mistaken in thinking Dan was the composer of this triangular-shaped orchestra? Or was I only now realising we were all in it together—each of us playing a vital role in finishing this piece of music?

I thought I needed Dan. But did I really just need them both?

No matter how hard I tried, the comforting tune was replaced by an anxiety-laden requiem. A singular drumbeat in my chest replacing the steady thump of my heart.

The silence between us swelled, like a string section on hold, waiting for the conductor to return.

Should I make conversation? Or keep my distance?

What did this mean? The whole thing felt... off.

If I spoke first, it might mean something. If he did, it might mean more. My wayward hormones weren't allowing for rational decision-making.

Was this about the flowers? Romeo buying that damn plastic gun instead of showing me how much I really meant to him? I had no idea what the hell was going on.

My best friend was gone. I thought Dan still had feelings for me. But why the fuck did that even matter when I had Romeo?

That's when it twigged. My body issues. The way I looked? Dan wouldn't care about any of that. I guess I'd convinced myself Romeo would. This wasn't just reassurance I was after. This was survival.

Dan sat back on the sofa carefully, Junior nestled in his arms—like this was his living room. His couch. And he was about to put sports on his TV.

Reminding myself all over again that his heart was playing games with mine, I crossed my arms over my chest, shielding the beat.

"So, who's the new woman in your life?" I asked, trying my best to keep it easy breezy.

He placed his fingertips on the baby's chest gently, rising and falling in rhythm with his breathing.

"No one important," he muttered. "That was a lie for Romero, right? You always loved my peanut butter."

As if that was the most important thing going on right now.

"Yes," I whispered—like Romeo had left the room and pressed a glass to the door. "You know why I had to lie."

Satisfied with my answer, he glanced down at his nephew, brushing the fullness of his cheek with a slow, tender finger. He seemed so comfortable. The delicacy in Dan's leaner frame just felt more fitting to cradle a newborn.

"Just think," he murmured, running his fingers slowly through the baby's soft curls. "He could've been mine."

I sank beside them, drawn in by our old flame that flickered everlastingly, refusing to die no matter how hard we both blew against the candle.

"I know you were excited to be a dad," I said softly, nudging him with my shoulder. "Sorry things didn't work out."

A fresh pang of guilt tugged at me.

Dan sighed, glancing at me from the corner of his eye with a softness only he possessed—letting me know this was a conversation, not a fight.

"Are you?" he asked.

Huh? "Am I what?"

"Are you sorry it didn't work out?"

It was like he'd pressed pause on my whole thought process. I just sat there, lips slightly parted, unsure whether I should be offering reassurance to him, of all men, sitting beside me.

Then, suddenly, it was too much for him. He handed the baby back hastily—like a game of pass-the-parcel gone wrong, only the prize had been revealed as a bomb.

Junior kicked his legs, fussing. His quiet squirm against my chest sent my heart racing.

Frantically, I bobbed him up and down, whispering nonsense to calm him. Now would be the worst time for him to start crying.

"Of course I am," I said, brushing my cheek against the baby's hair. "I didn't mean for any of it to go the way it did. And besides…" I looked up at Dan. "I could ask you the same question."

He shoved both hands into his pockets. Brows pinched.

"What question?"

"Are you sorry it didn't work out?" I paused for breath. "I mean, look at you. In a new relationship. Do you still have feelings for me?"

He looked at the baby. Then at me.

"I guess none of it should matter now. He's not mine."

The sound of a shoulder hitting the already cracked door sent it ricocheting off the wall, the vibration cutting across the room like a shockwave.

My husband didn't need to announce himself.

Gun drawn, Romeo entered like a blast of heat—boiling the paint off the walls with the force of his presence.

Once he'd scanned the room for threats and realised there were none, he holstered the weapon into the waistband of his shorts, bringing the boil to a simmer in a single blink.

"Shit. I was expectin' to fire at least two bullets. Nice to see you can keep your shit to yourself, Chloe."

Dan stepped away, tugging on his suit jacket. He fastened two of the three buttons, smoothing out the sleeves with methodical detachment.

"I was just leaving, Romero." His tone had dropped flat. Lifeless. Checked out. "Congrats again, brother. I'll see myself out."

He moved quickly, his shoes whispering softly over the floor. The shine of his leather dulled with each step.

When would I see him again? Or was that our goodbye?

The front door closed behind him with a hollow echo that rattled through the bones of the house.

Romeo scooped Junior into his arms, kissed his forehead. That single touch erased Dan's presence entirely.

Air shifted. Heat settled.

"Meetin' in an hour, Queen." His eyes glinted. "This is big. You best get your big girl panties on."

◆ ◆ ◆

And here we were, the 6:00 PM meeting in our bedroom I'd been waiting all day to attend.

I hadn't even needed to protest for an invite. Something in the operation had shifted. I was practically chair now.

The time I'd spent with Dan earlier had only added confusion to my already fried brain, but the sooner he left, the faster it faded. When that front door closed, so did my attachment.

Safe to say, Romeo made me toss the flowers in the bin, not before his ritual stomping, of course.

I joined in without hesitation. Petals stuck to the soles of my shoes, and the bitter scent of crushed stems followed me all the way upstairs.

Maybe he'd take the hint. Sometimes, a little thoughtfulness goes a long way.

Still, that wasn't what mattered now. Bleak as it was, no best friend, no backup, I had a marriage to fight for. And tonight? Being invited to this meeting meant everything.

Although, without snacks or refreshments, it was already far too masculine for my taste. The first one to fart or burp in my direction would have a whole other meeting with my fist.

The bedroom was dimly lit, curtains drawn against the early spring dusk.

I perched on the edge of the mattress, the dip in the memory foam reluctant—like even it wasn't sure I belonged here.

Tommy and Snake stood at the foot of the bed, hands clasped behind them. I settled into the sheets, hushing the baby.

Romeo, naturally, was already at the drinks cabinet, brooding over too many options. He didn't offer anyone else a glass.

"Aight, Tommy. Fill her in," he said into the rim of his first shot.

With a new recruit stationed outside our bedroom, not a single footstep was allowed past the door. No whores in the vicinity meant one thing: eerie silence.

Tommy didn't clear his throat. He'd been ready to deliver this intel yesterday. "Jamie and Harry. We've pulled some information. And it's not good."

Realising I was no longer pregnant, I clicked my fingers at the very attractive bartender who just so happened to be my husband.

"This sounds serious. Pour me one," I teased with a light giggle.

The friction needed cutting. As it stood, this was no place for a newborn. But Romeo wasn't in the mood. He slammed the bottle onto the counter like he was driving a sword into stone, then knocked back a gulp with a sharp smack of his lips.

Theatrical, of course. He hijacked the moment entirely.

Tommy waited for the nod to continue.

"Go on," I said, gently bobbing the baby—who'd had a milk moustache ten minutes ago and no good reason to fuss now, other than sensing his father's rage.

Tommy adjusted his stance. "Jamie and Harry are confirmed moles. Working for—"

Romeo stepped into the spotlight. Glass in hand. Ice clinking like a prelude. "Hold up, brother. I got this."

He took a sip, as if re-swallowing the news to speak it again.

Cheeks flushed. Knuckles white. "Benny. Motherfuckin'. English."

The bottle rattled against the glass, not from nerves but fury, as he poured another.

The next whiskey vanished down his throat. So potent, the liquor's aroma warmed the chill of the unthinkable.

The atmosphere plunged.

A drip from the bathroom faucet echoed in the dark corner. No other sound broke the silence.

Benny English had infiltrated our operation?

I clutched Junior tighter. "So you're saying he was behind the robbery? The pedal boat? Dan's poisoning?"

Romeo glanced to Snake.

Snake gave a slow, deliberate nod.

"Can't prove all that yet," Romeo said. "But what we do know is they've been feeding him everything since the day they joined."

Shit.

"So Benny was their client all along? I can't believe he wanted to work with me."

The thought stroked my ego.

"No," he snapped.

…Aaaand ego deflated…

"This ain't about you, Chloe. He wanted my attention. Credit to the cunt. He finally got it."

The idea that our impenetrable fortress had been breached hung heavy in the air.

Who was to blame? Our crew? Us?

A drop of milk leaked from my breast, unnoticed by the room. Then another. I was a new mother. This was… a lot.

I rubbed my forehead. "But why would he go to so much effort just to get your attention?"

"Because I said no to mergin' my business with his. My guess is he got wind of my deal with Bodu Manik through those two punk bitches. I've been avoidin' him too long. Now he's escalatin'."

The walls felt closer. The baby heavier.

I swallowed hard. "So what now?"

He huffed, glancing around like I was the only one not following. "Ain't it obvious?"

Kissing the baby had become a distraction. But Romeo's next words froze my lips to the crown of Junior's head.

"We kill 'em."

The curtains twitched in horror.

Outside, a storm of allegiance brewed as if the grounds themselves were being conjured awake to work alongside us.

Our son, suddenly sound asleep for the first time since birth, had been lulled by his father's words. Content in the chaos. Just like his dad. Written in their DNA.

"We?" I croaked, struggling to loosen the knot in my throat.

My body ached. Breasts too full. Postpartum pain lingering in the seams of everything.

"Yeah, *we*. Me, you, and the boy are goin' for a drive while the crew handles the preliminaries."

"Preliminaries?" I blinked. "What does that even mean?"

He looked at Tommy like I was something he'd stepped on.

"They're out on the loose. Need to close 'em down. And tomorrow? We send a message to English. Hell, I'll post their heads to him in a fuckin' box."

Romeo had spent the better part of the last ten minutes hunched over the back seat of his Rolls-Royce, wrestling with a car seat that—according to the instructions—was foolproof.

Impatient and exhausted, I pulled my jacket tighter and shifted from foot to foot beside him.

A mountain of baby gear still needed loading into the trunk.

"Come on, Romeo. Why don't you ask one of the staff to help you?"

He paused, lifting his head. Black curls appeared first, followed by piercing blue eyes that glowered with enough heat to shrivel the devil.

"This is man shit. Go sit in the car if you're cold."

That meeting had left the air cold—and neither of us was warming it.

I ignored the intimidation, a diaper bag in one hand, a bottle steriliser in the other. Overwhelmed didn't quite cover it.

"Do you think we need to start looking for a nanny soon?"

He stayed bent over the seat. "Yeah, yeah. We'll do that after tomorrow."

Like it was simple. After tomorrow. As if tomorrow didn't involve murdering two people in cold blood before lunch.

Hire a nanny. Bury a couple of bodies. On to the next.

Movement drew my eye. The SUV's back doors were flung open, boxes being loaded inside. All hands on deck. Preparations well underway. With all the new recruits, I wasn't even sure who ranked where anymore.

"So, who's shadowing this drive we're taking? Snake?"

"No, Queen," he said, like it should've been obvious. "Snake's leadin' on the snatch-and-grab. Tommy's comin' with us."

Snatch-and-grab? He made it sound like a supermarket sweep. But we both knew what it meant—Jamie and Harry dragged off the street and bundled into a van, just like I'd been at the club.

I placed a hand on Romeo's shoulder. When he didn't react, I reached up and brushed my fingers along the stubble of his cheek. His jaw was tight. His skin, usually warm, had cooled in the anxious air.

"This thing with English's bothered you, huh?"

He frowned, eyes still fixed on the car seat. "Fuck no. I been needin' an excuse to use my gun all week. Got myself ready to pop a cap in Daniele's ass earlier. Surprised I didn't have to."

We both knew he was lying. English had pulled the wool over his eyes —and Romeo hated being fooled.

We'd barely been on the road for five minutes. Tyres rumbled over grit, our favourite playlist murmuring in the background, white noise to fill the contemplative silence. The bass thumped faintly through my heels. My seatbelt felt tighter than usual around my neck.

I was unsettled. It was hard not to picture two body bags being zipped shut at every red light.

Dread lingered. But now that I was no longer pregnant, I could almost feel the weight of my gun again. My fingers curling around the grip. Raising it. Seeking revenge for my family.

Although… that wasn't all, was it?

I'd be lying if I said Dan's news hadn't spun my brain into chaos. His new relationship with some pathetic slut? Yeah, it was messing with me. Romeo was right—it wasn't my business. Not unless I wanted something with Dan.

Which I didn't. Not anymore...

My nostrils twitched. I couldn't ignore the sharp scent of alcohol circulating through the air conditioning. My husband and his addictions were always a problem. And I got it. At times like this, I really did. But with a newborn in the car, and at least three shots of whiskey in his system, the stakes felt different.

Sure, he had a high tolerance. No, his driving wasn't affected. But still... letting it slide didn't sit right.

Was I too tired to fight him on it? Or maybe letting a powerful man stay powerful, even under the influence, reminded me that normal rules didn't apply to him. And that kind of made him seem superhuman.

"Aight, what you not talkin' for?" His voice cut through the quiet. "You fuckin' love talkin'. Gets me on edge when you don't speak for four minutes."

I kept my eyes on the road. Headlights blurred through the windshield, streetlight glare smearing across the glass. My pupils stretched in the dark, then tightened in the light.

No way was I admitting that tomorrow was clawing at me. That this life wasn't a game anymore. It was real.

Still, the tension in his stare was building. I needed something to say. And for reasons I couldn't quite explain, my mind went to Dan.

The flowers. The thoughtfulness. The way he still didn't know what really happened to him on that plane.

Did we owe him that truth, at least? Or was I losing it?

Hands flat on my thighs, I tapped my middle fingers in a steady rhythm, trying to keep my breathing calm.

Should I bring it up?

His eyes kept flicking between me and the road, restless. Waiting.

"Come on, Chloe. Shit!" He squirmed in his seat.

"Okay, fine." I swallowed.

Any second now, I'd say it...

He turned the volume down on his favourite song. He wanted to hear every word.

The sudden silence made my ears buzz. The road grumbled beneath my seat, but the way the car sliced through the wind—sharp and fast—felt deafening now.

"Why did you lie to Dan about him getting poisoned?"

Romeo huffed. Not one of his big ones, but enough to snuff out the nerve it took me to ask.

"Here we fuckin' go again. Why is Daniele's name in your mouth?" His voice turned lethal. "You see him for an hour and what? Your pussy wet for him, is it? That why you don't wanna fuck me?"

My voice dropped to a whisper. "Forget it," I said quickly, tugging the seatbelt that kept trying to strangle me.

"No, no. Come on." He leaned closer. The reek of whiskey hit like a slap. "Let me know everythin' you got goin' on in that head of yours about my brother."

If the streetlights had been red, his face would've been cloaked in a devil's shadow.

Instead, cold white light sliced across his features, catching the wicked glint in his eyes. Just as demonic.

"Why didn't you tell him he was poisoned?" I fired back.

He smacked the car's console hard. The screen's pixels jolted but didn't shatter.

"Why the fuck do you care, Chloe? Why?"

He'd asked a question. And I knew the answer. But the truth wouldn't set me free. Not here. Not now. Not ever.

"I don't know why!" I snapped. "I just want to know!"

If there'd been an eject button, he'd have launched through the sunroof and straight into space.

He clicked the plastic casing back over the screen he'd just assaulted, composure gradually realigning. The shift from rage to reasoning was all performance.

"Aight, fine. Daniele's always relied on me to handle shit. As kids, I'd kick the fuck outta any little bitch who beat him down. I brought him in on this deal with Manik. He trusted the process. You think I'm gonna tell him he was poisoned on that plane 'cause of me?"

Oh.

When he put it like that, what could I say?

Romeo had a heart of gold wrapped in a Teflon shield. And the brothers, it seemed, just loved to hate each other.

He sucked the air from the space between us, like my words didn't deserve oxygen.

"You got somethin' else to say about him? What—are you gonna tell me his stroke game's better too? You prefer he jerks his dick with his right hand or somethin'?"

I flinched at the aggressive hand gesture.

I knew from the moment I found out he was left-handed that Romeo had been self-conscious about it.

His dad, twisted bastard that he was, had clearly made him feel like being different meant being weak.

Romeo licked his lips, impatient. "Come on, Chloe. Let me hear it."

"Don't be stupid, Romeo. Why would I care that you're left-handed? Is that why you never told me? You think it's a weakness?"

His eyes moved, but his head stayed still. Just a sideways glance. Barely an effort.

"We ain't talkin' about me right now. I wanna hear about you and Daniele."

That told me everything.

Only Romeo would be worried about something so minor.

His dad had been gone for years—yet his voice still echoed in the dark corners of Romeo's mind.

"Come on, woman. I'm all fuckin' ears." He tugged his earlobe to a stretch.

His pushing only conjured more thoughts of Dan. And as the minutes ticked by, it became painfully clear—I might not see Dan again for a long time. Maybe ever.

Romeo's pain rarely showed in words. It exploded in actions. He was hurting now. And dealing with it in the only way he knew how.

I took a breath, choosing my words carefully.

"The only thing Dan has over you, Romeo... is thoughtfulness." I kept my tone light. Soft. "It would've been nice to get flowers from you, you know? Just a thank you. For birthing your son."

There. I said it.

The indicator ticked on, loud and steady.

He used the turn to let the words land.

Then shot me a look. With a side order of heartbreak, he was too proud to show.

The blinker clicked off.

"When have I had fuckin' time to do that? I've been with you lookin' after our son since the second he came outta you."

I didn't answer. Didn't need to.

The silence became its own kind of weapon.

There was no difference in time between ordering that bloody toy gun and pressing 'Buy Now' on a bunch of flowers.

Of course, he took it personally. He always did.

"Fuckin' rich, you sayin' that to me," he muttered.

He flipped the sun visor down, yanked something from the card holder, then shoved it back up with a snap.

A business card landed in my lap.

It hit like slate, not paper. Heavy with meaning.

"You only gotta look at your finger to see how much I care about you. Even that fuckin' bracelet you're wearin'? Cost me a hundred and fifty thousand dollars."

The number sat between us like a third person in the car.

$150,000. He spent that. On me?

The card's edges dug into my palm. I flipped it. Some fancy jewellers downtown.

On the back, a handwritten figure: *$150k.*

His proof. My regret.

I brushed my fingers over the bracelet instinctively. Fragile. Cold. Expensive enough to buy a house. Or a life. And here I was, measuring love in flowers from a man who'd never truly won my heart—yet always had it.

It seemed silly now.

Me, wondering if Dan had spent more on Britney than Romeo had on me like that was ever going to be the case.

Was I the idiot?

An idiot to think a gift for birthing his son meant more than the time and presence he'd given us both from day one.

Whether it was the stress I'd caused him, or just his need to get the hell away from me, the engine suddenly roared louder—Romeo's foot slamming down, the pistons shuddering through the chassis. Like the car itself was trying to outrun the conflict.

"Sorry," I said. There wasn't a better word I could use.

His body language softened. Just a little. Like he'd made his point—and then some.

"Yeah. That's what I thought." He scratched the top of his head restlessly, like a yawning dog coming down from a fight he wasn't proud of. "Tellin' me I ain't romantic enough. Christ, woman. No one stresses me out like you do."

His fidgeting made the seat creak. He turned down the cabin temperature to cool the heat between us.

The console flipped. The music stopped. His phone rang through the Bluetooth, lighting up the screen and cutting through my daze with a flash of colour.

No caller ID. Just a photo of a pig rolling in mud.

I knew who it was instantly.

He frowned, fingers twitching on the wheel, tapping the leather like a warning. Processing.

A few seconds passed.

Then he jabbed the answer button.

"Who's this?" he said, voice clipped, as if expecting a report on the moles.

A beat of silence followed.

Then—

"Romey baby!" A woman purred through the speaker, voice crackling with static—like barbed wire dragging through the airwaves. "I believe congratulations is in order."

There was a long, almost painful pause. The pair of us stunned into silence.

I imagined Harper on the other end of the line, likely dressed in nothing but her underwear—vibrator in hand. She'd get her fix of my husband... and then finish herself off.

"Daniele just came home with tales of the new baby. I must say, I'm jealous I didn't get an invitation."

What!?

My heart stopped dead. Harper was the new, or should I say old, woman in his life?

Harper?!

The seatbelt was at it again, this time trying to slice my head off. I was tempted to let it.

"What are you callin' me for?" Romeo asked, gripping the gear shift like his hands were around her neck.

"Listen, Romey. Tell Chloe that if she follows my fitness programme—just thirty minutes a day, five to six times a week. That excessive baby weight she gained will come right off."

My eyes shot to Romeo. White-hot. Wordless. He didn't need me to say anything. He knew.

She did not just say that. Not when I was already broken by the way my body looked now, skin looser, curves unfamiliar, like I'd borrowed someone else's body and didn't know how to return it. I was already terrified he'd leave me.

"Speak about Chloe again," Romeo bristled, "and I'll end the call."

"Aww, Pookie..." she moaned, voice oozing smugness. "I didn't know you two were having a rough patch. Is it because she's overweight? I mean, based on the photos I saw online, I get it. I did tell her to get her thyroid checked."

For some reason, whether postpartum insanity or morbid curiosity, I kept quiet. It wasn't fear. It wasn't submission. It was calculated. Because if Harper knew I was here, I'd never get the truth. And I needed to know exactly how deep this went.

Romeo's features twisted with contempt. "What the fuck do you want, Harper? Last I saw you, you were stealin' my millions. Spent it all already?"

You could practically hear her eye roll. "Of course I didn't go through with it, silly. That was just to prove a point. I'm calling to congratulate you on the child. Dan and I are so happy for you. I know it's what you've always wanted."

His jaw clamped tight. Neck muscles tensed like a storm front gathering beneath his skin. "You don't know shit about me."

A sinister cackle cracked through the speaker, sharp enough to send a chill racing up my spine.

"Remember when we tried for a baby?" she cooed. "That was fun, wasn't it?"

No.

My brows launched into orbit. My jaw dropped to the floor. Somewhere near my ankles. What little I'd eaten today was on its way back up.

Romeo growled. Deep. Guttural. The kind of sound that could curl carpet.

The baby began to fuss, small choked puffs through his nose, barely audible but building. A warning. He was about to cry again. It seemed the more upset his father got, the more unsettled he became.

"I'm in the car with Chloe," Romeo turned down the volume. "And it's on speaker. I don't need this shit right now."

Silence hit again.

She was smiling. I knew it.

"Oopsy-doopsy, my bad." She giggled, unapologetic.

His hand jerked forward and stabbed the button to cut her off.

The engine's roar swallowed the quiet.

Junior let out a small, sleepy grunt in the back, but it wasn't enough to break through the fog of hatred wrapping itself around me.

I gave him ten seconds.

Then I let him have it.

"So, tell me, Romeo…" I turned in my seat.

The iced air between us sliced through the lingering heat of whiskey on his breath.

"You knew Dan was back with Harper, didn't you?"

He scraped his fingers through his stubble. Rough, scratchy strokes—like nails across a chalkboard.

"Yeah."

"That's why you didn't tell me about Britney, isn't it? You didn't want me to find out?"

He nodded. Tight. Guilt-stricken.

"So, tell me…" I inhaled, pressing back the burn behind my eyes. "You get mad about me and Dan easy enough, but what I want to know is—did you try for a child with just about anyone?"

His hands dropped from the wheel, landing on his thighs with a snap.

"Don't start, Chloe. Please."

I turned fully away. Arms folded. Eyes locked on the grey, wet world outside.

My heart cracked open. The two pumping halves bleeding sorrow into every inch of my body.

"I don't know why I thought I was special to you." My voice broke against the glass. The fog of my breath was the only proof I was still alive—still here—even though I felt like I was floating somewhere outside my own body. "Why did I think I was more than just a game to you?"

As if on cue, the sky broke.

Rain slapped the windscreen in long, dragging streaks as we sped down the freeway.

Sympathy from the sky. Was someone finally on my side?

How much could one person take?

Two hard blows to the chest. One after the other. Dan was back with Harper. The woman my husband used to be in love with. The one he'd also tried to have a baby with.

She was me. And I was her.

Both of us caught in the same vortex, side by side, yet enemies all the same.

"Chloe, stop. Now."

Wet tarmac clung to the tyres like glue. A low hum vibrated through the cabin. Between playlist tracks, static filled the space. A silence that felt too full of hurt.

My nails dug into the upholstery. The leather bit back—but I didn't stop.

"No, I won't stop it," I murmured, too far gone to pull back now. "I feel like a fucking idiot."

The wipers whipped back and forth, frantic—like even they couldn't keep up with this conversation.

He huffed. Loud. Frustrated. "Why?"

My voice cracked. "I just found out you tried for a baby with anyone who had a vagina."

I didn't mention the worst part. That Harper was back. That she was with Dan. The one man I'd quietly kept as a backup plan in the shadows of my heart.

That little detail? Straight into the box marked: HELL NO.

He kept his eyes on the road. But the emotion leaked off him like a slow puncture in a sinking ship.

"Chloe, please don't. I'm askin' you to stop. I don't wanna fight. Not after we just had a baby."

"Stop what, exactly, Romeo? Telling the truth?" I turned toward him. "Be honest. Was I just a game?"

The pause was longer than I was ready for.

It filled my throat with bile.

The rain simmered.

The wipers slowed.

It felt like the whole world was waiting on him.

He scratched at his stubble again, lost in reflection.

"Aight, yeah. I admit that… at first, because Daniele wanted you. It made me want you more."

Ouch.

Now we were getting somewhere.

My heart kicked up pace as anxiety lit up every nerve.

Fight-or-flight bubbled in my veins. My fingers curled around the door handle.

Any second now, I'd do it. I'd open it. I'd throw myself out.

"Why did you want a baby with me so soon? Was it to hurt Dan?"

"No. I mean... kind of."

No fucking way. I knew it.

My palm slapped against my chest. Horror bled through the cracks of vindication. A cold sweat broke across my overheated cheeks. My vision blurred as the world shifted around me.

"Oh my God. I can't fucking believe this."

As we reached the off-ramp and rolled to a stop at the light, he sat back in his seat, rubbing his hands together like he was trying to wipe the emotion off his skin.

The rumble of traffic slowing beside us felt like we were all on a start line, waiting for the gunshot that would launch us straight into the wreckage.

"The truth," he said, clearing his throat when his voice cracked at the end. "I thought my shit was broke."

I stopped breathing.

We both did.

"...Huh? What is that supposed to mean?"

He shook his head, disbelief in every exhale, like even he couldn't believe he was saying it out loud.

"Me and Harper were more than just fuckin' in the beginnin'. We were, you know—"

Like a newborn taking its first breath, I sucked in air.

My heart pounded loud enough to hear it. My lips tingled. My stomach flipped.

"What? Engaged?" I said through ragged breaths, clutching my necklace like it could keep me grounded.

"No. But I bought the ring. Was plannin' on it once her divorce with Daniele went through."

There wasn't enough air left in the cabin. Every breath was a battle. This was torture. Especially now—knowing how deeply he'd downplayed their relationship.

I clawed at anything I could grip.

My thighs. The seat edge. The door handle.

The ache between my legs, the place where I'd birthed his son, now felt tainted. Ruined.

"And?" I croaked, voice hollow.

He sighed, his whole body slumping.

Fingers uncurled like he'd finally let go of the lie.

"We both wanted a kid. She couldn't get pregnant after three months tryin', so I figured it was her. Things started goin' weird, and we split when Tat came along."

Harper was the first stab to the chest.

Tat was the sideswipe.

"Okay," I choked. "Then what?"

"Then I fucked Tat constantly, for eight months straight. Every month she weren't pregnant had me fearin' the worst. When she didn't get pregnant at all, that's when I knew there must've been somethin' wrong with me."

I frowned. "Wait… so did you know all along the baby wasn't yours?"

He nodded slowly. "I didn't know it was Saxon's until he confirmed it in the club. But yeah… she told me when I confronted her about cheatin'."

His face was pale, ghost-like in the dashboard glow.

Haunted.

My hand flew to my mouth.

"…Is that why—?"

He looked straight at me. Pierced clean through me.

"Why I killed her?" His voice didn't waver. "Yeah. I didn't plan on it endin' the way it did, but she mocked me. She said it out loud… that I couldn't be a father. You don't know how much that fuckin' hurt my heart, Chloe."

Raindrops slithered down the windshield like the tears streaking my cheeks.

He'd told me different versions of this story before—but for the first time, I knew. This was the truth.

This was what he'd been hiding all along.

I sat in silence, replaying everything we'd just gone through. Piece by broken piece, the half became a whole.

Had things been different, would his life have played on repeat—jumping from girl to girl, trying again and again?

One minute, I was desperate for reassurance. The idea that he still wanted a baby with Harper had my life hanging by a thread. A thread that, at any moment, I might snap. Might open that car door and let go.

But that desperation melted away. Slowly. Bitterly. As the full story unravelled.

We both learned something in that moment.

After all this time, it wasn't about the women. It was Romeo, chasing proof that he was man enough to father a child. Grabbing at anyone who would say yes—just to feel whole.

My fingers loosened around the necklace. The sharp edges had left little red dents in my skin.

The ideas unjumbled. They sat in front of me, clear as day.

This wasn't about him trying to conquer the world one womb at a time. His story mirrored mine. Two people making reckless decisions because they didn't believe they were enough.

Although, what baffled me was how Romeo didn't see it. How he couldn't understand why none of those women had gotten pregnant.

It was so fucking obvious.

They felt how I felt the first time I met him.

Unsafe. Out of control. Cornered.

He bulldozed his way into their lives, demanding babies with a force that made them say yes to his face while popping birth control behind his back.

Hell, I did the exact same thing.

Had he approached it differently, he'd have a dozen kids by now.

But the universe had other plans. We were so right for each other. So desperately in need of saving in our own ways.

We were so strong together. So weak apart.

With my back to him, I stared out the window, sighing against my reflection.

The woman looking back at me was sad.

But assured. And for now... That was enough.

"You got me pregnant first time, Romeo. There's nothing wrong with you."

He placed his hand on my thigh. The chill of anxiety transferred from his skin to mine.

"Chloe, look at me."

My leg flinched, pulling away from his touch.

His request was one I couldn't meet. Not now.

He needed to understand that his past couldn't keep bleeding into his future without it hurting like hell every time it did.

But he carried on anyway.

"Before you, I was scared I wasn't a man anymore. Once people found out my dick didn't work, it would've been over. When you got pregnant… I knew you were my angel."

He made it sound so romantic, but I wasn't sure he was ever that capable.

"So you just wanted me because I was proof of your fertility?"

He claimed my thigh a second time.

This time, he held on. Firm. Unrelenting.

"I loved you the minute you went to jail for me. You stopped bein' a game that day. Everythin' after that… I was already in love with."

I scoffed. Couldn't help myself.

The idea of Romero Giannetti being honest about his feelings only ever seemed… half true.

"Are you saying all this to get yourself out of the shit?"

He placed a hand over his chest. The throb of his pulse pushed against his palm like it was trying to escape.

"On my son's life, I've loved you longer than I haven't."

I sat back in my seat, trying to make sense of the bombshell I'd just uncovered.

The air hung heavy. No longer threaded with alcohol. Now it tasted of fear.

Fear of how much time he'd spent obsessing over his reputation. Fear that he was losing his grip on me now.

He thought he was infertile until I came along—

And now what? He saw me as heaven-sent?

How ironic. A Catholic man believing God had sent a hooker to save him.

I wanted to shake him. To wake him up to the fact that those girls didn't get pregnant because they were too high or too careful—not because he was broken. All that mental torment he'd been carrying was unnecessary.

But then again… if he didn't think that way, would I still be special to him?

I stole a glance at his side profile.

Tight jaw. Perfectly angular nose. So handsome, no matter the angle.

"While we're being honest, can I ask you something?"

He cast me a glance as the car slowed to a crawl around the corner.

"Of course. Shoot."

I played with a few strands of my hair, untangling the wording as carefully as the knots.

This question was loaded.

One that, months ago, I'd have been too scared to ask.

"Are you bothered that Dan is back with Harper?"

His reaction was calmer than I expected.

Too calm.

"I couldn't give a fuck about either of them. I mean that."

Did he?

I tucked my bottom lip between my teeth to keep the sorrow from escaping.

"None of it was ever really about her, Chloe. I didn't know what love was back then. Didn't have a fuckin' clue. I thought she was helpin' me. Pills. All that shit. T's helped me more in a few months than she did in years."

A memory hit me.

Pills.

That was her specialty.

"When I first came to live with you, I found some pills in the bathroom cabinet. I always wanted to know what they were for."

He screwed up his nose. "You mean the mood pills? You already know about those."

"No, these were different. A name I'd never heard before."

His arm twitched on the centre console. Fingers curled around the leather. Tight.

"Oh. Those pills." He stalled.

The words dropped into the silence like stones into deep water.

"They were somethin' Harper gave me to help get bitches pregnant."

Oh wow.

Her claws were six inches deep in his spine, and still hadn't been removed.

I toyed with my diamond ring.

Light refracted, bouncing across the dashboard in flickers.

The memory of the first time it slid onto my finger—in the back of a moving SUV—wasn't exactly Shakespearean romance.

"Do you still have her engagement ring?" I asked, unable to stop myself.

Wondering if it was as perfect as mine. The shape. The colour. The clarity.

The sky darkened with every passing second. Streetlights flickered past, each one making the stone on my ring gleam a little louder. Who would've thought a diamond could hold so much meaning?

He glanced at me before scooping up my hand.

Warm met cold.

Truth met lies.

"I don't have it. You do—right here," he said, eyes on the ring around my finger.

Huh?

Wind-swept. Side-swiped. Flattened.

"You what?" I asked, heart in my mouth once more.

Even the wipers offered a dry, solitary swipe like they were trying to clear my vision for me.

He continued. "Well… I never gave it to her. She didn't even know about it. So I figured…" He trailed off.

Then squinted—like realisation had just burned straight through his retinas.

My head turned toward him.

Slow. Too slow.

Eyes wide with the kind of fear that didn't want to hear what came next.

My finger felt like it was swelling. The ring was too tight. My throat tightened even more.

No.

What started as a squeeze on my hand had doubled down around my neck like a vice.

"Wait… Hold on." He smiled. Cautious. Raised his fingers in a playful gun sign. A Hail Mary for the tension. "I can see the look on your face. You don't gotta tell me. I've fucked up here… Fuck."

Elbow on the armrest, he massaged his temple, desperate for a way out of the mess he'd just exposed.

If I'd had a knife, I'd be dragging it across a sharpener.

Slow. Deliberate.

I could already taste the satisfaction of that first stab.

"I can't believe you've done this to me, Romeo."

He sighed. "Look, you remember what I used to be like? I was a prick—"

"Pfft. Prick doesn't quite cut it."

His lower lip caught in his teeth.

Between driving and fixing the worst mistake of his life, he was struggling to balance the two.

"I ain't disagreein' with you. But we can agree I've changed, right? I'm fuckin' nothin' like I was when I proposed to you."

The cloak of rage wrapped around my fear lifted—just slightly.

He wasn't wrong.

And he sensed my silent agreement.

"I'd already worked hard to make the change. But somethin' switched in me the second the boy came outta you. I see how you're mad over this. I'll fix it, okay?"

And while the sharpening slowed, the thoughts kept coming. Thick and fast.

Vivid images of him choosing that ring for her.

Laughing with the jeweller.

Talking through the proposal.

Flowers. Music. Lovemaking.

He saw the mistake. But it didn't change the fact that I was wearing another woman's ring.

"Look," he said, trying to fill the silence, "we got a big day tomorrow. Let's just see that through, then I'll buy you the biggest fuckin' diamond there is. You name it, I'll buy it."

Now, I'd be lying if I said that suggestion didn't interest me. A smirk tugged at the corners of my lips.

The idea of flashing something outlandish in Harper's face the next time I saw her? Very appealing.

A new ring would mean a clean slate. A fresh start. Something that belonged to me.

I arched a brow. "Even if it cost five million dollars?"

He laughed like I was a stand-up comedian.

"Baby, even if it cost fifty million."

Tugging on the band I was trying to remove only seemed to tighten it.

I had to get rid of it like I was ridding her from my mind.

"How much did this ring cost, anyway?"

He sniffed, flicking the tip of his nose in that gangster way he always did.

"Two and some change."

Wait.

Streetlights faded into the distance—less city now, more forest. Just him, me, and the baby in on this.

No witnesses to his murder…

"You spent two million dollars on an engagement ring for Harper!?"

The disbelief on his face, like I'd just accused him of a war crime, didn't help his case.

"Well… yeah! How many fuckin' times a day do we get papped? You think I'd let the world see my woman with a gumball machine ring?"

Ahh. Of course.

The ring wasn't a reflection of love. It was a flex. A message to America that he wasn't just the most handsome man alive. He was filthy rich, too.

The ground beneath us changed. Tarmac gave way to loose stone. A little eerie, if you didn't know the place.

But I breathed a sigh of relief as we pulled up somewhere familiar.

Nonna's cottage.

The engine cut off. Only the rustle of tree leaves in the canopy above remained.

"I know you've changed," I said softly. "I guess I believe you wouldn't do something so stupid now."

He smiled—grateful.

Relieved.

"Hand on my dick, I promise I'll buy you a new ring. Got it?"

I slumped back in my seat as his other hand found my cheek. The connection between us would never fizzle out.

"Got it," I said with a shy smile.

He pressed a soft kiss to my lips, then leaned in—forehead resting against mine.

"Tomorrow, at 10:00 AM, we show the world who we are. Me and you, Queen. Forever."

CHAPTER 14

1:01 AM

The hands on the clock seemed to move too quickly. Both of us too wired to sleep, Romeo and I sat together in Nonna's living room, wrapped in the calm before the storm the morning would bring.

Junior slumbered peacefully in his bassinet beside me. Its design, of course, perfectly complemented the curved woodwork and muted creams Lucy, our interior designer, had insisted on for the nursery in our recently refurbished cottage.

Credit where it was due—she'd outdone herself.

The club was practically finished, and it wouldn't be long before construction began on the new nursery at the mansion.

While I hadn't spoken to her since her part in the kidnapping, I held no hard feelings toward a woman who, it turned out, understood my husband's capabilities far better than I'd ever given her credit for.

Laid out on the new plush couch that still smelled of freshly manufactured brown leather, I nestled into Romeo's chest while we half-watched a sexy film.

The fire roared and spat in the hearth, hissing at us in protest—working overtime to keep the room warm against the draught curling down the chimney.

Talk of what lay ahead in just a few hours was non-existent. I'd tried earlier to bring up the subject. The hows, the wheres, the plan. But of course, Romeo's world was calculated for a reason.

Tonight, we were a new family of three. Tucked away in our cottage. Learning the ropes of parenthood with all the chaos that came with it.

If the cops came knocking in relation to two missing persons, our physical alibi—along with our emotional one—would be ironclad. Impenetrable.

Our crew was handling the setup.

We would handle the situation.

But right now?

It was movie night with my husband.

And for reasons I didn't fully understand, I felt... settled.

Romeo fidgeted, digging his hand into the popcorn bowl, spilling half of the buttery goodness across his lap.

"Look at this dude, thinkin' he's the shit in bed," he said, chewing with his mouth open. "Would help if his fuckin' dick weren't so small."

Distracted, I was still focused on the engagement ring that I couldn't get off my swollen finger. Even cooking oil hadn't helped.

He chuckled. "Did you fuckin' see that? Never used a gun in his life, this prick."

Only half listening, I trailed my fingers along the curve of his bicep through his T-shirt. Thick muscle. Softly pulsing veins. There wasn't a man on the planet hotter than Romeo—but, as usual, I kept that card close to my chest.

Soft moans from the female lead threaded through the air, straight into Romeo's waiting ears.

He was secretly loving this.

"I'm sure he knows what he's doing," I said, nuzzling my nose into his armpit and drawing in a deep, relaxed breath.

Leather. Oaky freshness. Perfection.

Romeo shunted me gently, careful to keep the wetness of his buttery fingers off the fine cotton of my bed shirt.

"Here, take some of this shit before I eat it all." He shovelled in another handful of popcorn.

Harper's words rang loud and clear, like the town crier's bell. I didn't need to see her face during that call. She was grinning, no doubt, when she said what everyone else was thinking.

I was overweight. She wasn't.

"No, thanks," I said, keeping my head nestled against the firmness of his chest.

His pecs flexed. "Why?"

He was insistent.

I was avoidant.

Together, we made a headfuck combination.

I wanted to ask if he noticed the way my stomach folded. The way my breath caught when she called me fat—and he didn't deny it.

But instead, I ate the popcorn like it meant nothing. Plucking a few stray pieces from his lap, I popped them into my mouth—savouring the satisfying crunch, cracking under my teeth like the silence he didn't know he was creating.

"There," I said, picking a shard from between my teeth. "Happy now?"

Quietly satisfied, he turned his attention back to the movie, laughing mockingly at the screen as he jutted his popcorn-filled hand toward the scene change—now set in a flower shop.

The FBI burst in.

Bullets flew.

Meanwhile, the female lead continued pleasuring her man beneath the register.

"Holy shit!" Romeo jolted in his seat as the guy took a bullet square in the back while mid-blowjob.

Relaxed against his chest, his fingers drifted lazily along the curve of my back.

The flickering light from the TV danced across the walls, its glow merging with the firelight above the mantel—wrapping the room in a soft, tranquil haze.

Each chuckle from him sent a ripple through his body, rocking me gently in a steady, comforting rhythm.

Something about the cottage always felt safe to me. And right here, in this moment, was exactly what I'd hoped for the day Romeo promised we'd hide away after the baby was born.

Another scene change.

This time, the characters found themselves in jail.

Why was the cop in charge naked?

No idea.

The visuals were stunning.

The script? Not so much.

I wasn't even sure why I picked this film. After the opening gunfight, it had just turned into sex layered on top of badly performed sex—and the giggler beside me wasn't about to let it slide.

Maybe, since I couldn't exactly fulfil Romeo's needs right now and his ever-present erection was digging into my side, it might give him a little inspiration to handle his own business when we climbed into bed later.

He laughed again, low and warm, the sound vibrating beneath my cheek. His hand rested loosely around my hip, thumb absentmindedly stroking the fabric of my shirt.

Relaxed and fully in control of his emotions, he pointed at the screen again.

"You can tell a fuckin' mile off when they don't really smoke. Inhale it, son!" He spoke to the actor who was enjoying his post-sex smoke like he could actually hear him.

With the amount of cigarettes Romeo got through, I figured it was fair to call him a professional in the field.

My nostrils twitched as I breathed him in again. Not a hint of tobacco clung to his clothes.

"Speaking of…" I peered up at him through my lashes. "You haven't had a cigarette in a couple of hours. Not bad for you."

I smiled at the thought. The idea of nicotine-stained fingers touching my baby was enough to make my fists clench.

"Told you I've been tryin' to cut down. Been smokin' since I was twelve. It ain't easy."

Something about that surprised me, and didn't, all at once. God only knew what that boy got up to in his youth. I'd barely turned the first page of that story.

The fire popped softly in the background, freshly chopped wood from the forest surrounding us feeding a slow, steady burn. A luxury I knew Romeo took for granted.

Fixated on the naked woman in the movie, his eyes stayed glued to the screen, far too interested in what she had to offer.

I hated to admit it… but it made me jealous.

Glancing down at my bed shirt, I tugged the fabric lower, revealing the swell of my engorged breasts through the open-buttoned collar.

"Are mine better than hers?" I asked, trying—and failing—to pull off breezy, carefree Chloe.

His attention snapped from the screen, fidgeting the moment he caught sight of my cleavage.

"You already know they are. She got them tangerine tiddies." He bounced his hands against his chest with a boyish grin. "You got them melons."

Satisfied in an instant. That was all I needed to hear.

Without thinking, my hand wandered beneath the sheep's wool blanket draped over both of us, seeking out the heat in his lap. He shifted slightly, hips tilting forward, anticipation flickering across his face as I slid my hand into the soft fabric of his sweatpants.

Excited and aroused, he reached beneath the blanket, pulled out his gun, and let it drop, landing on the rug with a muted clatter. Then, tugging his waistband lower, he helped me free him.

When I found what I was looking for, I wrapped my fingers around the thick weight of his cock, stroking slowly as the film played on. His stomach tensed, a tremor of restraint rippling through him.

Slouching deeper into the couch, he lifted the edge of the fleece to peek at my handiwork—watching silently as I worked him, hardening him until a soft pink flush rose along his cheekbones.

On-screen, the characters writhed beneath strategically placed satin sheets. There wasn't much left to the imagination, but Romeo wasn't paying full attention to the movie anymore. His focus was split between the screen and the rhythm I'd created just for him.

His lips parted with a soft exhale as his dick solidified, tension coiling in his thighs like a timer counting down to zero.

"So beautiful," he murmured into my neck, inhaling my scent like it enhanced the experience.

Inspired, he slid his hand beneath the hem of my shirt, raising it up and over my head in one fluid motion. Like the professional he was, his palm found the fullness of my post-birth breast—his touch soft, gentle.

He'd been needing this. Needing me.

When his lips closed around my nipple, the sensation was unexpectedly tender, less about hunger, more about connection. The flick of his tongue combined with the heat of his mouth stirred something deep in me. My spine tingled, breath hitching as something instinctive kicked in. Milk formed at the teat for him before making a direct connection between my legs.

"I've been needin' me some of this." His hand squeezed harder. "Feel how solid I am for you. So fuckin' sexy."

Tightening my hold on him, I pressed a kiss into his hair.

"That's it, baby," I whispered, inhaling the warm scent of coconut. Just feeling the sensations of this new exploration. It brought us closer in a way I struggled to understand.

In a hormonal state of confusion, my body wanted to nurture him. Claim him. Anchor us both in this impossible softness that only existed between people like us.

I ran my fingers through his hair while he stayed nestled against me, taking the moment he'd been so clearly craving.

Was this his way of asking for reassurance? For proof that I still loved him—not just as my husband, but as deeply as I loved our son? That I was still his, in a way that nurtured him?

The longer he suckled, the deeper the urges became. He was so erect for me. So lost in the moment, I knew it wouldn't be long. So close. Almost there.

Outside, the wind shifted beyond the cottage walls—travelling down the chimney and stoking the fire burning in the hearth. Hissing. Crackling. Wild shadows danced across the walls like they, too, were caught in our heat.

His breath thickened, hot and sweaty.

"Fuck... I gotta see this. See me come so hard for you." He tore the blanket away, exposing the full length of his cock to the open air. Flinching. Pulsing. Ignited red-hot like the flames beside us—his orgasm burning at the tip.

Still, I didn't stop. Strategic strokes kept him teetering, coaxing him over the hill, inch by glorious inch.

Breathless, he found my mouth, kissing me with so much passion it bordered on desperation. Like he needed more from me than touch alone.

"Can you taste it?" he whispered. "Your sweet milk on my tongue. You're so fuckin' beautiful."

I nodded my reply. Experiencing the faint sweetness he offered back to me. The intimacy of it folding around us, anchoring the moment in something stronger than just lust.

No amount of oxygen could fill the space between us. We were lost together in outer space, and still, somehow, guaranteed to find each other.

He was my needle in the haystack. I was his.

His mouth closed around my breast once more, claiming me, adoring me, while my hand moved over him, unhurried, savouring the moment.

A few more strokes, free and exposed for us both to see, and he trembled beneath my touch.

That's when he gave in.

Jaw clenched, his body unravelled in a quiet, urgent release—thick white spurts painting me in rhythmic waves of euphoria.

The fire in the hearth simmered with us, crackling low now, like it too was catching its breath. Even the cottage seemed to exhale, its old beams creaking in time with our slowing hearts.

Panting softened. The pressure in the room dissolved into something molten and warm. A quiet bliss.

The credits rolled in silence—white text drifting across a black screen—bathing the room in a low, restful darkness. Like a match just blown out, the light faded, but the smoulder of the night lingered between us.

I smirked, a little sweaty, hair clinging to the nape of my neck. "You needed that, huh?" I teased, biting my lower lip.

He huffed through a crooked grin. "I lose stamina when it's been a while."

The heat in the room cooled fast. My smile dropped.

Wind threaded through the refurbished wooden window frames, stirring the drapes.

Joking or not, he was bang out of line.

It might've been dark, but he sure as hell felt my glare as I shoved at his chest—slick remnants of his orgasm still clinging to my fingers, tangled in the hair across his sternum.

"You're joking, right? You keep bringing this up like we didn't have sex less than a week ago!"

"Over a week," he said, lifting a brow like that somehow strengthened his already invalid point.

The fire, now reduced to embers, matched the weight in my chest that only seemed to grow heavier still.

Lost for words, the electric energy in the room vanished.

Maybe because of our new bond, or the new way we loved each other, Romeo felt it, too.

"What did I do now?" He tucked himself away, suddenly exposed in a way that stripped the bravado clean off him.

Without missing a beat, he reached for his gun, waiting on the rug, and laid it on the arm of the chair. His hand settled beside it instinctively.

Not as a threat to me. It was his shield.

"I—nothing," I said, letting out a long, shaky breath. The kind that didn't feel like it belonged to me at all.

I dropped my gaze, but he wasn't letting it go.

He leant over and clicked on the lamp, bathing the room in soft light.

The heady scent of his arousal, mixed with the salt of his skin, fogged my already fragile senses.

His gaze met mine, shadowed by a seriousness that sharpened the air between us.

"Tell me, Chloe. What did I do?"

Only then did I remember I was still topless. I wrapped the blanket around my body, the sheep's wool itchy against my too-sensitive skin.

He watched, but didn't move a muscle.

"It's just..." I pulled the blanket closer. "You keep pushing me for sex. And... I'm... I guess I'm worried."

He slung his arm over the back of the sofa, gripping the leather like he was bracing himself—waiting for me to say something that would crush him.

He blinked, slow. "You think I became a dad, and what? Got shit in bed?"

My sensitive husband. So serious, and yet a laugh broke from my lips before I could stop it.

"No, Romeo. That couldn't be further from what I meant. I'm just… God, this is hard to say."

His white-knuckled grip on the sofa eased.

Changing tactics, he reached for my hand. Lifting my fingers to his mouth, he kissed each tip gently.

"Tell me," he coaxed—his voice less defensive now, laced with something more alluring.

I swallowed, heart hammering painfully against my ribs.

"I feel like my body is ruined. Like you'll look at me… and think I'm disgusting."

His lips parted slightly. He didn't even breathe as the words hung between us.

He brushed a strand of hair off my face.

"Queen, your body…" His voice cracked. "I worship you. Why the fuck would you think that?"

My arms folded across my stomach, hiding my biggest insecurity.

"I have stretch marks. My stomach is swollen…" I blinked back the sting forming. "I cried when I looked at myself in the mirror earlier."

His eyes shifted—like he was replaying events, searching for something he'd missed. A deep frown settled on his face, etched in further the longer he thought.

The cottage echoed his stillness.

The fire was long out—just a few faintly smouldering embers atop blackened logs remained.

"When did you cry?" he asked, already piecing it together before I even answered.

His shoulders sagged. "When I went out for that smoke… I came back, and you said you were tired… but that's why your eyes were red. God damn it, Chloe. You should've told me."

The baby, sound asleep, sighed in his dreams. So precious to me—everything I could've wished for. And still, I felt guilty that some small part of me wished my body hadn't been ruined by him.

I rolled my thumbs around each other, the knot in my chest tightening. Exhausted from motherhood, from lack of sleep, from everything. It had all moulded into one giant mess.

"I was worried your reaction would confirm it," I mumbled.

Romeo didn't argue. He simply peeled my arms away from my body and held them out wide.

Then, dipping low, he pressed his mouth to the soft roll of my stomach. Once flat—now two tyres. Lumpy. Ugly. Utterly disgusting.

But not to him. His lips were warm against the skin I hated most, as if he was trying to rewrite the way I saw it, one kiss at a time.

"Just lookin' at your beautiful body now… God, I fuckin' love everythin' about you."

Untrusting of his word, I squirmed out of his hold.

Sensing the fragility of the moment, he let go—but not before curling my wrist to his mouth and pressing a kiss to the back of my hand.

"Lie down," he said, command lacing his tone.

Already hard, he knelt over me, holding himself. The thick weight of his cock gripped tight in his fist.

Flat on my back, I stared up at him. This man before me. My husband. My everything. And yet… knowing he was looking at someone different now. Someone unsure of her own body. Unhappy with what she could offer him. It filled me with sadness.

Still slick from his orgasm, he didn't care, running his hand lazily along the shaft.

"Touch your sexy tits for me, Queen. Love them the way I do."

The soft curve of my belly rose and fell beneath the weight of anticipation, my pulse chasing each breath.

My hand moved with quiet devotion, tracing a slow line across my chest to meet the swell of my breast—resting there, thumb brushing gently over the peak like I was exploring my body for the first time. My compliance only spurred him on.

His pace quickened, breath catching as he struggled for control. He tugged on his cock, hungry and needy, the links of his watch snapping the silence into pieces with every stroke.

"You think I stay hard like this for just anyone?"

Huh?

My eyes followed his rhythm. I was mesmerised, but confused. Tilting my head, I shrugged.

He saw it. The doubt.

As I continued to massage, more of my body's own creation spilled from my tightened nipple. His eyes sparkled with desire. He loved it, adored seeing what my body could create for his son, a visible proof of what I was capable of.

He caught his lower lip between his teeth.

"Fuck." His head rolled back, lost in the moment.

Blood pooled low in my body at the sight of my husband coming undone for me. I craved our connection as much as he did. We needed each other—always.

"You see this, Chloe?"

His cock flinched.

I moaned. The heat rising between us.

"Before… when we talked about all that shit in the past—Harper, Tat…" He paused, sifting through the silence for the right words. "You think when I nutted, I could go again with them, straight after?"

My hand slowed. Pressure eased. I swallowed hard, a lump catching in my throat. Where the hell was he going with this?

Desire gave way to doubt. Just the thought of those beautiful women beneath him and how I no longer compared—

He leaned closer still. The unbearable tenderness of his weight hovering, cradling me like I was something precious. His sweet breath mingled with my self-doubt.

"The day I met you was the day I woke up. I felt everythin' you gave me. Sex with you… it's somethin' I can't even describe. How we fight. How we laugh. You're my wife. Fuck, you're my everythin'."

His hand stilled over himself. Dick swollen, pulsing beneath his touch —responding to his own words.

"You gave me a son, Chloe. My heart is yours. Do with it whatever the fuck you want. Without you... I'm nothin'."

My eyes shimmered, absorbing him. Truly hearing him.

"You're too sore, right?" he whispered, his fingers brushing the inside of my thigh softly, fleetingly, before his mouth closed gently around my nipple again.

He wasn't greedy this time. He was gentle. Nurturing in his own way.

I nodded my agreement, words tangled somewhere in my throat. His body hovered over mine, the heat of him wrapping me like a shield against the cold. Every part of him pulling me back to safety.

The warmth of his fingers set my senses alight as he brushed my cheek. "I can't tell you how much you mean to me, Chloe Giannetti. I'll die a thousand times over for you. For our son."

The tears I'd been holding back pressed harder against my chest. "But my body—" I started.

He let go of himself, folding forward until he rested gently against me —still careful, still holding most of his weight. His forehead pressed to mine. His breath fanned across my lips.

"Kiss me," he whispered into my mouth.

My fingers tangled in his damp curls, drawing him closer. The heat at the nape of his neck matched the fire blooming beneath my skin. And we did. Tongues entwining. Breaths mingling. The kind of kiss that felt like salvation.

I held on tighter. For dear life. Held his words, his breath, his whole heart in my hands.

His lips peeled from mine just enough to speak into them. A rush of his air caught at the back of my throat.

He flinched.

"Fuck, I'm comin'. Do you feel my love for you?"

Boy, did I feel it—the sudden jolt, the hot, thick wetness of his climax spilling across my stomach. Cooling instantly against my skin. Marking me. Marking the moment. His promise that I was good enough.

His mouth trembled against mine as his orgasm rolled on, our kisses growing hungrier and more desperate, as if neither of us could get enough.

The stillness of the room was disturbed only by our quiet devotion to each other.

"Your body means more to me now than it ever did before," he rasped against my lips. "Sexy as fuck, then. Sexier now. I love you, Chloe."

Overloaded with emotion, fear dusting the edges of my clouded mind, I felt him against me. Truly connected to the man I had literally killed for.

"You love me, don't you?" he breathed.

Like the gale turning the tide, we stared at each other. Funny, really, how when I needed reassurance most, he needed it even more.

I reached up, brushing a loose curl from his forehead to get the full, unobstructed view of his sparkling blue eyes.

"I love you more than I ever thought possible, Romeo."

6:00 AM

The alarm on my phone sounded before I was ready. Still dark out, the sun hadn't even made its first appearance of the day.

Romeo was already dressed in the outfit I'd seen a hundred times before. Black T-shirt. Grey shorts. Pulled-up socks. Sneakers. But today, I finally understood what it meant.

Today would be the first time I ever saw him kill someone. And that outfit felt far too casual for something so monumental.

Outside, crickets struck up the first notes of life beyond the cottage walls, the forest slowly beginning to stir.

Junior, finally asleep after his feed, let out a soft sigh—his tiny legs kicking like he was still in the womb, innocently responding to the rising pulse in the room.

The low glow of the lamp stretched long silhouettes across the walls, closing in the space like the anticipation already hanging between us.

As if reading my thoughts, Romeo stepped out of the closet, nudging the door shut with his shoulder. He looked over at me, a familiar jewellery box tucked beneath one arm, his knuckles white from the strain of his grip.

"I know you just had the baby," he murmured. "But you understand why this gotta be done now, right?"

Crucifix not yet worn. He was still with me—and it showed in the way he still cared.

I looked down at my saturated bed shirt, peeling the cold, damp fabric from my skin. A clammy reminder of how recently I'd given birth. The ache in my hips told the story I didn't want to burden him with.

Truth was, he needed this more than I needed to heal.

"God, look at the state of me." I giggled. "And this is with nipple pads."

He crossed the room in three strides. The mattress dipped beneath his weight as he leaned in. No liquor. No cigarettes. Just mint lingered between us as he pressed his forehead to mine. He closed his eyes and inhaled slowly.

"Tell me you understand, Chloe."

Matching the movement of his chest, I exhaled. "Yes, Romeo. I understand."

With a metallic click, he tossed the jewellery box onto the bed. The weight inside it was more than just the thick platinum chain. He exhaled a lungful of tension, releasing it into a room already holding its breath. His fingers brushed my cheeks, statically charged, cupping my face in both hands.

"I used to make the mistake of keepin' you out of this. But that made you the weak link. A target. Those bitches came to you behind my back 'cause nobody's seen what you're capable of. But they will. Today."

Like a flower squashed between the pages of life's morals, I nodded.

And there it was again. The chemistry. Buzzing between us, undeniable. Nothing but his body inside mine would silence it.

"Come here, sexy," he whispered against my parted lips.

The soft heat of his mouth melted into mine, warming the chill that clung to my cheeks. Our sexual connection only seemed to strengthen. Clit throbbing. Dick pulsing. I craved him—his hands, his weight, his breath.

Faint creaks from the bedframe snapped beneath us, anticipating a moment we both knew we shouldn't yet share.

My body bloomed, petals unfolding. My muscles drew tight, as if he'd pulled the arrow of my bow taut enough to tremble under the strain.

"Oh, God, Romeo," I murmured into his hair, fingers curling into the creased bedsheets.

His tongue rolled against mine, then he guided my hand to the thick ridge of his erection.

"Fuck, I need to be inside you so bad," he groaned.

I wanted to tell him I felt the same. Wanted to drown in the intimacy between us. Instead, I gripped him long and thick, the heated tip already spilling over his waistband.

"What's wrong with us?" I rasped, strangled by the heat of my own arousal.

His breath matched mine in pace, our rhythm building. "I don't know, but I fuckin' love it."

He shoved down his shorts. His erection sprang free, solid and ready.

"Suck it, Queen. I wanna feel your soft lips on my dick."

I shifted closer, all too willing. The intimacy we'd shared just hours ago still clung to my skin. He worshipped me without hesitation. Now it was my turn to worship him.

I kissed the hot tip. He flinched—his balls drawing tight.

A sound travelled up the staircase.

I ignored it. Licked the length this time. His hand scraped through my hair, desperate to feel more of me.

Then another sound splintered through the quiet.

I froze. Every hair on my body stood on end.

The crickets stopped. A solitary croak gave way to deafening silence.

From downstairs came the slow creak of the front door, stealing the moment entirely.

My heart thudded—two hard beats to match the footsteps that followed. Slow. Heavy. Making their way through the living room.

Like a winter snap in spring, the petals folded. The heat between us shattered like glass beneath a boot.

I let go of him, eyes darting to the crib.

"Did you hear that?" I whispered. "Someone's downstairs!"

I tugged the covers up over my body, the instinct to shield myself returning too fast.

Unfazed, Romeo dipped closer and ran the sharp point of his nose along mine.

"Relax. Just Tommy and Snake preppin'. It's all in hand. We know what we're doin'."

He pulled his shorts back up, adjusted the thick outline pressing against the fabric, and smiled the way he always did when trying to offer comfort.

It worked.

"Oh, thank God." I sagged into the pillow. "What are they doing down there?"

Tugging at the hem of my T-shirt, he peeled it over my head. The faint scent of sweetness lingered—grounding us both to the moment. A new life rested quietly in his bassinet, while two others edged toward their end.

"You just concentrate on focusin' your mind." He placed two fingers on my temple. "Everythin' else is bein' taken care of."

Goosebumps swept along my exposed skin, now covered only by a thin bedsheet. Him removing my shirt meant one thing. Now it was my turn.

I reached behind me and unclipped my bra.

Naked before him, with only a cover over my stomach, I thought he wanted more of last night.

Maybe I could give it a try. We always found a way.

Watching his every move, I kept my gaze locked on his through the veil of my lashes. He kissed the fullness of my chest, then pushed off the mattress. The coils creaked beneath him as he stood.

Wet shirt in hand, he lingered. His thumb traced slowly over the fabric—distracted.

"Listen, Chloe. I'm glad they interrupted us. I can't nut before somethin' like this. Like a boxer—gotta keep the testosterone 'til after the fight. You get what I mean?"

I did get it... but that didn't quell the throb between my thighs.

He waited for my response.

Truthfully, I was relieved I'd been spared more time before he saw the new me.

Eventually, I let out a soft giggle.

"What are you doing with that?" I nodded at his hand. "You're not going to wear it, are you?"

A look of relief loosened his jaw. He laughed, holding the shirt up to the light. It looked like it belonged in a wet T-shirt competition.

"Damn, those tits be workin' overtime, huh?" He grinned. "I'll go get that tittie pump thing from the car. Can't be havin' this shit distractin' me later on."

He said it in jest—like 'later on' meant a stroll in the park. But the gravity of it rang loud in my head.

By this time tomorrow, I'd wake knowing I'd taken another life.

6:59 AM

The forest beyond the cottage rustled in quiet discomfort, reminding me we were alone out here—but not quite.

Sunlight filtered through the leafy canopy, bathing the room in a muted glow that offered no warmth.

It was going to be a cold morning for all of us.

"Are you ready for this?" Romeo asked, standing by our bedroom door, waiting impatiently for me to get my shit together.

"Um... not really, no." My voice trembled ever so slightly.

We must've slept two, maybe three hours in the unfamiliar bed at Nonna's cottage. Junior hadn't helped matters, either. Sleep was what we both needed, not a bloodbath.

"Well, get ready," Romeo snapped, harder than usual. "This is where we show the world Giannettis are not to be fucked with."

If only it were that simple.

"Is my outfit okay?" I'd chosen a loose-fitting, knee-length dress and sneakers. Stylish, but comfortable.

As I shrugged on my light jacket, my fingers trembled. I zipped it up too fast and nearly caught the skin beneath my chin.

"It don't matter what the fuck you wear, Chloe," he muttered, refocusing on styling his hair in the vanity mirror. "It'll be gettin' incinerated after, anyway."

I stepped in front of my reflection and studied myself. Dark circles. Pale lips. The woman staring back looked like she was barely holding it together. Quiet. A little anxious. But she had no choice except to be ready.

"Oh," I breathed, barely audible. Eyes unfocused, I glanced at our son—dreaming so peacefully. "I guess there's more to this than I realised."

The diamonds in my crucifix caught the light, announcing themselves just when I needed them most. So delicate. So perfect. I clutched the pendant between my fingers and prayed divine intervention would keep feeding me the courage to go through with this.

It's one thing to kill someone in the heat of the moment.

A whole other experience when it's premeditated.

Romeo shifted toward the door, hand on the handle. His matching crucifix hung thick and heavy around his neck, chest rising and falling in a steady rhythm—but the darkness in his pupils gave him away. He glanced at his phone, then shoved it into his pocket.

"Aight. We'll eat first. Then handle our business. Got it?"

Gangster Romeo, or should I say King, was the only version of my husband I'd see today. The man who lay over me on the couch last night… even the one who helped with the breast pump earlier… nowhere to be seen.

"What?" I almost recoiled. "You're really going to eat at a time like this?"

He smirked like I was the crazy one.

Outside, the wind swept the porch, dragging leaves like a hand dusting moss from an old grave—like the grounds had seen rituals like this before.

Not a flicker of emotion stirred behind those ocean-blue eyes.

"Fuck yeah." He stared into my soul, giving the moment his full attention. "So are you."

I frowned into the mirror, willing Jasmin to the surface. Like holding my breath and inflating my cheeks might summon her sooner.

It didn't.

She wasn't here yet.

But she would be when it counted. I was certain.

"Before I step foot out of that door, I need to know the plan," I met his gaze through the reflection. "I'm not letting anything catch me by surprise."

Eighty degrees outside. It wasn't exactly winter, but my teeth chattered behind my lips as I wrapped my arms around my body, trying to thaw the ice block forming inside me.

Romeo, it seemed, had been packed away in a box. Lid closed. Locked shut.

"I'll tell you everythin' you need to know after breakfast." He adjusted his chain like he was readorning armour. With a final tug, the crucifix settled into place—dead centre over his chest. A soldier's dog tags before war.

This time, he really felt the weight of it.

"Does that necklace give you the same comfort as the last one did?"

His chiselled features stayed rigid as he scowled. Pupils blown wide, he gave me a full view of his thoughts.

"Comfort is for girls, Queen. This right here?"—he held up the cross—"Just my fuckin' pass to heaven. That's all."

7:45 AM

Sitting opposite my husband in a random diner in the middle of God knows where was not how I'd imagined this day would start.

With the four of us seated, Tommy and Snake included, the baby took his place at the head of the table, nestled in his pram. The most innocent member of this fucked-up gathering.

Cooking grease and meat fat clung to the walls. Once-white paint had yellowed with time. The place was your typical old-school American roadside restaurant—the kind you see in movies where the cop always buys the donuts.

We stood out like a sore thumb.

The doorbell chimed again as new customers strolled in, dragging with them a gust of air laced with burnt fuel from the standstill traffic outside.

I watched the old-timer closely, flat cap and walking cane, as he settled by the window and unfolded his newspaper. I could've sworn he caught my eye before I looked away.

Did he know what we were planning to do today?

"Why haven't we ordered?" I asked, shifting my attention back to Romeo. Just in time to clock the waitress, who'd definitely seen us walk in, stroll right past our table.

Cheap perfume floated behind her—faint but familiar. The kind carried on the back of a modest salary. I'd make sure Romeo tipped her enough to cover this month's rent, and then some.

Romeo smirked at Tommy beside him, rubbing his hands together in that cocky way he always did.

"Don't need to. We always come here."

Cutlery clattered. Fryers hissed. The server bell dinged again, announcing the next meal was ready.

Snake, seated beside me, fidgeted with his napkin—more heart than the other two. At least he shared my discomfort.

I leaned in. "Oh, okay. So you usually eat here before you—"

Romeo's fist sliced through the air and slammed the table. The jolt shot up my arms, lighting up my funny bone like a bolt of electricity. I flinched.

Not a single head turned.

"Don't start shoutin' our fuckin' business, Chloe," he muttered through clenched teeth.

The curl of his breath landed on my tongue—liquor and cigarettes at 7:45 AM was more than my empty stomach could take.

I swept a glance around the room from our corner booth. Red leather upholstery, chequered floor tiles. Way too busy to overhear us through the hum of coffee machines and the whir of an old ceiling fan caked in years of fryer oil.

He was being dramatic, to say the least.

8:05 AM

All too soon, a fresh waitress emerged from the depths of the kitchen, announced by the sharp click of her heels along the vinyl flooring, four plates balanced along the lengths of her slim arms. Dark-haired and beautiful, she made a beeline for Romeo, her scent arriving before she did—tacky florals and lavender, not unlike the perfume I used to wear.

"Hey, Daddy," she purred, offering the plate to him first, her red-polished thumb almost brushing the edge of his food. Her tongue slid across ruby lips, voice coated in syrupy sweetness.

The low hum of conversation dipped, like the whole diner felt the curse behind that word.

Arching her back, she nudged Junior's pram out of the way, giving herself plenty of space to flirt with my husband.

I raised my chin. Fists clenched in my lap beneath the table.

Romeo cast me a quick glance and took the plate—his fingers casually brushing her skin like they'd done this before. She practically folded over his lap, cleavage spilling from her low-cut gingham dress.

Paper rustled against damp skin as *Daddy* shoved a crumpled fifty between her breasts. And just like that, like a slot machine that had paid out, her smirk broadened and her back straightened.

The other three plates were tossed at us with a clatter of ceramic on laminate.

"Private booth's ready for you after breakfast," she cooed, like a pigeon pecking at scraps.

I sucked air through my teeth. Another private booth? Romeo really knew how to invest his money in all the wrong places.

He raised a hand, cutting her off. "Not today, Sally. Got business straight after this."

She leaned in like she had the right to know more—like I wasn't sitting right there. I watched her toy with the sleeve of his jacket draped over the chair, touching it like she owned his copyright.

There was never a time I didn't expect this. But still, it got to me.

Sally—with an 'I' instead of an 'A'—spelled silly. And that's exactly what she was being. Silly enough to keep pushing.

"Come on, Daddy," she whimpered, lifting the cuff to her nose. "You know I can make it quick. I can play with your—"

"No." He snapped like a bear trap.

Her confidence shattered.

"Erm... okay," she mumbled, voice small, eyes darting. "But we haven't slept together in months."

While she played with his jacket, I watched. And waited.

Waited for Romeo to say the right thing.

He didn't.

He stared down at the plate like it held more importance than my need for him to set the record straight.

Outside, the steady hum of traffic faded. Or maybe that was just the rush of blood in my ears.

I grabbed my napkin, ran the fork through it, scrubbing it like years of grease might come away... like she might disappear with it.

Heat surged up my throat. My blood fizzed, tingling behind my eyes like it had gone carbonated.

Something shifted. The final twig snapped.

The warm metal of my crucifix rested against my chest—a silent reminder of who I was. Of what I was capable of.

I grabbed her hand and pinned it flat against the table.

Her eyes flew to mine, wide and breath caught, and in that instant, she knew. I was not a woman to be messed with.

Gripping the fork, I pressed its points into the soft skin between her tendons.

"Listen here, you little slut," I said, pushing deeper. "If you don't want this fork through your fucking hand, I suggest you back the fuck off. Right. Fucking. Now."

Heart racing. Skin flushed. My whole body firing on all four cylinders—like being pregnant had shut three of them down. Until now.

Oh boy, was I ready.

Fighting to free her hand, she squirmed. But I rose from my seat, leaning my weight into the table. She wasn't going anywhere.

This fork was more than cutlery. It was every apology I never got. Every time I bit my tongue when I should've bitten back. My stepfather. My foster mother. Romeo's exes. Old clients who thought they owned me.

Junior stirred softly in his pram, a faint whimper slicing through the tension—reminding me why I was fighting.

"Please let me go," she begged, writhing now, her fingertips ghost-white from the pressure.

But she wasn't about to tell me what to do.

I'd release her when I was ready.

Another minute passed. The ceiling fan groaned overhead, its slow rotation sweeping a lazy draft over us. My adrenaline cooled. The burn in my arms turned to an ache.

"I'm going to let you go now," I said calmly. "And you're going to walk away. Got it?"

She nodded, eyes glassy and nose running.

I let go with my hand first, keeping the fork in place.

Then, with one tug, I yanked down the open neck of her dress and retrieved the fifty from between her tits.

"And I'll take that, you pathetic slut."

Car horns blared beyond the single-pane glass. A traffic cop's whistle blew. The world snapped back into motion as I withdrew the fork, leaving behind three deep marks in her skin.

Without a word, she spun on her heel and disappeared through the swing doors, clutching her hand as if it held the last crumb of her dignity.

I watched until the doors stilled.

Satisfied, I slid back into my seat—only to find Romeo, knife and fork in hand, grinning like a cat who'd watched the mouse get mauled.

"Told you," he said to his men, tucking his napkin into his collar.

I mirrored his smile, then narrowed it. "Told them what?"

Romeo focused on his plate. Bacon.

Eggs. Pancakes. Syrup. All of it.

He poured a thick stream of syrup over the stack like this was just any other morning.

"I told 'em you were ready."

I watched a lion as he devoured his prey. One piled forkful after another. I half-expected him to eat the napkin, too.

"Eat," he said, jabbing his knife toward me.

I ignored him. Sank back into the fake leather seat, arms crossed, skin peeling from the upholstery as anticipation leaked through every pore.

My brow arched. "You fucking planned that, didn't you?"

He cut into the pancakes, chewed slowly, then nodded.

The other brow joined in. "So you brought me here knowing she'd come on to you?"

Another smug bite. Another chew. Another nod.

"Not gonna lie," he said, swallowing. "Didn't think you'd stab a fork in her fuckin' hand... but I figured you needed firin' up. Get your head on right."

I shot a look at Tommy, half-hiding behind the menu like it might shield him. Then at Snake, who practically folded like a sheet of paper.

"All three of you in on it, then?" I sneered. "Can't say I'm surprised."

I tapped my fingers on the table's edge. "Alright. Since you're all so smart, I want to know the plan. Now."

The bell dinged from the kitchen. Another plate ready. Another normal day for everyone else.

Romeo's fork clattered against his plate. He looked at Tommy, then wiped his mouth with the napkin. Rolled it tight. Tossed it across the table.

"Aight, fine. Our package is waitin' for us."

Package?

I assumed he meant Jamie and Harry—unless he'd ordered another toy Glock for his two-day-old son.

"Okay," I said through clenched teeth. "So we eat... and then what? Dive straight into it?"

Romeo smirked. Elbows resting on the table, he leaned closer. The liquor on his breath had softened to something sweeter—syrup and coffee mingling on his lips.

I met him in the middle. Lips almost touching. Breath to breath.

"We eat, say a prayer... and then dive straight into it."

The pram jolted. Junior let out a cry.

Not a good time.

"What are we doing with the baby?" I asked, rocking the pram. The motion soothed neither of us.

Romeo took another bite, chased it with coffee, then thudded the mug down hard.

"The boy stays with us. Ain't never too early to have your first time."

The sentence landed like fat on bacon—thick, greasy, hard to swallow.

What I wouldn't give for a shred of normality. But no, of course not. While other new mothers rested, healed. I was preparing to commit a murder. With my newborn son as a witness.

By now, his faint cries had soaked through my T-shirt. Milk leaked down my front in a slow, warm trickle.

"He needs feeding," I muttered, eyes glued to the pram.

The push and pull grew more urgent. The squeak of the wheels cut across the silence.

No nanny. No family. No friend we could trust.

Just us.

And we had to be enough.

9:15 AM

The tyres hummed against the tarmac beneath us as I sat in the back seat of the SUV. Each pothole sent a sting between my thighs and a sharp pull in my breasts. A constant reminder I was a new mother. My fingers curled tighter around the edge of the seat, steadying the movement. Steadying myself.

Up front, a cell phone buzzed, unanswered. With every burst, a set of keys rattled in the cup holder, each clink marking a bullet point in the silence between us.

Junior, sleeping after his feed, suckled gently in his dreams. His tiny fists curled beneath his chin. The picture of peace.

I was anything but.

"We still ignoring calls, Boss?" Snake asked from the front, shoving the keys into his pocket to rid the cabin of the metallic rattle.

Romeo gave a curt nod, eyes locked on the view outside. His fingers tapped against his thigh, the crease between his brows deepening as he clocked a pair of crows pecking at a roadside carcass.

I let my trembling fingers drift over the diamonds on my necklace, eyes fixed on his profile. That perfectly angular nose. The shadow of stubble along his jaw. The way his tongue darted out to wet his lips, leaving them plump and glossy.

"She was good in bed, then, was she?" I murmured.

The words tasted like metal. I hadn't meant to say them aloud. But part of me needed to know he wasn't thinking about her now.

Romeo's head turned slowly. There was a look in his eyes I hadn't seen in a while—one that stirred something in my gut.

I held my breath.

"Who?" he said with a snarl.

My shoulders dropped instantly. I rolled my eyes. "Don't be annoying, Romeo. The fucking waitress you were drooling over back there. Silly Sally."

A smirk curled his lips, warming the chill in his features, but his eyes stayed devilish.

"Hell yeah," he said with a slow nod. "She sure as shit knew what she was doin'. I'll give you her cell—get you some tips."

Air whooshed from my lungs. My jaw dropped. The flesh of my chin may as well have been tearing from the bone along the freeway—he'd bowled me over that hard.

Stunned. Shocked. Beside myself. There wasn't a word big enough to hold what I felt.

My gaze flicked to the door handle. It shimmered like an invitation. Take the plunge. Disappear for good.

What use was I, anyway? It seemed obvious now; Romeo had rekindled an old flame when he shoved that fifty between her breasts. I knew he didn't find me attractive anymore. It was clear he'd been lying to me.

The baby exhaled—a soft, content sigh. I looked at him longingly. So innocently beautiful.

Clarity snapped back.

What was I thinking? He needed me. He needed his mum.

Romeo, relentless in his pursuit to ruin me, reached for his phone. Tapping contacts, he began to scroll.

The son of a bitch was looking for her number. Like stabbing me wasn't enough—he had to twist the blade, too.

Suddenly dizzy, a high-pitched ringing bloomed in my ears, drowning out the hum of the engine, the drone of the tyres, the last sounds keeping me grounded.

"Do you want her cell number or her Snap?" he asked, like it was a choice between ketchup or mayo at McDonald's.

The car shrank around me. The walls pulled tighter, like the glass was pressing into my cheeks from both sides.

My skin prickled. My airway closed. Bile rose—hot and sour—clawing its way up the back of my throat while his thumb kept on swiping.

The next thing I knew, my knuckle popped when I socked him square in the chin. The sound cracked through the car. Pain shot through my whole palm.

He barely flinched, but his face flushed red. Thumb paused mid-scroll. He tilted his head and looked at me.

We glared at each other. Panting. Seething.

"You're a fucking pig, Romeo," I spat through the sting behind my eyes.

He huffed—indifferent. Rubbed the spot on his jaw. Not to soothe pain, but to calculate his next move.

The sun burst through the trees, slicing through the glass in blinding flashes. Its harsh light caught the blue of his irises, cold as ice. And just as unforgiving.

"You can have that one for free," he said darkly. "Next one won't get a second chance."

Whether I lost my mind or chose not to listen, I swung again.

This time, he caught my whole fist in his palm.

"Chill the fuck out. Sometimes you just gotta face facts—she knew how to play with my nuts."

He shoved my hand back into my lap while I fought against him. A quiet tussle.

One that he won too easily.

He sniffed, flicking the end of his nose like the gangster he was—resetting the moment like flicking off a waste disposal after the finger got caught.

Was he for real?

"Maybe you should be with her then instead, huh? Let her deal with your relentless sex addiction."

The car began to slow. The tyres softened as we exited the freeway.

Romeo didn't flinch. Eyes locked on the view outside. Watching each tree pass like a road sign pointing towards our destination.

Tommy took a sharp right. We all swayed left.

Romeo's fingers twitched—just once—as he rested his hand on the grip of his holstered gun.

"Wait..." I said, squinting through the tinted glass. The fight drained from me with the sudden change in scenery. "Where are we going? I thought we were doing this at home?"

He didn't even dignify me with a look.

"You'll see when we get there."

9:48 AM

The faint squeak of the brakes as the SUV rolled to a stop marked our arrival.

Anticipation bloomed the second the side door slid open, and instantly, my nostrils flared with familiarity.

Cannabis hung thick in the air. Dogs barked in the distance. A run-down trailer stood in a sorry state, roof tiles missing, wooden cladding splintered and half-swallowed by overgrown trees and weeds.

We'd arrived at the trap house.

The same place we'd shared fried chicken all those months ago—before I really knew who he was.

Romeo gripped the door as he went to leave, but turned back to face me.

"Bring the boy," he said, studying every inch of my reaction.

Already scraping my hair into a ponytail, I peered down at my sleeping son.

"No way. He'll stay here with Snake."

Romeo's jaw ticked. He sat back down and slammed the SUV door shut, the sound ricocheting through the cabin—leaving Tommy and Snake on the other side with puzzled looks.

"Do as you're fuckin' told, woman."

The second his gaze dropped to the baby, I reacted instinctively.

"No!" I unbuckled Junior from the car seat and pulled him tight to my chest. His breath, warm against my collarbone, grounded me—gave me strength, even as my throat began to close from panic.

King ran a hand through his hair. No heavenly scent from his scalp. Just the musk of a cold-hearted killer.

Heavy breaths filled the space between us.

Beyond the yard, the dogs' barks grew rabid, one snapping its chain hard enough to rattle the fence line.

Doing what any mother would, I clung to my son. His safety mattered more than any revenge.

"Give me the boy. Now," King said, reaching for the baby.

His eyes, like glass, had lost their soul.

I jerked away, clutching Junior tighter.

"Fuck you!" I hissed, scooting farther down the seat.

King's hand sliced through the air before I could react.

The heat of it clamped around my throat, shoving me back into the leather.

"Now," he murmured against my parted lips.

Tears sprang instantly.

My first thought: he'd never strangle me. He'd never hurt me again.

Until I began to choke.

He squeezed tighter. His fingers burned against my skin, hot and trembling with rage.

My grip on the baby faltered.

Heat flooded my face.

My eyes pulsed behind the pressure.

Black dots bloomed in the corners of my vision.

And just when I thought he might actually go through with it—He let go.

9:55 AM

Drawing breath through what felt like a crushed windpipe was harder than they made it look in the movies.

The stale air between us seemed to solidify—catching at the back of my throat like cement dust.

King held our son against his chest with one arm. Only the dark curls atop Junior's head peeked out from behind the thick shield of his father's muscular forearm.

With his free hand, he shoved something toward me.

"Here," he said, thrusting my gun into my lap.

Heavier than I remembered.

Colder than I expected.

I held it in both hands. The polymer grip moulded to my palm like it had been waiting for me.

The SUV door slid open on the opposite side. Smooth. Well-oiled. It glided along the rail, slicing through the silence—a clean, mechanical warning.

Late-morning light spilled into the cabin, forcing my eyes into a squint. Dust drifted through the beam, ash suspended mid-air—proof the ending was already in motion.

Tommy stood in the doorway. Still. Waiting.

His blank expression didn't waver.

His stance shifted as if the timer had just hit zero.

"We're ready for you, Boss."

King gave a curt nod.

Then, over his shoulder, without so much as a glance, he snapped, "You better not embarrass yourself, Chloe. You have to do this right."

Of all the times Romeo had hurt me. All the times he'd disrespected me. Tried to control me. This time? The whole damn branch snapped—

and Jasmin clicked into place.

Eyes alight. I lifted my gaze and stared him down.

A sinister smirk tugged at my lips. No longer scared of him. Not anymore.

With a confidence I didn't know I possessed, I racked the slide of my Glock.

Metal on metal.

The sound bit through the air like a promise.

Every hair on the back of my neck stood tall.

Adrenaline sharpened my vision. I could see the grain of the leather seat. The blood beneath my skin.

"You'll be the one fucking embarrassing yourself, you prick." I leaned forward, voice flat. "I'll show you. And more."

9:58 AM

The quiet inside the run-down trailer rang out—hollow and grim, like a death bell marking the hour.

Old drapes clung to the boarded-up windows, letting only slivers of light bleed through. A leaky faucet dripped somewhere beyond the living room. Each slow drop ticked closer to the reason we were here.

Nothing about the place had changed. Same crumbling plaster. Same itch of old drywall dust clinging to damp skin. One stained couch. Bare floorboards that creaked under the faintest shift in weight.

But while the room stayed the same. I hadn't.

Gun in hand, I stood by the door, watching the man who'd just assaulted me cradle our son like he had the right.

Fingers curling tighter around the grip, I held firm. For once, confident we were doing the right thing.

Unsure of the next move, I waited in silence as Tommy and Snake dragged the couch to the back wall.

King, cradling our son, stalked the length of the room, perfectly in sync with the baby's tiny bobbing head as if they were one. I tracked every step. The way he controlled the tempo of his walk, like every beat belonged to him.

"Time?" he asked, not looking up.

Snake was already checking his watch. "Time, Boss."

King nodded.

Those code words between them always rubbed me the wrong way—this time was no exception.

Yet Jamie and Harry were nowhere to be seen.

I could've asked. Could've tossed a light enquiry into the room. But I wasn't speaking to King. Not after what he'd done in the car.

As I stepped deeper into the room, my sneakers added their own voice to the groaning wood.

The stench of damp plaster and dry rot dragged me back to a darker past—our secret meeting, the fresh ink around his eye, the way he fucked me... how he nearly attacked me for touching his chest.

Control. Fear. Violence.

Had he really changed at all?

He stopped in the centre of the room, just a few feet away from me.

"Who did the fuckin' clean-up last time?" he barked, just as the couch shift revealed an old bloodstain soaked deep into the boards.

Tommy looked at Snake, who was already checking his phone.

"Don't worry, Boss," Tommy said with confidence, adjusting his hold on the gun. "We'll get straight on it."

It didn't get more real than this. When he said he was off to 'handle business', this was what he meant.

The proof was right there on the fucking floor.

But whose blood was it?

Did they even deserve it?

God, there were so many things I wanted to say. So many questions I needed to ask.

Biting my tongue was the only outlet I had.

"Ready, Boss?" Tommy asked, slicing through my thoughts.

"Come here," King said, arms open to our group.

Needless to say, I didn't stand next to him in the huddle that followed.

Hot breath from four highly charged bodies mingled in the still air as we formed a tight circle in the middle of the room.

Tommy. Snake. King. Me.

Almost nose to nose.

Ready for the ritual to begin.

The walls pressed in.

A spider darted past our feet across the chalky boards—scrambling for cover.

I didn't know it then, but this room had witnessed far more than I could've imagined. The echoes of torture still lingered in the walls' decay.

Snake's watch ticked too loudly.

Barking dogs no longer howled.

The faucet had fallen silent.

Sweat pooled at the nape of my neck and ran cold down my spine.

Snake, eyes closed, exhaled through his nose—shallow but steady. A veteran in this field.

Tommy, cool and composed, raised his fist to the centre of the circle. Weathered knuckles on a hand, always ready for action.

"We got this," he said.

He didn't need to say more.

One by one, we knocked our knuckles to his, silently unified. Marking the path, we were about to walk together.

King's wedding ring caught a streak of light, glistening like it still held meaning.

It didn't. Not after what he'd done to me.

The silence thickened.

Time hung in the air like smog.

King rolled his neck—slow. His joints cracked.

Then, without a word, he raised his crucifix to his lips and kissed it. His eyes drifted closed.

"God… I ain't holy. Never claimed to be.

But you gave me a *famiglia—una regina, un figlio—*

and I'll protect 'em with blood if I gotta.

Watch my hands today.

Let my aim be clean.

Perdonami dopo.

I do what needs to be done.
Lead me and my wife into battle.
Keep my boy safe.
And if we don't come back… *portaci in paradiso.*
Amen."
We followed.
"Amen."

10:02 AM

A door at the back of the trailer's living room opened. Stained wood. Loose hinges. It groaned in protest as another wave of stale air filtered through.

Tommy and Snake moved together, dragging Jamie and Harry in before forcing them to their knees at our feet.

Hands bound behind their backs. Duct tape stretched across their mouths. Their eyes told the story their voices couldn't.

King held our son close to his chest. Gun raised, he aimed it square at Harry's forehead.

"Tommy, remove the gag."

The sharp rip of tape tore through the silence.

Skin. Hair. A chill ran the length of my spine.

Harry gasped—gulping air in ragged silence.

"Tell me who you work for," King demanded.

Harry closed his eyes, already surrendering to fate.

The barrel pushed deeper into his temple.

"I know you work for English. Let me fuckin' hear it!"

Even with King's voice raised, Junior didn't stir—lulled by the steady rhythm of his father's chest. His eyelids stayed shut. One small hand curled into a fist.

Before I could think it through, my hand shot forward. I tore the tape from Jamie's mouth, yanking strands of dark hair with it.

"What information have you shared about my family?" I snapped.

Same intensity as my husband.

Jamie's bottom lip trembled. A single tear slid down her cheek.

"Nothing, Chloe. We haven't said anything."

King's jaw ticked, but he said nothing. Just watched.

It was my turn now.

"Bullshit." I snarled. "You betrayed our trust. Came into our home with a motive. Now I want the truth. All of it."

10:04 AM

Tensions rose.

Barking dogs stirred the thick air around us.

A metal wind chime clinked in someone's yard—falling silent again the moment the wind paused to listen.

Heart pounding, I kept the gun pressed to Jamie's head.

King stayed locked on Harry.

"Our client just wanted a meeting, Chloe. That's it. I swear," she whimpered, sniffling.

King's grip shifted. His finger tightened around the trigger, pressing the barrel deeper into Harry's temple.

Muted light slanted through the boarded-up window, casting jagged shadows across the floor—uneven bars that made the room feel more like a cell than it once being someone's home.

"How much do you love him, Jamie?" King's voice was low—almost unrecognisable.

The room stilled.

A faint creak of steel echoed louder than it should've as his finger settled on the trigger.

"He's my everything," she sobbed.

Harry muttered something under his breath. A prayer, maybe. Or quiet surrender.

"Yeah? Enough to tell me the truth?"

She hesitated.

King fired.

The ringing in my ears pulsed in time with my heartbeat.

I'd read somewhere that time was a healer, but watching Harry's skull split open, I wondered how that could ever be true.

His body slumped. The dull crack of bone against wood sent a tremor through the floor beneath our feet. Blood sprayed the boards in a fine mist. One droplet landed on the toe of my shoe like a signature.

Junior twitched in his sleep. King cradled him closer.

A dangerous duo. So clear now—I'd birthed the devil's son.

"No!" Jamie screamed, the sob tearing straight from her gut. "No, please! You've got it wrong! Oh God, you've got it wrong!"

Her shoulders bucked with every breath. Wrists strained uselessly behind her back. The sharp scent of urine filled the air. But I'd seen this in movies before—the girl begging for her life long after the script was already written.

Fact was, she'd gone behind my husband's back. Infiltrated our home. Tried to fuck with our family.

We had a son to protect. A reputation to fight for.

"Last words?" I asked, pressing the barrel harder into her skin. "You got anything left to say to me?"

The gun in my hand grew heavier—like it, too, was waiting for this moment to land.

Jamie's bottom lip quivered.

"I promise you, Chloe... I'm not lying. But I know you've already made your mind up. I know you won't let me go."

King huffed beside me, bouncing Junior gently.

"I ain't never met a mole who ain't a lyin' piece of shit." His gaze stayed steady. His order was final. "Finish her, Chloe."

10:05 AM

I'd read somewhere that blood was the hardest stain to remove. Was it white wine on a bloodstain? Or had I made that up?

My ears rang, loud and deafening. With each slow blink, sound sharpened, bleeding back into the room.

That's when I saw her.

Jamie's lifeless body lay at my feet.

Dark, tangled hair veiled a once-pretty face.

Her eyes, dull and open—dead of sparkle.

I'd never seen a body this close before. Like really seen it.

Blood poured from her mouth, pooling at the suede of my shoe—sinking into the fibres like ink into paper.

Two dead bodies. Side by side.

I didn't move. Not right away.

Just stared at the stain spreading beneath me, like maybe it could be undone.

"Chloe." King shook my shoulder. His voice clipped. "Hurry up and take your clothes off. Put 'em in this bag. We're leavin'."

10:10 AM

Sitting in the back of the SUV, wearing a dress I'd never seen before. The trailer behind us smouldered—soon to be swallowed by flames.

Watching my husband buckle our son into the car seat felt like an out-of-body experience. Like we'd just climbed back in the car after a stroll in the park.

Different clothes. Different vibe.

Same ruthless man.

He'd planned this right down to the last detail.

My throat was dry. A glass of water and something for the headache pounding behind my eyes would've been just what the doctor ordered. But I wasn't about to share my thoughts with him.

Tommy climbed into the driver's seat. Snake followed, slamming the passenger door shut in sync.

A curl of paraffin smoke slipped into the cabin as the engine turned over.

"Poured accelerant all over the place," Snake said, casual as ever. "We'll need a new spot now, Boss."

King slid into his seat beside me, eyes fixed on the rear window, watching the place that held so many ghosts go up in flames.

"It was time," he murmured. "Clean-up crew need replacin'."

10:21 AM

King tapped his crucifix, casting me the occasional glance to check whether I was still pissed.

I was.

The weight of our decision to handle the situation was one thing. But the way he chose to handle me? That was something else entirely.

The A/C hummed low, blowing cool through the vents, tousling loose strands of my dishevelled ponytail as I watched my son sleep—so peaceful, so oblivious.

A faint curl of paraffin clung to the fabric of our clothes like guilt.

King shifted in his seat. "Listen, Chloe..."

There was that glint again, his wedding ring catching the light and scattering faint rainbow refractions across the ceiling.

He unclasped his crucifix and let it fall heavy into his lap, the metal clattering softly.

"... I took it too far. But I could see you slippin'." His jaw flexed. "I needed you angry."

Cautious and closed off, I folded my arms across my chest and turned slightly away from him. The sharp edge of the seatbelt pressed harder into my collarbone—like the car itself was on his side.

"Nothing excuses what you did to me, Romeo."

The young woman staring back at me in the reflection of the window was all Chloe. Jasmin was nowhere to be seen.

He sighed, dragging his fingers across his temples like he was losing a war with himself.

"I realise now I could've handled it different. But the way you forked that slut in the diner... I had to keep that goin'."

I caught Snake's eyes in the rear-view mirror. This time, I could tell he was on my team.

"Strangling your wife is not the answer," I muttered, rolling my eyes at his pathetic attempt to justify it.

My skin, still damp. Clothes clinging. The comedown from adrenaline felt like the spiral after a hard drug.

He leaned forward, bracing an arm on the driver's headrest.

A red flare of brake lights bled across the upholstery as Tommy slowed the SUV.

"Take a left here," he said. "We're goin' back to the Cottage."

10:47 AM

"Aight, listen up real good," Romeo said, kneeling in front of me as I sat frozen on the new leather couch in Nonna's living room.

He'd already tried to prise my legs open to settle between my thighs, but I wasn't having it.

"You can't fix this, Romeo. Not only did you put your hand around my neck. You fucking squeezed, too!"

His hands slipped off my thighs. He laughed, like I'd just told a joke.

But it didn't last long. The humour drained when he saw I wasn't smiling.

"Queen, what the fuck you talkin' about? I barely touched you."

The bassinet jolted. A not-so-subtle reminder that motherhood was my priority now. That every decision was about protecting my son's future.

Romeo rose. The couch leather sighed as he pulled me to my feet. His hands, firm and steady, rested beneath my ribs as he guided me to the mirror by the fireplace.

Standing behind me, he cupped my head with both hands. His fingers threaded into my roots, lighting up my scalp—for all the wrong reasons—as he tilted it left, then right.

The longer I looked, the more I realised... he wasn't wrong.

Confused, my fingertips drifted to my throat, tracing skin that felt bruised, yet not a single mark stared back at me.

His breath fanned warm across my neck, kissing the places I focused on the most.

"You think I'd strangle you for real?" he whispered in my ear. "I'd never hurt you like that."

Like clouds parting after a storm, a sliver of light crept in.

I turned to face him. Ocean blue to blue-ish grey.

"At the time," I croaked as reality dawned, "It felt like you were doing it for real. I could've sworn—"

He kissed me abruptly.

Slow. Reverent. Then again. And again.

Each soft press of his lips drew heat to my core. The kind of warmth that made me want to believe him.

"Come here, baby." He gathered me in. "Imma show you how much I love you."

He reached beneath me, scooping me up. My legs wrapped around his waist. I yelped, caught off guard, clutching his shoulders as he held me close to his chest.

Our breath mingled, warm and smoky, from the trace of tobacco, as our lips met again.

His hands kneaded my rear. My fingers tangled in his hair.

Then he moved.

One step toward the stairs—hollow beneath his feet, yet sure with promise.

Then another.

And that's when I realised what he was doing.

I breathed into his mouth, the warmth of his erection nestled between my thighs.

"Wait." I panted. "We need to bring the baby with us."

He broke away from my lips, glancing at the crib—torn between his desire as a husband and his duties as a father.

"He's sleepin'," he murmured, hands trailing slowly along my spine. "Tommy's right out front. He's safe."

His answer came with another kiss, soft but deep, before he placed his foot on the bottom step of the oak staircase.

Desire bloomed. The petals reopened, and I let him consume me—like a bee drawn to fresh nectar.

10:57 AM

By the time I registered the ache in my hips and the flutter in my chest, I was already beneath him. Laid atop our freshly laundered sheets, my husband hovered above me—exactly where I wanted to be. The blue of his irises shimmered in the light, bleeding through the parted drapes. He blinked, slow. Just looking at me.

"What?" I asked with a soft giggle, nudging him playfully.

He didn't budge, just brushed a strand of hair from my face with the kind of gentleness that came from a man who knew exactly what he had. He smiled then. That dazzling grin, perfect white teeth.

"I was just thinkin' how amazin' you are. We're a team. Handle our shit together. I was real proud of how you helped finish those bitches."

I narrowed my eyes, amusement tugging at the corners of my mouth. "This is because you like to fuck after you've killed someone, isn't it?"

He smirked, like I was about to be proven wrong.

"I love you, Chloe Giannetti. That's all this is."

Did I believe him? Maybe. The throb between my legs certainly did. But I couldn't have been more apprehensive if I tried.

Our connection crackled, amplified by the rustle of leaves against the eaves. The outside world was stirring with our heat.

Romeo peeled off his shirt and tossed it to the floor. A curl of lighter fluid chased the leathery bite of his cologne. Beneath it—cigarettes, sweat, and something unmistakably male. He smelt like a soldier mid-gunfire. Salty skin, oil and steel. My mouth watered.

Then came his shorts. No underwear, of course. God. That cock always did something to me—awoke a need so primal it bloomed low and hot between my thighs. I swallowed hard, throat dry, because I knew what was next.

He made the move for me. Fingers firm, he took the hem of my dress, lighting my skin like a fuse as he raised it to my midriff. Instinctively, I clamped my hands over my stomach, halting him mid-motion before he could reveal any more.

Desire between us dropped like autumn.

"What's wrong?" he asked, brows knitting as his gaze searched my face.

"I can't let you see me like this," I whispered, starting to sit up—to leave before I had to witness the disappointment.

But his body held me still. Gently. His weight grounding me. Then he kissed me with so much love I could taste it.

Tangled together, he let go of the fabric, trailing his fingers along my inner thigh. A slow, deliberate burn as his thumb brushed the edge of my hipbone.

I wanted him. Needed him. The tension in my lower back eased as my legs parted. He tugged on the band of my panties, peeling them down. The soft rustle of the period pad made me flinch.

"Maybe I should'a grabbed a towel," he said, arching a brow, that boyish grin tugging at his lips as he held the underwear—pad and all—like a trophy.

A laugh escaped me. He held them up, stealing another peek.

"Don't look at it!" I giggled, reaching to snatch them back.

He ignored me, tossed them behind him, then folded his body over mine. A hand braced either side of my head.

"You know that shit don't bother me," he murmured, kissing my forehead. "You're so fuckin' beautiful."

My toes curled. Every inch of me pulled tight with anticipation.

He nudged the head of his cock against my swollen flesh. Anticipation bloomed—then snapped shut like a flower in frost. I winced, sucking in a sharp breath through my teeth.

"Ouch… that's sore." I braced my hands against his chest as my thighs trembled under his hips. The heat of his skin burned beneath my palms like a roaring fire.

He stopped instantly.

We stayed like that. Breathing. Steadying. Calming one another in the quiet.

My hands softened, smoothing up to cradle his biceps.

"It's okay," I breathed. "Try again."

This time, he barely moved. The tip of his erection nudged gently between my folds. An inch first. Then another. Until he was fully inside me.

"You okay?" he asked, voice catching—thick with emotion.

He wasn't claiming me. He was honouring me, one slow thrust at a time.

I nodded, drawing his lips to mine as he rocked gently into me.

"Oh, Romeo… fuck," I breathed, hips swaying beneath him. His breath pulsed hot against my cheek.

"You mean more to me than anythin', Chloe." His forehead pressed to mine. "I'll keep sayin' it 'til you believe me. *Ti amo*."

Though the rest of me was covered, only my lower half exposed, I felt utterly seen. His words weren't for show. He meant every one.

A breeze whispered through the open window, branches rustling like nature itself was chasing its own climax.

His rhythm shifted. I felt every movement. The tightness in his thighs. The warmth in his skin. The slow build between us. His cock swelled—flushed with need.

"Can I come inside you?" he mumbled, still holding the pace. Patient. Steady. Needing my yes.

I nodded, trembling, my whole body alight. I pulled him back to my mouth.

"Yes, baby… come for me."

11:32 AM

"Do you need anythin'?" Romeo asked, naked, lying flat on his back with one arm slung over his stomach. A soft sheen of sweat glistened across his abs, catching the light pouring through the open drapes. The mess we'd made on the sheets was a clean-up for another day.

"Yes," I said, pressing a kiss to his chest. "Go get my son."

"On it." He sprang from the bed like he'd been plugged into the mains—energy suddenly restored.

A bird chirped as it flitted past the open window. The sheer curtains shifted in the warm breeze.

This was heaven. Reconnected to my husband in a way, I felt deep in my bones. And while he still hadn't seen my naked body in daylight, he couldn't have made me feel more beautiful if he'd tried.

The memories tied to that trap house—the fear he once evoked, the violence he wielded like a weapon. Mood swings. Chaos. The man before me now was different. We were different.

I understood why he'd pushed my buttons earlier. Why he'd dragged me to the emotional edge in order to deal with Jamie and Harry. He knew me too well.

Our souls tangled, so tight, so fused, we were becoming one.

"Did you hear me?" Romeo asked, brow arched.

I shook my head, clearing the fog from my thoughts.

"Huh?"

"I said—have we got any wipes to clean all this blood off my dick?" He gestured to the crime-scene matting his pubes. It needed more than a wet wipe, that was for sure.

"Grab Junior's bag when you go down." I smirked. "Plenty in there."

I watched him tug on his shorts, the muscles in his back flexing with every movement. So much strength coiled beneath the skin of a man already powerful beyond measure.

He was perfect.

He was mine.

"God damn it!" he snapped.

The flail of his arms sliced the romance in half.

A breeze sucked the curtain outward through the sash window—like the room itself flinched from the tension.

I shot upright. "What? What's wrong?"

Hunched over, facing away from me, he looked like a man who'd stubbed his toe. Then he twirled, one-legged like an out-of-practice ballet dancer, half annoyed, half smiling.

"Stood on your fuckin' pad. Forgot I threw it on the floor."

He flicked his leg, thigh muscles flexing as he battled what had clearly become the world's stickiest sanitary towel.

With a crooked finger to my lips, I stifled a giggle—watching the most handsome man alive make a mountain out of a molehill.

"Don't just sit there, woman. Help me!"

For a moment, everything else disappeared. No moles. No murder. Just a man, a sock, and a blood-soaked pad ruining his post-nut glory.

I scrambled from the bed, a little embarrassed, and peeled it off like duct tape from velvet.

"You best throw that sock out," I teased.

He laughed, genuine now, the tension of the day melting into the carpet beneath us.

"Good job I'm a patient man," he said, dusting himself off, resetting the mood.

I gave him a questioning look.

His chuckle rolled through the room, eyes creasing as the light returned to them. Then he dropped to his knees among the sheets, fists buried into the mattress, grinning up at me.

"Come on, get your sexy ass up. We're orderin' takeout."

CHAPTER 15

Romeo's playlist filled the cabin if the Rolls' as we drove home from Nonna's cottage the next morning. Hit after hit of throwbacks hummed through the speakers, lifting our lethargic moods just enough to keep us moving.

The sun shone brightly through a light dusting of clouds, softening the day's glare as it streamed through the windshield, as if the spotlight was still very much on us.

The air around us hung heavy with everything left unsaid. Our feelings. The clean-up. The repercussions. Romeo could deny it all he wanted, but the weight of what happened in that rundown trailer clung to us both, as close as the paraffin used to burn the evidence.

I turned the music down, letting the low rumble of the road fill the quiet.

"Any update from Tommy on the fire?" I asked, glancing at his side profile.

It wasn't a random question. Between Tommy and Snake, they'd dumped so much accelerant that the trailer next door went up too. Now it was all over the internet, morning news, social feeds, the lot.

Romeo shook his head without looking at me. "What fire?"

I frowned, replaying my question to make sure I hadn't jumbled my words—then realised.

"Oh, of course. Never mind." I smiled, playing along. "Any update from Benny English? He must've heard about Jamie and Harry by now."

The uneven road juddered the cabin. Even the playlist skipped a beat.

Romeo turned the volume up, gliding his fingers along my thigh before settling back on the wheel.

"Benny English who?" he asked, raising his voice over the thudding bass.

I glanced over my shoulder at the baby. He seemed to love it, legs twitching and fingers unfurling. His tiny chest rose and fell with the serenity I longed for.

"How's the boy doin' back there?" Romeo asked, stealing a quick peek.

"Still sound asleep," I said with a hint of pride, adjusting the cotton blanket he'd almost kicked off.

Romeo nodded like he expected it. "You see how he was in my arms when I pulled that trigger? I felt like he was part of me."

I smirked, lashes fluttering cutely. "Pulled what trigger?"

Two can play that game, buddy.

The low growl of the engine pulsed through the seats like a second heartbeat as Romeo put his foot down, accelerating at the first glimpse of open road ahead.

A nostalgic buzz stirred in my chest as the next track played.

"This song is us in a nutshell." I nudged the volume up.

Romeo screwed up his nose, turning it straight back down. "This is a chick song. You been addin' shit to my playlist again? Last time I had a client in the car, a fuckin' Britney Spears track came on."

My fingers twitched at my necklace. My mouth dropped open, then snapped shut.

'Client,' he says?

Did it say something about me that my first thought was whether this client was male or female?

Quick thinking kicked in. "Well, that certainly wasn't me," I said, like he'd accused me of leaving skid marks in the toilet bowl.

He chuckled. Light-hearted Romeo was my favourite.

"So you're tellin' me, Tommy added Britney Spears to my playlist?" He shook his head. "I'm a bettin' man, and my money's on my pain-in-the-ass wife."

Hmm. I hadn't heard a word past client. What I wanted now was a slick way to ask if the client was a woman. Something seamless. Something that told him I didn't give a shit who she was. I was confident enough to rise above it all.

"So... did your female client enjoy the music, then?"

I cringed the second it left my mouth, fingers knotting in my lap. Not smooth. Not even fucking close.

Romeo clocked it instantly, rolling his eyes.

"He. And no—Zhao Yichen didn't enjoy it." He leaned back, smirking. "Richest Chinese man I ever met. Bigger prick than me."

Romeo doing business with a Chinese billionaire shouldn't have surprised me, but it did. England. China. Maldives. He was casting his net far and wide.

Was that the same net he used to fish for women?

"So not a woman, then?" My fingers tapped the armrest. "Just to clarify."

He laughed like he'd seen me coming a mile off. "If he was a hoe, he was a fuckin' ugly one."

Interesting. The knots in my fingers began to unwind.

"Oh, okay. So not pretty like that waitress in the diner yesterday, then?" I stared down at my chipped nails. I was long overdue a manicure and better interrogation tactics.

The sun caught the edge of the windshield, flaring just enough to sting my eyes. Or maybe that was jealousy biting the inside of my skull.

He pulled down his sun visor, shading his frown.

"Forget her, Chloe. I just used her to fire you up. Nothin' more."

I followed, visor down, flipping the little shield over the vanity mirror to check the damage. The mirror caught a woman who looked put-together, even as she unravelled from the inside out.

"So she didn't play with your balls better than me, then?"

He shot me a brief look before focusing back on the road. "Ain't nobody suck my nuts like you do, Chloe. I mean that."

In the interest of keeping the peace after an emotionally fuelled couple of days, I slouched back into my seat. The expensive leather sighed beneath me, warm and form-fitting like a second skin.

That's when I gave myself a reality check.

So what if she did do better ball play than me? If that was a reason to leave your wife, he was a massive saddo—and I'd happily tell the world he had a weird ball-sucking fetish just to make sure he was the one who looked the fool.

I smirked at the idea.

"Anyway." I turned the volume up again. "This is Issues by Julia Michaels. Just listen to the lyrics."

After the second chorus, he tutted and dialled it back down. The back-and-forth between us had become a chaotic rhythm all of its own.

"What you talkin' about, woman? I ain't got no issues."

I dropped my chin, narrowing my eyes beneath my lashes.

The traffic lights flicked to red, and we rolled to a slow stop at the intersection.

"You don't have issues? If you say so, King."

The word lingered on my tongue like lemon juice on a paper cut. The atmosphere shifted. Neither of us spoke as the track played on, its melody now just background noise to the silence between us. I'd called him King in my head plenty of times, but it had been a while since I'd said it out loud.

"Wow." He rubbed at the tattoo on his neck like it was a scar from another life. "Sounds weird… you callin' me King."

I ran my hand along my forearm, trying to settle the nerves that flared. "It felt weird saying it. So much has changed, hasn't it?"

He nodded.

That name stirred something in both of us. I could see it play out in the tightening of his features.

A horn beeped behind us. Tommy, letting him know the light had turned green.

Romeo seemed to shake himself off, fingers tensing on the wheel as the car surged forward—joining the bumper-to-bumper crawl back toward the mansion neither of us was quite ready to face.

"You okay there, champ?" I leaned forward, trying to catch his eye. "Since I said King, you've gone all quiet on me."

A faint smile twitched. "Nah, I'm good. I guess that name just reminds me of my mistakes."

I nodded, stomach tightening as the back catalogue of everything we'd survived unfolded again. So much had changed—but there were still secrets between us. His inability to trust me with the truth.

"Romeo?"

He hesitated. "Yes, sexy?"

Normally, that word would've made me smile. This time, it barely curved my lips. A lump of dread lodged deep in my throat.

"I know you keep dodging the question, but… do we need to worry about Benny English?" My heart fluttered. "I mean… we killed two of his people."

His jaw ticked. Fingers whitened around the wheel.

"No, we didn't."

Hmm.

I stared at the dashboard, tracing the grain in the leather. Yes, we had. And it wouldn't be long before that crazy English son of a bitch found out.

"I just want to know that me and my son are safe."

Sunlight slashed through the trees in strobe-like bursts, splintering across Romeo's face like a disco ball in hell.

The car jolted as traffic slowed and he braked hard. His palm slammed the armrest in synchrony.

"Don't you fuckin' dare say that to me ever again." He turned to me, eyes wild, voice cracking like a live wire. "Do you know how fuckin' offensive that is, Chloe? I'm a proud man, and you expect me to sit here while my own wife questions whether I can protect my family. My own flesh and blood?"

I raised a hand before he could froth at the mouth.

"You've got it wrong," I stammered, clutching my necklace. "That's not what I meant."

His glare could've cut glass. "Yes it fuckin' is. Fuck you."

I sat frozen—blinking through the shock. Hormones still raging. Breasts aching. I felt exposed. Raw in a way I hadn't expected. My throat dried out. The necklace dug into my fingertips. The traffic blurred behind a film of tears that I refused to let fall.

He drew a harsh breath beside me, silence settling like a heavy fog.

I opened my mouth. Closed it again.

A new song began to play.

Gradually, his temper eased. His tight grip on the armrest relaxed. He reached over, lifting my hand from my lap and pressing kisses to each fingertip.

"I'm sorry, baby. But the sooner you realise who I am, the easier your life will be."

I snatched my hand back, heat flaring in my chest.

"No. You need to realise I didn't ask for any of this. I was just a working girl. Next thing I know, I'm married to my pimp and we've got a baby. This has been a lot."

He arched a brow, hitting the gas as the road opened up, pressing us into the seats. "You do know you're the pimp now, right? I mean, those girls are yours. Don't forget that."

My eyes fixed on the windshield as the trees blurred past like fleeting figures in a crowd. He was right. But it wasn't just that. My smile spread at the realisation: I was becoming the female version of him.

How did I even get here? Little Chloe Adams... married to one of the most powerful men in the world. And somehow, he made it all look so easy. Sure, I had to step up now and then—but the weight he must carry behind the scenes? Just thinking about it made my head spin.

I fixed a crease in his T-shirt, right over his heart. "Is that why you're trying to involve me more? You know, with the mole issue?"

He offered a slight smile, his gaze still fixed ahead.

"Difference between me and you? All I need to sleep at night is a decent nut. No matter what kind of day I've had, my head hits the pillow, and I'm out for eight hours."

He turned then, voice softening, catching my hand on his chest and bringing it to his lips. "But you? I've seen how you get when you're worried."

I blinked slow. "What do you mean?"

"Don't think I don't hear you talkin' in your sleep."

Oh.

I twisted a strand of hair around my finger. "Wait. I talk in my sleep?"

He nodded, changing lanes. "Figured if I bring you in on it, maybe it'll help."

My palms sweated, still stuck on the last part. "I can't believe I talk in my sleep."

Music filled the silence.

Then he dropped the grenade.

"Heard my brother's name come outta your mouth a couple times."

No!

My stomach flipped. The baby sighed in his seat, as if even he was disappointed in me.

"Really?" I squeaked.

"Mmm." Romeo flicked on the indicator, casual as ever. "Anyway, that kind of talk gets my dick limp."

Before I could even process that, he veered off.

"Where are we going?"

He smirked, letting the wheel slide loosely through his hand as the car straightened off the corner. "You'll see. When we get there."

The Rolls slowed to a quiet stop outside of a place I hadn't expected to see so soon.

That business card Romeo had tossed at me?

The fancy jeweller's downtown?

Well. Here we were.

The private showroom didn't scream wealth. It whispered it: *Bellari Figlio.*

Yeah—this place was fancy. You couldn't even get in without a gatekeeper and a surname with weight.

Tommy's SUV pulled up behind just as a call lit up the console screen. Romeo let it ring a beat longer than usual, finger hovering—then tapped Accept.

Static crackled. Tommy's voice came through. "What's the play with Junior, Boss?"

Gunmetal clinks and the faint echo of weapons being loaded filled the background.

Romeo's lips thinned like he'd just remembered that spur of the moment didn't exist anymore. Not with a baby.

He turned, leather creaking beneath him, and cast a glance at the back seat where Junior slept soundly.

"Get Snake to drive the Rolls round the block," he said. "You shadow me and Chloe inside."

Tommy didn't argue. He rarely did. But we all knew this wasn't one of Romeo's best ideas.

Cool. Clinical. Polished like a precious metal. The place screamed rich with a side order of pretension.

I was practically thrown into a high-backed chair beside the main display of Bellari's offerings. The legs screeched against the immaculate floor as Tommy urged me to sit quickly.

A young woman shining the glass cases looked up, startled. Heat rushed to my cheeks. I played it off, glancing around as if I were the one appalled by the noise. She smiled at me, then continued her spritz and wipe.

Crossing my legs at the ankle, fingers toying with my necklace, I straightened my spine—trying to look like I belonged.

Tommy pressed his earpiece. Nodded. "Perimeter clear, Boss. I'll wait right out front."

Romeo hovered by the door and pointed at me. "She armed?"

While he could've simply asked, I guessed it was my lack of natural discreetness that made him choose not to.

What did he think I'd do? Get it out and fire a few shots?

Tempting.

Tommy nodded. "Purse, Boss. Three rounds."

I clutched it a little tighter. Fine Italian leather was never meant to carry something so heavy, but at this point, it was starting to feel like a part of me.

Romeo followed Tommy out of earshot, and I watched them go as I tried to settle into this new environment, giving myself a shot at the whole rich and famous lifestyle.

A mist of soft florals floated through the climate-controlled air, delicately perfumed with something almost edible—like sugared orchids or candied orange peel. Only the finest, most breathable oxygen for the filthy rich.

The music, more like lullabies, offered the wealthy listening ear a tranquillity where spending millions felt more like a massage than a transaction. Even the bass seemed wrapped in satin.

Romeo strode back over, his stride commanding the floor without even trying. He dropped into the two-seater beside me—legs wide, arms slung over the back of the plush couch—completely at ease in a world that was never meant for him.

Beyond the single glass door, Tommy stood guard. Gun visible at his hip. A growing crowd pressed closer to the velvet ropes. I eyed them closely. Any minute now, the paparazzi would arrive.

Romeo felt my hesitation. His knee bumped mine, a small electric nudge.

When I finally pulled my focus away from the two-hundred-strong gathering, his smile nearly knocked me sideways. The room faded. For a moment, it was just him and me.

"The boy's fine, Chloe. Snake's loopin' the block. Minute he stirs—we're gone. Got it?"

I nodded, gripping my necklace tighter.

"Spend all my fuckin' money." He gestured to the cabinets. "There ain't a limit."

It was a strange feeling, being apart from my son, yet still wanting my husband to drop an obscene amount of money on a new engagement ring. I pictured throwing my hand in Harper's face. The diamond gleaming so hard it'd blind her.

Yeah. That's what I wanted right now.

The staff door clicked open behind the counter. A rotund man in a tailored suit, grey hair slicked back, shuffled around the perimeter of the display cases.

His fancy leather shoes tapped across the matching grey marble as he stopped beside us. A wave of expensive soap cologne drifted, mingling with the faint scent of fried chicken still lingering on his fingers from the rush of our surprise visit.

"Sorry about that, Mr Giannetti. Just on my lunch break. Such an absolute pleasure to have you back with us," he said, dabbing his glistening forehead with a silk handkerchief already damp with sweat.

"A real treat, sir. Tell me, what can I do for you today?" His tongue darted out, catching a hint of ketchup—confirming what I'd already suspected. A wing or a leg had definitely passed his lips just before we showed up, but Romeo was worth more to him than his lunch.

Romeo looked at his watch. "Listen up, Andrew. We don't got long. Engagement ring. Best one you've got."

Andrew's eyes bulged, and the seam of his trousers almost stretched. He was clearly excited about the commission he was about to receive.

Another suited man appeared. Tall, slim, and agile. This one holding a serving tray. Among his offerings, as he glided through the room, were a pair of crystal tumblers and a chilled decanter.

"Is sir ready for his refreshment?" he asked, setting the tray down on a specially assigned table. His chin raised and lips pressed, he was clearly used to being around people with money.

Romeo gave a quick nod and held out his hand to accept what I could only assume was whiskey.

"Ma'am?" the server asked mid-pour. The fall of liquid from a height into the cut crystal made for a satisfying melody—rich, deep, like a note from a cello.

I was just about to refuse automatically when I remembered. I wasn't pregnant anymore.

"Yes, please," I said, offering a smile.

Interlacing my hands in my lap, a flutter of excitement tickled the walls of my stomach.

Sure, I was breastfeeding. But a sip or two wouldn't harm the baby… right?

The sharp scent of aged whiskey curled in the air as the server poured my drink.

Romeo took a gulp and sighed, relaxing back into his chair, watching me with a hint of a smile.

Our server handed me a glass and placed a napkin beneath it.

"Thank you," I said, meeting his kind grey eyes.

I brought the glass to my lips. The liquor was so potent under my nose, I recoiled slightly.

"Smells good, don't it?" Romeo said, clocking the curl of my upper lip.

I nodded. "Although… is there some lemonade or something to go with this?"

Romeo chuckled into the rim of his almost empty glass.

"Pass it over." He curled his fingers at me. "She'll have iced water."

"What do you think of this ring?" I held up the centre fold of the glossy-paged inspiration catalogue.

White diamond, circular shape. I couldn't decide whether it was the woman wearing it that made it look good or if I actually liked it.

Frustrated, clock-watching for the baby, we'd been here fifteen minutes already, and I was no closer to knowing what I wanted.

Before Romeo could answer, the staff door opened again. The swing of the hinge echoed through the room—sharp, expectant. All eyes turned to the manicured hand that appeared first.

This time, it wasn't a sweaty, fat man.

Of course it wasn't.

A wind machine may as well have been aimed straight at her, with a slow-tempo sex track playing behind her strut.

A stunning woman swept into the room, wearing a tailored blazer and a pencil skirt that skimmed her knees. Glossy black waves tumbled around her shoulders. Her perfume hit a beat before she did—cool jasmine with an elegant bite. Every inch of her screamed expensive.

I already knew she'd fucked my husband.

My grip on the chair's arms tightened. Thighs clamped together.

The A/C suddenly felt colder. A breath of chilled air brushed the back of my neck like a whisper I didn't want to hear, leaving goosebumps in its wake.

Feeling foolish for having started to relax, my guard shot up like a reflex.

Romeo's eyes widened. The thick muscle in his biceps bunched as if this was a bigger deal than he was letting on. He set his third whiskey down on the glass top with a clink.

His hand raised high, like a red flag.

"Don't take another fuckin' step, Bethany. I'm dealin' with Andrew today." His words came firm. Final.

Yet she didn't so much as flinch.

Miss Bethany continued her sashay like she owned the floor. Each step was perfectly executed, like the roll of Romeo's hips when he made love. Purposeful. Confident. Sexy.

"Romero." Her smile gleamed. Bright white teeth and a slash of red lipstick. "Great to see you. I'm busy with a client of my own anyway."

She leaned into Andrew. "I need the key for the safe. I'm about to close on six figures." Her manicured hand pressed lightly to his chest. The contact made him blink twice and stammer.

From the corner of my eye, I studied Romeo. His reaction wasn't his usual. The cocky arrogance was nowhere to be seen.

This time, she held the power; she couldn't have cared less about him even if she tried. And he couldn't have made it more obvious that it bothered him.

She spun on her heel, casting one last look at my husband as she strode away.

"I always did like that cologne on you," she purred, waving slow—like a regal princess.

Her heels tapped down the corridor, each step a slow slap to my pride, until the door brushed closed behind her.

The room exhaled.

But Romeo's jaw ticked. His breath still hadn't returned when I crossed my arms and raised a brow.

"You still fancy her, don't you?"

His fingers flexed on his thigh. Then curled into a fist.

I barely waited for his answer before I kicked him in the shin.

He grunted.

Andrew cleared his throat beside us, shifting awkwardly in place.

My surprise attack did the trick. Romeo snapped out of it—blinking fast.

"Fuck no," he scoffed. "She was shit in bed."

The impatient gathering bubbled beyond the glass door. Tommy, no longer able to manage it alone, now had a new recruit to help. I hated how claustrophobic it made me feel.

Trapped inside and still annoyed that Romeo was keeping something from me, I wanted to confront him right here, right now.

I opened my mouth—

"We'll talk in the car, okay?" he said, reading my mind. Then he turned to Andrew with a smirk, like the last thirty seconds hadn't even happened. "Hurry the fuck up and help my wife spend my money."

"Certainly." Andrew bowed. "Ma'am, follow me."

Surrounded by diamonds and every precious stone under the sun, the display cabinets caught the fluorescent spotlights, sending cascades of colour across the room. Rays fractured into vibrant bursts that scattered like jewels spilled in slow motion. I didn't know where to start. Didn't even know what I wanted. But I knew one thing: it was going to cost my husband a fortune.

"Okay, I think I'll choose this one right here." I jabbed my finger at the immense catalogue of options glistening beneath the stark LED lights.

My fingertip left a faint smudge on the glass—silently noted by Andrew.

Romeo remained seated, sipping another glass of neat whiskey while he watched the pivotal moment unfold.

Andrew clutched his iPad like it was life support.

"I must say, ma'am, you have excellent taste," he said, already finalising his notes.

"So,"—he took a breath, like he needed a full lung of air to give this order its moment—

"We're going for a 15-carat intense pink radiant-cut diamond. GIA-certified, of course. Set in rose-tinted platinum to subtly enhance the warmth of the stone.

The diamond is, as you'd expect, VS1 clarity, cut for maximum brilliance, and flanked by two trapezoid-cut white diamonds—just enough contrast to draw the eye without overpowering the centre stone. The band is smooth. No pavé. Polished, sleek, and engraved with the word 'Romeo' in tiny script on the inside."

He glanced up. "Have I missed anything?"

I peered at my husband, who raised his glass with a smile.

"Um… how much is it?" I asked, suddenly feeling a little guilty.

"This gorgeous piece totals eighteen million dollars."

My eyes came out on stalks, darting to Romeo for his reaction.

"That all?" He huffed. "Order her up another bracelet to match. We ain't fuckin' around here, Andrew."

◆ ◆ ◆

Junior was sobbing softly when we returned to the car, his little tongue fluttering between each cry, fists curled tight beside his flushed cheeks.

Snake nearly leapt out of the driver's seat when Romeo opened the door, darting for the safety of the SUV waiting behind us.

With paps closing in and no time to argue, I slipped into the back seat, cradling my son against my chest while my husband—aka *Bethany's* former lover—drove us back to the mansion.

The car rolled forward, inching into traffic as silence unfolded between us like a drawn curtain.

Junior suckled at my breast, and the urge to fight softened. Each tug at my nipple eased the tension, melting it into something warm and grounding, a treasured connection between his body and my heart. The frantic rhythm of his jaw slowed as he settled, milk gathering between our bond.

"You hated that she didn't care about you anymore, didn't you?" I murmured, stroking the single black curl resting across our son's damp forehead.

The weight of his head in the crook of my arm softened me in a way nothing else could.

Romeo adjusted the rear-view mirror. His ocean-blue eyes found mine, slicing clean through the jealousy and the lingering sparkle of diamonds still crowding my thoughts.

"Aight, fine. Yeah," he said with a shrug. "I guess it did bother me that she didn't care."

He paused. "You wanna know why?"

I looked down at my almost naked ring finger. Only the wedding band remained after the jeweller had sliced off my old, stuck engagement ring. Or should I say, Harper's old ring.

We were told the new one would take two weeks to arrive. Fitting, really. Right now, I could've waited six months.

Maybe forever...

"Go on then, ass-hat." I took a deep sigh. "Enlighten me."

He merged into the bumper-to-bumper flow again, the Rolls gliding forward before easing to another stop.

Above us, the ceiling twinkled with ambient light—miniature stars stitched into black suede. Classic Rolls Royce. Soft. Surreal. Soothing almost, especially from the back seat.

Romeo ran a hand through his hair before sucking air through his teeth.

He hesitated. "I guess if bitches still want me," he said carefully, "then it means I'm still good enough to keep you."

Pfft. Please.

I rolled my eyes while rocking the baby. "You're really trying to lie to me like that?"

He eyed me through the mirror. "She's just another slut. I fucked her once in the back of my car. Her pussy had a weird smell. Put me off. I made an excuse—told her the paps were followin' us. That's it. Never touched her again."

Revulsion curled through me, triggered by the uninvited image of her legs in the air.

A 'weird smell', he says...

"What, like fish?" A flicker of amusement crept into my voice—offering him the tiniest way back in.

He sensed it. He knew me too well.

"Fish. Vinegar. Old socks… Somethin' like that."

I couldn't see his mouth, but the crease at the corners of his eyes gave him away.

He was smiling.

I was smirking.

"Ugh. That's gross."

I convinced myself I could smell it now. Like I was watching it all unfold for the first time. The image of him peeling down her panties and finding flies around roadkill was unfortunately vivid.

"You better have been wearing a condom."

He puffed out air as if I was the one who'd suggested raw-dogging the unwashed undead.

"You know me, Queen. Always rubbered up."

I shook my head, trying to scrub the mental montage of his cock buried inside too many women.

"Let's not delve deeper, shall we? Unless that's where you went wrong trying to knock up Harper and Tat?"

The corners of his eyes lost their crinkle. The joke landed. Just not well.

"Haha. Real fuckin' funny."

The traffic cleared, and we picked up speed. But just a quarter of a mile in, a roadwork sign forced us back to a crawl.

Horns blared around us in frustrated bursts.

"Move lanes, ass hole!" Romeo yelled through the windshield.

A phantom ache bloomed low in my abdomen—nothing real, but enough to make my hand drift instinctively to my stomach.

I caught his eye in the mirror again. "Romeo, you do realise I might be pregnant after yesterday?"

My voice softened as the reality hit. "Don't you think it's too soon?"

He turned in his seat, one arm slinging over the passenger headrest.

Confident. Composed. Purpose carved into every inch of him. His gaze didn't waver.

"If anythin', it wasn't soon enough. I told you I wanted another baby with you. Prayin' real hard for it."

I settled Junior back into his car seat, where, fortunately, he drifted instantly to sleep.

Heat shimmered off the car's hood. The sun burned behind Romeo, framing him in gold. In the wrong eyes, he could've been mistaken for holy. But there was nothing holy about my husband.

The baby snuffled, twitching like he sensed the shift between us.

It almost felt like we'd rewound time. Back to the start, when Romeo's idea of making a child came with a his-way-or-no-way policy.

I placed a protective hand over my stomach. Flat for now. Empty, maybe. But was a baby already growing inside me?

"Having a child is a decision we both make, Romeo. You realise that, right?"

Sirens wailed past in a blur of red and blue. Drivers shouted, waving their arms out the window at road workers who'd brought everything to a standstill.

"God damn it," he muttered, beeping the horn. Distracted. Agitated. "What the fuck are you on about now, woman?"

I offered my finger to the baby's tiny hand. He curled his fist around it, his grip surprisingly strong.

"I said, having a baby is a joint decision. You don't get to tell me what I do with my own body."

His voice rose, anger bubbling to the surface. "I fuckin' asked you at the time if I could nut inside you. You said yes!"

"Well, I—"

He cut me off, shaking his head.

"Or—more fuckin' accurately—it was, 'Oh Romeo, I love your massive dick. Please unload your bigger-than-average nut inside my sweet pussy.'"

He jabbed a finger against his temple. "I remember shit like that."

That wasn't exactly what I'd said. But my mind flicked back to that moment—him inside me, the way I'd clung to him like I'd never let go.

A tingle traced up my inner thigh, shamefully timed.

Maybe I had gotten lost in the moment?

Maybe I had begged?

My whole body jolted as a sudden vibration shot through my chest. For a second, I could've sworn his anger zapped clean out of him, straight into me.

Caught off guard in the heat of it all, it took me a minute to realise my phone was ringing.

"You gonna get that?" Romeo asked, fingers curling tighter around the gear lever. His thumb tapped a steady rhythm, like the caller might be a threat to him.

His narrowed eyes locked on mine through the reflection as I glanced down at the screen.

"Shit, it's Nelly." I fumbled the phone with slick fingers, nearly dropping it into Junior's lap. I hit answer.

"Hey, Nelly," I said, chirpy.

Last thing she needed was a play-by-play of our latest argument over women and thoughtless baby-making.

"Chloe Giannetti." She sighed. "I hope to goodness gracious you haven't forgotten about our session today? I've called you three times this week to remind you, but you didn't respond."

Hmm.

I could've told her the truth.

The first time—captured in the back of an SUV.

The second—hiding out at the cottage.

The third—pulling the trigger on a mole.

Instead, I went with my usual: avoidance.

Only this time, it was entirely justified.

"Sorry about that. The baby came a little earlier than expected. We're on our way to your office right now."

I gestured wildly at the turnoff for her building, like Romeo needed the extra push. I didn't need to repeat myself. He'd heard every single word.

"Ahh, wonderful," her voice softened. "I can't wait to meet your new bundle… I hope you remembered to prepare some questions for your mother-in-law. She's already sitting in my waiting room."

Fuck.

Shit.

Crap.

My arse crack sweated, palm damp against the phone as my blood turned cold.

I reached for my necklace again, toying with the pendant like it might download inspiration from the heavens. It clinked lightly as I twisted it between my feverish skin.

"Of course I have," I said with a nervous giggle. "So many questions prepared. Too many, in fact. See you in twenty minutes."

I ended the call and tossed my phone onto the centre seat.

"I fucking forgot that we have a fucking session with your fucking mother. Shit!"

My pulse quickened. Panic bloomed across my cheeks.

Romeo stayed quiet. Slouched in his seat, he took the corner with one hand on the wheel—casual, calm, like nothing touched him.

I tapped his shoulder, warm and slightly goose-pimpled. He was definitely feeling it, too.

"Hello? Did you hear me?"

He'd slipped into a trance the moment his mother's name was mentioned.

A beat later, he cleared his throat. "I heard you."

He paused. "No big deal."

One of these days, I might believe him.

But even the baby knew that wasn't true today.

The three of us, plus the baby, waited restlessly in the all-too-familiar therapist's waiting room.

A plug-in air freshener, mingled with Angela's old-fashioned perfume, pressed against my skull like a clamp.

The room felt too warm, too quiet, anticipation hanging heavy, sucking the breath from the walls. The cushion beneath me stuck with heat. Fabric clung to my lower back, sweat blooming in the small of it.

It hadn't escaped my attention that the usual vase of lilies had been moved across the room, swapped with the magazine rack. Why do that? I hated change. My fingers flicked restlessly over the armrest—a silent urge to move it back, to reclaim control of something… anything.

Angela, who had already tried to snatch Junior from the car seat at least a handful of times, wasn't helping my anxiety. But there wasn't a cat in hell's chance I was letting her win. No matter how much energy she drained from me, I was here to prove a point. She could fight me all she liked. I was going nowhere.

Her movements were animated. Theatrical. She flourished her hand like she was about to perform opera, jewellery catching the light like claws. Clutching her purse to her chest, she sniffed the air dramatically and muttered something in Italian.

I turned to Romeo, using him as a gauge for whether I should react.

He didn't move a muscle—just chewed on a stick of gum; the pace matching the twitch in his thigh. A vein near his temple pulsed, out of sync with the slow grind of his molars.

Her nose lifted again, inhaling like a bloodhound.

"Romero." Angela leaned over me and slapped his arm. "What is that smell? Did you bathe the *bambino* this morning? An Italian mother knows how to present her child to the world. This boy has your handsome features, but look at his clothing. Not acceptable."

My toes curled inside my sneakers. Even the short length of my nails dug into my palms. Under any other circumstance, I'd have smacked her round the head with Junior's changing bag.

Thankfully, we didn't have to wait too long. The imposing door to Nelly's office swung open. A breeze swept in, like someone cracked a window in a burning house.

Her kind face appeared.

"Giannetti family," she said, smiling. "Come on in."

This was about to get interesting.

Inside the office, the scent of fresh linen grounded me.

Nelly tucked strands of short hair behind her ears as she leaned over the car seat.

"What a gorgeous baby," she said, adjusting the blanket. "Look at those dark curls. Congratulations, guys."

A sense of pride swelled in my chest.

I giggled. "Thank you."

She smiled down at him, eyes soft. "Wow, Romero—doesn't he look just like you?"

She paused. Narrowed her eyes. "Hold on… what's this?"

Nothing ever got past Nelly.

She lifted something small from the seat, pinched between two fingers like evidence.

"D'you know," she said lightly, "we could have a full session dissecting why your newborn has a small plastic gun stashed under his blanket."

She peered up at Romeo through her lashes. "But we'll save that for another time, shall we?"

I snorted, trying to brush past the moment that confirmed my suspicion.

Nelly knew. She knew exactly who my husband was. And that damn toy was only going to make things more awkward when she eventually confronted us.

Romeo, unfazed, took his seat first. Leaned back. Legs spread. Having his moment.

"The only people who've got a problem with my son and his first fuckin' gun… are women."

He turned. "And yes, Mother, that includes Daniele."

Angela tutted, dropping into the chair on his left. I took mine on his right, placing the car seat safely by my feet—far from her reach.

She leaned across him. Romeo instantly pulled back in his chair, like the thought of their bodies touching made his skin crawl.

She pointed at me with a gnarled finger.

"Tell me. Why is she here? She's not a real Giannetti."

My mother-in-law had a way of spoiling the mood without even trying.

Romeo shoved her back into her seat. Then scooped Junior into his arms, settling him against his shoulder.

"This is what I have to deal with," he muttered. "Mom, shut the fuck up."

Nelly circled the desk and took her seat behind it. She adjusted her glasses, plucking a pen from the stationery pot.

"Mrs Giannetti," she said evenly, "you feel that your son's wife isn't part of the family?"

Angela scrunched up her nose in a gesture I'd seen Romeo do a hundred times.

"She's just a child. She's not capable of looking after my grandson, or my son, for that matter."

Nelly's lips tightened. "I speak on behalf of your son and his wife when I say—your mindset is not helpful in forging a relationship with your daughter-in-law. Chloe is ready for motherhood. There's no reason to call her a child. I've worked with this couple for a while now, and I've grown to adore each of them. It would be a great shame if you chose not to accept her as part of your family."

My fists unfurled as I listened to a woman I hadn't known long fight my corner like my best friend.

Angela huffed and dragged both halves of her woollen cardigan across her chest. "She isn't *Italiano*. Simple."

Nelly steepled her fingers. "And why does that bother you?"

The cardigan wasn't enough. Angela placed her leather handbag in her lap like a barrier.

"We have our ways and traditions that she knows nothing about. Romero doesn't seem to care, but it bothers me."

Nelly jotted something down. The scratch of pen against paper sliced through the silence.

"The fact that it doesn't bother him should be enough for you, Mrs Giannetti. Just look at that beautiful baby they've created."

Angela rolled her eyes. "*Figlio del diavolo.*"

Nelly cleared her throat, making another note.

"I studied Italian for three years. I'd take that back."

Romeo smirked as his mother swallowed the smallest bite of humble pie.

Like mother, like son—Angela turned agitated when challenged.

"Why am I even here, listening to these things?" she snapped.

Nelly didn't indulge her tantrum.

She finished writing.

The clock ticked louder, slower.

We were on her time now.

"I invited you here, Mrs Giannetti, to discuss your relationship with your son. It's a technique we often use in therapy to help the patient's inner child heal. From that point of healing, they can begin to flourish in adulthood."

"Pah!" Angela scoffed, yanking the wool even tighter. "Romero's problem is nothing to do with me. He keeps making the mistake of not being more like his younger brother, Daniele."

Nelly paused mid-sentence. Her eyes flicked between me and Romeo, then settled on Angela.

"Okay. Let's explore that further, Mrs Giannetti. What quality does your younger son possess that you think Romero lacks?"

Angela fidgeted. Sniffed like even the oxygen offended her. "Romero disgraced our family when he threw away his career for drugs. He could've been something."

Nelly tucked her bottom lip between her teeth. Fingers steepled again. "Romero, what do you want to say to your mother about that? We haven't touched on that part of your life yet, have we?"

He was already there. Mirroring her agitation. Clenched jaw. Wild eyes. One second from bolting. Fingers curled around the car seat handle like it was the only thing anchoring him.

"Why the fuck would I wanna sit here and listen to the reminder that my parents never thought I was worth shit?"

He leaned forward. Voice raw. "Yeah, I smoked a joint or two as a kid. So fuckin' what?"

Angela shifted in her seat. "Your father put everything into your boxing. You ruined it. You put him in an early grave."

"You ain't wrong, Mother." His words oozed venom. "I wished he would go to hell—and he finally did. I'm just waitin' on your turn."

Angela surged to her feet. Handbag clutched, she swung and slapped the back of Romeo's head.

He didn't even flinch.

"This is no good! You bring me here to a quack doctor saying all these things about me. I don't like it, Romero. I'm leaving."

She shoved her chair back, footsteps loud, arms flapping like the scene wasn't complete without her final flourish.

The door slammed shut, her perfume trailing behind like a bad omen.

I turned to him. "That's exactly where you get it from."

The air shifted as soon as she left—like someone finally cracked open a second window.

"What you on about?" he muttered, crossing one ankle over his knee.

I took the baby from him and settled him against my chest. His warm breath feathered my skin as he squirmed, then fell back asleep.

"Your theatrical side. It's from your mother."

He scowled, but didn't argue. He knew I was right. Maybe watching her storm out would make him think twice before pulling the same stunt next time.

Nelly tapped her desk lightly.

"That didn't go as well as I'd hoped. But I see what the problem is now." She turned to me. "Chloe, hats off to you. That must have been difficult to listen to."

"Guess I'm used to it now," I said with a shrug.

She looked at Romeo. "I'll attempt to reach out to your mother for a one-on-one session—if that's okay with you? Her refusal to accept responsibility is holding back your progress. And I won't let anything stand in the way."

She winked at me. That spark in her voice came from somewhere deep. We owed her far more than her hourly fee.

Romeo glanced at his watch. "Knock yourself out. As long as I don't gotta to be here when it happens, I don't give a shit."

I eyed him when he checked his watch again.

"Do you have somewhere to be?" I held the baby closer.

My emotional shield against the one person who could hurt me the most.

"Just an appointment, that's all," he murmured.

Something in his tone, guarded and clipped, made my heart pick up pace.

"Oh?"

It had been weeks since we'd spent any time apart. Now the baby's here, and suddenly I'm fending for myself?

He placed a finger to his lips. "Shh. We'll talk about it later. It's a surprise."

My skin mottled. Anxiety took hold.

Sweaty hands and short, shallow breaths weren't on today's to-do list.

Nelly stood, sensing the shift. Leaning forward on her desk, palms flat, her wedding ring scraped the wood.

"What's going on, guys? Open-door policy, remember that, Romero. If Chloe wants to know what the appointment is—why not tell her?"

His jaw tensed. Suspicion bloomed like a bruise.

That clock again.

Tick. Tock. Tick. Tock.

"It's a surprise," he repeated. "Can't be a fuckin' surprise if I tell her."

Nelly clamped her tongue between her teeth, thinking.

"Okay. That's fair." She raised her hands in concession. "But maybe next time, a little warning for Chloe would help ease her anxiety."

Romeo nodded too quickly.

I sighed and pressed a kiss to the top of my son's head.

"You know, Romeo, we keep paying for a full hour and only staying twenty minutes. We could've made so much more progress." I tucked Junior into his seat, fastening the straps with care.

The only response I got was the jiggle of his leg as he fished around in his sweatpants pocket.

Suddenly, I was tired. Done being the only one trying to save this marriage.

I stood, lifting the car seat.

My back ached. But not from the baby. From carrying the burden of fixing everything alone.

"Romero needs feeding anyway. Let's just go."

Nelly leaned over her desk, offering her hand to each of us. "No problem, guys. We'll pick up on this next time. Congratulations again. He's just perfect."

Humidity pressed thick over the parking lot, weighing down on all three of us like dead weight. The cool freshness from Nelly's office already felt miles away.

"Why do you have to ruin it every time?" I asked, securing Junior's seat in the back of the car. The strap from the change bag had left a red welt on my shoulder. I rubbed it, irritation simmering just beneath the surface.

Romeo lit his second cigarette, leaning against the hood. Smoke curled lazily around him as he watched me finish the job he should have done.

"Get off my dick, Chloe," he muttered, the words curling through a veil of smoke. "I've got an appointment. Relax."

He yanked the door open and dropped into the driver's seat with unnecessary force, jolting the car's suspension.

Behind us, Tommy, Snake, and the rest of the team waited in the SUV. The engine's low rattle had somehow become a source of comfort these past few months.

I gave them a curt nod before circling the back of the Rolls and slipping into the front passenger seat.

Clipped myself in. Said nothing.

The stale whiff of tobacco hit my nose—sharper than I remembered. It offended me.

I turned to the window. "You better not be cheating on me, Romeo."

My fingers ghosted over the button but didn't press it. I just needed something to touch. Something to second guess.

In the glass, my reflection stared back, haunted. My mind wandered, picturing him lighting a cigarette post-fuck. The scent, now a trigger, laced the air with accusation.

The words hung there, vulnerable and exposed, and I hated myself for letting them slip.

He knew how hard intimacy had become. He knew what my body looked like now.

Was he getting it from somewhere else?

That waitress from the diner?

The fishy, stank-pussy slut from the jeweller's?

He laughed—like it was funny. Like I hadn't just ripped my chest open for him.

"You think I'd be so fuckin' obvious? Just dropped eighteen mill at the jewellery store and get this reaction? Should've gone to fuckin' Dollar Tree."

With a sharp huff, I folded my arms across my chest and turned my knees away from him.

Could he really do that to me? Cheat?

He lowered the music a notch, trying to quiet the turmoil. "Don't go fuckin' my brother just because you think I'm cheatin'. We ain't playin' that game."

"As if," I muttered, though the thought had crossed my mind.

Something stank about the whole thing. Why was he so eager to leave?

His eyes darkened. That sharp flash of temper cutting through. "You keep tellin' me I can't see your body yet—but if I find out, you've let someone else... Daniele?"

His jaw flexed. "I swear to God, I'll lose my shit. I'll empty a clip in his chest."

My throat cinched. "I'm not the one cheating here."

"Neither am I, you fuckin' psycho. Shit!"

He slammed both hands against the steering wheel. The horn blared, sharp and violent, slicing through the car park.

The baby stirred in the back. Tiny legs kicked out in his sleep, blissfully unaware of the storm circling his world.

I knew I was provoking him. Knew it wasn't smart. But I refused to be blindsided.

As we approached the house, paparazzi lingered by the open gates, cameras raised. One lens caught the light and flared across the dash. A warning shot.

Romeo jerked the car to a stop by the front door, gravel scattering beneath the tyres. He left the engine running.

After a moment, he turned and placed his hand over mine. Hot. Dry. His skin thirsty for forgiveness.

"Chloe," he said, voice softer now. "Promise me you won't cheat while I'm gone."

Headlights glared in the rear-view as the SUV pulled in behind us. Tommy and Snake, waiting.

A tear slipped down my cheek, carving a cold line into the corner of my mouth. "Same to you."

He groaned, raking a hand through his curls. "I don't want you to cry. I'm tryin' to do somethin' nice here. Cut me some slack."

The engine growled beneath us, ready to take him anywhere but here.

Then the images returned—girls in the back seat, laughter, moans, him peeling off their underwear.

My stomach turned. I wiped my nose on the back of my hand and forced a breath. "Okay. Fine."

"Fine?" he echoed, scanning my face.

"Yes," I said quietly. My chin lifted, just enough to keep my pride.

But truthfully? I was breaking.

Had he looked at my body in the shower this morning and made up his mind that we were done?

With a chaste kiss, he dropped me off at the door. My son in his car seat. The change bag slung over my shoulder.

"I'll be a couple hours," he called, reversing. "I'll see you soon."

The scent of tobacco lingered on my lips. So did the phantom weight of his hand on my thigh. This was the first time he'd left me since giving birth. Watching him disappear through the gates, nearly taking out a pap or two, felt like more than just a goodbye.

I stood there, numb, and reached for my phone.

Should I call Britney?

My thumb hovered.

Hmm.

She hadn't even texted to say congratulations.

Everyone saw the photos. She knew.

I opened the front door, heavy in my one free hand, and stepped into silence.

A murmur of voices drifted from the kitchen, rich with Chef's spices. My stomach growled.

I shifted the car seat in my grip and trudged over the polished floor. No ring on my finger. No husband. Just me.

The ceilings stretched taller with every step. The hallway gleamed—pristine. Cold. Lonely. Nothing like the cottage.

I pushed through the kitchen door with my hip. The warm scent of garlic and saffron hit me just before the silence settled, a sudden drop into a pit of judgement.

Every girl froze. Darting eyes. Forks suspended mid-air. Even Lala paused her nail file.

"Evening, everybody," I said, voice steadier than I felt.

No one replied.

Chef's pan sizzled a beat too long, smoke curling in thick spirals.

My newly installed throne sat at the head of the table, a mirror to Romeo's at the other end. A symbol of our power and presence. But something held me back from claiming my place.

Then a hand touched my shoulder, electric and unexpected. I jolted and spun on my heel to find Snake: buzz cut, steel eyes, and an almost-smile.

"Follow me," he said, holding the door open again.

His boots thumped. Sure. Steady.

"What?" I asked, catching the clench in his jaw.

He stood to attention, hands behind his back. Always formal. Always distant.

"Word's out about the moles. They know you were involved. Give it a few days to settle."

My breath caught. A hand flew to my throat.

The girls knew?

"The club opens in a few days," I whispered. "I need them."

"They'll deliver, Boss." He rocked on his heels. "My advice? Go get some sleep. You look beat."

Maybe he was right. But sleep wouldn't come easy. Not with this much fallout waiting to hit.

I laid Junior in his bassinet and collapsed into bed, eyes locked on the whitewashed ceiling.

Yesterday still clung to my skin.

Every time I blinked, I saw Jamie. Her pale face. Her last breath. The sound of the gunshot wouldn't stop. The phantom recoil lived in my wrist, a tingle I couldn't shake.

Did I regret it?

Maybe.

But this wasn't something I could discuss with Nelly.

I killed Jamie. Me.

The thought of ending a woman's life stirred so many emotions—fear, guilt, confusion.

I thought of Alice. Hanna. Even Tatiana. Their deaths weren't my fault. Yet somehow, they still haunted me.

My body jolted.

I woke to Romeo kissing my forehead.

"Hey, sleepyhead," he said with a smile.

"Oh. Hey." My voice rasped.

But what I wasn't prepared for was a possible confession of adultery.

"Wanna see somethin' cool?" he asked, flashing a boyish grin.

If it was photos of the evidence, I wouldn't hesitate to rack the slide of my gun.

I sat up and rubbed my eyes, clearing the remnants of sleep from my lashes.

He edged closer.

"Wait—" I blinked. "You got a tattoo?"

Our bedroom was dimly lit as the sun dipped behind thick clouds, but I saw it clear as day.

He nodded, flicking on the bedside lamp. Warm amber spilled across the ceiling like melted honey.

"Yup. Take a look."

I watched closely as he peeled off the clear protective wrap, carefully revealing a thing of beauty.

His skin was a little raised and red against olive tones, but I could already tell it was a masterpiece.

"I wasn't expecting you to get another tattoo?"

He rotated his arm, giving me all angles. "Well, a sexy woman with a sweet pussy once asked me if this sleeve tat meant anythin'—and the answer back then was no. Since that day, I've thought about makin' it meaningful. Now it is."

Fresh ink curved into the original piece, skilfully blended. Mine and Junior's names, entwined with his date of birth, inked in elegant scroll lettering that matched the aesthetic perfectly. It was everything.

An emotionally fuelled smile parted my lips.

"Oh, Romeo. I love it."

My head lolled back slightly. It felt good to let my shoulders drop, to let my smile take over for once. The tightness in my jaw eased, and for a second, everything else just melted away.

Why, after everything, did I think he'd cheat on me? The thought felt stupid now.

"I don't have any tattoos yet," I said, glancing down at my bare arms. The hairs along them prickled with leftover chill. "Maybe I should get one, too?"

He arched a brow, raising my hand to his lips.

"Sure you do," he said, prising my middle finger from the rest. "Right here."

And there it was. The half of a heart I shared with a woman who slipped into my mind more times than I could count.

"Oh, yeah." I giggled, claiming my hand back. "I forgot about that."

"Pfft. I ain't. I see it every time you wrap your hand around my dick."

His eyes dropped to my finger, lips thinning slightly—until I pulled the blanket over me, covering the evidence of my past.

"Does it bother you?" I asked cautiously.

Bringing up old news was never comfortable for either of us.

"I guess it used to. But she ain't here anymore, so I got over it."

He rubbed the tip of his nose along the length of mine, igniting that spark that always seemed to live between us. "So, you didn't cheat on me while I was gone, then?"

I reached up, fingers combing through my knotted bed hair. "Um. Apparently I was sleeping."

He kissed the fullest part of my lips, and I felt the sense of relief in the way he exhaled. My mouth responded softly and willingly, opening to him once more. Like a flower in the meadow, its petals responding to light…

I wanted him again. Needed to know he still loved my body. That my worry he'd find someone better could be put to bed once and for all.

I pulled back just slightly, lips still touching. "While the baby's still asleep… do you wanna try again? To have sex, I mean. I won't hold back this time."

His grin spread wide. "Hell yeah," he whispered, planting soft kisses down my neck.

"Be careful, Romeo. I mean it."

And by that I meant careful with my heart as much as anything else.

That's when my brain panicked. Would he see me and run for the hills? Scream, cry… shoot me even?

"I got you, Queen. Tell me how you wanna do this."

He lay beside me on the bed slowly and carefully, as if trying not to startle a wild animal. Arms propped behind his head, his new tattoo was on full display—a perfectly timed declaration of love inked into skin.

I threw off the bed covers and planted my feet on solid ground. The lazy breeze through the open window swayed the drapes—until I slid the sash shut with a final click. This was a moment just for us.

I flicked the wall switch, bathing the room in light.

The baby sighed, shifting in his sleep—but the hood of the crib shielded his eyes from the glare.

The spotlight was on me.

Still in a loose-fitting dress cut at the knee, I gripped the hem and began to walk. Each small step closed the space between us.

Romeo's lips parted. His hands, resting by his sides, twitched with anticipation.

I paused with the fabric at my waist. "Are you ready for this?" I asked, hesitating.

He nodded, sitting up cross-legged as if this was the most important moment of his life.

I closed my eyes, took a breath—and went for it.

Peeling the thin material over my head felt like lifting weights in the gym. Breathless. Anxious. God, I was terrified.

I stood before him in my maternity bra and granny panties, one arm crossing protectively over my stomach.

The petals of desire clamped shut. My pulse held—waiting for his reaction.

"Holy shit," he murmured, fidgeting. "God, you're so sexy."

He licked his lips like he was starving.

"Do you mean it?" I asked, letting my arm slip a little lower.

He stood instantly and threw down his sweatpants, freeing the erection he didn't need any effort to get started.

"Just look at you. Fuck."

The heat of the room intensified like a furnace. Flushed cheeks spilled colour down his chest as he took hold of himself, almost losing control, then instantly let go.

"Fuck, I'm already there," he mumbled. "Lie down, sexy. Let me look at you."

And here I was again, looking up at the ceiling, but this time, for a whole different reason.

Exposed, vulnerable and a little scared. The brightness of the ceiling bulb stung the back of my retinas.

I swallowed dryly as my husband came to lie beside me. A hint of his last smoke. A recent spritz of cologne. My mouth watered the moment his fingers skimmed my thigh.

He'd stripped off all his clothes, leaving not a single barrier between us.

"Chloe," he said.

A catch in his throat dragged my attention away from the ceiling pattern instantly.

"Yes?" I whispered, locking eyes with the blackness of his blown pupils.

He took my hand, his grip quivering slightly, and placed it directly over the bullet wound on his shoulder.

"When you see this scar," he began, "what does it make you think?"

My brows creased as I felt the smooth hump beneath my fingertips. Memories of that day came flooding back in an instant.

"Um… I guess it reminds me that you saved my life. If you hadn't taken Hanna's bullet… I might've."

He smiled and nodded. Then, ever so gently, he placed a kiss against the stretch marks across my stomach.

"You see these little guys right here?" he murmured against my skin. "They remind me how much you saved me the day you gave me my son. I wanna see more of these when you carry the next one. You hear me, Chloe?"

The flowers were back in full bloom. The vines of my stretch marks tingled as his lips found each one. I heard him loud and clear.

He peeled down my underwear, both of us smiling at yesterday's memory of a similar image.

"This bad boy ain't goin' on the floor this time," he said, laying the panties—pad still inside—on the nightstand like he was setting down a coffee cup.

I sniggered. The kind of laughter that belonged to a woman who trusted the word of her husband.

The mattress tilted as he settled between my legs, his cock nudging the entrance that seemed so much less sensitive today than before.

He reached beneath me and unhooked my bra.

"Do you want to make a baby with me, Chloe Giannetti?" His voice was low, full of love, as he pushed the head just slightly between my slick folds.

My core convulsed, a knot of climax waiting to explode for him. I needed to carry his children. I had to feel the warmth of his orgasm mixing with mine.

"Yes, Romeo. Please." I clawed at his back. "Please."

My nails dragged along his spine as Romeo's chest brushed over mine. Leaking breast milk tangled with the fine hair on his chest, making for a sticky sweetness that only heightened the connection between us.

The bed frame creaked in rhythm with the roll of his hips. Lubrication flooded between my legs, giving way to an intensity I'd never quite experienced before.

"You smell so good," he said, burying his head between my breasts. He took a nipple into his mouth, sucking gently before getting lost in his rhythm again.

I barely heard him. His voice almost didn't register—my ears rang, and my heart thudded against my ribs as blood pooled between my legs. An ache to detonate around his cock. An agony to come for him consuming me.

"You ready, baby?" he murmured, pressing his lips to the swell of my breasts again.

"Not yet." My voice quivered. Thighs trembled.

"What do you need from me, Chloe? Tell me."

Confused by fireworks in my vision. The sensation of my body rocking beneath him, his dick rubbing against my insides in a way that took post-birth discomfort to out-of-this-world euphoria. I couldn't form words.

But my silence didn't stop him. He reached beneath us and pushed a finger into the sensitive, puckered opening between my cheeks.

"Fuck!" I called out.

I shot up, my mouth crashing against his as my orgasm ripped through my body. An explosion I couldn't contain.

He came too. Thick. Hard. His entire soul.

"Take all of it, Queen," he groaned into my neck. "God, I love you."

CHAPTER 16

"Shh, it's okay. Shh, Mummy's got you." I swayed like a shipwreck lost at sea, the baby's hiccupy cries warming against my collarbone. My arms ached from the effort, nerves fraying with each whimper.

Standing by the window, I let the sunlight warm one side of my back, the other still clinging to sleep's chill. A glint of brightness streaked through the half-drawn drapes.

"Shh. Come on. Jeez, he's being really cranky today."

Romeo, still flat on his back, let out a jaw-cracking yawn that startled Junior into a fresh squawk.

"I fuckin' know. I'm tired as shit. When do they stop cryin' all night?"

I shifted from a sway to a gentle bob, trying to reset his rhythm. "Hmm, I don't know. We still need to get a nanny—someone who can take over a couple of nights a week. How the hell am I going to run a nightclub and take care of a newborn?"

Romeo had already thrown on shorts and a T-shirt, but the sight of his dishevelled curls and hollowed eyes said everything. He moved toward the mirror, freshly spritzed cologne drifting in his wake—leathery, clean, and just strong enough to catch in my throat.

He opened his jewellery box with a crooked finger to his lips. Since the Maldives robbery, he'd replaced the stolen set with new custom pieces. That bloody dollar sign chain—still somehow a favourite—rested beside the crucifix. He peeled it out from the velvet lining. The diamonds caught in the sunlight, scattering light across his face. Then he pressed it against his chest.

He frowned.

And for a moment, something fluttered in my stomach. Maybe he was finally getting tired of the chains I'd never quite liked.

The sun pushed past a cloud. My arms tightened around the baby. I held my breath, waiting for him to make his announcement.

"You think I should get a new custom chain—of Romero's face?" he asked.

Oh.

The light dipped again. My breath slipped out in a disbelieving cackle as I took two long strides toward the nightstand, reaching for my coffee mug like a lifeline.

While I'd secretly hoped he was binning the chains altogether, his joker side had always been my favourite. "You really do make me laugh sometimes, Romeo."

But when I looked up, he wasn't smiling.

The light dulled further. The air shifted.

I dragged the curtains open to get a better look. "You're kidding, right? That was a joke?"

The crack of the jewellery box's lid snapped through the room like a mousetrap. "Forget it."

Shit. Didn't take much these days to offend him.

"I'm sorry, Romeo." I adjusted Junior's weight. "I genuinely thought you were joking."

"It's aight. I'm used to you bein' a bitch." He grabbed his phone without looking at me. "Anyway—get some clothes on. T will be here in a minute."

Huh?

"What do you mean, Tim will be here in a minute?" I clutched my coffee-stained robe tighter, the terry cloth scratchy against my skin. "Why is Tim coming into our bedroom at nine-thirty in the morning?"

I followed Romeo into the bathroom. Each step brought me deeper into the fog of his cologne.

He spat toothpaste foam into the sink, scrubbing his teeth so hard his shoulder blades flexed. The mirror fogged at the corners, his reflection a blur behind the steam.

"I needed a session with him but didn't wanna leave you and Romero again after the tattoo yesterday," he said, rinsing. "So I thought, shit, why not meet him in here?"

I sniggered, seizing the moment. "What, here? In the bathroom?"

Wiping his mouth with a towel, he stalked back into the bedroom. I trailed behind him.

"Good job I married you for that magic pussy and not your jokes." He tossed the towel toward the laundry basket. It hit the edge, tipping the lid like a house of cards. "You ain't that funny, Queen."

It was a beautiful spring day.

Curtains pulled back, sunlight spilled through the big bedroom window, casting the room in warmth. There was promise in the air, a good day ahead.

Tim had been sitting at the pull-out poker table with Romeo for the past half-hour.

I'd spent that time curled up in bed, watching the blossom-laced tree outside sway gently in the breeze.

From the driveway below, voices rose in a hum, crew chatter blending with the rhythmic clatter of tools. A faint beep sounded as one of the vans reversed out. Always working hard to please their boss.

Junior snuffled in his dreams. Sleeping soundly in his crib beside me, his eyelids fluttered. His little chest rose and fell, peaceful and steady.

I reached over to gently stroke his back with two fingers, then folded my hands beneath my chin. I prayed he'd stay that way until his next feed.

Romeo said something. Tim laughed.

Their sports chat had faded into the white noise of morning. If that was what passed for conversation between men, I was glad I wasn't part of it.

"You get what I'm sayin', T?"

"Mm-hm, sure." Tim shifted slightly, switching into the tone Romeo always seemed to respond to.

His notepad rested beside a half-drunk espresso. One elbow braced against the table, posture casual—presence commanding. The scent of roasted coffee mingled faintly with the breeze slipping through.

"First off, Romero, how'd you get on with your assignment?"

My gaze flicked to Romeo's leg. It jittered under the table.

Tim noticed too. "You haven't done it, have you?"

Romeo leaned back, stretching his arms above his head.

The chair groaned, shirt riding up just enough to reveal a sliver of skin at his waist.

A beat passed.

Tim's brow arched.

"Aight, yeah. I ain't done it. And what?"

I'd been told explicitly not to interrupt—but this was too good to miss. I raised my hand, tugging at the edge of the sheet draped across my lap.

Tim blinked away his irritation. His eyes softened when they met mine. "Everything alright, Mrs G?"

"Um... what was Romeo's assignment?"

His grin widened, like Romeo had just stepped out of the room. "Glad you asked. Since Italian is Romero's first language, he tends to revert to it mentally when writing longer sentences. So we're working on building full paragraphs entirely in English—for clarity and flow."

The sheet slipped from my chest. I hadn't realised I'd leaned so far into the conversation I was practically falling out of bed. One hand shot to the mattress to steady myself, the other pushing hair behind my ear.

"Can I see some of his work?" I asked, eyeing the folder thick with paper.

Romeo twisted in his chair. It rocked in protest—like it shared his mood.

His glare cut sharp.

"Keep your nose outta my business, Chloe. I mean it."

I ignored him and looked at Tim, hopeful.

"Sorry, Mrs G. Only if Romeo says it's okay—"

"Which it ain't!" he snapped back.

The swell of pride blooming in my chest wilted into a pit of annoyance.

"Well, if you can't show me, tell me." I crossed one ankle over the other, settling in for the scoop.

Tim stroked his chin, then smoothed out his page.

"Honestly? Once I realised the issue, everything flowed very smoothly."

I uncrossed my ankles and inched further down the bed, closer to the source but keeping just enough distance.

"The issue?"

Tim looked at Romeo.

Romeo looked at Tim.

Another beat passed.

Tim smiled, like he'd stumbled across a fond memory.

"When Romero and I first met, he wasn't using his dominant hand to write. Progress was a little slow. But once we ironed that out, it became obvious—Romero's incredibly smart."

"You heard him, Chloe." Romeo thumped his chest twice, gorilla-style. "Smart."

That's when it clicked.

Romeo, because of his father issues, had been forcing himself to use his right hand.

"So... Romeo told you about his childhood? The stuff with his dad?"

Tim opened his file like he was looking for something. A note? A shield?

Romeo's leg started shaking again.

Any minute now, he'd blow.

"Yes, Mrs G. I am aware—"

Romeo slammed his fist on the table.

Coffee sloshed over the edges, pooling beneath the espresso cup.

"Fuck you both. Don't talk about me like I ain't here!"

I recoiled under the covers. "Calm down, Romeo. If you wake the baby, that's on you. You always get sensitive when your dad's brought up."

Romeo stormed toward the crib like he meant to scoop up our son. But he didn't. He just stood there, staring.

Then, slowly, he adjusted the baby blanket. Just right.

"My father was a prick."

Tim took a sip of coffee.

"Why?" I asked.

"Why?" he huffed. "He used to strap my left arm behind my back. Force me to school like that. Humiliate me in front of everybody. So instead of doin' what he wanted, I did the fuckin' opposite."

He reached into the crib again. Adjusted the blanket a second time. "Made sure I did anythin' but fuckin' learn."

My jaw dropped. Eyes snapped to Tim.

But Tim was already smiling warmly.

"Thanks for sharing that with us, Romero. It's easy to understand why you never learned to read or write English when you moved to America. His Italian, though, Mrs G—it's perfect. His level of comprehension matches, if not exceeds, the age he left Italy."

Romeo swiped the tip of his nose, gangster-style.

So he was smarter than I ever gave him credit for.

Our eyes met. Ocean blue to bluish-grey.

"You're a smarty pants then, huh?" I giggled.

But Romeo wasn't laughing.

"Keep out of my fuckin' shit, Chloe. This is man shit."

I rolled my eyes. It was exhausting, always begging for information. Every day, something new surfaced. Some piece of him I still didn't know.

"For God's sake, Romeo." I turned slightly away. "Shut up."

The rage started in the pit of his stomach and surged upward like wildfire. Crawling up his neck. Fingers twitching. Eyes alive with fire.

His grip on reality snapped. Just like Tim's coffee mug, which he hurled across the room.

It exploded against the wall, shattering like a splash of paint. The echo shook the air. Vibrated the floorboards like the ripple of an earthquake.

Then silence.

Just his breath. And mine.

Tim didn't flinch. Didn't move a muscle.

I knew exactly what this was about. His father.

Tim calmly rolled up his sleeves, then stepped in.

He snapped his fingers once.

Romeo squared his shoulders and shot him a look.

"Sit down," Tim said.

Romeo obeyed.

My eyes darted between them.

The room, hot with rage, held its breath.

Romeo's chest rose and fell.

Then finally—

A long sigh.

Tim nodded.

The heat in the air began to cool.

"Now then, Romero," Tim said, turning the page—closing the chapter on that outburst without needing to say so. "Let's circle back to last week's hot topic: conflict resolution. Tell me how your week's played out so far."

A bead of coffee trickled down the wall. The conversation reset as if none of it had happened.

Romeo raised both hands in premature surrender.

"Look, T. I'll keep it real with you… I did kill someone on Monday." He took a sip of his coffee as if he'd just given an update on his taxes.

I shot upright in bed. My heart fluttered out of rhythm.

Did Tim know I'd killed someone, too?

Tim's lips thinned into a line. "I had a feeling you were involved in that trailer burning down."

Romeo squinted. "Wait… that was Monday?" He frowned. "I meant Tuesday."

"Hold on!" I interjected. "You killed someone yesterday?!"

I clutched my necklace, dragging the pendant hard along the chain. The more I tugged, the deeper it bit into my skin.

While I'd been worrying he was cheating, he'd been killing and stopping off at the tattoo parlour as if it were just any other day.

Romeo's jaw tensed. His fists curled at his sides.

"As I was sayin'…" He shot me a glare sharp enough to remind me I was supposed to be seen, not heard. "I killed a guy yesterday. But it was necessary."

He took another sip of coffee, mocking Tim as his drink soaked into the carpet. Then he slouched back into the chair.

Tim clicked the lid of his pen on and off, his way of battling between fight or flight.

I always knew Romeo spoke candidly to him. But unlike Nelly, our marriage counsellor, Tim was in on *all* the family secrets.

Hitching up his sleeves even higher, Tim sat taller just as the midday sun spilled through the open window, casting a spotlight over their table.

"Start from the top," he said, voice even. "We'll decide together if it was necessary."

Romeo shot up like his nerves were on fire. He paced the room, carving a path into the thick carpet as he replayed the scene in the theatre of his mind.

"I got a call while I was havin' my tattoo done—wait, T, check this shit out." He thrust out his arm, flexing like a kid proud of a gold star. "Sick, yeah?"

Tim nodded once, unreadable. His narrowed eyes tracked Romeo with something close to caution.

There was something different about my husband in front of him, excitable, almost childlike.

"Anyway, my boys told me about a late payer." Romeo stopped pacing, locking eyes with Tim. "So, I handled it."

A stiff breeze hissed through the window—just enough to chill my bones.

While I was still haunted by Jamie, Romeo had gone back out there and killed again.

Tim leaned back. His chair creaked, uneasy as he was.

"And by handling it… you mean you shot him?"

Romeo shrugged. "Well, I said, 'S'up, bitch,' first. Then I shot him."

He laughed at his own delivery—until he realised Tim wasn't laughing.

His smile dropped.

"You know what? You're gettin' just as bad as she is." He jerked his chin toward me. "Oh Romeo, stop fartin'. Oh Romeo, don't get a chain with your son's face on it…"

He threw his arms wide, full of exasperation. "I can't do shit in my own fuckin' crib!"

I knew I'd hurt him. My lack of support over the necklace, added to the father talk, was enough to tip him over. His feelings often ran deeper than he let on—much to his own detriment.

Tim placed both hands flat on the table, grounding himself. Ringless fingers. Not married. I wondered if he at least had someone.

"You know the drill, Romero. Let's take a step back and look at this from an outsider's perspective. "Tell me, how could you have resolved the issue without a firearm?"

Romeo ran a hand through his glossy curls, still refusing to look at me. I'd really upset him.

"I guess..." He dropped back into his seat, toying with a carton of cigarettes. "I could've given him a chance to pay before I shot him?"

Tim beamed. "Yes, Romero. Exactly that. Give people a chance."

Romeo's grip tightened, flattening the carton.

"I hear you, T. But it ain't that easy." He slouched deeper into the chair, rubbing his jaw. The scrape of stubble sounded like peeling Velcro. "You ain't walked the same streets as me. Bitches've tried to take my life too many times. I gotta get in there first, or I'm a walkin' dead man."

Tim shook his head. Calm. Unshaken.

"Nothing about your lifestyle has to be permanent. You could walk away from all this tomorrow. You, your wife, your son. You can leave it behind if you choose a different path."

Romeo sprang up again, launching into another round of pacing.

He stormed to the bedside table and yanked open the drawer. A fresh pack of cigarettes appeared. The cellophane caught the light like a gift, begging to be unwrapped.

I folded my arms and glanced at the crib.

"You're not smoking in here, Romeo."

"Chloe, get off my dick, okay?" he snapped, peeling back the foil. "I'm not gonna smoke it. I just wanna hold it."

I rolled my eyes and took a deep, cleansing breath. All this... because he was too sensitive.

He clamped the cigarette between his teeth and started pacing again, getting his ten thousand steps in for the day.

Tim remained a steady influence, watching him closely.

"Count backwards from ten, Romero," he said calmly. He raised his hands with the inhale, dropped them with the exhale—a calm demonstration for the storm pacing the floor.

Eventually, Romeo stopped at the foot of the bed, shoulders bunched high.

He took a moment to think about his words and then released a long breath. Fingers unfurled.

"Sorry, Queen. These sessions get me tense when I gotta start openin' up my feelin's."

Tim interjected, pointing his pen toward Romeo.

"That reminds me, Romero. How are you getting on with the lower dose of the medication?"

Romeo's eyes widened. Chest puffed. Classic defence mode.

"Err…" he hesitated, folding his arms. "I ain't taken the meds since the Maldives."

Another breeze caught the curtains, brushing cold fingers through my hair.

Well, that explained just about everything…

Tim rubbed his eyes, already bracing for the fallout.

After a beat, he sighed and lifted his gaze. "Can I ask why?"

Romeo removed the cigarette, holding it between two fingers—rolling it, fidgeting.

"When I jerked off, my piece kept goin' soft before I finished." He adjusted his crotch. "I wasn't sure if it was the smokin' patches or the meds, so I threw 'em both out."

My mouth dropped open. Even the baby's snuffles quieted.

I raised a hand to the room. "Can I just clarify here, Tim, that I had no idea he was off the meds? I knew he was acting up more than usual!"

The memory of Romeo's hand around my throat in the back of the SUV surged forward. Throwing coffee mugs and liquor glasses across the room like a sport.

Romeo's jaw clenched. "What are you on about, woman? I told you I threw 'em out!"

"No. You said you threw the patches out. You never said meds too!"

Tim stood, steadying himself against the tabletop. The weight of this session alone could've snapped the legs in two.

"Alright, everyone, let's take it down a gear."

He turned to Romeo, dragging a hand across his forehead, massaging the entire surface like he could squeeze the pressure out through his scalp.

"I'll order you some more of the mood stabiliser. We'll go back up to the higher dose while we fix this mess."

Then, to me, he offered an apologetic smile. "Mrs Giannetti, I'm sorry I've only just found out. If I'd known, I would've stepped in sooner."

Romeo flared. "There you go again like I ain't here. This is my crib y'all are standin' in."

Neither Tim nor I responded.

We'd both learned the same thing. Ignoring him when he was like this was easier.

Romeo switched tactic. He slammed his fist down on the table, inches from Tim's face.

The crash made the one remaining mug jump.

"Come on then, T. Smart ass. You tell me why my dick stopped workin'!"

Tim pursed his lips, unshaken.

He glanced down at Romeo's white-knuckled fist, then slowly lifted his eyes.

He held the stare.

"There are a number of reasons, Romero. Regularly killing people won't help your libido. I can tell you that for certain."

Romeo sneered, straightening to full height, looming over Tim like a bad dream.

"I don't give a fuck about killin' people. This is what I do. Why, after all these years, would that suddenly stop my dick workin'?"

Tim checked his watch.

The finality of the gesture sucked the heat from the room.

"I've overstayed our time slot. We'll pick this up at the next session." He gathered his folder, calm as ever. "The medication will be here this afternoon. Take one as soon as you can."

He paused, then opened his arms, expression pensive. Almost fatherly. "Come here then."

Without hesitation, Romeo stepped forward—and walked straight into a real embrace. Not the back-slapping contests he shared with his brother. This was different.

This was love. Admiration.

His eyes slipped closed, shoulders dropping just enough to let it show. I couldn't remember the last time I saw him let go like that. If ever.

I should've felt relieved. But watching Romeo fold into another man's arms made something shift inside me.

A reminder that he was still just a boy, bruised and angry, pretending as hard as he could that he was invincible.

"Take care, big guy. I'll see myself out," Tim said, patting Romeo's shoulder.

Romeo offered a curt nod. "Laters, man."

The bottom of the door whispered against the carpet fibres, then clicked shut.

I narrowed my eyes, waiting for Romeo to meet my gaze.

"What?" he asked, like the last hour hadn't just happened.

"I can't believe you stopped your meds."

He shrugged. Kicked the carpet like he was finally evaluating his choices, toes scuffing a path into the fibres.

When he looked at me again, I gave him a small smile.

"You and Tim are real close these days, huh?"

My fingers curled around the crib rail, responding to the microscopic flicker of jealousy crawling up my throat.

His eyes locked on the cigarette flattened between his fingers—channelling all that pent-up rage into paper and tobacco.

I sighed. "You're a real ass-hat sometimes."

He nodded, no argument. "We both are, Queen."

Right on cue, Junior stirred in his bassinet.

A second later, he let out a blood-curdling scream that sliced straight through my spine.

"Holy crap, this baby is really on something today." I scooped him up, the heat of his wriggling body pressing into mine, his head damp with sleep.

One hand patted his bottom as I rocked gently, his familiar scent —half-milk, half-dream—softening the tightness in my chest. "Don't forget, we've got his shots tomorrow morning."

Peace returned the second my nipple entered his mouth. Like father, like son. He let out soft, greedy whimpers as he latched and fed.

Romeo lit a fresh smoke, the hot snap of the lighter flaring between us.

He placed the cigarette between his lips. "I already remembered. Crew prepped." He tapped his temple. "Listen, I gotta go for this smoke. I'll be ten minutes."

He turned to leave.

"Wait!" I snapped, louder than I meant to, especially with Junior still in the room.

Romeo spun around, quick as a flash. "...Yeah?"

He plucked the cigarette from his mouth, shoulders lifting.

"I've got a final meeting with Lucy at the club this afternoon—before we open tomorrow night. You coming?"

He slouched on the spot, dragging a long breath through his nose before releasing it slow.

"What?" I asked, trying to read the exhale.

"You said 'wait' like you wanted some." He grabbed his crotch, tugging like it needed more attention than it already got. "Of course I'm fuckin' comin'. Why?"

I brought Junior's soft, dark hair to my lips. His smell, his little warm body, never failed to soothe my nerves. My eyes burned tight from lack of sleep.

"It's the girls... I've barely spoken to them since they found out about you-know-what. They're doing rehearsals. I just need some back-up."

He took a few strides over, standing beside me. The rough pad of his finger tingled my skin as he tilted my chin.

"You don't need me," he said softly, eyes sparkling. "But I'll be there."

He winked, then walked away, trailing the scent of smoke and aftershave.

I sighed, listening to the distant thud of bass from a car rolling up the driveway. Voices rose. Doors slammed. Whores on their way to work. Valet polishing up the vehicles.

Life never paused—not even when I needed it to.

"God, I hope he's right, Romero. I really hope he's right."

◆ ◆ ◆

As Romeo drove us to the club, I watched him, really watched him. Rays of light flickered off the platinum of his jewellery. His wedding band glittered.

Even now, in a plain designer tee and sweatpants, nothing about my husband was unattractive. The way his curls fell over his brow. The quiet flex of his hand on the wheel. The new tattoo wrapping around his forearm—it all suited him too damn well.

"You know what, Romeo?" I said, eyes tracing the ink. "I really love your new tattoo."

He grinned, glancing down at it while keeping one eye on the road.

"I'm glad you like it, Queen. It's my declaration to you."

His thumb tapped the steering wheel, a satisfied smirk curling onto his lips as if I'd just confirmed he'd made the right call.

I folded my arms in mock indignation.

"Did you see the photo of you online yet? Coming out of the tattoo parlour? The press got to see it before I did. Never mind the fact it overshadowed the club's entire advertising campaign."

He groaned under his breath. "That's one thing I'm fuckin' sick of—there's always a camera in my face."

He wasn't the only one tired of it.

We used the exposure when we could, but he'd always attract more attention than me.

"The club's post on Instagram got five hundred thousand likes. Your bloody tattoo got four million."

"I'm sorry about that, Queen. Bad timin' on my part."

"It's not just that though. The fact you killed someone, too…" I exhaled slowly, chewing my lip. "I worry one day you'll shoot a guy and the paparazzi will catch it on camera. I mean—did anyone see you kill him before you popped in to get inked?"

He sneered at a thought he didn't share.

"What's funny?" I narrowed my eyes.

"I reckon I've been papped emptyin' a clip maybe ten, fifteen times since I started my business."

The sky outside darkened. The sun was swallowed by a thick, brooding cloud. A weight settled over the car, dense and inescapable.

My jaw dropped. "No! Are you serious?"

He shrugged, casual as ever. "Must've spent close to a mil over the years keepin' my ass outta jail."

"A million dollars!?" I yelped like I'd been bitten, then shot a look over my shoulder at the car seat.

We both sat quietly, holding our breath… waiting for the tiny human in the back to kick off in a way only his father could compete with.

But thankfully, he didn't stir.

"Expensive lifestyle we're livin'," Romeo muttered. "Good job that I'm rich as fuck."

I'd spent hours mulling over what to wear for this moment—the moment I stood inside my brand new club, ready to give instructions to a group of women who didn't even want to be here.

In the end, the effort hadn't been worth it. I'd settled on the same style of dress I always wore these days.

Pants, given the state of my waistline, were still a no-go. The only saving grace was that my ankles had finally deflated enough to squeeze back into my heels.

Lucy, in her sharpest pantsuit, met me by the same platform we'd last sat on together.

A fresh blast from the newly installed A/C whispered through the room, filled with essential oils, lavender and something citrusy, meant to keep a harmonious balance between sweat-slicked skin and surface-level luxury.

The poles, now installed, glinted beneath the soft, deliberate lighting—ready and waiting for the show to begin.

Clipboard clutched tight to her chest, Lucy held it like a shield. The trust between us had gone. But she knew, as well as I did, I couldn't let her go. Not when I felt like I was drowning.

She smiled at me. Cautious. Guarded.

We hadn't spoken about her involvement in my husband's plot against me, but we didn't need to. It was water under a very rickety old bridge.

"Aight, Queen. Imma take Junior on his first security sweep," Romeo said, hot on my heels, pushing the pram behind me.

I'd almost forgotten he was there until I turned, and his smile pulled at my heartstrings.

He never did get those eighteen-inch rims he wanted for it. But it didn't seem to concern him now. The sight of him being a father made me want to do it all over again.

I glanced at Lucy, who was already smiling at the same view I had.

"Thought you guys were getting a nanny?" she murmured, flipping back to the itinerary.

My smile faltered. "Trust me. I'm regretting it too. We've just been so busy with… a number of things."

I nodded toward Romeo. "This one's insistent he'll keep the baby entertained tomorrow night. I guess we'll see."

He huffed. "There ain't no see about it. I'll show all y'all."

We both watched as he leaned slightly over the handlebar, whispering something under his breath to his son while he wiped spit-up gently from the corner of Junior's mouth. His finger moved with exaggerated care, as if the baby were more precious than air.

"What?" Romeo asked, a soft blush rising in his cheeks as he rolled the pram back and forth.

"Nothing." I smirked. "Carry on."

He rummaged in the change bag, no doubt searching for that bloody toy gun I kept hiding. Somehow, he always found new ways to keep it on the baby. The latest? Tucked right underneath Junior's bib.

A soft thud of footfall followed me as I took a few strides away from the chaos. I sighed, closing my eyes as a wash of light poured through the stained-glass window—Romeo's tribute to me.

The coloured glass hummed warmth against my skin, scattering fractured beams across the polished floor. It bathed half my face in a rainbow of colour. The other half in shadow.

"Lucy told me you organised this." I nudged my chin towards the mural of us.

But Romeo was distracted.

I caught him red-handed, shoving the little plastic gun down the side of the pushchair.

I'd deal with that later.

He tucked both hands into his pockets, chuckling like I'd tickled him. He knew I was on to his game.

"What did I organise? Oh, the window?"

Lucy joined us, her cologne clashing with Romeo's like a test I hadn't studied for. I didn't know whose scent I wanted to inhale more. "Beautiful, isn't it?" she said in awe all over again.

"I mean, I ain't sayin' it's what I ordered. Your big milky titties right in the centre was, accordin' to Lucy, 'Not appropriate' or whatever."

Lucy peeled her gaze from her notes. "Hmm. Neither was your other suggestion."

He thought back to the moment.

"There's somethin' wrong when a man can't order a glass window of him bendin' over his wife. Too many fuckin' rules about what's right and wrong these days."

Thank God for Lucy. Romeo's input would've had the place shut down on opening night.

"Thanks for your contribution, Romeo." I gave him a little push. "You and your son can go and play now."

He didn't need telling twice. A quick peck on the lips, smoky breath and warm skin, then he was off.

The wheels squeaked softly over the hardwood, the pram swaying as they disappeared down the corridor. A father and son duo. Off to conquer the world—one filled diaper at a time.

Lucy's eyes followed them briefly, the clipboard momentarily forgotten against her chest.

She exhaled beside me, steadying herself like she hadn't even realised she'd been holding her breath.

I watched her watching him. For once, I didn't feel threatened, just grateful.

I brushed my fingers over the stained glass, the cool surface ridged and smooth beneath my touch.

"This club…" I whispered. "It means everything to me."

I opened my eyes, finding hers. "We have to get this right."

"Alright, ladies, listen up." I walked the line of the last four standing. The only working girls still entitled to live at the mansion.

Standing in the centre of the room, spotlights beamed down on them, dust catching the light like glitter suspended in tension.

"You've heard some things." I stopped.

The snap of my heel on the wooden floor gave me the edge I'd been looking for.

"Yes, they're true. Doesn't change anything between us. Got it?"

Their slow blinks came one after the other, like a chain reaction of indifference.

Junior fussing just beyond the fire door got more of a reaction than the speech I'd spent all morning preparing.

Figures.

Yes, they were scared of me. They had every right to be. But there wasn't a fibre of my being that would let this club flop.

I tutted, already feeling my patience burn at the edges.

"Just get on the fucking stage and show me what you've practised."

"What the hell was that!?" I yelled above the music to the girl I'd actually had reasonably high hopes for.

Lala froze the second Lucy muted the track.

She folded her arms over her bare stomach, eyes darting for an escape route.

"Turn that bloody wind machine off," I snapped, already marching over to do it myself.

The room fell into a tense hush, punctuated only by the knocking sounds of the club's sign being installed out front.

"What was that, Lala?"

She scrambled to scoop up her clothes, clutching them to her chest like a makeshift defence.

"I'm just a working girl, Chloe. I've never done this before."

Lucy made a quick note beside Lala's name—adding a sharp, final cross.

My heart sank.

"We've got the rest of today to get this right. I've got four of you and only one who's done this before. Surely it's not that hard to swing around a fucking pole!"

Lala stammered something, but I didn't care to hear it.

"Next!" I hollered, flicking the wind machine back on as I collapsed into my seat, heels digging into the floor to anchor my rage.

The music burst to life again with 'Sexyback' by Justin Timberlake just as Tonya stepped onto the stage.

The overhead lights worked overtime, casting shifting shadows across the floor as the bassline dropped—vibrating up through the soles of my heels.

She moved in rhythm, her hair whipping around her face. She slut-dropped on the beat, but for lack of a better phrase, it didn't get me... hard.

"I don't think clients will go for her," Lucy muttered in my ear.

I leaned in, barely able to hear her over the sound.

The pole squeaked as Tonya's thighs slapped around the steel, her body contorting in ways I didn't know were possible.

Her bra strap slipped down her arm, teasing in all the right ways—yet the tingle between my legs was missing.

"This is a mess. An absolute mess," I said between beats. "We've only got Diamond Daisy secured, who actually knows what she's doing. And that's it."

The track ended with a crash of cymbals.

A climax without fireworks.

Tonya, crooked nose and all, scooped up her bra and panties. Dressing in front of us like this was just another day at the office.

"What am I supposed to say to that?" I murmured out of the side of my mouth to Lucy.

She clicked the top of her pen, marking another sharp little cross beside her name.

"Thanks, Tonya," Lucy called, standing. "But I think we've already filled the slots. We'll keep you as back-up."

In a strange twist of fate, Lucy and I sat on the same stage, legs slung over the same edge as we had the last time we saw each other. The same rhythm we'd adopted before was back in force—each foot kicking out in lazy synchrony.

I'd mistaken it then for an unspoken understanding, but now I wasn't so sure.

"I guess first we should address the elephant in the room," I said, eyes fixed on the colourful refractions of light bleeding through the patterned window.

She sighed, leaning back on her hands. "I'm glad you brought it up. I'm sorry about that. I really am."

Leaning slightly forward, I peered over my shoulder at her. "You are?"

"Of course. Romero asked me to help him with a situation, but he tends to leave out the details."

I leaned back to meet her. "He does?"

She nodded. "Told me to do whatever you asked. Said he wanted to test his security. It wasn't until after I crashed my own damn car that I found out they'd planned to snatch and grab you."

Hmm. The supermarket sweep again...

A hammer knocked just beyond the room, letting us both know the contractors weren't far from finishing their final task. Door signs.

The room felt a little warmer now that the chill between us had been addressed.

"So you didn't know?" I asked, shifting my weight a little closer to her. The wooden frame, not yet settled, creaked beneath my fingers.

She laughed softly, her legs swinging with a little more energy. "No. I didn't. I'm just sorry I had any part in it."

I relaxed fully, elbows buckling as I lay flat on my back, staring up at the ceiling. It was hard beneath my spine—but grounding, somehow. The lights above blurred into one long beam, their heat prickling across my skin.

"I've realised something," I said, mostly to myself.

Lucy lay back beside me. Her jewellery scraped softly against the stage as she settled, her finger skimming mine.

"Yeah?"

When I turned my head, I hadn't expected her to be so close.

"A five-finger glove won't fit four fingers."

She peeled her gaze off the ceiling, glancing at me as she lifted her hand in front of her face to make sense of it.

"Huh?"

She giggled when I smirked.

"Hookers and dancers aren't the same thing," I murmured. "I fucked up, thinking my girls could just do this without even trying."

I paused. Then said what I hadn't been sure I would. "Help me out, Lucy. Let me hire you as the club's manager?"

She blew out a breath through puffed cheeks. Mint gum. That man's cologne. It was hard not to be drawn to her.

"I'm an interior designer, Chloe. I don't have experience—"

I huffed. "You've got more bloody experience than me. At least short-term. Please?"

Lucy sat up suddenly, fire lighting behind her eyes. "I have an idea," she said, already pulling out her phone. "Let me make a call."

While Lucy stalked the length of the room, heels clicking in a rhythmic beat, phone pressed to her ear, Romeo sauntered in—hair a full-blown mess, curls wild with static and wind.

"You've been playing hard," I said with a giggle, plucking a leafed twig from his hair. He smelled outdoorsy, with hints of salt and sun-warmed leather.

"Me and the boy been busy," he said with pride. "Showin' him everythin' he owns."

I reached for his chain, tugging the heavy dollar-sign pendant from beneath his shirt and setting it square at the centre of his chest.

"I don't know how your neck survives this thing." I teased, letting the cold weight of platinum tingle the tips of my fingers. "So, you've been showing him his inheritance by rolling through the bushes?"

"Pfft. You ever tried off-roadin' with a push chair?" He frowned, dragging a hand down his face. "Ain't easy, I'll tell you that."

The fire door swung open, dragging a rush of brilliant daylight across the polished floor. A contractor stepped in, tipping his yellow hard hat.

"Just checking the quick release, sir. Won't be a moment."

Romeo nodded. "Already checked it, son." He adjusted his crotch with zero shame. "Need a hand with anythin' else? I got my work boots in the car ready."

His sweatpants sagged low on his hips, and his T-shirt clung in all the right places, just enough to hint at what lay beneath. A strong man, no doubt about it. But muscles wouldn't bring him wisdom.

The workman's eyes widened. "All done, sir. We're about to clock off." The door slammed shut behind him, stealing the flash of light with it.

Unfazed, Romeo's gaze swept the room again. Tongue flicking out, he rubbed his palms together.

"Anyway… where the sluts at?"

My calves ached faintly in my heels, but I wasn't about to sit down and give him the upper hand when he was scanning the space like he owned it. The man really thought he was slick enough to sneak a peek at a naked whore mid-squat?

"Don't make it so obvious, Romeo." I shoved him, letting go of his chain.

"Honestly? It's a disaster. The girls..." I trailed off as I sank onto the edge of the stage, the fresh wood sighing beneath my weight. "They're just awful."

He leaned beside me, foot propped. "That what Lucy's on the phone for?" He nodded toward our designer, who'd unbuttoned her jacket, face a little flushed.

"She said she knew somebody," I shrugged.

"While you're figurin' that out..." He eased upright, brushing the back of his knuckles down my arm. "You want anythin' from McDonald's? Gonna take him for a drive out—guaranteed he'll sleep an hour."

Lucy's ears pricked. Hand pressing over the speaker, she smiled. "Usual for me, Romero." Then she turned, continuing her call in a hush as she strolled toward the stained-glass window.

Romeo gave her a nod of approval.

Now, I'd be lying if I said him knowing her order right off the bat hadn't sent my demon into overdrive.

I smiled sweetly, rage poking its ugly head out of the box.

"I'll have my usual too, please." I plucked an invisible piece of lint from the sleeve of my dress, casual as ever.

The A/C unit above us clicked on with a hum, already sensing its role in cooling the heat rising in the room.

His hand tightened around the pram's handle.

"The usual?" he asked.

I nodded, chin lifted in expectation. "Yes. The usual. Is that a problem?"

He took a stride away from me, only to double back. "Hold on here. You don't got a usual. Every fuckin' time we go, I gotta pick for you."

I eyed him, careful not to let Lucy hear what I already knew. He just didn't love me enough to know what I fancied in the moment.

"Just get me a fucking cheeseburger," I hissed, then softened instantly as I leaned into the pram to kiss my son's head. Baby powder and warm milk. He smelled like heaven. "He's due a feed at four, so be back by then."

Tommy waited at the door, change bag slung over his shoulder—two men stepping into daddy daycare like it was the most natural thing in the world. Amazing, really, what a newborn could do to a family dynamic.

The boys left, the low hum of conversation fading as the door clicked shut behind them, just loud enough to drown out the construction workers packing up their final tools outside. Engines of commercial vans starting. Headlights flooding through the window.

Lucy ended her call.

"Okay," she said, clicking off her phone screen as she trotted toward me, energy renewed. "I know a chick who knows a chick. I've got three experienced dancers coming in the next forty minutes—guaranteed to blow our socks off."

I let out a long, quiet breath. "You're a lifesaver."

◆ ◆ ◆

"Numero uno," Lucy said with a playful chuckle, hovering near the wind machine again. "This is Tara Pom Poms. Dancing three years. Willing to go all the way if the client pays enough."

I leaned over, squinting at Lucy's notes. "Okay, that works. I've got two clients booked in for VIP treatment in the private booths."

"On opening night?" Lucy looked up from her notes. "That's brave."

Worry prickled under my skin, like I'd broken some unspoken rule I wasn't aware of. Suddenly, I was second-guessing every decision that had led me here.

I reached for my necklace. "It is?"

Lucy sensed the shift. Her voice softened. "Don't worry. It'll all work out."

But when someone tells you not to worry, of course you do—and more.

I chewed the inside of my cheek at the thought of having to refund the thirty grand each client had dropped for that special treatment.

"You ready?" Lucy asked.

I straightened in my seat. Full reset.

Tara's legs appeared first as she sauntered up the stage steps, landing in front of me in towering black stilettos. Tanned, skin glistening like glitter, there wasn't much left for her to take off—she'd shown up in just a bra and thong, half-hidden beneath an overcoat she was already shrugging off.

She chewed her gum with her mouth open, jaw working like she'd long since retired from giving a single fuck.

"What would you like?" she asked, popping a bubble. "I can audition like it's private room time, or stage. Money shot now, or at the end?"

A cloud of over-sweet body spray rained over me like April showers, cheap vanilla tickling the back of my nose like a sneeze I couldn't quite catch.

"Private room," I said, side-eyeing Lucy, who was very clearly judging me.

Tara took the thin strip of her thong between two fingers and gave it a deliberate snap, shimmying it in time with the sway of her hips. Each movement was fluid, controlled—like her body spoke more languages than her mouth could.

Lucy clicked on the fan.

A gust of wind caught Tara's hair, tossing it off her face like she'd just stepped into a photoshoot.

I sat back, intrigued by the way her cheeks shifted when she bent to touch her toes in time with the beat. Full confidence. Full control.

My fingers fidgeted in my lap.

I thought I knew how this all worked… until I met someone who actually had a clue.

Lucy hovered by the door. "Thanks, Kotton Kandy. See you tomorrow night. 9:00 PM sharp."

She threw me an enthusiastic thumbs-up. Both of us relieved we now had at least three solid dancers lined up for opening night.

Diamond Daisy. Tara Pom Poms. Kotton Kandy.

"Alrighty, third and final auditionee—Racey Casey. Come on in," Lucy called, stepping aside with a theatrical flourish, offering a light round of applause to keep the energy in the room alive.

I turned in my seat, one arm slung over the backrest, eyelids heavy and exhausted by it all.

A silhouette appeared in the doorway.

And that's when my jaw dropped to my knees.

Taller frame. Broader shoulders. Heavier footsteps.

"That's a man!?" I croaked, throat suddenly dry.

His bulge was the opener of his act, housed in a gold-coloured posing pouch that left absolutely nothing to the imagination. Not a thing. Not even the soft ridge of the crown of his circumcised helmet.

First thing he did was kick off a pair of black, suede-topped sliders, bare, pedicured feet slapping the floor. Then he strolled toward me like he already owned the damn show—a black towel draped over his shoulders like some kind of prop.

"Hi," he said casually, hopping up onto the stage in one smooth motion with no need for the stairs, like a cat leaping onto a windowsill.

His pecs bounced. Once. Unapologetically.

I blinked. Twice.

Well… okay then.

I cleared my throat, giving Lucy a sidelong glance.

"Um… I wasn't expecting a man." I chewing on my lip, thinking of all the other things I could be saying right now instead of the obvious.

He dropped to the ground from a stand—straight into press-ups. Two-handed at first… then one.

His muscles bulged, veiny and taut, as he got to work on his show.

Lucy pressed play.

The bass hit.

That's when he really got down to business, singing along low and husky, hips rolling in time with the beat as he dragged the towel back and forth across the back of his neck. His tongue curled around the lyrics to Pony by Ginuwine.

My thighs snapped shut the moment his cock swelled to a semi—thick and proud beneath that paper-thin gold pouch.

Jesus Christ.

Beads of sweat gathered at his hairline, catching in those thick curls that annoyingly reminded me of Romeo's. Only warmer. More golden. He had me hooked. If I'd had a dollar bill, it wouldn't have stayed in my hand.

He beckoned to Lucy, who tossed him a small bottle of baby oil from our box of props and supplies.

Pouring from a height, it dribbled down his torso in long, dewy streaks, tracing the ridges of his abs before pooling at the waistband—right above a smattering of pale-blonde pubic hair.

His hips circled with shameless ease. The towel twirled in one hand like a lasso.

My mouth went dry. Not from nerves, but from the unbearable urge to swallow. Heat gathered at my core, radiating between my legs. My thighs parting when he hopped off the stage, hands on my knees.

He looked me in the eye. Dark brown to blue-ish grey.

"Hey beautiful," he said in a husky, masculine drawl.

Next minute, the towel was round my neck, pulling my head towards his crotch.

Baby oil. Ocean-fresh cologne.

My lips parted. My breath hitched.

That's when I heard it.

A sharp crack, the unmistakable sound of knuckles meeting flesh.

Casey staggered, slipping on his own oiled feet as Romeo hit him square in the jaw a second time.

"Oh my God. Stop it!" I shouted, lunging forward.

No longer pregnant and painfully unafraid, I forced myself between them—palms pressed to each of their puffed chests.

Casey's nose gushed bright red, blood splattering across his torso like war paint while the music pounded on, oblivious.

"Cut it!" I barked, slicing the air toward Lucy. The bass collapsed into silence. Only our collective breathing remained—thick, ragged, vibrating with the intensity of what had just unfolded.

Casey wiped the tip of his nose, checking his fingers for fresh blood.

Romeo stood frozen. Black curls damp. Chest heaving. The McDonald's bag still clenched in his fist.

Then, with slow, deliberate intent, he let it fall. Fries spilled across the floor, landing in a pile, looking as sorry as I felt.

"Get the fuck out. All of y'all!" he roared, voice raw, practically rabid. The echo hit every wall twice, slamming back at us like thunder.

I pushed back my chair, ready to follow.

Tommy caught my eye—still rocking the pram with one hand. He shook his head once. Disappointed, I'd let it go this far.

"Sit the fuck down!" Romeo snapped, dragging the chair across the wood floor with a sharp scratch before tugging me toward it by the arm. His grip was firm, not violent. Eyes locked on mine. And in that moment, the room fell away. The heat from his fingers sank into my skin. Something in his voice, edged with betrayal, froze me to the core.

My arse hit the chair with a thump.

Romeo glared at Lucy and the male stripper. They didn't hesitate. Bare feet slapped the floor alongside the click of rushed heels—marking the getaway of their lives. No one dared to look back.

He turned to me, chest rising and falling like he'd just sprinted through hell to find me at the finish line.

"While I'm supportin' your ass, lookin' after our son, feedin' you, this is what you're doin'?" His arms flailed, voice raw. "Another fuckin' minute and his dick would've been down your whore-ass throat!"

My hand went to my neck, trying to cool the flush that climbed with shame. Speechless. Banged to rights. I had no idea what to say.

"Romeo," I whispered. "I swear to you that wasn't planned. Not even close."

He flicked a glance toward the exit. "The boy still asleep?" he asked Tommy.

Tommy peered into the pram.

"Yeah, Boss," he said softly, never stopping the back-and-forth motion.

Romeo's voice dropped—low, deadly calm. "Give me fifteen minutes. This slut needs teachin' somethin'."

Then came the soft twist of the latch. The door snapped shut behind Tommy and my son.

We were alone.

And I had no idea why.

Romeo scrolled on his phone, thumb tapping in slow strokes, until the bassline kicked in. 'Pony' by Ginuwine. The same track from earlier.

He dropped the phone onto the table, letting it play out. The beat throbbed low, deep, like a pulse between my thighs.

"Most new moms keep their swollen-ass pussy at home," he muttered, stepping forward. "Not my woman."

In one fluid motion, he peeled off his T-shirt, muscles flexing and tattoos shifting like waves beneath the overhead lights. His skin glistened—slick with heat and fury. The air between us felt charged. Flammable.

"Aight then. Let me show you somethin'."

He began his act.

If the male dancer had hopped on stage like a cat, Romeo was a panther. Silent. Precise. Every inch of him was ready to lethally pounce.

With calculated control, he knelt on the stage and placed his gun at his feet. The metal clunked against the wood, making its point clear.

Then, without warning, he dropped into push-ups. Two-handed at first... then one. His free hand rested at the base of his spine. Black coils of glossy hair flopped over his brow as his body moved with effortless strength—veins pronounced, shoulders squared. Ocean-blue eyes locked on mine. The tattoo on his neck flexed and pulsed, rising and falling in rhythm with the beat of his heart.

Ten reps turned into fifteen. Each one was smoother than the last. Slower. More controlled. Deadly sexy.

The heavy swing of his chain hit the floor in time, metal clinking and dragging with each rise and fall. Every breath he took seemed to steam the air between us.

Already, he was outshining the act from minutes ago. Skin glistening with sweat, his entire frame radiated raw masculinity and power.

I held my breath. The room did too.

The baby oil bottle left behind on stage toppled with a soft clatter. He rose to his feet, scooped it up, and poured a heavy stream down his chest.

His cheeks flushed as he watched me watching him. Each breath came shallow. The oil chased across his abs, catching the light as it pooled at the waistband of his sweatpants. It glided over muscle, turning him into something unreal.

No time wasted. He stripped them off and tossed them toward me.

Now, just in his underwear, he moved with effortless confidence. Each roll of his hips echoed the dancer before him—but with far more control. Far more command.

Then he landed two-footed off the stage, right in front of me. His hands settled on my knees. My thighs twitched as he spread them wide. My breath stuttered. My pulse skipped. The song played for a third time.

"Hey, beautiful," he said, voice low.

Ocean blue locked onto bluish grey.

I gulped. Emotion surged—embarrassment, lust, regret. A guilt-ridden throb tightened in my core. He'd watched more of the show than I realised. Now he was playing it out step by step, like an instruction manual. Only this time, the page was turned on me.

He rolled his hips closer, so close I could feel the heat of him press against my clit. I reached out, dragging my fingers across his slick skin. Everything beneath was muscle, tension, heat. His cock was already hard. Bigger. Thicker. Longer than his rival's.

With shaking hands, I hooked my thumbs into the waistband of his underwear and freed him.

His abs flexed as the cool air met the heat of his dick. The fabric pooled at his feet. He kicked it aside. The leathered skin of his balls tightened. His cock twitched—ready.

I took hold of him. My fingers curled around the weight of his length, squeezing just enough to make him hiss.

His hand found the back of my neck, drawing me in. No words needed. He needed to know, really know, that the only dick that belonged in my mouth was his.

I kissed the tip, soft, slow, letting my tongue flick and circle before drawing it into my mouth. Licking. Sucking. Flicking again.

His cock jumped, eager.

Then I took him in—deep. All the way to the back of my throat. The taste of salt and skin hit me all at once.

"Spit on it," he groaned, rolling his hips with control he barely held.

I obeyed. A slick string of spit slid down the length of him. I spread it with my tongue, coating every inch, then swallowed him again—greedy, determined, erasing everything but him.

"Imma fuck your mouth, you slut." His voice was rough. A little fractured.

He thrust deeper, pushing past my limits without apology. His cock hit the back of my throat again and again.

Tears pricked the corners of my eyes. My nails dug into his thighs. And still I let him, because this was how he healed. How we reminded each other we were still tethered to one another. Until death do us part.

"That's it, baby. Imma come so fuckin' hard for you... fuck—do the balls, suck 'em..."

His voice cracked with restraint. His thighs trembled beneath my hands, slick with oil, every muscle in his body coiled tight. The heat, the scent, wrapped around me like fire.

The swell told me that his orgasm was building. Instinct telling me to get ready.

And then he came. A thick, salty stream of his come hit the back of my throat. I swallowed it in one gulp, eyes locked on his.

He stalled—body jerking, head thrown back in euphoria, lips parted around a groan that never made it past his teeth.

"Holy fuckin' shit..." he muttered, dragging a hand through his curls, breathless. "You suck my dick so good. Shit."

I wiped the corners of my mouth with a slow flick of my fingers, then handed him his underwear—watching him float back down to earth.

We both smiled.

The tension in the room, the suffocating swell of walls stretched by his rage, finally relaxed, releasing a long-held breath. Relief settled over everything.

"So, are we friends again?" I asked, biting my bottom lip, fluttering my lashes for effect.

He stepped into his boxers, then his sweats, still riding the aftershocks as he looked down at me.

"If you didn't make me come as hard as you do..." He smirked, tugging the waistband up with a snap. "You'd be kicked to the curb by now."

I kept smiling and raised my pinkie.

"I guess we're friends," he said, leaning down to hook his little finger with mine.

Then he kissed me—soft, unhurried, the kind of kiss that sealed everything.

Thankful that at least one problem had been settled, I was already crouched down, scooping up the cold fries scattered like skittles across my brand-new floor. The paper bag rustled beneath my fingertips, still faintly warm. Salt clung to my nails. I swiped my hands together, like a job well done.

Watching me, he nodded toward the door. "Have you seen the signage out front yet? Looks real good."

"Wait—you really like it?" I asked, hopeful. My lower lip caught between my teeth. This was what I'd been waiting for. The finishing touches.

He nodded once, eyes soft. "Come see."

With his hands covering my eyes, he guided me out into the street. The thick downtown air clung to my skin, hot, humid, and familiar enough to tell me exactly where we were.

"Aight, Imma count you down. Ready?" His warm fingers over my eyes heated my cheeks.

"Yes—hurry!" I squealed, suddenly impatient.

"Three," he whispered in my ear. "Two." He kissed my neck. "One."

He pulled his hands away.

A white background stretched clean across the building. At the centre, a silhouette of a woman—curvaceous, head tilted back, one arm raised, holding a single rose between delicate fingers. The petals, inked in red, almost bloomed off the surface. Below her, in elegant cursive, the name *Jasmin's* curled soft and graceful.

It wasn't just a name. It was my promise.

And for the first time in weeks, I felt like I'd finally done something right.

I whipped around to see his reaction. He was smiling too.

"I love it!" I beamed. "It's exactly what I wanted. Eek!" I bounced on the spot, too giddy to stay still.

He chuckled, pulling me into his arms.

"Come on," he murmured against my hair. "Let's go home."

"We'd barely been back at the mansion five minutes when the baby cried for another feed, just an hour after his last."

Sitting on the edge of the bed, I cradled him to my chest, letting him latch again. The tug against my nipple came with a new kind of desperation—like he was trying to drink more than just milk from me. He was taking my soul along with it.

My phone lit up, dancing in time with the ringtone on the nightstand.

"Get that call, would you?" I asked softly, keeping my voice low. "I've just got Romero to stop crying. Bet it's Lucy—with the confirmed line-up of dancers for tomorrow night."

Like a dutiful husband, Romeo plodded over and scooped up my phone in his spade-like hand.

"Chloe Giannetti's phone," he said, all authority. "I'm her husband… Yeah?"

He took a step away from me, then another toward the window.

Outside, birds chirped an evening chorus amongst friends. The day was already almost done.

"Aight," he said. "Thanks for lettin' us know."

His tensed facial features sent a heavy ball of anxiety straight to the pit of my stomach.

"Who was that?" I clutched the baby closer.

Birdsong faded into the background—replaced by a silence thick enough to choke on.

He exhaled, eyes fixed on the floor. "That was the hospital. Bob passed away in the early hours of this mornin'. I'm sorry, baby."

He shuffled over and pulled me and Junior into an embrace, kissing the top of my head as he breathed in the scent of my hair. His hand pressed to the back of my head like a lid on a boiling pot—holding me together when I was ready to burst.

Numbness closed in, fogging my thoughts. I wasn't even sure how I was supposed to feel as I rested against his firm chest, its steady rise and fall so at odds with the shatter of my broken pieces.

"I'll look after you, Queen," he murmured. He kissed me again. "Don't you worry about a thing."

That was it.

His encouragement was my undoing—and suddenly, every single negative emotion I'd ever buried came hurtling toward me at a hundred miles an hour.

Tears flowed in uncontrollable, cascading waves down my sorrow-stricken face. My shoulders juddered as I sobbed into his rigid body.

The milk soaked through the edge of the blanket, reminding me that even in grief, the world expected me to keep giving. Junior continued to feed, sucking on my fractured life while strengthening his.

Romeo stroked my hair. His scent, his closeness, the weight of his presence... gave me hope. "Do you need anythin'?"

I leaned back, searching the depths of his soul.

"Can you take me to see my foster mother, Nancy?" My voice cracked, the air tasting almost metallic. "I don't want to go alone."

"Of course," he said without pause. "Whatever you need, I'm right here."

◆ ◆ ◆

I remained in a quiet state of sadness as Romeo drove me to my foster parents' house. Trees blurred by, evening sunlight slipping behind soft, white clouds. A normal day like any other—except now Bob was gone.

Was he up there? Looking down on me? On my son, the child he never got to meet?

I didn't really know why I wanted to see Nancy or what I was even going to say. All I knew was that I wished I'd listened to Nelly. Wished I'd had one last chance with Bob, just so he could've met our baby boy. My proudest achievement. He was so pleased when he heard the news of my pregnancy.

Why didn't I put in more effort? I'd regret that decision for the rest of my life.

Scenes of the past scattered my thoughts, as I viewed my childhood with Bob through the lens of a heartbroken woman.

The lake, our favourite place and last meeting spot, featured most heavily in my mind.

Nature was Bob's thing. We'd sit on our bench, watching the world go by. He'd lean into me. "Jassy," he'd say, "let me tell you a story." Tossing bread for the ducks, he'd recount the time he fed a rare orange-billed mallard and lost his footing at the edge of a pond back home in Tennessee —how his mother grounded him for a week after he lost his shoe to the silt at the bottom.

And I'd listen. Swinging my legs over the edge of a bench too tall for my feet to touch the ground, I'd let his voice carry me. Anecdotes, one after another. His storytelling voice was so soothing. So comforting.

Yet for reasons I didn't fully understand, I rarely let him past my protective barrier. Back then, I hated men. Bob, at first, was no exception to the rule. But his patience... his integrity... and most of all, his kind heart. They helped me heal. Enough to explore relationships beyond my therapist.

That lake, still vivid in my mind, no longer held the two of us on its bench. Just me, sitting alone. The mildew of lake water in the air, the same breeze ruffling my hair. A single duck feather floated across the murky surface, drifting into the space where he used to be. I missed him so deeply already.

Thankfully, at the very least, I'd given Bob the chance to meet Romeo. That was the one thing I had to cling to—when I wished so badly he'd met my son.

Romeo pulled the car, my G-Wagon, to the curb and cut the engine. The low rumble faded into silence outside the brick-built structure I used to call home.

Next door's dog barked from the front yard. The postman strolled by, tipping his cap at the old lady rocking on her porch.

Romeo peered out the window, eyeing the run-down exterior. "Still hard to believe you used to live in a dive like this. Really came from nothin', huh?"

With my upper lip pinched between my teeth, I sat in brooding silence. I had come from nothing. Still had nothing—except what my husband provided.

Hand on the car's door handle, my fingers twitched. I couldn't quite find the strength to move.

Romeo's warm hand landed on my thigh, levelling my anxiety. "You want me to come with you?"

I shook my head, flipping down the sun visor to check my reflection one last time.

"No. You stay with Junior." I drew a shallow breath. "I've got this."

I kissed him quickly, barely there, then stepped out into the heat, taking a long inhale as if I might not get another.

The breeze hit me like a memory. Thicker. Hotter. Smouldering garbage cans and poverty.

Feeling like a child again, I climbed the familiar porch steps. The tired wood groaned beneath my sneakers.

I knocked—three times for luck. A habit I used to reserve for clients. And waited for the beast to emerge.

Footsteps approached. A hollow echo through the lifeless walls. The old door creaked open. And there she was. Her crow's feet deepened the second our eyes met.

Behind us, an old Cadillac wheezed past, choking the air with fumes and smog. No doubt a drug deal was about to go down on the corner. I stood still, letting it pass.

Once the engine faded, the familiar scent of stale sherry and liquorice settled between us.

Then, without warning, she pulled me into a hug—knocking me completely off balance. Her arms cinched tight, pressing me into her like I was thirteen again. Her breath, thick with alcohol, warmed the nape of my neck.

My knees stiffened. That old scent wrapped around me like a net I couldn't slip through.

"Jasmin," she sobbed into my hair.

Goosebumps bloomed across my arms. Just hearing that name dragged trauma back to the surface—the kind I'd buried months ago. How far I'd come since our last encounter. How far I'd had to crawl.

The irony of it all was Nancy never gave me the courtesy of using my chosen name. Not until now. Not until I no longer needed it.

"Um… Chloe is fine."

Nancy's shoulders heaved as she opened her heart in a way I never thought she was capable of.

"Oh, Chloe. I miss him so much." She clutched something in her hand, Bob's old chequered shirt.

I'd almost convinced myself he was still inside. Waiting in the living room. Ready to crack jokes.

My eyes lingered on that shirt. "I'm sorry he's gone, Nancy."

She sniffled, wiped her nose with the back of her hand, then brought the unwashed fabric to her cheek.

"Do you want to come in?" she asked, stepping back. "I can make a pot of tea?"

I glanced over my shoulder. The black G-Wagon glinted at the curb. A symbol of everything Romeo had given me—the life we'd built. He raised a finger at me through the windshield. Watching my every move. Our entourage idling behind him in matching SUVs.

"Um… I can't, really. I've got my husband and baby in the car."

"You've had your baby then?"

The loose wooden planks shifted beneath my feet, unsteadying my core as I waited for her reaction.

Her lips lifted into a soft, bittersweet smile.

"Bob wouldn't stop talking about becoming a Grandpop. What did you have?"

My lower lip trembled. The thought of Bob missing out on his life's wish crushed something inside me.

"A little boy." My voice wavered. "Named Romero. After his father."

"That's sweet." She paused, blinking slowly, then took a breath—steadying herself. "Let me tell you something… Chloe. Bob's passing, and the journey to his end, opened my eyes to a lot of things. I haven't been a true Christian woman to you. And for that... I'm sorry."

I blinked. The air stilled. The house seemed to fall away around me. I was floating outside of myself.

I reached for my necklace, grounding my body in the weight of it.

She saw my unease.

"The thing was... I didn't understand why you didn't respect us when we took you in. Bob gave me a few home truths before he left. I promised him I'd apologise."

She'd completely taken the wind from my sails.

Was I dreaming?

"Wow, Nancy..." I stammered. "I don't know what to say. I'm sorry too —for all the trouble I caused."

Her chin tightened. Emotion twisted across her weathered face. "I should've never kicked you out."

"Honestly, it turned out to be for the best. It made me grow up, and of course, I met my husband. I owe you my gratitude for that."

She leaned in and hugged me again, longer this time. Bob's shirt, still clutched in her hand, brushed down my back as she wrapped her arms around me. His smell—so fresh, so familiar—it felt like it was him in my arms.

"I have something for you. I'd like you to have it." She dipped behind the door, then returned with an old tatty shoebox. "Bob was a hoarder. Kept a lot of stuff. One or two things in there he thought you'd like."

I took the box. Light in weight. Emotionally heavy.

"Thanks."

She gave me a pained smile. "Bob told me he gave you your stepfather's address. I think you should meet with him. I did once—"

My breathing stopped. The box felt so much heavier now. The swell of my heart tightened. That flood of pain dried up in an instant—leaving only drought.

"You met my stepdad?"

She nodded, her expression softening as she tucked a loose strand of hair behind my ear, leaving a sting in her wake like the brush of nettles.

"He begged and begged to see you, but CPS told us that wasn't allowed. So I decided to meet him myself. Just to get a feel for him… see what he was really like. I thought it might help me understand you better."

My stomach turned, flipped, and contracted. Heat flared behind my eyes. The porch beneath me felt like it might give way.

My mouth opened, but no words came out.

"I think he's changed a lot since you last knew him," she added. "He doesn't drink anymore, for a start."

Like a roller shutter slamming down over my chest, everything inside me closed off. Every instinct screamed: Run.

"Um… I really don't want to talk about him now." My voice came out stiff, clipped. "But I appreciate you letting me know." I forced a smile, taking a step back. "I just came to offer my condolences."

Adrenaline fired. I turned on my heel, blinking back tears before she could say anything else. I needed distance. Needed space. Needed the safety of Romeo's arms like air in my lungs.

Nancy leaned out from the doorway, her voice soft behind me. "Don't be a stranger, Chloe. Come by whenever you like."

The shoebox gripped in my hands. I sank back into my seat, pulling on my seatbelt with wide eyes and a dazed expression.

"What did she do?" Romeo asked, thumb hovering near the seatbelt clip. "I don't give a fuck what T says. I'll use my gun on the old bitch if I have to."

A laugh bubbled through my tears. "No, nothing." I shook my head in disbelief. "It actually went well."

"Yeah? What you got there?"

I tugged on the old Sellotape that barely held the lid closed. It popped, and I opened it—slow, careful. My eyes darted around the contents. A little musty. Years old.

Inside was a treasure trove. A time machine to Bob's past.

I dug beneath the surface.

A folded-up sheet of paper—yellowed with age, dog-eared.

To Bob.

Sorry I said those mean things.

From Jasmin.

Bob's writing scrolled next to my apology: *Chloe aged 12.*

Tears pricked my eyes. The burn in my throat strangled me of air.

"What's that?" Romeo asked.

I handed it to him, then dug in the box again.

A photo. Me and Bob by the lake. Right by our bench.

On the back read: *Me and our Jassy. Enjoyed an ice cream. Saw an orange-billed mallard.*

A feather was taped beneath. Evidence of our find.

Beyond that, there was an old veteran badge—maybe his father's.

But it wasn't until I saw an envelope with my name on it that it hit me like a double-decker bus.

I ripped it open.

Inside, a handmade card.

A drawing of a man on the front with a big smile, holding an ice cream. Chequered shirt. Beige pants. A big circle sun behind him.

The words scrawled:

Happy Father's Day.

Inside:

To Bob. Love Jasmin.

Inside the fold of the card was a neatly folded piece of paper.

A letter. Bob's writing:

"Dear Chloe,

I asked Nancy to give you this box. I wanted you to keep a piece of me in your heart, just like I'll always keep a piece of you.

I love you, kiddo. I always have. Made me proud in whatever you did, and I know you'll keep on doing.

I'm sorry I had to leave. Looks like God needed my help with something. Probably heard about my great cooking. Though, I doubt Nancy would agree.

Look after your head, keep up your therapy, and your heart will right itself.

You best believe we'll see each other again one day. I'll be sat at our bench, waiting on you.

Bring something for the ducks.
Enjoy your life.
Bob."

"Chloe?" Romeo nudged me.

The world rolled back into view.

"Huh?" My lashes fluttered. Tears soaked my cheeks.

"Come on, Queen," he muttered, slipping the car into drive. "Let's get you home."

CHAPTER 17

"Have we got everything?" I asked, frantically rummaging through the change bag at the top of the stairs. With a burp cloth clenched between my teeth, I dug through the bottomless pit, convinced I'd packed the bibs.

Natural light spilled across the landing, warming the freshly wiped oak banister. The housekeeper had just finished phase one of the deep clean I now insisted on weekly since the baby was born. Her signature clary sage and floral spray lingered—like our freshly laundered, summer-breeze-scented bedsheets. But beneath it, another smell crept in. My nostrils twitched. Still, I pushed on.

The housekeeper hovered beside her cart, holding the laundry hamper.

"Can I help, ma'am?" she asked, beginning to unload. Petite and wiry, she might've seemed delicate if you didn't know better. Her grey perm was the only real giveaway to her age.

I tugged the cloth from my mouth. "No, thank you, Mrs Knowles. It's about time *he* did something to help around here."

Three steps down, Romeo paused. One hand gripping the car seat, Junior snug and strapped in. He checked his watch, then looked up at me, expression unreadable.

"Don't talk shit, woman. I already helped you check that bag three times. Let's go."

Easy for him to say. What if I'd forgotten something? Letting Junior down wasn't an option.

Still, Romeo not stressing for once was surprising. He was usually the one who needed anger management and a Valium.

Today, it was my turn. A doctor's appointment for the baby—on the same day my club reopened in less than twelve hours, and barely a day after losing my foster father—would test anyone's limits.

My nose twitched again. No amount of clary sage was covering this up.

"Romeo, I can literally smell from here that you've farted. You can't just not do that for one minute, can you?"

Still frozen mid-step, he glanced between me and the housekeeper.

"You want to know why you smelled it first? 'Cause it was you in the bedroom two minutes ago. It's followed you out."

With both arms buried in the canvas bag, I froze. Glared at him.

I peered over my shoulder. The housekeeper was still fiddling with her apron—still listening.

"How absolutely dare you say that to me in front of the entire house?"

He arched a brow, eyes sweeping left, then right, finding nobody but the three of us.

"But it's alright for you to blame me? Face facts, Queen, you let out a rippler even I can't take credit for."

I stammered.

He smirked.

"Oh, I can't be fucking doing with this," I snapped, zipping the bag closed with a sharp jerk. "You—get back to work!"

Mrs Knowles didn't deserve that, not really. But with ass-hat cradling the baby like he was Father of the Year who'd never farted a day in his life, someone had to take the hit.

Romeo resumed his descent, shaking his head.

"We need a fucking nanny!" I snapped at his silhouette.

I slung the overstuffed satchel over my shoulder, wincing as the strap yanked a clump of hair from my ponytail. My scalp smarted. My patience wore thinner by the second.

He shrugged from the bottom step. "I know, and we'll get one. It's not like we ain't been busy."

I huffed and stomped down to meet him at the front door. Each step landed like a drum beat, the drama I was hoping to create muted by the luxury of thick carpet. Behind me, the bag scraped against the wall—but

I barely noticed.

"We should've been more bloody organised," I muttered, voice cracking. My cheeks burned, the air feeling too thick for a hallway this wide.

He didn't reply. Just stood there, eyes narrowed, focused on something behind me.

Curious, I turned to follow his gaze. And saw the damage. A long black streak across the freshly painted wall. Clear as day—like a black mark on a clean slate.

"As if you hadn't already pissed me off enough this morning. Was that you with the car seat?" I gestured sharply. "You're supposed to be careful with the baby, not wielding him around like a bloody bat. This isn't cricket, Romeo. This is real life."

A curl of breeze drifted in through the half-open front door. Its soft sigh was the only sound as Romeo blinked slowly.

He didn't say anything. Just looked down at the culprit.

I looked down, too.

"Oh God... did I do that?" My voice wobbled, vision blurring. "I've ruined the wall—like everything else. Everything I touch just falls apart." My throat tightened. Fingernails dug into my palms. "This day couldn't get any worse."

A hot tear slid down my cheek, stinging as it fell.

As if summoned by despair, the housekeeper emerged from the side hall. No words. Just the brisk hiss of cleaning spray and the steady swipe of a cloth, erasing the damage like she'd done it countless times before.

A pang of guilt settled between my pinched brows. But it was Romeo himself who said never apologise to the people who work for you.

Romeo leaned against the wall, twirling the car keys between his fingers like none of it mattered. The cheerful jingle couldn't have grated on my last nerve more if he tried. All casual, unfazed, foot propped. His brow arched.

"It's just a wall, Chloe. Chill the fuck out."

But it wasn't just a wall. It was a reflection of me, cracked, broken, ruined. If only someone could spray and wipe my mind clear of all the debris floating around in there.

"Don't tell me to chill out." My chin tightened. "Not today. If you were a bit more helpful, I wouldn't have to stress so much."

He caught the spinning key mid-air, defensive now, and slipped it into his pocket.

"I mean… you could've just changed the boy's appointment, no?"

I huffed. 'Changed the appointment,' he says. What a brilliant suggestion. Why didn't I think of that?

More enraged than before, I tossed the bag at his feet.

The slap of metal hardware against the stone floor clattered through the hallway. Another scratch on the house, another on me.

Ruined walls. Desecrated floors. I was on a roll.

"Baby shots are important, Romeo. You can't just change an appointment the morning of. And it wasn't just me who could've planned this better."

I jabbed a finger in his face. "You're a parent too—when it suits. God, you're a prick sometimes."

Sweat dampened my armpits. A single bead trickled down my spine. My foundation clung on for dear life.

Breathing fast, arms trembling as I folded them across my chest.

A door closed upstairs.

One of the girls darted down the staircase, shimmying past the housekeeper midway. The moment she clocked the tension, she made a beeline for the kitchen.

Romeo's eyes followed her until her footsteps faded… and the kitchen door swung… then settled.

"Get it all out, Queen," he said with a lazy shrug. "But with the fuckin' traffic on the 405, we should've left four minutes ago."

Ugh.

"Oh my God, why didn't you say so?" I slapped a hand to my forehead, eyes darting around the room, scanning for anything I might've missed. "Get the baby in the car. Now!"

Tommy was already propped against Romeo's car when we stepped out into the humid morning air, thick as a wet blanket draped over my shoulders.

Exhaust fumes from the idling engine clung to the stillness, settling like fog and leaving a bitter taste at the back of my throat.

"Boss," Tommy said, covering the speaker of his phone with one hand.

"What, brother?" Romeo muttered, tossing the baby's bag into the trunk.

A scrape across the gravel signalled Jack, hobbling past with his rake.

"Morning, folks," Jack said cheerily, resting his tired body on the handle. "Let me get a peek at the boy, then."

Tommy shifted his weight. Romeo eyed the phone. Jack remained oblivious.

"Look at him," Jack said softly, leaning into the car seat. "Nice to have new blood round here again, ain't it, son?" He turned to Romeo.

I prayed to God he didn't touch my baby with those filthy fingernails.

"Yeah. Listen, old man—we got shit to do. You need somethin'?"

Jack straightened. He tapped at his mucky coveralls until he finally fished something out from the left thigh pocket.

"Check this out. Found it in the pasture, three acres west."

In his palm lay a coin, dull and caked with years of mud. Maybe a quarter.

Romeo made an indiscreet attempt at an eye roll, then checked his watch—diamonds catching the light no matter where the sun pointed.

"Keep it," he said, lips thinning. "You earned it."

Jack flipped it in the air like a coin toss, heads or tails deciding who knows what. He whistled as he pocketed it, lifted himself off the rake and strolled by us, humming a cheerful tune.

His rake stopped dead in the dirt.

"Oh, also. Need you to order in some more lime." He removed his cap and swiped his hair back. "You know why."

The men nodded in silent agreement. Then Jack was gone.

As soon as he was out of earshot, Romeo cocked his chin at the phone.

Tommy stepped closer into Romeo's space, never a guaranteed safe move.

"I got B.E. on the line." He leaned in further. "Wants to talk to you."

Romeo's reaction was almost violent. The trunk slammed harder than necessary.

We all winced, bracing for the baby's cry. Junior only snuffled in his sleep, lips puckered in a dream-fed pout.

Romeo dragged a hand through his curls. "I ain't got time for that prick. Stall him."

Tommy cast a glance toward Snake, who'd just finished polishing the chrome on the front wheel. Neither of them flinched. Both unreadable.

"Boss." Tommy hesitated. "We've been stalling since the Maldives."

Jack's lawnmower kicked into gear somewhere on the grounds. The sweetness of cut grass drifted through the gasoline haze, clearing the blurred lines between them and me.

That's when I decoded the real meaning behind their exchange.

Gripping the strap of my purse, I felt the weight of my gun inside—just enough reassurance to keep my voice steady.

"Romeo," I snapped, watching him round the other side of the car. "Why the hell are you still ignoring Benny English?"

But Romeo and our son were already inside. Doors shut. Engine revved. Ready for departure.

Tommy looked at me, hand still over the speaker. A faint, scratchy voice crackled through the line. Just loud enough to make my fingers twitch like I might answer it myself.

Was that really Benny's voice?

Snake stepped in front of me, arm out like a barricade.

"Boss is ready for you, Chloe." His voice was a command. "You head on out now."

I opened my mouth to argue, but all that came out was a short, sharp puff of disbelief as I did what I was told.

Still flushed, strands of hair stuck to my damp skin, I caught Romeo glancing over—gauging my mood now that we were on the open road.

Eventually, he worked up the nerve. "You good?"

I blew out a sigh. "What do you think, ass-hat?"

Another minute passed. Cars whooshed by in muffled bursts behind the closed windows. Just an ordinary day for most of the drivers.

"English ain't a problem, Chloe. I'll deal with him when I wanna. Not when he does."

"Ohh, I didn't realise you were scared of him," I sneered.

He rolled his eyes as if I was splintering his last nerve, just as a shadow stretched across the driver's side, cloaking half of him in darkness.

We both clocked the police car pulling up beside us, matching our speed. The officer gave a quick glance through our window… then carried on without slowing.

"Who was that?" I asked, arms folding tighter across my chest.

"How the fuck should I know!?"

I shifted in my seat, jaw tight.

"So that's Benny English after us and the cops back on our tails. Do they know we killed Jamie and Harry?"

Romeo's biceps bunched, shoulders lifting like a drawbridge. His cheeks flushed red.

"You think if they had even a sniff of intel on us, they'd just let us be?"

I tapped my fingers against the dash, chewing it over. A splattered greenish-brown bug smudge distorted the view through the windshield —blurred and messy. Just like my thoughts.

Romeo's mouth opened. Then closed.

And to my complete surprise, he let the rage go.

"Pretty sure this has got more to do with Bob's passin' than anythin' else, right?"

Like curdled custard, my emotions thickened in the pit of my stomach. Now wasn't the time to talk about Bob. Not when I was clinging to what little focus I had left for tonight.

"Don't talk about him, please," I murmured, tightening my grip on the purse in my lap.

Romeo flicked a glance my way. "I can't support you if you don't let me in on it."

That… was unexpected. Romeo being insightful was a revelation in itself.

My voice softened. "It's just..." I swallowed, eyes fixed on the baby's reflection in the rear-view mirror. "I'm worried you won't be able to keep him settled tonight. And I've already got so much riding on this."

Both hands on the wheel, he let out a long, heavy sigh, as if trying to exhale my anxiety for me.

"I proved to you yesterday I can do it—and I'll do it again. First thing tomorrow, we'll hire help. Yeah?"

I rolled down the window and tilted my head out like a dog. Tears snatched sideways. Just letting the wind whip through my hair and blast a force of air up my nose helped settle the edge of my irritation... a little. The air outside smelled faintly of warm asphalt and engine fumes, but it did wonders at cooling the boil of my stress.

Eventually, I slumped back into my seat and rolled up the window as if nothing had happened—just a little more windswept than I'd planned for.

Romeo chuckled, fingers tapping on the steering wheel to one of his favourite Eminem tracks.

"I put money on you bein' pregnant again." He smiled. "You went normal for, like, two days after you had him."

Oh.

Call me sensitive, but that little comment rubbed me up the wrong way. Did he think me telling him not to talk about Bob meant it hadn't happened?

Speechless, my only form of retaliation was turning the music down.

His fingers stopped tapping instantly.

"Give me a break." My chin wobbled. "It was your stupid idea to tell the girls, right before opening, that I killed Jamie. If they didn't know that, maybe their performances would've been better, and I wouldn't have to rely on three strangers to rescue this mess."

He cast me a quick glance. "If they had it, best believe fear would've brought it out of them. If they didn't have it after they knew, they sure as shit didn't have it before."

"It's not just that." I toyed with my necklace. "I feel like I've lost them."

My bottom lip quivered. I'd lost them. I'd lost Bob.

"What's the problem with that? They ain't your friends, Chloe." He checked the left mirror, dodged a slowing car, then glided smoothly back into the right lane. In the rear-view, Tommy mirrored the move without missing a beat.

The faint click of the indicator cut out. Romeo eased back, one hand resting on the wheel. One thing I could never complain about was his driving. Even in the chaos of our arguments, he still made me feel safe.

A tight burn built behind my eyes. I pressed two fingers to each temple, trying to fight the sting creeping through my sinuses. My throat tightened as grief bloomed like a bruise from the inside out.

"They were my friends, Romeo. You don't get it, do you? The success I built—it came from trust. From respect. And now? I've got nothing."

He huffed like I was being naïve.

"You might not have their trust," he said, "but you best believe, from now on, you'll have their respect comin' out your fuckin' ass. I know what I'm talkin' about."

Arguing with him right before seeing the doctor wasn't smart. But with Romeo? I never could help myself.

"When it comes to those women, you don't have a fucking clue what you're talking about," I said through gritted teeth, fists curling tighter in my lap.

My oxygen supply seemed to shrink by the second as I locked eyes on his side profile.

His jaw flexed. Eyes narrowed. Tongue darted out to moisten those plush lips. He was pissed. Hell, so was I.

A whole five minutes passed. The radio hummed quietly in the background. The soft whirr of the vents and the gentle hiss of tyres on tarmac became the reluctant soundtrack to our latest fallout.

Then, like only he could, he reached into his sweatpants and adjusted himself. Only Romeo would get hard at a time like this.

"You calmed down yet?" he asked, a hint of sex still threaded through his tone.

I shot him a quick look, then hid my smirk.

"I guess," I murmured, grinning faintly at my reflection in the window.

He reached over, hand steady as it landed on my thigh. His palm was warm, heat seeping through the fabric. His thumb slid beneath it, brushing the crease between my legs.

"Stop lookin' at this like you're on your own. Whatever happens tonight, I'll be right there to help you. Got it?"

The energy in that small gesture, his touch, his tone, relaxed me in an instant. I smiled and placed my hand over his, lacing our fingers. His thumb brushed over my knuckle, rough skin over smooth, grounding me.

I nodded. "Got it."

He exhaled a long, cathartic breath, keeping hold of my hand as we merged lanes.

"Let's take one fuckin' step at a time. Get the boy what he needs. Then onto the next thing."

Calmer now, more in control, I turned to check the back seat. Our baby—our cherub—lay peacefully in his carrier, a soft snuffle rising from his nose as his chest rose and fell in rhythm with the road. The most perfect little boy I could've hoped for.

Romeo pressed his foot to the gas, sending us both back against our seats.

"Tomorrow mornin'," he said with a smirk, "you'll look back on all this and suck my dick."

I smiled, shaking my head. He could dream.

"Sorry we're late," I said to the doctor with a tight smile as we shuffled into his office and took our seats across from his desk. I shot Romeo a sharp look. "*Someone* took a wrong turn."

My hands were clammy. My whole body shook. We'd practically sprinted from the hospital parking lot to make it on time.

Romeo ignored the dig, hitching up his sweatpants as he dropped into the seat beside me—still sulking from the no-smoking rule I'd laid down the moment he lit up outside the car. The last thing we needed was to be judged as new parents, especially when one of us reeked of tobacco.

"No problem at all, Mrs Giannetti," the kind-spirited doctor said, turning to his computer screen. "Just going to pull up your son's record. This little guy's name is Romero Luca Giannetti the Fourth?"

Spoken aloud, the name carried so much prestige it echoed.

"Yeah," Romeo said, gently rocking the car seat to keep Junior asleep.

"Perfect. Let me scan over his birth notes. Won't be a moment."

While we waited, I fidgeted. The doctor's office was exactly what I'd expected. Clinical. White-walled. Slatted blinds filtered in just enough light to cast jail-like stripes across the linoleum. A fake plant drooped in the corner—because a real one, in a place like this, was impossible.

I set my purse down by my feet, careful not to reveal the gun inside, muting the clink of metal as it landed.

Not that it mattered. Romeo kept his tucked firmly in his waistband. His T-shirt had ridden up just enough to expose the polymer handle.

It just went to show—while guns were never allowed in hospitals, the rules just didn't apply to him.

I twitched again, impatient. This time, I wiped the baby's mouth as he began to stir, adding to the sweat gathering at the nape of my neck.

The longer the doctor scrolled, the more I worried he'd find something that flagged us as unfit parents.

"Okay, got it," he said at last. "Nice easy birth. Just what I like to see."

He slid open a drawer and pumped two shots of sanitiser into his palms, rubbing them together with a squelch that caught me off guard.

"So. Let's take a look at him."

A tannoy crackled somewhere in the corridor, followed by the slap of hurried footsteps beyond the door. I blinked, distracted by the sound. For a second, I thought he meant Romeo.

The doctor's grey fringe slipped forward as he leaned over Junior's carrier, brushing a clean finger across the baby's chubby hand.

"Oh, of course," I said with a small chuckle.

I popped the carrier straps and lifted my son out carefully. The newborn scent curled beneath my nose as the fine smattering of his black hair brushed my cheek. He squirmed and squealed at being disturbed, shifting in my arms—but calmed the moment I passed him into the doctor's waiting hands.

A whiff of alcohol from the sanitiser hit the back of my nose. No hint of cologne or fragrance. Just clinical sterility.

But oddly, it was the doctor's desk that gave me a flicker of calm when something caught my eye.

"Your family?" I asked, pointing to the silver-framed photo sitting neatly beside a signed hockey puck and a thank-you card. Proof that, beneath the coat and stiff trousers, he was no different from us.

He smiled, gently bobbing Junior. "Heather, the wife. Holly, my fifteen-year-old, and our Labrador retriever, Humper. Don't ask."

He gave a look that made me chuckle.

Romeo's fists and jaw clenched at the same time, checking his watch like he'd already had enough. My chuckle died in my throat.

"You know," the doctor said, gently swaying Junior side to side, "some kids don't look much like their parents at this age… but there's no denying he's your son, Mr Giannetti."

I smiled, glancing between my husband and my child. "Everybody says that."

The doctor placed Junior in a hospital-issued crib. A single white sheet stretched over a foam mattress—nothing like the plush bassinet he was used to back home.

I knew he was safe, but instinct had me scooting forward, perched at the edge of my seat, watching him closely.

A soft whimper escaped him, eyes screwed shut. But it wasn't long before he settled into sleep again.

"Okay, excellent. I like to get the baby settled first before introductions," he whispered with a gentle smile, breathing a quiet sigh of relief. "We need him asleep for this."

Romeo and I glanced at each other. Asleep?

"So, I'm Doctor Lanard." He extended a hand to Romeo first, then to me.

Mouth slightly ajar, I took it, still wondering what the hell we were doing here.

Parenting classes. It had to be. Did someone report us? Was it Romeo's smoking? The toy gun hiding under the baby's blanket?

"The look on your faces tells me you're wondering why you're here, right?" He chuckled. "I specialise in paediatric audiology. Today we're doing a routine hearing test—what we call an OAE."

Latex gloves already snapped on. He reached for a sterile packet on the tray beside him, unwrapping it with quiet precision. "That stands for otoacoustic emissions. I'll place a tiny probe inside each ear. It plays a few gentle clicking sounds, and the device listens for how the inner ear responds."

Hunched over the crib, the doctor glanced between me and Romeo, his voice calm and clear. "No needles. No pain. Just a quick check to make sure his cochlea's doing what it should. Takes around five minutes."

Relieved this was nothing to do with our parenting techniques, I side-eyed Romeo. Still mildly annoyed with him, but not entirely sure why.

His leg bounced, a restless rhythm I knew too well. Likely still sulking over the no-smoking rule.

Honestly, if he couldn't handle five minutes without lighting up, maybe he needed more than therapy. Electric shock treatment, maybe.

The doctor smiled gently, pulling my attention back.

"I don't mean to speak out of turn here, folks," he said, adjusting a fine wire on Junior's temple, "but… do I recognise you from somewhere?"

He didn't look up again, just kept his eyes on the baby. A subtle crease forming in his brow as he checked everything stayed in place.

We weren't used to questions like that. People just knew who we were. Period.

Romeo crossed one ankle over the opposite knee, his tattooed hand resting on the chair's arm. The lettering on his knuckles seemed to come alive as he flexed his fingers slowly.

Doctor Lanard's gaze flicked between us, gears visibly turning like he was trying to work out the square root of eight million. Then he nodded.

Foot on the bin lever, he dropped the sterile packaging into the trash. "Ahh, don't tell me. You're the owner of Giannetti Haulage."

The bin lid slapped shut like a bucket of water to the face.

Oh no.

Mistaking him for his brother was always going to land like a lead balloon.

Romeo's knee bounced harder. Closing his eyes, he took a shallow breath, then opened them again.

"You got it," he said flatly. "How much longer? I got… a phone call I need to make."

I rolled my eyes. By phone call, he meant shoving a cigarette in his mouth. Well, I had every mind to shove the whole damn packet down his throat.

"Just another minute. Not long now."

The machine gave a concluding beep, and the doctor glanced over at the result.

"Okay…takes a couple seconds to print the report, and then you'll be good to go. Let's see here…"

He held out his hand to receive the printing paper.

The faint, sterile hum of fluorescent lights grew louder the minute the room fell quiet. My back straightened. My breathing slowed.

Tension between me and Romeo vanished the instant the doctor hesitated over the paper in his hand.

"What's wrong?" I asked, my throat tightening like the grip I had on Romeo's T-shirt.

A distant cough echoed down the corridor, as if the hospital itself were clearing its throat to reveal the news.

Doctor Lanard leaned against the crib.

"Romero seems to have failed the test," he said gently. "We've got a refer result, which means we'll need to test a little further."

A chilled hand settled over mine. Romeo's skin said what he couldn't.

"More tests?" I asked, swallowing dryly.

The doctor rolled his chair forward and took a seat in front of me, placing a reassuring hand on my knee. He gave it a soft squeeze.

His voice even softer. "A lot of newborns fail the first test. In a week or two, we'll re-test using the ABR method—auditory brainstem response. If there is hearing loss, that test will help confirm the degree and nature of it."

Romeo's leg stilled.

"Now," he said firmly. "Do it now. I'll pay whatever it costs."

"Romeo, I'm scared," I whispered, watching the doctor prepare our son for his second test.

Neither of us blinked at the $2,500 price tag—it was nothing if it gave us peace of mind.

The room was silent, except for the soft clicking of the machine and the low hum of the air conditioning.

Junior lay still, his tiny limbs bundled tightly in his blanket. Blissfully unaware. He had no idea how terrified we were.

This time, Romeo stood beside me. Both of us with arms crossed. Both of us holding our breath. My heart thudded with every tick of the screen.

The doctor leaned closer to the monitor, eyes flicking over the results. Then again. And again.

My pulse roared in my ears. I reached for the edge of the crib without thinking, fingertips curling over the cool metal rail like it might stop me from floating away. Like it might anchor me to the truth I didn't want to hear.

This couldn't be real.

Finally, the machine fell quiet. He removed the electrodes slowly—carefully.

"I've run the test twice," he said gently. "There was limited auditory response detected in both ears."

I blinked, lashes fluttering as if that might clear the muffle inside my head. The whole room sounded underwater. I felt submerged, suspended, like I was drowning and desperate to reach the surface.

"So... we'll do the next test?" I turned to Romeo, grasping for logic. "Right? I mean, we have the money."

The doctor's lips thinned. "I'm sorry, Mrs Giannetti. There isn't another test. Your son... he's—he's deaf."

The word dropped like an axe to my chest.

Romeo's knuckles turned white beside me. He shifted his weight but said nothing.

Deaf?

I looked at Junior. Still asleep. Still breathing. His chest rose and fell with a soft, even rhythm, like nothing had changed.

"Are you sure?" My voice wavered. "Could the machine be wrong?"

I placed my hand gently over his chest. He was warm beneath my fingers. So alive. So loved. My breasts ached with the weight of that love, tethering me to him.

"The test is accurate," the doctor said kindly. "We did detect some response, particularly in the lower frequencies, but it wasn't where we'd expect for his age. Romero has what we classify as moderately severe hearing loss. In both ears."

I clutched my necklace, my anchor. Romeo looked up at the ceiling.

"W-what does that mean?" I asked.

Dr Lanard removed his gloves. "He'll likely struggle to hear normal conversation unless it's loud and close by. With hearing aids and early intervention, he can still develop speech and language, but he'll need monitoring."

Romeo sniffed, swiping at a tear. "How the fuck does this shit happen? Ain't nothin' wrong with her or my fuckin' ears."

Dr Lanard began filling in a form I couldn't even look at. His handwriting was soft and elegant. But every loop of the pen hit like a punch to the gut.

"There are a few potential causes." He moved to the next line on the paper. "In newborns, one of the most common is a virus called congenital CMV. Something the baby may have been exposed to in the womb."

Romeo sucked in a breath through gritted teeth, narrowing his eyes on me. His voice dropped—low and lethal.

"Tell me, Doc... how does a mother," he looked me up and down, "get this virus?"

I gulped under his glare.

The doctor finished writing, clicked the pen closed, and swivelled to face us.

"CMV is a bodily fluid-borne virus. Something as simple as kissing, for example."

Romeo stiffened. His eyes darkened.

"What about nut?" he asked. "You know, sex? Fuckin'?"

The doctor's brow arched. He rolled his chair back slightly. "Do you mean semen?"

The air thickened. Even the fan above seemed to struggle.

"Semen," Romeo muttered. "Yeah. That's what I mean."

Dr Lanard inched his chair even further back, careful not to hit the crib. "It's a possibility, yes. But any bodily fluids, really."

Romeo's finger twitched, then jabbed towards me.

"This is why I don't fuckin' trust anybody," he growled. "You and my brother… this is all your fuckin' fault!"

He snatched his jacket off the chair, turned, and stormed out. One last look at me. At our son. Then he slammed the door so hard the frame shook.

Junior stirred, but didn't cry.

My baby couldn't hear how upset his daddy was with me.

The silence was suffocating. Clinically sterile. Painful.

My heart shattered into a thousand pieces, scattering across the floor like spilled marbles.

The doctor cleared his throat softly. Rolled his chair back under the desk.

"I know that was a lot to take in. Are you alright?"

I nodded, still clutching my necklace like it might keep me from falling apart.

He leaned in slightly. "I want to reassure you, Mrs Giannetti. This diagnosis doesn't define your son. With early intervention, children with moderate to severe hearing loss can thrive. Romero is alert, responsive, and otherwise very healthy. That gives us a great foundation to work with."

I blinked, trying to focus through the ache building in my chest.

"Is this my fault?" I asked softly, a tear tracking down my cheek.

"No, Mrs Giannetti. It can happen to anybody." His voice stayed gentle. "We'll refer you to an audiologist. They'll run a more in-depth ABR, alongside imaging if needed. We'll also do bloodwork to confirm CMV, but we don't need that to begin support."

My hand dropped from my necklace as he passed Junior back to me.

"You'll have me to fall back on, Chloe. Every step of the way."

I moved on autopilot, settling Junior into his car seat. His skin was still warm beneath my touch. Still perfect. Still mine.

"And what happens next?" I rasped.

"We'll fit him for hearing aids, likely both ears. Designed for infants," he said, handing me the dropped burp cloth. "Speech and language therapy will follow. I'll give you everything you need to get him into early intervention services."

He softened. "You won't be doing this alone. He's lucky, you know. He's got a strong mother."

"But I have a club to open?" I blurted. The words sounded absurd, even to me.

He blinked. "A what, sorry?"

I shook my head, dazed. "Oh—um, the club I just finished renovating opens tonight."

He offered a small smile. "Rest assured. Your son's result won't impact that. Treat him as normal, because he is. Perfectly healthy. Children with asthma take inhalers. Children with hearing loss wear aids. No real difference, when handled correctly."

I nodded, looking down at my baby like I was seeing him through brand new eyes.

"God, I feel so lost."

He slid open the second drawer of his desk. "Have you hired any help yet? A nanny?"

I shook my head.

He pulled out a sheet and handed it to me. "This woman comes highly recommended. She's trained in infant hearing loss. Fluent in sign language. A really wonderful woman."

My hand took the paper automatically.

Sign language.

He added a business card. "Call me if you have any questions."

"Thank you, Doctor," I whispered. "Thank you."

"Please don't blame this on me, Romeo. We've no idea how this happened. Not until more tests are done."

Speeding down the freeway, he wiped away another tear as it slipped from his cheek. He sniffed hard, dragging his sleeve across his nose, then slammed his fist against the armrest, hard enough to knock his phone into the footwell.

"You fuckin' my brother is how this happened. Hell, you fuckin' everybody is how this happened!" His voice rose, almost to a scream.

I turned to check on the baby—so still. So content. His features were full of peace. Like he hadn't just been pulled into a world on fire.

Was this really my fault?

"What hurts the most..." Romeo's voice cracked. "I thought we had somethin', me and him. He seemed so fuckin' settled against my chest. I thought he trusted me."

He paused, breathing hard. His jaw clenched so tight it made his voice shake. "And now I gotta live with the fact my son needs gear in his ears just to hear me. How's that gonna look, huh? Romero Giannetti. Father of a kid who can't even hear his own fuckin' name?"

My breath caught. "You're ashamed of him?" The words burned my throat. "How dare you? He's your son. He's perfect."

I pressed a hand to my stomach. Nausea rose like a tide.

"I think I'm gonna be sick. Pull over. Let me out of this car. Now!"

He swerved hard into the next lane. A horn blared behind us. One of the SUVs flanked our side, security closing in, sensing something was wrong.

"Vomit all over the leather. I don't give a fuck," he muttered, eyes wild on the road ahead. "Might as well fuckin' shoot me now. It's over."

Bile climbed my throat. "What the fuck do you mean, it's over?" My voice shattered as the tears came.

The business card the doctor had given me was still crushed in my hand, but the harder I tried to read the words, the more the letters blurred, slipping out of focus like everything else.

We sat in silence. Crying.

"Listen," Romeo said eventually, voice more restrained, sniffing between words. "I can't do this right now. I need to speak to T. I need to figure out my shit."

Acting on impulse, I did what I always do—lashed out. If I couldn't make him feel it emotionally, I'd make him feel it physically.

I punched his arm as hard as I could. Pain burst through my knuckles. His muscle was solid steel; he barely flinched.

"I don't give a shit if you want to run off to Tim." I hit him again. "That baby in the back is your son. The same child you were showing off yesterday, telling him everything he'd inherit."

My chest rose in short, sharp gasps. "He needs us now more than ever." I hit him again, softer this time. "I need you."

The air stung my nostrils. A metallic tang coated the back of my tongue. The edges of the doctor's card sliced into my fingers, but I couldn't let it go. I'd clutch the blade of a knife if I thought it might help us.

Another tear slipped from the corner of Romeo's eye, but he tried to hide it. He was hurting. That much was obvious. But how far was he going to pull away before we were too far gone to come back?

"I'll drop you at the club," he said quietly. "I'll be an hour."

"What on earth is going on, Chloe?" Lucy asked, coming around the far side of a dressed table, walkie-talkie clutched in one hand. "You're an hour and a half late."

She adjusted the final candle centrepiece on the last remaining corner booth—giving it the full Lucy special treatment.

A gentle nudge. A tilt. A squint. Then she stepped back to admire her handiwork and turned to me for approval.

Her smile dropped the second she saw the redness in my eyes. "Have you been crying?"

I shook my head, swiping at the evidence.

"Just allergies."

I smoothed the edge of the tablecloth. The fabric felt too soft under my fingertips, too pristine to be mine. "This looks wonderful."

She nodded like she already knew it did, but also like she knew I was lying.

The walkie-talkie crackled to life.

"Hawk to Eagle. Hawk to Eagle. Over." A male voice burst through the speaker.

Lucy pressed the button and lifted it to her lips.

"This is Eagle," she said, flashing me a grin like she'd been made for this role.

"Crowd already gathering outside. Want me to put up the ropes?"

"Yeah, do that," she replied, adjusting the centrepiece one final time. "I'll be out to help in a minute. Over."

She clipped the device into the back of her jeans like a holstered weapon. Casually dressed, messy bun, Lucy was somehow even more disarming than her usual sleek professionalism.

"Allergies, my ass," she said, stepping closer and cupping my shoulder. Her palm was warm. Steadying. "What's wrong?"

There was no way I could tell her about Junior. Not yet. Not until I had to.

I placed his car seat gently on the freshly polished bar. Junior stirred, but stayed asleep. I ran my fingers along the soft curve of his cheek.

Opened my mouth to speak—

A crash at the back of the room stole the show. The tangle of panicked feet, a yell, and the unmistakable sound of glass shattering against the floor.

Both of us snapped our heads toward the noise. One of the young helpers had tripped, an entire box of glassware now strewn across the floor in jagged, glinting pieces.

"Jesus, Ethan," Lucy hissed, exasperated. "Last thing Chloe needs right now is you waking the baby with all that noise. Grab a broom. Sweep it all up."

Our eyes met again. My chin trembled. I could've told her not to worry. That my son wouldn't hear a shout from a stride away. Instead, I lifted my chin and swallowed it down.

"My father died yesterday," I croaked.

The moment I said it, the tide came rushing in. Bob's smile. His laugh. His smell. The comfort in his voice. I swore I could smell his aftershave—faint and fleeting, like it had clung to my memory instead of my clothes.

What I wouldn't give to hear him one last time.

Lucy's hand, still resting on my shoulder, fell away.

"Holy shit, Chloe." She inhaled sharply, hand pressed to her chest. "Why didn't you say? Do you want to postpone?"

I shook my head—almost violently. I needed this place. It was all I had left.

"Where's Romero, anyway?" she asked, glancing over my shoulder like a six-foot-four man had any hope of hiding behind me.

I turned slightly, catching sight of Tommy and Snake by the door. Snake gave me the nod.

"He's got a, um… gym session."

Her brow arched. High.

She didn't buy it.

"For God's sake," she muttered, rolling her eyes. "I hope you don't mind me saying, but he can be selfish sometimes."

She *had* bought it.

I rolled my eyes too, finally letting the trapped air in my chest escape. "Tell me about it. Anyway, he'll be an hour. I'll watch the baby until then, if you can keep things moving?"

She pressed a kiss to my cheek and jogged out to help Mr Hawk—whoever the hell that was. Not likely one of our crew. She'd probably brought him in herself, knowing full well I was currently less capable of running this place than the bloody drapes.

I caught Tommy's eye across the room and beckoned him over. He marched across the squeaky floor, heavy military boots striking with purpose—he was never anything less than prepared.

Out of habit, he placed a hand on the grip of his gun.

"Boss?" he said, stepping in.

Snake appeared beside him like a double act.

The speakers erupted. Lights stuttered, pulsing as the power surged. A sudden burst of music tore through the club, ricocheting off every wall.

I jolted like I'd been electrocuted. We all spun around.

Some guy in headphones was fiddling with wires behind the stage.

"Jesus Christ," I muttered, checking the baby. Junior's tiny hands stayed curled by his cheeks, unfazed.

Of course. He couldn't hear...

I turned back, hand on hip. "Why are you both here?" My voice sharpened. "Who's with Romeo?"

Tommy's eyes dipped to the grip I'd instinctively settled around my waist before he rocked back on his heels. Snake mirrored him. Two guilty schoolboys caught red-handed.

"He said he needed some time alone, Boss," Tommy mumbled. "Told us to be here with you. Said it's your big night, after all."

My stomach turned, folding in on itself like it was being wrung through a mangle.

The music flared again, louder this time, then cut out completely.

My hand flew to my chest as my heart skipped a beat.

"Romeo is having a session with Tim... on his own, no security?"

Tommy shot a look at Snake. Both of them nodded.

The sweat hit first. Then the anxiety. The floor tilted beneath my feet as dizziness closed in, air thinning like a vacuum had opened in my lungs.

"Tommy." My voice cracked like glass. "Do you know about the baby?"

He hesitated. His grip on the handle of his gun tightened.

"We do, Boss," Snake said quietly, stepping in. "He'll come around. Way I see it—he's doing the right thing. Getting his head straight."

Maybe he was. But still, when Romeo promised I wouldn't be alone... I believed him.

3:45 PM marked exactly an hour since Romeo left me at the curbside of my club.

Lucy sat beside me on the stage, kicking her legs back and forth while mine stayed stock-still.

"Give him a call, Chloe," she said, bumping my shoulder gently.

With one hand gripped around the baby carrier, nudging it softly to keep the baby asleep, I dug into my pocket for my cell.

His contact photo filled the screen the moment I unlocked it—his handsome face smiling back at me like everything was fine. It made me want to launch it across the room.

I hit call.

It rang.

And rang.

Voicemail.

A guttural noise of frustration escaped me as I tossed the phone. It slid halfway across the stage, skidding to a stop as if even it couldn't bear to be near me.

How could he? After all the promises. After all the effort.

How could he leave us alone at a time like this?

Selfish prick.

"What's this?" Lucy asked, slicing through my rage like a guillotine.

Confused, I tore my focus away from the passing server's fish knife—glinting at me like an invitation to teach Romeo a lesson.

She was holding something. An A4 sheet of paper.

I tapped my pocket. Empty.

Heat flushed my cheeks as realisation set in. The information sheet the doctor gave me about the nanny must've fallen out when I pulled out my phone.

She skimmed the page with a half-smile.

My eyes narrowed. Was she laughing? Was my son's diagnosis funny?

My fists were clenched, ready to defend him from anyone. With the way I felt, Lucy wouldn't stand a chance against me.

"Nice to see you've finally found time to research nannies?" she said. "This one looks very qualified."

The tension drained from my body like someone had opened a valve.

My fists unclenched.

Of course, she wasn't laughing. Why would she?

"Yeah," I said, voice barely a scratch of sound. I brushed my knuckles together to dispel the hurt. My right hand still ached from the hit I'd landed on Romeo.

"Honestly?" she added, handing it back, "I'd say give her a call. See if she can help you out tonight. When Romero does eventually show, you'll end up worrying more about him and the baby than your clients."

I nodded, scanning the sheet again. Words on paper had never held so much hope.

"Nothing to lose, right?" I offered a tight smile.

She retrieved my phone from where it had landed, wiped it on her jeans, and passed it back. "Nothing at all."

Next thing I knew, Tommy was outside with the baby while I tucked myself away in the women's bathroom—perched on the toilet lid, the door locked for privacy—as I waited for the call to connect.

The signs I'd had Lucy order, helpline numbers for women suffering domestic abuse, were now plastered on the back of every stall door.

One stared right at me. For a moment, it looked like I should be the one making that call.

The phone rang a couple more times.

I was just about to hang up, finger hovering over the end button, when —

"Hello, Rita Davies speaking."

Suddenly, I couldn't string a sentence together.

"Um, hi. My name is Chloe Giannetti. We, um... my son, um—sorry."

I winced. Chastised myself.

My hands were shaking so badly the phone nearly slipped through my fingers. The ridges of the case were the only grip I had to hold on to.

"Everything okay, ma'am?" she asked gently.

Her voice was calm. Professional. Laced with just enough concern to sound sincere without prying.

A final droplet plopped from the flushed toilet just as a strangled giggle escaped me.

"Honestly? No. I'm hanging on by a thread."

My toes tapped against the tile. Fingers fidgeted with the buttons on the tampon dispenser.

I drew in a breath and forced the words out before I lost my nerve. "Long story short—my newborn was diagnosed this morning with hearing loss. My husband hasn't taken the news well. I've got an important event tonight... no one to watch the baby... I'm screwed. The doctor gave me your information."

"A soft rustle echoed over the line, maybe fabric or a zipper." She was packing something. Already moving. Like she didn't need to know anything more.

"Doctor Lanard?" she asked.

The jingle of a car key rattled against the speaker.

I nodded, even though she couldn't see me.

"Yes," I murmured.

"Text me the address," she said, all business now. "I'll be over as soon as I can."

◆ ◆ ◆

Someone once told me—maybe therapist number two—that I had an uncanny ability to toss my biggest emotions into a pit at the back of my mind and seal it over with impenetrable lead. And this? This was no exception. My tears had dried up. My heart had returned to its usual rhythm.

I'd called Romeo two, three, four times in a row. Still no answer. The son of a bitch had let me down beyond the realms of tolerance. And if I was being honest, I wasn't entirely sure we'd make it back. All that bullshit about supporting me. Wanting to be the best father he could. Trying to get me pregnant again, like he had it all figured out. Then, as soon as the going got tough—he was gone.

Right now, as far as I was concerned, I was a single mother, alone in my newly refurbished office. Impatience gnawed at me while I waited for the nanny to arrive, an ache burning the back of my throat I refused to release.

Still, I was pleased with the new setup.

Lucy had stripped the space of all traces of its previous owner. It might as well have been brand new—right down to the classic artwork on the walls and the old-fashioned rotary phone she'd installed 'just for a bit of fun.'

I lifted the receiver, watching the coiled wire stretch as I brought it to my ear—imagining some billion-dollar deal waiting on the other end. Then I snapped it back into the cradle with a smirk.

Weird to think Romeo had ever used this space. Bet he spent less time hosting clients and more time fucking at least ninety percent of the staff. Probably more. Bent them over the desk. Over the chair. Had them sucking his dick while he reclined—hands behind his head like the king he thought he was.

I sank back into the chair, fingers curling around the leather like a queen reclaiming her throne. Only this time, a man would serve me. He'd crawl over broken glass. Walk through fire. Lick my pussy like the powerful woman I was. I'd show Romeo. He'd see exactly what he left behind.

Muffled voices drifted through the office door, left ajar—offering a deliberate, uninterrupted view of the VIP lounge beyond the glass wall. Another sound guy, or maybe this one was lighting, hovered near the edge of the balcony. Hard hat, a pair of safety goggles and a clipboard in hand. He shouted down to another tech about cable lengths and rigging. But none of it mattered. Not the noise, the crew or the lights, because Romeo wasn't here. And I was doing it without him.

If I did serve him divorce papers… Would he let me keep this place? Or would I lose this, too?

An assured knock startled me from my reverie. Tommy's straight face appeared through the gap.

I rose from my seat, hands braced on the desk as the office door swung open, flooding the room with light from the hallway. He stepped aside—and there she was.

Like a beacon, she brought instant clarity into the room. Tall. At least five ten, maybe more. Slim build. Long legs mostly hidden beneath an ankle-length skirt. Her look was plain, her dress sense old-fashioned. But those eyes? Doting, chocolate-brown, and trustworthy. Tote bag clutched in both hands over her thighs, a calm smile on her face—like she'd walked straight out of the solution I'd been waiting for.

She took a step over the threshold. "Afternoon, Mrs Giannetti. My name is Rita." She extended a well-cared-for hand. Trimmed nails, moisturised skin.

I took it. Sure and soft. The kind of hands I wanted my son to feel when she soothed him to sleep.

"Please, call me Chloe. Take a seat," I said, gesturing to the chair opposite mine. The crack in my voice didn't go unnoticed.

"Doctor Lanard is a phenomenal doctor. I've known him for years," she said, lowering herself into the chair with quiet grace. "If he gave you my contact, it's because he believes I can help."

Without looking, I reached for my coffee mug and took a sip. Stone cold. I winced as it slid down my throat, just like me, something forgotten.

"I really hope so." I clutched the mug in both hands for moral support.

She placed her tote on the floor. "I imagine it came as quite a shock?"

I nodded slowly. "The only thing I can tell you is that I feel numb. I lost my dad yesterday, and then this morning…" I exhaled shakily. "To find out my son is deaf… I don't even know how to process it."

Without a word, sensing what I couldn't bring myself to say, Rita rose from her chair, a whisper of fresh air shared between us as she came around the desk. With her big brown eyes locked on the baby, she gently scooped him into her arms—her skirt brushing the new flooring like it was sweeping up the crumbs of my despair.

He startled, squirmed, then nestled close to her shoulder like he'd known her all along.

"Are we talking profound hearing loss?" she asked softly. "No detectable hearing at all?"

I stared into the middle distance, eyes flickering as I tried to replay the doctor's words.

"He mentioned hearing aids. Speech therapy. Early intervention stuff…" I trailed off.

Rita nodded. "Sounds like moderate, then. Not total. But don't worry—I've cared for infants across the entire spectrum."

I slouched back in my chair, hands gripping the edge of the desk. "I don't have the first clue. I'm new to all this. But him being deaf—"

She placed her hand on my shoulder gently.

"I understand your concerns. Wholeheartedly." Her hand shifted instinctively, adjusting Junior against her chest like second nature. "My daughter, she's in her thirties now, was born completely deaf."

I watched the way she held him. The way it felt like she was speaking to him without words.

"Really?"

The harsh lights above seemed to soften, catching the silver strands in her hair like diamonds. My shoulders dropped—as if her arms around him had somehow lightened my load.

"Mm-hm. I've been through it all."

My grip on the desk tightened.

"Do you think you could start… now?" I asked, hopeful.

She checked her watch with the baby snug on one shoulder, then smiled like the timing couldn't have been more perfect. "Yes. Of course."

I pulled on my jacket, suddenly in a rush. "Are you comfortable enough in here? There's a TV, a small couch, drinks in the fridge—"

She made her way to the couch and carefully folded herself into the fabric, adjusting Junior in her arms. "This is perfectly fine for me. I'm used to working with families who travel, move around… you name it."

"Is it okay if we talk money tomorrow?" I edged towards the door. "I'll pay you whatever you want."

She smiled. "All I care about right now is knowing where your son's milk is stored, and where to find the remote for the television."

My lungs fully deflated. Relief swept through me like a silent exhale, plugging the leak in the dam before it could burst.

"There's a stockpile of breast milk in the mini fridge just under there," I said, pointing beneath the desk. "If you need anything, I'll be somewhere in the building."

She lifted Junior in front of her face and kissed his cheek.

"Chloe, we'll be just fine. You go do what you need to."

"Okay girls, one last time from the top," Lucy said, clipboard in hand, as our three showstoppers took their places against the poles. The music thumped, spirits were high—but it didn't go unnoticed by either of us that the fourth pole—standing lonesome—looked as out of place as I felt.

She cranked the volume higher. Candles flickered in centrepieces on unoccupied tables, casting soft, moody light across the stage. The girls twirled like their lives depended on it. Splits. Arched backs. Parted cheeks. They knew how to rouse a crowd.

Lucy bobbed her head to the beat, lips pursed like she was mentally scoring each routine. Gold thongs. High heels. Strobe lighting. It was all finally slotting into place—especially when Tara dipped low and bounced on the spot, eyes locked on mine like she had a shot.

I tore my gaze away, catching myself drawn.

We were ready.

The only thing not ready… was me.

"What time is it?" I asked, clutching the edge of Lucy's clipboard while she ticked something else off her checklist.

She reached into the front pocket of her jeans and tapped her phone screen. "7:45 PM. Doors open at 9:00."

I beckoned to Snake, stationed near the main entrance.

When he arrived beside me, the sharp chemical smell of parking lot fumes hit first, mingled with the scent of metal. He'd recently reloaded his weapons.

"You heard from dickwad?" I asked, trying—and failing—to keep my dignity intact.

"No, Boss." He stepped closer so only I could hear. "His location's still pinging at the mansion. Tommy sent a car, but it got turned away at the gates. You know what he's like. He just needs time. Anything I can help with?"

If Romeo needed time, I needed space. Selfish didn't even begin to cover how despicably he was behaving.

"Well, I need to get changed." I gestured down at the same old dress and battered sneakers I seemed to wear these days, creases worn into the fabric, soles barely holding on. Everything about me screamed tired. Used.

Snake's lips thinned. His jaw worked once—clearly torn between speaking and staying silent.

"We don't want to disturb him if we can help it. Maybe I could run to a store for you?"

The irony wasn't lost on me, especially since I'd only just earned back my credit card after the honey trap fiasco. The same card he'd once yanked from my wallet like a punishment.

I handed it over with a smirk. "Head to that boutique on Rodeo—ask for Gabriella. Tell her Chloe sent you. I want the most outrageously expensive dress in a size four, and heels to match. Got it?"

He nodded, already reaching for his earpiece. "Got it."

The bathroom lights burned down with surgical intensity, bouncing off white tiles and silver fittings, spotlighting the woman in the full-length mirror like she was on trial.

Sequins shimmered with every breath. My silver dress clung to the new swell of my thighs, cut short and unapologetic. The heels pushed me taller, spine straight, pain carefully tucked beneath pride. I looked powerful. Dangerous.

The clutch bag clicked open. I applied a sweep of gloss with the same precision I used to pull a trigger. Gabriella might've fucked my husband, but one thing I couldn't fault—she knew how to spend his money. Right down to multiple underwear options, just in case. Every inch of my body was accounted for.

Last came the diamond earrings. Classy. Expensive. Cold against my skin. Only then, as I secured the butterfly-backs in place, did I spot what was missing.

No engagement ring.

No Romeo.

I glanced at my Casio. 8:50 PM.

I'd already called him more times than I cared to admit.

My thumb hovered near redial, but I couldn't do it. Not again. Not when he couldn't even be bothered to text and ask if we were okay.

It took less than a second to make the decision.

My gaze dropped to my wedding band. I slid it off with a slow twist.

Tossing it in the bin would've felt good—cathartic, maybe—but I wasn't ready to let him ruin something else. I dropped it into my bag instead. Let it rot there.

But Nonna's ring? That was different. That held weight. Power. She never took his shit, and somehow I swore I could feel her strength pulsing through the cool metal as I adjusted it just right. It caught the light, fierce against the shimmer of my dress.

A mist of sweat clung to my hairline. Nervous. But ready. The kind of ready that came from pain and power in equal measure.

I checked the time again. 8:56 PM.

Tapping the watch face, I inhaled. "Come on, Chloe. It's showtime."

The bathroom door clicked shut behind me with a soft finality, like the universe closing a lid on everything I was leaving behind.

Music pulsed beneath the surface, low and steady, seductive as it threaded through a haze of lavender, candle wax, and warm bodies. Scent and shadow wrapped around me like perfume.

My heels tapped with confidence. My hips swayed. Every step anchored me to the floor, to the room, to this moment I'd built from scratch.

To my left, stained-glass light scattered rainbows across the floor with every car that rolled into the lot. A backhanded gift from my husband, the man I was beginning to question whether he had ever truly loved me at all.

To my right, centrepieces flickered in time with the bass—tiny flames dancing like they knew what was coming.

The strippers were warming up, limbs stretched, eyes locked on their reflections, adjusting routines that didn't need perfecting. They were born for this.

The only three girls left from the mansion, Sophie, Lala, and Tonya, who were now moonlighting as waitresses, stood by the lounge doors with trays in hand. Their painted smirks barely masked what I recognised as nerves. Eyes sharp. Heels planted. They were survivors, same as me. And whatever they'd heard—I could feel it in the way they held their ground. They hadn't given up on me.

Lucy stood by the main entrance, walkie-talkie crackling softly in her palm. She looked up the moment I approached, her face softening.

"Ahh, there you are." Her smile bloomed. "Wow. You look gorgeous. Like, stunning."

I gave her a slow twirl. My long blonde hair fanned out, sequins catching light like shattered glass.

"Thank you."

She grinned. "Word is, there's at least a thousand people waiting outside."

My fingers flew to my throat.

"Wait—really?" My voice cracked. "Holy shit."

"I know." She beamed, practically vibrating. "This is going to be a night to remember."

I turned away, heart knocking against my ribs. One last time, I pulled out my phone and dialled Romeo.

Straight to voicemail.

That was it.

The final straw.

I sealed my feelings for him in a box, snapped the lid shut without time for a label, and tucked it beside my heart the moment my phone slipped back into my clutch.

Now wasn't the time to break.

It was time to lead.

"Let's get this show on the road."

10:00 PM hit fast.

My feet ached in heels I'd already walked a lifetime in.

My breasts, swollen, sore, and heavy with milk, throbbed inside a bra that felt more like barbed wire. The straps cut into my shoulders, carving tension deep into the muscles of my neck.

Lucy found me near the bar, just as I eased onto a stool for five stolen seconds of relief.

"First VIP client is waiting for your introduction," she said. "Want me to settle them in?"

I stood up, breath catching. Brushed down my dress. Straightened my shoulders.

"No. I've got this." I smiled. "I want Tara on this one."

"Got it," she replied, already speaking into her walkie.

At the base of the stairs, with Tommy nearby, stood a man dressed like money. Tailored suit. Crocodile shoes. The kind of confidence that came from always getting what he paid for.

He smiled when he saw me. Cold eyes. Calculated. He looked like he already knew me.

But he didn't intimidate me. Not even close.

"Welcome to Jasmin's," I said, offering a steady hand. "You're in for a real treat tonight."

He took it firmly and businesslike, then leaned in, brushing the back of my hand with his lips.

"I don't doubt it, ma'am." His voice rasped with old smoke and expensive promises.

"Follow me," I said, flushing—just a little.

I led him up the staircase, hand gripping the polished railing. Not just for show, but to take the pressure off everything still healing inside me.

New carpet cushioned my steps. Fresh paint gleamed on the walls. This was the first official VIP ascent. And I was proud.

With every step, my smile grew. I'd built this. And now I owned it.

I sashayed like the ache between my thighs wasn't flaring with every movement. Like the dull throb inside me wasn't blooming into something sharper.

Every step was deliberate. Controlled.

By the time I reached the glass double doors of the VIP lounge, the pain pulsed like a bruise that hadn't healed yet—but I didn't slow down.

I glanced back to make sure he was still following and caught him watching my arse. The smile that broke across my face lit up the entryway brighter than the bulbs.

Waiting by booth one was Tara. Silky skin. Supple curves. She looked incredible. The push-up gold bra and matching panties didn't hurt either. Her hair was styled in soft waves, glittering like spun honey.

She spotted her client and rolled her hips in greeting—an enticing welcome that needed no words.

I tugged open the booth door. "Please, make yourself comfortable."

He loosened his belt.

Tara stepped forward, removing his coat with a practised flick. He sank into the plush recliner like a man well-acquainted with the rules.

I poured him a drink from our top shelf while his eyes roamed over Tara's body, lighting up with obvious approval.

"I'd like the full works, please," he said, pulling out his thick wallet.

I handed him the glass with a confident smile. "Sure thing, handsome."

My fingers brushed his shoulder. "On top of the thirty for exclusivity, there's an additional three-grand fee for an hour with one of my best girls."

The tap of his card against the reader triggered a satisfying ping—transaction approved.

I winked at Tara, then pulled the door shut behind me, leaving them to it.

Lucy was already waiting outside by the glass lounge doors. A little red in the face, clipboard still tucked under one arm, she'd been carrying the weight of us both tonight.

"Paparazzi are here," she said. "One of the magazines wants a quick interview."

An interview with me? They only ever wanted Romeo.

This was my shot at doing it alone.

As we passed my office, my head turned instinctively, eyes drifting to the closed door.

She stepped into my path and pressed a hand against it.

"The baby's fine, Chloe," she said, reading me like a book. "I already checked. Come on—this way."

A camera flash exploded in my face, momentarily blinding me. A wash of expensive perfume drifted past as a mic was shoved under my chin. Two, maybe three, journalists had me cornered by the main exit.

"Tell me, Chloe, how's opening night going?" one of them asked. Her eyes swept the room behind me, voice brimming with barely concealed envy. "Sure looks like a success."

Not a single empty table. The whole place pulsed with energy—bodies moving like silk in my peripherals. Ice clinked in glasses. Money changed hands like secrets.

"I'm very grateful for the turnout," I said with a polished smile.

Tommy and Snake stood posted at either end of the club, close enough to see, but far enough to keep me relatable.

As Lucy said—relatable gets you influence. Influence gets you popularity.

The bass thudded underfoot, vibrating through the soles of my heels. Even the reporter faltered mid-question, distracted by the seduction of it all.

"Is your husband proud?" she asked. "It goes without saying that our readers would love to hear Romero's thoughts."

My lips thinned. My fingers instinctively reached for the wedding ring that wasn't there.

For a moment, I'd forgotten about him completely—only the faint indent where the band used to sit reminded me he'd ever belonged to me at all.

"On dad duties, I'm afraid," I said smoothly. "Full-time job in itself."

She nodded, smile thinning. "Shame. Hopefully, he'll like this video on our socials."

Right on cue, the double doors behind her blew open, ushering in a gust of cool night air that curled around my bare legs like a warning.

Romeo?

The atmosphere shifted.

Laughter dipped. Bass softened.

A couple stepped inside. Tall. Poised. The kind who turned heads just by existing.

A question followed—something from the reporter—but I barely heard her. White noise now.

They stepped out of shadow and into light.

My stomach dropped.

Dan. And fucking Harper.

My chin nearly hit the floor.

"Excuse me," I said without looking at the reporter, already moving.

Dan's eyes found mine like they'd been trained for it.

His smile hit like a punch to the chest. Then came his little wave, and it knocked me sideways.

I caught myself with a step.

"I wasn't expecting to see you here," I said, brushing a kiss on each of his cheeks.

Harper rolled her eyes so hard it made my skin itch.

"His PR team told him to, honey. This has nothing to do with you."

I straightened, thrilled one minute and humiliated the next.

My hand swept across my dress, smoothing the sequins still bristling with embarrassment.

"Of course," I said tightly. "Well... thanks to your team, I guess. If you'll excuse me—I need to check on the bar."

Nudging the bartender aside, I poured myself a vodka.

Heavy-handed. Just a splash of coke.

I downed it in one go.

The unfamiliar bite squeezed my stomach like a vice. But right now, numbing the discomfort was a necessity.

I poured another.

Safe to say, I was tipsy within minutes.

The strobe lights slowed. Laughter hit louder. A camera crew weaved between tables, snapping exclusive shots of the place. That part had been planned.

What hadn't been?

Harper. Shoving her smug little face in front of the mic, all coy glances and fake giggles. She'd be soaking up the spotlight for a while.

If Romeo were here, I'd have told him to kick her out. But who was I kidding? I could barely focus past my trembling fingers without the urge to vomit.

My third drink burned its way down, setting my throat alight.

I watched her twirl a strand of her dull brown hair, giggling like she was marking her territory. I was so focused on her small-chested performance; I didn't notice Dan had stepped away.

A hand tapped my shoulder, magnetic in its connection.

My heart faltered.

I turned fast. The vodka spun the room on its axis.

"Dan?" I blinked, scanning him like I might be hallucinating.

"Hey, you. You look gorgeous." His voice was low. Familiar. "I stayed back thinking Romero was here. Where is he?"

Under the lights, his green eyes caught like glass—so alike in colour and sharpness, I could've sworn he was Romeo for a second.

My chin wobbled. But I swallowed it down. Took another gulp, then set the glass down—harder than intended. It clinked like it nearly splintered.

"I don't know. And honestly?" I met his gaze. "I don't care."

Dan gently took my hand, guiding me toward a quieter corner.

Snake clocked it. I saw him watching. But even he knew better than to question my judgement tonight. Not when the father of my child had abandoned me.

"What happened?" Dan asked, brow creasing with concern.

That familiar citrus hit of Tom Ford cologne curled around me, subtle but intimate. The brush of his fingers triggered a single tear, hot and traitorous, brimming at the corner of my eye.

I sniffed, wiping it away. No mascara smudges tonight. I wasn't giving Harper that satisfaction.

"We found something out this morning…" My voice cracked. "The baby… he's deaf."

Dan unbuttoned his jacket and perched on the edge of a barstool, stunned.

"Wait. Really?" He edged closer.

I nodded, eyes fixed on the centrepiece before me. Its tiny flame danced in rhythm with the strippers, their bodies bending to the beat.

"So Romero left?" His eyes scanned the room in disbelief.

My eyes followed his around the room.

The music. The movement. The noise. It all faded to background static.

Just the hollow in my chest remained.

I shrugged. "Looks like it, doesn't it?"

He reached for my shoulder. His hand lingered longer than it should have. The softness of it made my eyelids flutter.

I leaned in. Just a little.

His breath skimmed my temple. "Where's the baby?"

I opened my eyes as that little boy's face filled my mind.

"Upstairs." I frowned. "Why?"

Dan shifted his weight and unbuttoned the collar of his crisp white shirt. "Alone?"

Instantly offended, I leaned away from him.

"Of course not. I hired a nanny."

The next song kicked up a gear. A champagne bottle popped—shrill squeals of delight echoed off the walls as foam sprayed from the spout.

Dan's eyes drifted to Harper, watching her soak up every flicker of attention. "Can I see him?"

Suddenly, I really wanted to see him too.

"Sure," I hiccupped, catching the edge of the table to steady myself. "Follow me."

On the way to the foyer, I swiped a glass of champagne off a passing tray.

"Boss?" Snake said, stepping forward as he intercepted us at the foot of the stairs, one hand clutching his earpiece.

"Just checking in on my nephew, Mr Worm," Dan replied, giving him a condescending pat on the shoulder.

Too much alcohol had me snorting.

"His name is Snake," I corrected, gripping my stomach as laughter rolled out of me.

Another gulp of champagne fizzed behind my lips—sweet and sharp.

Snake remained unfazed. And unamused. "This isn't a good idea, Boss."

I raised a hand in his face, swaying slightly.

"Save that speech for the prick who didn't show. Come on, Dan. Let's go."

By the time we reached the top of the stairs, I felt… good.

The alcohol had numbed almost everything. The ache between my legs. The pain in my chest. Even the burning question of where the hell Romeo was.

Velvet silence wrapped around us. A stark contrast to the chaos pulsing below.

Dan's hand rested lightly on my lower back, steadying me.

Another man's touch after so long felt alien, yet my body responded as if invited.

I reached for the soft give of the door handle, but Dan gently intercepted me.

"It's late, Chloe. Let's not wake the baby by bursting in," he whispered.

I laughed—too loud. "He can't hear you, Dan."

He winced, putting a finger to his lips, nodding toward the private booths just down the hall.

Lifting my chin, a sharp prick of emotion bloomed behind my eyes.

My son was deaf.

And his father no longer wanted him.

Dan opened the door slowly. Cautiously.

A faint bassline trembled through the floorboards—soft as a heartbeat.

Inside, Rita sat quietly in the low glow of the TV, holding Junior in her arms. Her smile brightened the room the second she saw us.

"Mr Giannetti," she said, rising. "So nice to meet you."

She handed Junior over without hesitation.

Dan took him without question.

I swayed where I stood, lost in the surreality. Dan wasn't the baby's father. He wasn't even my husband. But there he was, taking a seat on the couch, cradling my son like he belonged there.

"Everything okay?" Rita asked gently, pulling me back into the moment.

I blinked.

Once—the room warped.

Twice—my head spun.

Third time—I landed back in focus.

"Yeah... it's going well." I stumbled slightly. "Has the baby been alright?"

She stepped beside me, arms folded, watching Dan with soft eyes.

"He's been perfect. Two feeds. Slept soundly." Her smile grew. "They look great together."

I hiccupped and nodded. They really did.

The moment snapped like a stretched elastic when Tommy pushed open my office door without knocking.

"Boss," he said, a little breathless. "Harper's kicking off. I need both of you downstairs. Now."

Dan stood, regret flickering across his face as he clumsily handed Junior back to Rita.

Harper was kicking off?

I bet she had a camera in her face while she did it, too.

Tommy pressed a finger to his earpiece again, voice tighter.

"Now, Boss."

Dan and I rushed out, swept into Tommy's urgency.

My heels clicked down the stairs with a stumble I pretended was intentional. Heat clung to the walls—thick with perfume, sweat, and rising chaos.

By the time we reached the bottom, Harper was already mid-meltdown.

"Where the fuck have you been, Daniele!?" She spat the words like bullets.

Champagne clung to the air, sticky and celebratory, now soured by her jealousy.

He leaned in and kissed her cheek.

"I was looking for you, baby, that's all," he said softly.

Baby?

Catching my glare, he flashed me an apologetic smile.

She noticed.

Her whole posture shifted the moment she clocked the hurt flicker across my face.

Dan wasn't mine. And I was completely, utterly, alone.

"Daniele!" Her shrill voice sliced through the music like a sword. Her chest heaved with theatrical rage. "Come on. We're leaving," she snapped—voice pitched like a tantrum.

Dan's hand found mine. His palm was warm. It melted the cold pit blooming in my chest when he gave it a gentle squeeze.

She saw it. Eyes narrowed. Lips curled.

Her gaze slid down my body like a scalpel.

"You haven't started my fitness plan yet, I see," she said with a sugary smile, dripping with venom.

I placed a hand over my stomach, steadying myself.

Willing myself not to crumble.

"Great to see you, Dan," I said with a soft sway. "I've got another guest I need to greet."

Then I turned away without waiting for a reply.

Lucy caught my elbow just as I veered toward the bar again.

"You're running a little behind," she said, gently swivelling me back toward the stairs.

"I've already settled your last VIP client in booth two for you."

I hiccupped again. "Okay, thanks. Which girl are we giving him?"

"I'll send Double D's up. Stall for two or three minutes—she's just finishing a lap dance."

Nodding was the best I could manage as the first step blurred beneath me. By the time the ball of my foot landed, I was nearly seeing double.

"You okay, Chloe?" she called after me.

I turned with a fake smile and an even faker thumbs up.

"I'm perfect."

Perfect—aside from being a single mother to a deaf newborn... whose backup relationship option was now dating my nemesis.

Tommy followed behind, silent as ever.

I knew he was judging me for Dan, but honestly? I couldn't give a flying fuck.

He waited, tight-lipped, by the double doors at the top of the stairs, holding one open for me.

Was it booth two or three?

Two. Definitely two.

An amber glow bled from beneath the door. Soft. Inviting. A muffled dance track curled faintly through the walls.

Before stepping inside, I ran my fingers through my hair and reapplied lip gloss—haphazardly, without a mirror. A feeble attempt at composure. At resetting whatever the fuck I was feeling.

I pushed the door open. My heel caught the threshold with an unbalanced scrape.

The client was already seated in the lounge chair, back to me. Fedora tilted low, trench coat draped across him like he'd stepped out of a noir film.

Old-school detective vibes.

But I didn't worry. No cop would risk stepping foot in a place like this without blowing up their entire career.

I circled behind the chair, fingers brushing his covered forearm, warm through the fabric.

"Welcome to Jasmin's," I said, voice slurred with vodka. "May I take your coat?"

He raised his head.

Plump red lips. Then lashes—long and feminine.

Finally, the sunglasses dropped—and everything shifted.

The hum of music vanished beneath the carpet.

The scent of cocoa butter curled in the air like a dream.

A memory.

My knees buckled.

I reached for the table, but my grip slipped as the room tilted on its side.

A manicured hand reached up, removing the fedora to reveal a cascade of golden hair spilling over her shoulders.

She smiled sweetly.

"Alice?" I whispered.

"Hey, bestie. Did you miss me?"

THANKYOU

To every reader who picked up this book, thank you.

Whether you've been here since the beginning or just stumbled into my world of chaos, heartbreak, and power plays, I'm so grateful you chose to spend time with my characters.

To those who rooted for Chloe, cried with her, screamed at Romeo, and maybe even cursed me along the way, I see you. You're the reason I keep writing. You carried this story as much as I did.

To my husband, who held my hand through rewrites and breakdowns, your patience and encouragement brought this to life.

And finally, to every woman who's ever been underestimated, pushed too far, or left to rise alone, I hope Chloe's fight reminded you of your own.

The story isn't over.

But for now, I'll leave you here.

With love,
Sam Douglas

Printed in Dunstable, United Kingdom